DISILLUSIONED

A Lay of Ruinous Reign

Book II

DISILLUSIONED

A Lay of Ruinous Reign

Book II

Briar Somerset

Welcome, Dear Reader.
This is the tale of sisterhood, chosen
family, misused magic, and what
happens to chivalry and poise when a
knight and queen fall to the blade of
their own desires.

Love makes fools of us all, especially
those with sharpened teeth and
hardened hearts.

One of bloud begotten and cleane,
　　She treads amongst shadows unseen,
　　Behind Three borne of the sundry seed.
　　Two Bound in Folly, One wrought by Need.
　　May no Fang nor Man rend this cursed bond,
　　Nor break the Night wherein they are donned.
　　A Crowne of Night, a regal wight,
　　Worn by the Daughters of the Harvest Light.

— BRANOC THE VEILED, THE HISTORIES OF THE
LASTING NIGHT, VOLUME III, CIRCA 13TH CYCLE
DURING THE EXILE YEARS OF THE WARLOCK

For Ella of Frell, who said no.
For Emma Woodhouse, who said too much.
For Buffy Summers, who wielded honor like a stake.
And For Spike, who never said the right thing,
but made it sound like poetry anyway.

Come forth, Dear Reader.
Thank you for trusting me to tell you this tale of camaraderie, longing, and what it
means to be bound by blood. The road is long ahead, the night enduring—
But so are our appetites.
And so are we.

PREFACE

Disillusioned is a work of speculative fiction set in an alternate version of early 16th-century Brittany prior to its annexation by France in 1532. While it draws from real geographical locations and socio-political structures, it is ultimately a work of fantasy. You will notice significant liberties taken with historical timelines, shifting borders, and the intricacies of court life and monarchial succession. Characters are inserted, ducal lines of aristocracy are rearranged, and some professions are imagined.

These deviations are measured and intentional.

The Ruinous Reign series explores Brittany's status as a once-autonomous Celtic kingdom, shaped by centuries of migration, war, and matrimonial negotiation with neighboring powers. The region's distinct identity—linguistically, culturally, and politically—provides a stunning foundation for the fictionalized landscape of Breton maritime and forested magic.

In reconstructing an imagined version of the past where supernatural creatures from local legend coexist with feudal politics, *Disillusioned* draws upon concepts of Late Medieval alchemy, botany, and my take on Brythonic fairy folklore through an anti-colonial lens.

Eleanor Trécesson (also known as Lilac by her father) is a monarch, daughter, survivor in her own right. More than anything, she's a tapestry woven from the lives of three real women who refuse to be forgotten: Constance of Brittany, who ruled as duchess under persistent opposition; Eleanor, the Fair Maid of Brittany, the Plantagenet heiress whose rightful claim to power made her a prisoner for the majority of her life; and last but not least, Anne of Brittany, the last independent ruler of the Duchy, whose marriages saw her rise to power and cultural osmosis/ loss. It was Anne's marriage to Maximilian which heavily inspired Act II of Disillusioned.

These stories of power denied and seized in rage breathe life into Lilac—Eleanor of Brittany, as we know her in the Ruinous Reign Series.

This is not a historical retelling. Rather, it is an imaginative reconstruction that blends archival silences, regional mythology, and speculative invention. Lilac's narrative explores gendered power, intergenerational trauma, and the enduring legacies of resistance through the scope of Medieval Dark Fantasy.

It is a romantic, violent dream of what might've been.

It is my hope, with the invaluable guidance of my readers and cultural consultants, that I've handled these topics of history and heritage sensitively, and appropriately.

Any inaccuracies or oversights are my own.

To learn more about the history of Brittany and their endangered languages today, here are some resources:

https://www.elalliance.org/languages/breton

https://icdbl.org/index.php

I currently use these books for my research on geography, legend, and the imaginings of Late Medieval life:

Antiracist Medievalisms: From "Yellow Peril" to Black Lives Matter

Trading Tongues: Merchants, Multilingualism, and Medieval Literature

The Time Traveler's Guide to Medieval England: A Handbook for Visitors to the Fourteenth Century

The Mabinogion

Le Morte d'Arthur

Legends and Romances of Brittany

Celtic Tales

Folk Tales of Brittany

Roscoff

Brest

Ambleside Sanctum

Brocé

Bay of Dougrnenez

Château de Trèce

Quimper

f Brittany

St. Brieug

St. Malo

Fougéres

rest

Rennes

Montgort-sur-Mey

he Mine

Cindergell

Trevelyan Farmhouse

Paimpont

CONTENT WARNING

Abuse
Abortion
Alcohol/ Drug use
Annexation
Arranged Marriage
Asphyxiation
Blood Play
Combat and war
Depression
Dub-con
Gore
Religious Trauma
Suicide

THE UNFORTUNATE AND SUDDEN VACANCY OF THE DUCAL SEAT

The selection of whores at the Rennes house had been scrumptious, particularly the pert tits of that Daphne. Armand tried to focus on the fogged memory of all those roaming hands, but every step from his carriage toward the entryway of his estate clarified the weight of his reality settling once again upon his shoulders. What was supposed to be an escape for one night had blurred into three, yet here he was, back in this hellhole clothed in every luxurious trapping.

Between the queen's barbaric orders of house arrest and the carousel of doctors treating his son's delusional moaning, it was with incredible willpower that Armand approached the heavy plank door. The pair of guards flanking either side of the steps remained silent and still. He'd paid them and his servants a month's wages to be sure word of his excursion didn't reach the palace, and the fact his own men were still here meant they'd well kept their end of the bargain.

A violent shiver rolled through him as he braced himself for Vivien's wrath and pushed the door open on well-oiled hinges. Darkness welcomed him, and he blinked several times in confusion. The silent black seemed to have consumed the expected whispered chatter of servants, the clinking of dishes being washed or stored, the raking of a broom across their fine marble.

Even his mad son was silent. *And where was Vivien?*

His guilt soured into fear. Armand's breath grew ragged. A warm breeze swept across the space, engulfing him in a sweet musk that made his skin crawl.

A faint babbling from near the stairs caught his ear as his eyes slowly adjusted in the pale moonlight entering through the hall's high windows. He shuffled forward and glanced up the stairwell, where the only answers to his silent plea were the echoes of his own labored breathing. Unable to break the silence to call for help or one of his goddamned servants, Armand followed the incessant murmurings to the small space under the stairs.

Two wide eyes glanced up at him, the black of his eyes blown wide. Sinclair crouched, balled up in the shadows. Armand put a hand around his son's arm, pulling him into the moonlight, only to retaliate at the crusted moistness of the fabric of his nightgown. Sinclair toppled to the side, the smell of vomit and piss wafting from him, as if the servants hadn't changed him out of his nightgown in days. His son stared blankly at him, no recognition dawning in his eyes. Then his gaze darted past as if watching, waiting for something. For someone else.

Only when Sinclair shifted did the moonlight catch on the ax head, its shaft clutched in pale knuckles streaked with grime. Blood, not yet congealed, gleamed along its edge. Armand opened his mouth to interrogate his son, but all that came was a frightened sob.

The front door blew open in a sudden gust of wind, jolting against the stone with a resounding *crack*. Armand scrambled away from Sinclair and finally found his voice.

"Vivien! Vivien, come here." His shouts rang out as he stumbled across the hall, and Armand could not bear the silence to come again. Could not bear what would surely *emerge* from the silence. "Guards!" he roared. "I need you!" And finally, when the armored imbeciles did not so much as move a limb, Armand's voice cracked as he yelled, "Driver! *Philip!*"

He limped left across the foyer and toward the open dining room, in misplaced hopes Godwin had left out a knife as he often did—the lazy fuck —and found himself slipping through a puddle of something thick and half dried. Arms flailing, he yelped and tripped backwards onto the rug, managing to swipe at the nearest corner of the table linen and taking with him several pieces of glassware.

Here, the curtains had been drawn on all but one tall window, through which the crescent moon shone weakly through skidding clouds. The duke didn't flinch against the shards of crystal, fixating instead on the form strewn on the floor before him that slowly swam into focus.

Godwin.

Clutching his throbbing hip, Armand shifted to his knees, compulsively needing to wipe his hands on the part of the tablecloth not drenched in the same puddle he sat in. Two crystalline eyes stared at him, unblinking among the porcelain. They were his wife's teardrop earrings, dangling from a crude gray lump at the center of the table.

Something shifted in the dark behind it.

"To what do I owe the pleasure?"

The smooth voice made him jolt, but the outline of a hooded figure lounging opposite him, seated in his chair at the head of the table, made him freeze.

Armand first heard that voice in the woods with Artus. The grating laughter as they'd chased it down, his father's expertly shot arrows it had dodged. The condescending smile in its tone now, and the way it shrugged its hood onto its shoulders as it lazily drummed its fingers upon the arm rest were all too familiar.

This was the closest he'd stood to the creature they'd chased for years, and now that they were face to face, he didn't know what to say. He'd first taken a shot at it on his seventeenth birthday, when he was but a boy and the beast was full grown, as his father had explained, damned in eternal youth. Tonight he was twice the age the monster's frozen years. Perhaps more.

And it was in this moment that Armand knew he would die at the Daemon's hand.

Such knowledge cast an odd calm over the duke, and he methodically wiped his hands on the fine white linen, leaving streaks like claw marks.

"We've met," Armand managed, a hopeless plea in the dark.

"We have," the shadow replied, the restraint in its voice sending waves of nausea through him. It leaned forward, elbows resting on knees, chin resting on knuckles. "But not like this."

Fine metal scraped against wood as the creature stood. Armand could make out the silver edge of his stoat-head cane in the shadow's hand, the one he preferred to leave at home, propped against the door, when he did not want to draw unnecessary attention to his bad leg. Swinging the cane so it rested upon its shoulder, the shadow strode around the table toward Armand, who did not move a muscle. He was frozen, a sinner stared down the pulpit by a priest.

The same cold that welcomed him in the foyer seemed to emanate from the shadow, following like a slow-moving draft as it stalked toward— and past—Armand. He closed his eyes, waiting for the blow. The bite. He prayed it would be over quickly.

Instead, something nudged him in the arm. The vampire was before him again, this time with one of the dull, rusted blades from the servant's armory in the nearby closet. It held the weapon out, and when Armand couldn't bring himself to move, it rolled its eyes and placed the hilt in his palm with the most pitiful sigh.

The duke quivered, clutching the blade even as he eyed the ivory hilt of his father's longsword hanging against the creature's back. Sinclair had told everyone he'd lost it in his efforts to recover the Trécesson girl, and that the vampire had scurried away with it stuck through its body.

Armand tried to clear his throat. "You want me to fight you?"

The creature took its time in answering. "I want you to be protected."

"From what?"

"Brocéliande." The creature turned, lifted his cane, and used the end of it to sweep a nearby curtain open. As if on command, the clouds fled, and the odd shapes on the table were cast into view as faint moonlight spilled over the entire room. "From the moment you run from me."

The blood.

The floor.

The bodies.

The head.

Armand bolted, running to escape—not the vampire, but what he had seen. The rusted blade clanged to the ground, forgotten, as he barreled past the stilled guards, leapt down the steps, and sprinted toward the gates that barred his property from the town beyond.

His bad hip gave out after three steps, and he let out a broken sob as he stumbled to his knees, desperate to escape the aroma of death still pungent in his lungs. Blood—there was blood crusting in the creases of his knuckles, under his fingernails, in the grooves of his rings. He retched, vomiting the remaining ale and food in his stomach.

He would never recover from what he'd seen.

As if God had finally heard him, the rattle and clomp of his driver's carriage came from his right. He pulled himself upright and waved frantically at Philip, who raised a gloved hand in reply as the carriage neared.

A glance back at the house showed its door wide open on its hinges and the driveway cold and empty. The estate would be a small price to pay for his life. He scrambled into the coach. His wife had warned him of this day —the day the girl realized her power and unleashed her unholy perfidy upon the kingdom. She would pay, now that there was proof.

She would—

As he reached to swing the door shut, a cool hand clamped around his fingers and squeezed. The duke's shattered cry broke the still of night as his bones crunched in the vampire's grasp.

"We're more alike than you think," it said, ignoring Armand's broken sobs, leaning against the door frame and blocking his only exit. Fangs glinted through its rueful smile. A large sack was tucked under one arm, the forgotten blade in one hand, while the other toyed with Armand's stolen cane—a gift from Artus.

Armand screamed for help, but Philip only turned in the driver's seat and nodded through the smudged window, smiling as if the duke had commented on the weather. The rusted blade clanged to the floor of the carriage, and Armand stared at it in disbelief.

"Please," he croaked, pressing his throbbing hand against the cold wall of the carriage. "I have—I can give you whatever you want." He shivered against the pain shooting up his arm, brain working on overdrive to forestall the inevitable. "We both served under the crown."

The vampire laughed, the sound of a death curse whispered into the night. "When I said we are alike, I only meant that we are both not opposed to bloodshed for the ones we love." Its head cocked in consideration. "I'm actually never opposed to bloodshed, but my point remains."

"I have not touched a hair on your queen's head."

The vampire grabbed both sides of the doorway with such force as it leaned in that the frame splintered. "Let's not pretend you haven't tried. And the same lack of success does not apply to your *wife*. She sent a forged letter to Eleanor to tempt her into the woods just after she murdered Laurent." Its eyes were glinting, and its voice shook. "She sent the princess into Brocéliande knowing I would be out for blood after our leader's murder."

"Ridiculous," Armand stuttered, blinking through the unfamiliar details. "Vivien would never do such a thing, nor could she have killed a vampire. You speak impossibilities."

Unmistakable humor flashed across the vampire's face. Its nostrils flared. "Surely you knew." There was a madness in its words. "*Surely.*"

Armand shook his head mutely; the weight under its ruby gaze was too much. He'd be crushed under it soon, but he couldn't bring himself to look away.

"Do not lie to me." So quickly that Armand felt it before he saw it, the vampire ground the end of the cane into his foot, pinning his ankle to the floorboard and snapping the tendon behind it. Bright heat seared up his leg.

"She couldn't have!"

The pressure on his ankle was gone. "I have proof from the Fair Folk."

The duke shook his head. His whole body trembled.

How could she? How would she? Vivien had never gone on any of their hunts, had never wielded a weapon in her dainty, curated life as an earl's daughter. Not once since they'd been introduced and paired together all those years ago, although... Her temper alone was a force to be reckoned with. Certainly, she'd envied his friend's family's power, always had some scorned remark to make in private about Henri's wife or their troubled daughter, but Vivien had done that with anyone she felt remotely threatened by.

"How?" Armand whispered, his voice barely a croak. "How did she do it?"

"That's what you're going to tell me."

"I have nothing to tell you."

The vampire scowled, its calm gone. There was nothing left of the convincing mask it had worn atop the ramparts for its wicked queen.

"Lie to me again, and I'll drain you right there."

Armand gripped the seat, his hand pounding. "I didn't know she was responsible, that she'd done anything." He snorted, a bitter sound. "If I'd known, I'd never have returned to my property."

The vampire considered him. The cane flicked up and rested under his chin, against his throat. "Are you saying she acted alone?"

To say that he did not think it was possible for her to pull it off was true, but her intent did not surprise him. Either way, she had acted without telling him or thinking of what might follow. Perhaps she hadn't cared. Armand was telling the truth, and he and their son would pay with their lives.

Perhaps the vampire could tell, either by his pulse or that he was seconds away from shitting himself, that this was the case. He exhaled, and his rage deflated. "Look at me."

Armand groaned and closed his eyes, one last gesture of defiance. If there was no one around to witness a heroic death, he could at least maintain his grip on his mind until he died. His breathing grew ragged as the vampire waited patiently.

When a minute passed, the duke looked up to find the brute smirking. It gripped his jaw, eyes boring into Armand's. "Forget what you saw; refrain from speaking of it for now. Go to the castle."

Armand scoffed and tugged against its vice-like grasp. Forget *what*?

"You will not move, will not attempt to escape. You won't stop for anyone—not for passersby, not for children or beggars. Not for your friend group at that pub in town. Your little militia cannot help you."

With each word, the dread filling Armand became stifled under a blanket of calm. The vampire was generous in letting him live. The carriage suddenly smelled of flora, ale, sweat, and sex. The fond imagery of the clean, bustling streets of Rennes at dusk filled his senses. "Yes."

"Seek an audience from Her Majesty."

He was meaning to do that. "What should I tell her?" His own voice sounded far away. He could use a nap about now. A long nap on a ride to the queen.

The grip on his face loosened.

"Your memories will return upon your hearing, and you can tell her whatever you like." The vampire's voice was like melted chocolate. "Tell her why you've fled your residence in the dead of night. Tell her about the unfortunate mess you've discovered. Tell her about Sinclair—but only after they know you're there to give her *this*."

The sting of his son's name was a distant lash on his cheek compared to the throb in his hand and chest. The sack was deposited on the seat next to Armand.

"This is your gift for her. *Don't*," it added when Armand shifted to peer down at it. "It is only proper if you open it in front of her and her court. This is what will gain her your sympathy." It paused and lifted its brows at Armand. "You will have her open it, or you'll impale yourself on your blade. Is that clear?"

He nodded, unable to look away despite the chill that ran down his spine. This vampire wasn't only sparing his life, it had given him a gift to present to the queen. It was kind. Why had he spent all those years in his father's shadow, trying to maim the poor boy for sport?

Moisture filled the duke's eyes. He nodded in gratitude.

The vampire pulled away, once again leaning against the doorframe, and dusted its hands on its robes. The aromas swelling around the carriage dissipated as it reached into its robe pocket and procured a handkerchief.

"In times of war," it said, taking each of Armand's hands in its cool fingers and cleaning the blood off. "We only bore the same crest, bloodied the same fields under the guise of monarchy. Today we, under the same crown, are bleeding for entirely different causes."

Armand's breath hitched as the vampire wiped his broken hand, the pain not entirely numbed. Was he... being lectured? It felt like it. There was a wave of something unpleasant that never quite broke the surface. "Henri is my friend," he said, defiant. "He is my family. I love him. I-I am faithful to Henri, I would never—" He stumbled over his words as the vampire regarded him coldly.

"And therein lies the *difference* between you and I, Armand." It picked up the cane, examining the blunt head of the silver stoat at the handle. "You and your late wife—gods rest her soul, she was beautiful, but her blood tasted like shit—were bent on convincing others of your fealty." It extended the cane so that the sharp tail of the animal rested under the duke's chin. "Your patriotism is meaningless. You love your own flawed idea of what this country should be as you actively hunt your own countrymen.

You command bloodshed to defend borders, yet the people and creatures within them mean nothing to you."

"I'm—"

"You are pathetic, human. You have no sense of purpose."

Armand sniffled. "And you do?"

The vampire twisted the stoat's tail against his shirt, nicking his skin. As Armand grunted against the sting, the Daemon's eyes flashed ravenously.

"I do."

Rage—rage was the feeling he couldn't place. It was a distant swell of anger that rose in Armand, but it remained caged within his ribs. He was stuck under this monster's spell, even when his muscles yearned to jolt into motion. "Is it her?"

The vampire paused his torture, considering the duke.

Armand held his breath. With each exhale, the tip of the stoat's tail dug farther into his flesh. "Is it Lilac?" If he died, he would not do it pandering to a queen so undeserving of her title and her pet of a knight.

The corner of the vampire's mouth lifted in a way that was neither wholly sneer nor smile. "You'll keep her name out of your mouth."

The duke glanced back at the empty manor, a shell of the vibrance that once filled it.

"Everyone has a home, Armand, and it appears you've done a bloody poor job at protecting yours."

Then, it pushed up the sleeves of its robes and swung the glistening stoat directly into Armand's temple.

"I assure you," Lilac said, resisting the most unlady-like urge to uncross her ankles beneath her thick chiffon gown and start fanning herself in the late spring heat. "No one is attacking."

The boy stepped up from the line of about one dozen townsfolk who had traveled to the castle for an audience. In the center of the Grand Hall, he had introduced himself as a blacksmith's son from *La Guerche*. He couldn't have been older than fifteen.

He clutched his cap to his chest. "But my father insisted I come and warn you." The woman behind him, who was accompanied by a handcuffed prisoner wearing a burlap sack over his head, nudged the boy roughly in the back. "Y-your Majesty. He saw plumes of smoke yesterday, just before dawn. Said they were signals."

"Well," she replied, her ears growing warm, unsure of the most appropriate way to argue with a near child. "He might've misinterpreted them. There are scouts already all over Fougères and Vitré, and it is warming up. Perhaps they were travelers," she said, noting the fortress villages within a day's trip north of his town. "Trust me, if there was concern—which there is not—I would have received word by now."

"This is why we waited a few weeks after your accession to accept inquiries at the King's Bench," John, the family scribe, muttered with a yawn. He rapped the desk from Lilac's left. "Next."

"Please, Your Majesty," the boy pleaded, wringing his hands.

One of the guards stood from the table against the wall near the courtyard entrance. Some of the crowd behind him began to whisper amongst themselves.

"*Gods*—there is no need for panic," Lilac hastily announced to the room. "No one is coming. No one is attacking."

"Is His Grace available?" the boy inquired, straining gently against the guard attempting to tug him away. "My father suggested I might appeal to him if there was any trouble."

"No." She'd specifically asked her father not to interfere, told him that his scribe was sufficient and had seen to enough of their family affairs to stand in place of a council or Henri's supervision during her first Court of Common Appeals. "No, he is not."

"Would you mind sparing your castle guards, then? Or direct some of the guards from Fougères to protect us and the smaller towns?"

Most of her kingdom's experienced militia were nearly aged out of service, with the last skirmish they'd fought being over half a decade ago. After the Raid led by Laurent and Garin, her grandfather had been forced to focus on quelling fear in the towns, meanwhile allowing for consensual vampire feedings to avoid something as gruesome from happening again. The Le Tallecs did not agree, and when Armand inherited his title as a child after his father went mad and was denounced, the training of a new army—the next generation's recruits—fell to the wayside.

Of course, efforts were not revived under Henri, either, and Armand's attention had pivoted to hunting Daemons since her father undid her grandfather's feeding law after her Daemon tongue was revealed.

She considered him carefully. Historically, that was what the fortress villages were purposed for. There was no harm in dispatching a few of the guards from Fougères, but doing so publicly would stoke panic in the towns.

"Until there is official word, until there is documentation of French troops at our borders, I will refrain. I cannot have the country in hysteria without reason, especially after my ceremony." She eyed the guard beside him. "Take him."

The guard dutifully escorted the complaining boy out into the bailey through the courtyard.

Lilac leaned into the scribe. "Send my order to increase the perimeter presence in Louvigne and Fougères. Quietly."

She sighed, rubbing her temples. The first three requests had been easy enough—not without trouble, but their complaints weren't entirely unexpected. The first two had blamed their drying crops on curses, due to the presence of the witches and warlocks allowed to live in the town. Lilac had asked them if they'd simply considered asking the witches they suspected if they were responsible, if there was some obscure vendetta one held over them worthy of withering cabbages. The answer, of course, was no. She invited them to perhaps see if those witches had anything to *help* their said withering crops.

The third asked if she could truly speak to Daemons, and when her answer was an unflinching yes, she had the nerve to ask if Lilac could then simply communicate to the creatures that the townsfolk of Paimpont wished to be left alone, citing a korrigan thievery that had long ago taken place at a bakery there.

She was reminded then of little Aife stuffing her mouth with the smooshed pastries from her bag and the korikaned's horrified mother, fearing terrible retaliation. Lilac's answer was straightforward, that these issues would only lessen because she intended to make changes to the treaty that gradually allowed for the Daemons to integrate into society.

That had silenced the room. Needless to say, no one had seemed satisfied with any of her answers so far.

"*Next*," repeated John, scribbling onto the piece of parchment unfurling onto his lap.

The woman who stood behind the boy dragged her prisoner to the desk, his hands tied with a familiar reddish-brown rope. She snatched the bag off his head—it was a man whose black hair had been chopped crudely as if with a knife, reminding her of her own lopsided haircut done by the blade at her thigh. She shifted, suddenly reminded how uncomfortable her scalp felt beneath the ridiculous towering wig that squeezed her head, thanks to her mother and Yanna, who'd insisted on cramming her into it for court.

Lilac tossed a pale yellow ringlet out of her eyes. "What are we looking at?"

"This," she croaked, reaching into her apron pocket and pulling out a sheet, holding it for the room to see. It was the WANTED illustration her scribe had drawn under Adelaide's spell. The pair on the poster resembled what could be described at best, a caricature of a vampire and witch—the former with huge fangs and wide ears, the latter with hollowed eyes and gaunt cheekbones. "Is one of your dungeon escapees."

John leaned forward, peering closer. He blinked. "Did I draw that, Your Majesty? I don't recall—"

"Yes, you did. We were all very shaken after my ceremony."

"How much is your reward?" the villager pressed.

Lilac held up a hand. This was absurd. "That is not him."

"Well," the man said, his words barely audible through the cloth wrapped around his mouth, "what might the bail amount be?"

"It resembles him perfectly." The woman slapped a hand on his back. "He entered my bedroom as I was asleep." She yanked down the collar of her dress, showing a large red mark upon her throat. "Tried to suck me dry, he did." She tapped the man again. "Didn't you?"

"I did."

"Is that so?" Lilac leered at the pair. "Is that... hawthorn on his wrists?"

"Yes." Then her eyes widened at the man's unaffected hands. "I-I mean no, it's not."

Lilac forced herself to swallow the sudden wave of frustration that rose. This formality had proven pointless. It might've helped if someone actually came in with an valid complaint.

No one had taken her seriously. Not one of them.

And why would they? a voice in the back of her mind asked. She had no real experience in ruling, no experience out in town except for that day at the Le Tallec manor, and Adelaide's marsh was the closest she'd been since then.

She trailed her clammy, sticky fingers over the worn cherrywood. Several decrees and rulings had taken place here, some that had changed the course of history for Brittany, for better and for worse.

Tonight would mark one more at The Fenfoss Inn, forever altering the history of her kingdom and completing her and Garin's bargain with Kestrel.

They'd settle and sign the Accords that would reinstate her grandfather's law and set a new precedent in defining the Daemons' rights as citizens of her kingdom. The faerie king had been gracious with his time—by the day of her coronation ball, as marked in their contract. It *had* been scheduled for the middle of summer, but shortly after her accession ceremony her parents advised she move the date up.

Lilac had protested at first, but once Garin informed her in passing—under the dramatic guise of uttering a prayer over her—that he came upon an agreed date with all their invitees, she had no qualms. The sooner she got both the meeting and her ball over with, the better—and so, her coronation invitations promptly went out for the end of May, and so did those for the Accords meeting at the inn on the eve of the third Sunday after she ascended the throne.

In two weeks, the crown would be bestowed upon her head in this very room, and Kestrel would be appeased, then relieving the threat of Garin's becoming possessed with the urge to kill her again.

By all means, she would've very much liked to avoid it.

"Actually," she began, and the small crowd and even the guards looked shocked to see her rise from her seat. "The two in question have been pardoned. There are no wanted witch and vampire; they were only prisoners in the first place under Sinclair's orders and not mine." Lilac gripped the edge of the desk. "And, might I remind you—*where* is Sinclair and his family today?"

She raised her brows. Lilac's rhetorical question hung uncomfortably in the still air. She nodded in answer, not caring that the heat was getting to her. "Prisoners in their own—"

The double doors at the front of the room flew open, and in barged a small brigade. Armand was at the front, *carried* by four guards, writhing, his face twisted in a gruesome grimace, mouth open in a silent scream.

Behind him, two more guards escorted a man she didn't recognize. Probably their family coachman, judging by his long coat and high boots.

Henri was at their rear, flanked by two men—Gondard and Perane, his councilmen of many years. He locked eyes with Lilac. "Everyone out! If anyone mentions a word of this, you'll meet your fate at the guillotine. John has your names, places of work, and residences documented!"

"Where to, Your Highness?" asked one of the guards over Armand's screeching.

"Anywhere but this room. This session is over." Henri strode to her desk, standing off to the side, almost protectively in front of her. The councilmen took their positions behind the both of them, on the bottom steps at the rear of the desk. "Bring them chairs and fetch Madame Kemble."

The guards dragged both men to the center of the floor, keeping them far from the desk. The room was silent except for the opening and banging shut of the doors as the remainder of the crowd was ushered out into the courtyard, one guard rummaging in the storage room in the far corner, and another darting into the keep for the infirmary.

"Father," she said through her teeth, but Henri silenced her with a finger in the air.

The duke's grimace had stretched into an equally terrifying smile, either at her or at least in her general direction, despite the grim expressions worn by the guards beside him. The coachman gazed off into the distance, his eyes heavy-lidded as he gave two slow blinks.

There was a sudden knock. "Come in," called Lilac and Henri simultaneously.

One of the doors opened, and in barged Madame Kemble, her long blonde-gray hair tucked into a bun, several cloths slung over her shoulder and a tool belt hanging from her apron donned over a nightgown, which indicated she'd been roused from a nap. She nearly stumbled under the weight of the bucket she carried, water sloshing as she made her way to the men.

Just then, the guard returned from the storage closet with two spare chairs, upon which both men were promptly seated closer to the patch of late morning sunlight pouring from the high windows.

Nausea burned Lilac's throat. Something was terribly wrong.

Kemble moved nimbly around them. She'd placed Armand's left foot into the bucket of water and placed a cold cloth against his temple and right eye, which was swollen, blooming in splotches of red and yellow. Yet, his smile-grimace remained.

Deep circles lined the purpling skin beneath the coachman's eyes, and

his lips were several shades too pale. He held a faraway gaze as if he were...
sleepwalking. Kemble noticed, too. She waved a hand before his eyes.

Before anyone could stop him he made to rise, only to fold at the
middle in an almost comical bow. Then, his knees buckled and his torso
followed.

The man hit the floor face first with a muffled *crunch*.

Armand made a strangled noise through his smile. The coachman
remained face down and did not get back up.

"Is he..." The words died on Lilac's lips.

Kemble was already shifting, patting her hands dry upon her apron
before placing a knuckle against the side of the man's neck. The shake of
her head was nearly imperceptible.

"Armand's driver," her father muttered. Then his voice rang out.
"Remove him."

"It'll take a bit to fetch the linen and stretcher, sir."

"You have hands and feet, don't you?" Henri left his station at the front
of the desk and moved to stand beside her. "Go. Take him out the courtyard door, quickly now, while everyone is at the chapel."

Two guards did as Henri said, hoisting the corpse by its blue arms and
feet and taking him out the courtyard door on the southern wall.

"What could it have been?" asked Gondard.

"People drop all the time," said Henri gruffly. "Armand will make everything clear once he snaps out of this shock he's in. In the meantime, no one
enters or leaves the room until we conclude this session."

Lilac dared a glance at Armand; he sat nodding, the remaining guard's
hand clamped upon his shoulder. There was no response to her father
calling out his inaction, something he would've absolutely revolted against
—if he were right in the head. Damp spots lined the collar of his white
shirt and armpits, and there was a visible sheen on his forehead.

He was not suffering from some normal ailment, some excess of alcohol. No, this man had been spelled. But by friend or foe? It was no secret
that Armand was not the same supporter of her as he had been of Henri.
Maybe Adelaide had poisoned him after the fact and sent him as a cruel
joke. Or were the Fair Folk behind his behavior? Lilac shuddered at the
thought of Kestrel; she was already dreading having to face him as night
drew near.

Only one way to find out.

"Your Grace," she said, welcoming him to begin.

John adjusted in his seat, readying his quill.

Armand's gaze cast to the floor, and he began to mumble under his breath. Kemble turned toward him, brow furrowed in concentration. Lilac cocked an ear but could make out nothing.

Kemble spoke quietly to him, kneeling and shaking her head as he slowly tried to spin in his seat, but the guard behind him grunted warningly.

Lilac waved a hand. "Yes, Armand? He may speak. Let him speak."

"I think he's saying he cannot speak with you until he gives you his gift, Your Majesty."

He'd brought her a gift. Something was certainly wrong. "Very well, then." She outstretched her arm, crooking her fingers. "Give it here."

The guard stepped back and released him, but not without a reluctant grimace, his hand sliding to rest at the hilt at his hip. The freedom allowed Armand to twist in his chair, swiping his arm behind him rather frantically. Kemble used her foot to push a long, narrow bag closed by a drawstring to within reach, and the man snatched it, cradling the package to his chest like a doting mother would hold her newborn babe. Then he turned his unnerving smile on Lilac and held it out to her.

She stood from her chair, and Henri's arm shot out to stop her.

"What if the same madness has infected him, Lilac?"

"That's what our guards are here for." *And his type of madness isn't catching.*

It was also what the jeweled dagger strapped to her outer thigh was for.

Ignoring the dread gnawing at her insides, she shrugged him off and marched straight toward the man who had fathered her worst nightmare. She stopped an arm's length away, and as she accepted the bundle, his fingers brushed hers. They were clammy, and cold. As soon as he released the bag to her, he slumped forward. She took two quick steps back, keeping her eye on him as she deposited the bundle upon her desk. It landed with a *thump*.

The duke took deep, shaking breaths, eyes closed, as relief and a mixture of other emotions washed over him.

Lilac smoothed her skirts with one hand and placed the other upon the hilt that rested on her right thigh.

"Why are you here, Armand?"

The words, like some sort of counterspell, washed over the duke, stripping away whatever deep enchantment had bound him. Eyes bulging, his entire body seized; then an unholy scream escaped his lips. He jerked and twisted until he toppled the chair, tipping the bucket at his feet.

Red-tinged water spilled toward her.

"My foot," Armand bellowed, causing the guards to circle closer. "My fucking—"

"Silence him!" Henri roared from beside her.

One of the guards grimaced and clamped a gloved hand over his mouth as Armand writhed, nearly sliding out of his chair. When the guard released him, the duke did fall to the floor, sobbing and clutching his leg with one hand, the other hand curled inward toward his body.

Kemble, with the help of two guards, hoisted him upright. They struggled to catch his flailing limbs, but the moment Kemble snatched his foot —the one that had been shoved in the bucket—he stilled.

"He's here, isn't he?" His gaze swept the room like an animal ensnared in a trap.

"Who?" Lilac glared down at him, forging through the unease in the pit of her belly. "Is *who* here?"

Armand trembled, the afternoon sun blinding him from the high windows like a torch held to his face, pressing the answers out of him. But he said nothing—until Kemble began to tug at his boot.

"No," he moaned, but the men behind him only tightened their grip on his shoulders. "Don't! Please, God. Don't touch it."

"The moisture will cause infection," Kemble shouted over him. She pulled a thin knife from her apron and slit the boot up the side.

He screamed.

"Oh my." A startled gasp escaped the nurse's throat, even as she moved to cut his hose away with her shears.

Lilac stepped around her father's warding arm.

Blooming in a mosaic of purple and red, his foot was bent in an unnatural form. The last two toes curled back, as if they'd been cracked off their joints, and his outer ankle was smashed in. Some of the skin had been torn across his shin, revealing the bones and meat underneath.

She glanced away from the mess of flesh. Her ears were ringing. There was no way he'd hidden pain that great without magic. Without faerie ether, a spell, or *entrancement*.

"What happened?"

He began to stutter, but every word turned into a whimper. Kemble fished in her apron and pulled out a flask. After a couple large swallows Armand groaned and, still shaking violently, said, "Vivien is dead. And she was killed by *your* vampire."

THE HALL ERUPTED WITH NOISE—THE COUNCILORS ASKING WHAT HE meant, what she knew, her father demanding the duke be shut up, Kemble losing all her normal decorum and shrieking about the vampire, retreating against the southern wall. It all seemed to fade into the background as Armand stared at Lilac, a sick grin that felt all too familiar on his sweat and grime-slicked face. A grin she'd seen on his son's face—one that told her the man she thought could be trusted was about to violate her.

One she'd never cower before again.

In one motion, she drew her dagger from her skirts and slammed its pommel on the desk. She cleared her throat in the moment of silence that followed.

"I will ignore your blatant accusation against the crown without a speck of evidence—for now," Lilac said from behind her desk, glad she had it to hide her hands against. Her nails were picked to nubs. "You expect us to believe that a vampire got past you, your entire guard and staff, and killed your wife? And you escaped to tell the tale? What of Sinclair?"

The duke's smile turned into a snarl. "My servants are useless, and my guards just stood there and watched! And my son was hiding under the stairs, clutching a bloody ax, likely from trying to defend his mother. Don't pretend to not know the wiles of vampires, girl..."

A collective gasp was heard around the room.

"You will address me as *Your Majesty*." She met his petulant glare with one of her own, even as her mind spun. Had it been Garin? "And where were you as this was occurring, Your Grace?"

For the first time, Armand's accusatory hysteria faltered. "I—I had been for a walk around the garden and only discovered the scene after it had occurred. The vampire was waiting to gloat."

Lilac's gut eased as understanding dawned, only to be quickly replaced with an echo of dread. "Ah, yes. I'm sure the air is refreshing so late at night."

Henri spoke next. "I'm not understanding, or perhaps you take us for idiots. You found your son bloodied and with an ax, yet your blame is on the vampires?"

Armand leaned forward. "I know what I saw. I know what I heard, Henri. The devil spoke to me. He urged me to come here, to give her *that*." His eyes flickered from the package on the desk to Lilac. "She knows of him!"

Lilac kept her face straight as she could. This was a simple game of words. "If you wanted to accuse my family of sending a vampire to assassinate Vivien, you could have at least granted us a private audience."

Armand's grimace turned into a scowl. He combed Lilac's face for some buried truth—for the smallest trace of the guilt.

There was none, she felt absolutely no guilt besides the shock. In fact, she couldn't help the small smirk that arose.

And that was when he lunged.

With his damaged foot and hand, he didn't get far, but she still fell back against her desk in shock. There were screams, but they faded into the background as the guards piled on top of him.

"You did this!" he snarled as they tugged him away, wrestling his arms behind him and snapping them into handcuffs.

Next to her, Henri was shakily returning his blade to its sheath.

You did this. If only. She could name several kings who would've had the whole Le Tallec family executed for interrupting an accession with a fit of hysteria, and no one would blink an eye.

Everyone waited for her order, but she could only stagger to her feet, shrugging off her father's offered hand. Her skin crawled under the weight of the duke's stare. Even after everything, the hatred in his eyes somehow still surprised her. Long ago, before she knew anything about how their politics worked, she had seen him and Vivien as an aunt and uncle, close friends and confidantes of her parents' court who had sworn to protect her and her family.

Now she saw in his eyes the same look of loathing Vivien had given Lilac as she passed her on the way to the keep at her accession. It was the same bitter astonishment from Sinclair from atop the ramparts just before he'd noticed Garin.

How did you succeed when I planned your downfall so carefully?

"Armand, it is a shame Sinclair was found holding the ax, but you have done the right thing in reporting him. What a commendable act of loyalty to your wife."

The guards held him in place beside the chairs. A puddle had formed beneath him as he trembled on one leg. It had been his good foot that was smashed in. "You think my son was capable of *that*?"

She pushed herself off the desk and approached him, ignoring Henri's warning grumble. "You don't want to know the things your boy is capable of." She looked down on him, and it felt good to watch his face drain. "As for this vampire, I think it reasonable to assume it was drawn by the scent of blood."

"*He* was the one who murdered Vivien. Cut her up and situated her like a Sunday roast."

"And yet you admit to not being there to see him in the act. The treaty states that bloodshed and murder are outlawed on both ends, unless in self-defense. What reason would a vampire have to attack a noble family, unprovoked? The raid was the last instance of vampiric violence recorded." She peered at him. "And why would he kill Vivien? What vendetta would he have against your wife, Armand?"

"I was—" He stopped, realizing what he would reveal. An unspoken recognition flashed in his glare.

"You were what? Where were you before discovering Sinclair and Vivien?" No answer came. She turned to her father and his councilmen. "I have decided he will remain detained for now. Meanwhile, please send a carriage of guards to their estate to assess the scene and arrest Sinclair."

"Have it leave after Lilac does," Henri grunted to the councilmen, to her surprise. "An investigation in town should not coincide with her visit."

They exchanged glances, but a cry of outrage from Armand brought their attention back to the duke.

"Such cruelty," he ground out as they wrenched him to his knees. "To arrest the one who came to you for help, who was your father's charge all these years. What law have I broken?"

"Where should I begin? You said you found her body upon returning to your home." Her temper swelled with each word. It was preferable to the anxiety building behind it. She refused to look at her father. He must be breaking to see his friend that way. "This means you were out of your home, does it not? Before the terms of your house arrest were lifted? This was before you falsely blamed me for Vivien's death and tried to put your hands on me."

"Your Majesty." He scuffled forward, the chains on his arms clunking taut.

"You cannot bargain for your freedom!" Her voice cracked across the room. "You didn't come to me for help." There was no room for mercy. It was strange, raising her voice at him. It should have been liberating, but cold unease filled her. "You came to accuse me."

"He ordered me to come here. To tell you of the scene I came home to, and to give you that." He nudged both shackled hands toward her. Past her.

The bag he'd brought lay untouched on the desk where she'd deposited it.

"I would have run far and never looked back," he choked out. "You would have never heard from me again, but he said I needed to deliver this gift to you. He en—" Armand's face twisted, the veins at his temple throbbing. "He *made* me."

Armand looked down, horrified at the memory.

"What is it?" Her ears were ringing. "What is it you wish to give me?"

"He did not tell me."

Something told her he was telling the truth. She reached for it, but Henri and his advisors grunted their alarmed disapproval.

"Lilac," Henri growled.

She ignored him and grabbed the drawstring corner of the bag, heart pounding. Knowing Garin, if any of this was true, it was probably a sword or relic of some kind. Surely it couldn't be worse than Kestrel's unopened letter awaiting her upstairs, tucked deep into her drawer.

Henri moved for the desk, but Lilac was quicker. She snatched it away from him.

"It's mine." There was no reason—none Henri or anyone else knew of—

that she should feel so possessive over the unknown item. She reddened. "He said it was for me."

"But if this is truly a gift from the vampires..." He passed a hand over his face as if he couldn't believe what he was saying. "I must ensure it is not meant to harm you."

Armand, whose hysterical demeanor had calmed into sudden relief, abruptly tried to get up. His eyes bulged when his friend took the bag from her. "N-no. It must be her. It must be Lilac."

"I won't look," Henri said quietly, doing his best to ignore the shouts of his friend. "We'll do it together."

In her absence, Sinclair had told everyone she'd run off with the vampires by choice. Did Henri believe any of it? Or was he just grateful she'd been returned alive and mostly unscathed?

Lilac exhaled sharply. "Fine."

Henri shifted closer, his hands on the lip of the bag. She nodded at him, then he tugged it open and tipped it out over the desk.

Something limp slid out, landing with a *plop*.

Her heart nearly stopped.

At first she couldn't tell what it was. For a second, she wondered if Garin had given her a large parsnip, but then her vision focused on the glinting materials that adorned one pale end and the nub of rot and filth at the other.

The stench made her gag immediately. "It's—oh my—"

It was an arm. A bruised forearm, chopped clean at the elbow.

She stumbled backward and nearly fell over Henri, who was already bent at the hip, vomiting. The councilmen had scuttled into the far corner of the room, one of them fumbling over what appeared to be his rosary. Madame Kemble was wide-eyed and entranced by the limb, not seeming as jarred as the others. Her face twisted in a mixture of disbelief and disgust as she made her way to the desk.

Armand had turned white as a ghost and was moaning loudly into a handkerchief one of the guards had pressed against his mouth. He was shaking violently again; suddenly he lurched away from the guards and his hands slowly raised—on their own accord.

"What's happening?" Armand shrieked. An invisible force lifted him as the guards retreated in panic, stumbling over each other.

BRIAR SOMERSET

The duke suddenly quieted, his groans reduced to whimpering as his shoulders shifted and the guards at his side began backing away. He was supporting himself, kneeling.

Everyone was distracted by the limb on the desk and the putrid aroma lifting from it. No one, and certainly not the spooked guards, anticipated the duke reaching into his shirt. Only Lilac seemed to register the rusted blade he pulled out.

Armand looked around the room one last time before he pointed the blade inward, on himself.

She choked out in anguish when he muttered something under his breath—a prayer, a last plea—before he looked up at her, eyes filled with terror, and cried, "Save me, Your Maj—" before cutting himself short, sinking the blade halfway into his own chest.

2

The surrounding guards lowered their drawn blades as the duke slumped over, the life still fading from his twisted face when he hit the floor and rolled, the hilt of the smallsword sticking out of him.

They stood, listening, watching him suffocate on his own blood. It trickled from his mouth, some soaking the front of his shirt. Eventually the wretched sound of his rasping breath faded, and there was a brief moment where it felt like a breeze swept through the closed room, a sigh of relief that the magic had departed.

John, who'd been still documenting the scene to her left, exchanged glances with her; at the look on her face his eyes widened, and he set the quill and paper down. It hung off the edge of the desk, his scratched scrawl spanning at least half a meter.

Sweeping the strands of her escaping hair off her cheeks, Lilac extended an arm and put her hand out. It eerily mirrored the hand on the table, whose jewel-adorned fingers curled daintily inward.

"Give it to me."

"B-but is court still in session, Your Majesty?"

"It is clearly over." She flexed her palm and he handed it to her, then scuttled away from the arm as if he'd been so immersed in jotting down every detail that he was noticing it for the first time. She grabbed it and marched to the top of the stairs. No one protested when she chucked the length of it into the roaring fireplace, where it was engulfed in flames.

No one in the room had seemed to actually believe the arm was a gift from the vampires before Armand killed himself, but it was now clear some sort of magic was at play. "He had many enemies," she said, doing her best to force the tremble from her voice as she stared into the fire. "He and Vivien live with the back of their estate surrounded by the Low Forest, and they proved to be traitorous to the crown. Who knows what trouble they were in, what vendettas were cast against them of their own doing."

It was so quiet, she heard her father exhale before speaking. "We cannot hide the deaths of the duke and duchess."

She turned. The guards stood motionless around Armand's lifeless body. "I said nothing of the sort. In his madness, Sinclair murdered and dismembered his mother. Armand and his driver came here to request an audience and deliver the terrible news."

Perane approached from the corner, huddled over his rosary. "But Your Majesty, others witnessed them enter the bailey in that state."

"Good. Grief is a terrible thing, isn't it? It can make people do things." She descended the stairs, preparing to leave the room, but her father beckoned her to the corner of the desk.

"What about the vampires?" Henri asked quietly.

"What of them? We have no proof. No bite marks."

"But they were certainly spelled; you cannot deny that." When she didn't respond, he glanced to their left, to the desk, where Lilac refused to bring her gaze. "What do you want done with that?"

"I want it gone."

One of the guards gingerly retrieved the limb and placed it back into its bag. Only after the guard exited through the courtyard door could she breathe again. She was distantly aware of Henri demanding everyone in the room swear their secrecy—that nothing of this would be spoken, and a public announcement of their death would be revisited post-investigation. Kemble, the last to leave for the keep along with John, muttered that she suspected there was not a drop of blood left in the limb due to its coloring. She left, promising she'd be back with some of the staff to tidy the room before lunch.

Now alone with her father, Lilac felt his gaze heavy on her. Face red, the lump in her throat the only thing holding back tears, she sidestepped him and walked toward the door she'd come through.

"You're still leaving this evening, aren't you?"

"Yes. There will not be any changes to my plans."

There was a sloshing of liquid as he slipped the flask hanging from his belt; she couldn't tell earlier if he'd been drinking prior to Armand's arrival, but if he had, he was certainly well sobered by now.

"You're going to buy a dress?"

At his tone, Lilac turned around. "I am. Mother and I agreed it would be a fine opportunity for me to find a gown for my coronation ball from the new shop in Paimpont."

"She did not agree. You told her, and she vehemently protested."

"That may be true, but the conversation I recall ended in me standing by my decision to visit the seamstress."

"It's a haberdasher."

"Her father was the haberdasher," she reminded him for the second time since she'd informed him of her plans in the middle of the week. "She kept the business name, having inherited the haberdashery from her father and grandfather. She's a clothier, and fashions mother's new hats and gowns as well."

Henri stared at her, his eyes rising to her head. "They're *wigs*."

Lilac raised her arms to straighten the towering powdered construction Marguerite had started wearing and even forcing upon her, and shrugged.

Henri's eye twitched. "You haven't *announced* a visit, have you?"

"No." She glared, waiting for him to continue. "But I'm not changing my plans."

"So you've said. But you shall bring a horseback guard."

"One of our steeds would indicate royal travel." She preferred not to bring an extra person that might end up being someone's dinner, but she had expected this demand. It would be impossible to leave without a guard on her father's watch.

"Then he will have a commoner's horse or ride on the driver's bench. But he is *going*."

"Fine. I welcome him and his horse on my journey," she ground out, determined this trip remain under her control. Her own planning.

Henri's mouth drew into a hard line, and he stepped closer, placing his hands upon her shoulders. "Lilac."

"Henri."

"Two men died in your presence this evening." It could've been the shifting shadows of dusk, but the bags under his eyes appeared deeper. His voice dropped to a whisper. "You must be careful. People are paying attention, Lilac. They are interested in you."

"They have *been* interested, Father." His warning felt similar to what Garin had said in her chamber. She flexed her fingers into fists. "I have fed the town rumor mill for years. You forget that this is nothing new."

"It is *all* new!" At his volume, she stepped away from him, and the former king lifted his arms, helpless. "And they are not interested in gossip. That is not what I meant."

Who else would be interested in... *What* else?

Heat flooded through her as his words sank in. "*No.*"

"Yes. It is time we had the conversation." His mouth was taut. He would not drop it.

And he was right not to, as much as she hated it. She was a girl who had been locked away as punishment for something she'd been taught to hate about herself, and when she'd finally escaped, she emerged as both a woman and a queen, with no time to sort out what either meant for herself.

Lilac might have been naive and young—and perhaps she *would* have been, Daemon tongue or no. But she hadn't asked for any of this. And she still had to face her duty. Even if the only way she knew how was with stubbornness.

"You have said to me before that there is no requirement of marriage."

Her father shook his head, and his mustache trembled. Shook it a little too hard. "And you are correct. But official requirement and prudent arrangement aren't so far apart, my dear. Marriage offers you safety and protection. It creates allies and strengthens borders against current and future threats."

"If I am entrusted to protect the creatures and people of this kingdom, then I would think I am able to protect myself, Father." Her voice began to tremble in anger.

He flinched at her mention of Daemons. "You cannot. You are a woman."

"Then why not assign me a fencing master? A cartographer in my lessons to learn how to navigate a map and arrange armies? Why was I stuck in a fortress with books and tutors and nowhere to go? Why not let me have both?" *Why didn't you prepare me for this role*, she wanted to scream at him. But they both knew why, and it was far too late to do anything about it now.

He had no answer.

Lilac straightened. "I will not marry, and I will not be forced. If you truly care for me, you will let this issue lie."

Henri's jaw tightened. He sidestepped to block her attempt to leave, loudly slamming his fist upon the desk. "Do not lecture a father on how to care for his daughter," he roared. "Here sat a dismembered arm from a murdered member of our house. A former member of *my* court. Two men *died* before you, in our very castle, this afternoon!" He looked around, even if they were alone, and lowered his voice. "France is likely scouting our borders."

She jolted and took a step back. "The boy—"

"Yes, that boy you ordered away, out in the hall? His father spoke the truth. Our guards received a pigeon in the early hours of the morning from the street sentries outside La Guerche, warning of smoke signals clear in the night. They investigated and found a small camp of soldiers."

Her throat tightened as he glared at her. "Were they armed?"

"Lightly. They told our sentries they'd gotten lost. Our men had them leave immediately, which they did."

"Perhaps it was just that," she pushed, wanting too badly to believe. La Guerche was right within her border. Anyone could get lost in the thick forests there. "A camp."

Henri rubbed his face, pinching the bridge of his nose. "You are this gullible. And you're telling me you don't need protection? And you're about to go to town? It's madness."

"I'm safe in the woods. I'll stay on the path," she lied.

He stepped back, the disappointment in his face very nearly disgust. "What have you seen in Brocéliande?" He swallowed roughly, as if any reminder of her time in that enchanted wood was still jarring for him. "What happened that made you so... so unmoved?"

"The friends you and mother considered as family, plotting to overthrow me. That's what." She watched her words sink in. "Vivien deserved it. She was a horrible person."

Henri neared, got in her face, his own now purple with anger. "Never repeat that outside this room."

She swallowed, tears loosening without her permission. Her mind spun with the new information thrown at her, compiled on her nerves for the evening. How was Henri so blind—how had both of her parents missed it? Even if they chose to remain blind to the fact that Daemons were no more inherently evil than humans could ever be, they still refused to stand against the Le Tallecs in a way that mattered. It was so difficult not to fault Henri and Marguerite for their lack of protection of her. They'd been too preoccupied with protecting their own reputation. He searched her face, but she pressed her lips together.

"What of the vampires?" he asked again. It was clear he would not let it drop.

"And what of men? What of serpents in one's own court who disguise themselves as allies and wait for the perfect moment to usurp the crown? What of boys who use their titles as shields as they terrorize whatever and whomever they want until they are satisfied?"

She bent, grasping the hem of her gown and tugging one side up to reveal the long scar that ran from mid shin, across her right knee and to her lower thigh. The bruises and scrapes were healed, but the shadows of scars were still visible, pink and raised. Her dagger was visible, tucked beneath her sheer stockings, but he didn't seem to notice or care.

Henri's eyes hardened.

"This is from fighting off Sinclair the night he returned to tell everyone I'd run off with vampires." She turned back to the door. "Vampires were never whom I needed saving from, Father."

Lilac found Yanna and Isabel waiting at the top of the steps.

She greeted them with a curt nod, not bothering to hide the sheen on her cheeks and swollen eyes as they trailed her to her bedroom. Taking turns speaking as if they had rehearsed their speech, they informed her a hot bath was drawn, her travel bag set on the bed, and her trunk loaded onto the trolley downstairs. It had been packed for one week's time at her request—even if, they reminded her, she would be gone only for a full day at most.

As soon as she reached her door, she bid her maids good night and requested they send up two staff members from the scullery before dismissing them, shutting the door, and locking it.

Lilac expected the knots of dread in her chest to unfurl once she was finally alone, but as she yanked her curtains shut and fumbled with the ribbons at her waist, they only grew tighter, constricting her from within. In the past week she'd barely eaten, her sleep schedule erratic as she'd dreaded the meeting and facing Kestrel. She was nervous enough.

Once out of her gown, she hastily scrubbed the thick layer of powder off her face and lowered herself into the bath, where rose hips swirled around her shoulders and clung to her skin. Willing herself to focus on the heat, inhaling the fragrant steam, she slid to focus on the smear of orange light streaming in from beyond her bed.

It was where he had bitten her. Where he'd held her. Even that thought made her stomach flutter.

The next day, Garin was roaming the halls as Father Guillaume's replacement again, throwing solemn, if not lazy, glances her way as if none of it had ever happened. He'd then disappeared for what felt like ages, only to show up again the next Sunday to assist the priest they invited from the Paimpont abbey with Mass, feigning all too well the appearance of a young, disheveled deacon—Budoc, they called him—who had learned too late into his vocation that he despised his work.

Henri was quick to suggest sending him back to the clergy in St. Malo, where he'd claimed to be from, and it was this dismissal that had cleverly brought Garin's disguised time at the castle to an end. She hadn't seen him in a little over a week.

How, then, had he done it? When?

Her hands shook as she washed herself, swallowing bile. She shut her eyes, trying to block out the image burned in her mind, not wanting to think of the state of rot or the stench of the arm, or the rest of her body.

The leader of the Brocéliande vampire coven was a lethal sort of showman, after all. That's who he was. He would not pander tact where he saw brutality more fitting.

But it was Garin she'd gotten to know during their short journey together. The vampire who made her laugh, who protected and challenged her. Who'd led her to his parents' farmhouse, knowing they'd be safe there. He'd taken her and made her come until she felt her body and soul would split beneath him. That night they left his home knowing more of each other, yet nothing at all.

She'd see him tonight and had no idea what to expect.

Teeth chattering, she dragged herself from the bath and threw a piece of wood onto the fire before collecting Kestrel's unopened envelope from her drawer. Handling it at the corner as if it might combust, she tucked it deep into her travel bag, which she'd packed with her little comforts. She could open it there, where she felt safe.

There was a dress the color of ivy laid across the chair near her vanity. Although the gold embellishment against it made it fussier than she preferred, it was light enough for summer travel and had a built-in corset, so she donned the dress herself. In front of the fireplace, Lilac slid her dagger down the side of her garter and pulled on one of the thick cloaks from her armoire, hoping to shake the cold that would not leave her.

Garin had killed Vivien in cold blood; that was, to her chagrin, the most believable part of all this. Why would he send Armand to her with an arm? Why hadn't he done it discreetly—why the need for this charade? If she was supposed to be finalizing the draft for the Accords tonight, a new treaty to protect Daemons from the cruelty and prejudices of her kingdom, why would he make his revenge such a public ordeal?

The sun was under the treetops when she was ready to leave. Lilac grunted, hoisting the travel satchel onto her back, when a rapid knock came at the door.

"You'll ruin your posture. *Further*," her mother squeaked, eyeing the bag as she pulled the door open, two fingers pressed to her lips in disapproval before waving them at the bowing pair of flour-dusted men at her rear. Two of Hedwig's aides, as she'd requested.

"Loading the carriage so early?"

Lilac stepped into the hall, taking her time before answering her mother. Uttering her thanks to the men, she gestured to the half bushels of grain she'd deposited next to her fireplace.

"Departing, actually."

Marguerite crossed her arms and watched them hoist the large bags out of the room and down the stairs. "You can always requisition your donations to the business in question instead of hoarding them in here like some paranoid peasant. I thought you told us you'd leave after dark?"

"I've got this one, thank you," Lilac told the last gentleman, who put a hand out for her satchel. She gave him a gracious smile to spite Marguerite's disapproving frown as he bowed and departed. "Well, I considered your strongly worded advice from yesterday, and I agree with you. It *isn't* safe to travel at night." Marguerite had begged her to cancel her trip. "There's plenty of sun out for another hour or so."

Marguerite's glare lessened. It faded altogether when she stepped back and regarded the queen's proper clothing and neatly brushed hair. Squinting suspiciously, she craned to peek into the cracked doorway of Lilac's quarters.

"Are you looking for something?" Lilac asked, edging toward the staircase. "For someone?"

"Where are Yanna and Isabel?"

"I dismissed them for the rest of the day."

The strain in the former queen's voice matched the vein growing more evident at the middle of her forehead. "They're here to—to—"

"To monitor me."

"*Protect* you."

"What is it they need to protect me from? Who? The two of them together don't do half the job Piper did."

Lilac waited, silently daring her to mention the Daemons or the vampires Sinclair had told everyone she'd run away with.

But Marguerite merely turned to face Lilac after glancing once more into her open doorway, her own fine gown twirling around her ankles, eyes slitted. "That Piper girl did anything but keep you from danger. I don't know what came over you to make these plans before I could help prepare you for a public appearance."

Her mother's forehead creased, her lip pouted. Years ago, a younger

Lilac would have fallen for it—believed that Marguerite was truly concerned for her safety and not her own reputation.

"I am the queen," Lilac calmly reminded her. "I can make whatever plans I choose."

Her still demeanor irked Marguerite even more. She scoffed. "A queen who knows *nothing* of the world."

"And whose fault is that?"

"Certainly not mine." Marguerite shuddered, as if the thought of shouldering the blame horrified her far more than any temporary comfort she could give her daughter. "It was not I who filled your head with whatever delusion caused you to learn to do *that*."

Marguerite's words stung like a slap.

"Learn?" Lilac gripped the bannister. "You believe I taught myself the arcana lingua?"

Her mother's eyes narrowed at the term. "How else would you have learned?"

She didn't have an answer. It was a deeply ingrained language meant for Daemons. She was an anomaly; that's what Adelaide had said. Either way, it didn't matter now—she was on her way to see Garin and those she dared call acquaintances. Friends, even.

Marguerite, on the other hand, had started to cry. "I admire Herlinde's work more than anyone, but why her when you can have anything custom made and delivered? Any designer would be honored. *Any* clothier would be thrilled to work with you, to come here."

"I would like to welcome her to Paimpont and support her new business venture there."

She shuddered. "This is your coronation ball, not a charity, for goodness' sake. And with how close we are to the date, you'd need to work with a *professional* seamstress accustomed to sewing finery for royalty on short notice; they often have partially sewn gowns on hand ready to customize." Marguerite cleared her throat, miffed. "For a coronation ball you should have a custom piece, but beggars can't be choosers."

She ignored her mother's jabs. "You seem happy with Herlinde's gowns. Does she not have any of these partially sewn gowns on hand?" The one Marguerite wore was beautiful—a morning glory blue with silver stitching.

"No." Marguerite made a face, crossing her arms. "I'm not sure, I've never been. I started purchasing from her last autumn, back when the Rennes location was her only shop. She'd agreed to sew for me based on my measurements and send the dresses to me, since I would have been laughed out of town if I'd visited myself, thanks to *you*." Her tear-streaked eyes widened, her heavy powder running down her face. "Perhaps you can do the same. Then you wouldn't need to leave tonight."

Appalled, Lilac reached past her to shut her bedroom door. Marguerite all but fell forward with a sob, nearly knocking her down the steps.

"*Mother!*"

Marguerite grabbed her wrist with an alarming urgency. "You are to find a husband soon, Lilac. By the time of your ball. If you do so, it will make a public statement of your intentions to marry, join forces—"

"Mother—"

"The ball invitations just went out. It's not too late. Many betrothals last barely two weeks. Some, days!"

She tried to shake the woman off, but Marguerite held on tight. "Let go of me." She'd told them she would be crowned without a husband, even when Sinclair and his parents had tried to impose themselves on her during her ceremony after there was real fear she'd been kidnapped or purposefully abandoned her duties. They'd never countered her marriage refusal before she left the castle—maybe that was only because Sinclair was the obvious choice, and in their minds he would become her husband, if not upon her taking the throne, then eventually.

Since her accession, not a soul had mentioned marriage to her until today.

She laughed, disbelieving. But there was not a glint of humor or even malice in Marguerite's expression.

"Is this about the scare this morning?"

"A *scare*? I would hardly call the possibility of France scouting our borders for the path of least resistance to us a *scare*. It should be taken seriously. Marriage will save you. The future of this kingdom rests on it. Your sovereignty rests on it." Her mother's eyes were hard as she released her. "We cannot afford another war."

They'd barely made it out of a century sandwiched between two of Europe's largest enemy forces. Dread over what she faced after the Accords meeting—how she was to ensure the survival of her country, the protection of her people and the Daemons—began to fill her.

"Has François not bothered sending someone? A letter, with his demands?"

Her mother shook her head.

"Is that not custom for such a powerful kingdom? He can't at least extend me a formal extension?"

"Extension for what?" Marguerite glared at her daughter skeptically.

"For marriage," Lilac snapped.

Marguerite blinked twice. Unlike Henri, her mother held nothing back. "No, silly girl. What aren't you understanding? He doesn't want your hand. He wouldn't try to force you into a ceremony. That would be merciful. Why do you think he'd send scouts in the first place? This is nothing new, France has had its eye on Brittany for centuries—you *know* this. Wars have been waged. In the past we've pledged allegiance to them and signed treaties with them, but we'd always remained our own."

Lilac began shaking her head, not wanting to believe.

"You're right. If he wanted to approach this formally, he would have sent a messenger or a letter. You are an unmarried woman inheriting a crown. Other men will be falling at your feet. Powerful, obscure. Rich, poor. And he knows that. He wants your *kingdom*."

Lilac held the banister for support, her mother's hysterics a heavier weight than the grasp on her wrist. She didn't want to think of what would happen to Brocéliande after the fires from the last war had blazed through the Argoat. During the century they spent in and out of battle, her ancestors were tossed between the rulers of England and France like a ball between angry children.

If it showed those watching one thing, it was that the Kingdom of Brittany, its duchies and its royal family could be powerful allies to any foreign power. She wondered if her ancestors on the throne had been so agreeable because it proved a boon to be attached to a larger, more powerful kingdom in some way or another. They'd stood on their own thereafter, but her parents were right...How long until that changed? How would her small kingdom stand in the great scheme of things if their sovereignty was something she wanted to keep?

An all too familiar fear thrummed through her. "I am not surrendering. Marriage would not help me."

"What do you think would happen to you, to our family, even if you surrendered peacefully to France?" Marguerite gave her hand a small, unfamiliar squeeze, her mouth lifting in a sad smile.

In her panic over marriage and the overthrow of her kingdom, she hadn't thought of that. They would likely be executed.

"You and I are *very* different." Marguerite's gaze lingered on Lilac, on the uneven ends of her hair that brushed just past her shoulders now. "I've never been in your position, but we women have certain qualities that give us power. You have the upper hand when you choose your battles and go forth in them. We may not have as much power in society, with or without a crown, but we can choose whom to turn our blades to. Whom we allow into our beds. So, marry someone. Anyone."

"*Anyone?*"

Marguerite released her with a soft snort. "You know what I mean. A king or any titled nobility with neutral relations—from an allied kingdom that is not France, of course. It can work a number of ways. If you give your hand to a king, your throne is shared, your power becomes his. You can also marry nobility in high favor of their king. That way, you might keep your crown with a prince consort at your side, and the ruler of *their* kingdom will align themselves with us, making for a more powerful combined army. A more formidable threat."

"Anyone," she echoed again, her voice faraway.

"Don't say it like that, Lilac. Anyone with the means to stand beside you, protect you. Anyone eligible who won't humiliate you. You refuse to relinquish your throne for a man, so you'll make it clear in your negotiations. Access to our ports and agriculture make for a more than reasonable dowry. As well as any children you may bear together."

Dowry. Children. She had barely learned what it was to rule. Her ears were ringing as she turned for the steps, doubt clouding her mind. "I will consider it."

"These are matters to discuss when you return." Marguerite's stare burned the back of her neck all the way down the staircase.

She did not follow.

Fearing the castle would swallow her up, she ran, and didn't slow once she reached the bottom floor. She exited into the courtyard corridor and shouldered the door that led outdoors, then marched forward. She would not be free until she'd left the grounds.

She wasn't safe until Brocéliande welcomed her again.

The carriage was parked near the stable, tucked in the inner corner of the bailey, where the bags were being loaded into the rear trolley. Two muscular, tawny horses waited at the front, and another, prepped for her guard, stood beside them.

As she approached, she marveled at the framework of wood and steel atop four wheels; what should have been a bitter reminder of her first and only time through Paimpont instead filled her with fascination, so much that she momentarily forgot her mounting fury.

A guard emerged from the stables and set his belongings atop the gate to the side. He approached and offered to help her up into the carriage. There was something familiar about him—his rough haircut and round face. Unable to place it, she took his hand and obliged.

"Shall the coachman stop in before we depart, Your Majesty?" he called through the window after shutting the door for her. "He's almost ready to go."

"There's no need," she said, realizing who he was as he spoke. He was the guard who'd caught her attempting to save Garin. He'd lost some of the cherub boyishness to a dutiful puffed chest, perhaps proud he'd been the one tasked with accompanying Lilac. She gave him a forced smile as he bowed and left.

It wasn't long before the coachman arrived, marked by the stomping up the step and a booming voice that floated through the front of the car walls. He knocked thrice.

"Permission to commence our journey, Your Highness?" the coachman shouted a bit too eagerly, rousing a grimace from the horrified guard, who darted a glance in Lilac's direction from atop his own horse.

Lilac couldn't help it. "Permission granted, sir," she laughed, his pleasant mood probably just what she needed to abate her building nerves.

She peeked through the curtains. Guards were lighting the bailey, starting with the torches lining the massive double doors before them. Stations were closing; sentries were changing the evening shift.

Finally, the carriage lurched, and she dug her nails into her palms as they rolled toward the open gateway.

Lilac was free. Free to leave her fortress, both in daylight and in a carriage. Free to travel to one of her towns at a moment's notice, so long as the main roads remained accessible and the weather, fair.

She closed her eyes and tried to focus on the slow rocking of the carriage as they burst into the glow of summer evening.

THEY EMBARKED WITH THE COMPANY OF A LIGHT BREEZE, AS WELL AS the crickets, emerging with the drier season and whose faint song quieted her nerves. Working against that was Giles, as her coachman had introduced himself with an eager shout. He spent the first few moments of their trip loudly telling the guard riding slightly ahead of them—no royal livery visible, to Lilac's relief—about a recent rodent influx in the stables and how he'd enlisted the help of a spoiled barn cat to deal with the matter.

She should've been grateful for any distraction, but she was too nervous, watching and listening out the window. Garin had told her to organize the carriage and that he would take care of the rest. He hadn't lingered long enough to clarify what that entailed.

Giles must have greeted half a dozen carts traveling in the opposite direction over their first hour. Despite her instruction on history and the economy, she was still shocked to find the road that cut through Broceliande so...occupied. It was the turn of the season when crops increased, and with that came an influx of trade. Travelers on horseback and those with produce-filled carts and yawning drivers rode by, possibly with goods for the castle. Or perhaps they'd veer north to Mauron, south toward the riverside estates of Campeneac, or continue west until they hit the sea. The Chateau de Trécesson—and Paimpont by extension—sat at an agricultural crossroads from the growing coastal cities, so the roads were bound to be busy.

It wasn't until they reached a point where the trees bunched together and a dense fog settled in, so thick that the sunlight struggled to reach anything past the road, that travelers grew scarcer, and the false feeling of reassurance from these passersby dwindled.

The road was empty for several minutes when, without warning, the carriage slowed. Giles had stopped talking some minutes ago. At first, she thought they might be allowing a faster carriage to pass, but when she peeked out the back window, she didn't see anything beyond the red-tinged fog of the sunset and dark masses of trees close on either side.

The guard suddenly shouted something unintelligible.

Gravel crunched under the wheels as they came to a rumbling stop. Lilac was already fumbling with the latch of the door when the guard's voice rang out once more, clearer this time.

"I said halt!"

She slipped through the carriage door and squinted into the haze. Nothing could be seen through the mist. She pressed herself into the shadows as her guard shouted again, and a form became visible—an advancing specter. It was obvious they were not interested in halting.

A cloaked figure sat atop an onyx horse with a obsidian mane, its hood obscuring any discernible features. The animal was not sleek like her Camargues or stout like the horses in town or the ones servicing her carriage and guard. The horse and its rider both towered, hulking toward them at a leisurely gait, right down the center of the path.

"We are traveling on official business," her guard shouted. "I command you to move out of our way!"

The figure pulled on the reins and came to a stop in the middle of the road, still blocking their course. Before she could move from her hiding spot beside the wheel, a sharp whistle cut through the air. There was a grunt—a male's voice—and then the mystery rider toppled forward off the horse.

The scream that ripped from Lilac's throat left her lungs raw. She hadn't seen the guard draw his bow; she should have stopped any further interaction before it began. She should have told them she was expecting company.

She darted toward the figure, despite the shouts of the guard and Giles, and dropped to her knees before him. She slid her arm under his neck, cradling him even as he groaned. The horse whinnied and shuffled back a few steps. Then, the man sat up as if there was a kink in his muscle and not a long shaft of wood sticking out of his shoulder.

"I agree to help retrieve your entourage, and this is what I get?"

That voice.

She yelped and shuffled back, dropping the hooded figure. With an irritated sigh, he righted himself and his hood fell back. Dark hazel-green eyes beneath cool blond brows sneered up at her.

The last time she'd looked into those eyes, they'd been red, and she'd been slapped in the face and nearly eaten. She watched from the floor, horrified, as Bastion gingerly straightened, gave her a half-hearted bow and extracted the arrow from his joint with a sickening squelch. He rolled his eyes and extended a calloused hand to her, but she refused, already back to watching the guard. The lad struggled with his bow and another arrow—which weren't made of hawthorn, based on Bastion's recovery.

Lilac shouted for him to stand down—for his own sake—when he raised it again.

It seemed either the boy hadn't heard her order, or he was too afraid for his life to follow. Another bow was shakily fired—but not in their direction this time. It whizzed over them.

"Come now," came a familiar voice, laced with dark amusement.

He was stalking toward them, hands in his pockets, seemingly materializing from the fog. She rose to her feet as he passed her and Bastion, walking toward the guard with a clean arrow in his hand.

Garin motioned hither to the guard. "Try again," he said quietly. *Encouragingly.* "One more time. Try me, I won't kill you. I'll stand still."

Giles gave a supportive clap and holler from the driver's box as the horses secured to the carriage and the one under the guard stomped nervously. All the blood drained from the poor fellow's face. His fate had been sealed the moment he'd been assigned to her journey.

Next to her, Bastion ran a hand over his face. "He is so dramatic."

Despite standing still with his arms out, the second arrow would have flown past Garin's body if he hadn't caught it too. He sighed and shook his head as he made his way to the guard's horse.

He hushed the nervous animal and, with what must have been an enormous amount of self-control, ignored the trembling arrow pointed in his face. Before the guard could react, Garin's hand was wrapped around the tip of the arrow he was struggling to nock.

He was trembling so hard that she barely heard him choke out a plea for his life.

She moved to approach them, but froze when the guard nodded at Garin. Blood was beginning to return to his face slowly but surely. Garin was speaking, slowly and quietly. With him, not at him. Her insides twisted, and she imagined the way a snake or cat toyed with their prey before devouring them, coaxing their victims to calm. It was what had happened with Piper. With Renald.

The guard then reached down to shake Garin's outstretched hand as if they were friends striking a casual deal. As if the boy wasn't so close to becoming someone's dinner. All fear had dissipated from the guard's expression.

Speaking of, Giles didn't seem caught off guard by the vampires' arrival at all. He was waving Garin over.

"Young lad, I brought your tool, as requested." He shook a palm-sized tin in the air. Its contents rattled along with it. He looked around before continuing his inquiry, tapping his fingertips together. "And I was wondering, erm, where might this er... this soup be?"

Garin suppressed a laugh as he retrieved the tin. "Patience, my friend. We're nearly there."

Friend? He seemed in an exceptional mood tonight, and the furthest thing from the bloodthirsty sort of creature capable of murdering the duchess and arranging her dismembered body upon a dining table. Perhaps he hadn't done it, and he would address it with her now. He would reassure her he was not involved, that his ravenous brother was instead to blame.

But when Garin turned slowly and their eyes locked as he made his way back to her, she knew she was wrong.

He wore a cream-colored shirt, this time with a tan vest tucked into a pair of canvas trousers and his usual black boots. The same baldric he'd stolen from Sinclair's guards wrapped snugly around his shoulder, and the ivory and gold hilt of the longsword he'd once pressed against the marquis's heart bounced behind him as he approached her, as did his mop of black hair. It was a bit less tousled than usual, some of it artfully swept to the side and maybe even brushed.

She couldn't help but watch the curve of his lips as he grinned. The air seemed to crackle as he closed the space between them.

"I may or may not have told him about Lorietta's mushroom pottage." Garin swept his index finger under Lilac's hanging jaw. "It is not very queen-like to stare with your mouth open."

"Told him?" She swatted his hand away. "You mean you entranced my driver."

The smile never left Garin's face, and it widened now. "Negotiated with. He drives a hard bargain."

With his hands behind his back, he bowed to her ever so slightly. The scent of summer hyacinths and woodsmoke wafted off of him, and she resisted the urge to throw her arms around him.

"Tell me," he breathed. "Who assigned that sorry excuse for your guard, and who is in the business of training them?"

She jumped as Bastion left their side—she'd somehow forgotten he was there—and sauntered toward the carriage. He held the bloody arrow out to the guard and muttered, "You probably lose these a lot," before swinging open her carriage door and hopping in, shutting it behind him.

Garin eyed Lilac expectantly with his arms crossed.

"My father assigned him," she said, face heating, "but it was the man who paid me an unexpected visit today to tell me of his wife's tragic death who was in charge of training them."

He released her. "I don't seem to recall."

"Armand."

"Ah, the duke." He nudged a sizable stone with the toe of his boot; it should have bounced, but instead, it launched like a pebble into the brush. "Doesn't that fellow have a bad leg?"

She ignored his inquiry. "He actively trained them before his carriage accident. Any incoming guards were supposed to be trained by Sinclair."

Garin's brows rose at her explanation. He hummed dryly. "My memory serves me differently. I thought his horse stepped into a clever korikaned trap as he and his riding troupe paraded a mutilated korrigan corpse down this very path. His noble steed landed on his leg."

"I..." She trailed off, unsure of what to say under his expectant stare. "We were only told there was a tragedy." She bowed her head, remembering the way the small creatures had so desperately fallen at her feet when she'd first stumbled upon them.

Of course Armand lied about the nature of his injury.

The winds of the forest picked up, ruffling Lilac's hair, then Garin's. His nostrils flared.

"No one should be hunted for sport," she croaked.

"Indeed. So, I don't know that I would call either of those accidents *tragic*. What I think," he said, beginning to circle her, "is that the duke and duchess received their dues."

The way the dying sunlight filtered through the trees, casting his dark hair in red and softening his features, made it difficult to look away.

Bastion shouted something out the carriage window, and Giles made an onward motion to the guard, then prompted his own horses. The carriage jolted forward. As they rolled past, Giles waved, and Bastion made an obscene gesture at her and Garin before he leaned back and yanked the curtains shut, safe from the last rays of sun.

Garin's eyes flashed in anger over her shoulder at him, but when they turned to her they were already softer. Kinder. He offered his hand.

Glad for the space, even if Garin's brother was perfectly capable of hearing every word if he wanted to, Lilac inhaled the evening air, taking in its damp earth and sweet flora. There were several scathing words on the tip of her tongue, but they all melted away the moment her skin touched his.

He lifted her palm to his mouth, and instead of kissing the back of her hand, flipped it and pressed his lips to the inside of her wrist as he dipped into a graceful bow. "Your Majesty. You look every bit as inelegant and delicious as I left you."

All she wanted was to feel his lips on her, but she returned his bow with a curtsy. "Our castle has been in turmoil without its patriarch. How will it manage without its impossibly young, handsome stand-in archdeacon?"

His lips slowly quirked. "I have a feeling they will manage just fine."

Garin ignored her withering look and beckoned for her to follow before sauntering toward the now halted carriage and guard a ways down the path, leaving her and the nibbling horse in the middle of the road. She groaned and made to follow them.

"Let's go then," she muttered to the animal.

Not to her surprise, it looked up and snorted dismissively, then went back to the grass.

Garin had circled to the other side of the carriage as he plucked flint, steel, and what looked to be a stout beeswax candle from the tin, then tucked it back under his arm. He shifted, using his shoulders to block the wind; on the third try, the wick burst into a bright green flame that danced violently in the strengthening evening breeze.

Garin lit the lantern dangling from the upper corner of the carriage. The flame in the lantern cage then burst into several shades of green before fading back into orange, causing the guard's eyes to widen—but he did not make the commotion he would have if not under Garin's spell.

He extinguished the candle between his fingers and slid it into the tin with the rest of its contents, then handed it back to Giles, who whistled a rather melancholy tune as he tucked it into the storage box beside the driver's bench.

"You haven't entranced my entire castle, have you?" she said as she approached.

"If I'd entranced everyone, that fellow there would not have been such a terrible shot. He couldn't even hit Loïg."

"Who's Loïg?"

There was then a hot breeze tickling her neck. A large snout appeared beside her, causing her to jump. The a horse—*Loïg*—sniffed at Garin from over her shoulder. She shifted out of the way, unable to take her eyes off the creature; its mane fell straight, reflecting the evening in a gloss that seemed to swallow the remnants of sun. Its tail was the longest Lilac had ever seen on a horse, falling magnificently to its back hoof.

She couldn't help herself. Lilac reached out—the animal seemed fine with this—to run her fingers along the intricate, unfamiliar patterns carved into the saddle. The large piece of leather was shaped differently than those from her kingdom, even distinct from the French or English varieties, sitting atop a thick tapestry spun in jewel-toned colors. Blues, greens, reds, woven between an astonishing gold.

Garin reached out, too, and barely removed his fingers in time to prevent them from being chomped off by its large front teeth. Startled, Lilac stepped back.

"He doesn't like you." The Camargue he'd stolen from Renald seemed to fancy him much more.

"No, he doesn't. I've tried to bribe him with sugar and carrots."

She laughed. "Someone finally not beguiled by your charms."

"He barely let Bastion mount. I'd say he's not a fan of the immortal variety. Perhaps it's the blood drinking." Garin shifted and set a gentle hand upon the small of her back. "Well?"

She withdrew her hand from the horse at his touch. "Well, what?"

"What do you think?"

Her pulse was already erratic, as it always was when his hands were on her. But this time, it felt different. Tonight, their time together felt different. Unhurried, and not urgent. "He's beautiful. Just like his owner."

"I would agree." He sounded like he was suppressing a smirk, but when she turned he was offering his hand. "Let's get you seated."

"Me?" Her gaze flickered between him and the horse. "Are you sure?"

"If you're too timid, he won't let you up."

"I did just see him try to bite you." But she took his hand.

At first, the layers of her dress wouldn't comply. She hiked her skirt up to fit her foot into the stirrup, the breeze refreshing on her bare thigh. She used his arm as leverage to hoist and swing herself up and over the saddle. Once she got adjusted, it hugged her bottom perfectly.

She took a moment, catching her breath. Then, she looked down.

As it had appeared from the ground, this horse was much, much taller than the horse she'd briefly ridden with Garin before. Her vision swam, and she pressed her front against its neck, burying her face in its mane. It didn't seem to appreciate her shifting weight and sputtered loudly, so she sat back up and groaned when it began to walk on its own, its legs shifting beneath her.

"Eyes open," Garin commanded from below, leading them by Loïg's reins away from the side of the carriage.

"It's so tall."

"Get used to it. Your father's Camargues are unfit for battle and should only be used for diplomatic business. The stables in Rennes are alarmingly empty." He spoke matter-of-factly; it wasn't a question. "Do you know if Henri has ordered more destriers to your capital?"

She was stunned into silence, feeling both attacked and shocked at his knowledge. She thought of the developments over the last few hours, her ears heating. There had been no confirmation of anything. "He hasn't. I don't plan on entering a war anytime soon."

Garin didn't seem to notice. "And you shouldn't. But to be caught unprepared is to write your loss in stone. No matter, the stables can be addressed. Loïg is from the north, primed for travel and battle, and his breed becomes attached easily to the right rider. At the moment, he is the safest horse in your personal arsenal." He turned his head partway, and despite the mild warning in his words, his slate eyes were light, his mouth pulled into an approving smile as he surveyed her. "You'll have to learn to ride someday. You'll start now. Loïg is your brute."

She stared at him.

"Happy birthday, Eleanor of Brittany."

Remembering to breathe, she gripped the small bars in front of the saddle for support. Loïg was *her* gift. She'd never learned to ride, and no one had ever gotten her such a... thoughtful, practical, yet unexpected gift. A horse. Her very own. She suddenly felt very far away.

Loïg. A means of the freedom she chased.

"Garin," she hissed.

He'd already turned away, guiding them forth. "Your Majesty?"

"Where did you find him?"

Instead of answering, he only steered them off the road to the right, allowing room for the carriage now slightly behind them to lurch forward.

"Right here, sir, in front of me," Garin called above the grinding wood and clomping horseshoes, holding his arms wide to the trees on the left side of the path. "Between that boulder and thicket right here. The smaller boulder. That's it now."

It was a small clearing in the trees he was pointing to, barely the width of a single horse, filled knee-high with half-dead vines, bluebells, and other tall flora.

Lilac made a sound of warning, but Garin shushed and patted the air. "Watch."

Giles drove the carriage forward, picking up speed before careening right just before them and swinging wide into the clearing, which was much, much too small to even fit the two horses side by side. The carriage

BRIAR SOMERSET

teetered slightly, resulting in a panicked yelp from what must've been a furious Bastion.

Refusing to witness the crash, Lilac turned her head—just in time to shield herself from the warm gust of air that exploded from the tree line, sending soil and grass flying in their direction.

Garin was laughing while Bastion shouted expletives out the window. The clearing was gone, and so were the thicket and boulder. In their place was a gaping entryway flanked by two stone pillars, gargoyles atop them. Beyond, there was a torch-lit cobblestone path, her horses and carriage—and a cheering Giles—rolling right through it.

3

"Ye of such little faith." Garin was suddenly behind her. How he had accomplished this when the horse couldn't stand him, she didn't know, but every thought fled her mind as his arms brushed her sides, his body molding around hers as he reached around her to grab the reins.

Already several trees down the path, Giles had resumed his excited chatter.

There was much to process, and it proved difficult with Garin at her back and the slow, rhythmic movement of the horse. Lilac was speechless.

"We'll find you an instructor." He spoke over her shoulder, inhaling against the curtain of her hair and causing her to shiver. "*If* you need one. Something tells me you're resourceful in times of need. Dire times of need, that is. Meanwhile, you have me." With a tug on the rein, he diverted them into the entrance, and they fell into a trot several paces behind the carriage. The guard then followed, closing off their small traveling troupe.

"Has this entrance always been here?"

"Since around the Hundred Years' War."

They were surrounded by torches—rows of them on each side, about a carriage length between each. The orange flames glimmered with the faintest outline of a wicked sort of green. They reminded her of the bright blue flames that had consumed them on their way to Cinderfell; the magic in them obvious. "Was it warded against humans?"

"By the witches against those not meant to see it." Garin spoke reverently, as if in awe of what the witches had done. "This entire path from entry to the inn, including some of its exterior, is protected by a second-level ward, and the building itself, a third-level ward."

As the trees grew denser, some of them bent over the path, creating a protective arch towering over them. Although the flames were much too close to their branches and leaves, they didn't catch. It all worked together to create quite a charming path.

"You're not going to ask me about the wards?"

She thought of the ward at the korikaned camp, about how she'd sensed the camp within it before the ward had dissipated entirely. A shift in the saddle pressed her closer against him, and she quickly shifted back. Giles was again talking the mouse issue and his heroic cat.

"Do second-level wards contain sound within their barrier?"

"Impressive. That would be a first-level ward—what the one around the korikaned camp *should* have done for you. Under a first-level ward, one can still bump into an object that will appear invisible, which is why the subject must be careful, but that is the easiest type of ward for non-magic folk to enact by way of a charmed object, such as Blitzrik's flint. A second-level ward not only prevents others from perceiving the spelled area, but also interacting with it, like it did for this path and its entry. It's been here for a century or so, and these days only Lorietta's merchants and other known carriages are allowed to access it."

"Lorietta deals with merchants?"

He paused for a moment. "Yes. How do you think she gets her ingredients? Granted, most of the time it's a fellow witch or two going to market days for her, but she does have them stop in from time to time. They know of the wards and have the charms to undo them." He patted the tin on his hip.

She absorbed this information, already hungry for more. "And the third-level ward?"

"Patience," he murmured, resting his wrists against her hips. "You'll see. Lorietta usually leaves it up to the inn."

Lilac turned to look at him, but he nudged her in disapproval. "Up to the inn?"

"Eyes forward. What did the inn look like for you? The outside, I mean."

She hadn't had the chance to study the exterior any longer than it took her to decide it would provide her shelter from the storm and the nest of ogres chasing her.

"Quaint."

"Oh, come now, that's royalty for 'shoddy.'"

"No." She laughed, unable to help herself. "It's royalty for *quaint*. To me, that means aged, well cared-for. It has stood the test of time. Cracked limestone walls, partially rotted wooden framing, chipped red-painted door, a sign warning humans against entering." She shrugged. "Okay, quaint with a side of shoddy."

Garin grunted, and to her surprise, they fell into silence. She hadn't meant to offend him—not this time. It was clear he was more than proud of his place of work—and it was more than where he worked, she reminded herself. The Fenfoss Inn was his home.

"The third-level ward," she reminded him softly.

"That one imbues the inn with a protective discernment charm. Not everyone can do this; it's part of Lorietta's and Meriam's ancestral magic. I'm surprised the inn even showed up for you, if I'm honest, given your family's history. Like with the second-level ward, it can also disappear if needed, and it's been known on occasion to change hats every now and then, depending on what travelers need. Their heart and intention."

"What does that mean?"

"Sometimes it's invisible, undetectable to whoever comes across it. Sometimes it appears as you've described it. And sometimes, she reveals herself wholly. Very rarely. Who knows what you'll see this time?"

It explained why she'd never known about an inn an hour east of her castle or why her parents had never warned her of it. "The night we met, Lorietta had said something about humans occasionally stumbling across it in their travels."

"It shows up for those in need. They are extremely hospitable people, Lori and Meriam—believe it or not. Wanderers in need of a drink, food, or safety can find it on occasion. There had to be some protection from humans like your ex-betrothed and his band of idiots."

She bit the inside of her cheek, chewing on the bitterness of a scathing reply, and decided against it instead.

"The ability to create them that well is rare. Lori and Meriam come from a rather gifted family of magic folk trained in Alteration. The *School* of Alteration, I should say. Emrys is always quick to correct me on proper terminologies. Speaking of, I do hope he is on time tonight. He's our warlock representative for the meeting, but he hasn't been to the inn in almost a week. It's not unlike him to disappear for a couple days, but he hasn't stayed out like this in ages..."

Lilac jerked back, unable to focus on his Emrys tangent. "Schools? Isn't magic inherited?"

"The predisposition for magic is inherited, but there are several subclasses of magic where certain skills can be honed. Five main branches of arcana. Alteration... Illusion. Those are the two I know of."

"Wouldn't a ward be an illusion?"

"Not these types of wards." Although he'd forbade her from taking her eyes off the road, she heard a smile in his voice. He enjoyed talking magic arcana with her. "At their core, they are all perimeter enchantments that alter the space within them. Some creatures and humans cannot interact with the inn or path at all." His voice grew rough, and he lowered it. "The duke's hunting troupe, for example. Anyone who poses a danger."

She thought of Kestrel and the Fair Folk. They were indeed dangerous, seemingly to all. Warding it against them would probably cause more trouble than it was worth. It reminded her of when she was young—the entire castle scrambling, her mother bitching at her father—all because he'd invited François over for an early supper. The king of France, two council members, and a portion of his guard had then sat in their Grand Hall. She didn't think they went over the terms of anything, no treaty or decree signed; it was just tea and a five course meal. Lilac barely recalled being shown to him, bowing with her mother, then being ushered back into her room to play with Piper.

It was perhaps wise to keep one's enemies, or allies suspected to live under a pretense, close. "What would they see if they came here?"

"Nothing. To them, all that fills this space is more of Brocéliande.

They'll walk right through it. Most of our human customers are people who never expect to find an inn in the middle of the woods or who aren't hunting Daemons. They merely seek a reprieve from the weather or the law. The ones that find us don't want us dead. Or even to bother us."

"The Fenfoss Inn found me," she remarked quietly. "It found me when I was running from everything."

"You weren't running. You were desperate for change, for solace. And you made it so. That's probably why the Inn showed itself to you. Either that, or it didn't consider you enough of a threat."

Feeling overwhelmed, Lilac looked up, letting her head fall back. Much of the remaining natural light of dusk was blocked by the archway of greenery above, but the torches and a warm light ahead provided more than enough illumination. Past the carriage and the guard, the dim silhouette of the two-story building came into view.

Ahead, Giles's excited shouting had finally settled, and the guard could be heard conversing back.

"You told me you'd come alone."

Something in Garin's words made her hair stand on end. "In what world would I ever be allowed to do that? Henri insisted I bring someone."

"I'm glad you took his advice. You're thinking of your safety. You should always have a means of protection—myself, or a guard at least—before you've learned to defend yourself." Before she could ask, he scoffed, and there was an edge to it. "It's important you know how if you're going to be with someone like me."

She was breathless at the thought of his hands on her. There was a pooling warmth in her cheeks that spread throughout her body at the sensation of his hardening length up her back. Garin cleared his throat and shifted himself off. Such a gentleman, despite everything. Lilac resisted the urge to arch into him.

"I picked that guard because I knew he was harmless."

"We know *that*."

She rolled her eyes. "What did you tell him earlier that he was so happy about? Before you entranced him."

"I only entranced the fear out of him. I told him he wouldn't be able to protect you from me, at least not with his current armory. I reminded him that ashwood is irritating to Daemons, but hawthorn is potentially lethal to vampires if it gets close enough to our hearts, and so the arrows he shot at us are no more effective than splinters. Told him a hawthorn stake is his best bet against vampires"—he clutched the reins tighter against the outsides of her thighs—"and that is only if, by some miracle, he is able to get close enough. That often requires stealth of hand and blade, neither of which he has."

She considered the mystery of Vivien and Laurent. "He's new. He hasn't had the same training as everyone else."

"Your duke should have taught him in good measure. It's a shame."

Gritting her teeth, Lilac held her tongue. She wouldn't mention it or argue now. Her irritation didn't last long as they began to slow beneath the shadow of the building. As the path curved widely left, their party finally came upon what lay at the end.

THE COBBLESTONE TURNED INTO A HALF CIRCULAR DRIVEWAY THAT wrapped around the front of the inn, simple but large enough to host a five-horse stable on the right of the building. To their left, an array of clay pots were stacked upon a patch of mismatched bricks. Beyond that, in the glow of several lanterns containing green spheres of flame, were the makings of a small garden.

All familiar, yet not at all—and the stable and herb garden weren't the most jarring details.

She moved to dismount the horse, using whatever part of the saddle she could grasp and nearly falling when her foot slipped; Garin, still seated, caught her by the wrist and helped her down. Lilac dusted herself off and made her way to the front.

The window to the right of the door where she'd once attempted to peek in was larger, taller, yet still covered by a maroon curtain, and below was a thick row of mint bushes lined with a thin flower bed of coppers, tangerines, and vibrant yellows. Marigolds.

The door before her was crafted in sun-worn redwood and inky iron; tonight, boisterous music did not float out from an ill-fitting frame, and the only sign read *The Fenfoss Inn, Established 1340.*

The building was clean, free of the clumps of moss that had grown on it before, its minimal framework shining as if recently oiled. The window she'd jumped from to escape Garin was closed. Nothing was the same as she'd left it, and there was nothing to show of her stay there—except for two broken vines of ivy that hung between the side of the building and a nearby tree.

There were footsteps behind her; when she turned, Loïg was secured to the stable and Garin was approaching. He handed her the plump travel bag, which she hoisted over one shoulder.

"Are you ready?"

A wicked dread coursed through her. "I'm ready to do what is right and not have Kestrel's threat hanging over our heads." She glared up at his teasing smile, one he probably meant to be encouraging. "Though, I might have felt more prepared if I hadn't seen two clearly entranced men drop dead in my Grand Hall today."

A flash of humor crossed Garin's face. Lilac opened her mouth to respond, but was interrupted by a scoff..

"*This* is where you work?"

The rest of the party had dismounted the carriage, and Giles and the guard were struggling to push it backward into the stable. With an annoyed glare at Garin, Bastion marched right toward them. His dark cloak swept the cobblestone, tied at the neck by a single rope over his dark tunic.

At the thought of meeting him at the Sanguine Mine and the bruise he'd left on her face, she dug her heels into the floor. She stared coldly at him.

"Bastion."

The look he gave her was flat, almost bored, as if he were a large cat trained over and over to avoid a piece of meat. He didn't bother bowing, only relaxing his shoulders a bit and curtly nodding once.

Then he stepped around her and gripped the handle of the inn's door. The door opened a crack before slamming shut again. "What the devil?"

He tried again, yanked, but even with his strength it did not budge. Dust rained down upon him from the stone and framework, but the door was sealed.

"Careful," Garin said, mouth twitching as his brother dusted himself off and whirled on them.

"What game are you playing?"

"It seems you don't have the permission to enter. You must ask."

"Fuck off," he growled. "*You* invited me here."

"Yes, but the inn is owned by the Aglovens, not I."

Bastion sneered and gave Garin a look that said he'd get him for it later. "How do you suppose I ask for permission, then?"

Just then, there was a *click*, and the window to the right of the door squeaked open with some effort. Two stunning orange-hazel eyes flicked between the three of them. A wide grin appeared, then altogether disappeared—only to reappear in the now partially open door. Although the light of the kitchen and corner hearth glowed dimly through, there were no sounds of merriment or of other inhabitants.

"You're early!" Lorietta bobbed down, then rose again, her eyes bright but cautious. "Your Majesty, so nice to see you again."

"It's an honor to be here." It was more than an honor. She felt at home.

"May I come in?"

The witch's gaze fell on the interrupting vampire, and her smile fell slightly. "Garin's told me all about you."

"Great things, I'm sure." Bastion advanced up the shallow step, and the door slammed shut, followed by a surprised yelp from Lorietta.

She opened it again, this time wide enough for them to see that the tavern was empty. Lorietta straightened her apron—light green today, with yellow and pink flowers roughly stitched in. "I haven't given you my answer."

Garin was behind them, watching with a bemused expression on his face. Lilac half expected his brother to lose his temper, the way he had so quickly in the Mine. But only Bastion sighed and crossed his arms, defeated.

"Look. I don't care if I'm not wanted here. Garin was the one who dragged me along to play representative. I'll gladly leave."

"Not so fast."

He was in the process of turning away, but Lorietta stuck a foot before the door, as if stopping it from closing again. "You are wanted here, Bastion. But I only need to warn you, as I do every vampire, that encroaching on unwilling donors is not allowed here."

"Oh." He sounded surprised, as if her stipulation should be obvious. "Fine."

"Garin has been in and out lately helping our queen, so we had to configure a replacement of sorts, a way to keep all denizens safe from assault or mischief of any kind. This is a newer enchantment we've placed on the inn. After our little guest here broke one of my windows to escape," she said, eyes flitting to Lilac. "I managed to turn it into an effective meddler chute."

Bastion and Lilac exchanged worried glances.

"Whenever Garin takes leave, the inn now has the capability of throwing any thieves, brawlers, or blood snatchers out the second story window of its own accord. Not that Meriam and I lack the means of breaking up fights ourselves, but why not enchant the inn so that our denizens think twice? I've not seen it in action yet, but I look forward to the day. So"—she scowled at Bastion—"don't tempt it." She swung the door wide open. "And with that out of the way, please do come in, Bastion."

Bastion slowly, carefully made his way into the inn, as if afraid it would throw him out for his personality alone. Lilac was trying to imagine what a meddler chute looked like when the aromas from the kitchen pushed everything else from her mind.

Like a child lured into a witch's candied cottage, she let the scent of pastry and soup carry her past the threshold into the tavern, to the bar where Lorietta had instructed Bastion to sit. While the exterior of the inn had changed, the inside was the same, albeit lacking the rowdy crowd and sticky floors.

The door swung shut behind her as she approached the counter. She turned—and Garin was nowhere to be found.

"He's helping the humans park your carriage." Lorietta placed a mug of something dark and a clear glass of what looked to be whiskey in front of Bastion before disappearing into the scullery doorway, the curtain of stringed silver beads swinging behind her.

Bastion chuckled to himself. He sniffed at the mug and made a face, then pushed it away, downing the amber contents of the glass in one swig.

"Cold blood," he said disbelievingly, wiping his mouth on his sleeve. "Fucking disgusting. I can't believe my brother drank this for years."

"We have plenty more liquor, then," Lorietta called out.

"I prefer mine warm, and I have no problem accessing it."

"Nonconsensual feeding is not allowed here." Lilac approached the bar, thinking of Piper and all the others imprisoned at his hands. That was at the top of the list she'd had John jot down during her Accords drafting sessions held in the library over the past week.

Bastion made an irreverent noise into his palm. "Wouldn't you know?"

"That means you'll have to convince someone to like you enough first."

He glowered in her direction, eyes narrowed, before Lorietta's head popped through the wall of tinkling beads.

"Some help, Your Majesty."

Lilac obliged without question. She dumped her bag at the bar with a warning look at Bastion before walking around it and parting the beads. They were heavy. "Silver?"

Lorietta was squatted near the far wall, where sacks of potatoes, wheat, and a couple crates of vegetables were stacked. She selected another potato and added it to the others in the crook of her arm. "Iron. Everyone might be welcome to eat and drink here, but no faeries of any kind are allowed in my kitchen."

The scullery opened up into a much larger room than it'd appeared from the outside; the cooking hearth sat in the nearest corner, and above it hung a large cauldron filled with the delicious-smelling pottage Garin had mentioned. Three large silk cushions lined the floor before it, colorful and woven with intricate patterns, while a small round table and chair sat along the wall, where a row of mismatched utensils hung.

Along the left wall, beside the crop storage, there was a tall cabinet filled with bottles of herbs and spices, and beside that, a smaller fire that burned green beneath a mini cauldron. There was a large woven rug at the back of the room between two barrels and a liquor cabinet.

Lorietta brought the potatoes to the table, where she began roughly halving them with the knife she plucked from the wall. Lilac stepped in, letting the iron beads fall behind her. During her journey through Brocéliande, she'd learned how several of the "rules" on interacting with Daemons had turned out to be superstitions. It was good to know that one was true—that even Kestrel and his terrifying jury of faeries had a weakness.

The house suddenly shuddered, the timber above them creaking in place.

The witch set down her knife. There was a book open on a stand between the table and the pot; she ran a finger down the open page. "Do me a favor and cut those last few for me, dear," she said, turning to the pot and lifting the gigantic wooden spoon that sat in it. "It's time for me to stir."

Lilac was glad to have her hands occupied instead of going over her memorized notes again. She picked her way around the pillows and began slicing the potatoes while Lorietta stared and muttered at her book. She began stirring counterclockwise with both hands.

"This is my grimoire," the witch said, feeling Lilac's eyes on her.

"It must be very old."

"A few years younger than Garin, I think."

Reminded of him, she glanced through the curtain of beads. Bastion was still alone at the bar.

The potato in her hand rolled, and a sharp stab of pain slashed across her knuckle as the knife slipped. Lilac dropped both and cradled her finger. "Shit."

A bead of blood—more than a bead—pooled at her knuckle.

"What's the matter, dear?" asked Lorietta without looking up from the pottage. "Nervous, are we?"

"Yes," she said, swiping her finger against her dress and sucking off the rest. "Extremely."

"Well, I can't have you bleeding into the food." But Lorietta turned her head ever so slightly and winked. "You can't start any discussion without all parties here—or at least Kestrel, if Garin's informed me correctly about your foolish faerie bargain."

"That's right." She knew the witch was one to speak her mind, but there was something about her comment that ate at her. "We had no choice."

"There's *always* a choice. While there may not be a way out of striking a deal with them, you as one of the agreeing parties can adjust or add to the terms. It's a gamble. It all depends on how much you're willing to divulge. Out of all the faerie courts of Brittany, the Court of the Valley is the most amicable."

Amicable? A violent shudder ran through her, imaging Kestrel's seemingly limitless power. There was nothing amicable about her experience at Cinderfell, Kestrel's manor.

Lorietta frowned.

"What is it?"

She cocked her head at the blank brick wall at the back of the kitchen. "There's an ingredient I seem to be missing. The pottage is nearly done. Will you retrieve it for me in the cellar?"

Lilac glanced around. "And... where is this cellar?"

"Move the rug."

She shifted the corner of the woven gold and maroon rug aside to reveal a wooden panel—a square of embedded into the floor. A single rung lay flush against it. A door.

"Oh," she said, attempting to hide her grimace behind a smile. "Could I maybe stir the pot for you?"

"No. My repetition spell has been set on the spoon, and it will stir itself every few minutes until it's of the perfect consistency, which, *if* I get that ingredient, should be around the time everyone starts arriving." She smiled. "We have time, but I do have to keep a close eye on it. *And* finish those potatoes."

What was the point of a spell to stir the soup for her if she couldn't leave the cauldron? But Lorietta wouldn't take no for an answer, so Lilac lifted the rung and opened the door, resting it gently on the wall. Shallow stone steps led down into the cellar, which seemed well-lit. It was hard to tell; the stairwell bent off to the right.

"And what is it I'm looking for?"

"You'll know. It's hard to miss."

She bent, bracing herself on the floorboards as she lowered herself down the first few steps. She had to duck after nearly whacking her head on the ceiling of the cellar, and as she descended, the glow of a flame grew brighter. It was much too bright to belong to a torch, or even several.

The steps led into a thin passageway. Lilac continued along it, hands on each side of the wall, until she finally came to a sharp corner.

When the room opened up, there was neither barrel nor bottle in sight.

❧ 4 ❧

Garin sat in a large, faded green armchair that looked like it had seen better years. Or centuries. In front of him crackled a cheery fire in a corner fireplace, the light gleaming the waves of his blue-black hair. She wondered, distantly, if his hair ever grew.

There was a neatly made bed across the fire, lush cream undersheets beneath a black duvet, and next to it, a short shelf containing books and several manually bound stacks of parchment. At the center of the room was a patchwork rug that appeared similar to the korikaned tents. His prized longsword from Sinclair was perched on a wall rack before her, and to the right of that, across the foot of his bed, was a thin door. A sort of cane with a silver animal glinting at the tip leaned next to it.

In the corner nearest her, a mounted shelf hanging with thick twine bore an array of strange potted plants, kinds she'd never seen before. She couldn't tell if they were from a different continent—or the Low Forest. It was hard to tell if any of them glowed in the flickering light. On the top shelf sat three of them, various shades of a gradient blue ranging from royal to periwinkle; they had *mouths*, or at least two prominent leaves that looked like mouths. On the shelf under them were three more dirt-filled pots with small green buds poking out of the soil. She could've sworn one of the blue ones craned in her direction.

Stepping further into the room and promptly away from the plants, Lilac cleared her throat. "Nice of you to share your space with Lorietta."

Garin looked up from the small, green leather book in his palm, turned so she could see his sharp profile against the hearth before him, and said, sounding alarmed, "What makes you think she shares my room?"

"Her plants make for some interesting decor, that's all."

He turned back to the fire. She waited while he finished his page, marked it with the ribbon protruding from the top of the book, and slid it into his pant pocket.

Garin stood, stretched, and sauntered over. She braced herself, waiting for the tender scorch of his touch, but he only brushed against her as he passed her and tugged at a string hanging from the plant wall.

There was a fluttering sound, and the shelves of pots were suddenly cast in a patch of soft, silver light. Above them was a rectangular ceiling window. The insides of the glass panes were covered in a thin layer of moisture, the outside flecked with soil and leaves framing a stunning scene of the moon and starlit sky beyond the canopy.

"How beautiful," she mouthed.

"Indeed," Garin whispered, a smirk ghosting his lips as he pulled back. "And they're mine."

"Yours?" She slowly turned to look at him, then back at the window, dubious.

"We only burn in direct light," Garin said, retreating. "Sometimes I'd open the window, lay back on my bed, and watch for hours when I couldn't sleep between shifts at the bar. It was once nice to see the sunlight helping my plants thrive, instead of fearing its ability to desecrate and burn. Now, it's not a problem for me."

His gaze was far away. She wondered what he was thinking about—if he was remembering the dramatic moment just before he realized he could walk in the day.

"Lorietta does have her garden, though. Just beyond the window here. We built it together. Well, she had the korikaned build the trellises and boxes, but we planted everything."

She remembered the way he'd critiqued Sable and Jeanare's overwatered carrots. It made sense he might share his parents' interests in botany, but this still surprised her. "Gardening seems like a reasonable way to keep necessary crops for an inn."

"It is. Meriam had mentioned starting one several years after I started living here, but she had no idea where to start. So, I brought Lorietta out there with me every evening, and we tended the garden together that way until she understood what to do. She's skilled now."

However aging worked for witches, Lorietta had been younger when Garin first showed up on the Aglovens' doorstep. Maybe even younger than Lilac. "Did they not know how to start a garden before?"

"Cultivating crops in the middle of the forest is a difficult task." Garin laughed, but it was tinged with bitterness. "You assume she would know how to keep a garden. Why, because she's a commoner?"

"*No.* Lorietta is a resourceful and talented witch. I didn't want you taking all the credit for her doing." Her cheeks burned, embarrassed at her assumption as she surveyed his fully furnished room and lush plant collection. "I just wasn't expecting all of this."

"She comes from a long lineage of arcane nobility from Germany and a successful mother from Paris. You were raised with a silver spoon, she with a bronze wand, and great manor before her parents died in an accident and her great aunt adopted her. The two barely knew a thing about gardening before I arrived."

She was silent as she processed this.

"You'll learn as she did," Garin said a bit sternly, a bit defensively, "that prejudice—the line between privilege and poverty—is not simply drawn by access to food, shelter, and wealth. Or even blood. Little would *you* know, it runs much deeper than that, and what she grows in that garden is still occasionally supplemented from the outside markets to accommodate all our guests. Your family and hers are different in that Lorietta was raised to turn no one away, within reason."

Face heating, she said nothing to fight him. He was right. About everything. She was finally beginning to understand, though she wasn't sure if she ever would fully. The Fenfoss Inn was more than an establishment for an overnight stay or an ale. It was where the lone traveler, Daemon or human, could find warm food, cold drink, and kindred conversation. They had little resources to feed themselves and those they housed, and whether or not funds were an issue, Lorietta could not simply stroll into town on any market day without being scrutinized, or possibly harassed. She didn't seem the type to hide or shrink herself for anyone, and rightfully so. Although magic folk lived scattered throughout Paimpont, surely they weren't treated fairly. Shifters themselves either lived in seclusion or became recluses because of it.

Under her rule, this would all change. Lilac turned on her heel and prepared to lead him up the stairs as she contemplated these things.

"Where do you think you're going?"

Something in his voice made her freeze. "Upstairs. Lorietta sent me to retrieve you."

"Are you angry with me?" There was a genuine curiosity in his words.

When she turned, he was watching her intensely.

The question surprised her, and her gaze dropped to the floor as she hesitated a beat too long. "No."

When she looked back up, he was smiling knowingly at her.

Her eyes narrowed. *Fine.* She would play along. Lilac stepped down and strode toward the middle of the rug—then slinked past him. She considered sitting on his bed, but it felt too forward. Which was ridiculous, considering he'd once made her come with the hilt of her own dagger.

He'd followed, naturally. She retreated, taunting him, her lips slightly parted and face flushed, taking him in.

Garin stalked her with a bounce in each step, slowly dancing them both, untouching, toward the end of his bed. Hands behind her to feel for the stone and keep herself from raking her nails into him, she came to rest against the wall. She was nearly panting when he cornered her.

"Do not lie to me, Eleanor of Brittany."

"Vivien is dead," she breathed, as if he'd drawn the answer from her.

"That she is."

Her hungry smile faded at his unapologetic answer. "Why? Why would —" She broke off at the look he gave her, stripping her bare.

"*Why?* She needed to be stopped. With someone like her, there is only one way that happens."

But there were so many things that could've gone wrong. What if the crowd at her Court of Common Appeals had been much larger? Some Sundays, she'd seen the entire room filled with townsfolk when Henri was king. What if she'd been hosting a dignitary, or someone from a foreign kingdom? She didn't even know if those who were there could be trusted to keep quiet until she had the chance to make an announcement about their deaths.

Lilac's chest heaved—desire, shock, wonder, rage all swirled inside her. "But you could have *told* me."

"Told you? Or asked for your permission?"

"Forgive me for thinking it would have been helpful to know about something that would trigger a rather public investigation, something that could have sparked anarchy if it was revealed the wrong way."

"You would have tried to talk me out of it. It wouldn't have worked."

"You cannot just murder everyone who crosses me," she said, unable to help her voice rising.

"*Crossed?*" His teeth were suddenly bared into a sneer. "She has more than crossed you. Vivien wouldn't have stopped until you were dead. She wanted all that was destined for you to go to Sinclair. She wanted it more than her own life." His next words came in a scraping whisper, dancing in the breeze across her skin. "Are you so unaccustomed to anyone fighting for you? Killing for you, Eleanor?"

Her body flushed at his mention of her name, the way his eyes danced when he said it. "It is I who you are avenging, yet I who will shoulder the consequences of it."

Her muscles tensed involuntarily as he studied her and let out a gust of air, as if it took some effort to control his breath. He took a step back.

"You are not the only one avenged by her blood." His words simmered with a rage so scathing, even if the threat behind them wasn't for her, it scorched her face and forced her gaze to the floor. The leader of the Broceliande vampire clan had his own vendettas to reconcile.

"And you will not shoulder the consequences," he added quietly. "I have made sure of it."

"You could have at least covered your tracks. You didn't have to make a spectacle."

An astonished frown parted his lips. "A spectacle?"

"Garin, she was in pieces. It's not funny."

Garin was suddenly in pieces, doing his best to hold in a surge of laughter. The skin of her neck was aflame. "There are public repercussions for a personal matter that could have been dealt with in private. The entire kingdom knows of Sinclair's behavior at my ceremony. I had reason to want her dead."

He collected himself before speaking. "Didn't you?" His gaze dipped to her lips, and the familiar hunger that occasionally made its way around his ability to reason with himself reared its head. "Why are you quivering?"

She glared up at him. "Tell me what you did. I deserve to know."

"I drained every drop of blood from Vivien. After I was done with her I entranced Sinclair, instructed him to deal with her body, then busy himself with tidying the dining room. What I *wanted* him to do was get rid of Vivien first, then dispose of Godwin. I suppose I could have been more clear, and the lingering effects of the toadstool could have interfered with my entrancement. When I returned to check on him last night to ensure Sinclair hadn't wandered off, I found her remains arranged upon the table like a Sunday roast. That was when Armand arrived." He waved a hand. "So, as humorous as that sounds, I regret I cannot take credit for the most creative display that upset him."

"Still, were you not the one who gave him an arm to present to me?" she said, frustrated he did not seem to grasp the reasons behind her fury. "Were you not the one who commanded him to impale himself?"

"I told him to have you open the bag; I couldn't trust any other circumstance. If you didn't, then he would kill himself. I figured you'd throw him in the dungeon if he succeeded."

"My father opened the bag for me," she informed him. "I still received your message loud and clear, in front of everyone. We're just fortunate it wasn't a public jury."

"You're wrong. The more witnesses, the better," he said matter-of-factly. He was so sure of his answer, so unremorseful.

If he wanted to quell her concerns, he was doing it all wrong. He only fed her anger.

"For *what*? To stoke your ego? To make everyone fear you more than they already do?"

"To ensure it was clear I am responsible for their deaths so that you would not shoulder the blame. If you were caught by genuine surprise, they would not think twice about your involvement with her murder. About your involvement with me."

"Armand tried to insinuate I was involved anyway."

"As I thought he might. How delicious, the thought of one of his last fears being that the queen of his country is in bed with his enemy." He reached up to tuck a lock of her hair behind her ear. "But he's dead now. So, you are free to pretend you are not involved, in any way you see fit, with the very Daemons you've sworn to protect. With the vampire whose room you stand in."

Lilac scoffed, but as he eyed her, his jaw set and his brows cocked, it became clear there was something she wasn't getting, a joke she wasn't grasping.

"How is staying away going for you, Eleanor?"

The subject change felt inevitable. Now that they were alone together, truly alone, something in the air had shifted. Pretenses were dropped, and so were formalities. She had never intended to stay away, had she?

She was selfish; she'd been called that before. Selfish for being caught speaking to Freya. Selfish for leaving a comfortable life at the castle and denying Sinclair her hand and body. Selfish for making her parents worry.

Lilac *was* selfish, and tonight was proof. "You're the one holding me here," she whispered.

"You're the one who walked into my room unannounced. And I have not held you anywhere—at least, not tonight. You're here of your own accord. You cornered yourself." He slowly closed the space between them, evoking a visceral reaction and sending a jolt of adrenaline through her body. He reveled in it, smiled knowingly as he placed a hand against the wall and two fingers of the other under her chin, then teasing one of them against the pout of her bottom lip.

He clicked his tongue. "If only Henri and poor Armand knew. And they don't, do they?"

When she shook her head, he gripped her jaw in a gentle vice.

Her lip was trembling again, which she hated because she knew he secretly loved it. Lilac coaxed his finger at the corner of her mouth onto her tongue; he watched, unflinching, as she wrapped her lips around it and sucked lightly. His breath hitched at the movement of her head, her tongue against the pad of his finger. She would play his game... and play it better.

His smile quickly fell. A low groan erupted from his throat as he released her.

"Is that what this is, then? Am I your revenge?"

"If you are my revenge, Your Majesty, then it is the sweetest I'll ever taste." He stalked away toward his plant shelf, leaving her aching for more. "Your hand," he said gruffly, without glancing back.

"My—oh." There was still a smear of red along her finger. The scrape had been deeper than she'd thought. She reddened further and wiped it on her dress, uselessly hiding it behind her back.

He returned with a white cloth in one hand and something long and green in the other. He looked more amused than hungry, but with him it was difficult to tell. He cocked his chin to the end of the bed. "Sit. Let me help you."

She slid off her cloak and settled onto the edge of his bed, again surprised that a vampire would keep his chamber so warm and cozy—though she supposed it was for the sake of his shelves of strange plants.

Garin reached down to peel her injured hand from her side, laughing when he met some resistance. "You think you could ever hide the scent of your blood from me? That, among the numerous summer aromas of Brocéliande, yours isn't the temptress that calls me forth?"

"This is what Lorietta gets for making me chop potatoes." She couldn't help but smile. "I honestly forgot it happened. I also wasn't sure how you would fare, after everything."

"Nothing about my desire for you has changed. If anything, it has been amplified." He lifted her palm to his nose and sniffed delicately at the gash on her finger. "Just as my ability to achieve that desire has been restored."

"Doesn't that make this worse for you?"

In answer, he squatted before her and drew out the green stem—it looked more like a long thorn than a stem—before readjusting his grip on her hand. It was a tapered stalk of some kind, covered on each side in a row of hair-like bristles. "What do you take me for? An amateur?"

She squirmed as he rubbed the slimy edge of it against her wound without warning.

His hand clamped around hers, stilling her. "Are you not used to an ounce of discomfort?"

She answered his inquiry with one of his own. "Did you get this from Adelaide?"

"No. She kills every plant in her care. Why do you ask?"

She didn't take the witch as someone bad at caring for plants, not with all the flora surrounding her cottage; the information threw her. "It looks like something out of the Low Forest."

"Oh. No, not this. Although it looks like one, it's not considered a fae-rooted plant at all." He cocked his head at the plant shelf. "Those blue ones are the only Low Forest species I own. My father would forage illegally in the outcropping of trees near Adelaide's cottage, and there were several patches of outliers that would grow there. He'd bring home seeds and plants but could never keep them alive, and the ones he did manage to maintain for a short while, my mother got rid of." He cleared his throat. "After I'd entranced Jeanare in the west wing, I'd poked around and found an unmarked bag of seeds in a box of belongings my father kept under one of his floorboards. It was still there. So, I took a sachet and planted the seeds that were inside."

Lilac stared disbelievingly at the plants. As if they'd heard him, the nearest one slowly swiveled its head in their direction. After all these years, it still took mere weeks for them to grow. She shuddered. "They seem so... so—"

"Not of this world?"

"Yes."

"I suspect that was at least part of what my father was trying to study without getting too close. Why the flora of the Low Forest only grew there, why the plant species had not naturally dispersed over time as other plants tend to do." He glanced back at his shelf. "I believe he overlooked one simple solution: the soil. I thought of how nothing had happened when my father tried to plant them in his best garden soils, so I went and scooped some from the edge of the Low Forest."

Lilac found this rather peculiar. "Why would the soil there be different?"

Garin only shrugged. "You ask me questions I ponder myself. Besides their odd coloring, they're almost identical to a mysterious plant I find fascinating from the New World, the *Dionea muscipula*." He withheld an impressed smile. "That's what the three pots below them should grow into in a few months, the mortal variety. They both survive on sunlight, water, and insects, though I have a suspicion the fae-rooted *Dionea* may have other appetites. I have plenty to learn of them."

She stared, fascinated by both the mystical plant species—and Garin.

She felt he could go on forever about his studies in botany, and she would gladly listen to them if it meant hearing him speak about what he enjoyed learning.

"And this plant, then?" She looked down to the thorn.

"This," he said, sealing her wound with a last pass of its warm, clear sap, "is *Aloe vera*, found in warmer regions, used for healing and medicine throughout the world. This one's from Spain, a recent gift from one of Lorietta's trades with her passing travelers. As were the seeds from the New World"

"A human trader?" she guessed, and her eyes widened when he nodded.

"There are much older, greater empires in other corners of the world who don't run screaming from the likes of us, believe it or not."

He unwrapped a corner of the cloth from the knuckles on his opposite hand and brought it to his mouth, tearing a long strip of it effortlessly with his teeth. She found herself rocking forward, unable to keep from staring at his full bottom lip.

He seemed not to notice, or at least pretended as much, but he cleared his throat as he wrapped the base of her finger thrice, loosely, and expertly tied it so there was enough room for her to flex her hand. "There," he said, looking pleased with himself. "The salve will allow you to heal normally."

"There will be a scar." She wasn't concerned with the scar at all, wanting instead to feel his mouth on her.

"My saliva only heals vampire-made wounds," he reminded her. "The scars we choose to wear are the ones that make us human."

"Like the ones on my legs." The words were out of her mouth before she could think better of it.

Lilac would be lying to herself if she really believed she hadn't said it on purpose. She leaned back onto her arms while Garin shifted to his knees and delicately cupped his hands on the backs of her ankles, just above her boots. He looked up at her softly, his brows raising in silent question for permission. When Lilac nodded, barely able to breathe, Garin's chest heaved as he slid his hands beneath her dress, along her lace stockings, from her ankles to her calves. His pupils were enlarged and fixated on her, his hands never breaking contact, and the bulge at his throat bobbed repeatedly as if his closed mouth had flooded with saliva.

"I'm sorry I brought it up," she said, voice barely a whisper, entirely unable to concentrate.

He silenced her with a shake of his head. "No, you're not."

He was ravenous and did a poor job of hiding it, but his collected calm immediately broke the moment his fingers brushed against her dagger on her right thigh. Licking his lips, he paused, carefully extracting it from between the material and her skin and placed it on the bed beside her. They both stared at it for a moment, its jeweled silver pommel winking knowingly in the firelight, before he slipped back under her skirts. He froze briefly when he reached past the lip of her garter and met bare skin. His fingers roamed her upper thigh, tracing lazy circles as his eyes slowly darkened.

He shut them, frustration seeping into his carefully crafted demeanor.

Lilac bit her lip to withhold a laugh as his hands rose and met her hip bones, his thumbs slowly reaching inward. The laugh escaped as a surprised moan when he dragged a thumb through her arousal, encircling her clit.

"*Modron*," he cursed, running his tongue along his lower lip. He ran his fingers along her inner thighs. "Where are your undergarments?"

She could barely answer with him toying gently with her cunt, stroking the sensitive creases of her inner thigh on both sides, making her blood pound through her veins. She savored the look of desperation on his face. "They're packed away."

"And I suppose tormenting me is your idea of fun?" His index and middle fingers found her next, stroking teasingly along her opening. She was already so wet, she could tell by the way his skin slid over hers, the way his breath stuttered as she shuddered at his touch. He gave a disbelieving laugh, the only pleasant thing about him in this moment, despite the greed in his eyes, which flicked up to hers. They narrowed.

"*You* were going to hold our meeting like *this*?" His fingers hooked into her garter, and he rolled the material of her stockings down, taking his time as he slipped her boots and the rest of the material off with them.

She flexed her bare feet as he courteously lifted one side of her dress, then the other to examine the fading bruises and scars on her legs. The one on her right leg—the one she'd shown Henri—made him stop.

His expression shifted from annoyance to something sinister as he reached beneath her skirts again, and two fingers found their way to her.

He made her wait, eliciting a growl of impatience as she wiggled, desperate for pressure—for relief. Garin shushed her and bent; before she knew it, his warm mouth was on her inner thigh. He inhaled, groaning low in his throat as he kissed along her skin, his tongue lapping at her arousal and causing her to shudder violently as his fingers encircled her cunt.

"I can leave a scar of my own," he growled, smirking against her thigh. "Right—" He broke off, as if kissing her couldn't wait a second more. "Right here."

He pushed his fingers in easily, groaning at her wetness, and curled them upward as he thrust into her. Once, twice—sending tortuous waves of heat through her body.

"Wait. The guests are arriving," she gasped. Anxiety warred with pleasure at her tightening core. "Upstairs."

"You won't take long," was all he said. He drove his fingers deeper, his throat bobbing as he rose and shifted the rest of her skirts up.

Her fingers curled into his thick waves as he came down on her, his tongue lavishing her clit, causing her to gasp, her toes curling in anticipation. She braced herself, had to remind herself to breathe as he thrusted into her and teased, sucked, flicked her until she began to come apart in his mouth.

He was right. It didn't take long at all.

"Garin," she whimpered, but he wasn't done.

She came alive as he rose again, climbing over her, his thick erection digging into her thigh through his pants. She opened for him as their mouths met, but not quite fast enough; he caught her bottom lip between his teeth. Shock flooded through her, mixing with sweat, heat, and salt as his tongue entered her mouth and swept furiously over hers. She tasted her own blood, and he groaned as his tongue greedily moved against hers.

Garin slid his fingers out to circle her flesh teasingly. Lilac whimpered into his mouth, rubbing herself against him. "Please," she begged, sliding her hands from his dark curls toward her stomach, struggling to reach for his belt. The meeting could wait.

But Garin pulled away.

"If I catch you flaunting yourself like that again," he breathed, his lips ruddy, keeping just far enough out of her reach, "I might not be able to restrain myself from taking you where you stand."

She could barely pull together her answer before he began slowly, gently stroking her clit again along the pads of his fingers. The tenderness of his touch clashed with the way he looked at her—into her.

He broke their gaze, only to slowly lower himself onto her collarbone, kissing up her throat. The movement still caught her off-guard. In defense, on instinct, she bucked against Garin, but this only seemed to excite him. His fingers entered her once more, and with his teeth tortuously grazing her skin, his shoulders pinning her down, she didn't know what to do.

Could he control himself?

Lilac shuddered, rocking forward into his hand, desperate to feel him deep inside her, desperate to feel his teeth pierce her skin.

Did she want him to?

"Drink from me, Garin."

A low, strangled sound escaped his throat when felt him shake his head *no*, somehow resisting her invitation. His other hand clamped over her mouth. Lilac whimpered under him, yearning to feel his teeth, the pain— her nostrils flaring for air as he silenced her with his palm, bringing her to the crest with his other.

Waves of fire and pleasure slammed into her. It was instinctive and vengeful all at once—his fangs teasing the side of her throat, too careful to break skin as his fingers thrusted into her, pushed her over the edge. Lilac breathed into her orgasm, convulsed under him, around him, and she tasted it before she realized what happened: the sweet savory of figs and honey on her tongue. Lilac shut her eyes and saw something other than darkness.

The gilded edge of a desk. A white quill, and the warm haze of a fireplace beyond.

It was so brief that she could have imagined it. It could've been her own memory, and she would have thought it was if she hadn't experienced seeing into Garin's mind before, when he'd prompted it in her room with his blood drawn by a prick of his finger.

It was a blink, less than a second, then it was gone. And so was he.

Lilac lay there, breathless, before rising to her feet. Even with him standing on the opposite side of the bed—his palm slicked in red—every inch of her body was flooded with sensation, as if his hands were still on her. She wanted to ask how his hand was, but when she approached him he held it out to stop her. It was barely a scrape, already healing.

"There's a commotion upstairs." His breathing was hard. "Please get dressed."

"I have clothes on." She hesitated. *Barely.* Her stockings and shoes were askew on the rug beside her, and her dress hung halfway off her body. "What kind of commotion?"

"It smells like Lori's burnt something."

Quickly, he crossed the room and threw the closet along the wall open. Tucked past his collection of cream and black tunics were several long garments in cloth, leather, and ribbon. *Dresses.* Velvets and corduroy, some of them mutely glimmering. He skimmed his hands through, trying to pick one.

The words left her tongue scathingly. "Are those from your other visitors?"

"Yes, nice of you to notice." Garin extracted one and tossed it at her. "Each of my mistresses coincidentally have your exact build and height."

She caught and unfolded a beautiful cream and forest green kirtle with a tan leather corset.

"There, that one matches the dress you've got on."

"What's wrong with the one I'm wearing?"

"These are different. *Protected.*"

Lilac glanced down at the piece of finery she held, willing her pulse to slow. The lace that ran through the built-in corset shone brightly in the firelight, silver and slightly glowing. "Where did you get it?"

"Shh." Garin wasn't listening. He was at the base of the steps cocking his ear, looking like he was struggling to focus.

Those garments hanging in his closet. Were they all for her? "What are those—"

"Lilac, if you don't put that dress on this instant, I'll make you regret coming down here tonight."

Heart racing, she stepped out of her gown and into the kirtle. The material had a generous stretch while the corset was light, seeming cosmetic more than anything. The leather was hand-carved in a curious pattern of filigree filled with angles, swoops, and leaves. It was pleasantly shorter than her castle gowns, falling mid-calf. Lilac donned her stockings and boots, then slid her dagger into the scabbard on the belt that sat at her hips.

When she joined him near the staircase, he was alert, eyes trained on the cellar ceiling. There was a loud *bang*, followed by a flurry of muffled voices and the scent of smoke. She blinked as they were cast in a beam of warm light.

"Have you been *eating* the queen?" The blond vampire's head popped down into the room. His nostrils flared. "Oh, thank heavens, you were just fucking her."

"What is it, Bastion?"

The inn shuddered before Bastion could reply—a low, resounding vibration that jolted the three of them.

Bastion jumped. "What the bloody hell was that?"

"A warning," Garin growled. "Of any threat to the inn. What is going on?"

"Whenever you two have a moment," Bastion drawled, "there's smoke coming from one of your bags, Your Majesty."

She and Garin exchanged glances. "Which one?"

"The one that isn't your inconveniently sized trunk. And your most diligent guard Hywell won't let any of us near it."

Before she could ask anything else, Bastion's head was gone.

5

"I told you hosting it here was a bad idea," Meriam snarled, just as there was a *thud*, then a shout from what sounded like the bar—the sounds of a struggle. Lilac straightened, her hand in Garin's as they emerged from the cellar into the scullery, the innkeeper's white curls taking up most of her immediate field of vision as the old woman glared daggers at Garin.

The scullery was empty besides the witch, the flame under the large cauldron reduced, the pottage simmering quietly. Meriam, wrapped in a nightgown and wool sweater, ushered them through the iron curtain. The smoke was stronger now, a gray cloud of it slowly leaking into the room, and Lilac bumped into Garin, who had frozen in the hall behind the bar.

She stepped around him, taking in the room—Lorietta was propping the front door open in attempts to waft the smoke out, Giles and the two korikaned, Blitzrik and Ra'arak on bar stools with their noses in bowls of pottage, Sable and Jeanare watching, frozen in the dining area to their left. Finally, at the foot of the stairs, Bastion was holding something—and some-one. Her travel bag was on the ground, the lip of it open and her contents spilling out.

In a delicate two-fingered grip, Bastion pinched her envelope from Kestrel, small clouds of iris blue smoke rising from the corners. With his other hand, he restrained Hywell the guard, who stared at the small white square with an unusual fixation.

"He smelled the smoke before anyone else did and began to fish in her bag. He pulled this out," Bastion explained.

"Give that to me." She marched forward, furious at herself for not keeping it on her body.

Bastion extended his arm, but Garin made a warning sound. "Wait."

There was something wrong with Hywell.

"I can hear it," the guard said, voice full of wonder. He reached across Bastion's body again, wiggling his fingers, but the vampire yanked him back by the neck.

"You can't have the *queen's* parcel. What's the matter with you?"

"Faerie ether," Garin said from beside her, his hand clamped on her arm.

The envelope suddenly burst into a ball of blue flames. Bastion yelped and released it as it fell to his feet. Hywell tried to lunge for it, but Bastion held onto him.

An angry wail came from behind the bar, where Meriam was gripping her knitted cap. "Get rid of it!" she shrieked as the ball of blue flames began to singe the planking.

Sable and Jeanare had scooped up Blitzrik and Ra'arak and watched from just inside the open door, while Giles had flung himself over the bar, the top of his head and bulging eyes barely visible over the counter next to Meriam. Lorietta burst out of the bead curtain brandishing a decorative bronze wand the length of her forearm.

"Reveal yourself," she cried, pointing it at the envelope, which was still intact amidst the fire.

What would have happened to her had she opened it earlier?

Garin's grip on her hand tightened, and everyone backed silently away as the flames died, leaving the envelope in the center of a circle of charred wood.

Everyone except Hywell, who wrenched himself from Bastion's loosened grip, landing directly on the parcel.

A deafening explosion rocked the room, and when Lilac found her feet again, Garin and Lorietta were shouting. A cloud of frenzied blue smoke filled the room before shooting toward the ceiling and funneling down into Hywell, who kneeled in the center of the char.

The envelope was gone.

The front door slammed shut, rattling the timber as the smoke entered him through his mouth and ears, the veins along his throat swelling as he inhaled against his will, until the room was clear.

His body seized, and the guard gave Lilac one last look of terror before he collapsed to the floor face-first. Body stiff, he continued to tremble there, his skull and joints rattling along the wood.

Lilac was not one to believe in souls, at least the church's version of them, but when Hywell—or whatever had hold of Hywell's body—rose to his feet, she knew his was long gone.

His eyes had *melted*, leaving streaks of red-tinged foam running down his face below two gaping sockets. His mouth opened loosely, as if his jaw had been unhinged from the rest of his skull, the entity possessing him forcing it open as it spoke in an unnatural cadence.

As it did so, a voice echoed through the room—one she would never forget no matter how hard she tried.

"Good evening, Your Majesty." It didn't come from his mouth, instead seeping up through the floorboards and vibrating into her skull, so loud it was painful. It was Kestrel's voice, echoing throughout the room, and by the horror on everyone's face, they all could hear it, too.

"You, the twice usurper, thief, and first of your kind, owe me something."

"Thief?"

"*Indeed!*"

Her knees buckled.

She'd closed her eyes, and when she tried to reopen them, everything was dark and blurry. The only clear figure was the shell of Hywell. Her hair whipped around her face as if she'd been caught in a vortex, and she couldn't decipher from the indistinct shapes around her if the wind impacted the inn or anyone else. A sudden pressure gripped her shoulder—the firm squeeze of an invisible hand. It grounded her, and she leaned into it.

"You agreed to a meeting," she roared, bracing herself against the wind. "That is all I've ever owed you, and you're not here!"

A deep chuckle spread into the marrow of her bones, nothing like the mirthful giggles from their first meeting in Cinderfell. "Careful, queenie. I agreed to release you and your friends once. We are *still* contracted by our bargain. Next time, you won't be so lucky."

"You called me a thief," she spat. "I haven't stolen anything."

"No, this debt is generational." There it was, the faerie and his riddles. "One you will end."

Another deal, when she hadn't even completed the first. Another to trap her into another debt.

"Tell me what I owe you," she shouted against the wind.

"*Don't you dare promise him anything,*" came Garin's voice, an echoing growl in her ear.

They'd planned on having Kestrel sign tonight, to have every party sign, but especially him. It was a clause in *his* deal they'd struck in Cinderfell. Why the change of heart?

Did this annul his bargain, or was there still the threat of Garin's urge to kill her over their heads?

A sick dread coursed through her. Lilac thought of Garin, the way Kestrel's power had possessed him before she began her accession ceremony. "I need your signature. We can't do this without you."

No answer.

She couldn't see the bar now, the tavern, or anyone else in her periphery, but could sense Garin's presence nearby. "Tell me you will sign, or I will never return whatever it is you're asking."

"A threat." Hywell's mouth finally cracked wide, his teeth gnashing together in an unholy grin. "Plucky little thing when you've got all your friends by your side, aren't you? Your promises in Cinderfell reeked of selfish resolve. I don't know that you would have decided to draw a set of Accords concerning the Daemons if it weren't for your vampire."

A pang of guilt resounded in her chest. She thought of all the harm her father had done, the unjust beliefs her family had upheld. "He helped me realize the changes that needed to be made. I would have eventually come to the same conclusion."

"Would you? Without the Trevelyan boy's ravenous affection for you?" He leaned forward and she tried to retreat, but her feet wouldn't move. "Without the threat of him tearing your throat out?"

She refused to answer, seething. Garin's presence glared over her shoulder.

"You kept your word for the first half of our bargain thus far. You successfully ascended the throne and your coronation ball looms in just under a fortnight. Keep what was stolen, as a prize."

Stolen? Debt? But he hadn't told her what it was. "What did my family steal from you, Kestrel? Land? Jewels? Weapons? You can have them, just tell me—"

"After careful consideration, I have decided it may prove more useful to me in your hands. Yet the debt remains, and I *will* tell you," he said, an impatient edge to his sing-song voice, "if you shut up and stop interrupting me."

Lilac gritted her teeth, waiting for him to finish.

"My bluejays report the coming of the Midraal Market. The caravan has something of mine—a chest, the size of a wardrobe trunk. You'll know it when you see it. Bring it to me unadulterated and unopened before your coronation, and our bargain will be dissolved."

She had never heard of such a thing. Her throat burned along with her face, mind spinning. "But what of the Accords?"

"Do with them what you wish. I don't see any parchment, any draft in your hand."

She'd written down several issues to be addressed and planned to draft the rest with all parties present. It didn't seem everyone had arrived yet, or chosen to attend; she didn't think she saw anyone there to represent the warlocks. Emrys wasn't anywhere to be found.

"I brought them. They're in my travel bag your smoking envelope ruined," she shot accusingly.

Hywell appeared to vibrate unpleasantly, and a choking sound could be heard from his mouth as Kestrel coughed into a laugh. "Ah, yes! That was rather clever, wasn't it? Don't fret, I would have jumped into the nearest mortal even if you hadn't chosen to open it at this meeting. But I knew you'd be smart enough to wait until you were back in the presence of magic and fangs to protect you."

That was enough. "Will you sign the Accords?" she asked, glaring into his empty sockets.

Hywell's corpse sighed. "I will sign them, *queenie*. When and if you get me the chest by your crowning. If not, your darling vampire will have his way with you—that still hangs over your head."

Lilac staggered to her feet. "That's all?" The simplicity of the request made her feel suspicious. She stared into those bottomless sockets, willing him to hear her and finding it difficult to read his responses without the faerie king's ethereal and expressive face.

The guard swayed, knees trembling, as if Kestrel's connection was faltering. "That is all."

"How can we deliver it to you? Will you meet me here?" A low warning growl radiated from Garin at her invitation. "Do we bring it to Cinderfell? I can..."

But Hywell's body began to shudder, and she trailed off. He remained standing, but his head lolled to the side, his body starting to sway like a branch in the wind. Kestrel's energy was gone.

Lilac spun on her heel, eager to get away from the corpse, and the blur of the room dissolved. Garin, Bastion, and Lorietta appeared around her, while everyone else was spread between the bar and stairwell, their faces wrenched in horror.

A firm hand grabbed hold of her wrist, and she looked back to find the lanky guard behind her, the blue smoke pouring back out of his body through his nose, mouth, ears—and even eye sockets this time. Lilac shrieked and tried to yank away from him, threw her weight into it, but Hywell didn't budge. His bony fingers only dug deeper into her forearm, and if she pulled any harder he'd tear into her flesh.

A sudden, strong gust of wind swept through, and all the smoke in the room swirled into a thin veil around him before billowing up the stairwell. The inn groaned again, and several chairs and napkins toppled in the gale ripping through the building. Everyone crouched and held onto something —a wall, the bar, the bannister, their hair whipping around their faces.

"The chute!" Lorietta exclaimed over the wind. "It's not working!"

Kestrel's voice sounded again in Lilac's head this time, except she couldn't make out what he was saying—or if it was speaking at all. The noise warbled as if travelling through water, loud enough to make Lilac groan. She clawed at her ears, desperate for relief.

The rush of the ocean, the sound of pounding waves in a conch rising to an unbearable volume.

Suddenly, everything went quiet.

There was a beat of silence filled only by her panting. Out of the corner of her eye, Garin started toward her. Then, Lilac was shoved across the room.

The impact against the wall beside the bar was softened by Garin, who was uncoiling his arm from around her waist by the time she righted herself, catching her breath. The force of her landing had knocked the wind out of her. She was barely able to regain her bearings when he gave her a gentle, human-strength shove, and she stumbled backward toward the corpse.

Lilac snarled at him. "What was that fo—"

But there was a flash of metal and a *thud*. Hywell was between them, trying to yank his broadsword out from the wall where her head had just been. He grunted, unintelligible, this time in his *own* voice.

It sounded pained, like a call for help, sparking a warning through every nerve in her body.

"It's not him," Garin warned, retreating toward the front door. "Don't let him fool you."

"Those are his defense skills, though," Bastion called, leaping over the banister and onto the stairs as Hywell finally pulled his weapon from the wall. "I'll bet you aren't so upset about them now."

Lilac fumbled with the hilt of her dagger, her palms slick with sweat. It didn't help any that it vibrated. She swore and scuttled back toward the hearth as she dodged a slow but heavy swing of his blade. *What could she do?* Her small weapon was no match against Hywell's sword, which had stuck, after his second attempt, into the floorboards.

She'd have to make her mind up quickly; he'd cornered her into the dining area. Even if he moved at a very human—very Hywell—speed and was preoccupied with retrieving his sword, there wasn't enough space for her to safely dart past him without risking being flown across the room again, or worse. Lilac stepped onto a chair and then a table along the front wall, keeping her arms out for balance. She stepped down onto the next chair, then leapt onto another chair a good two feet away. Garin was watching her from the doorway, his arms crossed, and the impressed grin he wore almost made her lose her balance. Both witches watched warily from between the bar and scullery while Bastion chewed his nails on the bottom step, looking ready to bolt up at a moment's notice.

"Thanks for the help," she bit out, glowering.

"We can't," Garin said, tracking her every move.

"What do you mean, you—"

A tug at her ankle and she went sprawling, most of her torso slamming against the table she meant to be climbing. She put her hands out to break her fall before spinning to face Hywell. Winded, all she could do was kick at him, and her boot cracked against his chest, sending him stumbling backward.

"He's a revenant."

"What a thoughtful, *useful* piece of information!" She scrambled to her feet, tipping the table between them, and tried to yank his sword out of the floorboards herself. It was no use.

"He's undead," Lorietta said. "A product of Necromancy. It's outlawed. And you're its target."

If they wanted to stand around and state the obvious, fine. She had no time to beg for help.

Lilac grabbed the smallest chair near her and swung it sideways as Hywell ambled toward her. It cracked against his body, two of the legs flying off, but at least the blow knocked him away from his sword. She hit him again with it, swinging in the opposite direction, and he teetered, this time falling onto his back.

Lilac growled, seeing red, her joints throbbing, and leaped onto him. She wiped her hands, snatched her vibrating dagger from her belt, and slashed it across the front of his throat. Hywell gurgled, blood soaking her hands and her new garment. She lifted the blade again and drove it into his heart.

Once. Twice.

That was for trying to kill her and ruining the clothes Garin had gotten her.

Sheathing the blade, she stood and stumbled away from his body as he sputtered, blood soaking the floor,pooling into the ends of her kirtle and into his hair. She darted toward the door, wanting to vomit, needing to heave—to feel the cold air of Brocéliande. But she looked up and met

Garin's stern gaze. He wouldn't move, his broad shoulders blocking the door.

"Where do you think you're going?"

She struggled to swallow. "Garin, it's not funny. Get out of my way."

His hand gently clamped onto hers, as if he noticed them inching up to claw at him. "The more assailants who act against a revenant who are not its intended target, the stronger and faster it gets. *You* have to be the one who kills it."

Lilac almost laughed. "Did you not see me slit its throat and stab it in the heart?"

"But he didn't die, did he?"

She turned in time to see Hywell righting himself in the pool of blood. Did her blade do *anything*? Terror tore through her as the monster slowly stabilized on his feet; some of the mysterious smoke surrounding him had shrouded the wounds at his neck and chest.

Healing him.

"So how do I kill him?" she spat, shrill.

Garin eyed Hywell. "How do you deal with corpses who don't want to stay down?"

He was slow but strong, and seemingly unstoppable. Lilac glanced around, panicked, hating feeling so helpless in a room of her friends anxiously watching her. Glower as she did, if their interference would make Hywell stronger and faster, she would rather them stand by.

When he started to shuffle toward her, she bolted for the stairs, but Garin was in front of her before she could dart past Bastion. "Think again."

At the sound of Hywell's grunting and shuffling behind her, she whimpered and ran toward the bar door instead, and again, Garin was there. Lorietta's hands were over her mouth as she watched. Meriam looked equally angry and horrified as Hywell shifted closer, swordless.

"Garin," Lilac growled, her fingernails digging into him, willing him to budge, to *help* her. "I just want time to think, to gain the advantage—"

"You don't have that time when stronger, faster enemies are after you." He was much too cool, too logical.

"Why are you so calm?" she shrieked, sinking back against the wall where the revenant's sword had first struck.

"Trust me, there would be little left of him if I put my hands on him. But he would regenerate, even from tiny pieces, and then he'd come back stronger, lighter on his feet. Even if we ran, he'd hunt you down. I don't think you'd like it very much if this revenant suddenly learned how to run and jump, would you?"

"At least let me kill him outside?" she snarled, stumbling back, barely skirting another swipe of Hywell's grime-covered fingers. Jagged, broken nails had sprouted in place of his short, stubby ones.

"I'm the only thing allowed to chase you through these woods."

Lilac only uttered a sound of protest, a wave of fear cresting over her bravado.

"Focus. He's momentarily forgotten his blade. You've discovered yours does nothing." Garin's brow rose expectantly. "What do you do when your blade falls to the wayside?"

Against that terrifying *thing*? The way it moved toward her—the way it chased no one else in the tavern, spared no one else a glance. *Run*, her very bones urged, every muscle in her body burning, her lungs gasping for air, exhaustion threatening to consume her.

"It would chase you across the entire continent until your heart gave out."

She glared up at Garin. He was enjoying this. She opened her mouth to snap at him when her dagger vibrated at her waistline. She spun in time to see Hywell lurching toward her with his hands outstretched to wring her neck. Lilac scrambled out of the way, but not fast enough. He caught her by the hair, and although his fingers were brittle, they were surprisingly powerful. By the hair, he yanked her to him and she lost her balance, her body falling against his, nearly toppling them both.

Scalp throbbing, Lilac let out a shriek that promptly cut off when those bony fingers wrapped around her throat. They clamped down on her windpipe, and she thanked the gods when she was able to lodge her fingers underneath his. She gasped for air, trying to force his grip to loosen with one hand while the other clawed and scratched at his face until there was blood on her fingers. None of it seemed to affect Hywell.

The smile had fallen from Garin's face when she wrenched away, stumbled, and found her footing. She raised one hand to him, one obscene finger, and caught a glimpse of a fanged laugh before she rocked *back* into Hywell with all her might and toppled the both of them into the nearest table and chairs. They fell onto the table, sending tankards and bowls of pottage flying. An inhuman roar pierced her ears. Terrified, Lilac peeled herself off him and noticed he was *smoking*. He turned, spinning frantically, but all she could see was the already cold, spilled bowl of soup that had soaked through his shirt.

With no time to ask about what had burned her foe, she swiped one of the tankards at her feet and cracked it against his skull. He stumbled back, but this time, his hand shot out and caught her, much faster this time, by the arm. She barely dodged his swipe for her throat as his fingers dug bruisingly into her flesh, and she used his grip to yank him close before trying to knee him. He grunted, but rammed his head against hers, his forehead slamming into her cheek. Blood filled her mouth, and before she could think, she kicked out. This time, her foot landed on the middle of his chest, and he skidded, landing another table away.

Whatever the soup had done to him, it didn't take Hywell long to recover. He righted himself and charged. Lilac grabbed the nearest chair and swung with all her might. Hywell stumbled into the corner.

"Finish him." The command in Garin's voice made her shudder.

As if she weren't trying. She would have swiveled to glare at him if she weren't so afraid of the ghoul charging at her again, but she did suppose his suggestion sounded like a better plan than pummeling him to bits with a bar chair. Lilac jousted him with the chair this time, knocking him with such force that his ankle caught onto the lip of the large hearth. He tumbled in.

The screams that came from him were inhuman at first. It might've been the adrenaline or the shock of it all, but some part of her deep down watched with both fascination and dread as the fire slowly consumed his body, spreading quickly over his clothes and limbs. He tried to gasp, to sit up, but Lilac had set the legs of the chair onto the thick stone surrounding him, digging in with her heels and leaning into it with her weight in case he tried to escape the cage she set around him.

There, she thought ferociously, hoping this was a clear message to Kestrel. *This is what you get for sending someone to force me into another one of your bargains while ignoring the agreement we had to come together and protect Brocéliande.*

There was Hywell's voice again, pulling her from the trance of watching his burning flesh. It was *his* voice, Hywell's boyish tone pulled into a high-pitched wail that could only come from someone burning alive. He cried for help. He cried for his mother.

Lilac moved to drop the chair, but she couldn't. Her legs wouldn't move, her arms frozen, heat rushing through her. It was as if an invisible force had thrust her forward, made her brace against the chair or she, too, might be thrown into the fire.

Finally, the force driving her forward dwindled and the chair dropped, but it was too late. Muscles burning, shaking, she stumbled back. The boy's haunting sobs faded as the embers consumed him, the unbearable stench slowly filling the room with dark smoke. Somewhere in the distance, the front door burst open.

With his dying breath, Hywell's mouth opened, and what was left of the upper half of his face let out a shuddering, wet gasp, echoing around the room and into Lilac's skull. Inhuman, not Kestrel's voice, neither masculine nor feminine but another sound entirely.

"This deal has been made in blood."

Then, he was gone.

LILAC TURNED AND DARTED OUT THE DOOR BEFORE ANYONE COULD STOP her and crashed into someone who smelled strongly of cloves and anise. There was the sound of several glass items plinking onto the cobblestone as they landed in the middle of the warmly lit driveway. Lilac gasped—the wind had been knocked out of her—and rolled off the person to plop upon the cool stone. She closed her eyes and let the dampness of the night soak some of the heat from her body. The ground felt so good against her palms, her ankles, anywhere her skin was bare against it, and she heaved, throwing up acid.

Had this horror been stored in that envelope the whole time, waiting to latch onto the nearest person to her? It could've been Yanna or Isabel. One of her parents.

Next to her, the other person groaned and sat up. It took Lilac a long moment to realize who sat across from her, wiping blood off her lip.

The last thing Lilac needed was Garin's temperamental ex-lover and damn good witch complicating things.

Adelaide took one look at Lilac, her ochre eyes scanning the state of the queen. "You." She reached for Lilac, but a figure stepped between them.

Garin bent, offering her a hand, but Lilac ignored it as she watched Lorietta approach Adelaide with a warm smile. She did accept the handkerchief Garin proffered to wipe her hands and face of Hywell's blood. Hywell, her father's youngest guard, whom she'd thought would need protection from Garin or Bastion, now dead at her hand. "What's *she* doing here?"

"She invited me," Adelaide said, accepting Lorietta's help with a nod before glaring at Lilac. She bent to retrieve the handful of small, multicolored bottles that had flown out of the tattered leather pouch attached to her belt. "I wasn't going to come—I don't care enough, and that Kestrel is so unnerving. It wasn't worth the risk. But I changed my mind once I realized it was a perfect opportunity to ask Her Majesty for a favor."

Lilac pushed herself to her feet, wiping her sleeve across her mouth. "A favor?"

"I want a horse." Adelaide glanced behind them at the stables, where the three tawny horses and Löig were drinking from a trough, her waterfall of waist-length hair whipping behind her. "That stunning steed will do."

"Not a chance," Garin said. "He's Lilac's."

To the side, Lilac glimpsed Blitzrik and Ra'arak leading a shaken Sable and Jeanare back into the tavern. Meriam watched from the window.

"What do you need a horse for? You couldn't find one in town?"

Adelaide gave a longsuffering sigh. "No one in town will loan or sell me one, not after they guessed it was likely me on those WANTED signs distributed by the castle. No one's got the balls to turn me in, but scarcely anyone has wanted to do business with me either way. Anyway, I need one fast. There's a carriage I'm tracking, a moving market."

Lorietta and Lilac exchanged glances. "The Midraal Market?" Lorietta said.

Adelaide shot a surprised smile at Lorietta. "Why, yes. Finally, someone with refined tastes. I've received word that it's entered the kingdom."

"Lilac and Garin were just about to track it down."

Adelaide's gaze disdainfully snapped to them again. Then she looked toward the inn, whose windows and door were still open. The stench of charred wood and burned flesh still seeped from the tavern.

"Lilac just made a blood deal with Kestrel through his revenant, which she killed. He wants a chest that the market is carrying to the coast. Don't ask," Garin added, when Adelaide opened her mouth to barrage them with questions.

She asked anyway. "A revenant? Here?"

"Is that not a common means of assassination?" Bastion's scathing voice floated from the door. He leaned against it, breathing heavily as if *he'd* done anything to stop it. "Seems pretty fucking effective to me."

"That's the thing I found strange," said Lorietta, tearing her lingering gaze from Adelaide. "'Revenant' is a broad term for undead creatures usually enchanted by a Conjurer, or reanimated by someone skilled in Alteration. But they don't attack indiscriminately."

Garin nodded. "When created, their sole purpose becomes hunting down the person who killed them, or if they died of other causes, those attached to a recent personal vendetta in their mortal life."

"But he died in front of our eyes," said Bastion. "Didn't Kestrel kill him? Why didn't it slink off after him?"

The adrenaline seeped from Lilac's body, only to be replaced with dread. "If Kestrel sent the revenant, transformed Hywell into one to give us his message, then why would he have it try to kill me?"

For once, Garin didn't seem to have an answer. They all looked to Lorietta, who looked uneasy. "Your guesses are as good as mine."

Lilac inhaled, willing the cool forest air to invigorate her. "Can someone please tell me what this market is?" She glanced sideways at Adelaide, who seemed on the fence of regretting the predicament she'd walked into. "And what do you need from it?"

"The Midraal Market is a nomadic caravan that can only be accessed by Daemons and magic folk," explained Adelaide, her oche eyes brimming with fascination. "It brings a variety of arcane goods—armor, spices, weapons, magic—from their origin in the east and other magical realms to the western kingdoms and occasionally overseas."

"Why can't mortals access it?"

She shot Lilac an annoyed glare. "Because they don't serve or sell to mortals. Could you imagine what trouble the world as we know it should fall into if humans had access to magic they themselves could not harness?"

"It would be like giving a small child a blade," Lorietta added. "But I hear they are talented Conjurers from an ancient bloodline, and I'm sure their market is warded heavily. It's the only way they'd be able to make it across the continent without being attacked."

Lilac's throat went dry as they all looked at her. *Could not be accessed by mortals.* "Well, it's a good thing we're stealing from them, then."

Lorietta and Batsion looked uneasy, while Garin's eyes flickered in excitement.

Even Adelaide's perpetually irritated expression molded into a reluctant grin. "Speak for yourself. I'm willing to pay or trade, depending on what they carry. Their meticulous schedule brings them throughout Brittany every three hundred years, and they were last here on their merchant pilgrimage in 1340."

Lilac could do the simple math. "It's over a century early?"

"Precisely."

"So... is that good or bad?"

Adelaide shrugged. "Depends on who you ask. I assumed they wouldn't be stopping to sell to clients this time around, but I figured if I caught up to them I could ask to view their wares. Or beg. Whichever they prefer."

"You have a point," Lorietta said slowly. "It seems by Kestrel's request that the market is in the area acting as courier, and he's having you intercept it for him."

Worry flooding through her, Lilac couldn't help but feel extremely ill-prepared. She barely defeated the slow-moving revenant on her own. She groaned inwardly and looked down at herself, hoping the damage wasn't too great—and gasped.

"When Garin told me he'd gotten your clothing made with fortifying and anti-staining charms, I laughed," Lorietta scoffed, an edge to her tone. "I stand corrected."

"I also asked for a subtle agility charm, but this was denied."

"Asked who?" Lilac asked, marveling at the like-new kirtle. She looked up at both witches.

"Don't look at me," Adelaide said, while Lorietta shook her head. "I don't waste my time with Alteration."

He grinned. "If I told you, I'd have to kill you."

He could keep his secrets. She'd charm it out of him eventually, because she could definitely do with more of these fine dresses.

"It's probably the reason she's still alive," Bastion mused, hands on his hips. "Right, well, I do hope you all have a fantastic rest of your evening. Stay safe, now. Don't upset the minions of some eldritch goddess and sink our tiny country into the sea."

"Where do you think you're going?" asked Lilac as he slinked toward the shadows.

The vampire turned halfway. "I'm not going to this Midraal Market, that's for certain." There was a defensive edge to his uneasy tone. "I'm going to go do what I do best."

"Complain?"

He shot her a furious glare that said he'd slap her again if Garin wouldn't drive a stake through his body. "*Eat.*"

Adelaide snickered, tucking the front of her long fringe behind her ears. "Are you sure? I think it would be interesting."

"I'm not risking my neck for *interesting.*"

"He's right," Garin murmured, regarding his brother with a knowing look. "He shouldn't come. We don't know how long this will take, and he has no defense against the sun. He'll stay here for now." He silenced Bastion's protest with a glare. "They could use the help in my absence, especially with what just happened with the revenant."

Lorietta made a reluctant noise. "I suppose I can find him a room."

As Garin gave Bastion a short set of instructions of what to do at the bar, Lilac turned her attention to Adelaide. "You said only magic folk can find the market. Does he count?" She gestured with a thumb at Garin.

The witch swept her dark hair over her shoulder and snorted. "They will likely be warded this time if they're transporting cargo. From what I understand, their main clientele includes magic folk and the Fair Folk. Vampires usually don't practice magic, though I have heard of a couple who study just for the sake of understanding their condition better at the Ambleside Sanctum. Either way, they typically wouldn't have interest in magical weaponry or ingredients." Adelaide trailed off as Lilac looked at her expectantly. "What is that chipper look about?"

The truth was, Lilac didn't hadn't known vampires held the ability to practice magic, didn't know what or *where* the Ambleside Sanctum was, but the heady rush of fear and adrenaline she'd felt before escaping her tower weeks ago had suddenly returned.

She had not accomplished what she'd set out to do this evening, and she wouldn't get the Accords fully drafted or signed tonight. That much was clear. But now that they had an out of Kestrel's original bargain so long as they successfully retrieved his chest—which, they would—Lilac felt a little better about returning home and devoting more of her time and attention to drafting the Accords. She would perfect her decrees and keep an eye on France.

But for now, adventure called.

Lilac was hardly surprised that Kestrel had asked her and Garin to track down a market they could literally not find, but she would not pass up the easy solution before her. "We need to get to the market but won't be able to find it without someone like you. You need to get to the market but don't have a ride. You'll come with us, won't you? I'm being serious," she added when Adelaide answered with a rotten scowl. "I'll get you your horse —I'll have a stable built near your cottage. But we'll find the market together."

Adelaide hesitated, still wearing her suspicious sneer. Lilac was just about to beg her when the witch scoffed.

"Whatever. I'm riding up front."

6

No one, not even Giles, said a word as the carriage jostled along the torchlit path toward the main road.

With Adelaide's agreement, the market party had formed quickly. Giles would continue to drive, with Adelaide sitting up with him. Despite a pleading look from Adelaide, Lorietta politely refused her invitation, saying she had the inn to look after. She insisted even when Lilac pointed out they should be gone for a day and a half at the longest, and Meriam was more than capable of handling things for one night. The two witches quickly worked together on a tracking spell for the market, with the result being a small green firefly currently floating just ahead of the two horses, guiding them toward the Midraal Market. Only the travel party would be able to see the insect as it directed them, and Giles would only have to stay alert to ensure the horses remained on track.

Lorietta had also provided a warm cloth for Lilac to clean her skin, a lined basket of bread ends and cheeses, and a beaten travel bag she told them contained magical essentials for their trip. These were shoved under one of the benches for easier access.

Before they departed, Sable and Jeanare had come to give their farewells. The korikaned had retired to their warded camp stationed behind the inn, Blitzrik's arms filled with pastries baked just for Aife. Sable slung her arms around them both and pressed a small scroll into Garin's arms before pecking him on the cheek. "For your troubles."

His brow had creased as he quietly shoved it into his pocket.

It was that pocket leg which Lilac tapped now, in the quiet of the carriage, listening to the muffled one-sided conversation Giles was having with Adelaide. "Well? Are you going to see what Sable gave you?"

"Nosy, are we?" Garin lounged against the partition opposite her, his head resting against the curtain-drawn front window, arms loosely crossed. A strip of moonlight slashed across his chest from the window, but other than that, she could only sense his smile in the dark.

"I'm only curious."

"I would joke about your own timeliness of opening letters and parcels, but I think you've had enough for tonight."

He wasn't wrong. In fact, nothing about the night had gone right. Instead, she left the tavern in a worse state than she found it—the Daemons were just as unprotected as before, and she'd invoked Kestrel's wrath *again*. Not to mention, she was now embarking on some quest to fulfill a generational debt to the faerie king. What had her family taken from the faeries?

She thought of the numerous scrolls and knives in her father's armory— now hers, she supposed. The jewels encased there, the brooches her mother owned, her dagger... but why would Kestrel once own something so useless? A dagger that didn't kill anyone, especially the Daemons Henri had claimed it did. Pretty, but completely and utterly useless.

Garin's hand rested lightly upon her knee, bringing her back. "You were incredible tonight."

Lilac grimaced, and for once she wanted him to be brutally honest. "I destroyed your tavern."

He made a dismissive sound. "The inn tidies itself in the early morning hours. I've seen worse after a korrigan brawl, but I'm sure Lori will put Bastion to good use."

The dark mood brewing inside her was not so easily assuaged. "My family ruined everything for Brocéliande. I promised Kestrel I'd fix it. I promised you—" She broke off, embarrassed afresh at her... naivete? Her evident inexperience in leading, in making swift decisions to protect others. Her audacity to hope that she could make some real change with the Accords, but instead, she'd spent the evening fucking around with Garin and then killing one of her own guards as Kestrel possessed him. She'd seen the kind of power the faeries held after striking her bargain with Kestrel, the moment Sinclair came much too close to stealing the throne from her. She'd heard what it had done to Garin, and was fortunate she'd been clueless that he was fighting the urge to rip out her throat that day on the ramparts.

And on top of her piling debt to the Faerie King and his unfathomable magic, she was a young, inexperienced leader of a small kingdom that was apparently doomed unless she announced her decision to marry by her coronation ball. If she didn't, the world would then see she intended to rule alone, and France would advance. She leaned forward and placed her head in her hands.

Her joints and muscles ached, but the greatest exhaustion was emotional, souring her growling stomach and gripping her chest. She'd planned and planned, worried and ruminated, but not for any of *this*. Kestrel and the threat he posed as she and Garin acted as his puppets—he was supposed to be the thing that scared her most.

It turned out that this was not the case at all.

"I'll remind you, your grandfather catered to both humans and vampires after our raid. It was not without flaw, but he was generous in comparison." He paused. "Perhaps that sort of thing skips generations. Empathy. Common sense."

It did, evidently. Her father's full reversal of her grandfather's law that allowed donors to willingly give vampires their blood—which somehow resulted from the Raid of 1482—came days after Lilac was caught in their kitchen speaking to Freya, shifter and mother of two. She would have to dig for information on where Sable's grandsons could be, maybe even issue posters and a reward for them if the old woman agreed to it.

Lilac dragged herself out of her circling overwhelm, preferring to focus on whatever information on Daemons Garin was offering. "When those humans frequented the inn, was the ward up for them, too?"

He was staring distantly at her hands on her knees, so she instinctively removed them and crossed her arms. "No. They came to us as donors, intending to help."

"Donors? That doesn't sound any better than cattle."

Garin looked up. "I'm sorry. Do you have a name suggestion you'd like to bring to the vampire council? Perhaps we can make some changes at the next meeting."

She ignored this. "Wouldn't they be considered your thralls?"

Something about Garin's grin shifted in the darkness. The low sound of his laugh made the hair at the back of her neck stand. "There are different types of victim proximity when it comes to interacting with us."

She straightened, prepared to listen.

"Donor is the preferred term for anyone who simply volunteers to be fed on and enjoys it. They remain free. Cattle is an unofficial term used in our coven by Bastion, for those imprisoned against their will," he said, staring out the window. "That has always been against Laurent's code of conduct, and it will be against mine. But donors and cattle are the same in that they hold no connection to a single vampire. They are food. Sustenance. Nothing more."

"What about vampires like Casmir?" She'd seen the foreign vampire romancing the woman at the bar the night she'd met Garin. Lorietta said he'd had his pick of human donors whenever he'd visited. "What are they to him?"

"He bounces between donors throughout cities, countries even. He's very old, very rich, but enjoys coming to places like Brocéliande because of the seclusion. They remain donors."

They swayed as the carriage shifted right to take a wide turn onto the main road. Lilac wondered about Garin. Did he have a favorite donor who gave their blood to be bottled? Maybe a preferred scent or taste. Had he seen any willing donors since his biting curse had been lifted? She frowned. How *was* he eating? A surge of hot jealousy ran through her at the thought of his hands—or teeth—on another.

"So they're not attached to each other at all? Regardless if they're having sex?" she asked quietly as the orange-green torches faded into the distance. After supper, that night they'd met, he'd brought her to her room and tried to entrance her. It was pointless to pretend she wouldn't have invited him in even without his vampiric powers or even knowing he was a Daemon, because that was exactly what she had done.

"Not attached in the Sanguine Magic sense. It's not the sex that binds them."

Lilac exhaled and rested her forehead against the window, letting the glass cool her, feeling so, so stupid. Garin *needed* to eat to survive.

To ensure something like the Raid would never happen again.

She'd meant her inquiry to sound careless, merely curious. The heat radiating off her would give her away; surely her ears would melt her earrings off. Hesitantly, she peeked at him through her hair, expecting him to ridicule her insecurity.

But if he noticed, he didn't acknowledge it. Garin's hands were clasped thoughtfully against his stomach, one foot propped upon the other knee as he said, "Whether they've been sleeping together does not matter. Ours are matters of blood, not the heart, though a donor technically could be romantically tied to any vampire, or several—and vice versa. But that alone would not tie them in the manner you're referring to."

"And thralls?" she asked, intrigued. Garin had demanded she pretend to be his thrall when he'd brought her to the Sanguine Mine. She'd received little to no instruction, but one thing was clear: they were supposed to be obedient. It was a role she'd certainly struggled with.

"Thralls are bound to us by the blood bond, which develops fully over three separate instances of deep feeding and blood revival—me feeding you my blood."

She remembered the way he'd confessed to needing to drink from her to the point of unconsciousness, then feeding her his own blood. "That's what you tried to do to me at the inn."

"Yes. Not fully, but a first-degree blood bond—invoked with a single blood exchange—would have made you agreeable enough to follow me from the inn to the Sanguine Mine without a fight. Or without running into Morgen-infested waters." There was an empty beat. He adjusted his collar, loosening it. "Second-degree blood bonds are more complex and introduce a stronger sense of belonging between the regnant and its victim. They'll feel agitated when separated for extended periods of time, and might eventually feel compelled to seek each other out. It also allows the vampire to entrance the thrall effortlessly, even when he is low on sustenance."

What could be stronger than that? "And the third-degree?"

Garin studied her face. "That is the blight of a regnant-thrall pairing. A true blood bond. It is inviolate and all-consuming, invoking feelings of passion most will confuse with true love. It does allow for the thrall to maintain their free will in some sense, seemingly more so than the first and second degrees; they are able to go longer periods without being in the physical presence of each other, not feeling as distraught over it—yet, the regnant will consume every thought, every breath. As long as they are within earshot, the thrall is susceptible to obeying their regnant at the drop of a hat, no eye contact or entrancement required. Any request, *any* demand. The willpower of the thrall becomes bootless, while the regnant's will remains openly exercisable over them." Garin paused, as if processing his own words. He grimaced. "At this point, the thrall will act in defense of the regnant regardless of what he has done—even going so far as hiding or denying his existence entirely, resorting to aggression to protect his master."

She imagined a corrupt vampire creating an army of devoted humans. "Can a vampire have multiple thralls?"

"No. Never. After the blood bond is built through three separate instances of deep feeding and *vitae* exchange, the active thrall must die or be released in order for another to be sired. Any attempt at siring additional thralls won't produce any effect."

Lilac picked at her nails, unsure of why this fascinating information made her so nervous. "And your entrancements?"

"What do you mean?"

She thought of Father Guillaume, wherever he was, and seeing Garin in the halls. About Armand impaling himself on his own rusty blade. "Must you maintain regular contact with those you entrance in order for them to continue doing your bidding?"

Garin hummed in understanding. "Sometimes, if our commands are for extended periods of time and depending on how well-fed the entrancer is at the time his victim is spelled. Entrancements are often shorter term, lasting anywhere from hours to days." He cleared his throat, sounding like he was suppressing a chuckle. "The guards I entranced at the Le Tallec estate were still standing obediently in front of the manor last I saw them, the night before Armand came to you. They'll probably drop from thirst and hunger as soon as it wears off. It is rare, but possible for those entranced to break out of it, unlike a thrall. The entrancement can end if we specify the achievement of a certain task or time period. If we don't, the effect weakens over time, and they'll continue performing the task or playing the part until it's worn off. Your priest, for example, is very old and without much vigor behind his willpower, so I only need to pop in every now and then. I haven't had to entrance him a second time."

Lilac thought about how Henri had told her Guillaume had been summoned to Rome and would return in time for her coronation, before Garin reassured her he was kept nearby. She decided not to ask, holding not one ounce of pity for that man. He deserved whatever fate befell him.

A muted, sharp reply from Adelaide made Giles laugh, which Lilac did not believe was the witch's intent. "So how is a thrall...released, then?"

"The most common method of thrall release involves the regnant leaving them in total seclusion. The bond will grow tepid, eventually fading, but it can take at least a week to start to weaken. At times, depending on the length of the bond, more."

"One week? That seems almost too easy. The victim could escape and, in a month, be free of the bond."

"Thralls are certainly not free, though it might seem like it to them. A fully bound thrall would never attempt to escape their regnant. They'd have to be physically removed against their will, and even then, no one in their right mind would knowingly kidnap a thrall from a vampire." Garin's look was faraway, and also astonished, as if such powerful magic shocked him as much as it did her. "They will try to seek each other out in distress if the release was not initiated by the regnant. It is easy containing a thralled human, but a vampire," he said with a despondent chuckle, "not so much. In this way, there is some consequence to the vampire for siring a thrall."

An involuntary shiver ripped through her.

"Laurent did his research and had his books, made sure we all knew the repercussions of creating thralls." Garin's fingers drummed upon his right thigh, where he'd pocketed the book he'd been reading in his armchair. "He did stress that, as the underlying force behind the ability to create them lies within the same arcane magic that gives witches, warlocks, and mages their abilities, there are exceptions to every rule. Each regnant and thrall pair is different; the terms of their bond privy to only them, in ways that cannot be controlled," he continued, lost in thought. "Such a volatile relationship is not one even the most power-starved vampire takes lightly. Thralls are usually created for combat. Espionage. Pleasure." Garin paused when Lilac shivered again. He shifted off the wall, leaning forward, the flash of his teeth in a subtle grin gracing the strip of moonlight. "Have I said too much?"

"It's cold," she lied, rubbing her hands together. Some of her nail beds had been picked raw. She cleared her throat and took her time before speaking again. "Are thralls ever consenting?"

Annoyance colored Garin's tone. "Consenting?"

"Are there any benefits to it? Are there people who ever *want* to become thralls? Without becoming victimized?"

He laughed dryly. "There are those who ask to be bonded to us in that way. There will always be those who beg for it, for a dance with immortality. But the things they're after are never truly granted. It is a very strong belief of mine that all thralls *are* victims, regardless of their initial willingness."

"But if the thralls made against their own will are dominated through arcane magic, would those *willing* be driven by something like..." She trailed off, reddening, knowing her wording was all wrong.

"Like what?"

"Like love?"

"No." He answered immediately, crossing his arms as if he'd been anticipating her questioning to go there. "That is not love."

He said no more on the matter. The air was too still in the carriage. She watched, unseeing, as particles of dust swirled in the strip of moonlight from the window.

Eventually, Garin leaned forward, looking tired from their conversation. "You should get some rest," he said softly.

She would have protested, except her eyelids had become heavy, too. They had at least several hours on the road ahead. "Maybe for a few minutes." She shrugged further into her cloak and leaned her temple against the cool glass, letting the soft rocking of the carriage lull her away.

Lilac had just closed her eyes when suddenly, she was being lifted. One hand under her knees and the other around her shoulders, Garin scooped and placed her onto his bench, against his shoulder, scooting to the far wall so she had the rest of the room to curl her legs. She shifted her bottom away from him, only to rest her head on his thigh.

He cleared his throat, and she thought there might've been a smile behind the noise. He rested his hand upon her head, his fingers beginning to gently knead the tension from her scalp.

Slowly, her eyes closed again. "I've missed you, Garin."

"I am never far," was all he said.

Anywhere that isn't right beside me, touching me, is too far, she thought. She would've challenged him further, but his hand had started moving again, roaming the taut spaces between her ears and down the stiff back of her neck that had silently bore the brunt of all the calamity these last five years in the shaken, divided kingdom left to her. Garin's slow breathing, and the steady bumping of the carriage, pulled her into the soundest sleep she'd had in weeks.

KNOCKING JOLTED HER AWAKE. GARIN STARTLED BEHIND HER WITH A snort, ripping the curtain behind them to the side and tearing it off its rack in the process. The muffled voices they'd fallen asleep to from the other side could no longer be heard. The tiny green firefly that Adelaide had conjured with Lorietta's help still looped in the air several feet in front of them.

The sky before them was a gradient of rich violets. Ahead of them on the road, pinpricks of flame danced in the distance.

"Where are we?" As she straightened, several short, puffing chimney stacks became visible against the sky.

"Nearing town," Garin rumbled.

Adelaide's voice came from up front. "While you two were snoring, *I* was trying to navigate us and keep the spell active."

"Why would you need to navigate us?" she asked, rubbing her eyes. "He just follows the glowing bug, right?"

Adelaide was silent.

It was then that Lilac realized there was only one silhouette on the driver's bench.

Garin swiveled and craned his neck out the front window. "Where is he?" Fury colored his tone. "Stop the carriage."

As Adelaide uttered something intelligible for the firefly to stop and pulled on the reins, Garin was already passing her, leaping out of the slowing carriage. Lilac jumped out and followed as soon as it stopped.

"The lantern, please," Garin shouted, sounding heavily irked.

Adelaide scowled and unhooked the oil lamp, then shoved it toward Lilac. She brought it back to him just as he was lifting the back door.

Laid across the top of her trunk of belongings with his hands and mouth tied in cloth was a tearful Giles. His downward-turned eyes lit up as soon as he recognized them.

She unsheathed her dagger and, before Garin could say anything, tore through the material binding his wrists.

"Careful," he said, hastily snatching the hilt from her, and she felt him slide it snugly back on her hip as she undid the knot at the nape of Giles's neck.

"I wasn't going to cut him," she retorted as Garin shooed her to the side.

"No, but I would like to return him in one piece."

As Garin lifted him out, Giles bowed and began to sputter his broken thanks to the both of them, to which Garin returned the bow and replied, "Of course, Father."

Halfway into a curtsey, Lilac froze, horrified. *Father?*

The old man was trembling. His cap had fallen off, revealing a haphazard, choppy haircut. "Father Guillaume is our coachman?"

When she said his name, the old man shivered and nervously met her gaze, though none of the undercutting disgust he'd once regarded her with was present. "You may call me Giles, Y-your Majesty."

"Does he know?" she mouthed, confused. She didn't think she'd ever witnessed anyone entranced before, and this wasn't what she thought it would look like. He seemed... present. She'd assumed Garin had given him a new identity and sent him off somewhere, or even had him tied up at the Sanguine Mine. He'd been at the castle this entire time.

Garin silenced her with a look and patted Giles on the back as he led him around to the front. Speechless, she stomped after him. The priest's beard had been chopped considerably, and she never knew what his head looked like, as he'd always worn some sort of hat or hood adornment when they'd interacted.

How had she missed it?

As Giles mounted into the driver's box, he turned halfway around and said, "Who is this Father Guillaume?"

"Apologies, sir," Garin said calmly. "I had confused you with a spiteful religious fellow from the castle."

"Oh. Is that why the witch tied me up?"

"It is likely. Let there be no mistake, Giles is our Master of Travels and now, keeper of secrets" —Garin shot a pointed look at Lilac—"and will not, under any circumstances, tell anyone in town that she is the queen. Thus, he remains leader of the reigns. Up *front*."

Behind Giles, Adelaide rolled her eyes so far back into her head,the whites of her eyes were visible. Giles grinned in response to Garin's announcement, and suddenly, something clicked. Lilac had never recognized him because Father Guillaume *never* smiled.

The man in front of her seemed proud, albeit embarrassed even, to be driving her. Father Guillaume had always been of the party outwardly regretful that Lilac was Henri and Marguerite's only child, that they hadn't tried for a future king. He'd become even more opinionated about her future reign when her Dameon Tongue was discovered, only holding the vile things she knew he wished to voice because of his duty to Henri.

Garin glanced down at Lilac, maybe to see if there was something she'd like to add. There was nothing. She was still shaken to be this close to the man she had spent much of her life avoiding. He'd treated her like most did —a stain upon her father's bloodline, and even defended Sinclair when he'd attempted to assault her on her birthday.

"Yes," Garin continued, holding his gaze when Lilac said nothing. "And do you remember how I told you we wouldn't tell anyone of the plans of our little excursion to The Fenfoss Inn until the queen made them known to her parents and their council?"

The priest nodded, sniffling, emotion seeming on the verge of spilling out of him.

"The secret we must keep this time is the queen. Understand?"

Giles nodded again with a small smile at Lilac. It was so unnatural. It was... grandfatherly. *Paternal*. But the man he was behind Garin's entrancement was anything but.

She swallowed. Lilac wanted him to drive them and nothing more. But as she glared at him, she noticed his face was more sallow than usual,

BRIAR SOMERSET

almost gaunt, even for an elderly man. His lips were chapped, and she'd felt his robes. They were thin.

"When was the last time you ate?" She couldn't help herself.

"Erm," he answered, and she felt Garin's questioning eyes on her as she reached into the carriage. "Your witch friend's soup. The friendly one," he added, glancing sidelong at Adelaide.

The bag Lorietta had given them was under one corner of her seat; it was a large cloth satchel pieced together with leather—a welcome replacement of hers from the castle. She thought she'd seen a garment there. Lilac climbed into the carriage and felt around until her fingers touched thick cloth. With a tug, a long, woven blanket crafted in fine threads of sunset unfolded. She then quickly grabbed a handful of what she could from the basket under the other bench, emerging with a cheese wedge and bread end.

"Get ready to move," Garin instructed, leaning against the frame, shielding her. "They've noticed us stopped for too long, and two of those guards are paying more attention than I'd like."

She squinted. It did look like two of the pinpricks of torches in the distance were slightly larger. Lilac hoisted herself all the way in and reached through the window to pass Adelaide the bundled blanket and food, which she reluctantly settled upon Giles.

Lilac caught Adelaide's irked grimace as Garin settled beside her. "What?" she snapped. "You're the one who tied him up."

"I'm not sure how these will work for you." Adelaide's hand shot through the open window. There was a small bottle of vibrant blue liquid in her palm. "I don't sell these to mortals."

Lilac accepted it. "What is it?"

"An illusory tonic. It will glamor you. Magic folk can dictate what the change will be, but the more complex the change, the more skill required. Sometimes it's a different hair color, a new wardrobe. Sometimes a new face or gender completely for experienced magic folk."

"And how do I do that?"

"Heavy concentration, but it doesn't matter. Your glamor will come at random."

Lilac turned it over in her hands and made a face. She didn't know how much she trusted another potion from Adelaide.

"Or don't take it, I don't care."

"They're discussing coming to investigate to see if we've broken down," Garin said quietly, placing his hand lightly upon Lilac's knee. "Start the carriage, Giles, or I'll have to do something about them."

"You will not." Adelaide's eyes glowed yellow and simmered as her head snapped back to them. "Some of us *live* here. We don't need either of you ruining everything for us again."

Lilac watched the torches stop, then slowly bob closer. "My parents and our castle guard know I'm supposed to be in town today."

"Yes, and they'll help *you*," Adelaide spat, fixing her hair. "The rest of us will be thrown in the dungeons for kidnapping you. Trust me, it'll be easier if these people don't know the queen is in this carriage." She glanced ahead, where even Lilac could now make out the silhouettes of the guards. "Although at this point, it won't happen fast enough." She groaned. "No, better to drink it. Swallow every drop. And don't look out of the window or open those curtains until it takes effect."

"Fine, and how long does it last?" Lilac asked, heart hammering.

"It fades the moment you consume food or drink, so don't do that."

"And you?"

"They already know me," Adelaide said, eyeing the guards. "They fear me, and that's enough."

Lilac looked down at the bottle in her hand, then at Giles. "No one will notice him, will they?"

"If no one recognized him at your stables, they won't here."

Adelaide had a good point. Garin was watching her expectantly, looking a little flustered as he peeked through the front window at the beginnings of Paimpont in the distance.

"Well?" he snapped. "Are you taking it or not?"

The carriage jerked into motion. Lilac popped the cork off and tossed it back. It tasted like burnt blueberry jam. "What about you?" Lilac managed, suddenly feeling selfish. He was probably the last person Adelaide cared about being recognized.

"No one will recognize me," Garin said quietly. "The last time I was in the area was when we were at the farmhouse. And the time before that, the night of the Raid. I haven't been back in the years since." His eyes were trained on the road ahead, but his hand slipped onto her lap and fumbled around a bit until she placed her free hand in his. He grasped it. "Easy now. We should pass through no problem, then veer off north or south."

"Or continue straight," Adelaide optioned. "Into the Low Forest."

She hoped not.

They passed the guards who had sauntered onto the path, and she pressed against the seat in case anyone could see through the slits in the curtains. There were no changes yet; she didn't feel any different besides a slightly sore throat from swallowing the potion. She wanted to ask how long it took but decided not to speak. They were all silent as they neared, and the tiny glowing bug led them straight into town.

The guards eyed Giles and Adelaide but didn't stop them as the dirt path turned into cobblestone.

"A bit early for foraging," one of them called out to Adelaide.

The other chortled as they rolled slowly past. "All that's a bit much, don't you think?"

Adelaide whipped her head in their direction. "I'm preparing for a blood sacrifice, and these are my loyal lambs," she shouted merrily. "Would you like to watch? Or to join?"

The guards didn't bother replying.

They rolled past a few streets of small houses and homes above shops before reaching the square with an ivy-covered fountain at its center. There was something eerie about witnessing Paimpont cast in the violet haze of dawn, barely anyone but the guard roaming at this hour. Lilac glimpsed the Hemlock Haberdashery across the square, the newly painted sign above, full in its letters and not peeling and aged like those which adorned the surrounding shops.

And then the carriage stopped. With an annoyed grunt, Lilac pushed Garin aside and peeked out the front. A stooped old woman stared at them, puffing from a pipe as she turned back to minding her business.

"Why have we stopped? Keep going, Giles."

Giles was already talking to the horses, clicking and manipulating the reins, but it appeared they wouldn't budge.

"Keep going," Adelaide urged, waving her hand at the bug, which circled back to her, looping around her head. "What's the matter with you? Don't make me put you back into this jar."

Garin reached across Lilac to peek out the curtains to their left. His lips snapped into a devilish smile, and despite his obvious nerves, he closed them again and opened his own door.

"What are you doing?" Something rippled over her skin, a shocking heat, and for a moment she felt faint at the rapid change in temperature. She gasped and leaned back in the seat. "Oh, Adelaide I…" She fanned herself, willing the dancing spots in her vision to leave.

"Ah, perfect, it's working." Garin was already slipping from the carriage without another glance back, closing the door to a crack behind him. "I'll meet you for a drink."

"A drink? Are you *joking*?" He didn't answer. Fuming, Lilac slumped, itching to pull the curtain, peek the door open. *Why had they stopped?* But the potion was finally working, and she couldn't risk anyone seeing. She took two deep breaths, bracing herself against the most unpleasant feeling of hot fluttering that continued down her legs. "What about the market?"

"With Adelaide's tracking spell, timing isn't as important. We'll be quick." There was a smirk in his tone, and Lilac wondered how his nerves had managed to make him more insufferable. "I'm asking you for a drink, Lilac. Not eternity."

Then he was gone, shutting the door behind him.

Ears burning, teeth gritting—she couldn't help it—Lilac lifted her curtain to see Garin stroll into the shop where they had stopped before. Above the door, the bug was flying in frantic circles, partially obscuring her view of the sign that hung there. A tankard and steaming loaf of bread were painted on it.

A pub.

"*Oh*," she shrieked, covering her mouth and releasing the curtain. A tingling sensation of warmth had suddenly spread from her center, shooting down each limb and up her neck, into her toes and to the top of her head.

"The horses won't move because the spell itself stopped here," Adelaide whispered.

Giles had gotten down to try to coax the animals forward on foot, but they wouldn't budge, instead intent on watching the insect flutter back and forth between them and the establishment to their left. As she watched, the horse on the right sat down, jolting the whole carriage.

"Might as well go. We'll wait here. I'm going to fix it."

She suddenly felt the snug fit of her leathers and blouse leave her body —only to be replaced by the soft feel of...

Of unmistakable satin. She looked down. A white gown covered her legs, while the most intricate designs were embroidered in sheer sleeves of muslin that hugged her arms, the bodice aptly supportive yet breathable and adorned in silk and lace.

In the premature sunglow and torches flanking the business, she bolted out of the carriage, not even needing to see her face to know something was *very* wrong.

Adelaide watched her approach, eyes wide. A bemused grin bloomed on her face. Giles had slid back into his seat, blushing immensely.

"What is this?" demanded Lilac.

"It's the glamor. Though, that's much too specific to be one the tonic chose for you. Without arcane concentration, for a mortal, it's usually something arbitrary, like different hair, a large feathered hat, or a mustache, or—" She pouted, disappointed in the lost opportunity to see Lilac in something comical.

This was embarrassing enough. "Turn me back."

"To follow him in there? You're better off dead. Stay in your glamor, Lilac. Trust me." The witch glared warningly.

No, she would not follow Garin anywhere dressed this way.

Lilac stamped back to the carriage door; she refused to join Garin for his glass of scotch or whatever it was at five in the fucking morning when they had Kestrel's quest to complete. Adelaide placed her hand on the frame, which scattered with violet sparks for a second. Lilac tugged at the handle, but it was no use.

"Adelaide, let me in."

"*No.* I need to reset the spell, and having you hanging around will just be an irritating distraction, if not a reason for townsfolk to come interrogate us. Go away."

A glance at the firefly showed that it was still circling the door, traveling from a pair of men who'd stepped out to share a drink on the stoop, and the torch that lit the peeling pub sign.

The Jaunty Hog. She knew it well without ever having been.

Lilac turned back to Adelaide with a frown. "What does this mean?"

"It usually does this around a roadblock, something preventing me from accessing the destination."

"But this is no roadblock. It's a pub."

"Right." Adelaide stood, leaning over the front railing, sneering. "It is a door, which you must go through in order to discover just *what* is causing the error in my spell, before I leave you all stranded and put your driver's organs in my ingredients cabinet."

"Dressed like this?" Lilac hissed. "I thought your spell would help me blend in."

The witch shook her head, her onyx hair falling around her face. "Illusory tonics and their glamors are only designed to help the wearer look *not* themselves. And you certainly," she said with a sharp cackle, "are most unrecognizable."

THE MOMENT LILAC ENTERED, SHE DEEPLY REGRETTED NOT BRINGING her cloak. She recognized the owner right away. Bog Abgrall, a stout fellow with beady eyes and a half circle of thinning brown hair framing the sheen of his otherwise bald head, stood behind the bar, cleaning tankards and chucking them into a wide bucket. He was often at the castle during her father's Court of Common Appeals, reporting the infractions of neighboring shops or requesting repair loans, by which Henri had been generous; one might wonder what needed repairing if not for the ancient cracked bar, sticky pocked floor, or the rickety tables and chairs that befell her nervous gaze now.

Bog didn't look up as she entered. "Be right with you."

Lilac muttered her thanks and approached Garin. He was seated upon a barstool with his back to her, another stool pulled closely to him. He didn't turn to look her way, seemingly distracted.

She followed his gaze to the right corner at the back of the room, where a group of men lounged in one of the booths to the left of the blazing hearth carved into the wall. Three of them were half asleep and the other four were actually snoring, their heads resting against their seats or slumped onto the table. Upon the two tables they'd pulled together were a couple tattered journals, a thin stack of parchment, a quill, and a large piece of paper that appeared to be some sort of illustration. One older couple sat at the other end of the bar. The pub was otherwise empty.

"Two cups of cider, please," Garin said, not taking his eyes off the table. He finally turned as she approached the bar beside him—and blinked. Garin's pupils widened, even as his brows rose. He glanced around, watching the elderly woman nudge her partner in the side as Lilac climbed upon the stool next to Garin. "She'll take a metal tankard, if you've got any of those."

Bog muttered something about special accommodations, then looked up at her. He double-took, and a wide grin spread over his face. He fished in one of the presumably clean tankard buckets, turned to the barrels behind him, finished with their drinks and brought it over, beaming. "On the house for the lovely couple. Congratulations. I'll bring some food."

Lilac pulled her drink the rest of the way across the counter, planning on bringing it to her mouth to pretend to swig from it. When she lifted it, she gasped, hiding her shock in the cup. She swallowed air and could see Garin in the corner of her eye, one foot up on his stool beam, one bouncing on the floor, watching her. He hooked a finger into the handle and then pulled his cup toward himself, expressionless.

She fumbled with the cup, holding it again in front of her to see her reflection. All the remnants of blood she'd probably missed under her nails and in the creases of her face were gone. Her hands went to her hair, which was no longer chestnut but a deeper shade of mahogany—the edges auburn, as if backlit by the sun—and gathered into a pretty, thick bun at the base of her scalp, loose curls daintily framing her face. Her full cheeks were primed in a vibrant wash of color as if bitten by winter wind, lips and eyelids painted in the same lovely shade of berry. Her chest was adorned in a lace filigree of branches and leaves with glittering crystal dewdrops upon a plunging dress that framed her chest, her arms covered in fitted cream sleeves lined in the same sheer material.

She'd seen the dress in the carriage, which was devastating enough, but *this*...

She'd witnessed this vision before, in her reflection at the Lake of Mirrors, where Kestrel had deposited them. This was some kind of mistake; it *had* to be. This disguise was supposed to hide her. The old couple across the bar and the men at the table were staring, but it seemed to be because of her dress and not her identity. Adelaide had been right; her features were so enhanced by the cosmetic trickery she stared at now that she wouldn't be recognized.

Was this a joke? No one else knew about the threat of France—and what her parents believed the solution to be.

Or did they?

There were no shadows under her eyes, which were clearer, sharper in the candlelight of the tavern. A stranger stared back. In her reflection, she looked sure of herself, sure of her decision. She looked beautiful, even in her devastation.

Eleanor Trécesson was radiant.

She was a bride.

7

It looked—and felt—so real. She gripped the sides of her stool.

Bog reappeared with a plate of bread, butter, and a jar of preserves. "For the beautiful bride, and"—he glanced sidelong at Garin—"her friend."

She frowned, mouth open as the barkeep left them. "Why did he say that? Why would he think we aren't together?"

Garin tipped the cup back, swallowing before answering. "That was delicious," he said a little loudly, wiping a dribble from his mouth, then tearing and popping a small corner of the bread into his mouth. "Oh, he thinks we're together. He just thinks I'm your paramour."

Lilac glanced around, reddening but too fascinated with watching him eat to pay attention to his second remark. "How are you doing that?"

The bar was getting fuller now, several overnight denizens from the inn on the upper floor emerging, yawning, from the staircase at the back. Other newcomers shuffled through the front, some joining the group in the back corner. Some of them noticed her, their gazes lingering a bit too long.

"Chewing," Garin answered through his mouthful. "Then swallowing."

He said nothing more when a second bar hand appeared—a towering maiden—and left a small plate of cheese between them without a word. Her stomach growled, and she shifted in her seat.

Garin gazed out at the slowly growing breakfast crowd over his tankard, his shoulders slowly relaxing. They might have sat at Bog's dilapidated bar, but he still looked like a prince who'd taken a wrong turn. Spoiled and a little dangerous.

They were just two people, two friends, enjoying breakfast together. One of them happened to be in a wedding gown. She remembered how easily she had assumed he was human, albeit a striking one. Was everyone here as fooled? Or had she just been easy prey?

Bile burned her throat as she watched Garin spread preserves over the piece of bread he'd plucked from the plate; she hadn't even had any of Lorietta's pottage and should have eaten on the way.

When he bit largely into the steaming rye and followed it with a corner of cheese, he looked more human than ever, a lock of his dark hair falling onto his forehead. "Blueberries in rye," he said, his eyes rolling back. He examined the bread. "My God. I'll have to tell Lorietta about this. An unorthodox pairing, yet entirely logical." He ran his tongue along his bottom lip. "Wouldn't you say?"

Lilac couldn't help but stare. "You... enjoy food, don't you?"

"All of our senses are heightened. We enjoy every version of food as an indulgence. At least I do."

"Won't it make you sick?" she said under her breath.

He pushed it toward her.

She shook her head, annoyed. But her stomach rumbled loudly this time, giving her away. "I can't."

The corner of his mouth twitched as he turned his head and took in her dress. "Pity. We all crave things we cannot have." Before she could reply with something scathing, he leaned sideways against the bar, eyes on her. But instead of the usual warmth in their depths, she saw only a taunting coldness there. "Did your parents prompt you to marry after that skirmish on the border?"

Lilac's face turned heated, and she scooted closer to him. "Lower your voice," she ground out. "It was not a skirmish. They were asked to leave and obliged. How did you hear?" Damn the loose mouths in her court. Had it been her father's weak councilmen?

"What did you think would happen once you rose to power?" He snorted. "I would not be surprised if your darling mother included

BRIAR SOMERSET

wedding invitations in those coronation ball parcels she sent out last week."

Feeling violated and nauseous, Lilac cleared her throat, smiling at the elderly couple indiscreetly staring as she tucked her hair behind her ears. She supposed posing as a man of the church, Garin heard all sorts of juicy tidbits, but she hadn't thought that would extend to state secrets. She'd dismissed him, but not soon enough.

"She did not," Lilac said, trying her best to foster calmness with all the eyes on them. Some from the corner table had started to stare, too. She placed her hand reassuringly on Garin's knee. "There will be no wedding."

He bent his head toward her. "You think they'll stay away for long?" He tsked, eyes snaking over her form again. "You do make a stunning bride."

His obvious insincerity took her by surprise. Did he think she'd hid France's border testing from him on purpose? It had been pushed from her mind the moment she was with him again. Maybe she should've mentioned it to him in his room at the inn, but she'd been so distracted by everything else—by the Accords, and his hands and tongue.

Fuck. Was he hurt? Angry?

Either way, considering the condescending evident disdain with which the vampire regarded her now, he could go to hell.

Lilac tilted her chin. "I do, don't I? One day, I'll make a regal adornment on my betrothed's arm."

"Indeed." His voice dripped with sarcasm. He looked around, seemingly unconcerned with the eyes his grating tone had attracted. He gripped her metal tankard and took a swig from it. "You'll make a pretty gift to..." He waited expectantly. "Whom, again?"

A gift? Lilac stood, her stool toppling back with a *crash* and garnering several heads turning in their direction. She never expected this to be his reaction.

His long leg casually stretched out at her side, subtly boxing her in. "Come, now. Don't I at least get to know who you're marrying?"

"I don't have a fiancé." She picked up her stool, her face on fire, her tongue dry as she eyed her tankard in his hand, furious. She could really use that drink.

Marriage. The word tasted rancid on her tongue.

"Yet."

How dare he interrogate her in the middle of a mortal bar, where anyone could hear. She sat stiffly down on the edge of her seat, not looking at him.

Garin took her silence as confirmation. "Clever girl. But you must have been propositioned by now. Who might it be, then?" When she didn't answer, his hand tiptoed across the bar, toward hers. "Scotland?" Her reality and his venom sank deeper with every word, every guess. "England?"

"Garin," she whispered. "Stop it."

"What king?" His fingers brushed her knuckles, and she pulled her hand back.

"Not a king."

"What prince?" He waved a hand. "What duke? Or... *marquis*."

"An eligible bachelor from an allied kingdom." Why was she telling him any of this? She had half a heart to give him answers—to prove wrong whatever it was he was trying to prove—and half a heart to dart out, into the square and away from a future she did not want to face.

"So *any* royalty?" His eyes tracked hers to the door over his shoulder. "Don't make me follow you into the square."

"Not just anyone," she said, lifting her nose and looking down on him. "Not necessarily a monarch or prince in line for the throne. Any foreign nobility with the armies to stand behind me in order to ward François off. I'm going to bargain to keep my sovereignty."

He snickered loudly, and she resisted the very strong urge to snatch the drink from him and toss it in his face. "So your progenitors have lowered their standards for you even further?"

"Why?" she seethed. "And no, I have not been propositioned. You're not offering, are you?"

His wicked smile faded. "No," he said coolly, "I just didn't think their standards could sink any lower than Sinclair."

"The bar has been on the floor for as long as I can remember."

"Wonderful." Garin's eyes flashed, so intense she was forced to look away as he took another slow sip from her tankard. "When it's in hell, you'll know where to find me."

All the anger and irritation in her swelled and had nowhere to go. She felt trapped. She would not let him see her cry.

"Then you are still unspoken for." He said the words plainly, quietly, like they were simple for him to digest. But the way his hungry gaze wandered over her throat and dress was unconvincing. His eyes dropped.

"I suppose I am." If Garin thought she *chose* this, he was an idiot. If he thought she wanted this, he did not know her at all. And maybe he didn't. "Surely none of this surprises you."

"It shouldn't have," he said softly, gazing distantly at her dress, not with hunger—or jealousy—but something else she couldn't quite place. "Not with the very real possibility of France gearing up for a real border skirmish. Your parents must have known. They've been eyeing your kingdom for years; someone must have suspected they would make a move once you took the throne."

"It's as if I haven't had everyone telling me I'd be a weak ruler because of my sex," she whispered frostily. "The idea of my marriage didn't catch you off guard, did it?" The thought made her sick, but rubbing it in his face felt good. In truth, she had spent little thought of the immediate threat posed by France until receiving news of the scouts yesterday morning. Upon returning, she'd inevitably be thrown into hours of meetings regarding the matter. Another issue to stack against her parents and her ill preparation, yet she was in no way surprised.

Garin said nothing.

"I didn't expect seeing me in a wedding dress would make *you* so angry."

He scoffed, his glimmering eyes snapping to her face. "It is not the dress." He tucked her hair behind her other ear and leaned in as if to whisper sweet nothings to her, elongated canines glinting in the firelight. "That dress is the least of my worries."

Heated, Lilac turned her head away from him, both horribly aroused by his evident jealousy and disgusted by how he dared use it against her. Even Garin looked far less than his usual, collected self, his hands balled into fists as he unabashedly stared.

A bold, bleary-eyed onlooker walked by, took one look between the two of them, and slapped Garin on the shoulder. "If you don't want her, I'll have her." Garin turned slowly to the man, whose smile abruptly faltered, and he quickly shuffled off.

Lilac was still trying to think of a proper rebuttal—or repair? She didn't know what she wanted, where she stood where Garin was concerned, and she wanted to understand why he seemed so furious—when someone started to play music.

Terribly.

A scruffy man in tattered brown robes came into view around the bar, plucking a lute and mumbling what resembled a sad tune, his beard dragging along the floor behind him. Some of the early-morning visitors swayed to his song while others jeered and booed.

The tavern owner emerged from the back of the room. "Emrys, for fuck's sake, give us a jig!"

Lilac did a double-take. *Emrys?* This man looked a far cry from the warlock she remembered leaving The Fenfoss Inn the first night she had visited. That man had been mysterious, regal—emanating power, even after an evening of imbibing. This man...was a drunken fool.

She glanced at Garin, who had frozen at the mention of Emrys. His eyes darted between the bard-warlock and the booth of men, many of whom seemed particularly entertained by the music.

Emrys, who had apparently not heard Bog as his dour tune continued, was just passing the corner booth when one of the older men shouted. A drink flew through the air, and the tankard cracked against Emrys's skull. Lilac winced sympathetically, but the warlock only rubbed his head and stopped singing, blinking in the direction of the thrower.

Garin cleared his throat, and only she was close enough to hear it was a low growl. "I know we were just arguing, and there is no one on earth I would rather continue that with but you, but I would consider it a great favor if you would distract that booth for a few minutes."

"Bog said to liven it up," the man who'd thrown the tankard roared, and the entire group and some around them toasted and laughed. Emrys swayed and glanced in Bog's direction, his eyes much too glassy and bloodshot. He gave a feeble smile and thumbs up, then began strumming a merrier jig, the first few notes so off-key that Bog winced in disgust.

"He's getting no supper tonight," Bog laughed, walking to the corner table with more drinks.

By the time Lilac looked back to Garin with her dubious reply, he was gone. Emrys had continued his stroll around the bar, and she spotted the top of Garin's head, several inches taller than everyone else, slowly making his way to the warlock like a shark.

Some of the men from the booth were watching as Garin met Emrys at the corner of the bar, and some booed as he handed the drunken man some bread. Emrys blinked up at Garin, and as his eyes widened and they began to speak, the men in the booth whispered to each other.

Time to move.

Lilac slinked off her stool, her almost empty drink in hand, and made her way straight for their booth. The huge illustration covering their tables was in fact a hand-drawn map, ink blotches, spills, and wrinkles marring its surface. Yet, its purpose remained clear.

It was a hunting map. There was the unmistakable curve of the Argent and her castle in the southwesternmost corner, and the rest was Brocéliande. The High Forest to the west, Low Forest to the east, and in the middle, sandwiched in between, were the farmlands, Paimpont, and Adelaide's marsh. Her eyes traced where she'd approximately found the ogre nest and then ran across The Fenfoss Inn, thankful there was nothing there to mark its existence. Nor was there any mark for the Sanguine Mine in the northeast of the Low Forest. There were several marks indicating a shifter or vampire sighting, but it wasn't clear how old these were or what the men's tracking methods were. Were they as inept as they looked, or a real threat? Were these the men Armand and Sinclair hunted with?

The hair on her neck rose as she surveyed the map, tiny wooden figurines, journals, and quills alongside it.

"What are you looking at?" one of the men seated across from her snapped. Most of the men at the booth hadn't noticed her yet; they were still watching Garin feed Emrys.

"Now, now," said Bog out of the corner of his mouth, setting down fresh tankards atop the map. "She's our guest. Our lovely, esteemed, probably wealthy guest."

The man who'd spoken earlier used his forearm to block off some of the map, but before anyone could do or say anything, she tucked her drink into the crook of her arm and plucked the nearest quill from its inkpot.

"Here," she said, pressing the nib to the parchment. She circled a general area well to the west of The Fenfoss Inn, unsure of how they calculated coordinates on a hand drawn map. The perfectionist cartographer Riou, who often assisted her father and Armand, would have pulled his hair out in patches.

Another, this man burly and shorter, peered around Bog. "What is *here*?"

"The largest camp of korrigans you have ever seen." She slurred purposefully, knowing all too well the way her words melted together when she'd had one too many ales. She winked at them when their eyes widened. "My father is a renowned cartographer. It seems like you could use one of those. Anyway, they are much safer to hunt than vampires or shifters, and easier to tie up, I'd imagine. They're smaller, so you'll catch more in one trip. Ten to twenty korrigans sounds like a more secure capture, doesn't it? Versus, say, all your men against one vampire."

The first speaker and Bog exchanged glances, while a couple of the men turned their attention to her. Bog chewed on his chapped lips. "It wouldn't take *all* our men to take down a vampire."

"Well." Lilac looked up at him through her lashes and ran a finger along his bicep. "How many of you are there?"

From the corner of her eye, she noted Garin slowly but surely making his way toward the front of the tavern, supporting the very inebriated Emrys. The other men whispering made her nervous, but not so much as Garin, who turned his head casually to see Lilac with her hand on Bog's arm.

His eyes flashed, brows slightly furrowed. Was that amusement? Confusion? *Disapproval?* She couldn't tell. And, she reminded herself, she didn't care.

When Bog seemed reluctant to answer, Lilac scoffed loudly enough for surrounding tables to hear while staying close to him. "It doesn't look like you have that many."

"We have a small militia," another of them with a bowl of black hair growled. "Led by—"

"We have enough." Bog glared at his counterpart.

"It would take at least *ten* men to restrain a vampire." Garin's head snapped to Emrys, who put his hand to his mouth and started to retch. "And I *barely* see ten here," she said loudly, causing all of those sitting around the tables to turn their attention to her.

Garin scooped Emrys into his arms when the old man stumbled.

"We have seventeen," the burly one said. "Eighteen sometimes, but—"

Lilac, who'd been leaning against Bog, slipped forward as Bog suddenly moved toward the door. The drink tucked in her arm spilled all over the map and off the edges of the table, causing the men at the table to yell and scuttle out of the booth.

"Whoops," Lilac slurred again, reddening, putting on the act of her life. "Looks like it's time for that cartographer."

Bog let out a sound of anguish, as if someone were kidnapping his first-born. "What are you doing? Put my warlock down this instant!"

Garin, nearly at the door, slowed and glanced over his unoccupied shoulder, dubious. "Warlock?" he called across the bar. "Don't you mean your bard?"

"No. I mean, *yes*—he isn't very good at singing, but he is our bard none-theless. *My* bard. People pay to see him. Let him go."

"Well, your bard's had far too much to drink, and his singing is going to empty the bar faster than any scuffle with my wife."

"Mathias! Lorenzo," Bog called, and the two men who had addressed her before stalked from their corner and through the crows, past Garin, stopping in front of the front door.

Mathias? Lorenzo? These were the men who had hunted Daemons with Armand and Sinclair.

Garin stood before the pair, tall and unrelenting. "He collapsed at my feet. Surely you can see he is unwell. I'm simply taking him to get some fresh air."

Bog stomped forward, while Lilac followed. "No, you're not!" He took hold of Emrys's arm and tried to heave him off Garin, but the vampire was already moving away, trying to dislodge the tavern owner.

"I am," Garin said, a streak of human-like bravado crossing his face as he tugged back.

When Bog finally stumbled back, his face was full of rage. "You take my warlock, you leave me your prize of a wife. I'll have her entertain us." A glob of spittle landed at Garin's feet. "In her wedding dress."

"Yeah?" Garin laughed, politeness crumbling away to reveal his open derision. "She'll insult your patrons, drink all your alcohol, and maybe draw you a better map. She won't bring you the crowds—"

There was a *crack*, and Garin stopped talking. He hadn't moved at all, but he blinked in disbelief as his hand slowly went to his jaw.

Bog had punched him. The tavern owner chuckled, his first still balled, seemingly proud of his own courage, and said, "She might not, but setting her up in one of the chambers upstairs would."

It all happened quickly. Garin slung Emrys across his back, and with a pivot of his shoulders, had Bog retreating against the door, Mathias and Lorenzo slowly easing away. Garin hadn't even touched him, but with the way he was staring Bog down, Lilac knew the tavern owner would have been through the door if Garin didn't have an image to maintain. A growl emanated from the vampire, and his back seemed to quake with the effort of refraining from pouncing.

Step by step, he closed in on Bog, whose instincts seemed to kick in and tell him *something* bad would happen if he ran from the tall, lanky fellow before him.

Lilac grabbed up two slices of bread, slightly steaming, that had been left at a nearby table. One bite, and she would turn back. She could do it. She would, for him. Her word might not hold much power in Brocéliande, but this was different. These were her people, hate her as they might. She would threaten them into compliance if it meant saving him.

She pocketed one piece of rye and held the other tightly, concealed in her palm. Garin was right. It smelled delectable.

As Garin reached for him, she brought the piece to her mouth. His hand wrapped around Bog's throat.

"So." The voice of a man boomed from behind. Everyone turned, including Garin, who'd started so hard he'd almost dropped Emrys. Lilac did drop the piece of bread, which clicked hollowly upon the plank floor.

The entire inn had fallen quiet. A few knocks and calls from outside, now that the door had been blocked for several minutes, went unanswered. Several patrons stood off to the side, looking nervous, probably eager to leave.

An elderly man stood in his nightgown—silk, Lilac noted, with a fur shawl over thick robes—at the top of the staircase. He clung to the banister with one hand, a wooden cane with the other. He looked like he would collapse the moment he released either support. An eye patch covered his right eye, but the left was gray and milky. It was hard to tell where he was staring, but something told Lilac he was staring right through her soul.

Bog began to stammer. "S-sir, I'm sorry. They were causing unrest."

A smile spread on the man's face as he turned and started a slow, wobbly descent down the stairs. "Which one of you," he asked, a word with each step, "disturbed my slumber?"

Garin breathed a low chuckle, but there was something tight about the sound.

The man finally reached the bottom and placed both hands on the cane. Anyone within five feet scurried back as he began making his way to the door. The cane scraped against the floor with each step.

"There are guests trying to steal our bard, my Lord," said Bog, his voice taking on an unusual deference.

My Lord?

The man seemed to ignore the tavern keeper as he stopped several feet away, his good eye fixed on Garin. "Better yet, who was it that allowed this vampire into my tavern?"

8

"Him?" Bog looked at Garin, deference for the old man replaced by slight skepticism. "A vampire?"

"Shut up, you buffoon." The old man took a final step forward and jabbed his cane at Lilac. "Grab them."

Garin stared at her warningly, shaking his head minutely as Lorenzo strode forward and gripped her by the shoulders. Mathias took him by the arm.

He was urging her to play along.

"Slice her," the old man ordered.

Lilac squawked in protest as Lorenzo tightened his grip on her. "Get your filthy hands off me!" When he ignored her, she tried to draw away from him, disregarding Garin's pleading eyes, and she was able to pry his fingers off the back of her neck before he coiled them around her throat, walking them back and pinning her to the wall beside the door. Furious, she looked to Garin, who wore an exaggerated expression of dread.

Lorenzo pulled a small paring knife and held it to her chest, and she had no choice but to still before the blade. He sliced her shallowly above her breast, and it stung enough to make her whimper. The sound of her own pain galvanized her rage, and the moan turned into a growl as she stomped his foot. He dropped the knife, cursing, but roughly yanked her hands and secured them behind her back.

Warmth trickled down her chest now, probably a violent sight upon the illusion of her wedding gown. Garin glared at the man, at Bog and the crowd as a curious circle gathered around them. When Lorenzo yanked her off the wall and brought her to him, he began to struggle impotently in Mathias's arms.

"What is wrong with you? All of you?" Garin snarled, twisting this way and that under Mathias's grip, his hair matted in a sheen of sweat against his forehead. "We are two innocent travelers passing through, and this is how we are treated?"

"Feed her to him," barked the man, spittle flying from his lips. "Show everyone! They'll believe me then. Let him drain her."

Lorenzo thrust her forward and Garin caught her as she tripped. His fingers were trembling as they gripped her arms, his face twisted in remorse, in apology. She stilled beneath his touch, wondering if he was going to drink from her in front of everyone as he refused to meet her eyes.

Feeding him felt like such an intimate act between them.

The thought made her heart erratic and made her thighs throb. *Do it*, was all she could think. *Do it and make them scatter like ants.*

Garin pivoted her, baring her throat to him, eyes black. The crowd of Daemon hunters and others watched in horror, unable to pull their eyes away. *Sick bastards*, she thought, shutting her eyes as she prepared for the painful pleasure of his teeth.

But Garin's grip on her loosened, and she stumbled back as something splattered her boots.

Garin heaved again as a second wave of vomit poured from his mouth, nearly dropping the warlock still somehow balanced on his shoulders, all the mead and bread he'd scarfed at the bar coming up unrecognizable.

She shrieked and scuttled back, as did everyone else. Mathias shoved Garin, grunting in disgust as the bile coated his legs. Hands on his knees, he heaved once more, but nothing else came out. He groaned and wiped himself on his sleeve.

"This is impossible," the old man spat.

Bog jabbed a finger at the door. "Throw them out," he barked at his men. "He will burn."

There was the sound of a latch lifting, and Mathias swung the front door wide open. He barked for the confused patrons outside—a small crowd now—to make way before dragging Garin out into the blazing morning sunlight, Emrys slipping off his shoulders. Lilac dodged Lorenzo's arms and scrambled out after them.

Mathias shoved the vampire to the ground, and as Garin fell, Emrys's limp form fell hard against the carriage before flopping to the ground. Adelaide's look of relief from atop the driver's seat quickly dissipated as she took in the state of the crowd pouring out around them and those that gathered from the square to see what the fuss was. Giles looked around from his perch beside the witch, oblivious.

The townsfolk had formed a circle around them. Everyone watched as Garin struggled to his feet, wiped his mouth and pushed the hair from his eyes—and *did not burn*.

Lilac feared he might massacre the town a second time, but he seemed to still be in control, in character, behaving weak and affronted.

"The devil's work," growled the old man, pushing his way to the front in the shade of the door. Several bystanders' eyes widened as if they'd seen a ghost.

"Monsieur Le Tallec," they muttered, looking shocked to see him outside. Some of them bowed.

Slowly, Lilac backed away. He was the mad duke. Armand's father had been pardoned early on, leaving the duchy to him at the mere age of seven. The reason wasn't clear, and her father had only said he was unwell when she'd once asked. Sinclair had mentioned his grandfather during his rant at the camp, but he'd also made it sound like the old man was sick, perhaps incoherent, noting that he spoke often of the Raid. The one here was aware and filled with such a simmering hate, there was no doubt in her mind that he was a driving force behind the Daemon hunts, along with Armand.

Garin bent to pick up Emrys. When he had the warlock secured—he was breathing, but still limp—Lilac whirled on Bog and his guards.

"We will never return to your tavern," she said, raising her voice for everyone to hear. "Accusing us of the most ludicrous things, assaulting your guests with knives!"

Bog chuckled nervously, gaze darting around the crowd as their whispers echoed throughout the square. "It was an honest misunderstanding. We thought he was a vampire," he said, pointing at Garin, who was pulling him into the shade of the carriage and dabbing the blood from Emrys's nose with a napkin.

The old man—Sinclair's and Armand's *relative*—bopped him on the head with his cane, none too gently. "He *is* a vampire."

"That man, not burning in the sunlight? The one currently tending to the poor warlock you've been exploiting?" she snapped, jerking her head toward where Garin ministered to Emrys.

"No, no." Bog chuckled, nervously patting the air. "He *wanted* to work for us."

"Or, he came for a drink and you never stopped serving him," Garin said, rage behind his quiet suggestion.

Bog shuffled nearer, lowering his voice. "You'll keep this quiet, won't you?" Le Tallec stumped closer to hear. "This was a terrible misunderstanding."

"This entire town will know of our mistreatment," Lilac said. "Other towns. Maybe even the queen."

"Please." He clasped his hands together, looking at Le Tallec for guidance. "Consider my warlock a gift."

"You've done enough. The warlock is just collateral."

He stepped back, reeling, and glanced helplessly at his crew. The lot from their booth was there at the front, behind Mathias and Enzo, looking ready to brawl in the middle of the street.

This time Lilac leaned toward him, her voice dropping. "I'm sure the queen would love to continue funding your secret trips to the forest once she learns where her family's funds have really gone. Certainly not to your pub." She cocked her head to the carriage, the fine working horses. "Where do you think my husband and I get our funding? We are never that sloppy, are we?"

She glanced over to Garin. Warning hesitation flashed across his face. *Ever the actor.*

"So readily giving away our secrets?" he chided under his breath.

Bog froze, and she stepped closer. Her eyes caught on the haberdashery across the plaza, where she could've sworn the curtains opened and then quickly shut at the top floor window.

"Others are watching," the tavern owner murmured.

"It's only a matter of time before the royal family finds out on their own, Bog. Imagine what little it would take for them to get a magistrate to come for your ledgers. It didn't strike me that *skilled* Daemon hunters would need to steal from the crown to fund their trips." She felt Le Tallec's and Garin's eyes on her and pointedly ignored them.

"The royal family would never fund them outright, in fear of conflict," he breathed. "Henri is too weak. His father was even worse. You said you come from a family of map makers."

"Who do you think it is we work for?" Lilac leaned nearer, pretending to guard their conversation. "My father works with the Trécessons and is paid handsomely to survey the land while scouting and documenting Daemon territory. There are certain maps he's made which are confidential, but *I've* seen them. I might've even tipped off Armand and Sinclair."

Bog said nothing as Adelaide stared annoyedly past them at the slowly growing crowd. Garin supporting Emrys, who was half slumped against the carriage door.

"Is she helping you?" Bog whispered.

"Everyone can use a worthy witch, from seasoned adventurer, to the seedy bar owner about to get his shop closed due to improper handling of royal funds."

He swallowed, watching Lilac cross her arms expectantly. "What do you want?"

Lilac fought the sudden urge to laugh at the thought of them being picked to pieces by hungry ogres. She placed a heavy hand on Bog's shoulder, spooking him. But he didn't move away. "Head to the location I'd circled if your map is still legible."

"Don't listen to her, Bog." Sinclair's grandfather's voice boomed from his position mere feet away. He stood tall, or as tall as the slight hunch in his back would allow. He looked to Mathias and Lorenzo, then turned his hardened glare at a fidgeting Bog. "You're going to let a band of strangers working with the village witch give you orders?"

"These orders were from the Le Tallecs themselves," Lilac pushed, heart racing.

She managed to peek a glance at the carriage; Garin was watching Lilac intently.

Le Tallec laughed. "No, they weren't." He gestured at Adelaide and Lilac exchanging glances, and Garin looking like he'd topple any minute. Emrys still leaned against him, but his hands were on his knees. "My son would never command our hunting troupe with the likes of you. With those who work with Daemons themselves."

"He wouldn't," Lilac said coolly, but inside she was panicking. She felt the enormous weight of all the eyes on her, the glares, despite people not knowing who she was. What if someone saw through her illusion? What if someone thought she looked familiar? She had to trust they wouldn't. "But Vivien would."

It was a shot in the dark. Those were all she knew how to take, but it looked like this one landed.

Le Tallec's eyes narrowed. "Vivien."

The clatter of distant horses' hooves and carriage wheels had the heads of the crowd turning in a wave. Then, a horn sounded. Bodies shifted to get a better view at whatever newcomer was gracing the town, and Bog and Le Tallec's crowd took one look and began to quickly retreat back into The Jaunty Hog. Thankful for the distraction, she strode over and took the other arm of Emrys. Up close, Garin looked ill—or was pretending too well to be ill. He too was glancing in the direction of the new carriage, and soon, the crowd began to part. Lilac swung the door open and tried to heave on Emrys's arm, push him and Garin up the step, but the vampire had frozen.

The top of a wooden carriage with gilded corners could be seen in the distance, and before it, the two sets of cream-colored ears.

"Come on." Throat dry, she adjusted her grip on Emrys and managed to at least tug them further into the shadows.

The royal carriage drew near, and hushed whispers spread throughout the crowd. As they rounded the cobblestone road, Lilac saw two more carriages following the first.

"His Grace," those around her were whispering. "Why is His Grace here?"

It was her father.

Garin finally shoved Emrys in. Anyone watching them would have seen him do so with the inhuman strength of a single hand, but no one seemed to notice.

The moment he hit the carriage floor, it lurched forward, the open door nearly toppling her and Garin. Adelaide's and Giles's surprised cheers could be heard at the front. The horses moved slowly through the crowd, the glowing insect resuming its loops through the air as if nothing had happened.

They jogged to catch up with it; Garin gripped her hand and pulled her through the open door with him. They both landed in the car, her on top of him and partially Emrys, who was still sprawled on his side. He reeked of onions and ale, and was in desperate need of a scalding bath. She groaned and shoved herself off, pulling herself onto the seat, dragging the warlock with her.

"What *happened* to him?"

Garin swore from the bench opposite, reaching past to slam the door shut. "I don't know. Lori said he'd stopped showing up and never re-rented about a week ago. I'm not sure if there was a fight or something that upset him while I was at the castle." A flash of regret crossed his face, and he wiped it away with a pass of his hand.

Gently, he lifted Emrys off of Lilac's lap and placed him against the wall on his bench, where he continued snoring, snuggling into his oversized robes.

Lilac's ears were ringing as the top of Adelaide's head popped up in the front window.

"Well? Was your support vampire not enough?" Adelaide growled. "Did you need an elderly chaperone?"

"Your tracking spell led us to him, the carriage only began to move once he was in it. *Go*," she urged. "Faster."

Giles prompted the horses, and their carriage increased its speed, eliciting shouts and jeers from the morning crowd.

Why was Henri there? He said there'd be an investigation at the Le Tallec manor, but he'd never mentioned attending. Did he come to ensure she was in town?

To preemptively announce her intent to marry?

"He's made an announcement," Garin said, concentrating. "His crier is shouting out the window."

"What is he saying?"

"They're passing through." He paused to listen, the smuggest smile she'd ever seen on him growing wider by the second. "They're coming for Sinclair's arrest."

THEY RODE OUT OF TOWN IN SILENCE. ACCORDING TO GARIN, WHO continued his surveillance of Henri's announcement out the window of their own carriage, Sinclair's arrest was the only thing her father's town crier had divulged to the public.

They exited the last of Paimpont through the northern path, finally steering right at Miss Quillrose's Tea and Spice Emporium, which was much further from the Le Tallec estate than the southern path that hugged the property. As soon as they were out of town, Adelaide demanded that Giles halt the carriage at her cottage. Garin teased that she wouldn't get out of the journey that easily, and at the witch's stony silence, Lilac realized that was exactly what Adelaide wanted. Garin apparently understood the same and told her that was an idiotic idea, Lilac adding that she was the one who wanted to find the market to begin with, when Adelaide promptly shut the communication window.

This did little to stop the argument.

They were silenced when Giles whoaed the horses as they approached her cottage, and the animals, ensnared once more by the fluttering insect, made no movement to do so whatsoever. With a final goad from Garin about jumping from the carriage, the matter was settled—Adelaide would be accompanying them to find the Midraal Market. The witch spent several minutes snarling on about how ludicrous it was the horses wouldn't halt for her when it was *her* tracking spell directing them.

Garin sat across from Lilac, supporting Emrys's bobbing head on his shoulder. When he began to stir, he tipped the warlock's head back and made him sip from a wooden flask he'd acquired at the bar to help him sober. He'd taken a few sips before pushing the flask away and retreating back into his cloak once more. Parts of the concoction, which contained oats and eggs, had dribbled out and dried in his beard, which was so long it coiled over Lilac's feet. It didn't take long as the morning grew warmer to notice the carriage reeked of sweat, ale, and maybe some kind of cheese. Out of both disgust and guilt, Lilac reached down and set the mound of Emrys's hair onto his lap so it at least wasn't touching the floor. After a bump on the road, it slid off his legs again, and a hand darted out. Garin tied the beard into a loose knot, which hung effectively above Emrys's lap as he drifted back off to sleep.

From Lilac's nervous peeks through the curtains, for which Garin cursed everyone, it seemed they would venture into the Low Forest. But before they broke into the dense thicket of winding tree trunks and twisting roads, the horses took a sharp turn to the right, jostling everyone as the carriage teetered one way, then the other. Garin's arm shot out across the aisle to keep her from being flung against the wall, but his hands were off her as soon as they were righted.

Garin frowned, and when he lifted the curtain on their right, she saw they rode along an iron gate. Within it was a slightly overgrown garden. They were behind the Le Tallec estate, sandwiched between it and the edge of the Low Forest.

The curtain was dropped once more, and she forced her thoughts to her father and the scene they'd left in Paimpont. Sinclair would finally be brought to her dungeon, where he belonged, ruined by fire or not. The blacksmiths had hammered at least a couple of the four damaged cells brand new, as far as she was aware. He could sit in the smallest cell and await the fate she decided for him—the gallows or guillotine. Which one depended on how much she felt like making him suffer.

Lilac absentmindedly rubbed at the scar on her leg, thankful for the belt from Garin that now held her dagger. Her father had publicly covered for her. He didn't have someone else do it or leave room for speculation; he had done it himself. For her. Sinclair was guilty to the public, the Le Tallec family soon to be found guilty for treason. There was no mention of a trial or her audience, no need to show her scar to a jury of people who might not have believed her otherwise.

Garin's voice broke into her musings, though he seemed to be talking to himself as he glanced outside. "How odd that we're headed south, away from the path that would allow the market to sell to the Fair Folk." He glared out the front window, retreating into his thoughts again. His chest moved noticeably, as if he were focusing on controlling his breathing.

Then, he methodically pulled a second flask from his pocket, brought it to his mouth and gulped. She looked away, knowing by the small sounds of satisfaction he made that it wasn't alcohol he was drinking.

Even in the semi-darkness of the curtained carriage, she could feel his intensified gaze shift onto her, then away again. Each time, a buzz of anticipation coursed through her, only to feel deflated when he made no move toward her.

Lilac slumped against the seat, crossing her arms and bouncing her foot until her gaze fell upon Lorietta's bread basket beneath Garin's bench. Suddenly remembering her hunger, she dove for it, and Garin started back with a grunt, as if witnessing her bending to reach between his legs had caught him off guard. She greedily pulled the basket onto her lap and found a bread end. A small sound of satisfaction escaped the back of her throat; they were still *very* warm. The basket was enchanted.

He watched as she dipped the tip of the knife into the small bowl of butter and brought it to the bread. It was as if he'd never seen a girl butter bread. Maybe it was the wedding dress she still wore. She was wrong—this was the best glamor she could have hoped for. *Serves the asshole right*, she thought, silently thanking Adelaide's tonic. She looked up through her lashes, meeting his gaze and smirking.

It might as well be his first and last time seeing her in one.

His eyes narrowed. "Just what do you think you're doing?"

"Eating." She frowned under his glare. "I'm starving."

"Why are you breaking your glamor before we find the market?"

She waved the blunt knife in his direction. "Who knows how long it will be until we find it? Besides, you've eaten," she said, looking pointedly at his pocket.

Garin leaned in. "I don't believe being in a confined space with a hungry vampire is something you want to experience."

"I've done it before." She paused, the loaf halfway to her mouth. "Maybe I enjoy it."

"And how do you expect to proceed once you're recognizable again?"

"Just as I'd planned before. Pure luck and delusion."

He leaned back in his seat and scoffed under his breath. *"Unbelievable."*

"What do you care if I'm seen?"

"We're conducting a heist of a foreign market—an arcane market. You cannot be seen." His hand darted out as she brought it to her mouth once more.

Lilac stared at his fingers wrapped around her wrist. She imagined them sliding down her arm, down her body. It had been hours, yet she missed the way his hands felt.

What would it be like to hold them, be held, without fear of scrutiny or retaliation?

"What do you plan to gain by revealing yourself to the Midraal Market, Lilac? To anyone else we might encounter before you're safe at home?"

"What makes you think my home is safe for me?"

His nostrils flared. The way he looked at her was torturous.

"They might sell their goods to us at a lesser price." They both shot a look at Adelaide, who peered back at them through the partition. "What? She's the queen. The *Guài* are perfectly political creatures, commonly holding positions of power and wisdom in the eastern empires. Even in the *mortal* world, they are respected as much as they are feared. They are likely diplomatic enough to understand the importance of trade with royalty. Maybe we'll be lucky."

Lilac tugged her piece of bread away, and he only gripped her tighter. "I'm tired of being kept hidden, Garin."

"As long as you're alive, you're a target. Even without your arcana lingua, this would be true. What's a little pretending if it protects you?"

"When do I get to be myself? Appear as myself?" She gripped his hand with her other and slipped her fingers under his, almost annoyed he let her win so easily. "I was just in a tavern, in the nearest town to my own castle, with a bit of rogue on my cheeks and my hair up, yet no one noticed me."

He laughed darkly, infuriating her. "It is certainly more than a bit of rogue."

"What is that supposed to mean?"

"I would not have noticed you, if it weren't for your infuriating scent. And it is a good thing no one did. You saw what that tavern was like."

"I did." Lilac shoved his hand off, furious with his ability to insult her with his logic. "They don't respect me, or my family. When does it end?"

"You're the queen. It doesn't."

She searched his face, and he gazed back at her, completely unremorseful. Garin opened his mouth to say something else cutting, but the carriage abruptly began to slow, causing Emrys to fall into Garin's lap. The horses began to whinny and stomp.

Garin attempted to right the warlock, his head swiveling.

"Why have we stopped?" he called to the front.

Adelaide only hushed them, her hand on Giles's mumbling mouth.

The forest had grown silent. No bird, no rustle of wind in the eaves could be heard. She expected to hear the bluejays, Kestrel's most trusted scouts singing in the canopy, but she did not. All was still.

Garin yanked the curtain back to reveal an overcast sky quickly becoming obscured by a thick mist that began protruding from the trees. The glowing insect was nowhere in sight, but it seemed they'd emerged onto the path that ran south of Paimpont and the estate. The bug had just started to pivot them into a wide right turn.

There was a loud whistle, then the sharp cracking of wood. A searing pain—an actual heat—scorched Lilac's knuckles, and she shrieked as the piece of bread was knocked from her hand and stuck in the plank to her right. She blinked, pressing her back against the seat. The blueberry rye had been skewered upon the shaft of a glowing red arrow.

A hole, rough and singed in its edges, smoked on the wall to her left. Warmth spread down her knuckles—a throbbing pain—and she pressed her hand into her dress as the pounding of heavy hooves neared. She startled when a tingling sensation rippled from the crown of her head, down her face and neck. The sensation was not slow crawling, like when her glamor had first materialized. This was quick, and jarring.

The beautiful dress she wore smoldered away in a violet border of flames that quickly engulfed her body, revealing her kirtle beneath.

"We found him!" came a female's echoing voice from behind, muffled through the carriage walls—along with the clomping of several heavy hooved.

"Is the tracking spell still active?" Garin was also flat against the wall, eyeing her in alarm.

"No," Adelaide shouted, frantically searching for something within her robes, then within her bag.

"Then onward, Giles!"

"Yes, sir. Which way?"

"Away from the arrows!" he roared as Lilac shrank away from the one stuck inches from her face.

"Back west it is." The carriage sprang forward at Giles's command, and without needing to change directions, he quickly got them up to what felt like a dangerous speed. "But what about the market?" Giles shouted.

"We won't be able to find it if we're dead." Adelaide held on for dear life, looking like she was on the verge of trying to climb through the tiny partition. "Did none of you bring weapons? Really?"

Garin snarled in frustration. "None that are long range. What about your vials?"

"What do you think I could have picked up when I asked the carriage to stop at my house?"

Lilac was already elbow-deep in the bag Lorietta had provided. She pulled out the first hard thing she felt: a round, narrow-necked bottle that fit in the palm of her hand. It felt heavy, like there was liquid inside, except none had spilled out even in the jostling of the carriage. A piece of cloth hung out of its open mouth.

"What do we have here?" A wrinkled hand shot out. Emrys took it from her, fully awake now and leaning forward from Garin's lap. "A light-and-toss."

"A what?" they said in unison.

"A light-and-toss," he said matter-of-factly.

"And what do we do, Emrys, with this light-and-toss?" Garin asked.

"I'm... not sure. I was never allowed to have one at the Academy. As far as I know, you light it." The warlock held his index finger and thumb and pinched the corner of the cloth. It burst into a slow crawling flame that climbed the material. He handed it back to her. "And toss." Pleased with himself, Emrys peeked out the window at their attacker and dropped the curtain again, his face suddenly pale, eyes bulging.

"I'd do it quickly if I were you," Adelaide snapped, climbing onto her seat to get a better view. "Height helps with dis—" Her eyes widened as Lilac ducked under the arrow shaft, holding the smoking bottle and cloth away from her body. "Why did you light it?" she screeched, her black hair whipping around her head.

"It was Emrys!"

Whatever it was that didn't register for anyone else clicked for Emrys almost immediately. He opened the door to their right and gripped Lilac firmly by the waist before hoisting her right out of her seat. Garin seemed so taken aback by the movement, he didn't stop the warlock in time, and when he did move, she was already halfway out of the carriage.

Her stomach lurched, and she shrieked, cussing at the warlock as her hair whipped around her face. She held the flaming cloth as far from herself as possible and clung to the top of the door with her other arm. The flame had already burned a third of the way up the material.

"Let her go!" Garin shouted, and Lilac gasped as Emrys's hold loosened for a moment, then gripped her tightly as he adjusted her so she was seated on his shoulder. Emrys was surprisingly strong for his age.

She could hardly see anything through her hair, but could feel Garin jostling him below, trying to pull them back in without toppling Lilac. "Stop it, you two," she screamed, scrambling for purchase and steadying herself on the roof. "I'm going to fall!"

"You have one chance," Emrys bellowed from below. "Don't miss!"

With a final shake of her head, her eyes were clear—and she almost wished they were covered again.

Charging toward them through the mist was a stunning black and red carriage pulled by a single animal. The magnificent broad creature, long and off-white in coat, with two thick horns, was nearly the size of the cart itself, wide as two horses side by side. A woman with two long black braids stood in the driver's box, steering the animal toward them, while another followed beside it on horseback, wielding a thick bow and arrow.

Her heart dropped. A retractable awning jostled along the left side of their cart, various charms and symbols swinging wildly in the wind.

"What does the market look like?" she yelled.

From behind her, Adelaide's panicked shriek pierced the howling wind. "It's the market, don't throw it!"

The flame was nearly at the bottle; there wasn't any time to deliberate.

"Lilac," Garin commanded. "Throw! Throw it or we'll get blown to bits!"

She arched her arm back, but another arrow whistled through the air, this time hooking the bottle in the opening. It flew out of her hand, which got soaked in the bottle's contents and erupted briefly into flame. She shrieked, but it was lost to the wind as a burst of light and air exploded ahead of the carriage. Another shout from an unfamiliar male voice, screams from Adelaide and Giles, and a chilling unison of horse neighs were almost simultaneous with a deafening crash.

Then, Lilac was airborne.

9

Hands were fluttering over her when Lilac began to slip into consciousness. She couldn't see anything, couldn't tell if her eyes were open, but the hands... She knew they were Garin's by the slow, steady breathing above her. She could feel them, but barely.

It was everything else she felt. Pain—excruciating agony—spread down her back, up her neck, and into her pounding skull. She could barely move her arms; she twitched a finger, or at least she thought she did. There was a loud exhale of relief above her. A hand lifted hers, cradled it, but a chest-shattering moan came from her mouth at the ripple of fire that it sent into her shoulder.

"Garin, don't *touch* her," Adelaide snarled, her voice trembling and broken. "Don't—" She trailed off, gasping. "I found him. Your driver."

Then, the witch was silent. There were no discernible sounds coming from Giles or even Emrys.

"You hit the girl instead." It was an unfamiliar, echoing female voice she heard now, off in the distance, cold and laced with blame.

"I shot him eventually," a second voice replied. She was clipped, aggressive. Younger. It was the one she'd heard shout earlier, the horseback archer.

"He wasn't even your target," Adelaide shot from nearby. There were footsteps.

New fingers, soft and smaller, gingerly palpated her collarbone—then her sides, and the pain there was so great it caused Lilac to inhale sharply. She couldn't do anything, couldn't move to swat those hands away. Her gasps turned into sobs, breaths feeling much too shallow. Each time her ribs expanded and contracted, a jolt of agony ripped through her.

Adelaide cussed, backing away.

The first voice spoke again, low and apologetic. "I don't understand. Our scout is never wrong."

"Well, it was," said Adelaide. "She's not just a *girl*. She's our queen."

There was a moment of silence. "She tells no lies," said the first voice to her counterpart. "Is she yours, blood drinker?"

"Yes—n-no." His hands lifted off of her. "She is my charge."

"A vampire and the mortal queen," the second voice mused, growing closer.

Lilac tried to move, to sit up, to see. She felt herself blinking—at least she thought she was—but all she saw was darkness.

"Stay away." Garin's response was pure warning, his voice inhuman. "You've done enough."

The shuffling slowed as it neared. "She is suffering from her injuries," said the second voice. "We have nothing on our cart that will heal her momentarily, but you can simply offer her the kiss of death. She will be renewed."

"No." His answer was curt, leaving no room for protest. "She's awake. She can hear us, I can tell by her pulse. But she won't open her eyes. What is wrong with her?"

"My arrow was imbued with a spell that strips a person of all active glamors and illusory magic. It's just a wound to her hand."

"Do not speak the obvious to me," Garin snarled. "She is still partially glamored, and her body is pulsing with magic, but she won't wake."

Still glamored? What did he mean?

Adelaide interrupted them from near her head. "Her breathing is quick. Drink, then feed her your blood, Garin. It'll heal her."

"*No.*"

No? Somehow his answer shocked her. His hesitation to turn her was understandable. She wasn't sure it was something she would choose over death, either. But healing her? Why wouldn't he do it?

Paralyzed, Lilac itched to move, to scream. Others would suffer without her; the Daemons and her kingdom needed her, but that wasn't at the forefront of her concerns.

She was selfish. Angry. How dare life be ripped so violently from her fingertips. She had a kingdom to fix, a job to do. Everyone to prove wrong.

A vampire to bed again and again. His hand to hold, his mouth to kiss. She'd barely lived. She focused on the pain in his voice, on the fury and spite surging inside of her—anything was better than allowing herself to crumble under the stifling agony.

Save me, you bloodsucking asshole.

"The blood exchange alone would not save her," drawled the second voice. "She's not exactly dying. Her pulse is there, enough to buy you time to make a decision. You should be able to hear it, vampire."

"Not exactly dying." His words were venomous. "I can also hear the rattle in her chest. I refuse to believe there is nothing you magic folk can do."

The first voice replied, "We don't have magic folk where we're from. We are the *Yao Guài*. We reign over arcane ingredients and transport for Emperor Shizong and other influential parties, though the fugitive we seek is of personal interest. He is a most powerful warlock, eternal in his youth, golden hair. Born of an incubus and a sorceress. We've tracked him across continents."

"And what do you want with him?" spat Garin.

"He owes us after paying with counterfeit coin."

"That's it?" Adelaide made a skeptical noise. "And you thought that drunk warlock was him?"

"We were traveling to the coast when my sparrowhawk began tracking him," said the first voice, tinged in regret. "She led us to your carriage. She has never been mistaken."

"Well, she was," Garin said, his fingertips caressing Lilac's arm, her shoulder. A tingling numbness had set into her hands. "This is a clear mistake. She's not supposed to—" He took a deep breath, and by the shuddering sound Lilac knew there were tears. "This wasn't supposed to happen. There are potions, spells. Ones that can heal her from the inside out."

"Of course there are," the second voice interjected dryly. "And there are those who can heal with their hands. Bonemenders, such as Feiyan. But to stop any bleeding, you would need some sort of tonic or a talented Blood-smith. Alas, I am only an archer."

The first voice—Feiyan—interjected. "You are so much more than an archer, Na. Even if Xiu was mistaken, the warlock *must* be in this area, lurking in the forest somewhere. He is the only person I have known to have come back from death, over and over."

"My sister is right," agreed Na. "He might be able to heal her. If *you* paid his debt to us, he would be required to fix your queen. Or, if he cannot, he would fulfill any duty, however you see fit."

"How much does he owe you?"

Adelaide made a sound of disgust before they could answer. "Don't pay them! We don't even know what he looks like or where he is—"

"Here," said Garin. A bag of coins clinked near Lilac's head. "Is that enough?"

"It is plenty," said Na.

"You chased him across continents for *that*?" said Adelaide.

There was a warning edge to Na's tone. "No one gets away with theft from the Midraal Market without paying. Not even death itself will erase a debt to us." The bag of coin jingled as Na retrieved it. "But now his debt is paid in full, and he is released by...?"

"It doesn't matter." Adelaide's answer was frosty.

"We simply must know who released the almighty Myrddin of his debt."

There was an intake of breath from Adelaide at the warlock's name. "*Myrddin?*"

"Trevelyan. Garin," he bit reluctantly.

"*Trevelyan*," Na crooned the name as if inhaling it, and the sound of it on her tongue jabbed a distant spike of jealousy in Lilac's chest.

"You're sure?" Feiyan sounded taken aback.

"Yes," said Garin roughly. "To ensure something like this doesn't happen a second time. So no one else falls victim to a carriage accident or worse over a ten-shilling vendetta."

There was shuffling near her again, to her left. "May I?" Feiyan said.

Garin was silent but remained by her side as she approached.

Then, a light pressure upon Lilac's abdomen. Two palms and a dull ache. They moved outward, reaching her ribs and causing her to wince.

"Well?"

"Her ribcage is shattered. Part of her spine as well. The type of spell I can do to mend her bones is not the same," Feiyan said, her hands moving down Lilac's abdomen, "as the tonic we'd give to stop her bleeding. I don't have one on me, but either way, those together will corrode her body. Mortals are not meant to sustain such amounts of arcana."

Fear spread slowly like molasses through Lilac's veins.

"And the warlock?" Garin asked, on the brink of hysteria.

"We don't have time," Adelaide said softly.

"She's right. And that much magic in the queen's body might kill her anyway, with how weak she is. Myrddin is powerful, but not specialized in medicine."

"But," added Na, sounding amused, "your vitae would heal her tissues and bleeding quickly, with almost no consequence at all."

Garin's laugh was scathing. "No consequence?"

Gentle hands brushed the hair off her forehead, smelling of anise and satsumas. "Na is right. Sanguine magic is different, not as abrasive as general arcana. It deals specifically with the soft tissues of the body—the mind, vessels, and arteries of a mortal. It would not affect her bones, would not overwhelm her with magic. I can heal her spine and ribs, but it will do nothing for her internal injuries. Bone mending magic is hard enough on a healthy mortal body, with no other affliction. Your queen is hemorrhaging, vampire."

"Yes, and this is your doing."

Na made an angry sound of protest. "We pursued you as we tracked our warlock, but I shot the second arrow trying to help. There was a human man traveling on horseback ahead of you, coming from the opposite direction. It was he who was not paying attention."

Garin and Adelaide were silent, and there was a sudden burst of warm wind—sunlight and breeze danced across her skin, warm and golden behind her closed eyelids.

Their mist—likely some sort of ward—had dissipated.

"See?" said Na. "He was on the wrong side of the path. He could have crashed into anyone. Just be thankful it was you and that no one else in your troupe was harmed."

Suddenly, Garin's fingers slid under her, hands prying between her rigid body and the ground. She exhaled, bracing herself as she rolled against Garin's chest, the pain excruciating. This was not a torment she could ignore. She breathed through a whimper, tears leaking from her eyes. She wished for it to be over and remain in his arms, cradled like this.

Despite Adelaide's protests, Garin lifted her carefully, and Lilac rose until she could tell he was standing.

"*Garin*," Adelaide said in warning.

"Not harmed?" His anger was palpable, she could feel it radiating off him. "Her spine is broken. You killed our warlock and coachman."

"Only your warlock. The driver still lives," said Na. "As does your precious queen. It did not escape us that *you* had a tracking spell of your very own. Why were you seeking us in the first place?"

He answered with some effort. "There is a chest you carry. Kestrel, of the Court of the Valley, wanted her to retrieve it from you."

There was a noise of recognition. The *guài* said nothing when there were footsteps, the sound of someone walking away.

"I'll do it," Garin called out disbelievingly. "Heal her spine. I'll do the rest. Just tell me what I owe you."

The creaking and slamming of a wooden door—that of their carriage.

Na, who'd lingered behind, suddenly giggled. "My, my. Fate is a fickle thing, isn't it?"

"This is not her fate," Garin snapped. "Not as long as I'm alive."

Feiyan returned, her footsteps heavier. Something large clunked with each one, the sounds of wood against metal. "This is for you." She set the item down with a grunt.

Lilac's heart fluttered. *The chest.*

"What's in it?" asked Adelaide.

"We weren't told."

"What do you want for it?"

"It's yours. The vampire's, I mean," Feiyan said. "Bring it to your faerie king in good faith. Normally, I would charge a string or two of copper coins for something that does...nothing. But your servant's life is collateral. And it doesn't surprise me Kestrel wants it back. What would that faerie like more than a gift that was supposed to go to someone else?"

Even with her mind clouded by the rush of adrenaline, something didn't seem right. They were giving the chest to them for free? With nothing in exchange? Garin and Adelaide were speechless, but if they felt the same suspicion they didn't dare express it.

There were sudden hands on Lilac's chest, and Garin lurched back. "Take your hands off—"

"Silence, vampire." Feiyan's soft demand sounded just as lethal.

"Lay her back down," Adelaide urged.

"Yes, place her against the earth."

Garin bent his knees and gently did as he was told. The *guài* bent with him, her hands in contact with her abdomen. Without any warning, Lilac's body suddenly went cold—frigid, as if she laid in a tundra—then warm, her skin tingling. Then, Feiyan's nails dug into her, pressing her ribcage together.

Lilac let out a bloodcurdling scream and felt herself seize involuntarily. *Movement.* Her shoulders jerked up toward her ears, and she breathed through the unimaginable searing pain flooding her chest.

"There we go. Roll her over," Adelaide directed, and Garin's hands pivoted her body onto its side.

Lilac coughed, bile and vomit shooting up from her esophagus into her nose. Garin began rubbing her back, patting it while she emptied her stomach.

"Consider it a favor," said Feiyan.

"And this," Na added.

Behind her was an enormous creaking and scraping of wood.

Muted golden light flooded her vision, and Lilac blinked against it. Everything was hazy, as if she observed the scene from underwater. There was Lorietta's bread basket demolished in the dirt, and beside that, a bloodied pale foot peeked out from worn robes. *Emrys.*

Large hands gripped her and ripped her toward the surface. Toward the light.

She started to struggle, but Garin refused to put her down. "You're weak. You'll need to rest."

She itched to reach up, to brush the hair from his forehead and put her lips to it. He looked pained, like he ached to do the same. But she pushed and eventually he gave in, setting her down gently. Her legs were shaky, her thighs feeling like she'd trekked leagues, dark spots marring her vision.

Once she supported herself, she was instantly dizzy. Lilac looked down and saw her neat, clean kirtle and leathers from Garin. Her glamor *was* gone.

Their carriage was also upright, their horses grazing the tall grass off to the side.

Adelaide stood behind her, hovering over two bodies. Two men, Emrys and Giles, lay side by side.

Giles looked like he'd rolled. There was dirt and debris in his hair, his eyes softly shut, chest almost imperceptibly rising and falling. Emrys laid on his side, tangled in his own beard, a red glowing arrow buried in his chest.

Adelaide offered a despondent smile, her face streaked in grime and tears. She was dragging a large wooden chest—Kestrel's—to the back of their carriage. Those women, their large creature and the market, were nowhere to be found.

Lilac opened her mouth to ask, but a startling cry escaped instead. "What happened?" she sobbed, turning away from Giles and Emrys, feeling like she might collapse.

Garin reached for her again, but his head snapped up and locked on something just before there was a faint rustling behind their carriage.

"*Salvēte*," came a voice.

A man in traveler's robes limped toward them. He couldn't have been more than thirty with dark brown hair, a thick mustache, and a trained smile despite his appearance. Burgundy soaked the side of his fine pant leg, and half of his face was blooming with bruises.

Nobility or a diplomat—or both—she could tell by his clothing and the Latin in which he greeted them suspiciously.

"Salve," Lilac said. "*Bona dies*."

He paused, his brows rising. "You speak Latin?"

"Were you not the one who greeted her first?" Garin said, in perfect Latin. "It is the *lingua franca* in our region."

Lilac reddened as Garin glared at him, immediately understanding the man's questioning. Responding to him had been second nature, but in her kingdom, commoners only understood so much as was recited in the church. "He is my guard and a man of God," Lilac reassured the man, blinking rapidly and making an effort to stop herself from swaying in the wind.

He raised his hand, and in it was a thin, leather-bound stack of papers. A large leather satchel hung from his shoulder.

"I was hoping you'd be able to point me in the direction to... *Pem-pont.*" He stopped when he reached the end of their unscathed carriage and turned to look at it, scratching his head as he surveyed the gruesome scene before him. As his gaze fell upon Adelaide, who had begun to drag the body of Emrys by the feet toward the back door of their carriage. The man swayed a bit too, pausing to steady himself. "Shit, what a mess. I was reading my map and all of the sudden, I toppled off my horse. I don't know what hit me."

"Who are you?" Lilac approached him, ignoring and walking away from Garin's strangled warning. He looked important.

The man puffed his chest, evidently proud she'd asked. He pulled one of the loose scrolls from his satchel and unfurled it for her to see. Intrigue won out over annoyance that he couldn't just tell her, and Lilac walked up to him to read from his parchment.

Order from the Holy Roman Empire was all she was able to glean before he chuckled and tucked it away again, as if he weren't supposed to show anyone but was proud of doing such a naughty thing.

"You're an emissary."

"Yes," he said as she stepped back, reeling. He looked her over once and said, "Women don't wear belts or blades where I'm from, but"—his eyes roved hungrily over her hips—"I certainly think they should start."

"State your business." Her voice and gaze instantly hardened into the suspicion she couldn't hide, but he seemed to enjoy the attention.

He leaned in. "I would love to see you when I've concluded my errands, but it might take a couple of weeks." He was the kind of man she might have thought mildly handsome if she'd never met Garin.

"She asked you what your business is," Garin said, and she could sense him nearing behind her.

The man's eyes darted beyond her right shoulder, and his smile fell. She didn't bother turning to see what look Garin was giving him.

"I—I really shouldn't say." He winked at her. "But maybe you could point me to the nearest inn. You and your troupe are welcome to join me. Maybe after you've taken care of this..." He trailed off, perhaps for the first time realizing he stared at what might be the bodies of two men, marks in the road, and the debris of a crash site. "Was there another carriage here?"

Lilac stepped closer, ignoring Garin's low growl. "You seem like a fine diplomat. If you're headed for the Chateau de Trécesson, I'm afraid you're traveling in the opposite direction."

"Well," he said, blinking through his air of offense, "I know the emperor wanted me to depart in two days, but I insisted on giving myself extra time. I heard of a fine clothier in town, and I—"

"*Emperor?*" Lilac, Garin, and Adelaide spoke in unison.

"I should not have spoken." He turned on his heel but Lilac chased him down, quickly catching up with his brisk walk.

Behind their carriage, the dirt path was disturbed, hoof marks and splatters of blood everywhere—but no horse to be found.

Her mind raced, desperately grasping at an alibi—lest she snatch him and jostle the truth out of him. "I ask because I am the daughter of the royal cartographer, and we were headed in that direction."

At this, the man slowed. "*You* are the daughter of the queen's cartographer?" He did not hide his excitement well at all. "What are you doing all the way out here?"

"My father sent us to town for more parchment," she lied.

This simple answer seemed to suffice. The man looked this way and that. "You've heard the rumors, right? About France."

Her brows knotted as the gravity of her situation—an emperor's diplomat confirming his kingdom's knowledge of it—sank in. She knew all too well of the reports of those smoke signals. But she had to pretend otherwise.

"France?" she said in alarm. "Will they advance?"

"That is what we suspect." The emissary looked both ways. The roads had remained empty. "And their king is not offering marriage."

Lilac immediately stiffened. "The queen would never accept. She would not surrender."

"Perhaps not, but she'll then require a stronger foothold on her land to keep France at bay. Her small army would never last." His chuckle was grim.

"What does that have to do with why you're here?" Garin snapped. He was right behind her now, his breath on her ear.

The man gulped and averted his eyes, keeping them fixed on Lilac. "This knowledge is sure to spark a flurry of proposals once made public. Of course, Maximilian has demanded complete secrecy, so his offer will stand first."

"And what makes your leader so bold to send you two weeks before her coronation?" said Garin.

The man couldn't help the smile that bloomed upon his face. "Maximilian hopes to be married by her coronation ball. If she accepts his proposition and signs the contract," he said, patting his satchel, "then he will marry her, by way of me."

Lilac said nothing. Neither did Adelaide or Garin, but his hand immediately reached for her waist, settling firmly on the small of her back.

"Maximilian offers what no other ally will: a proxy marriage through myself to prevent France from annexing her country. She doesn't have to see him, but if she wants to solidify her people's continued protection, she'll visit Austria to eventually bear his children, and—" He frowned at Lilac, whose limbs had gone numb. "I'm sorry, does that rogue have fangs?"

Before Garin could reply, the man stumbled back, his face wrenched in horror. The hilt of her dagger stuck out of his chest.

It happened so fast; a strangled noise slipped from her throat as she stepped back, warm blood covering her hands. She obviously didn't do a very good job at stabbing him, because he sputtered a cry for help before stumbling away, screaming.

Behind them, Adelaide was cursing. Garin was frozen in place beside her, his look of terror rapidly consumed by a dark disbelief she'd never seen. He whirled on her.

"Lilac, that was an emissary from the *Holy Roman Empire*." Rage gripped every word.

"I know who he was. I'm not marrying him or his king," she snarled, or at least wanted to snarl. It came out more like a whimper as her breathing became labored. Her body felt exhausted, as if the act of bravado had leaked the energy out of her.

"So you tell the emperor by letter!" Garin shouted, fury mottling his carefully crafted calm. "You send a formal apology, Lilac, you don't murder his representative. Not in broad daylight."

Clutching her dagger to his middle, the man had broken into a slow sprint in the opposite direction of the town—off the path into the trees.

"There will be people looking for him."

Shaking violently, Lilac had no answer. *What had she done?*

Garin tore his murderous eyes from her and bounded into the woods, Adelaide shouting after him. The last thing she saw was the witch's terrified face as the world turned to darkness once more.

WHEN LILAC WOKE—OR THOUGHT SHE HAD, ANYWAY—BROCÉLIANDE was cast in the orange-violet glow of twilight. Strong arms lifted her from a carriage, and she buried her nose into a red-stained shirt that smelled of wood hyacinths and iron; it made her homesick, made her stomach churn with a distant want as they carried her from the chill to warmth, up a set of stairs, and down a dimly lit hallway lined with doors, several of which creaked open to reveal curious eyes. They slammed shut again upon a furious, barked command.

They brought her to the second door on the left and placed her on a bed, pulling the covers up around her, and when they tried to leave, Lilac reached out and grabbed the owner of those arms by the shirt and asked him to stay—and everyone else fussing over her to leave.

Without question, he curled around her, his body molding around hers even with the blankets between them. As hard as she struggled to wake, as this seemed an important moment to savor, his warmth and the way his thumb kneaded the tension out of her neck and shoulders made it impossible.

He was gone, then he appeared again with a couple books tucked under his arm, like an apparition with impressive taste. He read to her from the *Lais of Marie de France* and a newer collection of stories—one, about a chivalrous knight called Gawain. After he gently informed her that those were all the books he'd brought from his room, she begged for more. Chuckling, Garin placed the books down upon the chair and made his way to the bed, climbing in behind her. He began to recite a tale from memory. One his father used to tell him when he was young.

"Once upon a time, during an age when magic and mortal coexisted more freely in the world," he murmured into her hair. He shifted his hand and laced his fingers between hers with a distracting gentleness before continuing. "There was an island kingdom feared by sailors and revered by the Morgen. A legion of wicked creatures lived there, warded from humans and protected by a dyke with a strong gate to keep the sea and other intruders out—ruled by Gradlon the Great, who had a lone daughter.

"Although he often traveled between his island and Brittany, his daughter was forbidden to leave. The Church had told Gradlon she would bring imbalance and destruction to the world with her unmatched powers, impious ways. One day, during a walk along her shore, she spotted a Breton sailor through the gate, whom she fell in love with. That night, the princess stole her father's key as he slept and opened the gates to let her lover in, submerging her kingdom in the dead of night.

"Gradlon mounted his enchanted horse, Morvarc'h, and barely escaped with his life—and his daughter. When they reached land, the clergy, king, and army waited for them. Gradlon told them of his intent to disappear into the woods, remaining untroublesome to the kingdom and its mortals. They forbade the princess from coming ashore, and so, at the urging of the Church, Gradlon tossed his daughter into the sea, along with her underwater kingdom."

Lilac drifted asleep before Garin told her what happened to Gradlon, if the princess had ever found her escape. Her happy ending.

Darkness swept over the queen like a beckoning shroud. A veil of in betweens, neither here nor there.

When the excruciating pain came, coupled with a terrifying searing pain against her windpipe, she almost wished to sink deeper into the abyss. The void was was peaceful and expected nothing from her; there were no clause-tethered offerings, no threat of war, or rulers who would fight for her hand and womb only for the gain of a monarchy and naval dowry.

Waves crashed over her, the pounding of a lapping, greedy ocean.

Let me be one with the sea if blood cannot hold me.

Beyond the onyx waves, there were glimpses of...something else. A cathedral of shimmering turquoise. A ceiling that mirrored a star-speckled sky. Black and red velvets, silver candelabras, jewel embellished tablecloths, and a vast feast laid upon a table that seemed to stretch infinitely before a twirling crowd of dancers and their glimmering eyes. Firebreathers and jugglers roamed among them.

It seemed hunger still existed in the abyss, for her stomach burned, her throat aching against the bile. Before she could reach for the dishes lining the table, a pale hand appeared at her side, holding a single fig dripping with honey.

Lilac bit into it, a stranger unto herself—yet never more whole—tasting the salt of iron that was replaced with an unholy, unnamed sweetness.

She opened her eyes to Garin setting a chair down at her bedside. He propped her up on a pillow and spoon-fed her soup with soft vegetables and a strong taste of garlic. Thinking of something she'd read in her studies, she groggily asked him about an aversion to garlic, to which he only responded with a chuckle, shifted to the floor, and smiled at her with kind eyes the shade of rubies before kissing her forehead and murmuring apology after apology—some of which she understood, some of which made no sense at all.

"I'm sorry, Eleanor. I'm sorry for all that's happened. I am sorry for what's to come."

With his nonsensical murmurings and terrifying eyes, there was no

BRIAR SOMERSET

doubt in her mind that she was still dreaming. So, Lilac placed a finger to his full lips to silence his apologies, and asked the question that had hung in the back of her mind for weeks.

"Are you sorry for wanting me?"

"Yes." Garin shuddered through the answer, his gaze on the bed past her. "Yes, I am. I'm sorry for what it means for you to be wanted by someone like me."

It was a good thing this was a dream. The worst thing it could turn into was a nightmare. "What about loving me?" Lilac asked. "Are you sorry for that?"

He looked up at her again, and as in most of her dreams, Lilac did not stay up long enough to know how it ended.

10

She was alone as she sat up among the mess of maroon sheets. Her clothes had been changed, and her hair had been brushed, falling in thick waves, brushing her shoulder blades; she wore one of the simple cream nightgowns she'd packed, nearly too comfortable with no undergarments beneath. As she stretched the kinks out of her upper body, there was a tug at her left hand; her last two fingers and knuckle were wrapped in some sort of gauze, though there was no pain when she flexed those fingers.

Curiously, she unwrapped the gauze. Whatever injury the arrow had left was gone, as was the shallow slice from her potato mishap in Lorietta's kitchen.

The half empty bag the witch had given her was set at the foot of her bed, now filled with what looked to be several folded garments gifted from Garin.

She was at the Inn, in the room she'd rented on the first night she'd stumbled upon it, the darkness out the window evident despite the curtains being pulled. But there were no sounds of debauchery outside her door. No voices or clinking of glasses. None of the loud korikaned tunes she'd grown to miss. She rubbed her eyes and stood, prepared to gather her belongings and step out, when she noticed an absence. Her dagger wasn't on her body. Lilac swept her hand into the bag beneath the linens and found the belt and leather sheath empty. Then she checked under the bag —nothing. Garin had no reason to hide it from her; wouldn't he want her to have the only method of defense she owned?

Especially after the past day.

Yesterday. The last couple of days? The fogged memory she clung to, of her body pressed against the warmth of Garin's, was replaced with panic. Her parents had been expecting her back, and when they ran into the merchants, it was already a day counted into her journey.

Had it happened? Had she dreamt it all? Her imagination wasn't that vivid, she thought, turning back to the door, especially to conjure—

She came face to face with her blade. Her hand flew up, fanning before her and knocking it from the hand that steadied her. She blinked against Garin's sudden and overwhelming proximity.

"*You*. I was looking for that," she said, breathless, as he crossed his arms and silently watched her retrieve the dagger from where it had landed beside the hearth. He said nothing as she approached the bed, lifting her leg to place the weapon against her bare thigh and remembering she didn't have her garter or belt on. There was nothing to tuck it into under the loose nightgown that swirled just above her ankles.

He scoffed under his breath, and she narrowed her eyes. "Whoever dressed me couldn't have given me my undergarments?"

"You did have them, but you removed them yourself. You were half conscious, but you insisted."

She scowled, heat and humiliation climbing her face. "Did we...?"

"No." Garin's expression was stormy, unreadable. "Whenever necessary, I restrained you until the witches intervened. They kept you asleep most of the time with a draught in the soup we fed you, so you could rest and heal. But your wakefulness was reassuring. Albeit troublesome."

"Kept me asleep? How many days has it been?"

He counted on his fingers and hummed. "This morning's the fifth day. Bastion's been watching the path from your castle, and no search party has been initiated yet. We'd planned to intervene if necessary, but there's been no reason to so far."

Five days. She suspected her parents were slow to dispatch the guard because she couldn't afford another scandal, but this was the least of her worries.

Garin took her hand and helped her sit on the edge of the bed and, dizzily, she allowed it. He sat next to her upon the chair she remembered him reading to her from.

"Lilac."

She would have smiled at him, at the tenderness in his gesture and voice. But there was something else there—a hesitation just beneath the surface. "Garin?"

"I'm sending you home."

She pulled away from his hand, still holding hers. "*Sending* me? Why?" Of course, she could not stay at the Inn forever.

"Giles readied the carriage last night. He was able to repair it with the help of the *Guài*," he added sourly. "Those creatures were quick to do so when they learned who we were. I was going to allow you to wake on your own, but I thought it'd be much later in the day."

Giles. Guài.

She remembered those women, stunning, glittering, and deadly as they had chased them down. She rubbed her eyes, trying to remember everything that had happened. It all came to her in fragments. Being thrown from the carriage. The incredible pain. The corpses—

"Giles...is alive?"

"He is alive. You have nothing to worry about here," he replied, more stern than reassuring.

"But I do. The Accords are a work in progress, and we need to get that chest to Kestrel. We *did* get the chest, right? Maybe we can attempt a meeting again now that we..." She trailed off as Garin crossed his arms and leaned back. Away from her.

"Lilac," he said, slowly.

Why was he looking at her that way?

"We all agreed it would be best for you to focus on things at the castle. I imagine your parents are very worried."

We all? "When have you ever been concerned about my parents?"

"My concern is for you. You will return today. There is no question."

"I will return when I please."

"Lilac." Garin glanced briefly at the door. "You need to convene with your council."

"I don't have a council."

His voice was even, reasoning. "See? What is a queen without her council? Without an advisor or ladies-in-waiting? You'll have to appoint them when you return. You've much to do."

She didn't understand. Her memories of the past five days spent in recovery did not match how he treated her now. She *remembered*. He'd held her, laughed with her, or at least *at* her. He had kissed her forehead as she lay in the crook of his arm, whispered the things he wished to do to her, followed by strange apologies as she drifted back to sleep.

He looked at her quizzically, resting his chin on his hand.

"I think I've done fine without a council thus far. I have you, and I suppose Adelaide, Lorietta, and my dutiful scribe, John." Lilac forced conviction into her voice, which wavered at the memory of him cradling her to his chest on this very bed. She did not want to think about returning.

Unmoved, Garin nodded against his knuckle. "That, I agree with." But that was all he said.

"What will you do without me?" The desperation in her voice was sickening, but she couldn't seem to stop it. "How can I be of service here?"

As if sensing her thoughts, he said, "I don't want you to worry about anything unnecessarily when you have many mortal affairs on your plate already. When you've already been through so much here." As his words sank in, he scooted the chair back and stood. "Bastion has already sent a note to Cinderfell from the nearest hawthorn tree, and I'll keep you informed as things progress. For now, you must return to your castle."

She stared at him, incredulous, as he extended a hand and mustered a despondent smile. Lilac didn't take it.

"Well? Are you ready?"

"That's it?"

"I suppose."

She stood from the bed, her hands shaking. Her voice was hoarse when she next spoke. "Are you coming with me? To the castle?"

"Not this time. The witches will. It's not best to have you return alone, as the sound of the carriage crash apparently carried to Paimpont, so there may be more thieves lurking along the roads than normal. Plus, I still think they'll be more receptive to magic folk returning you than I, especially after the arm. And with all those ridiculous rumors Sinclair spread of you running off with vampires." He crossed the room and lifted two logs from the pile to nestle them among the dying embers."

Why was he avoiding her gaze?

"Plus, what exactly would I do there, Your Majesty?"

She didn't quite know how to answer that when all she wanted to do was stomp over and force him to look at her. "You were there after my ceremony. I saw you several times in the halls. You came to my chamber."

He continued to fiddle with the logs. "I wanted to ensure your safety and needed to ensure Giles remained entranced in his new job as stable-hand while maintaining my own cover at the castle." He straightened and dusted his hands. "He will remain under my influence until I figure out if he is fit to return as priest, or if another need be appointed. If there are any issues, I'll come to remedy them. Otherwise, there's no other reason for me to involve myself, is there?"

"*No reason?*" As he moved toward the door, she sidestepped, blocking it with her body. She couldn't even name the emotion pounding through her veins. It felt like there was a fountain of words to be spewed, all of it stopped by the lump in her throat. In the short time they'd known each other, Lilac had felt hated, despised, yearned and hungered after—but she never felt *unwanted*. "You don't want to see me."

"That is not true." He moved to reach past her for the doorknob, but she gripped it with her own hand, forcing him off.

"You laid with me just there," she whispered, anger mounting, pointing at the bed. "You read to me several stories, told me one from your child-hood. You laughed with me. You knelt and apologized to me for..." She frowned, her memory distant, as if it were years ago. *No*, she thought regretfully. Even decades would not erase the memory of Garin's trembling breath against the nape of her neck, of his too careful fingertips drumming upon the blanket he'd tucked around her. "For wanting me."

There was no glint of recognition in his eyes—just guilt, or maybe concern. "Lorietta had me entrance you back to bed every time you jolted awake or had a night terror. Doing so can invoke strange or violent dreams." He looked down at her fist on the knob. "She said she couldn't keep feeding you the sleeping draught without risking your health."

"I don't believe you." She glared up at him and wiped her cheeks hastily against the back of her hand, clutching her dagger. *How could she be crying?*

Had none of it been real? None of his caresses, and care, and... love?

It felt so real.

Garin took her hand and nudged the blade along his extended wrist. "Just a taste will tell you all you need to know."

The offer wasn't sincere, she could feel it. Her limbs were buzzing, they ached to move. In a flash, she moved the dagger, pointed it at his throat.

Shocked at her speed, at the motion, she jerked back. The blade clattered to the floor.

The stern mask Garin wore faltered. There was a glimmer of surprise, but all he said was, "How much do you remember after you woke? After we crashed."

She didn't know. Everything was muddled. There were glimpses of what had happened, but none of it felt real. All she could remember—all she could think of—was Garin. Hearing everything, being trapped in the darkness of her own mind, the cage of excruciating pain that was her broken body.

Waking up in the dirt to him hovering above her, cradling her, his eyes filled with real terror, his remorseful, devilish face twisted into some intoxicating combination of the heavens and hells.

Then, him, next to her in that very bed.

"What *happened?*"

He nodded slowly, like she was a feral animal liable to snap at any moment. "We're not entirely sure. Like I said, your body was loaded with magic. The merchant's archer hit you in the hand with an arrow imbued with a disillusionment charm, meant to lift any and all enchantments. They weren't after you, but Emrys." His voice grew tight with fury. "The idiot paid them in counterfeit coin years ago, so they've been tracking him. They shot him in the chest."

The *Guài* had said they were tracking someone. A powerful warlock... but from what she barely remembered of the argument she'd overheard, Emrys hadn't been the target. What she did remember, *vividly*, was that she hadn't undone Adelaide's tonic. She was about to. That's when the searing pain had bloomed on the knuckles of her right hand.

"He died," she croaked, blinking away the image of his corpse.

"Yes, but it wasn't the arrow that killed him. And he didn't stay dead for very long."

"What—"

"The arrow obviously dissolved your dress," he grunted, forcefully swinging the topic as she gazed past him, unseeing. "Your bones were broken in multiple places. The *Guài* warned us about overwhelming your body with magic. We had no choice but to wait for it to be let out of your system. For a few days, Lorietta fed you, washed, and kept you clean. And I ensured you kept your privacy as much as possible," he added when her gaze dropped to the floor, hot humiliation flooding through her.

"But I woke up. I was awake after the crash...Wasn't I?" She shut her eyes, rifling through shards of memory, not wanting to remember but *needing* to. She couldn't recall much else, but there were jolts of emotion—relief, rage, then terror. Being able to only hear, then suddenly blinking against the sunlight. "There was so much pain, then none at all. I remember seeing the carriage there. Giles and Emrys, on the ground. Their bodies twisted in the dirt." She swallowed past the lump in her throat. "Where are they?" she asked quietly. "Are they here?"

"Emrys is...alive," he said with an annoyed grunt. "He's a few rooms down. Bastion has been in and out, helping us nurse him back to health. Giles was completely unconscious for two days. A head injury. We thought we'd lost him, but Emrys brought him back with a spell once he had recovered enough."

Lilac started to say something, but Garin silenced her with a look.

"As a parting gift, the *guài* performed a bone mending spell on you, but it only fixed your spine and ribs." He was speaking quickly now, as if the memories were too painful to linger upon. "You did wake, then, briefly." He stopped to eye her sidelong.

"Then?" Her heart sank. "What else?"

"You were bleeding. Internally," he explained. "Healing your bones and veins required two different spells from the *Guài*. Both would have been too much magic for your mortal body. Between how weak you were and how much arcana might've been left over from Adelaide's tonic and the arrow, we didn't know." His voice cracked. "I had to choose."

What was there to choose?

She felt she might make herself sick, trying to pull at memories that refused to surface. Uncomprehendingly, she looked down at herself. Her muscles ached only slightly, her body tender in some places, especially her shoulders. But she was alive. Here, with him. "It seems you made the right choice."

But he only gazed at her with a mixture of scrutiny and sympathy. "I was forced to make an impossible decision."

What was that look? Regret? "What did you do?" She hadn't meant the question to come out accusatory, but his eyes had dropped reluctantly to her throat.

"A blood exchange has the power to heal a person's bleeding, their veins, anything related to their soft tissues, depending on the extent of their injuries. So, I drank from you. Then, I fed you my blood." Lilac drew back from him, pressing against the cool of the door as he continued. "Lorietta and Bastion monitored us to ensure I didn't get carried away. It was a miniscule exchange, but it healed every wound in and on your body."

Suddenly, she understood his hesitancy. "Was a bond created?"

This would explain why she couldn't imagine leaving his side. Her body flushed at the thought of being bound to him in that way; it was a concept she hadn't been able to fathom when he'd explained the process to her in the carriage, and she certainly couldn't now.

Confusion warred with the want that dared entertain the possibility. She couldn't be bound to Garin. She was the queen.

"No," he said brusquely. "According to the witches, the amount of blood we exchanged was not enough to warrant a complete bond. Whatever you're feeling now is temporary—something that's easily dissolved by time spent apart."

Several emotions warred inside her, the strongest of them fury. Then behind it, regret. She was just fortunate to be here. The way he looked at her now, she wasn't sure Garin felt the same.

"That's why you need me gone."

Irritation flashed across his face.

"I'll have a meal first," she said firmly, chin up. "Say thank you and goodbye to the others—"

"I'm sure there's a whole feast awaiting you at the castle. Lorietta has closed the bar and kitchen outside of evening hours the past week. She wanted to keep the inn as peaceful as possible for all of you to recover. Everyone is in their rooms." His response was curt, impatient, and he gestured for her to move away from the door.

Lilac peered up at him, incredulous. "Garin, my injuries would have been fatal had you not done the blood exchange. Right?"

His nostrils flared in answer, as if he were losing patience.

"Do you *regret* saving me?"

"We need to leave." He shifted, his arm snaking around her waist for the knob.

Lilac gripped it tightly with her free hand, again blocking his attempt. In a flash that startled a stifled scream from her, his lips slid against hers. His hands moved against her arms, her waist, his tongue teasing her bottom lip before forcefully entering her mouth. Her worry and anger settled at his scent, his taste enveloping her entirely.

Woodsmoke. A bluebell wood, strong and sweet.

Nothing else mattered. All she wanted was to be under him, around him. She'd dropped the blade and curled her fingers into his hair, and—

Garin pulled away and tenderly wrapped one arm around her waist, the other jostling the knob at her back. The silver in his eyes began to shift, and the room began to shimmer.

Lilac shut her eyes, gripped his shoulders, and kneed him in the groin. Garin grunted in shock and spun her, pinning her front against the door. Lilac squirmed, shocked this time at her reaction *and* reflexes.

"Don't fight me," he said, sounding breathless. "Not now. Not like this."

For the first time since waking, Lilac noticed how her whole body thrummed with energy, with vibrant life. Everything felt enhanced. Yes, she had aches, and her anger and sadness had felt particularly vile... but she also felt strong. Invincible. Was this the magic he'd mentioned that hadn't quite left her body? It was more than the adrenaline that had fueled her survival through Brocéliande. She wanted to fight, seduce, and draw blood, preferably all at the same time.

Lilac could have stopped fighting him, as he'd advised. She could have turned back and kissed him again. She could have invited him to fuck her.

Instead, she elbowed him, hard, in the cheek.

"Fuck," he said, his voice trembling against his restraint. "Stop it—"

Pushing them off the door gave her just enough time to see him stumble back, then lunge for her, eyes wild and dark. The movement wasn't slower than usual, but she could somehow track it, giving her just enough time to react. Heart pounding, Lilac ducked and rammed him around the waist.

Garin landed on the floor at the corner of the bed with a soft *thud*, still with the grace of a cat, and in the next second, she was straddling him.

"Or what? Or else you'll snap my neck?" she snarled. His hardened cock strained against her ass, only fueling her anger. "Or else you'll entrance me? Control me?" Her voice wavered with emotion, looking down at herself, at her powerful limbs. "Is *this* why you're so angry you had to save me?"

He tossed a dark curl out of his eyes. "I am not angry about saving you."

"Then what? What was the cost?"

He said nothing under her, absorbing her fury in silence.

She looked down at herself, pressed against him, bare beneath her thin nightgown, willing herself to stay focused. "There was a cost, was there not? Something is bothering you. Is it why I am able to do this?" She brought her hands before them. "Fight you? Are we bound, Garin?"

She did not know whether to laugh or cry at the thought of being *his* thrall. Every emotion she felt was most unpleasantly rampant.

"I told you, it's all the magic in your system. The witches both agree that the *Guài* remedy and my blood are still a volatile combination, even if it did not kill you. And *you*," he said, slowly propping himself up on his elbows, then his palms, chuckling. "Fight *me*?" He didn't take his eyes off her lips, and before she knew it, their mouths were barely brushing. His aroma enveloped her senses again, and her anger dissolved; she leaned in to kiss him, utterly unable to help herself, but Garin's hand rose to caress her cheek, then lowered and wrapped around her throat. "Look at me."

Want and fear warred inside. When she tried once more to shove off him, there was the cool of a blade—her blade—against her neck.

"I *said*, look at me, Eleanor." This time it wasn't tender, and there was no question.

The urge was too strong. She was drowning in him, in his scent and with her body against his. It wasn't even because of the long, lethal fingers wrapped around her throat or the blade that made her instantly stop struggling against him.

It was his voice—both the tide and the raft—coaxing her further out to sea.

Lilac's eyes rose to meet his. The room once more began to shimmer around them.

"You're going to follow my instructions." He spoke softly, and somehow this was much more terrifying than any command he'd barked before. He raised his brows, gauging if she was listening. "Nod if you understand."

She gritted her teeth, and there was a flame of anger that burst somewhere in the distance, but that was all too far away now. She nodded.

"You're going to get off of me and put your cloak on." He cocked his head pointedly over his shoulder at the coat rack in the corner of the room, to the right of the hearth, where her wool cloak hung. "It's rather cold outside this morning."

She hated how he spoke to her, like she was an insubordinate child. However, he was right; the mornings were often chilled at the castle, and she couldn't imagine how much colder it would be in Brocéliande. She moved to shift onto her feet, but he released her jaw and caught her by the forearms again. His thumbs moved soothingly against her flushed skin, trailing down to her hands.

"I wasn't done." Garin spoke around his fangs, his eyes like muted starlight filling her with hope and a distant dread that floated further by the second. "You will do it on your hands and knees, please."

There was a stab of rage as she strained against his will. But he showed no anger back; his features were softer, gentler. He'd said *please*.

"Now, get off."

She slipped under his spell and did as she was told.

Before she adjusted herself, Garin was already striding across the room, and he came to stop beside the coat rack. He tossed her dagger onto the bed next to her bag and folded his arms. "Go on then. Crawl to me."

Lilac felt her body act, but by now there was little protest in her mind to something so ridiculous. On all fours, mildly aware of her thighs rubbing together beneath the thin layer of her nightgown, the queen crawled through the dust to the tapping boot awaiting her. In the time it took her to get there, his control began to wane; her ears grew hot, and humiliation began to find its way into her buzzing subconscious.

Garin bent to meet her eyes. She tensed her muscles to get to her feet, but Garin only hummed in disapproval. "*Mmm.* I did not say to get up."

"You ass—"

"Stand."

She immediately obeyed, and when he offered a wolfish smile and praised her, a rush of relief flooded her body, momentarily quelling her fury.

Then, all that was left was betrayal.

She stood still, the room spinning as it returned to normal with every breath, every blink, the shimmering quality of the air dissipating. Garin unhooked her cloak and strode behind her, the heat of the fire easing its way into her aching, buzzing joints as he patiently helped her into it. One arm, then the other. Then, he circled to her front, assessing her.

"It is temporary. Whatever this is, it is a meaningless side effect of our blood exchange that will wane with our separation."

Meaningless. Her chest felt like it would crack in half. That was not the word she had in mind. *Separation.* She didn't like that, either.

"I have never had a thrall myself or seen it done, Your Majesty, but if we were bound to each other—*if* you were my thrall—I wouldn't have had to entrance you just then. Imagine me being able to do that to you, control you, with a mere whisper. I could command you to crawl to me from across a ballroom full of people, and you would obey. Without question." He took her right hand and examined it. Turned it this way and that—and in that moment, his stern expression, that cold façade, broke.

Garin closed his eyes softly and cradled her palm in his hands before pressing his lips to her wrist. He inhaled, as if wanting to devote her scent to memory.

"There is no cost too great," he said, and it took Lilac a breath to understand what he spoke of. He lowered their hands and reopened them. "I would save you in a heartbeat, one thousand times over, even if it meant risking making you my thrall and revoking what little, true freedom you have. Anything to keep you here, right here in front of me." His gaze dipped to the pulse hammering in her throat. "To keep you breathing, that harmonious heartbeat pulsing—*just for me*. Don't you see why this is wrong? There is no cost too great. For *me*. What then, are you to pay?"

She wanted to pull away from him but couldn't bring herself to, and this time it had nothing to do with his sanguine magic. She didn't care. She could rule from the inn, from this very room, with him.

He reached up and stroked her cheek with his thumb. "I want you to go home and consult with your council, with your parents, on everything regarding protecting your kingdom from France. Consider your options and your best propositions."

There it was. Lilac ripped herself from him, but he caught her in a second, grip iron hard.

"There's been a skirmish on your eastern borders, Lilac. Bastion has caught wind of it while you recovered."

She froze, torn between anger at him for actually pushing her to marry and the need to know about her kingdom's safety. "When?"

"Yesterday. Your father and his men are dealing with it as silently as possible, not wanting to draw attention to the fact you are not at home."

She wasn't thinking clearly—these were clear concerns to have, and she *should* be speeding home with all haste possible. But all she could focus on was that she would be dealing with everything without him.

That he would be here, without her.

As if reading her mind, Garin took a step back. "We'll see each other again. We still have to deliver Kestrel's chest, though it might be safer for Bastion and I to do it."

She was so angry, she couldn't see straight. "How is it so important to you that I keep my free will, yet you are ordering me to marry?"

"I am not ordering you, but I am urging you with my deepest wishes."

"Oh, *fuck off*."

"*Why* do you refuse to marry? Help me understand." Garin studied her, holding her at length. "You are the queen. You may have been able to avoid a Le Tallec betrothal, but do you really expect to remain unwed forever?" He shook his head uncomprehendingly. "This happens all the time— borders shift, armies jostle. Leaders must protect themselves."

"You are no better than Henri," she said, her ears burning. "Than Marguerite. If giving my life to someone I do not know is the fate that has befallen me," she said, hoping every shaking word dug into Garin as hard as she threw them, "then I will throw myself upon that blade when and how I see fit. *You,* of all people, will not order it done. How dare you!"

"Your marriage was bound to be transactional, was it not?" He exhaled, forcing himself to release her and keeping his distance. A tremor passed through his body before he continued. "You knew from the day of your birth that you would not have an ounce of true freedom, did you not? You are the wombed crown of a country with a small army and an abundance of trading ports. Are you blissfully unaware that you are one of the most underestimated pawns in the world? Did you think we would fuck and fancy each other, and society would change its mind on your eventual marriage because of your station?"

Lilac grabbed the empty candelabra from the mantle and chucked it at his head. He caught it and tossed it aside, sending it clanging into the corner of the room and leaving a sizable dent in the wall.

He took a small step toward her, and she shrugged her cloak further onto her shoulders, closing her body off to him. "Do you not study your own histories?"

"I have had *all* the time to study, Garin—that is all I've ever done with my life." Her throat was tight as she thought of the ghosts and books that had kept her company and the friends she had now. She rubbed at the moisture brimming her eyes, drawn by pure loathing. "You cannot be upset with me for wishing to live *my* life in a way that isn't laid out in the histories. Times are changing and I intend with every fiber of my being to be part of it."

"I am not upset. I am merely asking you to spend time at your castle, tending to the matters that are most important. I am asking you to wed, as is done in the order of your kingdom. It *will* keep France at bay. It will dissuade their king. He is smart. He would gladly spend the minimal resources required to acquire a smaller kingdom like Brittany, but would not think to challenge larger, more equipped forces over your crown. Not now. Not after the war we fought against them with England."

"There have been no propositions. It's been weeks. No one will proposition me, not with my history and the legend surrounding our kingdom."

"But there will be. Your kingdom has too much to offer for trade, and agriculture. And you…" He closed the space between them and slid his fingers between hers, not bothering with slowness or gentleness. "Anyone—

king, commoner, Daemon—should be ready and willing to offer you their hand and aid."

"And you?" Her voice was barely audible.

"I will be there. To protect you, to advise you when warranted—"

A confusing burst of hope unfurled in her chest, but the desperation in his eyes gave him away.

"You'll be there?" she said, unable to shed the mocking edge to her tone.

"I will."

"You won't be affected when I am rifling through proposals to sign away my life?"

The corner of his mouth twitched. "No."

"And at my wedding?" she said numbly. "When I am sent off for the ceremonies? Or if the wedding is here?"

"Either way, I shall."

How was he so calm when she felt she might burst?

"And," she said, the lump in her throat on the verge of choking her, "you will be there when I am given no choice and France inevitably brings its skirmishes closer, and I am forced to bed the king or prince I marry—"

"Eleanor," he warned.

"And bear his children?"

The crack in his composure was gone. He nodded slowly. "You have my word. And your offspring, too, will have my protection." His expression was stern, otherwise open. As if he thought these things should be no question of him at all.

If Garin considered her protection his duty, then he would not show her what he truly felt when it came to matters of the heart.

But she had to know. "You told me that night in my chamber," Lilac said, almost unable to finish the sentence, feeling so foolish, reddening further as she wiped another tear from her cheek. "You said you would always want me."

"Yes." His answer was unflinching. "Nothing about that has changed. If anything, it has grown even more true."

He should have lied. She wished he did.

Even hearing what she wanted, the rage inside her stoked hotter, and she stamped her foot. "Then why? If you are willing to go through all those things, why would you watch me proceed with a betrothal?" She paced away toward the mantle, her trembling voice rising. "How can you entertain watching me marry a person I do not love, be forced by the threat of war to bear their offspring to secure my place and secure their dowry of land and ports, knowing that I never wished those things for myself? How can you, Garin, if you feel as you say?"

His reply was slow and sure, void of any hesitation. "Because it's the life you deserve. You deserve someone to match your stride and back you with forces that keep enemy powers at bay."

"And if the life you believe I deserve is not the life I want?"

"What other choice do you have?" His eyes blazed into hers, finally angry at her questioning. "What else could you want?" He crossed his arms, quietly assessing her, then spoke skeptically. "You don't want those things? Never dreamed of them? With anyone?"

"Does that bother you?" she whispered back.

He only exhaled in answer, swallowing whatever he was going to say with his jaw clenched. He laughed briefly and ran a hand over his face as he strode away from her, toward the corner of the bed.

Then, he stopped when she began to speak.

"There were days spent in my tower, Garin, where my grief felt so heavy that I could not picture a future for myself at all. Sometimes I could not even picture the next day. It is hard to hope for things when you are caged inside your own mind and tower. So, forgive me for not knowing what it is I want. What future would I possibly have dreamt of, when the only one ever optioned to me was Sinclair?"

"He is not your only option," he retorted, but his face twisted. That, he could not mask. "Not now."

"If my only options are Sinclair and anyone *not* Sinclair, then why bother?" she shouted. "I should have married him! Their family already heads my local armies, unprepared as they might be—it would have been less of a burden on you to worry about." She didn't mean it, of course, but the words cut him deep enough.

"All right, Your Majesty," he said with a mocking bow, motioning at her. "What is it you want?"

The question caught her off guard.

"Tell me. More time with me? Forever?" He clicked his tongue. "Forever in your delicate, mortal terms? Or on the other side of eternity?" he offered coolly, glancing back at the chamber door. "You think I won't give that to you? You'd be enslaved then, but at least it would be to your own bloodlust and not mine. At least then, there would be no concern of me thralling you. You know what? I'll get Bast in here right now. My brother would happily slit your neck with his blood forced down that pretty throat of yours. I'll only have to say the word."

A set of sharp raps came at the door, as if the others had been listening all this time. Meriam's voice floated through. "Garin Trevelyan! I will *not* have the death of the queen under my roof!"

"Ready the carriage," Garin barked.

Lilac marched up to him, snatching her bag. She would not be forced out and humiliated further. "I would rather suffer the poor consequences of being *your* thrall than marry a stranger."

"Oh?" His brows rose mockingly, humming, as if he'd considered something new. Lilac moved to pass him, but his arm shot out, catching around her waist.

His lips grazed her ear. "Do you truly think I would hesitate on an invitation to snatch Henri and Marguerite's precious daughter from right under their noses? Do you think I give a bloody fuck about France? The only stake I have in this is Brocéliande. François would do what your family never had the heart to and burn all of the woodland in the Argoat to ashes."

She pulled back, glaring. "Brocéliande is your only stake?"

"Stakes involve shared interests. I don't share what is mine." His voice had dropped to a seductive whisper, and she was forced to look away. She did—down at the dagger glinting on the bed. "I will see you again."

"When?"

"Give me one week at least. One week to ensure any magic in your system filters out in the absence of other arcana. And to make sure that any of this," he said, eyeing her arms and fingers that had been so inhumanly nimble against his own reflexes, "is gone. Then, we will commence our Accords. Meanwhile, I'll work on contacting Kestrel about his chest."

She *did* she feel like her heart would shatter at the mere thought of a week away from him.

She nodded curtly, but as she tried to move away from him, her chest ached. She couldn't get enough air. Her hands rose, letting the bag fall to the floor, fingers curling into the soft fabric of his shirt. She wanted to stay, between his storytelling, her hallucinations of the haunting, glimmering cathedral, and the dream of his sincere tenderness—the last thing Lilac wanted was to leave.

He surveyed her, and with every passing moment of silence between them, his expression smoothed into that calculated calm she'd grown to *loathe*.

In the back of her mind, she knew this wasn't right. This was unlike her. Unbecoming, as Marguerite would say. She would not beg for his affections, would not make her yearning known more than she already had. She was far above it—or so she believed.

Maybe it was for the best. There was a kingdom to save, a greedy king to ward off. A powerful leader out there who might make a loving husband one day.

The thought immediately repulsed her, only driving her to look upon the bed again. She imagined slitting her palm and bringing her dagger, dripping, to Garin's full lips. Staining his mouth in her, dragging the edge along his tongue. Watching as he slipped in and out of his mask of self-control.

She *wanted* him. She wanted him now and felt she always would. No matter what it took, regardless of the cost. But what she wanted most, more than anything in the world, was impossible with France at her throat, too.

Garin's smile faded immediately as he eyed her. Before Lilac could react to his words, the air around him began to shimmer.

"Look at me," he pleaded.

Lilac fought against the urge, but it was no use. Despite the unusual strength in her limbs, he was much, much stronger.

"Go home, Lilac. You will consider your options. And you *will* marry."

"My," came Isabel's high-pitched voice, her ringlets tickling Lilac's nose. "This powder is something else." She was scrubbing so hard, she feared her skin might start peeling. "Are you sure there are no oils in it?"

"Yes," Lilac snapped, her shame and tact long gone, only exhaustion and confusion left in her body. "That is because I am not wearing powder, nor oils, as I am reminding you for the..." She counted on her fingers.

"Third day," Yanna said from her perch on the end of the tub.

"Third day now." She lounged back in the tub, leaning away.

"And your skin has a lovely flush about it. It is more even. How?" Isabel lost to her impulsive thoughts and swiped a finger down her cheek. Lilac swatted it away, equal parts glad and disappointed her burst of inhuman strength had seemed to fade quickly in the time since she'd left Garin, just as he said it would.

She'd been so blinded by anger that she hardly remembered what had happened after he'd entranced her. She remembered it in glimpses.

Bastion and Lorietta had escorted her out of the room as Garin sat at the edge of the bed with his head in his hands. They'd led her downstairs to the waiting carriage outside, where Adelaide sat in the innermost corner, complaining about being forced to accompany them, until Lilac began to yell expletives out the front window.

Lorietta then nudged a mug-shaped flask in her direction, and, too riled to fight anymore, she got one last, "*You bloodsucking, big-eared coward!*" out the carriage partition before gulping heavily from Lorietta's proffered cup —milk and lavender tea, mixed with a powerful calming tonic, she was sure.

She'd spent the rest of the ride with her head on Lorietta's shoulder, hiccuping through her tears. Even Adelaide couldn't bring herself to make fun of her.

Lorietta had nudged Lilac awake as they rolled through the bailey gates; Lilac woke in terror and tried to brace herself, both palms on either wall, hooking her fingers into the lip of the windows and readying for the violent force that might expel her from the carriage. She fought to conceal her horror as, instead, she felt her fury shift, her refusal slowly turning to indecision, then consideration while the witches took their time in opening the carriage door.

Garin's words, some of his first to her during their first meeting at the inn, echoed in her memory. Faerie ether, imbued in their arts and music, imprisoned one in their body. A vampire's entrancement dealt with the mind, making its victim a *willing* slave.

Peeling herself off the seat, Lilac had cursed them both before stepping out, ignoring the astonished greeting by her guards already surrounding the carriage and stomping through the front doors of her castle. She barked an order for all in her party to be left alone and that they remain unhanded.

Her friends—at least, those she'd begun to trust as friends—had betrayed her. The witches couldn't possibly have been under Garin's entrancement too; though, the faraway smidgen of logic she'd retained reasoned, they would be idiotic to go against the vampire's demands with how determined he was to get her to leave.

Yanna hovered over the tub, scrutinizing her counterpart's work. "Isabel, that is *enough*." She slapped Isabel's cloth away from Lilac's face. "Nothing on your eyelashes, either? No rouge?"

"No," Lilac bit out.

Yanna—and by extension, a very curious Isabel—had brusquely cut off any attempt to interrogate Lilac as they'd flanked her, Giles, and the witches. From the carriage through the bailey, into the courtyard, and past the Grand Hall door they journeyed, where they met a small crowd: her father and his council, her mother, several guards, John, and their family cartographer, Riou, who glanced up and did a double take from their kingdom map.

Seeing two witches nervously bowing beside their puffy-faced, tear-streaked daughter at the courtyard entry aided greatly in distracting anyone from questioning her further than necessary. Her parents immediately ambushed her, her father pulling her into a bear-like hug as her mother stood at a near distance. Marguerite's eyes were rimmed in tears while she informed her coldly about the murmurings of a loud carriage crash heard from Paimpont in broad daylight, with no marks or debris to be found.

There were also reports of a wandering lone horse that had been spotted without a rider who would take off every time someone approached. She could at least truthfully claim to not know anything about that.

Not thinking clearly, she first intended to tell her parents she'd been safe at The Fenfoss Inn. The thought of Garin instantly brought angry tears to her eyes again, and all that came out were broken words and a sob. Lorietta quickly interjected by introducing herself as the owner of a nearby tavern and Adelaide, one of the witches from town, both of whom Giles and Lilac had graciously saved in their travels when their horse escaped from them. It was then that Giles chimed in as if rehearsed, informing everyone that he would be dropping them back off in their town before returning that evening. They left with haste, leaving an open-mouthed Henri and Marguerite to stare at their daughter as she weeped into her dress, the tear stains magically disappearing.

Through her sobs, she began to mumble that the clothier from The Hemlock Haberdashery would have to fit her at the castle—when a stifled gasp from Marguerite stopped her.

Her mother marched over, took one close look at her, and decided there was something unsettling about her appearance; after demanding everyone else from the room, Henri said it was her hair, that maybe she had dyed it with ink and minerals. Marguerite suggested, looking faint, that she thought Lilac might be with child.

Lilac was so taken aback by the suggestion, she silently stopped cursing Garin and instead thanked him for his inability to father children, offering to urinate upon barley with them acting as witnesses—to which Henri had responded by actually fainting.

At this point, her determination to immediately fulfill Garin's demands was suddenly replaced by a slow burning horror that ate at her from the inside out. Feeling ill, Lilac quickly excused herself and dashed down the corridor, up the foyer stairs to her tower, Yanna and Isabel huffing behind her.

She'd swung her door open, gripped her vanity, took one look at herself, and saw what everyone else had seen—understood what Garin had meant when he was snarling at the *guài*. Lilac went to the tub and grabbed one of the cloths placed on its rim, then grabbed the fresh pitcher of water that had been placed upon her bedside table. Eliciting a small, sad cry from one of her handmaidens, she dumped half the pitcher onto the cloth and began scrubbing her cheeks upon returning to the mirror.

The only progress she'd made was ensuring her already beet red face was even more inflamed. Panic rising in her chest, she chucked the pitcher across the room; half hoping she'd shatter it against the wall with her unusual strength, Lilac was simultaneously relieved and irked when it flew only halfway across the room and broke into two large pieces upon the floor.

Her glamor on her skin and hair had indeed not worn off, and it did not do so even when she tipped back the rest of the pitcher water into her mouth—even as she snatched one of the croissants Hedwig delivered shortly after her outburst. She was *stuck*, the subtle but profound effect from Adelaide's tonic not yet faded.

Tearfully, she ordered Yanna and Isabel out and spent that first night in bed praying, begging for sleep to come. It never did, wakefulness causing her to toss and turn with what started as a tightness in her chest that grew into a most uncomfortable sensation of unease throughout her body—the unbearable feeling that nothing was right in the world, and the dreadful knowing that it would not be improved by any amount of sleep she chased.

Then, she attempted to push *him* from her mind, facing the fool's task of shielding herself from his influence head on. She imagined announcing her official intention to rule without a spouse, as she supposed she should have done at her ascension. She imagined throwing herself into another public scandal so large, it would dissuade even the most desperate of nobles and kings.

It didn't take long for her skin to start to crawl. She sat up in fright at one point because she thought she'd seen a shadow move in the corner of her room. The dread began to set in, then—a slow, seeping horror accompanied by thoughts of *him*. His ruddied mouth and hands.

In the silence, it seemed impossible to rid her mind of Garin, not when desperation and turmoil so often found one in the night.

At some point before dawn, Lilac dragged herself from bed, her back cold with sweat, and pulled on her robe. She left her room, only to be startled by none other than Yanna, who sat leaning against the wall outside her door. Roused from sleep, the usually colder, judgmental handmaiden said she sent Isabel to bed, but couldn't bring herself to leave while hearing Lilac's sobs echo throughout the second floor.

She escorted Lilac to the library, where Riou's map had been placed for the night, and reluctantly went to fetch the cartographer, John, and both of her father's councilmen at the queen's behest. By the time the group arrived, looking disheveled and concerned, Lilac had already tidied the corner desk she'd recently claimed as her temporary office while drafting the Accords and ball invitations with her poor handwriting. She grabbed her notes on Daemons and stuck them beneath the tomes and manuscripts she'd previously acquired from her room and the library shelves. Then, she ordered her newcomers to be seated along the table that divided the eastern half of the library as she surveyed the map.

From then until dawn, Lilac launched herself and her small, confused team into a set of administrative tasks. Riou spent the better part of their meeting assessing the map and explaining the markings to her; there had been one other smoke signal sighting just north of La Guerche yesterday, but by the time the guards had arrived, the camp was cleared. Lilac ordered fifty men to the area—half to scout and the rest to stand by in camps around and north of the border town. They would monitor it for several days, make their presence known, and then return.

When Riou suggested this might be seen as escalation, she pounded her fist upon the map and demanded it so, turning to John, who watched Lilac with a mixture of fear and admiration above his quill.

With John's help, she then began to draft the beginnings of a decree announcing the requirement of all able-bodied men between the ages of eighteen and fifty to register with their respective duchies, effective immediately and without any mention of pending war.

Lilac would abide by Garin's commands—she had no choice, especially if it was going to affect her ability to rest—but she was thrilled to learn, even in her sleep-deprived state, that this did not seem to affect her ability to take other related matters into her own hands.

She would set up defenses, even if her father's men were hesitant to, even if advised against it. She would try, because everyone—rich, poor, human, and Daemon—deserved a queen who did.

Also, because it seemed Garin had agreed with the general consensus of her country's military being unstable and unorganized. She would prove him wrong, even as she found and took a husband.

In hindsight, the thought of marrying a stranger should have made her as angry as it had mere hours ago when she was chucking candelabras at Garin's head—but the horrifying thought of standing at the altar with a powerful stranger began to entertain her if it meant devastating Garin.

By the time sunlight streamed through the tall window, Isabel joined them, bringing with her a plate of baked goods and sliced apricots from Hedwig's pantry.

Too heated to eat, Lilac found herself in the middle of her second argument with Riou—and this time, Henri's council. She'd demanded John draft a letter to Henry VIII, seeking possible aid in the event of a war, believing he would accept as their former ally and protector in war.

This immediately drew sounds of protest from all of them, the councilmen citing very sternly that the King of England would too gladly launch into a full-fledged war with France again. They had the resources and the men, they'd said—which was her point. But, according to them, without a marriage or betrothal in place, even their longstanding friendship would not secure a solid enough relationship to be worth a war in her stead; England could then decide at any time they decided to retreat at the price of the Breton crown.

No one, not even her kingdom, wanted a repeat of the Hundred Years'

War, or one to that scale, that much was true. She was in the middle of arguing that she would perhaps explain the nuances of her situation and he'd merely send her several brigades, when the sun on her back felt suddenly unbearable. She sidestepped into the shadows, but this didn't seem to help much.

The heat was getting to her. Lilac barely ground out that she would revisit the option of outsourcing troops without marriage at a later date, before she found herself being lifted off the library floor by two sets of hands, one at her head and one at her feet. Her shoulders and back of her skull throbbed, the sharp voices of Yanna and Isabel ringing out above her as the councilmen carried her up her tower stairs.

She spent the rest of the day—what she remembered of it at least—dizzily being tended to by her handmaidens, Madame Kemble, and Hedwig, who spent several hours pressing cloths to her head and staving off any pending fever. She did recall her parents coming to the door, only for Kemble to usher them away. Her caretakers found it most concerning that the usually breakfast-ravenous queen had not thought to request food be brought to their early morning meeting, but she hadn't realized she was starving until it was too late.

Even with a full platter beside her bed, Lilac's first inclination was not to dig in under Kemble's watchful gaze, but insist on her privacy. She had the girls draw her curtains against the sunlight before they left, and as soon as the door shut, she shakily bit into a sausage, devouring the entire thing along with an apple and half piece of bread, washing it down with a glass of water.

As she'd feared, this did nothing to quell the ache in her chest and churning in her gut, the general feeling that *something* was wrong—and, for once in her life, that something wasn't nerves or fear. Or hunger.

At least for food.

She'd laid down and, again, forced herself to shut her eyes. She lay there in the silence, hating being inside her own mind and once again willing rest to come easy, but all she could think of was Garin. How cross she was with him, what she would say to him if he were there. What she might do to him.

There would not be much speaking or fighting, she knew. Her hands slipped beneath her nightgown and she cursed him. Cursed herself and her humanity.

When the sun dipped beyond the trees, casting her room in fire and gold, Lilac finally slept, the last of her energy reserves spent by making herself come to the mere thought of him next to her. It was a poor semblance of sleep, riddled with broken dreams of Garin's hands and teeth. In her dreams, he was pacing the length of his room at the inn.

He was a monster who needed comforting. Shaking, shivering into his quilt, the bottom half of his face and teeth smeared in burgundy, eyes shut tight against the world, the embers dying before him.

Lilac woke the following morning with a start, rays of sun peeking through her curtains, her nightgown drenched in sweat and her hair a bird's nest atop her head.

She'd prolonged it as much as possible. If Garin's sanguine magic, his entrancement—whatever it was—continued to torture her this way, who knew what might happen? It might drive her mad. She had set her defenses in place as much as was reasonable without any true provocation from France.

She had a choice... or wanted to believe she did. Lilac could continue as she had and not do anything. Continue to suffer and allow Garin's magic to work around her—against her. Or, she could do as he demanded and make him regret every moment of it.

She could watch him beg for her blood and body, and revel in it.

Lilac had then leapt from her bed before her dutiful handmaidens could stop her and marched downstairs, nightgown drenched in sweat, to the Grand Hall. She'd swung the doors open and doubly shocked her parents by demanding all propositions received by the courier in the days she was gone. Marguerite had then slowly glanced up from her breakfast to exchange a glance with John, as if it hadn't been a topic of conversation as of late.

The scribe then cleared his throat to announce in front of her parents, near dozen staff and scullery either taking their meals or helping organize it, and the six guards lining the room that there had been none thus far.

No proposals.

For the first time, Garin was wrong.

Lilac had her mother repeat the news, just to confirm. Begrudgingly, Marguerite did as she requested, along with a strongly-worded suggestion for a bath. By the time her mother began nagging on about the next thing, Lilac had turned heel, her ears ringing. She could not marry if there were *no* offers for her hand. Impossibly, she felt something shift, an immense pressure off her shoulders and chest. The sensation of restless dread in her chest had begun to dissipate. Lilac grabbed a tart from the incoming breakfast cart she met at the door and marched back up to her tower, followed by the baffled gazes of her parents.

Lilac had simmered in giddy rage as Yanna and Isabel arrived had drawn the bath she sat in now.

Garin was a monster with a sweet tongue, wielding a terrible kind of magic. He would never hold this kind of power over her again. This had made the first and only other time he'd entranced her feel like *nothing*; the way he'd had her hold her vibrating dagger to herself, bringing her to a swift and shattering orgasm—though, that had not been a request she'd intended on fighting.

But being humiliated, made to crawl across the floor...

Heat blossomed upon her cheeks, moisture stinging her eyes.

How *dare* he entrance her, strip her of what little freedoms he'd spoken of.

A spark of defiance brought on an abrupt wave of vigor, her strength returning with her anger as her mind finally started to clear enough to consider the repercussions of Garin's betrayal.

It was time. She had played his game, a little too roughly for her liking. Now, she would play her way. She would make him pay, risk of a blood bond or no.

She rose from the bath without warning; there was no sense in staying any longer if Yanna and Isabel were going to prod her like some experiment. Isabel toweled her hair while Yanna slid her into a pretty kirtle of muted pink over a cream shift, and a fine eggshell corset patterned in roses and leaves from the back of her armoire, duly ignoring the folded stack of clothing Garin had gifted her at the bottom of it. This was one of the pieces of clothing her mother had acquired in the past year, should she one day return to society—as if fashion would suffice as any kind of bandage over her Daemon tongue.

Perhaps in the past few days, in Lilac's hysteria her handmaidens hadn't had the chance to examine her properly. They stared at her in the mirror as she combed her hair, which brushed the bottom of her collarbone and had mysteriously deepened in color, dancing in several shades of oak and auburn and framing her full, flushed cheeks. Lilac rifled in her vanity drawer for her powder and rogue to try to cover some of it up while they styled her in a pair of half-up braids that softly crowned her head and balanced the intensity of her gaze.

"Are you... expecting someone, Your Majesty?" Isabel asked, stepping back after her hair was fashioned.

"No." Lilac untucked a couple chunks of hair around her crown, just like she liked it.

Yanna remained by her side, watching the queen with her arms crossed. "Who are you going to see?"

She didn't answer right away, already busied with dabbing a deeper shade of rouge on her lips and cheeks. "I'm not seeing anyone. They're going to see *me*."

She retreated from the mirror, swallowing nervously and brushing her skirts down. Yanna promptly swatted her hands off and tightened the front lacing of her corset. It was exactly the touch she needed.

She was ready. She had to be ready now, or she might never be. Lilac thanked them one last time for all they'd endured before uttering one last request, to which they dubiously agreed.

The queen emerged from her chamber anew on the third evening like some exhumed thing, blade strapped to her thigh, breasts plumped toward the gods, and an appetite for vengeance.

HEDWIG AND HER HELPERS WERE PUTTING OUT ROASTED GAME AMONG plates of fruit and bread. The chef did a silent double take as Lilac walked by and took her seat at the head of the table, where every pair of eyes in the room followed, and whispers commenced.

To be fair, Lilac felt more different than she looked; at least, she thought so after examining herself long enough at her vanity. If her towns-people were going to talk, it should be over something worthwhile. A carriage crash, a bar brawl... Her dealing with vampires. Those rumors, likely circulating now, were far more entertaining. For the first time in years, the whispering around her had nothing to do with her *arana lingua*.

Surprisedly pleased with the different kind of attention, Lilac took some turkey and cheese onto her plate and began to eat just as her parents and their own small entourage were the last to enter. Usually it was Lilac who arrived halfway through the meal, and so they squinted at the head of the table as the doors slammed shut behind them.

Her mother's hair was sticking out of a hair cover, as if her maids had attempted to wrestle it into place; as if she hadn't slept last night. Where she usually regarded her daughter with a disapproving tilt of her mouth, Marguerite now offered her a tight smile at her rosy appearance in both her complexion and ensemble.

"You're rather dressed for dinner," Lilac commented.

Despite her hair, her mother wore a sky blue gown with puffy sleeves, and it looked like she'd put all of her shiny silver trinkets on. Henri pulled out a chair to Lilac's left as his wife let out a strained chuckle across from him.

"Oh, I could say the same of you," replied Marguerite.

"Are you hosting someone?"

Looking peeved that Lilac had avoided the inquiry in her statement, Marguerite placed a small bunch of grapes and a corner of bread onto her plate before answering. "As a matter of fact, yes."

"Oh?" Lilac leaned over her plate and took a dainty sip of water.

"For now, some of the ladies of the court—my court," she corrected, "are on their way, just in time for Hedwig's baked custard. My ladies-in-waiting arrive tonight."

Lilac coughed into her glass and placed it down, wiping the dribble off her front before it soaked into her dress.

"Keep yourself together," said Marguerite, as if her old friends were already present.

The women who'd served on Marguerite's former court resided in surrounding towns, some in different duchies. The closest in Marguerite's circle, besides her two ladies-in-waiting, had been Vivien herself. She'd skirted holding a distinct role, however; Vivien would've kissed a Daemon before sitting at an official station *beneath* the queen consort.

She'd always wanted the position for herself.

Marguerite's ladies-in-waiting were also a pair she'd learned to remain cautious around. Even before her *arcana lingua* was revealed, Lilac knew them to be terrible gossips. They hadn't lived at the castle since requesting to be relieved from their stations in light of Lilac's scandal. In the midst of it all, she remembered being shocked her mother let them leave so quickly —but as she got older and noticed Piper's absence more and more, she understood. A lady-in-waiting was a queen's confidante, advocator, and assistant, but often became more than that. They were her mother's friends. Marguerite preferred to lose her personal companions than force them to serve her against their will. Doing so might have stirred additional gossip surrounding her family—Marguerite's second worst nightmare following stale fashion.

"They're coming here tonight? For dessert?"

"For your coronation," Marguerite corrected. "They'll have arrived by dessert, yes."

Her parents were staring blankly back at her, looking just as confused. Lilac pushed her plate away.

"Might I remind you, guests from out of country and across the kingdom will be arriving throughout the week. Some will be staying at nearby taverns, some at the available manors and estates of willing hosts. But those closest to our family are invited to stay here. You *know* this." Marguerite peered at her daughter, as if trying to ascertain her sanity.

Lilac swallowed her biting reply. Her mother was right, this was customary. "Gertrude and Helena are nearly here. Will they stay in the north wing?"

"Yes, we had those quarters cleaned and prepared while you were gone. This is what is usually done when hosting esteemed guests. In case you've forgotten."

The thought of hosting many strangers in the same castle where she'd hidden from the kingdom was nearly too much to bear. "It's been years, thanks to you," she shot. "With France at our border, I haven't quite been focused on our guest list, or their accommodations."

"We did mention it in passing a day or two ago," said Henri.

"You were still bordering hysterics," added Marguerite. "A bath with the girls did you well."

All she'd been able to think about was Garin. Even when she'd forced him from her mind, momentarily distracting herself by tending to her duties, she'd *felt* it. Him, his dark absence. His power over her.

"And what of the investigation at the Le Tallec estate?" Lilac eyed Henri, who slowly looked up from his plate while Marguerite shifted her glare to him. "We agreed on one after Armand killed himself and I just assumed others might already know about it." Lilac stuffed her irritation down and feigned confusion, lowering her voice. "Did it not occur yet?"

"It did the morning after you departed. The evidence was irrefutable. Sinclair is in the dungeon with double the guards." Henri bit into a dripping turkey leg, quick to change the subject. "You didn't see our caravan of carriages roll past in the square?"

"I suppose I was busy being fitted. Herlinde did not have anything to my liking, by the way," she lied, for Marguerite's benefit. "I've requested her to come fit me here. She will have it finished in plenty of time."

"So you've mentioned," said Henri. "We passed your carriage on the way to the estate. Outside of the Herwick Haberdashery."

Lilac hummed, as if she'd simply forgotten. Henri was lying for her. They might've spotted Lilac's carriage far ahead, but Giles had been driving them out of the square by the time Henri's carriage pulled in.

"The *Hemlock* Haberdashery," Marguerite corrected.

"That's it, now."

Lilac took her time chewing through her fig and cheese-covered bread as her mother waited for her to respond. "I must have been inside the shop at the time."

Marguerite all but shuddered into her custard, and as an afterthought, said, "It is a wonder Herlinde bothered settling her second shop next to that pig's trough."

She said nothing as she finished the last scraps on her plate, grateful for the warm meal she could finally eat and keep down. Several unpleasant memories of the past three days flashed through her mind. The cold sweats and gnawing at her stomach, yet no appetite to eat when food was placed before her. The muscle spasms and heat. The unbidden images of Garin.

No proposals. It had brought great relief to her that morning, solving her most immediate problem of completing Garin's demand of marriage.

There were, in truth, many reasons a king or noble should want her hand in marriage, offering Brittany immediate protection from looming crowns. Her kingdom had plenty of room for expanding agriculture, and would provide port access in exchange for quality agriculture, fishing, and coastal farming. Perhaps her arcana lingua had affected her prospects. Maybe other kingdoms also regarded her as a queen shrouded in dark myth and legend.

And if not? If a suitor eventually came along—was Garin truly willing to sacrifice what they'd grown to have? Did he not feel what she'd grown to feel?

Uneasy, her mind swam with questions. Was the Garin she remembered —who'd laid beside her, read to her—truly a figment of her dreams? Was this uncharacteristic kindness, tenderness from him something that only existed in her imagination? Even if it was, the vampire who had guided her through the worst of the woods last month, brought her to Adelaide's cottage, was not. He was real.

She was queen, the topic of her pressure to marry should have occurred to either of them far earlier. But she was just as guilty, not wanting to believe it would come down to this. She'd assumed she had time. That they had time.

Yet, he'd demanded her to wed, and Lilac remained without any offers to consider. What came next? How much longer before that dreadful feeling of sickness and unease returned, all because she had not signed a marriage contract?

She stabbed her piece of turkey angrily, not bothering to cut it, bringing the slab of it to her mouth to tear off.

Lilac worked to steady her breathing as she swallowed the rest of her supper, gulping the rest of her wine and slamming the glass onto the table. Garin did not tell her he did not want her. He'd done far worse—*demanded* she marry someone else.

If fate was not so cruel, she would have ridden him during that first night at The Fenfoss Inn. If only he'd left her alone, if only he hadn't intended on using her as his pawn, she could have left and never seen him again. He might've come to mind on nights when the bed got cold. During winter months when the frost reminded her of his eyes and the hearth's warmth, his touch. But she would've survived. Eventually.

At the very least, Garin could have pretended to not care for her. Then, keeping her distance from the one person she wanted might not feel like it was maiming her, and this meal would not be the first real one she'd consumed in a week. She wouldn't have spent the last three days throwing herself at every administrative distraction, just to collapse in bed and chase sleep in a sweat-drenched stupor. She wouldn't have battled an exhausted mind that refused to rest, in her deepest delusions willing Garin to appear on her balcony, just so she could push him off.

It might've been easier if she would just admit to herself one heart-wrenching truth: Lilac was but a girl—one of many—yearning for someone with dark hair, sharp teeth, and a lethal smile who did not yearn for her in the same way she did him.

She hated the thorough fire with which Garin consumed her, yet could not bring herself to douse it.

"*Lilac.*" Her mother stared at her. Henri was frozen over his plate. "Your guard is speaking to you."

The queen blinked, and the guard who stood at the corner of the table came into focus.

"Your carriage is ready, Your Majesty."

A prim smile of relief found its way onto her face, which she dabbed free of gravy. "Thank you. I'll be right there."

Marguerite wore a panicked grimace. "Dear."

"Yes?"

"A carriage?"

"My carriage, Mother." Her racing thoughts could wait. It had been Garin's magic that had tormented her—would continue to. It could wait, everything and everyone could wait until she was with him again. "Yanna and Isabel were kind in preparing it for me at such short notice."

Her mother let out a strangled laugh, eyeing the others dining in the room. "You haven't told us of your plans for the evening. Why don't you join us for dessert? We have a busy week ahead of us."

"But if I am present, then what would you all talk about?"

Her father placed his hand on Marguerite's knee under the table, but she shook it off.

Lilac's chair scraped against the floor as the room watched her rise. She curtsied in place. "Mother. Father. Good evening."

Marguerite stood. "But you have an important meeting tomorrow."

Lilac didn't care. Her mother couldn't say anything to deter her from her plan to leave. Whatever they were scheming could wait a day or two. She'd already stepped out from the table. Every head followed her as she stalked toward the courtyard door.

"There is a diplomat who wants to see you."

At her mother's words, Lilac froze halfway across the room. The guard bumped into her, and she waved away his apology.

"Tomorrow morning," Henri clarified, washing his mouthful of food with a swig of ale then skewering more roasted potatoes upon his fork. Glimpsing his daughter's infuriated stare, he turned to Marguerite. "However, there's been many a meeting I've attended after an evening of dancing and imbibing. The past several days have been difficult. She's in need of reprieve."

Marguerite shot him a look. "She is a *queen*, Henri. She cannot be seen tossing back tankards as she's done here, throwing up in a pot, sneaking off with the nearest sentry doing God knows what just hours before hosting."

That shut Henri up. Lilac reddened immediately as everyone else in the room diverted their gaze, the staff busying themselves and pretending not to hear.

"Lilac must not only be present, but coherent to greet him upon his arrival." Her mother looked like she might collapse. "Imagine, he arrives and our feral queen is lost to the woods yet again."

"No one wanted to inform me of this earlier?"

"After realizing you were in crisis, we were advised against it. Until you improved." Her father swallowed the last of his potatoes. "As you might imagine, the past few days were not the most ideal for our attempts at communication."

"I've been ill. Traveler's illness."

"Yes," Marguerite said before Henri could stop her. "We had Kemble determine it was *that*, and not anything else concerning."

Lilac's chest constricted. "When?"

"She took your urine from the pot during one of your tantrums, before you ordered everyone out to rot in bed."

"You tested me?" Her body began to quake with a silent fury. "Without my permission?"

"Why?" Marguerite squinted. "There is no concern for pregnancy, is there?"

"*No*," she answered truthfully, lifting her lip in disgust. "Not at all."

"Good. Because the last thing you need is some bastard child before you're even crowned."

Henri's face was swallowed by his tankard. "Fortunately, none of the barley or wheat sprouted," he commented into it.

"Still, she hasn't been herself. What could it be?" Her mother began to count on her fingers, reciting the options and turning back to Lilac. "Is it the season? The heavy bloom? The heat? The weather has been favorable, it is bound to be a joyous summer. Has the food not been to your liking? We can change anything on your menus."

Ears ringing, Lilac shook her head. *A diplomat. Barley.* This was why she was so upset with him. Upset was not the word. She never put it past the likes of her parents to cross a line, yet it was the last thing she expected from Garin. She needed to see him, to understand his reasoning. To make him regret pushing her to marry.

To feel him again.

"Is it a boy?" Marguerite's clipped tone cut through her reverie.

Lilac held her tongue and the wave of anger that followed.

"Forget him quickly," her mother advised with a darkened glance at Henri.

"Some privacy, please," Lilac commanded to the room, her face aflame, too stunned to say much else. Everyone but the guard behind instantly rose and obliged. "*Who* is coming here? Tell me now."

Hands shaking, Marguerite sat again and took a slow sip from the teacup Hedwig had placed before her shortly before being ordered out. "We've received communication from one of the counts in the Austrian court. The courier brought a letter by."

A count? They'd received it while she was at the Fenfoss Inn, recovering. The room suddenly grew hot. "By courier? From Austria? Wouldn't he send a pigeon?"

"We received it the third morning after you'd departed for the haber-dashery, when you failed to return. He's already in country and has been staying at a local inn after arriving ahead of time." Marguerite gestured jabbed a hand toward her. "Can you imagine the upset, the anxiety it caused us? It is a wonder you even chose to return."

Of course, it was her absence for a foreign count that had concerned them. This was probably why they'd refrained from sending out a search party; drawing attention might affect this count's perception of her family. Of her.

"Which inn?"

"He did not specify," said Henri.

There had certainly been no Austrian count present at the Jaunty Hog. "What's his name?"

"Albrecht Fritsch," her mother said, reaching for her teacup again but knocking it over with her knuckle in her excitement. "He's on the Habsburgs' court."

The Habsburgs. He was one of Maximilian's men. An important figure. Highly favored.

"We can fetch John to retrieve the note, if you wish," her mother offered.

"Did this not seem too important to keep from me? You told me at breakfast that I received no propositions."

"You *haven't* received any propositions. Not by letter." Henri leaned forward and raised his eyebrows, willing her to listen. "No leader is willing to claim a public stake in a war against France unless your hand and dowry are secured in private."

Lilac laughed dryly. "You mean they aren't willing to risk their standing if they aren't certain I'll accept and that their return is secured, because becoming France's enemy might not be worth it otherwise?"

Henri gave a disgruntled shrug. "That is how this works, is it not? Information can be gleaned or even ambushed from a courier, they scarcely travel armed enough. Albrecht has made it clear he would like to meet with you and sent a letter ahead of his expected arrival come Monday. *Tomorrow.* That was all it relayed, among other fine details."

"He sent a letter *on* his travels? He didn't bother sending a request of any sort beforehand?"

"He must be confident in his offer."

Now everything was starting to make sense. She *had* thought her parents seemed a tad too calm that morning.

What would she do? What of Garin? "Send it back. Tell him I—" Her hand flew to her mouth as she launched into a sudden coughing fit, throat tight. *Deny* was the word that failed to make it out. "I have too much to lose," she managed. "I will not give up my freedom and name for a count."

"Marriage to a noble might give you more of that than you think," said Marguerite. "You do not have the time nor resources to be selective. Marriage to anyone in the emperor's court will still highly benefit you."

She wanted to shrivel into herself at the thought of some decrepit noble making his way to her castle on his pudgy old steed. "I can't marry just any —" She exhaled. Any broken attempt to explain that this was not what she wanted for herself would fall on deaf ears.

"Well dear," Henri said, "Albrecht's name would come with its own benefits and protections. He is in favor of the emperor, and you'd become one of the ladies of the Holy Roman Empire. Think of the benefit to you, to your kingdom. He's already nearly here, why don't you hear what he has to say? He is expected at some point in the morning."

Marguerite steeled herself against her daughter's burning glare. "If he has anything to offer you, he will be welcome to remain at our castle until you've made a decision. Hopefully before your coronation ceremony Saturday evening. He will be in attendance at the ball following. You will get to know him. Maybe even grow fond of him."

"But what about the Le Tallecs?" she pointed out. "No one knows that Vivien and Armand are dead. We haven't made an announcement, have we?" Garin had listened to the proclamation from Henri's carriage window and said that they'd proclaimed Sinclair's arrest. To her knowledge, it was all that was said.

"We haven't," Henri confirmed, lowering his voice. "But a statement must be made since they won't be in attendance. Any delay will stoke suspicion. You can make a preemptive announcement to your guests, so they are not caught off guard. Then, we will send out a notice with the town criers."

She imagined what the notice might say. "After discovering Vivien, murdered and dismembered by Sinclair, Armand traveled here and killed himself on the floor of our Grand Hall. Their son is in my custody and not a threat to society any longer."

"Precisely," Henri said. "Simple. Brilliant."

Her father was right; any effort to hide their deaths would be suspicious. It felt like he was covering her, but she reminded herself, were she accused, Henri and Vivien would shoulder the same blame. It was the truth, so far as her parents knew. The only thing he hadn't spoken a word of was Armand's insistence of Lilac's involvement with the vampires. She would not mention it any further. More Daemon scandal would not help her in boosting morale in the case of a war; luckily, it hadn't seemed anyone else in the Grand Hall at the time of Armand's accusations had believed him.

What did Henri believe, though?

"So it would behoove you to remain here to welcome everyone coming to celebrate you. Maybe even proposition you." When Lilac didn't answer, her mother intently sliced her grape in half, popping it into her mouth on the end of a fork and savoring it.

Even before Garin's caution over a possible bond developing—far before their journey and the crash—her mind had been consumed by concern over the Accords meeting and seeing him again.

She'd been distracted from the matters at her castle, the matter of her hand; she'd been a fool to think denying Sinclair was the end of it. Now that everything was forced into focus, she couldn't help but feel jarred into an unbridled anger.

Anger at her parents, surely with Garin... but she had no one else to blame except herself. The past few days had been spent throwing herself at other matters of duty in order to distract herself, making herself sick with the effects of prolonging Garin's demands. All she had to do was enter a marriage that might save her kingdom from war.

If she just did as she was told, it would make everyone happy. The thought made her insides coil, but her kingdom was at stake.

Really, a small voice at the back of her mind said. *Was it Garin being selfish?*

It had been impossible to make a sound decision with the incessant gnawing at her insides, and apparent the inability to focus or remember small details. She needed to see him. It would quiet her body and mind.

"I am leaving for some fresh air and privacy," Lilac announced. "If anyone follows me, they will find themselves rotting beside Sinclair."

She turned the knob and strode out into the early evening, willing herself to forget the open-mouthed glare of her mother, and her father's face half hidden in his cup, deciding not to mention she intended to return by the end of the night. Maybe she shouldn't. Maybe she should never return and spend the rest of her days waking up in the arms of the man who infuriated her.

She was not the only pawn here, so far as she was concerned.

"Let them send search parties. I'll order them home," Lilac drawled to the guard as he trailed her along the courtyard corridor that lined the patch of grass and imported greenery, riverstones surrounding the duck pond at the center. For a fleeting moment, she thought basking in the deep amber light and pondering her woes until the torches lit might be a better idea than the one she had in mind.

Then, she saw *his* eyes in the stars, just visible in the gradient of dusk—winking, vicious demons of time—and stomped all the way through the shaded passage to the bailey, where Giles greeted her with a wave. The horses and plain carriage were once again prepared for departure, just as she'd sent her handmaidens to prepare in urgency. She swallowed, marveling at the way her racing heart and bubbling nerves seemed to subside the closer she strode to the stable.

Lilac allowed the guard to help her up the carriage step, then thanked and dismissed him. She'd brought no bags this time, only her dagger strapped to her thigh, and the inescapable, unholy need to see *him* again. The last few days might've seen a moment of weakness from her, but the moment she'd discovered there were no propositions for her to consider, Lilac decided it was time. When she thought she could try to push through the unsettling sensations her body and mind betrayed her with under Garin's entrancement, the feeling had surprisingly lessened.

Her nausea had mostly subsided by the time she'd joined her parents for supper, and now, in the breeze, it felt as if she'd just removed a particularly tight corset. She exhaled and took in the night, savoring the lightness on her body.

For the first time in days, she could breathe. The worst of the soul-crushing anxiety was over.

Garin had entranced her, demanded she return to the castle, consider her propositions, and marry. She'd done so. She'd obeyed—and indeed, did not marry while lacking a proposition.

His horrid hold on her was over.

BRIAR SOMERSET

Lilac felt naked without her cloak, but the relief quelled her slight shiver, providing plenty of warmth; she wouldn't need it this time to protect her from the frost, Daemons, or nosy onlookers.

Let them see me, she thought. *Let the world know that I am free—that no one controls me, not God, man, nor monster.*

This was her realm. If her kingdom once considered her wicked enough to lock away, and if Garin felt he needed to entrance her to marry, then Lilac was a formidable enough force to be seen imbibing at a tavern—or leading her men into war.

I f Garin felt so strongly about not seeing her, he did a poor job at revoking access to the inn. Gaining access to the gate wasn't her goal as much as seeing him, being near him again was, but she could only assume The Fenfoss Inn was where he'd remained in order to avoid her and stop any potential blood bond from developing further.

Who knows, she thought, fiddling with her dress ribbons and chewing her lip, careful this time not to make herself bleed. He might be across the kingdom by now. He might have boarded a ship for the New World.

The thought made her uneasy, but as she willed herself to stop squirming and Father Guillaume—*Giles*—prompted the horses to slow before the thin clearing on the left side of the path, she knew she'd made the right choice.

There was no way to explain it, but she could feel it. A buzzing in her joints, a hitch in her breath. He was here. She would see him.

And even if she met the same fury with which he left her, Garin shouldn't have expected any less. If he didn't have the witches strengthen the wards against her, he could have at least hidden the tinderbox that would allow her to access the path and pop in for supper and a drink, after all.

Since Lilac was his only passenger, she'd felt there was no need to ride in the carriage alone and had decided to sit up front with him. The ease with which they found and revealed the gate on the main path would have been more surprising if Giles hadn't taken that moment to pull a plump gray cat—an orange-eyed chartreux—from the driver's box to his right, just before they made the tight left turn into the hidden entry.

Lilac spent the start of the ride through the brightly lit canopy swallowing her shock and stiffly holding the creature, which Giles had placed on her lap.

It was evident that this was the barn cat that he had mentioned early on in their first trip. Lilac didn't know where Giles might've acquired a barn cat, as they weren't known to need or utilize one until recently. If she didn't know better, she would've thought it was one of the strays that used to frequent the bailey and courtyard several summers ago, chasing the birds and ducks that lived there.

The funny thing was, Father Guillaume had *hated* cats—so much, in fact, that he had convinced Henri to hire a pack of small hunting dogs to chase them away.

It was a hair away from digging its claws into her chemise, so she continued awkwardly stroking it until she eventually felt it calm and curl up against the warmth of her stomach.

Lilac asked him where he'd found it. It seemed an innocent enough question that wouldn't upset him or trigger any specific memories, but her heart sunk when she looked over to see his unkempt eyebrows knitted. The way his hands tightened on the reins. Lilac told him gently that he could trust her, that he could certainly keep his newfound pet and that they could discuss it more over a warm bowl of Lorietta's potage. This instantly made his eyes soften.

Apparently, Giles had acquired her—she didn't have a name, so he decided in the moment to call her *Bisousig*—near the import stores on the eastern wall of the bailey after noticing her flouncing after the mice. This made sense, since the rodents could have come from any of the incoming agriculture, certainly the shipment boxes from the shore.

When they fell into silence again, Bisousig purring against her belly and licking its paws, Lilac fought the urge to ask him about Garin, curious about the terms of their own entrancement. However, she refrained, fearing any mention of Garin might cause his spell to break.

Fortunately, she didn't have to.

"You look lovely tonight, Your Majesty," Giles said with a nervous clear of the throat, probably eager to change the subject. "Are you off to see Mr. Trevelyan?"

Lilac turned, surprised Garin would've given him his surname. "Yes. I mean, I wanted a night at the tavern. If he happens to be there, then so be it."

"But Mr. Trevelyan is there every night, working," he replied matter-of-factly. Then he made a face, backtracking. "Erm. *Most* nights. On the nights he doesn't spend at the castle. Those days, he's working at the bar in the mornings, and Lorietta takes nights."

They rolled along for a bit before Lilac turned to glance at him. Giles, who was staring straight ahead, spared her a brief look before he smiled, his eyes seeming sharper tonight in the bright orange-green light.

Lilac shifted in her seat, suddenly nervous about what he might know—what he might expose about Garin that she wouldn't necessarily want to know. It wasn't her business, after all. She considered telling him the vampire hadn't done so since a week after her ceremony, but decided to keep her mouth shut as a wave of anger hit her like a brick. "He doesn't spend nights at the castle," she finally spat, feeling her face climb with color.

The coachman leaned his head back against the carriage, his brow furrowed. "Ah. Perhaps I made a mistake in saying—"

"Saying what?" Giles only groaned at her grating tone, but she couldn't help herself and pushed further. "Well? Where does he spend his nights out if not with me?" The words tasted so bitter on her tongue, tinged in regret and an emerald jealousy.

"On your balcony," he sighed. "He watches over your bedchamber."

Lilac startled, then yelped when the cat dug its claws into her thigh at her sudden movement. The horse shook its head and snorted.

Giles uttered a noise of comfort for the animal, his eyes widening as they fixated back on the road. "In that case, he does *not* do that. He positively does not sit on your balcony with his back to the stone, just out of sight and concealed by your curtains, staring up at the stars and the canopy of his home." He glanced sideways at her again. "And, when he's bored, Mr. Trevelyan certainly does *not* climb down to the stable with stolen drink and plates of bread and fruit from the stores to have a chat with me."

Silently, Lilac stared ahead at the now looming building, its windows and rooms aglow as they rattled and clomped into its shadow. She didn't know if she believed Giles. He easily could have been entranced, trained by Garin to gain back her favor.

"He is a generous friend," Giles said thoughtfully after some time. "He watches over you like a dragon does its horde of gold."

Lilac's throat was dry when she finally replied. "Do you know if he's been there the past couple nights? Since you and I have been home?"

"No, Your Majesty. He hasn't."

Lilac was silent the rest of the way to The Fenfoss Inn.

THIS TIME, THROUGH THE WINDOW, THE MAIN ROOM APPEARED LIKE THE first time she happened across it. There were silhouettes of a moving crowd; the sounds of uproarious laughter and the jolly picking of a mandolin floated through the still night air. Loïg was tethered, grazing in the grass just past the stable. Her horse looked up, gave a snort of acknowledgment, and returned to munching on clovers.

She stood as soon as Giles pulled into the driveway, an almost unpleasant excitement seeping its way into her bones. She ignored his warnings and shoved Bisouig back into his arms before climbing out and jumping down onto the cobblestone.

Lilac smoothed her dress, pulled her corset down slightly, and asked Giles to meet at the front door after he'd parked. She'd worn a new perfume tonight, one her mother had given her years ago that she'd then thought made her feel old. Tonight, she didn't mind it. This one headier, with notes of musk and vanilla, the scent filling the air as she began to sweat.

Just as she reached for the knob, the door swung open. It was Adelaide, her black hair thrown into a tight, high bun, her cheekbones flushed, and the skin under her eyes primed in a new wash of dark glitter. She scowled at the sight of the queen. Then, her glassy eyes grew wide.

Lorietta craned her neck from the iron-bead curtain behind the bar, which was full of korikaned and several magic folk. There were a couple human-presenting patrons present she hadn't seen before, both men and women. Either donors or shifters, she thought distractedly, probably less surprised to see them than she should have been. Some turned in their stools to look her way.

No faeries were among the crowd tonight. Neither was Garin.

"You're here," Lorietta said, sounding equally shocked and relieved. Then, her face twisted into the same mask of concern Adelaide wore as she finished pouring a waving Blitzrik his drink. "What happened? Are you all right?"

Lilac moved to pass Adelaide, but the witch continued to block her path.

"Where's Garin?" Lilac asked.

"Not here," replied Adelaide.

Lorietta gave the other witch a pointed stare. "*Adelaide.*"

"What? I'm not getting my throat slit tonight."

Lilac neared, gripping the doorframe, still processing Adelaide's answer. "Did he leave for Cinderfell?"

Loïg was right there, yet Hywell's horse was missing. Another thorough glance at the main room and she didn't see Bastion. Or Emrys. She stared uncomprehendingly through the door as the witches watched her, briefly remembering the other hazy parts of her and Garin's argument upstairs; Emrys had been killed by the *Guài* but hadn't stayed dead for long. "Did they all leave to deliver the chest?"

"Keep your bloody voice down," Lorietta said sharply, marching over to them, the long pink robe draped over the apron swishing behind her. "No, the thing's still upstairs."

"The vampires tried to contact Kestrel again," Adelaide added. "It would be a risk to travel to Cinderfell unannounced to deliver it. They're awaiting a response, but if it comes to that, they're taking the warlock with them."

Her body was buzzing, her hands growing numb. She suddenly couldn't focus on anything else but laying eyes on him, ensuring he was safe with proof of her own.

"Fine. Where is Garin then?" When the witches exchanged glances, the sinking feeling in the hollow of her chest turned to panic as they regarded her with uncertainty. Maybe he *was* here. Maybe they were keeping him from her. "Let me see him."

Adelaide crossed her arms, the powerful scent of mead and cloves wafting off her. "He was adamant we didn't allow him to leave the inn for the next week. I was against babysitting a vampire from the start, but *she*"—she threw a displeased scowl at Lorietta—"insisted we help him."

"We tried to restrain him," Lorietta said. "But we should've known the inn's magic wasn't enough to keep Garin."

"Keep him from what?" Lilac asked.

Adelaide stared. "Are you slow? From *you*."

Her heart dropped. She imagined him showing up at the gate and growing furious she wasn't there. Searching the castle for her. Reeling, she stepped away from the doorframe.

Lorietta approached them, standing beside Adelaide. Their shoulders brushed, and Adelaide, whom Lilac thought would have flinched at closeness, didn't notice.

"Before you panic," said Lorietta, "he did leave, but I don't think he went to your castle." She gave Adelaide a pointed look. "If he traveled in her direction, he would've found her by now. On her way here."

Lilac would be sick. "You were responsible for him. He asked for your help..." It was difficult to mask the tremble in her voice. "And you lost him?"

"He and his *friends*," Lorietta replied, matching the frost in her tone, "were in his bedchamber when Bastion and Myrddin sprinted up the cellar stairs. They claimed that Garin and Casmir had bolted out of his cellar door. They then dashed out the front to follow behind on horseback."

"Casmir? The vampire from the bar?"

Lorietta nodded.

Lilac rubbed her temples, trying to understand. "So, he's with them now?"

"We hope so," Adelaide answered. "They left together. The nomad vampire, the violent one, and that warlock." She reached up, unbothered, to smooth a loose lock that sprung out of her updo. "And Garin."

"Earlier this afternoon, the former three had gotten raucously drunk and burst his door open. They collected several of my wicker baskets and brought down a whole feast to *spruce his mood*," Lorietta quoted. "The vampires brought spirits and bottled blood. They were tired of him sulking in there."

"I told you it was a horrid idea to let them do that," Adelaide said.

Lorietta grimaced. "I thought it would be good for him. Garin struggles with loneliness as it is."

Lilac thought of the fragments of dreams she'd had in her bedchamber. Garin, pacing the floor, then wrapped in his quilt. Everything felt far away —pieces were starting to come together, but nothing was making sense in a way that comforted her. She felt unable to place the details into a coherent picture. They fuzzed in her brain, which only focused on one thing: locating Garin. "No one knows where they went? No one heard?"

"No," Lorietta said, and Lilac thought the witch's orange eyes flitted quickly over to Adelaide. "Meriam was tending the bar tonight. We've been taking turns since Garin began locking himself in his room after you returned home. She was the one who alerted us they'd left."

She thought of the last few days, the hell they had been. Feeling prisoner to her own desires, yet unable to act on them, truly, until she did as Garin had asked and found out there had been no propositions for marriage. It had almost seemed too easy. Once she'd decided to try to leave to find him, most of her physical symptoms had eased.

Had he felt the same tortuous restlessness, the confusion she had? Was it also alleviated by giving up on trying to stay away?

If he'd left, supposedly to find her, and hadn't... then where was he? "He told me I had to stay separated from him for a week to be cautious."

"He is right in his concern," admitted Lorietta. "This behavior of his didn't start until after he sent you away." She side-eyed Lilac and rubbed her forehead. "Have you two exchanged any amount of blood before the carriage accident?"

Lilac's red face answered for her, and the way her voice cracked on her "*No!*" solidified her lie.

"When, how, and how much?" asked Adelaide, a shocked grin blooming.

"We haven't," she hissed, composing herself, her face scorched. "Not in an amount that would matter."

"Your Majesty," Lorietta said slowly, stepping closer and dragging Adelaide forward with her. With a wave of her hand, the front door to the inn swung and clicked shut, blocking out curious ears. "This is important and could cost lives if it hasn't already, so I encourage you to answer in full transparency." She looked this way and that and lowered her voice to a threatening whisper. "As long as you are on my property, your answers are safe here. But I need your honesty."

"I can poison the truth out of you," Adelaide optioned.

"That won't be necessary," Lilac snapped, feeling stripped bare. "In my bedchamber, at my tower. He visited me one week after my ceremony. We talked, and he fed me a drop. A prick on his finger, to reveal the memory of me walking into your tavern the night we met."

Lorietta's brows creased for a brief moment before the expression smoothed. "He used his magic on you?"

Lilac scoffed. "I don't think he has a problem with that."

Then there was that second time when she'd bitten his hand as she came, when his blood had shown her the view of a familiar desk—her father's study, books and papers askew. It had looked like it, but in the moment she'd been so shocked she hadn't thought of what it might mean. Another question for the vampire. "That's what their blood does, doesn't it? Shows you their memories?"

"Sometimes," said Adelaide, looking to Lorietta for confirmation. "With intent, they can send vivid memories through to the consumer. They show you what they want to, a past vision from their own eyes. It's part of their Sanguine magic."

"I thought that only referred to their entrancement," Lilac said.

"Their entrancement, their ability to host thralls, aromatic lure, and even the strange effects of their *vitae* are part of it," explained Lorietta. She closed her eyes as she spoke, almost as if quoting or paraphrasing something from memory. "Sanguine magic, though limited in the scope of arcana, is still powerful as it is mystical. Sending visual memories through their blood is how they can recall their own memories that might be lost to time if they're extremely old or weren't paying attention in the moment; for them the memory might be something obscure, vague, but it is as if the drinker experiences it for himself, usually under entrancement. *Histories of the Lasting Night, Volume I*," she recounted. "Long ago, Meriam had me read up on vampires if we were going to take one in. Since you left, Garin has been on edge and threatened anyone who has tried to enter his chamber. Had Bastion up against the wall on the first night."

"A textbook." Lilac thought of the human-authored texts and manuscripts on Daemons that had her making a fool of herself her first time in Brocéliande. The vampire manuscript, which she'd been meaning to search for in her Accords planning. "Is there anything in it that might tell you what's been happening to him? To us?"

"I've searched and seemed to have misplaced it. I haven't seen that book in quite a while, though I am usually able to dig it out." Lorietta sighed laboriously. "Did he drink from you, too? In your tower."

"Yes, moments after," she admitted quietly. Just to get it over with, she added, "I had his blood once more, accidentally, the night of the Accords meeting. Downstairs in his chamber before everything happened, and it was also a very small amount. A smear, but it wasn't an exchange. He didn't take my blood from me then. We were—"

"I don't want to hear it, don't make me cast a deafening spell on myself." Lorietta threw her hands up, exasperated. "And those were the *only* times, outside of the exchange that saved your life? You are sure?"

"Yes," Lilac said defensively. "He told me how it works. It has to be a significant amount of blood. He did tell me our exchange might cause some effects that would decrease with our time apart."

"And were there?" Lorietta pressed.

"Sickness without fever. Restlessness. Sleeplessness. Nausea. Now gone," she lied. The restlessness had certainly returned, morphing into something else entirely.

"You must be drained a large amount, to the point of unconsciousness but not death, which is a very fine line. Then comes the challenge of the vampire bloodletting into the victim's mouth, getting them to ingest it. That is why it is always the vampire's *choice* to enthrall a person, one with astute self-control and ample knowledge of what a dying pulse sounds and feels like." Lorietta eyed Lilac decidedly as Adelaide stared nervously between them and the trees. "A drop, a smear, not even the amount he took from and fed you the other night comes close to what would need to occur to trigger the thrall bond at any level. If it did, there would be thralls running amuck."

"Plus," added Adelaide, "the effects of a first-level blood bond would have eased over the course of the three days you've spent away."

Lilac forced her quick, shallow breathing to deepen as she quietly assessed herself. She thought of the inhuman strength that had surfaced when Garin had challenged her upstairs. He'd said it was a result of the volatile combination of his sanguine magic and the arcana still in her body. Was that truly a product of both? Or either? She wouldn't dare mention it now.

"He entranced me to go to the castle, consider my options, and marry. I did as he asked—*except* marry," she clarified as the witches exchanged glances. "I had no proposals awaiting me. After learning such this morning, I made the decision to see him. And now, here I am. His entrancement has dissipated."

"It seems it has." Lorietta placed her hand to her lips, as if there were more to say. She refrained.

"But she is still in her bridal glamor. All but the gown." Adelaide shifted her black knitted robe further onto her shoulders. "It even withstood the *Guài* arrow's enchantment."

"I have no explanation for that," Lorietta admitted. "Arcana, even Sanguine magic, is at times uncertain, skirting the rules society pretends makes it predictable."

"And he hasn't been sleeping, or even come out of his room to feed from the blood whores—"

"Donors," corrected Lorietta.

"That's right," Adelaide said. "*Blood whore* is what Lilac is to him."

Lilac didn't bother responding, couldn't even listen to their bickering; they grew quiet once they observed the dark fury that surged across her face, the shame and flash of jealousy again at the thought of his fangs in another's neck turning into panic once more.

In all this time spent talking, she could've found him by now. "I'm leaving." She started in the direction of the carriage.

"Don't be ridiculous. There's plenty of room for you here, and we can revisit this in the morning, Your Majesty. Come now, it is the sensible thing."

"I'm not waiting until morning to find him." She couldn't. She had a meeting tomorrow just to tell a man who had traveled across a kingdom and a half *no*. Lilac nearly couldn't see straight, panting into the cooling air, the wind whipping past her face in the dark as she marched toward the stable. Giles was just now hobbling toward them, cat tucked in his arm, the carriage crookedly parked in front of the stables.

"Why does your priest have a cat in his arms?" Adelaide said, giggling.

"Honestly, I'm not—*get back in, Giles*" Lilac commanded furiously as Giles squinted and saw the queen stomping his way, freezing midstep. "We're leaving."

"Yes, Your Majesty—"

"No," Lorietta snapped, confusing him further. "Stop. No one is going anywhere, certainly not to seek Garin out. Not with that vampire in this state."

Lilac shot a glare over her shoulder at the following witches. "What state? Is he angry? Hungry?"

"I wouldn't exactly call it hunger," Lorietta began to reply.

Lilac turned to confront the tavern owner as a loud *pop* sounded in front of her, followed by a puff of billowing white smoke. She coughed against the strong aroma of black powder—and screamed.

A man stood between her and the witches. He flopped his long golden hair out of his face, making a startled noise upon spotting the perplexed witches, and then spinning, doubling back at Lilac as he fixed the royal blue velvet robe that dusted his loafers. The material shone in the night, a pattern of white stars mirroring those speckling the clear sky above.

"Funny seeing you *here*, Your Majesty," the man said. "I was afraid I'd end up in the middle of your dining hall." Relief flooded his long face. He couldn't have been more than in his early thirties, with piercing blue eyes and a short, neatly trimmed beard.

He held his hand out.

"Don't touch him," Lorietta snarled at Lilac—she wasn't planning on it, already shrinking away—then turned to the man. "Where are they?" She craned her neck, glancing around as if expecting to see Garin watching from the trees. "You left him?"

He ignored Lorietta's inquiry, still glancing at Lilac. "Pleasure," he said, offering his hand again.

She didn't recognize him, but his voice and accent much were too familiar to ignore. "*Emrys?*"

"Myrddin Ambrosious Wyllt," said the man, retracting his arm as if the name should have been familiar. "Myrddin the Great?" His impish grin fell further when Lilac gave him an astonished grimace. "Emrys. Ambrosius. I've gone by a few names in the last few centuries, but you can call me Myrddin."

Lilac blinked at him. The voice was his, yet warmer, fuller. Younger. Much less gruff. Garin had said he was alive and seemed annoyed about it, but hadn't mentioned *this*. "You were the warlock they were after," she said accusingly, expecting to feel more anger toward him. But all her fury was focused on finding Garin. "But how? How are you alive?"

"It wasn't the arrow that killed him, but the impact of the crash. Myrddin woke and stabbed himself in the arm with the merchant's arrow stuck in his armor shortly after we got to the inn," said Adelaide, looking equal parts terrified and impressed as Lilac remained at a loss for words. "He had a chest plate on."

"I had become stuck in my own glamor after living in it for a few decades, hiding from the *Guài* and other... prominent figures. Using the *Guài* arrow I'd so easily acquired seemed the simplest way out."

Lilac frowned, glancing him up and down. *This* was the drunk old man with the filthy beard they'd rescued from the Jaunty Hog? "You don't even look like a warlock anymore."

Myrddin stepped back, his eyes roving over her tight corset and pink kirtle. "And you certainly don't look queenly tonight." When Lilac crossed her arms over her chest, he snorted. "I'm not complaining. You've certainly dressed the part for our destination."

"She's not going anywhere." Lorietta marched over.

Adelaide was close behind. "It wouldn't hurt to hear what Myrddin has to say."

"*He's* the one who got them into this mess. You're not bringing her anywhere near him."

"You know where he is?" Lilac urged.

"That, I do."

Lilac neared him, eyeing his outstretched hands. "Please, take me to him."

"Myrddin," Lorietta said, her cat eyes flashing bright in the night.

"Is he safe?" Lilac asked, unable to focus on anything but knowing Garin was well and alive. Her heart dropped when the warlock made a face.

"It's not *his* safety I'm concerned about," said Myrddin.

Lorietta leaned past her, into Myrddin, causing him to recoil into his beard as she jabbed a nail toward his chest. "We cannot have the queen enthralled to Garin Trevelyan, of all people. If you want to help, do what you should have this entire time. Convince him to come home and sever any existing connection between them before it is too late. Consider how difficult it was to keep her from him, and to keep him from leaving. She left the castle! We're just fortunate he didn't find her first, or that he didn't end up at the keep gates. There must be a way."

"There are very few ways to end the beginnings of a possible bond, however it was formed," Myrddin said, politely shooing the witch's finger. "One of which you've tried. The others, I don't imagine will interest him in this moment."

"Thanks to *you*," Lorietta said, shrill.

If the fear of thralling her or the mere possibility of a blood bond was preventing Garin from wanting to see her, be with her, then she would prevent it. Break it. She would do anything.

"How?" Lilac asked. "I'll do it."

"These methods involve great sacrifice and must involve both of you, except for the most obvious: death of the regnant."

"No," Lorietta and Lilac said in unison.

He squinted, then turned to Lilac. "Have you ever considered the benefits of a regnant-thrall companionship? There can be certain powerful attributes in—"

"I will banish you from my property forever, make it invisible and inaccessible to you, Myrddin," Lorietta threatened, shaking a fist at him.

His brows rose, considering. "If I help, do I get free drinks for life?"

"You're immortal," Adelaide pointed out.

"Exactly. Either way," replied the warlock, sidestepping a fuming Lorietta, "the first step is to get Garin back."

"*You* were supposed to bring him back—why couldn't you have teleported him and Bastion here?"

Myrddin scratched the back of his neck. "Erm. Garin, at the moment, is not accessible. I must take her to him. I will return them both in one piece." Myrddin held his hands out toward them again, forcing the witches to back away. "One touch and you're *all* coming with me."

Lilac glanced back at Lorietta, who looked like she had half the mind to swing at him. She gave Lilac a warning glare as Adelaide watched, wide-eyed. Adelaide looked at the queen from over Lorietta's shoulder and gave one minute nod of approval.

Without a second thought, Lilac slammed her palm into Myrddin's. There was a jerk behind her navel, and the world began to spin.

13

U nlike Kestrel's method of portaling, Lilac's feet never truly left the ground. This was worse. She swallowed part of the dinner burped in her mouth and couldn't help but close her eyes tight, her fists balled. As the spinning slowed, she became aware of other sensations—Myrddin's hand clamped firmly around her forearm, her palm wrapped around his. The smell of musk, sweat, and long worn perfume. A steady thumping and strumming that grew louder every second. Suddenly, the spinning stopped altogether as the sound of drums and strings and flutes filled the dank air, and she lurched when they stopped; her vision began to adjust to dim light, and she couldn't help but shout in panic for the warlock, who yelped in anguish somewhere near her head.

Disoriented, Lilac shifted onto her elbows and realized she was laying on something soft; she blinked in the dappled dark, and found herself partially wrapped in Myrddin's royal blue robes. He shouted again, muffled this time—beneath her. She abruptly righted herself, turned and opened her mouth to apologize, but gasped as a set of hands and back of a head appeared before him, roving up Myrddin's thighs as he, too, sat up.

They'd landed on an alcove with a large chaise, which was filled with limbs and mouths, some faces adorned in glittering masks. Someone's wet mouth grazed her earlobe, and she shrieked; there were bodies, both fully dressed and naked, *everywhere* around them—very much alive, grinding and brushing into them. Myrddin sat between two women spilling out of their corsets and the glistening, shirtless gentleman kneeling in front of him. One of the women and the man wore masks beset with glistening beads and feathers.

"N-no thank you," the warlock said, his cheeks pink. He held his arm out in alarm to Lilac. She sidestepped the man on the ground and yanked the warlock to his feet. He took a moment to gather himself, giving Lilac a moment to process the whimpering and groaning going on around them.

"A *brothel?*" she shouted over the tantalizing beat, not caring who heard. The music at the front of the room drowned her out anyway. "Where are we? Where is he?"

"Rennes. The Fool's Folly." Myrddin gave her a regretful smile, then pointed behind her at the nearby staircase. A pair of giggling women, both unmasked, nearly fell over themselves as they descended it.

Lilac stood on her toes, immediately scanning the room for an exit. All she saw was an upper floor. The glimpses of a long bar at the back of the room, several shirtless barkeeps behind it. Beautiful masked women carrying trays of food and drink. A stage.

Her vision was then blurred by the tears stinging her eyes. "Why did you bring me here? I thought he wanted to see me."

"It is rather complicated," explained Myrddin, dipping his head in apology. "At the moment, he does not want to see you, Your Majesty. But he does *need* you."

She didn't know what to say. Previously, the thought of him alone with a donor made her feel uneasy, but the thought of him drinking from—*in bed with*—another woman filled her every pore with the searing heat of jealousy.

"He can have his whore," she spat, envy flooding her.

The warlock made a little sound and poked a finger in the air. "Er, *whores*, which was the point of this excursion."

Blinded with anger, Lilac grabbed him by the front of his robes with one hand, and the next moment, her dagger was in the other. She held it in his face.

Myrddin looked only mildly alarmed, but not at her. She followed his gaze up to the three chandeliers that hung from the ceiling, dimly lighting the open portion of the floor, and the small torches lining the walls and the staircase. The flames flickered, danced violently, as if an undetectable gale had blown through the building.

A gentle hand pressed against the small of Lilac's back. She dropped the warlock when a stunning woman with a towering pink wig came up from behind her. "Keep the knife play upstairs, you hear me?" she shouted over the band at the front corner of the tavern. "You can wait for a room. Where is your mask? You know the rules," she barked.

"My mask?" Lilac said, realizing belatedly what the mask must indicate. Many women and men scattered throughout the dance floor wore them. "Oh, I'm not—"

Myrddin's foot stomped onto her toes, and she stifled a yelp. "She lost it in our evening spent together," he said gruffly.

The woman rolled her eyes, her own face decorated in heavy powder, rogue, and jewels, and pressed one into Lilac's arms. She disappeared into the crowd, muttering under her breath.

It gleamed gold, crafted in what felt like linen padding and soft metal, adorned at the corners in tufts of greenery and Baby's Breath, curving tastefully upward at the ends. A short row of glinting beaded tassels dangled from the bottom to conceal most of the wearer's cheekbones and nose.

Sheathing her dagger, Lilac scoffed, threw the mask to the floor, and turned to leave. She would find the door; find her own way home.

Myrddin grabbed her hand; his eyes were urgent. "Your Majesty," he said with a little bow of the head and another nervous laugh that made her want to put him through the wall. "I understand how upsetting this must be for you."

"*Upsetting?* This is humiliating, Myrddin."

"Look, Garin is only here because of me. *And* Bastion. And Casmir." At her look of utter loathing, he continued urgently. "We were having a night at the bar when Bastion finally convinced Garin to allow us into that dungeon of a room he'd barricaded himself in—at least without him smiting us. It was a grand old time. We got him drinking until we started playing at something with a little more... stakes."

"You were gambling," she figured.

"I wouldn't call it—" he began, but under her glare ended up folding. "It was Casmir's suggestion that we bring out the coin. I have somewhat of a habit, I admit it, and have run myself dry time and time again, but I couldn't help it. Those vampires are so competitive! And they were mixing blood and liquor—it skirts their high tolerance and inebriates them."

She would be sick again. "How did this lead to Garin coming *here?*"

"No one enjoys having a hungry vampire around, especially as hungry as Garin seemed, so, after a few card games, I bet him that Casmir could obtain more consenting donors without the use of their vampiric influence. I told him that Casmir was more educated, from a wealthier background, and those attributes would likely help him gain the upper hand—"

She stepped to him again. "You *what?*"

"They bolted out of his room, ended up coming to The Fool's Folly! Admittedly, the older, foreign vampire was less drunk than Garin at the time of their departure, and I imagine Casmir would have helped curb Garin's temptation to engage in any foolish, public antics. Bastion and I followed on horseback with our own tracking spell not knowing where they would end up, where we would be transported if I used my magic. Once we realized where he'd arrived, I teleported myself to you. But something is *wrong*, Your Majesty," he added pleadingly, gripping her shoulder when she turned again to leave, stopping her. "Something is very wrong with Garin, and no one realized it until he left the inn."

"And you brought me here to beg him to return." Lilac was shaking.

"You don't understand, I brought you here because I made a terrible mistake suggesting this in the first place and don't want anyone to get hurt."

"No, apparently I'm not understanding," she snarled. "So he's on a rampage at a brothel because he's drunk on liquor and blood?"

The warlock cocked his head. "Erm, something like that."

"Garin wouldn't do that. He wouldn't hurt anyone," she breathed, swallowing at whatever dark thing he was implying, even as uncertainty plagued her. "Whoever jumps in bed with him is doing it of their own accord."

She tried not to think of the past three days, the influence he'd held over her, but it was no use; the memory was imprinted in her bones, as was the way she'd allowed the fury and illness to build until she decided to leave to see him. She'd made the decision to leave in madness. She'd never forget it.

Lilac felt as if she would never comfortably eat, sleep without setting her eyes on Garin again. As the witches and Myrddin had seemed to confirm, maybe he had gone through the same kind of torture. She'd braved Brocéliande to see him, risked rejection again.

Yet here he was. Lost in a brothel.

"He's not himself," Myrddin insisted, watching her thoughts churn. "Your time spent apart has somehow not eased anything for him. He'll hurt someone if he hasn't already. He'll listen to you. You are the *only* one who can convince him to leave."

Fear pulsed through her body with the pounding beat of the mandolin and drums. "That doesn't make sense. You're a powerful warlock," she said, the bravado from her anger already faltering at the warning in his words. "He won't hurt anyone," she insisted, not knowing how much of that reassurance was for her own nerves. "You don't know him."

"Do you?"

There was a pop before she answered, and there was a sudden pressure on her forehead and nose. She cried out, and her hands went to her face—the mask she'd thrown was pressed against the top half of her head, the soft silk fitted perfectly against her cheekbones and the bridge of her nose. She swore and went to undo the tight knot at the back of her head, but the more she struggled with it, the more the string tightened on its own, squeezing her already throbbing temples.

"Ouch!" The pressure lessened when she stopped tugging, the tips of her fingers and nails stinging. "*You.*"

Myrddin was watching her through the holes of her mask, his features twisted in regret. "I'm sorry, Your Majesty. Bastion should be arriving any minute now on that horse; we'll be waiting outside for both of you. If anyone else could stop him..." His shoulders fell in regret. "Just get him out of that room, into the streets, and the mask will come off. We'll find you."

"You and Bastion?"

"Yes. You have my word."

She glanced at the stairwell again. It swirled to the second floor, which cut off at a balcony overlooking the dance floor. There was a door at the start of the hall, closest to the bannister and apparently locked, as told by the lone unmasked woman knocking, listening in, trying the knob, then leaving in frustration.

There it was again, that deep sense of knowing in her body. The building anxiety over Myrddin's words left her in a rush, warm relief replacing it as she merely laid eyes on that door.

He was there. She knew it.

Fear struck her as soon as she looked away to see Myrddin also staring at the balcony door.

There was something obviously critical that she was not understanding —that no one else was bothering to explain to her. "You got him into this, you're going to help me." She lunged for him, but her hands only grasped air, the thin cloud of smoke wisping around her.

Myrddin was gone.

Lilac waved the biting scent of black powder away and stuffed down her panic, freezing and allowing herself to be swallowed by the dancing crowd, holding her breath against the suddenly overwhelming stench of the room. The sounds of sex, the stifling perfume, the stench of sweat that invaded her nostrils and mouth. She ended up being pushed along, her feet finding motion as a new song started at the front stage to the right of what seemed to be the door, where a trio of fiddlers had replaced the mandolin players and drummers. She found her fingers brushing another wall and turned, pressed her back against it, coughing, willing the wood to soak the heat from her body.

Two women brushed past her, the same ones she'd seen descending the stairs—those stairs that first led to Garin's room, if her gut feeling was to be believed. They dragged an unmasked blonde along with them this time, one who hadn't been there before. Arms interlinked, they tugged her toward the stairway, giggling coyly into the woman's ear with the stems of drink glasses in their fingers. One of them had what looked like a large bottle tucked under her arm.

She should warn them. They were clueless; they had no idea what they were dealing with if what Myrddin said was true. But she would not save them, or Garin.

What was there to save him from? Pussy and fresh, pumping blood? He'd spent years unable to drink from people. He should indulge, shouldn't he? She'd wanted it for him, although she hadn't been able to dwell on it long without feeling most envious.

Lilac turned this way and that, clinging to the wall, suddenly burdened with the pleasant thought of marching up to them and yanking them back down the stairs by their hair. She almost could not bear the thought of his mouth on another woman's neck, possibly buried deep inside her... even when he'd refused *her* throat as he'd fingered her in his chamber.

Giggles erupted from the balcony. There was a clink of glass, and cool droplets rained down on the crowd. No one else seemed to notice. Lilac cursed and wiped the liquid from the mask as some dripped into her eyes. She licked her lips, salty-sweet from her tears and whatever drink had spilled.

She gritted her teeth when she heard a door—Garin's door—open, and the laughter continued before it clicked shut again.

Lilac had never felt jealousy like this. It came in waves of sadness, then ebbed out in white-hot fury. She was sweating.

One of the masked women walked past with a tray of drinks. Maybe *she* needed liquor. Even a tankard of ale would do—anything to take the edge of envy off long enough so she could focus on leaving. Finding the bar required her to leave the spot of safety she'd just uncovered, but she felt like she'd burn up without something to drink, and soon.

A couple brushed past her, a woman pushing her masked partner into one of the alcoves that lined the wall next to her.

Lilac held her breath, bit her tongue, watching the man stroke the woman's hair, one hand cupped against her throat as they both settled into the round booth. The woman slid into his lap as soon as he was seated. Then her eyes met Lilac's, and she beckoned hungrily with her finger.

Lilac turned away, blushing immensely, only to spot another masked man stalking past her from the far corner. The first man felt the bulge through the newcomer's trousers and slipped his cock free, beginning to slowly jerk him as the woman began to bounce in his lap.

She should join them. With this mask she blended in—no one would know. The swirl of temptation in her stomach danced at the thought of being sandwiched between all three of their beautiful bodies.

No sooner did she consider it, when the image of *him* spiked in her memory, an unwelcome intruder; the thought of his hands slipping between her thighs, of him tasting her. As much as she hated it, she wanted Garin. Needed him. *He* would know it was her if she went to him despite her mask.

But his attention was elsewhere. Angrily, she shoved the thought from her mind.

The crowd shoved and pulled against her like a current as she peeled herself from the wall, the candles high and bright, surrounded in golden halos. The music sounded like it had grown louder, faster, but she could still hear everything, the groaning and whispering. The bodies around her seemed to be pulsing, and soon enough the pounding beat of the jig played on stage was in her chest, behind her navel. Between her thighs.

She blinked and found herself at the front of the tavern, at the door, hesitating with her hand on the knob. Rennes was a large city, after all; she could catch a carriage home without trouble. Bastion and Myrddin were here. They could deal with him.

An arm appeared next to her, a hairy hand slamming and pressing the door shut just as she'd opened it. Lilac spun and came face to face with two mesmerizing red eyes, so dark they would've appeared black if not for the torch near her head. He smiled and stepped back to give her room, but his aroma of fine wine and blueberry cologne had already enveloped her. Her sensitized body reacted to his closeness, her feet immediately following; as soon as he offered his arm, she linked hers through, and he pulled her back into the heat of the crowd. They came to a stop, and to her own surprise, she leaned in.

"Your Majesty." His breathy accent tickled her ear, sending chills down her back.

Lilac softly shut her eyes, hearing her own syrupy voice. "Hello, Casmir."

Casmir chuckled, pulling away just enough to peer down at her. He towered over Lilac, glancing down at her with a soft smirk. "Why good evening, Your Majesty."

He was dressed handsomely in a black leather vest, hand-carved filigree across his broad chest. His shoulder length hair was half up in a bun, the rest of it falling in umber waves. An amused, fanged smile was sandwiched between his thick mustache and beard. He inclined his head and barely pressed his lips to the back of her hand before releasing her.

"Both a worrisome and lovely surprise seeing Trevelyan's pet here tonight."

The mention of his name filled her with a tumultuous anger, the heat in her body causing the mounting need she felt to spill over. She tilted her head, glared up at him—and rose on her feet to kiss him.

Lilac closed her eyes. She kissed him because she was angry, because she had gone to the inn to upset Garin in the first place. Because her body was on fire, and she needed someone—anyone—to put it out. Still, it took her by surprise, just as much as it did him. Casmir's lips were stiff at first, the rest of him rigid against her, but then he quickly opened for her, his soft mouth cupping hers. His hands found her waist, and he allowed her to push him as she placed her hands on his chest, walking him back through the crowd to the nearest wall.

Casmir was not sweet and smoky, flora and woodsmoke, like Garin. He tasted bitter, like mint and strong tobacco. When his ankle hit the shallow step of an empty alcove, he stumbled back onto the seat. Lilac released him, and before he could right himself, she climbed onto his lap, her skin flushing at the sensation of him hardening beneath her.

Casmir propped himself up on his arms, the beginnings of an appalled smirk overshadowed by his shocked glare. "That," he breathed, eyes flickering down to her legs spread over him, his stiff cock pressing against her inner thigh, "is involuntary."

"Well this isn't. And I am *not*," Lilac said, leaning down and brushing her lips against his, "Garin's pet."

Even as he opened his mouth and their tongues briefly met, her body didn't react the way she thought it would—the way she wanted. He was startlingly handsome; there was no questioning her attraction. Still, as she slowly rubbed herself against him, there was a strong tug behind her navel. A *warning*, one she duly ignored—in fact, the tinge of regret only made her want Casmir more. How funny it would be, if Garin walked out of his room and glanced down to see her riding the vampire's cock.

Suddenly, her thoughts were no longer muffled by the painful desperation to be touched, and a rush of adrenaline washed her eagerness away, momentarily clearing her mind.

She broke off, sickened and panting. *What was this?* Must her conscience be so prudish? Lilac fought back, dug her nails into the cushions on either side of her and leaned toward him again, hoping to drown out the resurfaced thoughts of Garin upstairs, with his whores... But Casmir planted his hands on her shoulders, gently holding her back.

"I can see you are hesitant," he purred. "What is it you want?"

"I want you." The words felt foreign as they exited her mouth. Her shaking fingertips trailed her collarbone, where she pulled one of her sleeves off her shoulder, exposing her throat.

Casmir's eyes narrowed warningly. "That's not what you want."

She ignored him, rocking forward onto his erection and willing him to put his hands on her.

He only steadied her in place again. "As much as I would love to," he breathed, "I cannot, Your Majesty. Have you had anything to drink tonight?"

Her face fell as she pulled back and studied his sobered expression. "I haven't. Why?"

Casmir's nostrils flared in her direction. He was scenting her.

"Stop it. Stop that."

"You've had the Dragondew Mead."

Lilac leaned away, scowling. "The what? No, I haven't had anything to drink. Not since before Myrddin portaled us here."

"He didn't *portal* you," he repeated, lifting a hand and smoothing her hairline. "That's what the Fair Folk do. He teleports." When he pulled his hand away, she caught a glimpse of shimmering moisture on his fingertips. *The spilled drink from the balcony.* "Dragondew Mead is what they offer the ladies and gents who work here. It's optional, but it's not unheard of for patrons to get their hands on it by bribing someone at the bar. It isn't hard to obtain on busy nights such as this."

"It was only a few drops. Someone spilled it from the balcony." Her hand went to her hair, her mask, attempting to wipe the rest of the moisture off. "What is it? What does it do?"

"It is made from the Sea Holly honey from Brest. It encourages arousal, only very slightly. Improves one's stamina in bed, their performance. Their climax."

"People drink whole cups of those?" A dribble into her mouth shouldn't have been enough to make her feel this way, like she needed to be touched.

"Sometimes two." Casmir cleared his throat, regarding her warily. "I'm not sure you need any more, though."

She reached down, considering, and began to fumble with the large silver clasp on his belt. "Then make me come." It would be a welcome favor, and she wasn't sure if doing it herself would help. Her muscles were seizing, burning.

His growing grin, the long fangs beneath them were all too tempting. He gazed up at her, his striking red eyes studying her. There was a look there that made her stop.

Pity.

"You're lovely, Your Majesty, and I would be honored to participate in whatever devious scheme of revenge you are out for tonight." His hand found hers, his fingers trailing up her forearm and giving her goosebumps as he lightly squeezed on her wrist. "Yet, I regretfully must refrain."

The pressure on her arm made her jump, her core quiver. Lilac gasped at the reaction his light touch sent throughout her body.

Her cheeks burned. She would not beg for his attention the way she had Garin's. "Of course," she said, her heartbeat palpable in every part of her body. She pulled her arm away, hating the words at the tip of her tongue. "I am sorry for acting this way."

Casmir quickly waved off her apology. "Don't. It's the mead, and your obvious attraction to vampires. It is something you cannot help—and neither can we. Unfortunately, you reek of the Trevelyan boy."

She... reeked of him? Lilac gripped the table and slid off him, head pounding. The thought of Garin again, him with another woman—with multiple women—undressed and covered in blood flashed through her mind again, unbidden.

"His essence, his scent covers you." He smiled, and while his mouth might have been teasing, his eyes were kind. "And you cannot stop thinking of him, can you?"

She glanced around. No one was watching them, but she wanted to go back to the door. She was embarrassing herself. She needed air. To her surprise, Casmir gently sat up and scooted back to make more room for her on the bench.

"See?"

"I don't understand. It's been days since I've seen him." Casmir's words haunted her. She motioned at herself, at the rose-colored kirtle and the absent oils Yanna had washed from her hair under scalding water—recalling all the grime Isabel had scrubbed from her nails after she'd pushed herself to exhaustion, attempting to manage the kingdom through the toils of

Garin's punishing influence before languishing like some love-burdened specter.

Yesterday, after her fainting spell, she vaguely recalled Madame Kemble suggesting a trip to the shore might fix her in time for the ball. She would love one now, if not to walk into the sea. "What do you mean, I reek of him?" She glared at Casmir, tugging her dress back onto her shoulder. "I've *bathed*!"

"It does not matter, young one. Not when a vampire has claimed you. You are off-limits."

"Claimed?" A sound of disgust escaped her lips.

"You belong to him. Or, will by the end of the night," he said from the corner of his mouth.

"I do not *belong* to anyone," she said, but blood flooded her cheeks, her ears. "Myrddin was the one who ordered me to convince Garin to leave the brothel before he stuck this mask on me. Permanently, until I complete his task." She scowled, unable to help herself, knowing she shouldn't divulge any more information to the vampire than she already had.

"And yet you came to find him on your own accord. Just how do you think you were able to leave?" Just then, he looked past her. "Ah. *Merci, mon amour.*" Lilac turned to see him reach past her and retrieve a tankard from the tray of the masked woman who'd appeared at the table.

"My pleasure." The woman smiled at Lilac before flouncing away.

"I left because his entrancement on me lifted the moment I'd tried to obey his orders of accepting a proposition that would save my kingdom. There were no propositions." She purposefully didn't mention Albrecht's letter.

"Is that what it was?" Casmir made a little noise in the back of his throat and lifted his drink. A toast. "And you were about to romance me just now. To prove what, exactly?"

"Don't flatter yourself. I wasn't trying to romance you. I was trying to fuck you, if it wasn't clear."

"You both are fitted for one another, that's certain," he said with a rough laugh. "Anyway, I won't be the one to bed you tonight." He lifted his brows in consideration. "You should get a human to please you. They aren't upheld by vampiric law, and better he killed them than me."

She'd been so determined to fuck Casmir, it hadn't occurred to her what the consequence of her spite and lust might be—other than Garin's jealousy, and getting back at him for entrancing her and then ending up here.

If she had somehow skirted the bounds of Garin's entrancement, she'd still left the castle to find him, hadn't she?

"If a vampire encroaches upon someone else's *property*," he explained, waving the tankard at the fearful realization dawning on her face, "then the regnant is allowed a duel. Personally, I wouldn't balk at the opportunity to lay the lad on his arse, but then I'd never be allowed at his family's cozy little inn again. Plus..."

Lilac followed his gaze to the staircase across the tavern, up to the balcony.

"No one in their right mind would dare challenge him tonight." There was an edge to his tone, a concern matching Myrddin's.

As the words sank in, he took a swig, and when he put the cup down, his lips were tainted in red. He licked them clean. "It isn't uncommon that blood bonds go awry, especially when inadvertently formed and the first thing the regnant wants is to be rid of his thrall."

"He did not want to be rid of me," she snapped, willing the fearful anger rising with every heavy breath to fade. He wanted to get a rise from her. "Garin explained what thralls are, how they work and what he did to me in order to save me." She was unsure of how much Casmir knew, and it was impossible to tell with the way he watched her with intent patience. She lowered her voice. "He and the witches both confirmed it wasn't nearly enough to invoke a blood bond, even of the first degree."

Casmir reached out—all of the suaveness and hunger with which he'd touched her arm just moments ago, gone—and awkwardly petted her on the shoulder. "I would agree, and he'd said the witch and Bastion had monitored his process. Yet, I do find it alarming that, what are supposed to be the mild symptoms of an incomplete blood exchange appear otherwise."

It was hard to tell in the low light, but it looked like the curiosity with which he was eyeing her had morphed into wonder.

"Lorietta said the rules of all magic are arbitrary," she said softly.

Casmir only shook his head in answer and took a swig from his tankard again, but Lilac's arm shot out and grabbed the handle. In shock, he released it and watched her slam it back down onto the table.

"Tell me what you know," she demanded.

"That's the thing," he said, hesitant. "I am very old in comparison to your friends, Your Majesty. Traveling became my one true joy in life after mine was ripped from me in an instant. I am four and a half centuries old, have walked and sailed every mapped corner of this world and still yearn to discover more, feel more. That is the curse of the vampire. The Church believes we are evil because we are shamelessly lustful. From my own experience, vampirism has merely made me a glutton for everything I loved as a human, and what I learned to enjoy as a Daemon. Travel. Shameless romance. Books. The Trevelyan boy has his plants, his research. His love of caring for the inn and its denizens. But in all my years visiting, I've never seen Garin more invested in anything like he is with you. I don't know much of *anything* about what is transpiring tonight. I have never seen it."

Her heart was pounding so loud all of a sudden, along with her core—her upper thighs—but none of her want was for Casmir any longer. She looked around again, afraid someone would see her in such disarray. The fear faded quickly.

Lilac gripped the table, digging the edge into her palm. "He insisted there was no bond, that nothing was ever started because he hadn't drank deeply enough, or fed me enough of his blood."

"*Nothing was ever started.*" Casmir gave her a condescending frown. He ran his hand over his face. "You must understand this in order to begin to understand your vampire: we are obsessive creatures by nature—even outside of lust or interest for one thing or person. This is how I've learned to travel and spend time amongst so many of my kind without getting mauled, taking the time to understand the things they protect, what they guard most carefully. Most covens don't take well to strangers, as Garin does not care for or trust me. Wisely." He laughed lightly, despite the dark warning tone of his words. "Because of this nature, we spend so much of our time existing in a state of restraint. Garin exercises that restraint around you."

"We've—" Lilac stopped herself, her face aflame. "Garin has had my body and my blood. And I, his."

"He has known what it is to taste you. A blood bond is to *own*." Casmir sighed and offered her a small smile. "Whatever transpired between you, between the carriage crash and in that room at the inn has made that restraint all the more precarious for him to carry. He is usually very skilled in at least pretending he does not care."

Lilac balked at this through a body-quaking shudder. "I wouldn't call doing all he has for me *not caring*."

"He would do far worse if he did not feel the need to mask anything he felt for you. Nothing that already *exists* need be started, by the way." Casmir carefully slipped his fingers through the tankard handle, ensuring she wouldn't knock it out of his grasp again. He sipped his drink. "Any condition can alter the strength of a blood bond. Sickness. Depression. *Love*. He has been terrible since banishing you. More than usual."

"We cannot be bound." She had nothing else to say.

Casmir tipped the tankard back, his throat bobbing as he finished the liquid. "All I know, with absolute certainty, is that your absence has utterly destroyed him."

She didn't want to hear any more; she couldn't focus on anything but the pulsing that had moved into the tops of her hips. She couldn't bear to think about Garin, about how much he wanted her—anything to prolong the inevitable in entering that room.

Lilac squinted as he wiped red off his lips. "What's in your cup, Casmir?"

"Fire Ale. It's expensive, but you can ask for it at the bar and bring a cup to him," he suggested. "An offering, just in case. Then he might spare you."

"He'd never harm me."

"Not on purpose." His eyes flitted to her thighs. "Still, it's smart of you to bring that blade."

"I used it on him once. I wouldn't need to use it again."

"Then you're more of a damsel than I thought. It's made of metals. Won't do any real harm, as you've probably discovered, but it might jolt him enough to realize what he's doing. What you should be carrying on you at all times, is this." He leaned in and revealed the sharp tip of something marbled and textured out of his coat pocket.

At first, she blinked, unsure of what she was staring at.

Then, she jerked, scrambling out of the alcove and slipping off the bench. "*Never*. I would never use that on him, Casmir."

"He's dealing with his hunger in ways tonight that will not suppress it. I believe it grows worse."

"So the only option you had was to *stake* him?" Her anger did nothing to quell the aching need that had begun to spread through her body. Fingers flexing at her side, she had half the mind to wrestle it from him.

"It would only kill him if it entered the heart. Other than that, a hawthorn stake will disable him."

Lilac stared at him. "Why did you do this? Why did you bring him here?"

"I did nothing. We both agreed to a challenge set by your warlock. Your vampire left on his *own* accord. I didn't have to lead him here." Casmir laughed before sobering quickly. "Once I realized this was where he was headed, I stopped trying to dissuade him. I thought it was a good idea, a responsible one, due to the potential number of willing donors who frequent this place and how discreet it is. I did not realize at the time the extent of his hunger, or your connection."

Lilac swallowed a stab of jealousy.

"Oh, don't look so glum, Your Majesty. It's you that has a spell over him now."

"A brothel, more discreet than The Fenfoss Inn?"

"By number, there are not as many donors there. The vampires and people concerned with ethics and morals go to your beloved's inn. Donors who wish to be anonymous and protected by magic folk if things go awry. But why not mix pleasure and feeding together?" He leaned in. "The way it's supposed to be, isn't it? You're acting like it was hard to convince Garin."

She looked over her shoulder, expecting to see him watching from over the balcony.

"When he darted off, I kept a close eye on him, ensuring he wouldn't suddenly change course to Paimpont or to your castle."

"So gracious of you." Lilac was only half listening to him. The room closest to the balcony opened a crack, and the pair of giggling women stumbled out—the same ones she'd passed earlier. They didn't seem to be laughing now.

"Tonight, Garin is riding high on his instincts, Your Majesty. Everything the devil himself created us to do—to seduce, drain, and hunt—has flooded his senses. But anyone he drinks from or tries to seduce will only make him want you *more*."

At his words, she turned slowly back to him.

"You now understand our concern. You're the only one who can reason with him. Myrddin and I would help, but anyone entering the room with you will be seen as his competition. He would attack me without thought. Us going in there as a group, with or without you..." He trailed off, exhaling. "That's how your kingdom would witness its second raid."

She didn't need to hear any more. Lilac said her thanks and stepped away from him, ambling away toward the crowd.

"One more thing," Casmir called out. She didn't bother looking back. "Please give him my condolences. For losing our bet."

14

S hrugging off offers from men in both traveler's tunics and fine clothing, Lilac shoved her way to the bar, her hair sticking to her forehead and the pins in her half-up braids falling out. She'd tried to squeeze her fingers under the mask again, until the tips of her fingers were throbbing. There was no use, but she wasn't concentrating on that. She'd liked to think the pain helped distract her from everything else she felt.

Her body burned, as if soaking in the body heat from each person she passed.

She exhaled in relief when she emerged from the crowd, clinging to the counter and relishing the cool against her skin as the warlock's and Casmir's warnings resounded in her mind.

She understood their hesitation completely; not even she wanted to face a potentially aggressive Garin. But what reasoning would she bring that another vampire and powerful warlock could not?

If Bastion and Myrddin had left the inn on horseback, and Myrddin teleported to her on the journey, then Bastion should be here by now. She could use the help since Myrddin and Casmir had proved useless; he seemed brave and if nothing else, restless enough.

And yet, no matter who stood beside her, she'd still have to face him.

A shirtless man with a rippling back and waist-long black hair worked behind this bar, which was wide and spanned the length of the back of the room. He turned, the delicious cut of his waist visible just above his trousers. He acknowledged her with a finger in the air and quickly finished up with the patrons before him.

"One Fire Ale, please," she said, forcing an impatient smile when he finally approached her. She didn't recognize the frost in her voice, but there was a building urgency at her core making her limbs buzz.

The man laughed, but his face quickly fell when her forced smile dropped into a cold pout. "We're out of Fire Ale," he said curtly.

Something told her he was lying. "I just saw someone sipping on some."

"And? You know the rules."

"I'm new," she managed, finding it shockingly easy to lie and think on her feet while actively imagining running her tongue along the beautiful stranger's bare waistline. She blinked, the thought shocking her. "Remind me."

"Courtesans are to reserve themselves for the patrons of higher class."

"That doesn't sound very good for business."

He scowled, looking this way and that. "Leave."

"Aren't we to serve them as long as they're able to pay?"

"Courtesans are banned from feedings," he whispered, leaning in. "If you're interested in defiling yourself, you'll do it after your shift." With his nose in the air, he turned away.

"I'm not going to feed him from the vein—"

"Shut your mouth, girl."

She bit back a scathing remark. "He just mentioned wanting a drink from the bar, and a Fire Ale is what he ordered. That is all."

"And that's swell. But you're not one of my barmaids. Not dressed like that." His gaze dipped to her corset, and back up to her mask. "I'd get one of them to do it, *if* we had any Fire Ale left."

Lilac managed a cool shrug. "I just thought I'd keep my client happy."

The man ignored her, picking up a towel.

She thought of the unmasked women guiding the blonde upstairs, and the liquid they'd spilled onto her from the balcony. The distant ache and need to feel pressure against her clit—inside her—growing more prominent. "Since you're so concerned about the rules," Lilac said, watching him run the cloth along the inside of a glass. "It would be a shame if anyone discovered Dragondew Mead in the wrong hands."

The barkeep stalked back to her without missing a beat. "You want to feed your vampire?" He looked left and right and dipped beneath the bar, clanking around and returning with a small golden saucer, upon which sat the wide base of a matching goblet, the mouth covered entirely by a red cloth napkin. "Good luck," he muttered, then stalked away without another word.

That was easy, she thought, balancing the heavy cup atop the saucer in the palm of her left hand, mimicking the graceful way Hedwig would do it. She headed in the direction of the stairs. It was much harder than it looked, and she had to stop it from falling off with her free hand several times. No one batted an eye in her direction.

There was then a flash of unmistakable honey blond off to the right, and she nearly spilled over, wobbling in place. "Bastion?" She turned, frantically rising on her toes and craning her head; he'd just passed her, a couple grinding bodies away. "*Bastion*," she said, raising her voice.

Bastion was already gone. She swore it was him. Even if the crowd and music probably drowned her out, how had he not smelled her? Lilac swore under her breath, looked back at the nearby staircase, then moved forward in Bastion's direction, steadying the goblet again. The last thing she needed was to enter his chamber covered in someone else's blood.

Then, there it was again. That feeling, the tug behind her navel. This one threatened to take the breath out of her, so prominent she could almost name it. It was familiar, an echo of the emptiness she'd felt tossing and turning in bed the last few days—except this wasn't coupled with the dread of the world crumbling beneath her. This felt different, urgent. Instead of a warning pull on her wrist, this was a choking fist upon her throat.

It was a demand.

She might've been able to fight it, but trying would only draw attention. Seething, she turned back around, gritted her teeth and climbed the stairs, one stubborn foot after the other, finally moving in agreement with the dark sanguine magic urging her forward.

At the top were several other courtesans and denizens in the hall; two of them stalked out of another room and didn't even blink in her direction as they passed her on the way to the stairs, while another sat outside a room, humming to herself and puffing at a pipe. The force pulled her attention to the left, and her body pivoted, following suit. Leaning against the wall to the left of the balcony and cast half in shadows, were the two women she'd first spotted upon arrival.

The third—the last to join them—was nowhere to be seen.

One was in an ivy-green knitted shawl with her glass held loosely in one hand, and the other, a pretty brown kirtle that came up to her knees. They watched her coldly as she approached, and one of them made a noise of shock when Lilac turned toward the door on her right. She reached for the knob. Fighting it was no use, even when it was obvious the door was locked from the inside; she tried to turn it this way and that, but the door would not budge. The moment she tried to tug her hand off, a wave of nauseous dread hit her.

Lilac blinked, stunned by the peculiar sensation, and continued jiggling the knob.

"He didn't order *you*," one of them said behind her.

She reddened and turned halfway. "And how would you know that?"

The woman's eyes widened in surprise, her scoff deepening. "Because they're not supposed to eat the whores here."

"Perhaps he ordered me to sate his other appetites." At this, the force driving her arm seemed to wane slightly, but not without one last embarrassingly violent shake of the knob. Lilac willed with all her might for her hand to release it, tugging hard. She stumbled back before finally rapping her knuckle upon the door of her own accord.

No answer. Only muffled voices from within, a thump and scrape here and there, although neither sounded like sex or a struggle. Lilac glanced at them again from over her shoulder, just as she finally pried her hand free from the door. They regarded her with a mixture of wonder and disgust.

"Where's your friend?" Lilac asked as she faced them.

The one who hadn't spoken yet shifted against the wall. "What friend?"

"The woman you brought here. I saw," she added, so they wouldn't bother lying.

They whispered to each other, and the second one nudged her friend.

"*Stop it, Nellie*," the first speaker snapped.

"But Elona," Nellie groaned, looking nervous.

"She's in there with another guest," Elona said, her eyes narrowing. "What of it?"

"Just wondering," Lilac pried, sick with envy, though they didn't seem to notice. They seemed only concerned with the competition she presented. "It's obvious he hasn't been satisfied since I was summoned to help," she said, managing a suggestive smile. "Have you considered going in there with her? Maybe three is better than one? Four even?"

"It wasn't *us*." Elona's lashes batted in offense. "He was so hungry, he couldn't sleep with us. And he certainly wouldn't want to fuck *you*."

"You're probably right about that."

"He was adamant," explained Nellie. "He said he couldn't do anything until he had blood."

"When we first heard there were two vampires here tonight, we thought it'd be easy," Elona said, her pupils hazy. "But the older one is downstairs dancing, and no one seems to be able to get him to a room. We thought that was what they were here for... having sex *and* feeding. The sensation is like no other."

Lilac felt like she needed to vomit. "Why didn't you offer him your necks?"

"Because," Nellie said, frowning at the door, her face shifting in confusion. "He insisted he *only* wanted to feed. That the only appetite he'd entertain tonight was for blood. And that..." Nellie looked down, picking at her nails. "He said—"

"He said when he was done with us, w-we wouldn't be able to continue anyway," finished Elona, looking uneasy.

"You mean you wouldn't be able to have sex?"

"In the condition he'd have left us in," said Elona quietly. "Yes."

"And you still thought you could convince him otherwise."

They both nodded.

Lilac's pulse was erratic, anger spiking with the jealousy that shouldn't have been at the forefront of her mind. This didn't sound like Garin was being funny, or even chivalrous.

Shrugging uncomfortably, Elona adjusted the shawl hanging off her bare shoulders. "We even brought him a drink."

Her heart sank. This was wrong. Garin was vulnerable, and maybe he did need help.

How dare you, should've been her next words. *He's not himself.* Maybe a punch to the face would have sufficed. Several options flashed through her mind before she opened her mouth. "What was he like?" was all that came out.

She couldn't help herself.

Nellie sniffled while Elona cleared her throat bitterly. She was probably not used to being turned down. They were both beautiful. "Polite, but at the same time ill-mannered. Maybe paranoid. Kept watching the door, as if expecting someone, or something else. He seemed distracted."

Lilac couldn't quite concentrate on their conversation or anything in the hall for that matter, but only because she was suddenly all too present in her body. Her stomach churned, and as her hand went to her neck, she realized she'd been sweating; all of the powder, rogue, and perfume she'd put on just to torture Garin, gone.

Her gaze flickered down to the glass Elona was holding. Had the women before her felt the effects of the mead, too? Did they also feel this pulsing at their core, the need to feel something? *Anything?* They seemed a bit fidgety, but perhaps that came with the nerves of trying to seduce a vampire like Garin.

If they'd had any, how did they look so calm when Lilac had been fed only a few drops and felt like she might rip her clothes off if she didn't come soon?

She looked down at the cloth-covered chalice in her hands, filled with what might be four or five large gulps of a stranger's blood for him, hoping it would be enough.

Nellie was eyeing her chalice as well. "What did you bring him?"

"Stop entertaining her, Nellie," Elona snapped. Her grip tightened on her half empty glass.

Before Lilac could answer, the door creaked open to reveal a well lit room. She could just make out the corner of a four poster bed, the glow of firelight.

No sight nor sound of Garin. Or the woman.

They hunched together behind Lilac, craning their necks to peek past. "Move," Elona sneered, pushing off the wall and gripping Lilac's shoulder, shoving her away. "Where are they?"

Lilac's ears burned. "Get your—"

"Get your hands off of her." Garin's voice floated from inside the room, just as there was a tug at Lilac's skirts.

"P-please," rasped a female voice, wet and weak.

Nellie made a fearful noise and Elona did as she was told, falling back against the wall once more.

No.

Lilac forced herself to look down. The third woman the pair had escorted up to Garin's room was at her feet, pulling herself into the doorway, fully clothed except for the high lace neckline of her pretty gown, which now laid across her chest in red ribbons, looking like it had been slashed open with a knife. Or teeth.

The pair's startled cries were drowned out by the rush of blood in Lilac's ears. Without thinking, she bent to pick the girl up—but Garin's black boots appeared before her as he slowly positioned himself behind his prey, whose gaze bore into Lilac's, pleading and filled with horror. Blood flecked her head, some of it matted into her hairline as if it had been smeared across her head in an attempt to put up a fight.

Lilac couldn't bring herself to look up at him, even under the guise of her mask. Instead, she placed the saucer down beside her and reached out to support the shuddering girl over her forearms, but Garin's voice slid over her.

"Leave her," he said boredly, as if helping his victim were an unnecessary favor.

Strangely, Lilac felt herself strain a little stronger now, able to resist his demand. "She needs help."

When she slipped her hands under the girl's armpits and knelt to get a better grip on her before hoisting her up, Lilac jolted in shock; in the poorly lit hall, she hadn't seen the pool of blood beneath her—also spreading warmly now onto her own front. She shrieked, unable to help it.

He *hadn't* drained her blood. This girl was still alive, bleeding to death before her eyes.

Lilac stumbled back. Blood spurted from the puncture wounds from Garin's teeth on the girl's throat as she coughed, attempting to speak. Lilac moved, intending to grab the cloth from the saucer she'd placed at her side and press it to her neck, but in her agony, the woman writhed free, looking panickedly at Lilac, then up at her friends—her *friends*, who, in their desperate state, had sacrificed her to Garin. Now, she knew, it was in hopes he might then have had enough restraint to sleep with them without killing them.

Elona and Nellie were backed against the wall, their expressions wrenched in horror.

Lilac's will finally broke, and she had no other choice but to look up at him. Garin gazed down upon her coldly, bracing himself against the darkened doorway. His mouth, and even part of his nose, were smeared thickly in a deep red he hadn't bothered wiping off.

Did he know? Surely he recognized her? Did he look upon her with such disdain now because he couldn't smell her beneath his victim's blood and her layers of new perfume? Was it an act, like it had been several times before? Her face burned as she imagined his distant, exasperated demeanor in The Fenfoss Inn, as he asked—*commanded*—her to leave out of concern.

This was nothing like that. It was distant and foreboding.

She gritted her teeth and moved to hoist the woman up again, whom he roughly snatched by the arm. The girl had stopped fighting.

"Be *gentle*," she snarled softly as Garin lifted the girl from her. Lilac wanted to try to stop the bleeding with her cloth now that the woman had stopped moving, but with the way her eyes were glassy, rolling, and half-lidded, she could tell she was past any help she could offer.

Garin held her limp form out to the two others, who shrank away. His nostrils flared, his voice low and on the verge of impatience. "Take her."

"Y-you—" Nellie stammered, leaning away as Elona reluctantly accepted her from Garin, lip curled in disgust and stumbling under her weight.

"I what? Killed her?" Garin barked a laugh as they flinched. "It appears her heart is on the verge of stopping in *your* arms, is it not?"

"There is a warlock here," Lilac interjected, tearing her eyes away from him with effort. "Somewhere downstairs, in the crowd. Gold hair, young, deep blue robes. Go find him; he'll help her."

Surprisingly, Elona sucked her teeth as if she'd forgotten Lilac entirely. "Why? So that you can have him all to yourself?"

Jaw slacked, she slowly backed away. What kind of terrible magic was in that Dragondew Mead—in the sea holly or in the bees? No naturally occurring aphrodisiac would make someone offer a friend, or even a stranger, to a vampire just for a chance at bedding him.

She'd done her job in offering. Lilac shook her head and tried to wipe the woman's blood off her hands, but it was fruitless with all of it smeared on her front and down her arms. When she looked up, Garin was studying her, shadows from the flames framing his sharp profile. He ran his tongue across his lower lip, sweeping a lone curl off his forehead and smearing it in blood; in the heat and sweat, her heavy heartbeat pulsed in time with her core—for she'd had the mead, too.

Suddenly, she wasn't sure she wouldn't kill to fuck him, either.

"You didn't even eat her," Elona muttered as they dragged their friend toward the stairs.

He said nothing, folding his arms and watching them leave. When he turned back to Lilac, his glare faltered. He looked tired. "That's because she wasn't to my taste."

Unable to help herself, embarrassed by the enthusiasm her racing heart made it impossible to conceal, Lilac crossed the dim hall and bent to recover the saucer and covered chalice atop it. When she stood, Garin was already gone and the door was creaking shut.

15

"Was that necessary?" Lilac stuck the toe of her shoe into the door and shouldered her way in, letting it fall shut behind her.

The room was spacious, draped in gold and maroon linens she could tell were worn and not dusted in months at least—but in contrast with The Fenfoss Inn, it was near luxury. There was a red settee centered before a crackling fire and Garin braced himself against the back of it, facing the hearth on the right hand wall.

He wore a loose cream linen shirt that had been untucked from his trousers. His shoulders were relaxed, but the veins on his hands were visible as they gripped the frame of the chair.

The room was sweltering, or it at least felt like it. She craned her neck, looking around for a window. There was one opposite the fireplace, covered in drapes on a door that appeared to lead onto a balcony. Then, there was the four poster bed, an armoire, and a closet.

"You're lecturing *me* on morality? They were the ones who brought me their friend to eat just so I was satiated enough to bed them."

"And were you?" she asked quietly.

He either didn't hear her or chose to ignore her question. Without a glance in her direction, he reached for something dark that sat on the bedside table between the settee and the bed. Before she realized it was the slim neck of a decanter, Garin had filled the stout glass beside it and tipped it back against his mouth.

He hesitated after emptying it in a couple swallows, picking up the decanter and studying the bottle. Then, he placed the glass down and took another long swig straight from the decanter. A strangled sound escaped Lilac's mouth, but the warning died on her lips.

"You should leave," he said simply, his glance toward her fleeting before making his way to the front of the settee and taking a seat. When she said nothing and just stood there, he leaned into the lush back of the chair, settling in. "Well?"

"Well what?"

"I'm not in need of your services."

Refusing to look at him, numb at his words, she made her way over to the table at the corner of the settee. She didn't stop to glance his way as she swiped the decanter off of it.

Lilac held it to her nose. It smelled like Scotch, but it was hard to tell. Lilac tossed it into the fire just in case, and skittered back when the flames jumped at her, the backs of her knees bumping the chair.

Garin was watching, open-mouthed. His eyes, now that they were in the light, were the shade of rubies like they had been in her dream. There were deep shadows around them, as if he hadn't slept in days. "God, woman. If you wanted a drink, you could've just said so."

"I think they poisoned you."

His hair was messy, sticking up in odd places as if he'd been yanking at it. He gave a dismissive grunt. "Those wenches? Poison *me*?"

"It was probably in your liquor. Or in that woman's blood. Some fell from the balcony onto the crowd—onto me, and some got into my mouth."

He hummed, disinterested. "Unfortunate. Well, I'm immune to most poisons. When will you die?"

"I won't."

"What was it?"

"Dragondew Mead. It's what they serve to the courtesans here."

Garin frowned. "That doesn't sound familiar. Nor does it sound like a poison if they serve it to the courtesans."

"It was given without your consent or knowing—i-it's made from some sort of plant. It was..."

She tried to think, to remember, but all she could focus on was his mouth, the way his teeth nipped his bottom lip and his brows lifted as he watched her squirm.

"Yes?" Garin drawled.

"Sea..." His expectant expression made it impossible to concentrate. "Sea something. Sea—"

"*Silphium*." Garin's eyes flickered as he rifled through his knowledge of plants. "I've never heard of it infused into a mead before, though. That's no poison. It's a contraceptive. Responsible of them to have on hand, but you wouldn't need it with me," he said, smirking at her heating face. "I appreciate the concern. As long as it wasn't hawthorn, I'll process it quickly."

He seemed more interested in her now, so she didn't bother correcting him even if she was certain *Silphium* wasn't the herb. Lilac swallowed. She thought he tracked the movement of her throat, although it was hard to tell with the flames dancing in his irises. "Hopefully."

"Yes, hopefully. As long as I've had something to eat." There was something mocking in his tone. He'd assaulted her with his hungry gaze and sarcasm many times, but tonight something was off. "Isn't that why you're here?"

"It is." Fumbling with the saucer, Lilac took the corner of the blood-stained cloth that covered the chalice, some of it from the girl, some of it from the spilled—

Lilac frowned. Empty. The chalice was empty, dry, with not a drop of blood in it. But there was *something* in there.

She reached in and pulled out a small, silver object, and held it up to the firelight.

The barkeep downstairs had been telling the truth, after all. In her panic, in the haze of the mead, she didn't understand exactly what it was she was looking at—or why it belonged in the empty chalice.

It was a blade. A scalpel.

"*A vessel.*" His breath swept the back of her neck, jolting her. "One that you are meant to fill."

Lilac started and caught herself on the edge of the settee, the chalice and saucer clattering to the floor. She hadn't seen or heard him stand.

Scalpel gripped in the other hand, she pulled herself up onto the seat as Garin advanced on her, and didn't stop until she'd slid all the way back. She couldn't help but tremble as he knelt before her, one knee up and an elbow propped onto it, examining her. Up close, there was no warmth in his gaze. No familiarity, no fondness there.

"You came to bloodlet for me."

His taunting lilt coupled with his intoxicating scent made her dizzy. "I came to convince you to leave."

"Leave?" Garin chuckled, the ominous sound sending waves of nausea through her. "Now, why would I do that, when I have you here? All to myself. A glamored hire sent to lure me out."

She shook her head vehemently. This was a misunderstanding he would not take lightly. "N-no, I am no hire. Myrddin transported me here to come get you."

"You work here." His lip curled away from his fangs in distrust. "You're a product of that blasted warlock. He transmuted you. This is your glamor." His gaze roved over her, lingering on every detail with sharp scrutiny. Her eyes. Her mask, the flowers on it. Her lips.

She fought back a violent shudder, realizing Garin's implications. "It's *me*."

He reached toward her face.

"It won't come off," Lilac said when he tapped the corner of her mask. "Myrddin is here, downstairs, and he bewitched this blasted mask onto my —*ow*," she said, slapping his hand away after he'd tried tugging it harder. It would rip her skin off. "He spelled it onto me, and it won't come off until you leave this room."

He gave a thundercrack of a laugh. "They don't want me to leave this room. Not right now. Not tonight."

"*I* do, Garin."

"Do not speak my name if you have been bewitched to not only convince me to leave, but that you are her," he said, eyes darkening.

She didn't fight him, knowing she was in no place to challenge him. Instead, she asked, "What's stopping you? Why are you here?"

"I am here because I made a grave mistake. I cannot leave without revisiting a past I have put behind me, and not without undoing so much of what you—what *Lilac*—is accomplishing this very second. At her castle. Far, far away from here. From me. As she should be."

She couldn't help herself, not with how his voice cracked with desperation. This was a Garin she had not yet seen. His forehead was slick with sweat. Lilac reached out for his knee, to place her hand there, but he shifted away—and she stopped at his warning glare. "Lorietta and Adelaide said you hadn't been eating well."

"Have they now?"

"It's what they told me when I went to the inn in search of you."

He exhaled through his nostrils, deliberating, probably trying to decide how much information he could divulge to whom he thought was a stranger.

Garin's throat bobbed. He was eyeing her lips again. "I cannot talk to you. You should leave."

He stood to get away, but her hand shot out to grab his. Fortunately he didn't retaliate, only looked down at their hands in wonder.

"Even if it was true, what you believe—that I am not me, but one of the lovely courtesans who work here," Lilac said, choosing her words carefully, "then someone compensated me for my time with you. You may use it as you wish." Garin ran his tongue over his bottom lip, watching her intently, still as a statue. "You can talk to me, if you wish to do nothing else."

Slowly, he neared and knelt before her once more. "I have been ill," he said quietly, as if afraid someone would hear.

"Since the crash?" she urged, despite the menacing look he shot her. "Since you saved me?"

"I refused to take a donor at the inn because of my bloodlust. I haven't felt myself since—" He stopped himself, speaking hurriedly when he continued, as if displeased by the memories. "Something told me if I took a donor, I'd end up breaking many of Lorietta's feeding rules. So I drank myself *sick* on cold blood. That backfired. I drained a lone traveler on the way here. I couldn't help myself. I was blinded by it, not unlike the first thirst. By the time I arrived in Rennes, it felt like I had not had blood in weeks. It was then I discovered that something was very wrong, and yet I couldn't bring myself to return to the inn, to my bedchamber, where I should be. If I turned back, I knew without a doubt I'd end up at her castle."

The room had gone very quiet despite the noise downstairs. "What would you do, then?"

He flashed her a threatening scowl and decided not to answer her question. "When I got here, I stumbled into the nearest room and realized feeding makes me *hungrier*. The more I take, the more I want. It took everything in me not to drag the nearest bystander into the alleyway outside and bleed them dry as I'd walked up those steps and put myself in —in a brothel, of all places, where everyone's inhibitions are already low. When it is already easy, easier than usual, to do as I please. *Take* as I please." He looked down at his hands; they were shaking slightly. He closed them into fists. "I've never known a hunger like this, one that keeps growing. And they dare dangle their little decoy before me, and..." He cleared his throat, his nostrils flaring, his tongue flitting out to the corners of his mouth. "Fuck. It was *Sea Holly* in that mead, wasn't it?"

Lilac sat absolutely still, a mouse between the paws of a cat. "Yes. I couldn't remember the name at the time. I tried to tell you before you interrupted me."

Garin cussed under his breath, anger flashing in his eyes.

She flushed and looked away as he shifted, not missing how he fluidly adjusted himself at the front of his trousers, so quickly she wouldn't have noticed if she wasn't already on the verge of looking there. Lilac scrambled for anything to distract herself from the urge to stroke him over his pants. "Is this the same hunger you felt at the end of Kestrel's deal?"

This seemed to distract him. Garin regarded her warily. "They prepared you well, haven't they? The feeling isn't the same, but in a way it is worse. It isn't a sensation of frenzy. It is a slow burning, steady hunger that strives to outlast me. That will wait me out until I have no choice but to give in."

She tried not to look as dubious as she felt. "What will help it pass?"

His eyes darkened. "I will be fine," was all he said.

He certainly did not look fine. Garin had never looked more like a vampire. Tonight he was more like the ones they described and illustrated in her books. A handsome ghoul, slightly gaunt, the shadows under his eyes prominent, his dark brows and lashes making the red of his eyes even more striking.

Even with his biting curse from Adelaide, he'd never looked this starved or depraved.

He seemed to sense the churning fear in her. She'd forgotten it excited him. Garin gave her a lazy smile, but it wasn't friendly. It was knowing, like a guard who was proud of himself for cornering a petty thief.

Couldn't he smell her? Sense her in the way she did him? If there was some sort of magic tethering them, the connection Casmir had hinted at, then how could Garin not tell it was her?

He cocked his head, the motion animalistic. "Bastion coached you to ask me about our deal with Kestrel?"

She began to shake her head in protest. "He didn't have to coach me about anything."

"I'm done playing their games. I'm going to send your head back to them on a platter."

"You told me you were sorry for wanting me," she blurted.

He froze, listening.

"In the room at the inn. You said it was a dream, but you held me. Read to me." But her words—her possible proof of identity—only seemed to anger him. "It was real, wasn't it?" she pushed.

Jaw set, Garin rocked back onto his heels, speaking methodically. "I am sorry it had to happen this way. That you're caught in the middle of this. They've sealed your fate by telling you far too much." He refused to meet her eyes as he took his time rolling his sleeves up to his forearms, revealing streaks of reddish brown across his skin she hadn't noticed before. The woman *had* fought him.

Lilac blinked back tears.

"If you want this to be painless, I suggest you stay very still and shut your eyes. I can also entrance you to feel no pain. Please let me know what you prefer."

"No," she snarled softly, glaring at him through her blurry vision, her ears ringing. This was not how it would end.

"I understand you're upset. Blame the warlock and vampires for ensuring your death."

"No," she said past the lump in her throat, hyperventilating. Myrddin had had too much faith in her. He'd sent her to her death. "Garin, it is *me—* your queen, and I order you out of this room."

There was no answer at first. Just the unsteady hitch of his own breathing as he worked to steady it. "I am trying to give you options for pain, for your demise. Not many of my victims have ever received an array of choices, so I would consider myself lucky if I were you—and above all, please try to calm your heart." He inhaled through his mouth, his fangs dripping saliva. "I am concentrating on not tearing into you, and your terror is making it all the more difficult."

Staring past him into the orange blur of the fireplace, she shuddered violently when he slid his palm flat, under her hair, along the right side of her throat.

She wouldn't die this way. Certainly not at the hands of the man who'd helped her realize there was more to life than stone towers and the imaginary monsters they kept out. She jerked and made to stand, but Garin restrained her with a simple shift of his fingers, his hand clamping over her collarbone. He could crush her shoulder with a twitch of his powerful fingers. She lifted her chin to open her airway while her mind raced to think of anything only she would know—or a way to beg for her life that wouldn't make her last moments so pathetic.

"Giles told me you sit outside my room some nights," she rasped. "That you watch me sleep but never come in."

At this, he refocused on her. But the liquid garnet of his eyes shifted in a way that made her skin crawl. "Did he, now?"

She stayed silent.

"Did he also tell you it was out of loyalty? Chivalrous duty?"

Lilac flinched at the way he spat the words, like they were dirt in his mouth. His other hand suddenly slid over hers, which had been gripping the scalpel handle *very* tightly. His long fingers encircled her wrist.

"Did he make you think it was out of some valiant effort of protection, instead of the nature of what I am? Who I am—the inescapable yearning to possess my current obsession?"

She'd play his game. "Was it this same yearning that urged you to command her to marry someone else?"

Garin frowned in disbelief, thrown by her inquiry. "Not you, too. Imagine this kingdom, one of this size against France."

She shrugged. "I think she'd put up a fair fight."

"Do you know anything about the histories of the last war, the countless fires that decimated the Argoat? There's been activity at our eastern border in the last week, several small camps scouting the area. They'll send another soon, and another, until they choose to advance. Until there are casualties. They're testing her." His face shadowed with regret. "Her parents have dealt with it swiftly, avoiding drawing attention to Lilac's absence at the castle, but it is concerning that she's currently without a duke or noble beneath her who can lead her country into battle. There is much at stake, far more than I think she realizes. She's fortunate she has Henri alive in this circumstance, someone to guide her." Garin barked a laugh. "But the man has never fought a war."

Hearing his doubtful take struck a chord of irritation in her, even if she was egging him on. "You think she cannot lead her men?"

"I know she cannot. Not without moral support within her kingdom—not with the way they've protested her reign in the past over her *arcana lingua*."

She'd known Garin wanted to protect her, but it felt like the same skepticism she'd met at her meeting in the library. A confirmation that he also questioned her abilities. "What about a Daemon alliance?"

He glanced at her, doubtful. "Elaborate."

"Would the Daemons help in case of a war?"

"They certainly wouldn't side with the French, if that's what you're asking. It is our unanimous want for Lilac to retain her sovereignty, as well. However, our involvement in the current state of the kingdom would prove a hindrance to any attempt Lilac makes to rally a campaign among her mortal subjects. To support a war any leader would first need extra bodies, resources, but most importantly the general support of her people. After the last five years, I am not convinced the threat of France would be enough to swing their favor."

Lilac swallowed his answer in reluctant silence. It might be the mead getting to her head, but the implications of her question regarding a Daemon alliance were foolishly far more profound than the tangent Garin had swung their conversation to. But he was right. She could use his expertise and the unmatched power of the Daemons—Kestrel and his faeries, even—but it still might not mean much without the support of her people. "Common ground, our home, is everything we stand to lose if France successfully annexes our kingdom."

"It is not that simple. Look at how her mortals have treated her over something as simple as language." The topic had seemed to center him, but his fury remained. "Part of it is her parents' fault. They could have silenced anyone at those riots and protests of her reign with a row of guillotines in the streets. They too did not know what to do with her, how to protect her. Cowards, the lot of them." Garin removed his hand from her shoulder and hesitated as he brought it down to his side, looking like he might place it upon her knee. He didn't. "I would not be so bold as to assume Daemons will fight blindly, risk their necks for a crown which historically has not done the same for them. It will come at their discretion depending on what the queen chooses to do. Rallying the humans to stand with her will take some time. Even if, in the best scenario, she is allied with a ruler who allows her to keep her sovereignty, Lilac could stand to gain the favor of both mortals and Daemons. Marrying someone powerful would then allow her time to do so instead of hastening the process under the pressure of war."

Hearing his honesty was terrifying. She tried to keep her voice steady. "And you're planning on holding that over her head?"

"No. I wouldn't need to. A Daemon alliance would come at far too great a cost. She'd instantly lose most if not all of her moral support in the towns —a fatal flaw. This is the reason she must marry someone powerful. Delicious idea, though. I might fancy seeing her beg." He stared past her. "The queen can fuck whomever she wants, but even if she did push for Daemon support, I doubt it would solidify until a public alliance is established."

Despite his sound advice, she clung to his last statement. "Even Casmir?"

Garin's eyes narrowed. "Casmir?"

"Can you not smell him on me?" she finally asked.

His nostrils were already flaring the moment she'd uttered the other vampire's name. "I haven't been able to smell or taste anything but *her* since I ordered her away." There was more disbelief than shame in his admission. "The queen has done nothing but torment me with visions of her tender touch and wicked mouth these last few days. I've dreamt of begging for her return. She is within and without. All of it is her, and—and... what of Casmir?" he said gratingly, as if remembering himself. He wiped the sweat from his brow.

Lilac smiled. She couldn't help but feel a rush of victorious relief that he'd suffered in their time apart, too.

Whatever was tethering them, whether the leftover magic in her body or an obscure partial bond, it had seemed to amplify their need to be near each other, while the effects of the mead had made her starved for touch. If there was any of it mixed in that decanter—she was certain there was—then he would soon start feeling the same. A volatile combination in a vampire, hunger for blood and body. The lust threatening to take him might soon be enough to dissuade him from killing her. Maybe then she could lure him outside.

"*Well?*"

Lilac leaned forward. His eyes flickered to her cleavage, then quickly back to her flushed face. "I was in his lap earlier tonight. Just after I kissed him."

"Kissed..." He glanced down.

"Yes. He's passionate."

Garin's look shifted from hesitant to murderous. "Did he touch you?"

"He did," Lilac breathed, her mind filling with thoughts of Casmir's erection under her just moments ago. "But what would it matter if you believe I am not her?"

His jaw clenched, as if he were debating whether to be furious about it. "Was it what you wanted?"

"Yes it was."

Garin's expression was unreadable.

"But he refused to fuck me. He said that I *reeked* of you." Lilac stilled, trying to ignore the pressure at her core as he neared again. Her entire body pulsed under his conviction. His heat.

Garin bent his head and delicately slid her hair out of the way. Then he pressed his nose to the side of her throat and inhaled deeply against her skin.

If he couldn't sense Casmir on her before, he did now.

Garin's grip on her wrist tightened immediately, and in that moment, her blade began to hum at her thigh. If she were thinking straight, if she weren't already drugged on his proximity and the effects of the mead, it would've sent her into a panic.

Instead, she moaned against the vibration.

His pupils widened against the red as he pulled back.

Lilac shifted against the seat, already feeling how wet she'd become in his presence. Not taking her gaze off him, Lilac reached for her right thigh and bunched the material in her palm to lift the hem of her chemise. Garin released her and shifted back; she bit her lip as he swiftly widened her legs with his knee, letting his fingers trail over the material at her calf. He looked up at her questioningly, just as he had in his bedchamber.

Lilac nodded. She was a fool.

He dragged the hem of her dress up her bare leg, revealing the dagger strapped at her thigh.

Delicately, he plucked it from the sheath without touching her skin. Garin held it straight up in the light, suspending the blade between them and marveling at the intricate adornments. He, too, must be remembering the way he'd entranced Lilac to make herself come with the vibrating hilt.

He lowered the blade, and just as she prepared to feel him shove the rest of her skirts away to press it against her center, there was a prick above her bodice. Garin held the tip of her own blade against her chest. One swift move and it would pierce her heart.

"You are a cruel and wretched thing. A willing instrument in my undoing."

"Garin." He was beyond reason, so convinced that he was being tricked. "Put it down."

"I have to believe," he said quietly. "It cannot be true. You are a courtesan Myrddin sent to retrieve me. And if not, then you are a demon sent from the deepest circle of hell to torment me."

"If you're going to kill me," she said, chin lifted, "then do it. But do not pretend your tremendous anger would be misdirected at some courtesan. Do it because you cannot bear to think of me—"

"*You are not her.*" His face twisted with desperation and something else she could not place. His shoulders quaked as he stared at her, murderous. "I don't know what is happening to me. I will drain you, and move on to everyone in that fucking tavern. Do not lie to me!"

She stilled, pressed back as far as she could against the settee as Garin's chest heaved. *Heartbroken.* He was heartbroken.

They stared at each other in silence, the music and voices outside filling the gaping void between them. No knock came, no shout or acknowledgement from Bastion or Myrddin, if they were paying attention at all. If no one heard Garin's shouting, no one would hear if she screamed for help.

"She is leagues and leagues away from here, under my command. Safe from *me*." Garin looked down at the blade, still processing that it was in his grasp. "I have done my part so Lilac has a fighting chance."

She blinked through her blurry vision. "Done your part? Do you mean against France? It is her part and hers alone. You said so yourself."

"That isn't what I mean." His breath was shuddering. He shifted his weight back, taking her in. "My newfound ability to daywalk has garnered me more purpose, more hope to this life than feeding and slinking in the shadows. But as soon as those curses were lifted, there was another awaiting me on the other side. You see, I have made the beginner's error of falling into a precarious trap." He laughed, a hopeless sound. "She exacerbates my very condition. But it could never be. Not without anarchy." Garin exhaled, the weight of his confession visibly leaving his chest.

It then crushed hers. Lilac's glare only hardened, tugging her trained armor over her exposed heart. "You cannot possibly feel that way if you willingly shove her off to someone else."

Garin's lip curled away from his teeth. "Any assumption otherwise would be ludicrous considering what I cannot help but feel for her. It is infuriating, a burden and a medal I willingly wear. So is the hope that she and I could ever exist in the same room, in the scope of the public eye, without wielding blades at each other. Without performing, ruse after ruse. I would do it till the end of days, but the humanity in her will grow weary and tired. As it should." Again, he pressed the tip of the dagger against her skin. "She knows that deep down. She wouldn't be here tonight, she's smarter than that. I have made sure everything is in order," he reassured himself. "I have done my due diligence, and will ensure she marries if it is the last thing I—"

There was a ripping noise, followed by a squelch.

Lilac winced, then smiled at the sting of pain at her upper thigh.

16

GARIN

He should make them pay. *Bastion. Casmir. Myrddin.* He thought he'd get drunk on a couple of pretty girls and forget the woman for whom even the darkest parts of his soul bent the knee. Now, he was just drunk on blood and scotch. And Dragondew Mead, apparently.

And he was *still* ravenous, his cock now annoyingly stiff in his trousers.

He did not want to harm this girl for merely looking like Lilac. His idiot friends had probably offered her a hefty coin bag since it didn't seem they'd entranced or spelled her. Even Bastion should have known this was a step too far.

What did they think would happen? That he wouldn't figure them out? That he'd be tricked into somehow believing Lilac had managed to escape her gates and travel so far from her castle after her prolonged absence? What were they intending, besides solidifying this courtesan's certain death?

He could snap her neck like he said he would. Then, and only then, would her glamor dissolve. He could slip undetected onto the balcony. The staff would find his mess, the bodies, and then, and only then might the establishment seek to ban vampires, as they should have long ago. His kind didn't belong here. Not with drinks like this Dragondew Mead floating between unsuspecting hands and mouths. Feeding from the vein was more ethical under Lorietta's strict watch.

And if it were her, if the girl before him *was* the queen... it meant that Lilac had somehow belied his entrancement. *How?*

The night was cruel, the darkness crushing, and Garin would do almost anything for solace. To crawl into the light, bloodied and barren, where the vast forest and reason awaited him. Where he'd be held accountable for his actions.

But he was stuck here, cornered by a hunger and lust he'd never before experienced.

Garin swallowed, throat burning. A glamor of Lilac felt exceptionally personal, because in the split second it took for her to cut herself, understanding flooded his senses.

The girl shoved the wet scalpel against his hand, clumsily pushing it against his palm. He finally fumbled with it, an unwelcome chill rolling off his back when her fingers brushed his.

Garin brought it to his nose and inhaled, and several images flashed through his mind—a steaming loaf of speckled bread. A vase of dried Cornish lavender on a clean mantle. Sunlight streaming through a window, and a green armchair before a crackling fire.

He was going to kill her.

Garin's stomach painfully lurched as she watched from the settee—he, transfixed on the blooming splotch of red on her skirts, and her, on him. Slowly, her fingers tiptoed, bunching the fabric of her kirtle and revealing the gash just above her garter sheath. A rivulet of blood trailed down, toward her inner thigh.

He'd lost her dagger and scalpel at some point, barely able to cling to his sanity. His restraint.

"What have you done?" The words escaped from a desolate place. From the husk of the person he was, the monster within already rejoicing for what he'd do next.

Her breath trembled, her words floating on air. "Perhaps it isn't just blood you hunger for."

Garin swallowed the saliva flooding his mouth as she shifted her skirts the rest of the way. Her pussy was glistening beautifully for him. His throat went dry as she trailed a trembling hand inward, past the hem of her skirts.

　　　　BRIAR SOMERSET

"Lilac," he groaned in warning.

Her bright eyes danced at the sound of her name on his tongue, surprise flitting across her face and relieving that expectant, curated look of Lilac's that this girl had replicated with uncanny precision. Her cheeks still deepened in the most delicious shade of currants as he unabashedly took her in.

How he'd missed that look.

But her expression faltered as he rose to his feet, took a step back and braced himself against the mantle.

"This is impossible." This *couldn't* be his queen. Lilac could not be here, because if she was, it meant everything he'd feared as his thirst had grown in his cellar room, was true. That their time apart *hadn't* dissolved whatever this connection was, like the witches said it would.

Before he realized what he was doing, Garin dropped to his knees.

The look on her face was hungry, none of the fearful hesitation that had been there before when he'd refused to entertain the possibility. Her demanding smile was the last thing he saw before he slid his arms under her, dragging her forward. She whimpered at the sudden movement, as if she had the right to be shocked at all after baring herself to him—letting blood for him. A daring offering.

He flattened his tongue against the soft skin of her inner thigh and dragged it upward, lapping the rivulet of blood along the self-inflicted stab wound.

She tasted like an oasis of all things absent: the week he and Bastion had spent in Roscoff trying to process the vampirism that plagued them, breathing in the ocean air for the first time, knowing that this was the seaside trading town his mother had intended to make their new life in.

Carts of cloth, salt, and wood.

She tasted like trips to the long-gone Paimpont bakery, whose owning family was killed in the Raid; warm nights in front of the fire, before memories of that mantle were stained in blood; drifting off in Aimee's lap with a piece of warm bread in his hand.

She tasted like emerging from the Trecésson dungeon and feeling sunlight upon his face for the first time in two hundred years.

Lilac jerked, as if to shift herself against his mouth, but he wrapped his arms around the outsides of her thighs and secured her in place.

It was her.

It was her.

It was her.

Her blood was a lone beacon shone upon his sinking raft, his only options to drown in it or be swept away, forever lost by the tide.

He would not let her go. Not until he was finished with her.

First, he needed to heal her. She yelped as he sank his teeth into her without warning, right over her wound, her skin and flesh giving way like butter. He was close enough to her pussy that she could have ridden his face anyway. But he held her down.

"*Garin,*" she growled at the shock of pain, taking a fistful of his hair in her grasp; she tried to push him off at first, but after his first swallow, she let out a gasp and pulled him closer.

The relief he felt was immense. Her blood rushed into his mouth and down his parched throat, like warm milk on a harsh winter's night. Swallow after swallow, there was a shift in the atmosphere, and the world went quiet. His ears were no longer ringing and his other senses were *immediately* relieved of her, no longer tainted in her essence; he could smell the embers of the fire crackling away behind them, the overpowering aroma that most certainly belonged to the bud and leaves of the Sea Holly. The room was no longer stifling, and he could even feel a cooling breeze coming through the crack under the balcony door.

He swallowed once more, then carefully unsheathed his fangs before he could get carried away.

They both stared, panting, at the marks his teeth left; the slice she'd made with the scalpel was still there, but blood dripped more noticeably from the deep puncture holes he'd left. His bite wound was messy, the skin around them already bruising. He could wipe it all away in an instant, but he couldn't tear his eyes away from the pooling red.

He wanted every last bit to himself.

Guilt ate at him. He was already feeling better, and she was feeding him from her thigh. But there was no trace of fear or hesitation there, nor could he smell it on her. Only encouragement and a dangerous excitement. Quickly, Garin bent and ran his tongue over the marks, her curious gaze burning him.

He straightened, embarrassed, attempting to wipe his face off and ready to utter what semblance of an apology he could string together.

"Lilac," he said, his face burning. Garin took her hands in his. "I'm not myself. Nothing has been right. I—"

She hooked a finger beneath his chin, and forced it up. He finally looked at her, and she locked eyes with him. Her pupils swallowed him whole.

Her blood had quelled his need to feed, sobered him. But another want surged within him—an effect of the Sea Holly, no doubt. The plant's effects should not have been this strong; he cleared his throat at the sudden urge to lift her from the chair and place her upon the four poster bed. Pound her into the mattress. He forced his breathing to slow, silently reasoning with himself as he gently grasped her hand and lowered it from his face.

It didn't matter, he thought, attempting to smother his worry with the fact that Lilac was safe. She was here, in front of him. It didn't matter how, they'd figure that out later. She'd offered her blood to him in full transparency and he had taken it. She was safe. He could finally think, breathe without tasting her at the back of his throat upon every tortuous inhale.

She is safe with me, he told himself again, his stomach knotting as the very nature of him, both man and monster, yearned to covet her for himself —the woman who belonged to the kingdom.

Bride. Eternal muse. Gilded pawn.

He might not have kingdoms or armies for her, but she had not yet seen an ounce of what his strategy or sanguine magic looked like at full power. It might frighten her. Whether kingdoms apart or with her in his grasp, Garin would never be released from the kind of torment she inflicted on him.

He cleared his throat, desperate to dislodge those thoughts. Both their minds were clouded with the Sea Holly. Enchantments and flora mixed together often fostered dangerous consequences.

Garin would stop now, while he was ahead. She was about to meet the emissary. She and her parents would meet Albrecht and hear of Maximilian's offer, he'd carefully arranged the pieces to align. Lilac would soon be the emperor's wife.

The emperor's wife. The thought took his breath away. He had done away with those concerns days ago, when the whisperings of French scouts and the path to bolster her armies had become clear; he had thrown Lorietta's little book into the Argent and watched several pairs of white-green hands fight over it before dragging it down. Nothing legitimate could ever occur between them that would benefit her—not with the current threat presiding over her.

He had decided this firmly in the nights he'd spent by her bedside as she clung to life at the inn. He should have known it from the start.

Garin was capable of making the right choice. He would stand, clean her off, and escort her out of the brothel. He would—

Lilac cleared her throat, yanking him from his foolish daydream. The woman who looked up at him was no emperor's wife. No forlorn bride, no damsel.

She was his, within and without.

Her hungry gaze raked over him, from his face to his trousers as she trailed her hand beyond her skirts and ran two fingers through the residual blood left on her thigh. She then brought her hand to her center, smearing the red there through her wetness.

Garin watched, horrified, the thump of her heart drowning out every other sound, quieting the world for him as it had since they'd met. The queen then rose in her seat and brought those fingers covered in her wetness and blood to his mouth.

He felt like running through a wall.

He loosened his grip, his cock straining against his pants as he bent and brought his mouth to her. Garin lashed at her clit with his tongue, exploring, gently pacing her until her knees began to shake under direct pressure. Not lapping at her like a greedy animal took tremendous effort. It didn't her take long at all.

Her body clenched under his grasp. "*Garin.*"

Lilac gripped at the seat too clumsily to find purchase, and Garin slowed but did not remove his mouth from her as he coaxed his first two fingers in. She opened up for him beautifully, so warm and tight as her head fell back onto the frame, hips rocking into him.

She was his Lilith, his deity to revere and resent. Garin was a mere man spelled by her luminosity and struck down by her lightning. Try as he did, he had not been able to think about anything, anyone else but his servitude to her these last few days. He'd forced himself to sleep, or at least laid with his eyes forcefully shut in an attempt to quell the hunger ravaging his insides. And even then, there in the darkness, Lilac's haunting, sweet face never left him.

And when he did sleep, in the fragments of his dreams, Garin didn't think of reaching for his trousers before ensuring she'd finished thrice on his tongue and twice more on his hand.

Lilac gripped the settee cushion and her other hand wrapped into his dark curls again, gentler this time. She whimpered as he stretched her slowly, changing the quick flicks of his tongue to broad, flat strokes up the length of her dripping warmth as he curled his fingers inside her.

If her blood tasted of sunlight, her pussy was the dancing darkness that beckoned him back, reminding him that he was still a man of chivalry but a Daemon in need first, and *fuck*, how he'd missed the sound of Lilac panting his name as if she could not bear to keep it to herself.

They'd had to keep quiet in his room at his farmhouse, but tonight, he didn't care who knew it was him making her come.

She began to tremble again, but instead of pulling his head against her, Lilac pushed at him. With restraint, he pulled back. The notes of pleasant amber and vanilla floated above the natural scent of her skin.

"Get up," was all she said.

He did as he was told. She quickly pulled off his belt, and as she shifted his trousers down he wondered, followed by an instant stab of guilt, how many times Lilac had done something like this. She was free to do as she pleased. He hadn't asked her before, and it did not occur to him when they'd first made love. It certainly didn't matter now; it was a mere carnal question, fleeting, one of selfish greed that yearned to belong to her. One that merely wanted to ensure all the hands and mouths who'd ever worshiped her had feared and cherished her, just as much as he.

He chuckled darkly to himself. Of course, they hadn't.

"Garin?" Her voice was husky.

The sound of his name broke his reverie and caused him to look down in answer, just before she took his length in her palm.

"What are you thinking of?" Lilac glanced up at him as she stroked him, just as she had on their first night together. He exhaled, recalling how difficult it had been not to tilt her head back and coax himself past her lips then. He wouldn't do that now, but he also wouldn't stop her. Tonight, Garin would do exactly as she wanted.

"You," he finally said. It was all he could say after everything he'd accidentally just confessed to her. *It is always you.*

She laughed, a whimsical sound, just before she slid to the floor. He twitched in her hand as her warm tongue met the tip of his cock, coaxing her thumb against his sensitive underside. She locked eyes with him and ran her mouth down his shaft.

Garin let out a strangled sound and stumbled back as she took more than half of him into her mouth. He felt her throat constrict around him; it had been a few years since he'd been with a woman this way, but that wasn't anything close to whatever spell the queen had him under. She didn't even look up when he grasped the mantle to keep them from falling into the hearth. With his cock in her mouth, she didn't seem to notice, only following him on her knees as he shifted them to safety against the wall to the right of the fireplace.

Not knowing what to do with himself, Garin reached down to collect the strands of her hair. It was everywhere, escaping her braids in loose waves; eventually, he gathered all of it in his left hand.

"Tighter," she removed herself to say, then bobbed down on him again.

Garin flexed his fingers, and she reacted almost immediately to the sensation at her scalp, moaning. The sound vibrated around his shaft as she started to suck him deeply, with her mouth and her fist enclosed around the rest of him.

"*Fuck.*" Once he found her encouraging him to control the movement of her head, he knew he wouldn't last long. He felt himself losing control, and it was a battle he'd willingly lose.

She rocked back to look up at him. Her face was reddened, and she laughed as she wiped her lips and chin, so gloriously messy. Her eyes flashed with such a hungry mirth, Garin wanted nothing more than to drop to his own knees and beg to be the one who worshiped her at the altar.

Gods. Modron made him *just* for her.

"Not yet," she said, and moved to stand.

He kissed her on her way up, his lips meeting hers fervently, aching to be in constant contact with her. He needed her, but this—this was so wrong. She'd soon be crowned. Married. He had done all in his power to urge her along that path of destiny.

Lilac nipped softly at his bottom lip and giggled into his mouth. This woman was single-handedly beating her own destiny back with a stick. Or perhaps a dagger.

She was the beginning and end of his demise.

"I need to feel you." She tugged him by his shirt off the wall. She continued their kiss and pivoted him, guided him until the backs of his knees hit the settee. Then, she shoved him. There was none of that unusual strength there from the other early morning, Garin noted, distantly pleased. But he played along and sat back for her.

She was already slipping her dress off, looking entirely ethereal and soft, framed by the firelight. He watched, mesmerized, and thought about how her curves and divots felt beneath his palms, the way her romantic waves of hair brushed her shoulder blades. How soft her skin felt beneath his fingers calloused by time and the blade.

Garin leaned back, smiling appreciatively as she glimpsed him with his cock in his hands. Lilac pivoted to the flames, as if undressing for him still daunted her.

Finally, he thought. A healthy dose of fear.

He scooted aside to make room as she approached him, eager to feel her quaking under him again. But Lilac just leaned over him, lifting one leg, then the other. Straddling him.

She positioned herself in his lap, her dripping cunt bare and rubbing against him. Garin reached up, tenderly cupping and planting kisses upon her breasts as she leaned into him. He braced himself.

Out of nowhere, the amplified scent of her blood hit him again.

Garin grabbed her by the shoulders and sat up. He felt his pupils dilate before he even processed what she had done. Lilac sat back, red dripping onto her bare stomach, down past her navel, pooling between their thighs.

"Shit," he heard her mumble, though he could only focus on the blood running down her torso, a surge of ecstasy and vile hunger rattling his soul.

She dropped the scalpel he'd thought had been lost to the floor and brought her bleeding wrist toward his mouth, unknowing of what she'd just done. Some of it dripped onto his white tunic, spreading in blotches of burgundy on his shoulder. "*Whoops*."

"Lilac," Garin sputtered, catching her arm in his shaking fingers. He couldn't even get a full sentence out without her temptation invading his nostrils, the hunger ramming him like an ox. He held his breath, only to learn it didn't matter.

He could taste her so violently on his tongue he thought he would be sick. It shouldn't have hit him this way. The sensation was *back*—that overwhelming hunger, the one that had caused him to rip through more throats in a single night than he had during the Raid.

The feeling which first drinking Lilac's blood tonight had cured. Or, so he'd thought.

Garin wanted *more*. He shut his eyes.

The wetness at her wrist began to run through his fingers, so warm and inviting. "What are you doing?"

"Feeding you."

He froze. He could hear the quickening of her heartbeat, inwardly cursing her, working to slow the numbing rush of adrenaline that began to flood his body.

"No," he said through his aching teeth. "I can't."

"What do you mean?" She glanced down at him, her cheeks flushed. "Why can't you?"

The instinct in him that yearned to indulge in his carnal pleasures roused at the challenge. Garin had respected the women he slept with, at least enough to not make them his meal at the same time. He'd fed from them before or after, sometimes both, but never during. Other vampires thought differently, such as Casmir, who regularly brought eager donors to The Fenfoss Inn; little did they know, feeding while having sex was a risk for even the most experienced vampires.

It was a dangerous fantasy, a game of predator and prey. It wasn't a matter of morals for Garin. He simply knew himself too well; try as he might to suppress this trait, he brought a certain fervency to every endeavor he pursued, including lovemaking and feeding. He wouldn't try to combine the two now, not under the influence of the mead. With Lilac, he would lose himself.

"I haven't. It is too much of a risk."

"There's a first time for everything," she said simply, though the little hitch in her breath and crease on her forehead told him this surprised her. *Excited* her. "Take what I am offering, Garin."

She was so foolish, so greedy, the way she looked down at him. Beckoning. Didn't she know he wanted it? Didn't she know how difficult it was for him to pretend he didn't? Once the blood touched his mouth again, it would begin all over. Being sated only to thirst again.

What was this hunger driving him mad?

"The first time we slept together, I was bound by my biting curse. Forbidden from taking from you. I don't think you realize how easily I could take from you now. Continue to, even when you've decided I've gone too far."

"Okay."

He glanced up at her, how quick she was to respect his wishes. "Okay?"

Lilac held out her hand. "Then let's go. Leave with me."

Garin didn't know how to answer, or even begin to explain what he felt —just what was barring him from leaving this room. He hungered for *her*, certainly her company and her body, but there was something more. He had craved her since the moment they met, but he'd never sought her blood in a way that concerned him for her own safety.

He could not bear the thought of her in anyone else's possession. He'd forced her from his family's inn, said things he'd immediately regretted.

What lay beyond these walls? Beyond the night? What was their future together, with or without the threat of war?

Garin slowly removed his hands from her; they were shaking again. This couldn't happen. What about all he'd done to ensure she make the right choice? What about seeing that she had a second chance to at least hear Maximilian's undeniable offer at her castle, before her parents and council, where she could not attempt to assassinate him?

What about Brocéliande, his coven, and his family at the inn? How would they fare in a war against France, if not prevented in time?

He closed his eyes. Tonight, Garin was not himself. He knew nothing of reason.

"Will you let me leave?" she challenged as he reluctantly glimpsed her. "Would you let me get up, dress myself, and walk out of this room? Away from you?"

He felt his muscles twitch, the tremendous energy there coiling, excited for the chance to spring. The thought alone made his throat burn, thirst like a fist around his airpipe. If she walked away, he wouldn't let her get within a few feet of that door. They both knew it.

"I am a pawn to my desires tonight. More than I have ever been."

There was no hesitation on her face, no tremble in her voice. "Then drink."

Hesitantly, Garin slipped his hands under her and gently lifted, guiding her over his cock. This felt good. It felt right, the way she squirmed and released her weight onto his hands.

But he stopped her, his voice hoarse. "Do you want me to fuck you while I feed from you, Lilac?"

Her mouth tightened with impatience, her rapid pulse deepening as she brought her dripping wrist over his mouth.

Garin sank his fangs into the underside of her wrist, accepting her cruel offer, the monster in him rejoicing in mocking praise as he gave in.

This is what it should be. Could always be, if only you gave in.

His eyes rolled back into his head, and he drank generously.

Glorious sunlight. A warm, salt-dusted breeze.

She was his Lilith, his maker and destroyer. The beginning of the end, the night that beckoned him forth. Especially when his tongue was slicked in her.

17

There was something wrong with them. The both of them. The Dragondew Mead had worsened the effects of their connection, whatever magic that had not waned in their time apart, partial bond or no—but Garin's mouth against her wrist impossibly dragged her mind from those concerns. Fire faded to ice.

It was twice as intoxicating as he held her over him.

Garin took one last pull from her wrist then removed himself, quieting her frustrated snarl with a short tug of her hair, causing her to moan. "Is this what you left your safe abode for tonight, Your Majesty?"

She could hardly concentrate on an answer with the head of his cock at her entrance. Lying would only prolong his torment. "I wanted to make you regret entrancing me."

A guttural laugh escaped his throat. "By fucking Casmir?"

"By any means necessary," she choked out, desperate to feel him.

He chuckled again, the sound sweeping across her spine. "There are far worse things you could do to me. Consider this a lesson in revenge."

Garin slid his hands onto her hips and slammed her down onto his cock.

Gasping, Lilac's head fell back, feeling herself abruptly adjust to him. His next thrust was so painstakingly slow, there was no doubt in her mind he meant to punish her. His grip on her was unrelenting as he controlled every movement. She reached down and dug her nails into his wrists.

"I want to ride you."

A wicked glimmer crossed his face. "I have given you what you want. Now, I'm going to take what I need."

He shifted her, angling her chin up before sinking his teeth into her throat with no warning. Lilac scraped her nails along the back of his neck, instinctively cradling him closer. Encouraged, he bit down harder, sucking deeper, the heavy pull against her skin causing her to rock onto him. All thought, all memory and concern melted away as she convulsed, soaking the settee beneath them.

Garin groaned, taking a shuddering inhale before lifting his fangs from her. "That's it, now. Look at you."

Lilac burned, hungrily raking her fingers into his shoulders. "I would hardly call this revenge."

His lips brushed hers as he thrusted into her from beneath, wetting her mouth in her own warm blood, not quite kissing her. "You haven't the faintest idea the torture you unleash upon me." He reached up, his thumb gliding across her cheek. "I never thought it was possible for you to look more beautiful—yet here you are, covered in the blood that I've drawn. You make it increasingly difficult to do the noble thing."

"The noble thing," she said, voice thick, "would be to ally yourself with me."

"I wasn't thinking that far ahead." Garin's eyes drifted up from her lips, excitement dancing behind them despite his sad smile. An *apologetic* smile. "The noble thing to do tonight would be allowing you to leave this room without my nature getting the best of me."

Realization slowly sank in. She nodded, desperately trying to smother her alarm. She'd thought he'd begun to see reason moments ago, when he'd first drank from her thigh; she'd also fought to keep her thoughts coherent through the process of trying to convince him to leave.

She'd tried seducing him, making sure he was fed. She'd thought it was her blood he'd craved. Maybe it still was, but how much of it did he need? How much to wash the effects of the Dragondew Mead away?

How was she supposed to sober him when they were both drunk on each other?

He bent his head, sniffing at the unscathed side of her throat, as if searching for another vein. Lilac clutched his face with both hands and firmly pushed him away before he could bite her again. Fortunately, he obliged.

"Look at me," she said softly. His skin was hot, and her hands came away slicked in beads of sweat.

She'd come to make him pay and still intended to, but she would do so another time, when they were out of the fire. He had suffered enough for now.

It was hard to concentrate again on her plan—her plan in the making—when he was still hard against her, his erection now resting against her stomach. She didn't understand; if Myrddin was as powerful a warlock as they'd said he was, couldn't he at least have given her a tonic or anything that might make this mission of hers easier? He hadn't had *any* specific advice to spare?

"Look at me," she said, cradling his face. "Please."

Garin craned his head back. His dark eyes, bleary in fear and hunger, were rimmed in red, like the edge of sunset without the promise of tomorrow. He kept his mouth shut around his fangs as his gaze slowly floated from the hearth, to her.

Stroking his jaw and dragging her fingers through the blood, Lilac planted a kiss at the corner of his mouth. "It's going to be okay," she said, wishing it desperately to be true. As she spoke, she swept her leg, then her arm off to the right, where he'd dropped the dagger. The scalpel might've been there, too; either would do. "We're going to walk out of here, and Bastion and Myrddin are going to help you. We will figure it out, whatever this is. Together."

Her heart dropped. There was no shape of a blade, no brush of cold metal against her skin—any weapon to have on hand, just in case. Casmir's warning and offering of the stake played in her mind as she shifted, moving her foot around to feel further.

Garin abruptly stood.

They were walking; he was carrying her away from the hearth. Away from *both* weapons. Securing her legs around him, Garin began to shake his head, his frown pitiful as he pressed his lips into her hair.

No. This wasn't supposed to happen. She jolted when her back hit a wall.

"You told them where you were going, didn't you?" he asked, his brows knotting in desperation. She inhaled sharply as he placed himself against her again, one arm supporting her under her thighs, his other hand against the wood beside her head as he pressed her into the closet door. Aromas of summer night and woodsmoke invaded her senses, causing her to slip between fear and ecstasy.

She opened her mouth to answer, but the sound came out garbled as he sheathed himself into her. He thrusted *hard*, rattling the door frame behind her. Again. Then again. And *again*.

Garin bent his lips to finally kiss her, and there was nothing urgent or rushed about it. His mouth was lazy, intentional. Possessing. When his tongue swept and teased hers, Lilac came almost immediately, tasting the salt and iron that drenched him.

He broke away. "Please tell me you told them."

"Told who what?"

"Your guard," he panted. "Your protectors."

Coming down from the waves of pleasure cresting over her body, she tried not to think about the increasing probability of her dying in this room at the hands of a vampire who was very clearly spiraling out of control—because why would he ask her that? Why would she mention to anyone at home she intended to travel to The Fenfoss Inn and possibly disclose its location?

But as the beginning of a cold smile ghosted his mouth, she realized his inquiry was rhetorical. "Does anyone besides my imbecile brother and his friends, anyone who *should* know your whereabouts, know where their precious queen is tonight?"

"What would that matter when you were the one who sent me away?" She challenged his mocking gaze. "I could be anywhere tonight. With anyone. What would it matter if anyone knew? What would you do if there were dozens of my guards waiting outside this very brothel? That wouldn't stop you, would it?"

His thrusting slowed. He eyed the warmth trickling down her throat, noticing the bite wounds he hadn't healed. He moved to put his mouth on her, but she pulled back as far as she could in his arms.

"What is it you want to do?" she asked, carefully trailing her fingers across his bloodstained lips. "Take me far away from here?"

Garin's forehead creased, his throat bobbing. Gently, he unsheathed himself from her, continuing to cradle her.

Lilac only continued. "Hide me in your Mine? Would you fuck me in that cage of yours?" Her body began pulsing again at the teasing of her own words, hoping to keep him agreeable. "Protect me? Would you make me yours there?"

"*Stop.*" He grimaced. "You're right. What would your family and their guard know of protection when their leader is in my arms, instead of where she belongs—safe at her castle? Even more reason for you to marry a more powerful king."

His last comment was the end of that. Lilac pushed off the closet door, righting herself against him. She accidentally must've opened the other side, as something—clothes, or perhaps bags of rye or cotton, based on the muffled thumps upon the floor—tumbled out. She didn't know. Didn't care.

Sensing her discomfort and instant change in mood, Garin stepped away from the wall. He didn't stop her as she untangled herself from him and snaked her legs out from his grasp.

"Lilac." His voice was tight.

"*No*," she said, her irritation growing as his words registered. She set herself on the floor. "Do you believe a ring on my finger, hundreds if not thousands of soldiers at my gate, would stop you from finding me?"

"I would not need to if it was I who wants you to marry."

"Yet you seem to think those defenses are enough to deter an entire kingdom."

Garin only laughed. "There is no comparison between François and myself. A king who wants your kingdom will spare his own men and resources to have it. It is only me, and I only want you." He dipped his head to her. "And I am no gracious king or benevolent emperor, Lilac. There is no limit to what I would sacrifice."

This admission was all she needed. "And that is how you ended up here, is it not? You dragged yourself to Rennes because you knew that you would tear an entire castle apart to find me in your thirst and turmoil. You might have started a war yourself." She took everything he had thrown at her at the inn as her own ammunition now. "You weren't sure what you'd end up doing if you set so much as a foot west, so here you are. Cowering in the corner of a brothel."

It was evident his own reasoning being proved unsound displeased him. Garin held his tongue, though she could tell by his shallow breathing and glare that his words would not be kind.

"It is true," she continued, "if I hadn't felt the undeniable urge to come and find you tonight, I would have gone on to meet the Austrian count who has requested my attention. My parents received a letter, announcing his arrival from the Holy Roman Empire tomorrow." She savored the subtle shock that flashed across his face. "To think I might've been propositioned by him while you ravaged the city, striking my capital down with yet another Raid. This one, inflicted by you, and you alone. This endless hunger you feel."

She braced for his reaction to her particularly low jab. Garin absorbed it, and if it angered him, it didn't show. He seemed to still be processing the vital information regarding Albrecht's letter, but his lack of response annoyed her. "But then, in your eagerness to be rid of me the other morning, I'm not sure you considered what it would mean for me to be married to someone else. If not then, it certainly should be taken into consideration now, with whatever magic has bound us—"

"There is no bond," he snapped, echoing her own denial when she'd spoken to Casmir.

"It doesn't matter that you are convinced that this is so outside the realm of what is possible; you are oblivious to what's *been* happening. I don't have to tell you how miserable the last three days have been."

Garin looked to the floor.

"I don't have to tell you how I struggled with restlessness, distracted even as I tried to carry out my daily tasks, and those you commanded of me. I couldn't sleep, couldn't eat. It wasn't food I hungered for. It was not subtle. Everyone noticed. They tested me for pregnancy." A lump had formed at her throat, and a slow and cadenced anger had seeped into his expression. She'd felt violated by *everyone*, needing help, all while trying to keep them out—keep what had happened a secret. Blame laced her twisted features as she remembered how terrible it was to be away from him. The thought now made her ache, even as she was so upset with him.

His voice was hoarse. "You should have been able to do what I asked."

"I did. And still, I suffered. And so did you."

For once, Garin was speechless as he watched the shadows dance across her bare body. She suddenly felt very naked before him.

Lilac crossed her arms over her chest. "Simply look to the future that you have demanded of me. You might have been able to stomach the idea of sharing me with a king before ordering me away. But how does that thought fare *now*?" she stared him down as he digested her words one by one.

"I told you, I..." He trailed off, perhaps struck at the thought. His eyes darkened. "There will be no sharing of any kind, regardless of what happens. Your duty to your kingdom and their fealty to you remain. They are just that—duties you must fulfill in order to ensure the safety of your kingdom, at least long enough for François to realize he cannot annex you."

"Long enough?" she said, intentionally playing into what she hoped were his deepest concerns. "So I am to play the part of someone else's wife while you are able to take of me as you want? As shall whomever secures my hand?"

"Lilac, that is not what this is."

"But what if Albrecht offers me his hand tomorrow?"

He watched her, expressionless. "That is likely to be the case."

"What if he is kind?" she pushed. "What if he is a good and loving husband? A patient and protective father one day?"

He took a hesitant step toward her, his arm extending at the elbow as if he wished to stroke her face. He stopped himself. "I want you to have all the things that fulfill you. That you deserve. All the things I cannot give you, Lilac. That is what I want."

She'd meant her inquiry to hurt him, to draw blood. His response was the last thing she expected—an echo of what he'd reassured her at the inn when they'd fought. None of his reassurances brought her peace, not then and not now.

"I am too young and inexperienced to know the things I want and require to be fulfilled as queen, Garin. As a woman, even. But I do know one thing well. I will not be cornered or coerced into giving my life or womb to anyone. Marriage sounds horrid, but if I ever do marry, I will do it on my own terms. For love, and not under your or anyone's demands. I do not care what is at stake; if Brocéliande wants to be saved, they will stand with me, and I will work with my people to do the same. No one, not even *you* will force my hand. Your sanguine magic will kill me before I do so."

"Will it?" Garin was laughing. It was menacing and quiet, a warning sound her body shrank away from even as her core *still* ached for him. Lilac resisted the shocking urge to jump onto him again, even as he stared her down, still fully erect, bloodied, his fangs glistening. "To be freed of your torment is a gift I'd welcome with open arms." Garin took one unsure step toward her. Then another, as if retraining his reflexes to approach her with gentleness.

"Then why not be done with it now?" Lilac mirrored his movement, backing away. The balcony door was visible from the corner of her vision. "I'll have you know, I look forward to meeting that Austrian count tomorrow, just to tell him to get back onto his fucking horse and go to he—"

Lilac's heel caught onto something, causing her to lose her balance. She teetered before plopping down, the impact softened by what she expected to be cloth, or a bagged bushel of something.

She rolled on her side to push herself up, and instead of meeting cloth or rye, her hand met something else—cold and unmoving. Rigid, but soft. *A hand*, streaked with blood along with the body attached to it.

A pile of corpses. She'd landed on them.

Lilac opened her mouth in a stifled scream and actually yelped when two hands yanked her up from under her arms. Garin's hands were off her the moment she was righted.

"You," she couldn't help but say, looking down at the mess before her.

Four bodies—two women and two men, their clothes askew in ribbons around them—laid in a tangle of limbs on the floor before the open closet. They were gray in pallor, their throats mangled, their skin torn open.

Lilac scuttled back, startling as she bumped into Garin.

"They were the original occupants of this room. I fell upon them as soon as I opened the door." His hair was wild, his clothes half off his body. Instead of a fallen angel, Garin looked like a disgruntled demon who had accidentally stumbled out of hell and was most displeased by it.

She pivoted and retreated from his unruly stare, trying not to look at the corpses behind him.

Garin began to follow her, head low, eyes black and tracking her every movement as he soaked in the aroma of panic that must've been pouring from her body. She was running out of time. She hoped he could sense her extreme annoyance and anger under the fear, hoped he knew she would fight back. Lilac began to shift toward the door that led to the hall, but he was suddenly before it.

"Together we would bring your kingdom to ruin." His hands went back, bracing himself against the door. "Do not tempt me any further."

What would she do now, if any quick movement might solidify her demise? He couldn't follow her out of one of the doors if he kept blocking her exit. If she moved toward the balcony, he'd do the same. Lilac stood in the middle of the room, the bed behind her, the hearth and settee to her left, and the only other exit of the balcony door on her right. Past the corpses and open closet.

As she considered her options, Garin surveyed her throat—which still slowly bled onto her front. *How could she win?* They'd continue in this dangerous dance of sex and blood, lust and Garin's hunger, until one instinct won out—and if she didn't act fast, there'd be no chance for her or her kingdom. If her lineage ended tonight, with her, François would have his way with her kingdom.

She and Garin were trapped between the effects of the Dragondew Mead and the magic that held them close. Whatever it was, *something* awaited them on the other side.

"Or perhaps we'd make it whole," she countered, refusing to let the dread and nausea overtake her as she rode the fear. "Because even in the shadows, here we are, cornered. Drugged, aroused beyond comprehension, standing over your corpses—and *still* fighting for each other."

Still hungry for each other, a small voice in the back of her head echoed. What better drove leaders, warlords—poor and rich, human and Daemon —than hunger?

She darted toward the hearth.

Garin was merciful in restraining himself enough to not run after her. Beat her there. She thought it'd be worse, the consequences of actually running from him, as he'd warned her before not to do. Still, she scrambled, sweeping her hand across the settee cushion and peering over. Where was the scalpel? Her dagger? The most useful thing it did, besides vibrate at impending danger for the wielder, was to appear magically on her body at times of need. It did not do so now.

Lilac dropped to the floor, her arm shooting under the chair before Garin's boots stopped beside her. He had pulled his trousers back up, she noted—before his hand fisted into her hair.

"Let me go," she yelped in protest, shocked, her scalp throbbing as she rose to her feet to alleviate the immense pressure.

He spun her to face him, her nails raking against his hand. Disbelieving, Lilac snarled and thrashed, but the more she moved, the more agonizing his grip on her became.

He'd lost control.

Lilac thrived on too much pride and spite to beg for her life. Muscles burning, she stopped fighting as Garin waited her out. Hunger flashed in his eyes as he dragged her closer. "I tried to give you a fighting chance, didn't I?"

"By sending me away? By forcing my hand in marriage to a complete stranger? To leverage me, just as my parents have?" She forced her breathing to remain even as he bent over her.

She wasn't sure he heard her. Lilac stilled in his grasp. This was exactly where she needed to be. Where Myrddin intended for her to be.

She planted a kiss at his temple, feeling him inhale deeply against the corner of her jaw. She forced her muscles to relax, even as they ached to flee. He dipped her and cupped the back of her head, cradling her waist close.

The familiar burning then shot through her veins, mounting with the warmth of the fire behind them. The pull at her throat and insidious sound of him gulping flooded her ears, grotesque now that he wasn't pumping himself inside her. Now that fear had consumed her. She stared off into the distance, letting her vision slip out of focus.

She slipped a hand up his chest as it all turned to ice, tugging him closer by his shirt. Garin groaned against her throat. Being fed from felt so *good*. She fought a shudder, listening to his slurping, noticing how easily the fear faded. It was no wonder people came to do this here, and at The Fenfoss Inn.

If there was a way to choose her fate, let it be this. With him, by her own hand.

"You are worth the risk, Garin Trevelyan," she whispered against his hair, finally feeling the freeing tug of darkness at the threshold of her mind.

With the last of her energy, Lilac reached up and slashed the scalpel against his collarbone. She rammed her mouth against the wound and bit down, her blunt teeth scraping through his flesh.

Liquid honey poured into her mouth, down her throat as the world shook around her. She sputtered, forcing herself to swallow, almost gagging. Then, she swallowed again. There was a ragged gasp and Garin's anguished bellow, but it was already far off in the distance.

LILAC BLINKED AGAINST THE HARSH MIDDAY SUN. WHEN HER VISION adjusted, she wasn't quite sure what she was staring at.

She spotted herself first; she was there, in the enchanted dress and leathers from Garin. To their right was their carriage, intact, although the wheel marks and debris from the crash were still visible around them, at least from what she could see.

She—Lilac in her vision—was standing, hands clenched, scrapes and bruises all over her body, before a well-dressed man. She didn't recognize him. This man was tucking something away into his satchel as she watched before him.

Lilac tried to advance, to survey her surroundings, even flex her fingers —forgetting she had no control, no feeling of her arms and legs. This was *Garin's* memory. He turned to the right then; Adelaide was several feet away, standing beside the large chest the *Guài* had gifted them. The witch exchanged a worried glance with him.

The strange magic folk were nowhere to be found.

Her vision whipped back around when she heard her own voice, clear as day. "You're an emissary."

An emissary?

Sickness gripped her as this emissary began to speak again, mentioning her belt and dagger. It sounded like a compliment; with her own ears ringing, she wasn't sure.

Her voice pulled her attention. "State your business," Lilac in the memory said.

The man began to mumble about seeing Lilac another day, but then they grew closer—Garin was walking toward them. "She asked you to state your business," he said.

The man looked in her—in Garin's—direction, appearing slightly alarmed. He glanced back at Lilac. "I—I really shouldn't say." He winked. "But maybe you could point me to the nearest inn. You and your troupe are welcome to join me. Maybe after you've taken care of this..." He trailed off, glancing past them. Her vision then followed his gaze. There were corpses of two men among the debris behind them. Emrys—Myrddin, in his not-yet shed glamor, and Giles. Although she'd known of this, seeing their bodies again was still alarming. She tried to close her eyes, but couldn't.

"Was there another carriage here?" asked the emissary.

She watched herself step closer, and Garin's low growl sounded loud in her ears, coming from his chest. "You seem like a fine diplomat," she'd said. "If you're headed for the Chateau de Trécesson, I'm afraid you're traveling in the opposite direction."

The emissary waved her off. "I know the emperor wanted me to depart in two days, but I insisted on giving myself extra time. I heard of a fine clothier in town, and I—"

"*Emperor?*" Lilac, Garin, and Adelaide said in unison.

"I should not have spoken." The emissary turned and briskly walked away, but Lilac chased him down, catching up to him despite her limp.

"I ask because I am the daughter of the royal cartographer," she'd called, "and we were headed in that direction."

The man slowed and turned. Her lie had impressed him. "*You* are the daughter of the queen's cartographer? What are you doing all the way out here?"

"My father sent us to town for more parchment."

The man looked this way and that. "You've heard the rumors, right? About France."

"France?" she'd said in feigned alarm. She only would've said it to encourage more information from the stranger. "Will they advance?"

She felt Garin's fingers flex at their side, shocked to feel a surge of bitter rage—a wave of cresting jealousy in their body that was not her own.

"That is what we suspect." The emissary looked both ways. The roads were empty. "And their king is not offering marriage."

Lilac's reply was cold, defensive. Rightfully so. "The queen would never accept. She would not surrender."

"Perhaps not, but she'll then require a stronger foothold on her land to keep France at bay. Her small army would never last." The emissary laughed, dubious.

They were moving again, and they didn't stop until their arms were nearly touching Lilac's. She felt Garin's balled fist open, his hand twitching near hers.

"What does that have to do with why you're here?" Garin snapped.

The man averted his eyes from him, keeping them fixed on Lilac. "This knowledge is sure to spark a flurry of proposals once made public. Of course, Maximilian has demanded complete secrecy, so his offer will stand first."

Maximilian. Albrecht wasn't the one planning on communicating with her. It was the emperor of the Holy Roman Empire. They were to host his *emissary.*

Suddenly, she couldn't breathe. She wasn't sure if the sensation belonged to her or Garin, or both. Panic struck her square in the chest. Had she suffered a head injury in the crash? No one had mentioned it. Hadn't Garin told her their blood exchange healed all?

How could she not remember any of this?

There was another sound—a loud rushing, faint thumping, but they were nowhere near the Argent. She didn't know what it was, but refocused on the conversation with some difficulty; it sounded like Garin had argued with him. The emissary was replying now. As the man spoke, their arm shifted, settling on the small of Lilac's back.

"Maximilian offers what no other ally will: a proxy marriage through myself to prevent France from annexing her country. She doesn't have to see him, but if she wants to solidify her people's continued protection, she'll visit Austria to eventually bear his children, and—"

Garin looked down at Lilac, and the rushing sound grew louder. It took a second for her to realize it was *her* heart. Garin, listening to her pulse.

The emissary's eyes flitted up and looked at them—at Garin—straight into his soul. The emissary squinted. "I'm sorry. Does that rogue have fangs?"

The words were barely out of the man's mouth before he stumbled back from Lilac. Her dagger was stuck halfway to the hilt in his chest, blood spreading rapidly over his fine clothes. Garin was shouting, his bellowed words heated, directed at her.

Lilac saw herself step back, her fists drenched in blood; she was in the middle of shouting back at him when she saw herself trail off, blinking at the ground. Their own vision shifted again, snapping onto the emissary, who had scrambled for the woods to their left of the path, screaming.

As Lilac faded into the corner of her vision, Garin was moving into the foliage, eyes trained on the emissary's back. In several large strides, she saw Garin's large hands dart out, his legs springing as he pounced.

She took a shuddering breath. Lilac was back in her body, coughing—but not on blood.

She stared at the ceiling, where a slow-building layer of smoke floated above Garin's shoulders. She was pressed into the floorboards, him above her, her hands grasping the rug beneath her, waves of stomach-churning pleasure slamming into her through Garin's slow thrusting and the pull at her throat.

He was splayed over her naked body, his hands on either side of her head as he bent, pressed into the side of her throat, slurping her blood obscenely. Like an animal, in the way he drank and fucked her. Her arms went up and she dug her nails into his shoulders, and as her core began to tighten in that welcomingly familiar way, she froze.

The edge of the bed near their feet was in flames. Lilac lifted herself partway onto her arms; small pockets of fire had bloomed in other corners of the room—the closet, part of the dresser, the table that previously held the decanter, now knocked over, glass shattered across the floor. On the garments of the bodies piled next to them.

"*Garin*. Garin, the room is on fire," she managed between gasps. The feeling of his teeth in her as he drank this time was entirely different. It made her forget her fury. None of it was ice or fire; she felt it all, and it *hurt*. He had ripped into her, but balanced by the pressure of his mouth and him deep inside her, Lilac found herself panting loudly, a sound she could not smother.

It was blinding, the pain and pleasure not canceling each other out—but *mounting*.

She tapped him, said his name; fear blossomed, consuming her wholly, unadulterated by any drug or bond. She was afraid for her life but never wanted this to end. Never wanted them to end.

His grip on her tightened suddenly, and Garin cursed into the side of her throat. He detached from her, his tongue running flat up the side of her neck as his release covered her inner thighs and lower abdomen.

"Garin, the room."

Lilac said his name again, and again. No response.

Garin hovered over her, deliberating, his darkened eyes inhuman and holding no remorse or understanding. As he bent to her throat again, she shifted both arms under his chest, hands pressed against him. She managed to curl her leg beneath him and pushed with all her might, grunting and bucking him to the side.

Garin *flew* off. Lilac marveled at her hands and legs—that inhuman strength she'd felt in the hours after the first blood exchange had saved her. Her power had returned as she'd hoped.

He'd landed to her right, his back slamming into the side of the settee, which sat further than she'd remembered. In their raucous tandem feeding and fucking, they'd at some point shoved it across the room, off to the right of the roaring fireplace.

Garin immediately rolled over, blinking at the room around them, which slowly filled with smoke before their very eyes.

Her blood was everywhere on him—his face, dribbling down his chin, matted in his hair and smeared over his hands. She grimaced, and when she did, she felt the thick layer of Garin's blood dried in patches over her own lips and nose. She tasted it on her tongue, slicked over her teeth and gums.

Iron. Salt. Honey.

The skin on his neck where she'd stabbed and drank from him appeared smooth beneath the layer of ichor.

Reminded, her hand flew to the side of her own throat. Through the grime, the indents of his teeth were already gone. And despite all the blood she'd lost, her mind was clear. She felt strong. Herself.

More herself than in what felt like ages.

Garin's gaze had followed her palm, his face shifting in realization. Then, disbelief. His eyes were glassy as he surveyed her and the room.

There was a crack; a beam dislodged from the corner of the room, flames spreading down its length. They had to get moving.

Lilac crawled to snatch her bundled dress at the corner of the rug, stood, and held her hand out to him. He didn't move, didn't bother looking at her. Staring at the pile of bodies, Garin shifted his feet beneath him and rose, leaving her hand outstretched. He sauntered past her and slowed when he reached the balcony door, sweeping the pale pink curtain aside. It had just rained; the panes of glass were fogged, covered in a sheen of dew despite the clear evening hours before.

Even as he said nothing, even as he silently turned to face her—his angular, bewildered features lit by the flames surrounding them—she *felt* his anger. It was a barreling force, slamming her head-on.

"*What have you done?*"

She feared answering him.

"What did you do, Eleanor?" His shout rattled her bones.

Clutching her dress to her front, eager to shield herself, she stormed up to him—and she could've sworn she saw him flinch.

"I risked my life," she snarled, shaking so violently she might fall over. "You could've killed me. Would have killed me."

"*You* were the one who kept urging me to drink from you like some deranged addict." He grimaced, face shadowed with regret and blame. "*I* was in control."

"In control." She laughed, the sound like a whip. "Neither of us have been in control. You killed four people in this room alone. Another on the way here. You would have kept going if I didn't. You wouldn't have stopped drinking, killing. Fucking." Myrddin had sent her to mend Garin's immense thirst, made worse by both of them consuming the mead—and there was only one way to do that while ensuring she'd become strong enough to fend him off. Another shot in the dark, and this one had stuck. Barely. "I did it to save us both."

"You think you saved us?" He glared at her, disdainful, as if he hadn't been on his knees, drooling for her just moments before. "By bonding yourself to me days before you take the crown? Marry?"

"Don't act as if I haven't just done you a favor. I have only made myself more agreeable to your whims."

Garin's nostrils flared. "My *whims?*"

"This makes your task of ensuring I do as you please, much, much easier!"

"It has done more than that, Lilac." His voice trembled. "It has changed everything."

She had never seen him look more disgusted. With her. He was going to make her hyperventilate. She began to sputter and cough in the thickening smoke, but refused to back down. "Forgive me for not sparing you a worse fate."

Garin laughed, low and dark. "There is no fate worse than being bound to you."

His words rocked her. She couldn't feel less connected to him, the way he regarded her with such hatred. In fact, she wanted nothing more than to get away from him.

She held her dress and glanced at the door, realization sinking in as she mapped the layout of the tavern in her mind. He was blocking the balcony exit, but she could escape into the crowd downstairs and leave with the rest, help usher them all out. Someone needed to knock on all the doors down the hall, too. The flames seemed to be contained to their room, though they were spreading slowly. There was time to alert everyone.

"You won't make it far, will you?" Garin said, as if reading her mind. "Not with you being so newly bound to me."

Her throat burned. "What about everyone here? Downstairs?"

"Not with me *dripping* down your legs." He cocked his head, narrowing his eyes against the flames dancing across his face. "Not with you as my thrall."

She shuddered, bracing herself against the threat of his words. "This was our first instance of a deep feeding and blood revival," she said, quoting what he'd told her in the carriage. "Even with our blood exchange at the inn, we'd then be connected at the first or second-level at best. It'll be fine, w-we'll stay separated and... I'm going to alert—"

Garin was laughing. "Put your dress on."

Lilac nearly lost her balance when her arms and legs moved instantly; the next thing she knew, she was bending, stepping into her bloodied dress.

It was the same tug at her navel—the same convincing force that had walked her up the stairs and to the right room, had her knocking upon his door. The same force that eased her from the castle and had guided her to Garin, but stronger. Much, much stronger.

Lilac glanced over her shoulder at him while her body obeyed, feeling like she could fight it. But she was too stunned to focus on it properly. Shaking, her fingers fumbled with the material as she tried to resist, her muscles aching to pull the sleeves on.

Garin took a step toward her, disbelief marring his anger.

"Stay away from me," she ground out, hardly able to speak as the smoke filled her lungs. Unlike before, it *hurt* to fight his command. Her biceps cramped, the force knocking the wind out of her as she strained.

Her eyes burned, moisture flooding them as they stung in the soot and heat. She tried not to think about the pile of bodies and pungent burning flesh.

"Lilac," he said sternly, withholding whatever other command was at the tip of his tongue. "What will you do? Escape this room unclothed?" He extended a hand. "I'll help you." Despite his offer, he looked as though it pained him to even address her.

"I don't need your help." It was harder to breathe now; she coughed into her arm, trembling under the immense power that controlled her. "Don't come any closer, Garin, or I will throw myself into the flames."

"*Come.*"

Her body obeyed, legs first, pivoting her hips toward him and lurching her into his arms. Garin caught her. She steadied herself against his chest, and before she could push off—or stab him again, as she considered—his arms coiled around her. The moment their bare skin touched, warmth flooded through her and the trembling ceased. He breathed against her, cradling her head to his chest, and soon, her breaths slowed to match his despite her fury.

Then, he stepped back. "Stay still and allow me to help you," he said softly, and all the fight left her body.

She watched silently as he helped her into both sleeves, made quick work of the lace at her front, and then dropped to his knees before her. The smoke was nearly blinding her now. Lilac held her breath as he gently hooked the lone garter strap onto her foot and slid it up her thigh, hating the way he took his time despite the walls climbing in flame around them. The smell of burning flesh singed her throat when her chest felt like it would explode and she was forced to inhale; she moved to sidestep him, blinking against the tears, driven by the need to breathe clean air.

Garin clicked his tongue. "Not yet."

"*Please.*" She would choke on her own breath, but her feet remained firmly planted on the ground as she strained. "You ass."

"Don't move." He reached back, procured her dagger from his pocket and slid it into its sheath beneath her skirts, his fingers scrupulously brushing her inner thigh. "You will not be without protection, useless or no."

He straightened, their mouths barely brushing on his way up before he loomed over her. His thumb brushed her cheek, wiping at the tear-streaked blood and soot staining her face. Lungs aching, Lilac launched into a coughing fit again. She released a single broken sob as he waited patiently for her to finish.

Then, Garin bent and pressed his lips to the corner of her mouth. Blinded by the smoke and heat, feet stuck in place, Lilac lunged for him and snapped.

Stunned, he pulled back and wiped his knuckle across his bottom lip. He'd moved out of the way before she could make him bleed again, but her mouth had scraped against him.

"There we are," Garin said as Lilac panted into the smoke. "Ruthless is the creature who resorts to teeth when her blade is out of reach."

Ignoring her lethal glare, Garin slowly strode to the balcony door and swung it open, causing all the heat and smoke to billow out in a rush.

Voices and shouting could be heard outside the alley, toward the street. He cocked his head, listening. "Bastion and Myrddin have been escorting people out. Go."

Chest throbbing, the invisible weights around Lilac's ankles released— and she threw herself onto the balcony.

18

L ilac's lungs burned as she stumbled into the night, swallowing the clean air gasp by gasp. Once the tears from her stinging eyes had allowed her to wipe away most of the soot, she peered down, nose dripping. The alley below was dark, lit only by the blaze behind them and the lamps on the bustling street to their left. There was an occasional uproar of laughter and shouting as the drunken denizens filed outside, away from the brothel fire.

The balcony was small and made of rickety wood, probably decades if not centuries old. There was barely enough room for two people. She took hold of the banister before her and shook it to check its stability. It rattled under her touch, and there didn't seem to be a gate or ladder leading down to the first floor.

Her stomach lurched when Garin's weight shook the entire structure; his arm slinked around her middle without warning. She shrieked and clung to him; one moment, he was lifting her, and they were climbing onto the thin banister like large, perching cats. The next, she was scrambling for purchase against him as they fell into the dark alleyway.

Garin landed soundlessly. Lilac wasn't so stealthy, jerking with the impact and stumbling out of his arms as he released her. Gasping, she bounced on the cobblestone and fell forward, barely catching herself against the far wall.

She pushed off the rough brick to glare at him, jostled but otherwise unharmed. "You *dropped* me."

He was dusting his hands and looking up at the flames now creeping out onto the balcony. "I was tempted to see how indestructible this bond has made you, seeing as you and I have somehow skipped *all* the steps," he said, his words laced with mocking fury even as he gave a lackadaisical shrug. "I could've thrown you off and you'd have lived. Most likely."

She snarled and marched in the direction of the street, but his arm shot out, catching her by the wrist. In one fluid, gentle motion, he yanked her close, his hands sliding up to her face—to her mask. She batted them away, but Garin's reflexes were still faster.

Their chests moved as one as he contained her with one hand and grabbed the corner of her mask with the other. She would look ridiculous, the skin where the mask had lain likely cleaner than the rest of her face.

But Garin didn't seem to think so. His breath hitched as he pulled it off, slinking the string up and above her head, as if he hadn't truly believed. As if he were still expecting someone else, after everything. He tossed the mask aside and his jaw clenched into that infuriating stare of disapproval again.

She'd encouraged a blood exchange, a true deep feeding, because it was the only thing that would stop his hunger—and keep her alive—by granting her this unnameable strength. She hadn't known it would do *this*. Her chest heaved in mistrust and betrayal. Had Myrddin known this would happen?

Then again, the only reason they were put in that position in the first place was the carriage crash, and the blood exchange that had begun their uncontrollable need for each other and set them on this course. The crash, where she'd...

Where she'd—

Lilac stared down at her hands, imagined them covered in blood. The blood of the emissary she was supposed to meet tomorrow.

She was never supposed to be propositioned by a count. She looked up at Garin, who was watching her with his arms crossed.

"I stabbed Maximilian's emissary." Her voice was as unsteady as she felt. "I stabbed Albrecht. I don't—How did I—"

But she trailed off as the corner of his mouth quirked. There was no pity or shock there. Of course, he was not surprised. He'd *been* there.

"Why do I not remember?" She shut her eyes, rifling through the poor memory he already had of the crash. The corpses, the pain. The shouting and being stuck in her own body. She couldn't recall anything else. There were no true, organic memories of her own—only what she'd seen through Garin's eyes. "*How?*"

"He told us he came to proposition you for the emperor."

"I know what he did. I saw it when I drank your blood."

"And that was your choice, wasn't it?" He reached out for her slowly, as if not to spook her.

Lilac was well past that. She moved out of his reach, her chest aching, thinking of the vision of her father's study that had flashed before her eyes when she'd bit his hand. The way she couldn't conjure even the faintest memory of sinking the blade into the emissary's chest.

What had she felt in that moment? Why she'd done it was obvious, but *stabbing* him? Guilt and pride warred in her, knowing she'd do it again.

Covered in blood and soot, his hair ruffling in the slight breeze scattering leaves through the alleyway, Garin was gazing at her unremorsefully. It was the first time tonight where his eyes were not shadowed by that overpowering hunger.

In fact, she noted, taking a curious step closer—they were gray again.

"Did you kill him?" she asked, remembering the vision of him bounding after the emissary.

"No," he said curtly. "I saved him. I saved him so your country wouldn't be demolished by Maximilian's army, as it would be if he ever found out the queen of Brittany stabbed his dignitary to death."

"Where is he now?"

"Safe at the inn. Kept away from you until your meeting, where you cannot harm him and preemptively destroy your allied relations."

She couldn't contain the shock and hurt any longer; the confusion would soon overwhelm her. Lilac spoke slowly, the words simmering off her tongue. "Why don't I remember?"

"Myrddin helped me."

Lilac stared at him, her jaw slack in disgust. "You had Myrddin remove my memory?"

"You would have regretted it."

Lilac spat a laugh. "You do not care about the things I might come to regret. It was and is my only proposition. My killing him would have ensured I did not marry," she said, speaking through her own reasoning. And his. "This went against your own interests."

Garin's expression darkened. "I was protecting you."

Knowing he was a fucking liar, that she wouldn't have known about any of it if she hadn't swallowed his blood, made everything he said all the more difficult to believe. Her parents had claimed Albrecht's letter was received three days into her journey.

The crash and stabbing had occurred on the first full day.

"Turning a count down would have been far too easy for me, wouldn't it?" she shouted. "You knew it was not enough to sway me, even under your entrancement. *You* wrote to my parents, didn't you?"

He didn't even try to deny it. Garin picked an invisible piece of dust off his collar. "Fortunately, the fellow carried a bundle of their official stationery in his satchel."

Sickness and dread overtook her. "You wanted me to believe it was Albrecht coming to propose to me. You made no attempt to mention Maximilian at all."

Garin jabbed a finger in her direction. "Precisely, Lilac. Do you know why? Catching you off guard was the only way you and your parents would end up hearing Maximilian's offer. He is the most powerful ally you have on the continent. Henri and Marguerite would never let you pass it up, but if you knew it was Maximilian offering marriage, you would have bolted. Wouldn't you?" He bent his head, condescending. "I might write your dear parents again, telling them of how you're about to throw everything away for—"

Garin stopped.

He froze, frowning. Listening. Garin's face then twisted, lips curling around his fangs in a snarl as he turned.

Casmir stepped out of the shadows from behind him. The vampire said nothing, made no noise before bringing his closed fist in front of his face. At first, Lilac thought he was drawing back to hit Garin. The scream that stuck in her throat released into a large palm that clamped down over her mouth. The familiar aroma of tombstone and iron flooded her nostrils.

Casmir opened his fist and blew, sending a cloud of brown dust into the air—into Garin's face, the scant remnants drifting over her and her assailant.

Lilac instinctively shielded her eyes. Nothing happened to her that she could feel, but Bastion yelped, his hands sliding off her face. He held onto her, tugging her body in his recoil, yanking her off her feet.

"Fuck's sake, Casmir!" Bastion growled from over her shoulder.

But it seemed the powder had mildly affected Casmir too. He shook his palm, dusting it frantically against his lapel and scuttling back.

"I'll kill you!" Garin choked on the dark dust, his eyes shut and drool dripping from his open mouth as he snarled and grabbed for Casmir, who easily dodged him. Even in the dim light, she could tell there was something wrong. Blood was running down Garin's face, from both his eyes and nostrils.

It was sawdust. *Hawthorn* sawdust.

Garin lunged blindly and slammed Casmir against the opposite wall. A flurry of soot and dust rained down. Casmir grabbed hold of him and yanked Garin sideways, pummeling his head against the wall.

"*Stop it*," Lilac cried as they grappled, nearly breaking free from Bastion's loosened hold on her. There was a *pop* and cloud of thin smoke between them, followed by the scent of black powder; Myrddin stood between her and Garin, frantically fumbling in his robes. Bastion caught her then, and wrapped his arm around her once more, this time much too tightly for her to throw herself from his grasp.

They watched in horror as Myrddin threw what appeared to be a ball of leaf-dappled vines in Garin's direction; the moment the vines made contact with Garin's body, they snapped across him, pulling his arms behind his back and ensnaring his wrists. The same happened around his ankles with the toss of a second ball of vines.

"Hold him still," Myrddin shouted at Casmir, hand outstretched.

Rolling his eyes, Casmir adjusted his hold on Garin; the more he struggled, the tighter the vines grew, pulling so tautly it looked as if they'd cut into his skin. Lilac fought down the urge to break free from Bastion, knowing it was probably for the better that Garin was restrained after the events of the night. Still, her body strained against his brother, as if defending Garin were ingrained into her reflexes. Maybe it was.

Casmir pulled a long piece of wood from his cloak and tossed it at Myrddin; the stake flew into the warlock's hands. He adjusted the stake in his palm while the foreign vampire held Garin steady.

Wasting no time, Myrddin rammed the stake into Garin's lower back.

Lilac gripped Bastion's shirt and turned her face into his shoulder as he awkwardly petted her head. She would faint. She *wished* to be unconscious as they watched Garin struggle for a moment, the bright hysteria in his eyes fading as he slumped forward into Casmir's arms. His head rolled to the side as Casmir adjusted him. Garin's tired gaze flitted up to the flames making their way onto the balcony, then locked onto Lilac.

"Save them. Save the brothel." His face twisted in agony. "My mother worked here. Lilac, don't leave..."

His voice trailed off, his eyes crossing. Then, they fluttered shut.

An all-consuming mixture of fear and rage struck her as she watched him go limp. Lilac suddenly understood what drove kings to do cruel and mad things.

"If he is dead," she heard herself bark, her jaw trembling, "*all* of you are ordered to the gallows with a bounty so high on your heads, no one in all of Brittany would be able to resist searching every nook and cranny for you."

"Relax. He's not dead," answered Casmir. "But we had to sedate him, just in case."

Myrddin was shaking. "I did it. I—"

"You stabbed him in the kidney." Bastion gave a disbelieving laugh.

"He told me I'd have to do it as far as possible from his heart!" Myrddin jutted a finger at Casmir. "Where else should I have staked your brother, in his buttock?"

Knees trembling from the adrenaline, Lilac unslung herself from around Bastion's shoulder as Casmir unremorsefully dragged Garin over to them. Bastion readied to receive him, but Lilac shoved him aside, her arms out.

Casmir glanced at her skeptically, then Bastion. "You're sure?"

"Give him to me." Her voice shook, but she'd never put more conviction behind a single sentence. "Give Garin to me, now."

Everyone watched as Casmir gently deposited Garin's limp form into her arms. She easily adjusted him onto her shoulder, careful not to touch the stake sticking halfway out of his back. She hugged him close, listening, paying attention to his chest, the slow beat of his heart and shushing Bastion when he opened his mouth in alarm.

Bastion marveled at her as she supported his brother without a breath of struggle beneath his dead weight.

Casmir was also eyeing her, brows risen.

"Don't look so surprised," she snapped. "You knew this would happen." Lilac's glare shifted to Myrddin, who watched them expectantly.

"Is this what you were arguing about in the room at the inn?" asked Bastion. "Your strength?"

"Partially. That is none of your business."

"I think most of the inn heard bits of your fight," he retorted. "Particularly when you were slamming each other around."

"After he'd healed me, I didn't feel any different. But during our conversation we discovered I could not only strain against him, but *move* him. It faded by the time I got to the castle, almost as soon as we'd left him," she admitted. "And just now, after he'd drank from me, and I from him, I was able to shove him off me."

Bastion said nothing, but his hand went right to his mouth. Casmir and Myrddin stared at her, but they didn't seem too surprised.

She failed to suppress a shudder at the memories, everything blending together into the pinnacle that was their blood exchange. The one she was awake for—the one *she'd* initiated. "I was able to stop him from feeding on me." There was nothing more frightening than the uncertainty of his control in the moment. "That was why I did it."

"This is nothing short of intriguing," said Casmir, exchanging a look with Myrddin, as if her strength had been a topic of brief discussion before. "It appears you have maybe siphoned some of his strength and speed, if it occurred with both blood exchanges."

"Maybe. Is it temporary?" she asked.

Casmir rubbed the shadow of stubble on his chin. "The bond or your gifts?"

The question caught her off guard. She had no answer.

"As for your strength and improved reflexes, I am not sure. It could fade again, the moment you two are separated. It could exist as long as he is your regnant."

She distantly absorbed his answer, hating the thought of being away from him again despite her fury. Her mind was already on his form in her arms and the words he'd croaked before collapsing. His mother had worked *at* The Fool's Folly. She had healed people in town and in the war, but she supposed that didn't mean Aimee couldn't have also served as a courtesan.

She considered the possibility void of judgment, only clutching him tighter, willing her body heat into him as if it would help. Lilac bent and swooped her arm under the crook of his legs, cradling him.

"The queen. Enthralled. Fully thralled to Garin," Bastion was groaning, his face craning to the sky in realization. "We're all fucked. *Fucked.* When he wakes, he's going to kill us all. He's going to get Myrddin, then me." He sighed, oblivious to the ash raining down on them. "Do you think if I stand beneath the balcony just here, then it will collapse on me?"

"I never thought I'd see the day I appreciated my immortality," Myrddin said, side-eying Bastion. "Casmir was the one who directed me to stake him."

"Better you than me." Casmir dusted his hands off, which had already healed from the sores the hawthorn dust had brought. "It'll keep him down until you're ready for him to wake. Unstake him when it's time, not a moment before, but I suggest you don't delay it. The longer you wait might worsen his reaction in realizing Lilac is not present. It is only what I predict. I won't be around to know."

Lilac raised a finger to stop him. "You are mistaken. I intend to be present when he wakes."

"No," both Casmir and Bastion said together.

Myrddin cleared his throat at the irate annoyance that had flashed across her face at the vampires' response. "Although I can understand your now natural urge to want to protect him, Your Majesty, it is my strong recommendation you are not around for the moment he comes to. Not when the last thing he remembers is us ambushing him with a stake. He will be safest back at the inn."

"Indeed." Casmir gave Myrddin a nod of agreement, and without warning, began to retreat into the alley.

Lilac quickly cleared her throat. "Casmir?"

He looked over his shoulder.

The flames hadn't wholly reached the balcony yet, but black smoke belched from the opening and rose high, disappearing into the night. "Help them. Ensure everyone's been evacuated. Especially the courtesans."

"You're asking me to help these mortals?"

"I'm not asking."

Bastion and Myrddin snorted, but they were silenced as Casmir glared. But he pivoted and stalked past, toward the light this time and into the street beyond.

Myrddin's face had broken into a concentrated smile that faded as soon as he caught Lilac staring him down. "Is there anything you can do to put the fire out?"

"If I were able, I would have by now."

"What do you mean?" Lilac frowned, what little tact she'd held exhausted by the eventful night. "They said you were all-powerful."

He blinked, as if offended by her question. "I'd need to access a body of water nearby to draw from to deposit on the fire."

Irritation grated her. Surely he was joking. "You summoned those flames, but you can't extinguish them?"

Myrddin's nervous, polite disposition, which she was beginning to feel might be a facade, disappeared. "Summoned? I cannot simply draw the elements out of thin air. Only mages can do that, and I am not one of them. Even those who practice in the School of Conjuration call items— and gods forbid, creatures—from a known place."

"But there was a hearth there," she argued, confused, knowing she would lose but doing it anyway.

"I did not summon those flames," Myrddin insisted. "We thought it might be your—your lovemaking. Or your grappling."

"Shut up, the both of you." Bastion's head swiveled, listening. Voices could be heard shouting in the room above now. "There's no need. They've brought buckets of water up."

"Fine." She'd lost track of what happened when she was in the vision, witnessing her own attempted murder of the emissary. This only partially relieved the many questions overwhelming her. "Could you at least teleport us home?"

The warlock looked down his nose at her, then pointed his chin at Bastion. "Your horse is still out front, is it not?"

He strode toward the street in the direction Casmir had gone, but Bastion moved, blocking his way. "You can't leave. We need your help."

"Do you? It seems your queen feels my benevolence was not enough."

"Benevolence? *You* started their bet. You dumped me in that room without protection or advice," she snarled, remembering the powerful pull against her throat and how she wouldn't have been able to fight him off unless she'd known about the strength she'd come to acquire. Even then, she hadn't known for sure. "You helped Garin wipe away my memory of that emissary."

"Here we go," muttered Bastion.

Myrddin's defensiveness shifted to anger, his blond beard quaking. "I would have been a dead man to tell him no, Your Majesty. He would have tortured me until he got his way. I might have my pitfalls, but *I* am the reason Rennes is not steeped in blood tonight." His eyes flitted to Bastion, who glared at them both. "Indeed, one of my powers is clairvoyance, but I am bound by the laws of the Old Faith from telling anyone of the future. I am only allowed to advise and direct, but that hasn't stopped the great kings I've been indebted to from trying to extract the information from me, however they see fit."

"So your great advice was to trap them together until she ended up dead or enthralled," Bastion spat.

Lilac said nothing, shivering against the sudden cold.

"I did what I had to. As did Lilac and Garin. I can tell you things about events passed, and possible outcomes that are no longer. What I can tell you is that Garin would not have stopped here. He would've stayed a few more hours, drank his fill. Then, as he slowly realized the blood he spilled did not fill him, he would've fled into the night, killing as he went, diverting to your castle at the end. He would have struck your army down until you had nothing left to fortify yourself against France. Then, their country would be the *least* of your concerns."

"He wanted my blood."

"He wanted," he corrected, "with an uncontrollable desperation and hunger, to simply find you. It seems you both were driven by the same urges." He craned his head, contemplating. "You broke through his entrancement, did you not?"

She thought of Garin's words. Those tonight, and the threat she'd thought was empty, meant to scare her when he'd cornered her in his grotto. She was unable to help herself from imagining it.

She closed her eyes, only to discover a vision—

Garin, striding up to the chateau gate, unarmed, asking to see her. He'd ask once. A glint of blades in the moonlight as the guards refused, laughed, and in a flash of black, him tearing through their flesh with his teeth and hands before they got close enough to see the red of his irises.

Lilac tried to open her eyes, but the vision remained.

He was in the corridor before the Grand Hall, veering right for the throne room, where her parents often entertained their closest guests.

"Stop," Lilac begged Myrddin, as Garin—the ghoul of him—stalked toward the stone doors. "I understand."

The vision eased. Bastion stood next to her, looking just as unsettled.

"Better here than there. And through all that chasing, his bloodlust would have grown so great that when he finally cornered you, he wouldn't have been able to stop himself. The urge to complete the bond drove his endless hunger, but your death would've been another solution to free him, wouldn't it?" The warlock's question hung in the night grown silent.

"We both had the Dragondew Mead tonight," she added. "I, no more than a few drops, him, possibly more. Two guests who'd tried to seduce him put it in his drink."

"Ah," said Myrddin, understanding immediately. "That certainly would have complicated things. The effects of the plant were likely made more potent. But it probably saved you time, if not your life. His lust for you would have recentered him from his hunger, but not for long."

There were shouts for water in the background, and she thought the blaze dimmed slightly, the hiss of a suffocating fire and billowing smoke sounding above them. But she couldn't look away from the warlock, both intrigued and terrified at the unyielding magic that had befallen them tonight.

"Why was there the urge to complete the thrall bond in the first place?" Lilac said, her voice barely audible.

,"There usually exists some form of yearning for one another's company once a first level bond is initiated, thus the need to watch and keep the potential thrall and regnant apart," he explained, stroking his beard. "But an instant bond like this is rare, if it has ever existed before. Either way, it was better you found him early."

She steeled herself against the mixture of emotions that followed, even as the weight of being Garin's thrall bowed her shoulders. The memory of his control over her upstairs made her insides clench with both fury and longing. A shard of pain spiked at the right side of her throat, where Piper and Garin had sunk their teeth into her—where Kestrel had dug his inch-long claws into the bloodied meat there and held her windpipe shut at Cinderfell.

She looked down at herself, distantly wishing she'd worn one of Garin's self-cleaning kirtles. She was *covered* in blood, hers and his.

Myrddin's outstretched arm appeared in her periphery; she blinked the tears away and looked at him questioningly.

"May I?" he asked, holding his hand out.

"Don't do anything to hurt her," Bastion warned. "You've already signed our names in blood by staking Garin in the fucking kidney."

"Don't remind me." He gave a curt nod to Lilac. "Your Majesty, would I steer you wrong?"

She refused to answer his irony, but waited for further instruction.

Myrddin waved his hand in the air, first in a circular motion, then what looked like half a square before he pushed his palm toward her. She flinched as a tingling sensation enveloped her feet, then began climbing up her legs.

Lilac gasped; before her very eyes, her shoes and skirts were clean, perhaps even more neatly laid and freed of wrinkles than they'd been when she'd left the castle. The sensation continued up her torso, her arms, chest, all the way to the top of her head, until not a speck of dirt, sweat, or blood was felt upon her body.

She spun, regarding herself. "That is quite impressive, Myrddin."

"It's only an illusion. Nearly the same type derived by Adelaide's tonic. The same disenchantment rules apply—the moment you ingest food or drink, it wears off. This is to get you home without needing to answer questions."

Bastion made a noise of relief. He was looking up at the balcony. "The fire's out." He concentrated, listening. She hadn't noticed, but they had been cast in near darkness, lit only by the torches on the street. "Everyone seems to have made it out."

Myrddin shifted, placed himself between them and held his hands out, palms up. "On the count of three."

They both nodded.

"One."

Lilac braced herself, readying her palm above his, shifting Garin in her arms. Bastion did the same, looking utterly skeptical and ready to recoil, probably thinking about Kestrel's unpleasant portaling experience.

"*Two...*"

Myrddin clamped a steel grip on her outstretched forearm. She heard Bastion scream somewhere off to her right, and her stomach dropped as the ground disappeared and the world started spinning. She hugged Garin tight and shut her eyes.

THERE WAS A RUSH OF WARM AIR, AND A SET OF NEW SCREAMS. THE world—the room they'd landed in—had slowed and eventually came to a stop, but they were contained within a vortex of wind that loosed every piece of parchment and shuddered the hanging pots suspended by the beams on the ceiling.

They'd teleported into a firelit room shrouded in potted, hanging greenery, amber and cobalt bottles galore—no Low Forest plants to be seen this time. Adelaide shot up in a small bed tucked in the right hand corner of the room, cussing and pulling the covers up over herself, her bare shoulders barely visible above the knitted comforter. Lorietta was dressed in a pretty, puffed sleeve white gown with a hem adorned in pink roses, in the middle of pulling a pair of brown boots on.

She dropped the second shoe and stumbled back. "*Modron!*" Lorietta squeaked as Myrddin dipped into a bow, seemingly unbothered by the way his vortex had promptly floated the bottoms of his robes.

"Stake me now," Bastion said, shielding his eyes with one hand and tugging Myrddin's robes down with the other. "You couldn't bother to at least wear your braies?"

"Greetings and salutations," Myrddin shouted above the wind that continued around them, several pieces of crumpled paper and leaves making their rounds. "A delivery for you. Two vampires, intact. Mostly."

"*Myrddin*," Lorietta screeched, her large eyes falling upon Garin's limp form in Lilac's arms—the gore staining his face and body. "*Not my chamber!*"

There was a large lump on her bed, under the covers, where Adelaide had been.

"If I'm teleporting within a property's walls, I can only teleport to *people*. Or Daemons. An arcane law meant to protect... ethics?" He waved a vague hand. "Seems rather counterintuitive in this particular circumstance. I hate to deposit this dormant, rather deadly vampire and his aloof brother on you, I truly do. My apologies, my friends."

Lilac wanted to close her eyes again, on the verge of throwing up, but she kept them open out of burning curiosity. The air around them had slowed considerably, almost making the spinning sensation worse. Myrddin shook Bastion off, and the vampire coughed and stumbled out of the vortex onto Lorietta's rug next to the pit-style hearth in the center of the room.

The warlock then elbowed Lilac but clamped his now free hand over hers, which had been tucked under his arm. "Well, Your Majesty? What are you waiting for?"

Keeping her distance, Lorietta refused to get any closer but craned her neck to get a better view of Garin as Bastion gingerly righted himself before her. Lilac held him close, a carnal feeling of distrust flooding her body.

"It will be okay," Myrddin shouted over the wind. "I promise."

"I can't." She shook her head, clutching him. "I can't leave him."

"You can. This place is his home," the warlock said with a reassuring squeeze of her hand, his crystal gaze warming her even as she held tears back. "You will see him soon. You have no choice."

"I thought we were severing their bond," Lorietta interjected.

Myrddin glanced knowingly at Lilac, unmoved by the sickening motion. "We can try. If that's the case, I'd prepare for more casualties, though."

There was a simultaneous exclamation of fear and protest from Lorietta and Adelaide. "That goes against everything he wanted for her." Lorietta glanced at Garin in horror. "What made him change his mind?"

"It was me." Lilac shifted Garin forward as they all looked to her. "I did it. I made myself his thrall." Gingerly, cradling his head, she leaned over. "Be careful with him."

Bastion took him from her, and the moment he was out of her hands, she attempted to follow—tried to step out from the vortex. She was yanked back by the collar by Myrddin, who held her close around the shoulders as the wind picked up.

The room dissipated into blurs of orange and green.

19

L ilac made the mistake of shutting her eyes again, opening them moments later when she felt dew on her face and the ground beneath her feet. She stumbled into the dark when the spinning stopped, nearly launching herself into the brush before Myrddin caught her by the arm and led her to a nearby oak trunk. Her stomach heaved as she steadied herself against it.

"There now," Myrddin muttered, releasing her. "For all the things you could've inherited from Garin, you'd think he would have spared you some of his grace, too."

When the feeling passed, she straightened to see Myrddin watching her from several feet away, dusting his robes and grimacing. "What will happen to him?"

The warlock finished brushing himself off, glared up at her, then nodded toward what appeared to be a break in the trees. "That is the least of your worries at the moment, Your Majesty. I assure you, he is safe."

She pushed off the trunk and poked around, bumping into bushes and brambles before making her way out of the trees and finally onto wheel-and-hoof-flattened earth.

To her left was her keep flanked by its towers; he'd teleported them to the edge of her chateau grounds. She never thought she'd be so happy to see it. The gate to the bailey was open, and no guard presence was visible from where they stood.

"Were you expecting visitors?" Myrddin asked.

She wasn't. Her mother's friends should've arrived hours ago; they wouldn't be caught traveling in the dead of night unless absolutely necessary. Lilac started down the path, Myrddin shuffling close behind.

She slowed, suddenly considering how odd it might seem that she'd arrived without her carriage. Without Hywell, or Giles...As the fog continued to clear from her mind, she realized this was the least of her concerns. Lilac turned to Myrddin. "What about Garin? Truly. I worry for him."

Myrddin's hand went to the back of his neck. "Well, they won't do anything without me there to protect them, that's certain. He won't wake as long as the hawthorn is in his body." He watched the open gate, picking a leaf out of his beard. "That doesn't look promising. Tell you what I do know—if I let you walk through those gates alone, Garin will kill me. He'll find a way."

Days ago, she would've been hesitant to arrive with a warlock in tow. "Don't do anything strange," she said, and beckoned him forth. From what she could see as they neared, the main keep was still well-lit, even at this late hour. Her mother had been expecting Helena and Gertrude, hadn't she?

But why were the gates open and unattended?

She took off at a run across the field and through the path. Dread tore through her as she half-hoped to be met with a blade in her face once she reached the gate. At least it would mean *someone* was watching the place.

But none came.

A lavish, two-horse drawn carriage was parked in front of the stable, one she recognized as Lady Gertrude's. Helena must have ridden with her.

But there was another unmarked carriage she didn't recognize parked just before the front doors to the keep, as if its occupants had abruptly abandoned it.

She circled the carriage and marched up the steps, into the shallow archway. Just as she reached for the nearest rung, both doors swung inward.

Two astonished green eyes stared back at her, framed in loose red waves and ablaze with profound irritation. There was a guard on either side, and

Lilac could sense more voices and hurried movement beyond—but nothing else mattered. The world stood still as she gazed into a most displeased round face that brightened at the sight of her.

"See? *There* she is," Piper said, yanking her arms out of the guards' grip and motioning at Lilac. "Good evening, Your Majesty."

Both guards looked so shocked to see Lilac and Myrddin—who'd fallen behind—that they only remembered to bow once Piper dipped into a shallow curtsey.

Speechless, Lilac returned the gesture, meeting her guards' eyes with frost and attempting to mask her shock. How well she managed to hide it, she couldn't say.

"Well?" Lilac snapped. "Don't just stand there. God forbid I might access my own keep."

"Of course, Your Majesty." They retreated, tugging Piper with them, until they were well inside the foyer.

"Why are my gates open and unattended?"

"We were preoccupied," one guard stammered. "As you know, our numbers are momentarily limited; your father sent some of us to supervise the sightings in *La Guerche* and *Fougères*." He eyed Piper, careful not to say too much. "There was an unexpected arrival we rushed to attend to. *She* was caught wandering your tower as the keep was being secured." He jostled Piper, whose hands had balled into fists.

"Stop that," Lilac sneered, squinting at the smear of blood and blossoming patch of blue-green at the corner of his mouth. "What happened there?"

The guard wiped his face. "She put up a bit of a fight."

"I'm sure she did. I'll have you know, I sent the guard to those bordering towns," Lilac retorted curtly. "And she fought you because I've been *expecting* her. This is..." She'd want to use an alias. "Philomena, was it?"

Piper's face twitched in disdain. "Phoebe Allard, Your Majesty."

She *would* come prepared.

"Phoebe Allard, yes, my apologies. Gentlemen, meet my new lady-in-waiting."

They muttered curses under their breath, glaring daggers at each other and bowing deeply. The other guard grunted. "We didn't know you chose one, Your Majesty. Henri never said—"

Lilac snapped her head to him like a wandering shark who sensed blood. "And is it Henri's business when I bathe? When I change? When I relieve myself?"

He reddened. "No, Your Majesty. I suppose not."

"Then my lady-in-waiting she is." The guards said nothing more on the matter as Piper failed to conceal her own shocked grin. Lilac cocked her head at her. "What's so funny?"

Piper shook her head, allowing her hair to curtain her face. "Nothing, Your Majesty."

"Very well. I've been anticipating her arrival after my second visit to the haberdashery," Lilac continued. "She's arrived early and was probably forced to let herself in after you all abandoned the gate." She shot a look at the other guard who'd begun to say something, silencing him. "Unhand her and restation the bailey. Have your men secure my gates." She took Piper by the arm and stared the guards down. "Now."

They promptly released Piper.

"Your Majesty," one said as Lilac took several steps in the direction of the foyer staircase. "You were at the haberdashery? In Paimpont?"

"In Rennes." Lilac regretting the words before they were out of her mouth, cringing inwardly as they tumbled out anyway. She'd been gone for several hours at the most. It was not near long enough for a trip to either town and back, even on the main roads.

She clutched her friend's hand, eager to escape to her tower, but something else pulled the guards' attention out the door.

Lilac had forgotten all about Myrddin. "And this is—"

"Herlinde," came a light, dancing voice as a woman entered the doorway. She was wrapped in a fuzzy black robe over a pink nightgown adorned with green tassels that swept her beet-red boots. Her shoulder-length curls were a dazzling shade of black, so vibrant they were almost blue, and when she shifted in the torchlight, it was as though the light itself sashayed through them.

She smiled in a strikingly familiar manner, her cheeks rosy and welcoming. "Herlinde of The Hemlock Haberdashery." She bowed as she stood in the doorway, stifling a yawn.

"Come in," Lilac said, highly impressed. She'd never known what

Herlinde actually looked like, but the disguise Myrddin had taken on was uncanny.

She strode in, reached past Lilac and Piper, and unflinchingly shook one of the guards' hands. The guard jerked back, wiping his palm on his robes. Herlinde—*Myrddin*—then pivoted to Lilac, opening her arms for a hug as both guards retreated.

Lilac accepted her stiffly.

"You and that warlock owe me," Herlinde growled into Lilac's ear, patting her daintily on the back. The witch pulled away, her light brown cat eyes twinkling at the crystal-studded iron chandelier. "Your castle is marvelous. Thank you for having me. It's a rather quick ride back when magic is in the air and the breeze is right." She winked at the guards, nudging her head at the door. "Your driver just parked the carriage at the stables, Your Majesty."

"Th-thank you."

"The pleasure's been all yours."

Reeling, Lilac stepped aside to see what Herlinde had motioned at. Piper leaned over to see, too. Impossibly, Lilac's own carriage, horses, and a grinning Giles sat just outside the stables, waving quietly from his seat. When the guards craned their necks out the door, Herlinde shot Lilac a knowing look behind their backs and winked.

An illusion? It had to be. Myrddin had glamored himself as Giles.

And it was Herlinde who stood next to Lilac.

"You're a witch," first guard said, gazing into Herlinde's vertical pupils.

"She is," Lilac said. "What of it?"

"Was this witch also stranded without her horse?" The second guard eyed them dubiously, probably remembering her and Lorietta's half-baked excuse when she and Adelaide had showed up in her carriage. He also likely wondered why Lilac would bring Herlinde to the castle at what must be near midnight by now.

She was honestly stumped. Her body felt strong somehow, muscles burning with energy and the memory of Garin's hands, but her mind was exhausted and all out of lies.

"No," Herlinde answered for her with a snort. "Me? Stranded? You see, Lilac had visited me to check if I'd received the imported fabrics she'd requested on our first visit. I hadn't, not yet, but I invited her in despite the late hour," she explained. "We had some tea, and I expressed concern with her not taking a guard with her, especially after the last one abandoned his duties—" Herlinde glared at the guards—"in favor of a tavern stop." Herlinde sighed in pity. "Anyway, we get along splendidly. Still without guard, Her Majesty was so kind to invite me to accompany her on the way back, and I suggested I might take a peek at her wardrobe for her fitting and style preferences. Although, I am glad to return at a later time, though." Herlinde bowed again, taking a hurried step back toward the door. "I feel I may have walked in on something."

"Wait," Lilac blurted before Herlinde could escape. She had questions, and the witch would answer them. "Herlinde, you came all this way. You are welcome to peruse my closets any time. At the very least, come in for dessert before Giles brings you back." She ignored the irked gleam in Herlinde's eyes—she had to be at least distantly related to the Aglovens—and turned back to the guards. "Are Hedwig and Mother still awake? We'll take dessert upstairs, if so."

"And some of her croissants—" Piper cut herself off, the constellation of freckles across her face nearly disappearing in her increasing redness. "If she has any, that is."

"How assuming," Lilac gritted through her teeth.

"I said, *if*."

"Hedwig is wide awake," the first guard replied, warily observing the three of them. "But she's busy with your parents and their guest in the Grand Hall."

Lilac turned her attention from Piper. "What guest?"

"He arrived just before we found Phoebe. Refuses to leave until he's had a word with you."

She swallowed her nerves, nodding. "Show us the way, then. And never," she added with a fixed glare, grasping Piper's hand as they followed the guards into the west wing corridor. "*Never* handle any guest, especially one of mine, again in such a manner."

Despite being fully lit, the halls were quiet and void of their usual evening inhabitants, no staff nor scullery maids closing down for the night. Just when they reached the end of the corridor, the double doors to the Great Hall swung open. The guards leading them stepped aside as crowd filed out: at least one dozen sentries, a whispering Lady Gertrude, and her often present accomplice, Lady Helena—tankard in hand—at the rear. The first guard who'd escorted them uttered silent orders to the ones that emerged.

Past them, she could see two tables had been moved to the center, but her vision was blocked by her mother's friends.

They startled at the sight of her, stopping to bow. Lilac returned the gesture and exchanged a kiss on the cheek with each. They eyed her hungrily, taking in every detail they possibly could—her bright eyes and deepened shade of her hair. The taller and more brazen of the two even took in a sharp breath at the healthy sheen of berry that frosted the edges and center of Lilac's face.

"You look so...so healthy," Gertrude commented as they slowly continued past, motioning aggressively for the guards to continue. The doors shut with a

"Thank you, Gertrude," Lilac said. They looked surprised, but not as shocked as her mother did the first time she'd returned. They'd already been discussing the queen and her altered appearance, no doubt. "Are you two off to bed so soon?"

"Yes, actually," Helena said with an apprehensive glance back at the now closed doors. Her cheeks were red. "Henri's pours were *much* too heavy. And they—"

"That's it now." Gertrude took her slurring friend by the hand. "All of you have a good night," she said with a lingering glance upon Piper.

Normally, the former handmaiden stood a few inches taller than Lilac. At the moment, however, she slouched behind Herlinde, as if aiming to make herself the smallest person in the room.

"Tomorrow, then," said Helena.

"Tomorrow," said Lilac. She waved them off toward the northern wing and pushed the doors to the Grand Hall open before the guards could get to them.

Both tables split the room, with the remaining ones pushed against the walls. On the right one, half was covered in a small feast and dessert spread. Hedwig's signature pastries and tarts, a tea cart nearby with a half-eaten bird and what appeared to be sausages and cheese at the end. On the left-hand table, Henri sat at the far end, his back to the stairs and fire, his expression unreadable as he greeted her with a minute nod. Wearing an uncomfortable smile, Marguerite was seated to his right. Four of their guards surrounded them.

But someone else sat at the other end of the table with his back to Lilac —also surrounded by four of his own men. Two of them were Armand's guards, dressed in the familiar red and gold of the Le Tallec estate. The other two were Mathias and Lorenzo, although she barely recognized them under several layers of bandaging. Large ribbons of gauze wrapped around both of Mathias's arms; Lorenzo's right foot and calf were encased, too. Heavy blades and bows hung from their scabbards.

One by one, they all turned to face her.

The last, the seated stranger, was Monsieur Le Tallec.

"Good evening, Your Majesty," he said with a yellowing smile. "So nice of you to join us."

"There is nothing to join." Henri glanced up at Lilac. There was a clear glass of what she assumed to be water and a cup of tea before him. He'd attempted to sober up. "Artus was just leaving."

Lilac remained where she stood, her eyes locked on Sinclair's grandfather. "What are you doing here?"

"I came for a drink. For a chat." He stared at her from over the rim of his teacup, sipping his tea. "It is a pleasure to finally meet you and your mother, and to see your dear father again." His attention shifted behind Lilac—to Piper, Herlinde, and the pair of guards that flanked them. "Erm, is that a witch?"

"Order your men to surrender their weapons," Lilac began. She was keenly aware of her parents' eyes on them, Hedwig watching mutely from the head of the pastry table. "Or there will be no chatting of any kind. It's been my rule for every visitor since your grandson attacked me."

Artus sat back, extending his hands in mocking welcome. "Have your men come and take them from mine."

Loosing the indignant rage burning inside her would only fuel his insolence. She refused to give him the satisfaction. The room was dead silent as Lilac observed Henri's warning stare from over Artus's shoulder.

"Of course, you Trécessons must be used to taking things from me and my kin by now." He gave Lilac a pitying glance, then turned to face Henri head on. "Our families have a long history, don't we? First, Francis stripping the Ermengardes of their titles over a trivial misunderstanding. Shortly after, banishing me from my own duty of birthright and installing my son prematurely. Then your daughter's escapade with those vampires my grandson nearly lost his life to. The kingdom has not forgotten so easily."

Some of this was new information to her, particularly this business about the titles. The Ermengardes were a prominent noble family; when were they ever dismissed? Lilac opened her mouth to reply, but her attention caught on her father's trembling, red face.

Henri stood so fast his chair knocked back with a crack. He swept his arm across the table, his and Marguerite's glassware smashing to the floor. "Misunderstanding? The Ermengardes were caught siphoning royal funds to finance their lavish vacations without Francis's knowledge!"

"Your father was cruel to banish my daughter-in-law's family," said Artus. "They were loyal to your father. Gratienne with was pregnant with Vivien."

"Vivien's parents were sentenced to ten years of serfdom during the court session you interrupted. They remained here. Francis could have sent them to the dungeons. The Ermengardes' titles were eventually reinstated in Vivien's tenth year, and my parents even granted them a trip to the coast before they resumed their duties at Father's side. They were not banished entirely from my parents' court. Not as you were."

Artus's eyes narrowed. "Ah, yes. They were fortunate for the chance at a trial."

"You broke into the Grand Hall, screaming nonsense about Daemons at the court and jury—including the row of French diplomats in their jury who'd come to monitor the Ermendardes' trial. You made a spectacle of my father's authority in front of them, and you've the audacity to question my father's decision to deem you unfit for duty? Although, I do suppose congratulations on your remarkable recovery are in order—you seem plenty well enough to travel to my castle in the middle of the night with your accusations. Have you clawed your way out of the depths of your madness, or is it simply that it only troubles you when you're asked to do your job?"

This was the first Lilac had heard of the reason for his dismissal. He'd interrupted Vivien's parents' trial. But the subtle triumph in Artus's smirk led Lilac to believe not everything had come to light. What more had Artus done to warrant losing his title? More than that, what else had he managed to get away with? Had Francis feared Artus's interruption would leave a certain impression on the French diplomats? Just how unhinged was his rant?

Even she thought it seemed a harsh punishment to come from her notoriously docile grandfather.

Despite Henri's response, Artus looked amused. "You know, Francis took pity on Armand after my wife died. He was gracious in refraining from revoking their statuses. Helped him become a fine duke. You were fast friends, you and my son. All for Sinclair's right to greatness to be stripped from him."

"His *right?*" Blood boiling, Lilac started forward.

Artus's guards immediately covered him, one of them drawing his blade. Robes shifted and metal sang as both guards at Lilac's side mirrored them.

But there was a quicker flash of movement.

"That won't do." It was Piper. She stalked past Lilac and held her hand out, holding eye contact with the Le Tallec guard before her. "Your weapons, please." He placed his blade in her hand without question while she looked over at the other one. "You too, give it here."

Herlinde's laugh was barely audible behind her. "Modron. Would you look at that."

Lilac's mouth hung open. The room exchanged confused glances as Piper tucked their blades under her arm, leaving Artus's guards silent and blinking. In the same fashion, she collected Mathias and Lorenzo's bows, quivers, and daggers. Smiling to herself, Piper strode over to one of the far tables against the wall and laid them out neatly, one by one. She dusted her hands off and promptly returned to Lilac and Herlinde's side.

"Who is she?" Artus asked the guards beside Lilac. "Were you not just apprehending her?"

"Yes," one of them answered, looking hesitantly at Henri, who had shakily seated himself once again. Marguerite was rubbing his shoulder. "We were mistaken."

"She's my new lady-in-waiting," said Lilac coldly. "I've been expecting her but wasn't sure when exactly she would arrive."

Artus squinted at Piper as Henri's eyes flitted briefly to Lilac, then back to Piper. "I've never seen her before," said Artus. "Where did you find her?"

"*I* did," Hedwig responded, flicking one of her peppered brown braids over her shoulder. "I handpicked her earlier in the month."

Piper began to fidget at her side; Lilac stopped her with a brief glare.

"But ladies-in-waiting are chosen from prominent families by the Stewardess." Artus laughed, as if this was all some ridiculous scheme to rob him outright of some truth he was owed. "She's in charge of your kitchens."

"We never replaced the one we had after my father died. Lilac has promoted her," Henri said boredly, taking a swig from his new water glass brought over by Hedwig.

Lilac understood Hedwig's quick thinking; the chef had covered for Lilac many times. But why was her father lying for her? *Again?* Did he actually pity her, or was he equally tired of the scrutiny? Surely he wasn't doing it out of love or loyalty.

She willed the telltale heat and blooming red in her face to calm, but she couldn't believe that after such a night, Artus was here—and that after everything, the Le Tallecs had still managed to weasel their way into her castle. At least now she seemed to have allies willing to stand against them.

Lilac didn't dare look at Hedwig, who unsurprisingly spoke as she returned to her spot at the head of the food table.

"He wouldn't know, Your Grace. Living in his little pub like he does."

Artus's ridiculing smile fell. He ignored Hedwig. "I hear your borders have been threatened."

"I've handled it," Lilac retorted, trying not to sound as defensive as she felt.

"Your father has handled it while you've been... elsewhere." He eyed Piper then, and Herlinde, who'd remained patient and silent in her shadow. "Haven't you?"

Her answer was simmering. "My whereabouts are none of your concern."

"It is natural, given the prison you've finally broken yourself out of, that you want to explore. Every young ruler should know their kingdom front to back, now, shouldn't they? And your parents did their best ensuring your literacy and education of the world within the boundaries you were given. They even encouraged you, rightfully so, to consider my grandson as your husband. He would have made a worthy partner."

"Do not patronize me. There's not a decent bone in Sinclair's body. He was never in my consideration." The mere thought of him made her want to shrivel within herself. She hated remembering now, her thoughts unclouded by any partial bond to Garin, that he currently resided under the same roof.

Even as her prisoner, it wasn't enough. She wanted him dead. The only reason he was alive was because he deserved a worse fate.

The way Artus looked at her now, as if their very interaction were a joke to him because he considered her unworthy of his time underneath it all, reminded her much of the marquis. Sinclair was much more like his grandfather than Armand.

"He would have provided for you, kept you in France's good graces and safe from those blasted creatures."

"Those creatures you hunt and murder unprovoked?"

A silence hung in the air. Artus's subtle smile deepened his wrinkles as her mother whipped her head at Lilac, glaring over pursed lips while her father disappeared into his cup of water. Apparently, her father's support didn't yet extend to the Daemons.

Lilac turned to the guard to the nearest guard. "Will you please fetch John?"

"At this hour?" Marguerite said from across the table.

She shot her mother a silencing glare.

Artus interjected with a clear of his throat, his smile widening at the mother-daughter back and forth. "Your Majesty, given the bloody history of Paimpont that I'm sure you're aware of, I would not call the active management of these Daemons unprovoked. And yet you seem to care more for their wellbeing than the security of your kingdom, which simply required a marriage to Sinclair."

Lilac resisted the urge to launch herself at Artus. She could strangle him. With her freakish strength, she could *literally* strangle him, probably both his men and his guards. But Artus knew better. He, like the Le Tallecs, *knew better*. Knew she wouldn't. From birth, Lilac had been placed on a pedestal, held to a different set of standards to begin with.

As the world watched the girl with the Daemon tongue, everyone else got away with murder.

"I can see some benefits of the marriage weren't explained to you. What your parents might have failed to clarify is that marrying my grandson would have secured your distance with France, at least for several more years. Possibly generations, your entire reign, if you gave Sinclair a healthy son or two."

Lilac did not miss Henri and Marguerite's exchanged glances, but she remained intently focused on the old man in front of her.

"You see, my mother was born to a viscount during Charles's reign, and Vivien's paternal bloodline is of junior French aristocracy, long existing in favor of the kings with several generations of pristine peerage. Entering into a marriage contract with Sinclair would have protected Brittany because France would have been a natural ally, leaving them uninterested in annexation. Instead, you've antagonized your most powerful neighbor by not only turning Sinclair down but arresting him with a public announcement. Humiliating him. Not to mention the type of company you've been concerning yourself with." He gave Piper and Herlinde a pointed once-over before returning to Lilac with a pitying grimace.

Marguerite gripped the tabletop, looking as if she were about to faint. Henri exhaled but said nothing.

"Your grandson deserves everything that has befallen him. You don't seem as high caliber of a man yourself if my grandfather revoked your duties prematurely, leaving them to a seven-year-old boy. One who turned out to be no better."

She wasn't sure what the old man had been hoping for—if he honestly thought she would have plucked Sinclair from his cell and summoned a priest—but she wouldn't have married him even if he had come with all the power and security in the world.

Artus's condescending expression had shifted into a snarl. "Sinclair was your best chance at retaining your sovereignty."

"I'd be careful with your implications if I were you," Lilac warned. "You wouldn't want it to appear so blatantly that Sinclair was France's intentional way into Breton nobility and the crown, would you?"

Artus leaned forward in his seat. "And if it was? What would anyone do about it?"

She should have him thrown out. She could have him arrested for the threats he'd made.

Instead, Lilac turned to her guard and looked him in his bewildered eyes. "My scribe, *please*. And while you're at it, please also request the company of our coachman, Giles. He's outside in the bailey."

He frowned. "The coachman? Why?"

"I won't ask a third time."

The fellow nodded without another word and left to fetch them both.

"I don't owe you or anyone else an explanation of whom I spend my time with or why I'll never marry your grandson. It is not your business, Artus, and you will not question me in my own castle."

"Ah, but what *is* my business are the goings-on in my fief. Such as the increase in Daemon activity west of Paimpont, in the region between my home and yours," he suggested, eyeing Lilac. "Two men were recently snatched up and eaten."

Artus wouldn't dare mention her and Garin's appearance at the Jaunty Hog, or her suggestion on where to hunt next; doing so would be admitting mistreatment and manhandling of the queen. She could bring it up herself and have him locked away with his grandson... But she also wasn't eager to have them in the same dungeon together, where they might figure out a way to scheme.

"Korrigans or ogres?" she suggested, withholding a triumphant smirk. Mathias and Lorenzo shifted uncomfortably, wincing with their movement, glaring sidelong at Artus. "I've heard they are both especially feral this time of year."

Artus's eyes narrowed. "Is that what your cartographer told you?"

"I'm sorry." Henri held a hand up. "What does Riou have to do with any of this? And this is your fief no longer, Artus. My father made sure of it."

Try as she might, Lilac could feel her sorry attempt at composure slipping. Realization sank in as Artus smiled up at her. That was his purpose in coming tonight. He wanted them to know of his connections to France, to remind her parents of it or inform them if they didn't already know.

This was what Sinclair's family had dangled over their heads for so long. Lilac's father was wed to her mother of Breton nobility, and didn't have the same opportunities to fortify his kingdom against such militant threats through marriage.

She was the queen; an unclaimed bride, as far as the world knew.

Artus looked down, chuckling to himself. "Henri, your daughter is in bed with Daemons, running away from her responsibilities while France is at her door, and my family is your concern? Transfers of power occur all the time. Some by marriage. Others by force."

Artus wasn't even addressing her directly, speaking of her like she was an afterthought in the room, still the young black sheep of her family to be reprimanded with a slap on the wrist—or the snatching of the crown yet to be placed upon her head.

With her arcana lingua, she was bound to be.

Her stomach growled, and Lilac eyed the platters of pastries and tarts that Hedwig had worked hard to prepare for Marguerite's early guests. It looked as though Artus had arrived in the middle of their dessert and made everyone else so uncomfortable that they left.

"If she merged our families like she was supposed to, like the whole kingdom expected her to, she might not find herself in such a predicament. My grandson is no madman; he's been *poisoned*, and you lot had the nerve to remove him from his rightful place of care under his parents' watch until a cause and remedy were found. They've hired the best physicians from Paris." Suddenly, he gripped the table and hoisted himself to his feet. "Seeing as you have no other propositions, because who else would want to—"

The doors swung open to admit first the guard, then John, looking aghast and a bit frightened in his pale blue nightgown and warm cap. Myrddin—still glamored as a confused Giles—trailed in last, shrugging into the hood of his robe and glancing hesitantly around the room.

Lilac greeted them with a solemn smile. It was time to make her intentions clear once and for all.

But first, food.

Lilac moved toward the table with the sweets. It appeared Myrddin had briefed Herlinde well on Lilac's glamor; the witch stared warningly at her while the rest of the room tracked the pair who'd just entered. But the queen ignored the witch's glare.

"Good evening, John. I'm sorry for waking you. I'm glad you and Giles could join us," Lilac said, tiptoeing her fingers along the fruit and pastries, and landing on a still warm piece of bread. "There have been some changes I'd like to announce. Please, help yourselves and have a seat." She offered a prim smile at Herlinde, Myrddin, and Piper as she took a plate of custard tarts, jam-slathered bread, and a plump apple to the chair at the head of the table.

They watched her dumbfoundedly. Myrddin nudged Herlinde.

"Your Majesty," Herlinde offered hurriedly, covering her colorful night-gown with her robe when all eyes in the room shifted onto her. "Perhaps you would want to wait until after your announcement to eat?"

"I'm ravenous. Thank you, though."

Herlinde silently stalked to the seat to Lilac's left and sat. Myrddin mumbled something about having had something to eat on the carriage ride there, then lowered himself next to Herlinde. Piper still hovered over the spread at the other end of the table, cutting off a piece of roast fowl and slathering it in jam. She piled a few pieces of rye onto her plate, then a dollop of butter, taking the serving knife with her. Smiling contentedly, Piper strode over to sit at Lilac's right, where the queen tapped her fingers upon the table.

John had shuffled awkwardly off to Lilac's side and stood at her armrest.

"Would you like something to eat, John? A cup of tea?" Lilac motioned to the iron kettle on the tea cart off to the side, but the scribe shook his head.

Watching over her spread, Hedwig was losing the battle of hiding an enormous grin. Deciding for John, she rolled the tea cart between the tables and poured him a steaming cup anyway, placing it to Piper's right.

At Lilac's second motion toward the bench, John looked tempted. He leaned in, clutching his quill box and parchment to his chest. "What about privacy, Your Majesty? Your notes?"

Across the room, Artus and his men were muttering among themselves. Lilac ignored them. "There is no need for privacy tonight. Thank you."

The scribe bowed and seated himself next to Piper, who'd already finished one piece of bread and was piling pieces of the roast and jam onto her second.

Lilac directed her first statement at the scribe, who was ready with his dipped nib over the parchment. "Saturday, on the 21st of May, I will be married."

Artus steadied himself on the back of the chair while her parents exchanged glances.

"*This* Saturday?" Marguerite said, kicking Henri under the table. "But that's the day of your crowning."

"It will precede my coronation. The wedding and coronation ceremony will be one in the same. My ball will follow in the early evening as previously scheduled."

Henri coughed into his fist when Marguerite's alarmed gaze darted to Artus. Her mother laughed. "Married, to..." She trailed off, observing the former duke who had risen from his seat looking as if Christ himself had come to him. "On second thought, we'll need time to prepare. It might be too late to amend the invitations, after all, and you never know who else might be interested in your lovely hand."

Lilac hummed. "Funny. Was it not you who suggested it before I departed for Paimpont last week?"

The muscle under Marguerite's eye twitched. "That was before you decided to extend your trip, dear. And I'd meant *announcing* a betrothal at that time might be useful." Marguerite, once assuming Lilac's willingness to marry Sinclair, ironically balked at the concept now that she still thought it was Albrecht interested in proposing to her. "And what of the decorations? The performers? Not to mention the feast. Hedwig will *kill* you."

"On the contrary, I am happy to provide as requested," Hedwig interjected. "Anything for Her Majesty."

Lilac's heart swelled. She wasn't used to this kind of outward support. "There's no need for decorations beyond what we'll already have. This will be a smaller wedding; it will have to do for now."

"For now?" said Marguerite.

"Yes, until a large celebration can be organized in the future." Her mother drew in a sharp breath, finally picking up on her hint. "For now, the coronation ball will serve as my reception. There will be the feast table we can always extend, and the musicians we've already arranged are highly talented, I'm sure. You hand picked them, didn't you, Mother?"

Henri met her gaze from over Marguerite's shoulder, but Lilac looked down, suddenly shaking, willing herself to ignore the abrupt tug at the base of her throat where she felt the slight pressure of Garin's mouth. The burn of his teeth. Did this sensation signal his approval?

This was what he'd wanted, wasn't it?

Even with her announcement and the ache in her chest behind it, the longing to go to him was there... but it was *distant* this time. It didn't feel any less significant, but there was no burning need to act upon it, no dreading the consequence if she didn't. Maybe it was because she knew Garin was safe and in good hands. Maybe it was because he was still unconscious somewhere deep in the bowels of The Fenfoss Inn. Maybe his magic, through the completed bond, had somehow eased up.

Maybe it would return tenfold.

They were connected, and in that horrid knowing, there was a strange relief. But this lack of symptom did not excuse anything that had happened, the way he'd exercised his power, tugging her around like some marionette of his affections.

Her parents had been expecting her to run away from her duty. So did Garin, apparently. Enthralling her to leave and consider her propositions was bad enough; he'd had Myrddin tamper with her memory too, stripping her of yet another choice—*another* freedom—knowing that it was what she'd chased in the first place. A cure for her Daemon tongue before she understood it, yes. But she'd yearned for freedom, the ability to make her own decisions all the same, and thrusting herself into Brocéliande had given that to her. It was the very reason they'd met.

Lilac would guard her kingdom—mortal and Daemon—despite their thrall bond, and despite France. That was something no one would ever take from her.

She picked her apple off the plate.

"This weekend?" Artus was saying. "That's only four days away. Sinclair will need to see a physician—several. What was his state when he was arrested? The last I heard, the doctors my son had hired were useless in—" He trailed off. No one was paying attention to him.

Every pair of eyes had drifted onto Lilac. Even her own guards were busy watching her.

Lilac was examining the apple, turning it this way and that in the fire-glow. She ignored the narrow-eyed glare from Myrddin, Piper's hesitant stare and the way Herlinde held her breath.

"Did you hear me? My grandson will need time to prepare."

Lilac sank her teeth into the fruit, shrugging out of reach of Myrddin, who had lunged forward, nearly toppling Herlinde from her seat. There was a brief rush of warmth that puffed around her, a climbing and falling heat, just as there was when the *Guài* arrow had nicked her hand.

Let them see me as I am.

The apple was even sweeter as she chewed, some of the blood having rubbed off from her fingers. Nearly everyone at the other table had risen to their feet at the sight of Lilac's unglamored rose and cream kirtle, sweat, soot, and blood coating the material and her skin. She was duly impressed by the illusion's ability to cover the awful stench that now wafted up from her revealed form.

Henri backed away, stumbling over the bottom step behind him. Marguerite followed, almost tripping over her husband's feet. "Halt," he commanded several of the guards who had started backing away.

"*Lilac*," said Marguerite, tears dragging through the powder on her cheeks. "Are you—"

"Am I what?" She dared her mother to ask the question. "Am I *what*, Mother?"

But Marguerite only reached a trembling hand out to point. "You're bleeding just a tad."

At the back of the room, Artus's men had retreated toward the double doors. Only the old man remained seated, his widened, surprised eyes quickly narrowing into consideration, as if seeing her covered in blood was all the confirmation he'd needed to believe the worst of her.

Like she gave a fuck.

"Secure both doors," she ordered. Without question, her guards shifted to the entrances.

There was a whimper at her side, softening Lilac's hardened gaze. It was Piper. Her eyes were fixated on Lilac's throat. On the drying red upon her sleeve cap and down her front.

"I will be married on the day of my coronation," Lilac repeated to the room, hoping this news would be enough to keep Piper distracted. "*Not* to Sinclair. I will wed Maximilian I of the Holy Roman Empire. Here, in our church."

"*Oh*. Oh, that *is* wonderful news." Marguerite placed a hand on her chest, looking more relieved than shocked. Then, she fainted.

Henri caught his wife before her head hit the steps. Several stifled gasps and murmurs rippled among the guards.

Artus's face had turned purple, but he began to laugh. His men echoed him, chortling nervously.

Henri looked down at Marguerite, as if Lilac's presumed mistake would be enough to wake her. "I think you mean Maximilian's *count*. The letter and request to meet were from him. There is hope, but we cannot be so bold as to assume that this is why he wanted to meet."

"It is no assumption. I heard it myself." She paused as the room took in her lie. "I stopped in a tavern tonight for some food and drink, and over-heard the barmaids whispering of a recent guest who'd been loose-tongued regarding his business in the area once the ale started flowing. He spoke Latin, was well-dressed, and said the emperor had sent him on his behalf to proposition the queen."

The murmurs died down. Everyone stared. Her father steadied himself upon the nearest step.

"This Albrecht arriving tomorrow is Maximilian's *emissary*."

The nervous laughter among Artus and his men cut off abruptly.

"That is—" Henri struggled to find the words, his face growing red despite his skeptical grimace. He groaned, wiping the sweat off his lip. "Is Maximilian traveling as we speak? The trip from Vienna takes weeks."

"No. He offers me a proxy wedding and sent Albrecht to claim me. I overheard this when passing them in the halls," she reassured her father. He looked like he might collapse. "There was no one else around."

Artus's fury melted into hopelessness as his men side eyed him, probably anticipating an outburst.

Defeated, her father exhaled and motioned to her. "Are you hurt, Lilac? Are you bleeding?"

"No. Most of it isn't even my blood."

Henri fell silent then. Piper's gaze was fixed on the table, but Lilac could've sworn there was a glint of mistrust behind it.

She should've stopped there, but the shock on Artus's face was too good to pass up. "I will also be working on making amendments to your law regarding Daemons, Father. I'll be releasing my own decree." She looked to John, who continued writing all this down. "Perhaps we can discuss this over tea tomorrow?"

"Indeed," said John, without looking up.

Henri shifted, allowing his wife's head to rest more comfortably on his broad thigh. He twisted this way and that, his hands brushing his belt. Not finding his flask, he swore under his breath and finally spoke. "Tomorrow morning, there will be many things happening at once. You'll have your meeting with the emissary—after you've had a bath," he added roughly. "I am also awaiting another briefing regarding the bordering towns."

"The meeting with Albrecht shouldn't be long. Just a document to sign —I assume," Lilac added. Her voice was thick with building grief, but she kept a tight, hopeful smile. "These amendments will be effective immediately."

Wood scraped against stone. Artus was standing. As he started toward her table, one of her guards swiftly blocked him with his blade. "My son will never agree to any of that. He'll demand an audience!"

"He had one last week," Lilac said.

The former duke's face fell. As she'd hoped, word of Armand's demise hadn't reached him. He straightened, retaining his composure through sheer force of will. "What was the audience for? Sinclair's appeal?"

"Sinclair is not granted an appeal at this time, Artus," Henri said. "Your grandson is guilty of assault on my daughter on multiple occasions."

Artus gave a skeptical laugh, but Lilac turned to him, stone-faced. "Armand came last Sunday during my Court of Common Appeals. He claimed he found Vivien murdered in their kitchen and Sinclair holding a wood ax. He then proceeded to blame me for her death before spilling his own guts all over this very floor. That, if you were wondering, is the reason Sinclair was moved from his home to my dungeons. Once this is all over I intend to appoint my own council, with whom I will convene to decide his fate."

Artus slumped, his knees hitting the ground. "Armand is dead?"

"Yes," she said, as Henri passed a slow hand over his face.

"We'll aid in funeral proceedings," Henri offered, "if you seek a Christian burial, but it will have to be held at the Paimpont abbey, given your family's standing."

"And what about a magistrate?" Artus asked. "For a property exchange?"

"You don't have access to the Le Tallec estate, with or without Armand," Lilac said, eager to end their impromptu meeting as quickly as Artus was to swing the subject of his son's demise. "Neither does Sinclair, given his criminal status. You may not be aware, but your family's standing with mine is now *very* public, so don't get any ideas. There will be no transfer of noble property or funding to you."

Artus said nothing.

"John will be sending a notice regarding their burials," continued Lilac. "Where should he send it?"

"You know where."

"How would I know?" She waited for his answer, daring him to reveal he'd had his men put their filthy fingers on her. "All I know is that you've been banished from both my castle and the Le Tallec estate. Where are you residing?"

"The Jaunty Hog. Send it to the Jaunty Hog," Artus answered through his teeth.

"Ah, yes. I believe my father is familiar with the owner."

This was followed by a short grunt from Henri. Artus remained on the floor, saying no more.

She realized how starving and lightheaded she finally felt; it was impossible to tell how much blood Garin had taken from her. It was impressive that she herself had not collapsed.

Lilac took another bite of her apple and followed it with her fig jam spread over the piece of toast. It was delicious. This was much needed—the warm food, but also everything else. The moral support from those around her. The validation of her wariness of the Le Tallecs now come to light, now rightly justified. The unsettling strength now coiled in her limbs due to Garin's Sanguine magic, and the conviction that drove her tonight.

She did not expect being granted the things her soul had yearned for to be equally as taxing.

By the end of the weekend, she'd be married to one of the most powerful leaders on her continent. The emperor, not his emissary. Her name would be his. Her title, too.

It was what Garin had pushed for. It certainly was a far better option than the one Artus Le Tallec had tried to corner her into.

But she'd be married to one, and enthralled to another. Two things she did not want for herself. Two paths that ensured her freedoms were not truly hers. One that pleased Garin so greatly he'd betrayed her to ensure it —and the other that had infernally tied them together. It infuriated him. He'd made that very clear.

Either way, this was how she would protect her kingdom. This was the cost. An end to justify the means.

Numbly, Lilac accepted the second plate that someone placed in front of her; she saw a swish of Hedwig's robes in her periphery, Herlinde's hand pushing the fowl and maple carrot covered plate to her with another cup of tea. She felt like she needed to lie down but couldn't imagine being able to shut her eyes. Lilac stared unseeingly at her plate as she ate, her breathing slowing.

She attempted to push Garin from her mind, the worry of him at the inn, and instead thought of the hungry Daemons and Lorietta's small garden. The way they made do with too little stretched too far, in both sustenance and protections. Lorietta was one person, part of one arcane family skilled at Alteration and setting wards; the vampires, shifters, and korikaned were still hunted despite her help. They shouldn't have to hide of live under the pretense of glamors.

Lilac thought of riding the winding path to The Fenfoss Inn, the aromas of the kitchen where she'd nicked her finger. She could hear Garin's low, heat-rousing chuckle, the aroma of a dusk-fallen bluebell wood as he'd bandaged her hand and told her about her scars. That not all of them needed healing or hiding.

Remembering the way she'd hazily discovered her healed knuckles just before their argument at the inn, Lilac glanced down at her left hand. Then, she checked her right, just to be sure. *Gone.* The scars on her hands were gone.

Heart thudding distantly, she walked her fingers back on her thigh, gathering the material until the hem bunched into her hands and ignoring the abashed comments made by Henri. Her legs were mostly clean, save a thin layer of soot...and void of scars. *All* of them. The ones left by her fight with Sinclair, even the ones she'd sustained in her childhood—the little divot in her left knee from learning how to climb up—and tumble down— the stairs. The deep scrape she'd gotten climbing one of the fences in the bailey.

The scars we choose to wear are what make us human, Garin had said.

She swayed, suddenly dizzy, falling back to rest against her chair.

"Eat," the witch urged, nudging the plate closer and grasping both of her smooth hands. Even her mannerisms were like Lorietta's. "You'll be sick if you don't, making even more of a mess on yourself."

Lilac chewed, each swallow blurring her vision a bit more as moisture flooded her eyes. There was some conversation, low and firm, but she couldn't focus on any of it. She was mildly aware of Myrddin, briefly stirring her new steaming cup of tea from Hedwig with his fingertip after the first one had grown cold before offering it to her. Lilac accepted it gratefully and put it to her lips, the heat bearable as she washed the last of her meal down.

It wasn't until a door slammed shut that she looked up, refocusing on the room.

Herlinde sat to her left, knitting what looked to be a starting piece of clothing or blanket, the ivy-green yarn trailing from what seemed to be the inside of a pocket on her fuzzy robe. Hedwig was busy at the end of the table, nearly finished with stacking the dishes onto her cart. Myrddin sat next to Herlinde, watching the fire and fiddling with his thumbs, seeming lost in his thoughts. So did Henri, who sat in Marguerite's chair he'd righted, pivoted toward the door.

Her mother was gone. As were Artus, his men, and his guards.

Piper was nowhere to be found.

"Where is everyone? Where is Phoebe? Artus?"

"I had your mother taken to bed." Deep shadows danced under Henri's eyes as he turned from the fire. "I ordered the guards to lead Artus and his men out, but he'll tread carefully from now on. Your Phoebe left to prepare your room."

She set down the last bite of bread she'd been holding, regretting her exhaustion. It was shock and survival that had pushed her to this point. "You let him *go?*"

"There was no punishable offense."

"He leads Daemon hunts. Specifically against vampires and korrigans."

"There has never been any proof of that."

"He just admitted it. No human has ever bothered reporting it, and you've never bothered supervising your funds that go to Bog."

He looked up, as if surprised she remembered the tavern owner's name. Henri stood.

Lilac mirrored his movement, her chair knocking against the bottom step as she pushed it back.

"Come now," Myrddin said, tapping her gently on the arm. The warlock had stood, now waiting patiently to her left as Herlinde knitted away.

But Lilac ignored him. Her voice was barely a whisper as she said, "Why are you and Mother more afraid of me than those like Artus, who actively hunt innocent people?"

"They are not *people*, Lilac. They organized bloodshed upon our town not even a century ago." He glanced at her sidelong, his face etched in disappointment.

She was used to the look. She didn't let it stop the scorn with which she regarded him. She glanced down at the scribe's now-empty chair. "As of tomorrow morning, assault, harassment, or murder of Daemons will be equivalent to that of those crimes afflicted upon a human person."

"They are animals," Henri suddenly shouted, causing Myrddin to jump and Herlinde to look up from her knitting. "*Daemons*. Exactly as they are called. Unholy when they killed those families in Paimpont and unholy when they steal bread from the castle larders, and you bring public disgrace to your family by associating yourself with them without refrain."

He snapped his head at the remaining guards at the doors and motioned for them to leave. They did so without question. By the time they swung shut again, she was marching up to Henri to stand toe to toe with him.

"When have I ever been a beacon of religion? A beacon of anything to this kingdom?"

"Since your birth," he snapped. "Certainly not of religion, but of your own code of morals, if it can be called such. You spew gluttony and indecency. You run around careless, and without covering your tracks. Do you think I didn't know you were at Bog's tavern instead of with the seamstress? Is that why you had to go a second time tonight?"

Lilac said nothing, glaring at Henri as he looked over her shoulder at Herlinde, then Myrddin.

"I have held my tongue long enough. If it were I on the throne instead of you, I would have the both of them interrogated under oath. It is a wonder Artus did not bring it up when he very well could have."

"Well, you are not. You insisted on passing the position down before I was ready. Before discovering if I'd ever be ready."

"I made the decision unaware of your alarming stances," said Henri unflinchingly.

Habit took over. She wanted out. A fight with her stubborn father had never ended well, never resolved in mutual understanding, but he usually moved on with muttering into his alcohol by now. She moved to sidestep him for the door, but Henri wrapped his hand around her bicep.

"I don't understand this change of heart, Father. You've been protecting them. You must continue to," she urged him, biting back the fury at his grip on her. "Please. They've done so for me, time and time again."

"No, I've been protecting *you*. Tell me, Lilac, what father enjoys seeing his daughter questioned? Doubted in such a way?" He brought his face close. "I do not. But when you do it to yourself, there is nothing more I can say in your defense." He gestured helplessly at her ruined dress, her bloodied skin. "Look at you."

She did not cower. She wasn't afraid of him. Little did he know, all the questioning and doubting, both within and from those around her, tired her, too. But instead of challenging those doubters, instead of helping change society's understanding of Daemons or at least starting with his own perception of them, he expected her to change.

And change she would, but in none of the ways he wanted.

"Yes, *look* at me," Lilac said, voice full of conviction. "I am done hiding."

Henri held her simmering gaze. "Is this why you're letting your vices come to light? With the nerve to enter this castle clothed in such filth? I-in magic and blood?"

"Why not? Everyone knows of yours," she spat in a seething whisper. "*You've* resided under this hallowed roof for years, an adulterer—" Her father scoffed but she pressed on. "A gambler. A murderer. Look at your drinking habits, your ill-supervised funds and the unjust causes they go to. Your whores. Are there any illegitimate siblings I don't know of? If so, please take care to send them my way. Maybe then I wouldn't feel so alone." Henri flinched, deflecting his watering gaze toward the double doors. "You and I are torn from the same cloth, Father. Filth teaches filth."

Ripping herself from him was effortless. Henri stepped back, looking at his own hand, marveling at her arm. *Her strength.*

She'd have to be more careful.

"If it is of any comfort to you, I don't feel I am qualified to lead anyone. But I will protect those I love and care for, and even those who might not deserve it, with or without a crown on my head—at the head of a throne room, charging into battle, or at the gallows."

"You will focus on your own affairs. *Our* own affairs," he breathed, staring at Herlinde. "You will leave your newfound acquaintances alone until your coronation is finished."

"She is my seamstress," Lilac said. "She is sewing my ball gown."

"It will now be her wedding gown." Herlinde spoke without looking up from her project.

"There will *be* no wedding if the emperor, or anyone else considering you, changes their mind. Understand that a nobleman representing an emperor in his travels, especially in the context of a proxy marriage, has the power to suggest otherwise to his leader. If Albrecht finds you unstable, unsuitable, then he may choose to communicate so to Maximilian and return before the ceremony."

"Then let him," she said, teeth bared. "I left this castle in the first place to ask the magic folk to fix me. They couldn't do it, so do not think I haven't tried to magically morph into the woman that meets your and Mother's expectations." Her father's throat bobbed at the unexpected confession. "But in my quest, I was defended and accepted by those whom you would never expect. I will stand up for them either way. They are considered abominations that walk amongst us only because we refuse to see them as kin. They are Brittany just as much as they are Brocéliande. I *will* protect them, even if it means standing up to France on my own. Even if it means standing up to Artus. To you."

The room was quiet as Henri bowed his head in defeat. Lilac looked to Herlinde and Myrddin, who'd too eagerly stood from the table. She nodded, dabbed her mouth on her napkin, and proceeded toward the door.

Before she could lead them out, her father spoke again. "Where did you find her, Lilac?" he said quietly.

Reluctantly, she slowed. "Who?"

"Piper."

Lilac swallowed. "Her name is Phoebe. You shall call her Phoebe Allard. And it was she who found me." Lilac fixed her expression before turning to him again. She smiled despite her father's look of alarm. "Why? Is there something wrong?"

He was shaking his head. "It's been a long week. I might pay Madame Kemble a visit."

"You should do that, Father. You look pale. As if you'd seen a ghost."

He lowered himself onto the stairs behind him as she beckoned the witch and warlock out. A final glance before the doors shut behind them showed Henri with his head in his hands.

21

Herlinde and Myrddin refused Lilac's offer to accompany her upstairs, quietly citing the limits of the illusion outside that was her horse and carriage. The real carriage and Giles were still at The Fenfoss Inn, and Myrddin informed her before they strode into earshot of the foyer guards that her coachman would dutifully return by the next morning, fed and bathed.

Herlinde promised she'd return with her assistant later in the week with her gown—impressively, even for an enchantress clothier, no measurements needed.

This quelled Lilac's quiet concern over her ball-turned-wedding dress, but by now that was a distant worry compared to everything else that piled upon it. France. Meeting the emissary and hearing Maximilian's offer. Garin, and what they'd done at the brothel. Kestrel's deal, and their Accords.

The *Guài* chest at the inn, yet to be delivered to Cinderfell.

Silently she watched, suddenly feeling very alone as the guards opened the gate. Myrddin climbed into the driver's box, Herlinde carrying her kitting project into the carriage, and they rolled forward, past the bailey gate and onto the path until they were swallowed by the treeline.

He'd disband the illusion and teleport them once out of eyesight.

There were many burning questions she'd wished to ask them—how had Herlinde known so much, and how was she related to Lorietta? The tavern owner had never mentioned other family in the area. What was the plan for Garin when Myrddin returned to the inn tonight?

But there were guards flanking the door, and so the witch and warlock had only answered Lilac's curious gaze with a parting smile before leaving.

Upstairs, she found her chamber door ajar, tub filled and steaming, the doors to her balcony propped open to a pleasant night—or early morning—with one of her book stacks.

Yanna and Isabel were still nowhere to be found, and must have retired to bed—she hoped. Lilac hesitated in the doorway, glimpsing her lady-in-waiting pacing the length of the room, with half the mind to check the shared second-floor handmaidens' quarters next to the library.

"Well?" Piper demanded, pacing away. "Where is he?"

Lilac stepped into the room and watched Piper stomp past her. She shut and locked the door.

The vampire, besides her healthy glow of pink and full cheeks that no longer showed her bones since the last time Lilac had seen her, didn't look like a vampire much at all. Now that she could focus past dolling out lie after lie, Lilac noticed the olive shift Piper wore was familiar. As the vampire paced between the vanity and the balcony doors, growling profanities under her breath, she also noticed a pair of her own shoes upon her feet.

"Thanks for drawing my bath." Careful to stay out of her way, Lilac made her way to the tub, watching Piper's nostrils flare.

"Where is that coward?"

"It's nice to see you, too."

Piper slowed her pacing, much like Garin did when he was upset. Maybe it was something to do with a vampire-type of restlessness.

Lilac wasted no time undoing the lace at her front; she would have waited for Piper to settle down, but couldn't stand the feeling of crusted blood on her skin and soaked through her clothes another minute.

"Did *he* do that to you?" Piper asked quietly. She was facing the vanity, surveying Lilac's reflection in the mirror.

"He did," Lilac replied hoarsely. She added, "but I did it back to him," when Piper's eyes flicked dangerously up to her.

"Good." Once Lilac had loosened her corset and clutched the dress to her body, Piper faced her again. "We must scrub that stench off of you."

"I know." Lilac grimaced. "Sorry. If I smell like corpses, it's because I was in a room of them."

"Corpses? All I smell is—is *Garin*." Piper tossed an arm her way, nose wrinkling. "You—"

"Reek of him?" Lilac lifted her arm and inhaled, gagging on the aroma of her own sweat, blood, and flesh. "I think Garin smells like bluebells and a crackling hearth. Trust me, there is none of that here."

Piper's laugh was sharp. "Just before he killed me, he stunk of pond water and death."

They'd been sloshing in the Argent River with the Morgen before reaching the Sanguine Mine, where Bastion had egged Garin on enough to make him snap Piper's neck in a decision of pity. He'd slipped Piper some of his blood off his thumb just before—and that, according to Garin, was what had facilitated her transformation.

"And do I smell of pond water and death to you now?" Lilac asked.

The vampire made a face, contemplating, nostrils flaring. She opened her mouth and inhaled, as if tasting the air.

"Stop that," she said, unsettled.

"It is no single aroma," Piper replied decidedly. "His blood and yours—as you are no doubt covered in it—but there is something more. An aura. His. The scent is pure possession, and I know—I just do—that it is him." Her voice shook, tapering off at the last of her words. She gazed at the fire, reluctance and hatred burning through the moisture in her eyes. "He is my... my—"

"Garin is your sire," Lilac offered softly.

"Yes. That. And in that way, I will always be connected to him. In my worst moments, when I was lost and afraid to go to the town, I thought of finding him. Not for council or his help, but because I knew I'd likely find you there. I refrained, afraid I'd meet his unruly brother if I didn't stay hidden. My urge to seek you has been far greater, so I came here."

Lilac absorbed Piper's fury and was met with deep guilt; Piper had been a vampire for less than a month, but she'd been wandering the wilderness with no one to guide her. It must've felt like forever. She'd confirmed what Casmir had said, and if he could tell Lilac was somehow tied to Garin before she'd entered that room, Piper could definitely sense it now. She couldn't have known what a thrall was.

"Well, Your Majesty?" Piper was sliding both sides of the curtains further open, poking her head outside the balcony doors and inhaling into the night. "If you've nothing to say and if he's not here, then where is Garin?"

Lilac slipped down her loosened corset and kirtle, wincing as she peeled off the parts where the material clung to her skin. "He's at a Daemon tavern in Brocéliande, less than an hour east. That's where he lives."

"A tavern? He hasn't moved into that underground prison he's now in charge of?"

"No." Lilac stuck a toe into the tub, testing the water before stepping all the way in. "He may oversee the coven at the Sanguine Mine, but he's still residing and working at the tavern. The Fenfoss Inn. Witch-owned," she added, at Piper's glare.

"Fine. Not that it matters." The vampire strode to the middle of the room, cradling her face with her hands and gazing at the floor.

"Piper," Lilac said, suddenly grateful for the water she'd splashed on her face as she used a small cloth to scrub the blood off. The tub water quickly turned the color of rust, smelling strongly of iron, and her stomach churned. She forced herself to look up. "Why don't you remove your shoes?"

"They're yours." Piper's face was instantly tearful. "I've stolen them."

"You haven't. They're yours," Lilac said sternly, blinking back the moisture in her eyes. "Do remove them, though, and make yourself at home. You make me anxious with your pacing. Take them off, and stay a while. Unless you plan on escaping into Brocéliande anytime soon."

Piper made a noise of contempt. "I prefer to be anywhere Garin is not. With you, I'm not sure that can be helped, though."

Lilac chose her words carefully. Honestly. "It cannot. But he's far away from us tonight. Either way, you will speak, think, act candidly. You are under my protection."

"Whether he's at the Sanguine Mine or not, I'm not going back." Piper slid one shoe off, then the other, and pressed her heels into the edge of the fox fur rug beneath her.

"You won't. I promise."

Piper's eyes narrowed at her consolation. "How do I know that when you've been with him?" Lilac's chest constricted as her friend's mouth opened, framing two long fangs on her upper row of teeth. Everything she must've been holding back at the Grand Hall flowed out. "How could you? How could you leave me behind? Leave *with* him? *Be* with someone like him, and h-his brother, who had imprisoned all of us for years?"

"They had no choice. Feeding ethically was even a risk that would get them hunted. And Garin was trying to help you." Lilac looked down, her face on fire as she gripped the tub. The words had slipped out without thought.

Piper angled her chin at Lilac, her gaze glassy.

What was wrong with her? How easily this strange protectiveness had crept up on Lilac, as if it were her second nature to jump to not only Garin's defense, but his entire coven—even when Lilac in fact *agreed* with Piper's fury.

Lilac pried her fingers off the lip of the tub. Chips of wood plinked to the floor and into the water, not unlike the night in the Trevelyan farmhouse, when Garin had gripped the back of the chair and demolished it. She hadn't exactly pulverized the rim but small pieces still came away, the wood planks cracked down to the center.

"Help me?" Piper's forehead creased as she surveyed the damage and Lilac's trembling hands, which she sank beneath the water in shame. "Is that what he did to you too?" Piper strode to the tub as Lilac shook her head—and gripped her face. The pressure of her fingers forced Lilac's mouth open.

"Ow, unhand me," Lilac snapped, but she stilled as Piper examined her blunt canines.

Piper's nostrils flared as she searched her face. She smeared a hand over Lilac's cheek, then stuck a finger into her mouth and scrubbed at her teeth vigorously before Lilac swatted her hand and jerked away, tearing herself from the vampire's grip.

"I am not a vampire," Lilac snarled.

Reeling, Piper cradled her hand to her chest and said nothing, retreating to the middle of the room again. "Then why do you look as if you've spent the week laying in the sand? Like you've been eating cherries

—" Piper looked down at the crumbs of wood before the tub. "What *are* you?"

"Peeved," Lilac answered. "Tired. Just as confused and unsure about everything as you are." She gave a despondent laugh. "What I do know, at the very least, is that you are undeserving of everything that has befallen you. That I have wronged you."

Piper's lower lip quivered. Her head swiveled to the keep door, then to the balcony as she wrung her hands. Looking for another way out.

Lilac would not lose her again. The several children born to the staff had remained under the strict instruction of Hedwig, starting with mild tasks in the scullery or bailey. Piper had been introduced as her hand-maiden, almost as if Henri and Marguerite had brought her in as a preemp-tive Lady-in-Waiting. Almost as if they'd anticipated the concern the kingdom would hold regarding her gender alone, and thought she could benefit from the company.

Where foreign princesses often had a fleet of handmaidens in rotation, there had only ever been Piper, and she'd only ever served Lilac. "My family took you in. They raised you as a child servant and failed at protecting you from the system that is a result of the very prejudice we upheld. They failed you. *I* failed you. I will make it up to you, and you will live here again as my Lady-in-Waiting."

The vampire stopped fidgeting, no longer looking like she was at risk of hurling herself off the balcony. "It cannot be, Your Majesty. I am no noble. No daughter of a Viscount or Lady. I am the mere daughter of farmers."

"It does not matter. As you've seen in accordance with my kingdom, titles mean very little here. I want you in my court." The thought of a second chance, for her and for Piper, filled Lilac with hope despite the night's chaos. "As long as you want to be."

Piper scowled, doubtful. "That is too gracious an offer, Your Majesty."

"*Lilac*. Outside court, please call me Lilac."

Piper chewed on her lip, and Lilac's heart swelled. "I'd rather burn in the sun than go back, but I am still at a loss. If anything, my presence will only complicate things for me. And for you."

"It will not change anything, Piper. It will not erase the horrors you have endured. It will not give you your old life back and it won't cure you of the

BRIAR SOMERSET

hunger and power you wield now. It won't make up for the time lost in our friendship. But I want you here. Need you. We might both be connected to Garin in ways that are too difficult to fathom, but I cannot bear the thought of losing you again. Although I do not deserve you." Piper sneered and wiped her face, turning to the wall as Lilac slid up to the edge of the tub, sloshing water through the cracks her angry hands had left. She meant every word. In fact, Lilac had never been more sincere. "It is your choice. But if you stay, you are to accompany me on trips. To soirées and balls. You will have your own wardrobe, and access to books and any lessons you so choose. To an education. You'll be my Lady-in-Waiting. Handpicked by myself. I will have it no other way."

When Piper whipped her head back around, her eyes had narrowed into slits. "You think you can demand my loyalty, my service to you, just because I would want for it, had you not?"

"Then where will you go?" Lilac countered selfishly. "The woods? To Rennes? Your parents' farm?"

In answer, Piper only slid the vanity chair out and curled up on it as Lilac moved on to massaging the soot from her hair, working the soap through to her scalp and down the smooth sides of her neck.

What else was she to expect? Of course Piper was upset and afraid. Lilac swallowed her grief and frustration. "There are several properties throughout Brittany where the noble families reside. Some in towns, others outlying cities. Some in the countryside—luxurious cottages and manors. I could send a letter to one of the families of lower nobility informing them of a new, direct heiress that had fallen in her favor. You could be a distant cousin, or niece. I could have you inherit one of them. There would be plenty of room to keep you safe."

It would cause a small uproar, but everyone already despised Lilac enough for other reasons. Her heart fluttered at the striking realization that one more would not do her harm.

Rinsing the now discolored soap from her hair, Lilac thought of the Brocéliande vampire coven, of Garin and the others. *A manor...*

A manor would do them well, wouldn't it? One with many rooms and thick curtains. If she truly needed to, she could search for one with no assumed heir. Surely there existed one that was already vacant or was soon to be.

"And what would I do there, exactly?" the vampire mumbled into her arm. "Frighten everyone away? Become the town terror?"

"That doesn't sound so bad, does it?" Lilac said, poorly withholding her smile. "Lurking in the windows once the sun's gone down. Emerging on foggy mornings, remaining naught but a shadow in the haze and pouncing on unsuspecting men."

Piper burst into a fit of giggles before she shook her head, her scowl tightening. She removed the ribbons that held her braids and snaked her fingers through several loose knots, finally pulling her hair around her. "I would help you dress, Your Majesty, but I cannot. Your bath has only made the odor stronger. It smells like he's in this very room."

Lilac lifted herself from the tub and toweled herself off, went to the drawers of her armoire, and pulled out two of her most comfortable night-gowns. She balled one in her hands and tossed it at Piper.

Piper only looked at the fine garment and frowned. "I said I'm not dressing you."

"You are entitled to my closet before you are provided your own wardrobe. I'll ask Herlinde to fit you," Lilac replied, perching on the side of her bed to slip hers on. "You are not to dress me. For the things I prefer to wear, I can dress myself. Plus, Yanna and Isabel—" She paused, looking around the room. "Where are they?"

"The two women waiting outside your door like dogs? They wouldn't leave me alone once they discovered me, so I asked them to leave and not say anything. At that point they were on the verge of hysterics so I had no choice—"

"No choice to what?"

"I grabbed them then *suggested* they should go to bed—after I begged them not to call for the guards, that is. It took a couple tries, but they finally heard me." Piper sniffled again. "If I'd known all I needed to do was convince them to go to their bedchamber, I would have done that in the first place. I was afraid I'd have to strangle them unconscious."

Lilac felt for the edge of the mattress and plopped onto it. Piper had *entranced* them to bed. "At least you didn't eat them," she offered, swallowing the sudden urge to laugh. How could she possibly find humor in anything tonight after her drive to survive Garin's madness had changed everything?

Yet, so did her friend's arrival. She was just happy Piper was back.

The vampire's bottom lip quivered. She snickered, composed herself with an alarming swiftness and said nothing more, hugging the tops of her knees, hiding behind a cascade of thick copper hair.

Relief cast over Lilac, mingling with her fading adrenaline. She needed rest. To shut her eyes and drown the world out, to find sleep before Garin's insidious influence gripped her subconscious and body once more. She braced for the crushing paranoia that had come nightly since he'd banished her—but as she slid back the covers and yanked them over herself, she only felt her aching joints sigh into the mattress.

She yanked her feet from the edge, as if he were the monster waiting to drag her into the abyss, and cocooned her body in the duvet. She savored the warmth after the night had drawn much of it from her veins.

Piper had not moved, gazing into the mirror. There were many burning questions that would wait for another day. For now, Lilac didn't care if they were ever answered. She only hoped Piper would make the right decision, the safest for herself. She might be stronger, faster now, but she too had spent years locked away, even more alienated than Lilac had been.

Lilac had had the luxury of her tower. The help of her household staff and guards, her parents and their court. A means of warmth. Nourishing food and clean water. Piper had none of that, and no one.

"I'm going to have the private quarters on the second floor prepared for you tomorrow. The room shares a wall with the handmaiden's bedchambers, but it should be fairly quiet since only Isabel and Yanna sleep there." At the end of the hall, next to the library and past the infirmary, the room was often forgotten. It was fully furnished, the fineries in it protected by thick linens and reserved for the monarch's lady-in-waiting or valet. "Until then, you are not spending the night in that chair." Lilac turned to face the tub. "If you can stand the stench."

She let her gaze drift to the circular patterns on her ceiling, which wove beveled petals through vines and leaves, shadows shifting in the firelight as the chair scraped against wood. There was a reluctant grunt and shifting of fabrics as Piper changed out of her shift and into the garment Lilac had thrown at her.

Behind her, the bed sank, and Lilac rolled onto her back to see Piper propped against the pillows, arms crossed, gazing out at the clear sky through the ajar balcony doors.

"This position will require me to do many things during the day, and I won't be able to fulfill your requests as I used to."

"I'll only need your company in the evenings. You are free to do as you wish in the day. As for travel, I prefer to do so at night."

"Surely that cannot be." Piper gave a doubtful scoff. "Everyone will suspect me sooner or later."

"My staff would learn to accommodate you, just as you've done for me all those years. Plus, some continue to believe I've involved myself with vampires, anyway. There was a witch in our Grand Hall just an hour ago, and two more from Garin's tavern who had accompanied me here earlier in the week."

How easy it was for her to make these promises and mean them especially when it involved protecting Piper. The public would learn of her involvement with Brocéliande soon enough. It wouldn't take long, not with the changes that would come with the Accords and the steps toward justice she intended to take for Brocéliande.

Her mind drifted to Garin and Bastion. Myrddin, who should be arriving at the inn any time now after teleporting Herlinde back home. Adelaide and her new alliance with Lorietta, and what horrors Albrecht might be waking up to as they nursed him back to health for tomorrow. Unless he was accustomed to dealing with the Daemons in his own country, they surely had to entrance him; Adelaide might have a mind-altering tonic to put in Lorietta's soup. They'd at least asked Myrddin remove the memory of Lilac stabbing him.

She thought of Garin, and what he might've woken up to. Whom he tried to strangle. He hadn't marched up to her gate yet, to her knowledge.

As a vampire's thrall separated from her regnant, Lilac thought she might feel lonely, even distressed returning to her tower. But the worry she'd felt when Myrddin had teleported them outside her gates had been smothered by the shock of Piper, then Artus's unwelcome presence. The despair she feared and braced herself for—the knotting in her throat and ache in her abdomen—hadn't yet made itself known.

The room was too silent. Perhaps Piper was already asleep. "I went home," she said, just as Lilac thought she might close her eyes.

BRIAR SOMERSET

They popped open again. "To your parents' farm?"

"Yes," Piper answered dully. "For the first time since I've worked for you, yes."

The day Piper and her parents had arrived in their foyer, Lilac was no older than six. She'd been told the the week prior that a great surprise was on its way. She'd been expecting a horse, or at least a pony, even if her parents had insisted she was too young to learn. Surprised she was, when the guards opened the doors to a plain-looking couple whom Lilac had thought she'd seen before. The woman was the cousin of one of his viscounts from Saint Malo, Henri had explained, as the couple then parted to reveal a girl with striking red hair slicked into a braid coiled neatly at the back of her head.

Piper Krenn, she had introduced herself when her own father had nudged her, as if they'd rehearsed it many times. She then dutifully said she was seven and a half, the daughter of the man behind her, an esteemed sheep farmer—the owner of Krenn Farm, which was sandwiched northeast of their castle, between Brocéliande and Rennes.

"Did they understand what happened to you?"

"Not fully, I don't think. I had waited for some time to pass. It was close to a week, over three days since I'd last seen you. The red in their eyes—our eyes—fades after that long. I figured that out a while ago, it was how long we'd have between our feedings in the cages. So, I waited." She pulled the corner of the duvet over herself. "Mother still nearly fainted at the sight of me. Father eventually let me in when I begged." An unnameable sadness crept into Piper's expression. "And I *did* beg."

"What do you mean you begged?" They'd made their own daughter, who'd been missing for years, beg to be welcomed into her own home?

Piper shook her head, still lost in thought. "On second thought, maybe I'd entranced them, too." A small sob escaped her throat. Her fangs had grown in again. "Oh, I don't know."

"What were they thinking? They didn't rejoice at the sight of you?" Lilac snarled, her voice wavering in incredulous anger. She found herself lividly considering their arrest. "Were they not happy or relieved to see you?" She sat up against the pillows when Piper only sniffled. Lilac had spent so many of the days after her fifteenth birthday moping about her own punishments, she hadn't paid attention to what had happened to

Piper. *Selfish*, she was so selfish. She recalled being informed the next morning that Piper had been relieved of her duty. "Didn't my father send you home with a letter of some sort? Anything explaining what had happened?" Lilac's inquiries were probably not helping, but she needed to know.

Piper closed her eyes and exhaled, long and slow, before answering. "He did. He had John write one for me. I traveled some way east when the vampires found me. It was that one," she said with a soft snarl, "Bastion, and another male. I dropped my bag of belongings, scattering them on the road—including the letter, hoping someone would find it—"

"Wait," Lilac said, her insides curdling, hoping and praying she was misunderstanding. "What happened to the carriage? Or the—the horse? No one found them abandoned, suspicious?"

Piper met her widening eyes with a quiet smugness.

"The coachman? The guard?" Sickening heat swept over Lilac. "My parents sent you home alone on foot?"

Piper laughed, a forlorn sound. "They imprisoned you over your Daemon tongue. You, their own daughter. Do you really think anyone cared about what happened to me? Furthermore, would it have mattered?"

Lilac remained silent, her face and chest burning with the heavy heat of self-disgust.

"My parents were alarmed when I showed up at their door, anyway. I'd tried to wash off in the river before, but it was woefully hard to remove your blood from my dress and apron. Yours, and that of the man I'd taken in the vestibule. My *maman* eventually woke up, and once she was herself, offered me one of her gowns. They tried to feed me. I denied the food they gave me, not knowing what would happen if I ate it. We chatted a little, not much was said. They didn't really ask questions. Father was quiet as all else. I stayed for some time, a couple weeks. Eventually I grew hungry, but I feared leaving in case they decided against allowing me in a second time. A few days passed before I gave up."

"How did you eat?"

"I had some of the bread and stew they'd offered me, especially since I didn't want to stoke their suspicions. My *maman* is an impressive cook. Always has been." Piper picked at her nail beds, which had turned red.

Without thinking, Lilac slapped Piper's hands off her lap; the vampire yanked them away.

Piper growled. "*God*. You've become Marguerite."

"I have not," Lilac said, appalled at the comparison and rather shocked at the sound that had just escaped her friend's throat. Her mother had prodded her many times for doing the same in her nervousness. It had been out of habit. "Sorry. I was wondering about your...bloodlust."

"Oh." Piper shifted a leg up, forcing her hands—fingers already healed and no longer inflamed—to her side. "My craving for blood returned at the end of the first week. I considered venturing out at night, feeding on anyone nearby enough to fill myself without killing them. But I didn't know if that was possible, or what my limits were since last feeding from you and from the other man." She made a face. "He didn't survive, I don't think."

A week seemed like a long time based on Lilac's existing knowledge of the vampires' physiology. Garin had been able to go several days without blood when they'd first met, but she supposed his options were limited at the time. And he'd been weaned off of vein blood for years. From when he'd drained Mathis and Enzo outside Sinclair's camp to the farmhouse, it hadn't even been three days since he'd followed her from the inn.

Even then, he'd admitted he'd been fighting his hunger throughout their journey. She recalled the way Garin had fallen upon Renald at her request, as if he'd been parched.

I am a pawn to my desires tonight. His words at Fool's Folly raked a chill across her skin. She could hear it—hear him. Lilac fought down a violent shudder, only noticing Piper watching her warily when the vampire addressed her.

"Are you all right?"

Lilac tucked a lock of damp hair behind her burning ears. "Did it not bother you? The hunger?"

Piper studied her a second longer before replying. "It did, eventually. It grew enough for Father to suggest I take an evening stroll. I think they assumed I was restless, or had developed some sort of sickness, or intolerance to heat. So, I began to do so every evening. A walk for my health." Piper sighed. "I ventured further each time, telling myself I'd try to take a drink of someone without slaughtering them if I came across a ripe opportunity. I think I purposefully avoided the commonly walked paths, and instead started carefully mapping my way around. We had traveled by carriage the day they'd brought me to the castle to live with you, and so I'd tried to recall the way we'd taken. I discovered our home was quite far from the main roads—strange for a sheep farm, now that I think of it." She wrinkled her nose and rubbed at it as if the pollen had gotten to her. But the hitch in her voice and the way it warbled gave her away. "It took me a few days of searching. Two nights ago, I finally found the path to the main road and went back, terrified of the choice that lay before me. This morning I made the decision and informed them I'd be leaving again."

"What did they say?" asked Lilac. "Did you tell them you were headed here?"

"I told them I was off to serve the queen once more. No other specifics were given. They didn't have much to say and at least didn't stop me. In the end, I asked them not to tell anyone I was there or what had happened. Told them I might not return for a very, very long time. They were rather agreeable to that, too. My father did comment that I was not allowed to take either of their horses with me."

Piper exhaled, turning slowly to Lilac, surveying the rage that must've been etched upon the queen's features. Her friend's lip quivered, her nose and cheeks pink, and for a moment it was uncertain if she would laugh or cry. She then brought the corner of the duvet to her face, and her shoulders sank into a heart-wrenching sob.

Nothing could have held back the tears that came. Lilac's nostrils flared, chest quaking painfully as the ceiling dissolved into a blurry, tear-filled vision of a childhood that had fleetingly been ripped from between them. What could have been their best years together as friends had turned into a nightmare. Lilac felt horrible for ever complaining about anything, weeping as Piper cried into the blanket beside her.

Because the Henri's letter hadn't made it to them, had the Krenns not known their daughter was relieved of her duty and no longer residing at the castle? Had her parents *ever* been expecting her? Is that why there wasn't a larger uproar when Piper had gone missing?

Lilac hadn't even known Piper never made it back to her parents' farm, not until it was much too late. No one had known. And so no one had saved her, either.

She wanted to throw her arms around Piper. She wasn't sure if that or a

BRIAR SOMERSET

pat on the head was appropriate or would get her her head bitten off, considering Piper's fangs were still elongated. So, she offered, "You should have entranced them to let you take a horse."

Piper leered at her.

"You did it to Yanna and Isabel."

"I wouldn't know how to do it now, on command." Piper looked down at her hands, which had begun to shake. She tucked them under the blankets. "I don't want to try and I don't intend to learn. I am the furthest thing from those monsters."

"You're right. You are not them." Lilac nodded, settling down against the soft pillows behind her. "Well, tell me how you got here, then. Did you follow the road west?"

Piper wiped her nose on her arm, seemingly grateful for the topic change. "I left their farm and soon came across a caravan of magic folk headed in the opposite direction. Two women and an odd, hulking animal. I would've ran, but they approached as if they recognized me. I didn't intend on telling them who I was, but they somehow knew where I was headed. They fed me and—and *why* are you looking at me like that?"

"They fed you?" Lilac propped herself up on her elbow. "You *fed* from one of them?"

"No," Piper said through her teeth, making a sound of disgust. "From the magic folk? Can we do that?"

Lilac's mind immediately went to Garin, and Adelaide's family. Then she instantly regretted asking. "I'm not sure. But what did they feed you, then? Did they have bottled blood on hand? People?" she optioned, frowning at the last part.

"No. They fed me warm bread with meat in the middle. A rich, simmering broth of bird and berries." Piper licked her lips. "They waited patiently as I ate, then sent me on my way. They told me a pair of carriages filled with rye and livestock were just ahead, headed to the castle for a celebration. They advised me to follow far behind. Just in case they diverted, they told me which paths to take especially if I encountered a fork in the road."

The *Guài* were mystical creatures. The dishes Piper described didn't sound familiar, but perhaps it was bewitched food for vampires. Lilac considered asking about the sensation that followed, what exactly happened after a vampire's body rejected mortal food shortly after consuming it. But Piper was eyeing the ceiling, her hardened gaze softening as she traced the floral carvings outlining the chandelier above them, just as she used to upon her bed when Lilac would sit at the desk with her tutors.

"Garin sometimes eats," Lilac said matter-of-factly, unsure of how to approach the topic with much tact. "I think he enjoys it for the taste. But it doesn't seem to nourish him. It makes him ill afterward. He vomits."

Piper either chose to ignore this or didn't hear, her mind probably faraway.

Lilac rubbed her eyes, turning back to the hearth. Tonight was not the night for more questions or shocking revelations, or else her head might explode. She supposed even the weight of her and Piper's conversation was better than being kept up, distraught by thoughts of Garin. Even as the night progressed, none of what she'd felt being separated from him after he'd sent her away plagued her now, but she still feared its gradual return.

Lilac didn't want to think about it; didn't want to remember the blood-stained mess of The Fool's Folly, or the days preceding it. Didn't want to think about Fire Ale, or the Dragondew Mead, or how it had clouded every sense of hers. She didn't want to dwell on Garin's possessive grasp on her, or his mouth on her throat. How he'd claimed her, through and through, as Casmir had warned. Devoured her.

Her head spun, body throbbing at the thought of him, feeling the waves of wanton distrust building again. Of sadness and regret for the days to come, but Garin had said it himself—this was her duty. He'd gone so far as to entrance her to leave him, strip her of her memory of stabbing Albrecht.

Lilac sank further into her sheets, refusing to let fury wash over her relief of Piper's return. She wouldn't do this, wouldn't let it ruin the fact that her friend was back. All that mattered was that Garin was safe at the inn again, under the watchful eyes of their friends—hopefully more carefully this time. What mattered was that Piper was alive and back home. That Bastion hadn't found her first and sent her back to the mine, or worse.

"It was kind of the *Guài* to point you in the right direction," Lilac finally said, eager to escape her ruminations. "I'm glad you're here."

"Who are they? Where do they come from? When I asked, they only told me they were headed home."

"They're a sort of magic folk from the East. Powerful acquaintances of mine."

She felt Piper shift behind her. When Lilac peeked, she was propped against her pillow, shoulders pivoted to Lilac, eyes wide with curiosity.

Lilac shrank back. "What?"

"Will you marry him, Your Majesty?" Piper blurted.

"I must." Lilac looked at her firmly. She really did not wish to talk about it, but it was inevitable, and Piper's concern was fair. "It is the only thing that will stave off France."

"Garin." Piper's forehead creased. "I meant, Garin."

The question was unexpected. A surge of disgust tore through her. "*No.*"

She expected a noise or sense of relief from Piper, but there was none. The vampire looked down through her lashes. "Oh."

What was that look? *Disappointment?* "You heard Artus. I have no choice. France's threat is real."

"You haven't even been propositioned," Piper pointed out.

"My hand will go to Maximillian, *when* he proposes to me. By way of the emissary."

"Yet it was foolish of you to mention it in front of everyone when you haven't even met with him. Did you truly overhear it in a tavern?"

"Something like that." Done with their conversation, Lilac laid back and closed her eyes. She reopened them again when Piper said nothing.

The vampire was chewing on her nail, staring into the distance.

"Foolish, I may be," said Lilac, more than happy to continue if her friend insisted. "But I must do what is necessary to secure our kingdom. I haven't heard of any offer or consideration on Garin's end. He's been too preoccupied with ensuring I wed a powerful ally to reinforce our defenses."

"He is an idiot, but it makes sense that he'd be hesitant."

Lilac's stomach soured hearing Piper might actually agree with him. "Garin insists that publicly aligning myself with Daemons will malign any effort I take in encouraging my towns to support a war. On the other hand, he suspects Daemons will not expend their efforts for me. Understandably."

"Not because of that." Piper slid out of bed and made her way to the vanity chair, rummaging in the bundle of kirtle she'd changed out of. She held up a book.

Deep umber leather with fraying pages. As familiar as the wry smirk on Piper's face.

A couple weeks ago Lilac had pulled the written accounts on Daemons, poorly organized and filled with misinformation, from the between the library and the book stacks that sat in her bedchamber—one of which currently propped the balcony doors open. She'd skimmed through the parts her tutors once had her study, using the half truths within them to draw her Accords notes.

The vampire manuscript was the only one she couldn't find; a thin collection comprised of firsthand observations strung together by several authors. *Skin cast in a concerning pallor which improves upon heavy feeding*, she recalled reading. *Sharp canines that grow with heightened hunger or arousal.* Lilac hadn't laid eyes on it for some time and eventually assumed it had been misplaced somewhere among the shelves.

She immediately recognized it as the book in Piper's hand. "You were in my library."

"If only," Piper snorted. "This book nearly killed me. Again." She returned to the bed, manuscript in hand. "It was tucked between the bricks to the left of your balcony. I grabbed onto it while climbing up. Almost lost my balance and fell. Was about to chuck it into the fire before recognizing it as one of your books from Rolet and Eugene." Piper slid back under the duvet. "You know, the ones I had to pretend to aid in tutoring you with in order to read."

"Yes, I remember. You have access to them now. The entire library," Lilac said, her entire body buzzing.

"Oh, I know I do." Piper flipped the book open and skimmed, flipping open to a page past the middle. The top corner of the page had been folded in. She pointed at a tangle of scrawl, a crooked penmanship certainly different from the rest. Her finger landed upon the first word on the page.

"*Vampires*," Piper read, her cadence cautious. She'd mostly been taught to read alongside Lilac. *"Are are a species of Daemon that participate in the rituals of matri... matri—"*

"Matrimony?" Lilac shot up and snatched the manuscript from Piper, continuing the passage out loud. *"Vampyres—"* She'd never seen it spelt that way, with a *y*, before. *"—occasionally wish to wed, but the process is often over-complicated by permissions and hierarchy. This is especially true for rogue or unin-*

formed vampyres who sire their betrothed for the sake of eligibility—or, their spouse for the sake of eternal companionship—only to find their newly-turned lovers distressed and wholly unfamiliar with the feelings of romance once shared, regardless of how deep, with their sire." The writing grew messy here. There were also several blotches of running ink, as if the parchment had gotten wet in the rain, making the script more difficult to read.

In his bedchamber at the Mine, Garin did say it was against his species' law to create one's own mate. She'd never known why, or the consequences; this was why he'd threatened to have Bastion turn her at the inn.

"How horrible," Piper whispered. "Siring someone you love makes them fall out of love with you? You'd think that's important to know."

"Shhh," Lilac said, scouring the parchment. "*In most cases, fledglings become too attached to their sires to even consider claiming loyalty to their partner once they've Awakened. This attachment, not to be confused with love, falls within a spectrum between authoritative respect and hapless, utter submission. In a similar fashion to mortal nobility, Vampyres will still insist on marrying to form alliances or bring peace between long-rivalled clans.*"

"Clans?" said Piper. "They mean covens, don't they?"

She flipped through the first half of the manuscript, which contained the studies that were used in her lessons overseen by Rolet. "That's what Garin and Bastion refer to it as, and so do all the other contributors of this manuscript." Lilac turned back to the folded page again, continuing on. "*For those who persist against the many odds, Vampyric matrimony may serve the purpose of securing a dowry, including estates, claim on hunting land, or gaining rank within the clan—the last, only at the approval of the involved Doyen.*"

Doyen. Clan.

Vampyre.

These scrawled notes were obviously written in by someone from another kingdom. *When?* Lilac wondered. *Why?*

She didn't miss the fact that the passage seemed to touch briefly on interspecies marriage. Mortal and vampire. It was a wonder she and Piper had never been prompted to read this section of the manuscript; Rolet had probably thought it unimportant, if not entirely inappropriate to teach the future queen.

Her eyes adjusted quickly as they flew across the remainder of the page.

"Despite being the highest order of Sanguinary Rite, a coupling willing to pursue a true Blood Vow is rare. However—"

Lilac flipped the parchment, where it appeared a new section on blood drinking started, the previous penmanship resumed. It had seemed the section on vampiric matrimony was unfinished. The text she'd read from had stopped abruptly, leaving the last quarter of the page blank—except for a single note at the very bottom, in the same rushed scrawl.

"See 'The Histories of the Lasting Night.'"

She never recalled reading or encountering such a tome in her library, but she could've easily missed it, even with her leisurely research. If she had, she'd remember such a striking book title. Maybe she'd ask John to procure it for her later. "This isn't Garin's doing, is it?" Lilac had never seen him write, nor had she read anything he'd written.

Piper ran her fingers over it and sniffed, nostrils flaring. "No. This ink is aged with the parchment. Even those tear stains or whatever they are, those aren't new. Decades, at least. Maybe a century?"

Lilac started to flip the page again, but decided to fight the temptation to continue on. *Garin had been reading the manuscript.* A passage on *marriage.* She shut it, sliding it beneath her pillow and gritting her teeth.

"Good idea, we won't get any sleep if we continue. Tomorrow, we will hear the details of your proposition." Piper chewed on her lower lip, suddenly seeming unsettled. "Do you really think Garin has not at least entertained the thought of asking for your hand? Although he didn't write those notes, the pages in particular also smell of him."

"Entertained at most. He was doing his research," Lilac said, her face hot. Piper definitely heard her heart skip a few beats; the vampire's brows rose when she doubled down. "He's been convincing himself that pushing me to marry Maximilian is the best option, as he has been." She refused to even consider the possibility he'd entertained it, especially when she had alluded to an alliance in the brothel and Garin outright ignored it. "To have me carry through with his intentions."

"Speaking of intention, Artus came here to frighten you into marrying his grandson using their distant blood as a threat. But you must remember, he was once on your grandfather's court—the *Breton* court."

Piper was right. Monarchs were known to keep their enemies close, whether they knew it or not. Even those in denial, as with her parents and the Le Tallecs. "You believe this would have alienated his family from François?"

"Yes," said Piper. "Even if he was in denial of it. Marriage to Sinclair is unlikely to save you, and Artus's family does not have the French influence he implied they do. Yes, he might share their lineage, bu his bloodline nor public denouncement would have affected whether or when France advanced." Her hand abruptly shot out and snatched Lilac's fists from beneath the blanket. "You hypocrite," she hissed.

Lilac glanced down at her own finger nail beds, picked raw. A bead of red bloomed along her pinky nail; wide-eyed, Piper grabbed and brought Lilac's wrist to her mouth. Lilac shrieked and pulled away in alarm, but not before Piper lapped the droplet of blood off her finger.

Piper immediately released her, face twisted in concern. "*Oh.*"

"*Oh?* A warning would have been helpful," Lilac snapped, nearly falling off her side of the bed, cradling her hand and pressing the wound into her gown. "Asking for permission, even better." It was as if her body had acted of its own accord, recoiling from Piper's movement before she could even think. Her skin crawled, the same sensation she'd felt while kissing Casmir—even if the motion hadn't been intimate. "What's that look for?"

"Why do you taste like that?" Piper's lip lifted in disgust. She made a violent sound and wiped at her mouth. "*Eugh.* You *are* his thrall.

Lilac stared at her.

"You weren't before, when I first saw you two together. But now you are. Right?" Piper was astoundingly astute for someone who was once juvenile staff, then imprisoned underground. "Is that why you're not so...frail anymore? Why you're quicker and stronger?"

"How do you know what a thrall is?" Lilac asked, cautiously sliding back under the covers. Garin might've mentioned it when he and Bastion had argued in the Mine vestibule.

But Piper nudged her elbow at the bedside table. "Before your hand-maidens came barging in, I'd started skimming the manuscript once I'd realized what it was. I thought, well, how useful—a guide for the monstrosity I've become thanks to your plaything-turned-master. I thought I'd wait for you to return from whatever you were doing, assuming you were at supper. '*Another's thrall becomes unappetizing to others once the process is completed*," she quoted. "Evidently true, though I didn't expect it to be that bad." An expectant glare followed.

Lilac's silence was confirmation enough. "Even if I am his thrall, that is all I am to him."

Piper's look of scrutiny faded to annoyance. "Your Majesty, there is no use in lying. Even when you first wake as a vampire, you have a different sense for things. A deeper knowing. I knew I had to consume human blood without any prompting, knew I had to do it to survive. I tore into the person nearest me, an old man snoring against his cell door. He was weak, there wasn't much to him and he didn't fill me for long. Shortly after leaving the Mine, I sensed you in the woods and intended to seek you out for help, but my hunger got the best of me. Tonight, I could tell something was off the moment you bit into that apple and all the blood and dirt appeared."

"It was an illusion. Eating made my glamor wear off."

"That's why I asked you if he was here. It is why I left the Grand Hall. He is everywhere you go, less an aroma and more an essence, a dark veil of warning for other vampires to heed. Even when I first saw you with him, I could tell he'd wouldn't ever let you out of his sight. The only reason he didn't sense me after I escaped the vestibule was because he was distracted looking for you." Piper stared at the ceiling. "My desire to find you was easily overwhelmed with the urge to feed. Too easily. I would've never hurt you had I known."

"None of it is your fault," Lilac said firmly, remembering it all. Garin was at her side within moments of the fledgling vampire finding her. She'd assumed she hadn't made it far enough from the grotto, and that Garin had heard their scuffle. She didn't know he'd followed her. For what? To protect her? To tell her he'd changed his mind—to drag her back to the mine?

Lilac turned to Piper; her friend was tracing the patterns on the ceiling with her faraway gaze. "How do you feel now? Do you need more blood?"

"No," said Piper quietly. "Definitely not from you. I actually haven't felt that way, that unnameable thirst, since last drinking from you. I was so distracted by how hungry I was, I suppose I hadn't realized your taste. The bad hunger pangs, the burning in my throat and gums...None of that has resurfaced, even in the days I spent at home." Piper looked somewhat defeated. "Our discernment is strong. You know—sometimes too much—

the things you wish to *not* know. Who people truly are. Where your place is in the world. It's how I knew I had to leave Krenn Farm and return here. From the moment I arrived, my parents' cottage no longer felt like home."

"They didn't welcome you as they should have. They didn't celebrate your homecoming as you deserved."

A small smile spread upon Piper's face. "Yes, but that's not why I left them. I knew you needed me, Your Majesty. I had no choice but to come."

"I do need you." Lilac laid back, urging the tension in her shoulders to release, struggling to accept it all. Piper's presence. Artus's reminder, contrived or not, of the very real threat looming over her head. Garin's fury and overwhelming influence, their new bond. The absence of the heaviness she'd dreaded—strangely, even with her change of heart at the thought of marriage.

"Piper, do you think great kings have ever questioned their destiny?" Lilac whispered.

The vampire hummed. "Several have abdicated. We learned in your history lessons, of Richard II of England. Sweden's Afonso V. Then, comes your father."

That was fair. Lilac's father's decision to pass the throne down in the prime of his reign, good health and all, still baffled and irked her. "I mean in their early days at the throne. Or even before they're officially crowned."

Piper's head snapped down to her. "Why? Don't think you can back out now, in the limbo between your accession and coronation. The throne is yours, you already sit upon it and wield its power, the crown and ball are merely the end of the formalities. Don't tell me you're questioning your place."

"If you suggest such a thing again, I'll have you banished to that manor house," Lilac replied, matching Piper's frosty tone. "I'm not questioning anything. It's just..." She shrugged, her worries seeming silly as they rose to her tongue. "I wonder if these kings ever question their own qualifications to lead? Do you think their minds are clouded with concern over their roles as sons, friends, and new leaders of a country? Do you think they fear letting their kingdom down?"

Piper took her time digesting the question as she sank onto her pillows, too. "I am not born of royal blood, Your Majesty. I have only touched a silver spoon and known a hint of privilege because of your parents bringing me here, plucking me from my farm. I was not allowed to accompany you on your journey to the town or the Le Tallec estate with Marguerite, nor attend the soirées you did. But I do know from my observations—from comforting you and watching that *boy* send you letter upon letter when you wished to be left alone—that by your gender and birthright, you have been subject to the pressures of not only leadership, but etiquette, kinship, education, daughterhood, and the growing pressures of marriage and creating an heir. Among other things. So, I say your fears are valid."

"Fears? Piper, I am terrified." Lilac closed her eyes, chest aching, eyes burning. She scowled, chills shocking her body at the truths Piper had spoken aloud—and the others compiling at the back of her mind. She might have been queen for less than a month, but she knew better; she was already scrutinized enough within her own kingdom, and any wavering determination might seem like hesitation or weakness. "I am terrified of making the right decision for my kingdom and the wrong one for myself. My heart should be with my people, and with any good-hearted ruler intent on offering me his name and aid. I should be grateful."

"Gratefulness for all he offers doesn't mean you will come to love him." Her friend smiled grimly, reaching down and giving Lilac's hand a light squeeze. "I am in no position to advise you on alliances or marriage, but one thing is clear: Regrettably, you belong to Garin, whether you are queen of this country, or the next, or both," Piper said, swallowing the disdain of her sire's name. "You belong to Garin in a different manner than I do. It is merely an issue of hierarchy for me, I am his fledgling. His subordinate. You are *his*."

"I am his thrall." The realization said aloud made her tremble beneath the duvet.

"But your place is beside him, and he will ensure it is known. The way he spoke of you, to you in that vestibule in front of Bastion. That wasn't real. You were playing along with him." At the look of dread on Lilac's face, Piper laughed unexpectedly. "I could tell, even before being turned. I know you. You detest the idea of marrying Maximilian for this very reason. Sometimes your heart, your blood, knows before you do."

Lilac bit her lip, willing her body to calm. Enthralling herself to Garin had indeed changed everything in the blink of an eye, including the concepts of marriage and belonging.

To whom. With whom.

Her kingdom was threatened by annexation and the only clear solution was one she detested. She'd caused this. But she'd done what she had to in order to survive, just as she had time and time again, and would continue to.

Even if Garin hadn't ever spoken of a Blood Vow, he'd at least cared enough to research it. But that didn't matter, Lilac decided, shoving the thought from her mind. After realizing his intentional, planned betrayal, she knew better than to let tonight's discovery fester into hope.

She wouldn't put it past Garin to order her all the way to the altar, command the vows from her very tongue if he had to.

He had no qualms in forcing her hand, and who knew what he was capable of—to which depths the head of the Brocéliande vampire coven would sink—in order to ensure France did not win? And Artus was brazen enough to suggest that a marriage to Sinclair would prevent France from advancing. She had tried to do it on her own, but to her dismay, Garin was right; the countrymen capable of forming her army and fighting for her crown might not only refuse, but revolt, *again*, when she amended the Daemon law in Brocéliande's favor. Which she would do, without question.

Riou and her father's council also held fair points—England was too much of a risk to involve, especially in the early stages of war, when her marriage alone would stop the threat without wasting the resources and blood of outlying kingdoms.

Lilac would oblige, but she'd do it on her own terms. She swallowed and wiped her tears away. She would never be backed into a corner again, not by France nor Garin. She would not make a decision that would reign over her title, body, and land in a single moment of fear.

She'd make a stunning, devoted bride. She'd have Herlinde design the most breathtaking gown that would have Marguerite and her court falling over each other.

France would watch. So would Garin.

Lilac would do it afraid, her crowned head held high.

"I am to be married this weekend," was all she said.

Piper rolled over to face the balcony doors and yanked the covers over her head. "Then I pity the kingdom who stands between you both."

22

L ilac stared down the length of her table at the Grand Hall doors, sweat beading on her forehead, fingers gripping the corners of the table too tightly. Her slumber had been peaceful, finally void of nightmares of Garin, yet she'd woken with a growling belly and enough anxiety to power a horse.

"Has your food gone cold?" Isabel said from behind her. When Lilac didn't answer, she tried once more, but a deep toll drowned her voice. The bells had begun to ring, marking the liturgical hour. Yanna was already removing her plate to the nearby cart. She was careful to sidestep Piper, sitting at Lilac's right, with a wide enough berth as she silently refilled a second plate for the queen.

Not even Hedwig's impressive spread laid upon their finest dishware could pull Lilac from the shock of the morning—of waking to the bells, discovering Piper with half the blankets kicked off, doused in morning sunlight from the balcony door they'd forgotten to close. Snoring. Her skin perfectly intact.

Piper had just opened her eyes when Lilac screamed. They'd leapt out of bed shouting, Piper batting at imaginary flames and Lilac falling over herself to shut the curtains, the ruckus masked by the deep tolling that rang throughout the keep.

Without another word, Piper had staggered to the door and opened it to a shocked Yanna and Isabel, mid-knock. The vampire slipped out between them before Lilac could stop her, Piper's quiet sobs echoing throughout the stairwell. With no time to dress herself in anything ornate, Lilac ordered the two to go after her. Reluctantly, they'd obliged, and she tugged her comb through her hair, slid her shoes on, and dashed after them.

The four descended the steps to the second floor in order to avoid the bustling kitchen, Lilac snatching Piper's hand and urging her to breathe. To her chagrin, there were several maids putting up ribbon and flowers in the foyer anyway; Lilac swore and urged the group along, but her staff still stopped working to acknowledge the queen and her entourage, if only to stare.

In the Grand Hall, they'd found Hedwig and her staff weaving the final touches—bouquets of roses and elderflowers from her mother's garden—around the breakfast spread.

"Her food's obviously gone cold," Yanna said, eyeing Piper when the last of the bells echoed off. "Neither of them have touched their breakfast after the commotion this morning."

"It's very nearly lunchtime." Marguerite lounged on Lilac's throne at the top of the steps behind them, fanning herself in the sunlight. She squinted down her nose at Piper, who had also barely touched her breakfast, distracted with turning her palms this way and that under the table, checking her exposed wrists peeking out from her canary pink sleeves.

Unsatisfied that none of the girls had acknowledged her comment, Marguerite sighed. "I assumed my daughter's impressive record with punctuality and appearance might actually be remedied by having a lady-in-waiting." She examined her nails. "I suppose I was wrong."

Piper only frowned, turning her head toward the doors.

"Yes, because yours have remained so dutiful," Lilac commented. She hadn't yet seen Gertrude and Helena, but was momentarily grateful for their absence given the morning's events.

Marguerite had never cared for Piper, and there was no way Henri hadn't told her mother whom he suspected *Phoebe* might be. It was still Piper after all, despite her redder hair, eyes the color of spring, and her glowing, healthy appearance. It didn't matter what they thought. Piper was her charge now.

Marguerite stared in disapproval at the both of them, tucking a lock of her hair into the blonde wig balanced precariously upon her head. "The last thing you need is a bad influence. Or, whoever gave you both the idea that wearing your nightgowns to this meeting would be acceptable." She waved a finger at Yanna and Isabel. "Is there no way we can dress them? We've waited long enough. They both could have donned three gowns by now."

"No," Lilac said, immediately shooting the idea down. She'd been riding her nerves so high, if they went to her tower, it would be a challenge convincing her to leave again. "He could arrive at any time."

A proxy wedding was risky business as it was; hopefully her future husband and those in his circle would not fuss over trite matters such as a woman's appearance in relation to her worth.

As Garin had said, this was transactional; she was a ruler making a deal, a contract with another—although, she'd barely gotten her feet wet in terms of doing any real ruling since Henri's abdication. She'd inherited a kingdom who did not want her in the first place.

This was her fate, the fate of many women before her. She was a willing pawn for the good of her people. A stalemate, and the thought probably unsettled her more than it should have. She washed down her nerves with a swig of cider, which she'd recently requested to be served at the castle, and was reminded of Sable and Jeanare. She thought of their grandchildren— wherever the boys were. The thought of Freya still made her uncomfortable, but it no longer brought her to her knees, because she could *do* something about the systems that had harmed them. She *would* do something. This role was much bigger than her.

"If this emissary was sent all this way to propose for Maximilian without either of them ever meeting me, then I doubt he nor the emperor will care about me spending the day in a nightgown," Lilac said.

"We don't know for certain that's *why* he's coming." Everyone— including Lilac—turned to Piper, who shifted in her seat. Her lady-in-waiting nudged the fruit around her plate with her fork. "We won't know until he's here."

What was she doing? Lilac glared warningly, deciding this was the time to bite into her salmon baguette in order to hold her tongue.

"Where did we find her again?" asked Marguerite, staring down upon Piper in disdain.

"She is the second daughter of some baron." Lilac waved a dismissive hand, intentionally choosing a junior rank, already put off by the morning.

Marguerite straightened, almost falling out of Lilac's throne. "A baron, you say? Which baron?"

"One from the coastal towns," Piper answered. "Our village is small. Insignificant." She took a sudden interest in the wedge of Camembert on her plate and happily bit straight into it, eliciting an eye roll from Marguerite.

"Perhaps it is better I *don't* know this baron. No matter. The emissary is late." Marguerite grabbed the bowl of grapes Yanna had brought her. "We were told to expect him in the morning, just past the first bells."

"Anything could have happened to slow him," Lilac replied. "Weather. Busy roads. Animals. Thieves."

Marguerite let out a disgruntled snort. "If we're launched into war and our kingdom is not tightly aligned with Maximilian or anyone else, I will strangle you and place you at the front of the army myself."

"That is where I would march, regardless." There was no doubt she should have shared the same concerns her mother had—and she did, all things considered—but Lilac could not help being distracted by the fear that Piper would burst into flames at any second.

Why was she not affected by the sun? *How?* Was it because Garin could now daywalk, as he'd called it at the brothel? This didn't seem likely, considering he'd turned Piper into a vampire days before Adelaide's magic allowed him to exist in the sun. Made apparent by Piper's reaction, it was something she was shocked by as well.

Her newly immortal friend had picked her way through a plate and a half for the last three hours, and didn't seem to show any signs of sickness the way Garin would have by now.

"It is a possibility," John said from the seat opposite Piper, "that he ran into some sort of obstacle. Anything is possible." He fidgeted with the quill hovering over the scroll before him, refocusing upon the law she'd spent the earlier part of the morning drafting—not the full set of Accords, to avoid breaking the seemingly vague rules of Kestrel's deal preemptively, but a single law ensuring the basic safety of Daemons to begin with.

By royal decree of Queen Eleanor Trécesson, no person within the Kingdom of Brittany may inflict unjust injury, assault, or murder upon a Daemon. Each case will be elevated to the King's Bench. Those found guilty will face charges most serious and potential consequences most fatal, John's notes read.

They'd stopped their decree drafting when Marguerite had earlier returned from overseeing preparations for the elaborate display in the garden ahead of Lilac's coronation, wondering where the emissary might be. It was nowhere near done enough to go to the town criers, but with Garin's sobering opinion on Daemon alliances and Artus's visit, it was crucial she start somewhere—beginning with the very right to protection against targeted violence from those like Artus's family.

Sinclair's grandfather was no madman. They'd played it that way, but he was a mastermind. She'd relieved her glamor before him last night, in partial hysterics, in hopes he would react in a way to get him and his men jailed. He knew she couldn't imprison him for running the hunting troupe out of the Jaunty Hog, because revealing so would let everyone know she'd been involved in the near-altercation that took place there.

Lilac couldn't possibly focus on further lawmaking, not now with her mother's fretting. Plus, her own worry Piper would burst into flames at any second. Still, Marguerite's concerns were valid—and Piper had no right to antagonize her just because of her reluctant loyalty to Garin. The emissary *was* late. By three hours. Garin had said he was recovering, and she could only assume he'd meant at the inn. Had he changed his mind? Was he having trouble entrancing the fellow?

Had Albrecht woken in a fright and decided that he would report her to the emperor?

Lilac looked down at her nightgown and simple leather turn shoes, wondering if not excusing herself and Piper to get changed into their finery was a mistake, when the courtyard door banged open. It was Henri with an open envelope and a piece of unfolded parchment in his hands. He'd been absent all morning after drinking his anxieties away following Artus's departure—and who knew if he'd actually paid Kemble that visit—but Lilac had assumed he'd stayed in bed.

He said nothing as his glare landed on her and Piper, marching straight for her end of the table. Henri's ruddy face and pursed lips under his mustache said it all.

"Can I help you, Father? Do we require another shipment of ale?"

"The courier came by. You wonder why your emissary isn't here?" He slammed the parchment and envelope at her setting. There was a dark red blob on the envelope—a wax seal stamped with a tiny design that resembled a coiled serpent framed in flowers.

She picked the letter up and unfurled it.

Greetings,

I am requesting funds in the amount of 200 gros to repair the hearth, floor, armoire, and bed for one corner room and balcony following an isolated fire last night.

Signed, *Madame Pearl Toranaga, The Fool's Folly.*

Brief and to the point, no pandering or flowered wording the way most would write a personal request for funds to the monarchy. No blame. Still, Lilac's mouth went dry.

Henri stood over her shoulder, rereading the letter, the muscle under his eye twitching. He snatched it from her before she could fold it again.

"A brothel, Lilac?" he growled as Piper locked eyes with her. She flinched when Henri raised his voice. "A fire!"

"What's the problem?" Lilac frowned in feigned confusion. "They need our help, and straight away."

Henri passed a hand over his face. "I don't think we've ever received a letter from the whorehouse. Not in my reign. Have we, John?"

"No, not if my memory serves me correctly, Your Grace."

"Even your father considers himself *above* the harlots of that house," her mother spat, inspecting her fingernails as Henri fell silent.

"What exactly are you accusing me of?" Lilac hissed. "Fucking someone there? Starting the fire?"

Nevermind that it was the truth; she just wanted to hear them say it. Her parents didn't know what they thought either, or were hesitant to voice it. They exchanged peeved glances with each other. They'd *seen* her covered in blood and soot.

Marguerite lifted a helpless hand. "Then why would they bother contacting us?"

Her parents had been willing to provide aid to Bog without much pushback at all. "Because everyone deserves the right to ask for help. It is a right for all that shouldn't only be reserved for nobility, or those close to them, or in bed with them. Or inebriated bar owners." Lilac angled her head to glance at Henri, shielding her face from the window. "Don't get me started on who we've laundered money through, Father."

Henri's mouth hung open. Lilac pushed her chair back and carried the parchment and envelope to her scribe. "Approve it for disbursement. Please double the asking amount by the end of the week. I would also like to issue my decree today."

John's hand stopped sliding across his notes, scribbled in a separate book. He peered down, shifting the sheets of parchment to survey her draft. "As in, by this evening?"

"As in, as soon as possible. Alert the town criers."

John chewed on the nib of the quill as he sometimes did, staining his bottom lip in ink. "I suggest a partial release. I can send this first bit to the town criers, if you're sure. But the rest, including the other clauses, can be finalized and released at a later date. That is, if you feel more preparation is required."

"That is precisely what I meant," she said. "We will start slowly." She had informed John beforehand that there would be several clauses to the decrees she planned on passing—the latter ones containing her Accords. He'd balked at some of them and had quietly approved or disapproved with a hum or tilt of his lips, but otherwise obliged and kept her plans confidential. "We will release this decree today. The rest is the portion that requires signatures of external parties."

John nodded dutifully.

Henri craned his neck to read the scribe's scroll, but Lilac quickly stamped her hand over it. "It is not for your eyes until release. You can read it with everyone else."

Henri took an affronted step back, crossing his arms and whipping his head at Marguerite, who only scowled at him.

"And these are punishable by imprisonment?" John asked. "Just to be sure."

"By either imprisonment or death if a trial isn't warranted. Thank you." Lilac took several steps toward the door, and when she didn't hear any movement behind her, spun and motioned to her scribe and Piper. "Well? This decree isn't going to release itself."

John and Piper exchanged glances. "I thought I'd take care of it, especially since you're preoccupied at the moment, Your Majesty," he said.

"Well, I am not making myself very useful here, am I? We'll finish this in the library."

"Are you positive? We can wait," said Piper half-heartedly, her poorly hidden scowl lessening. "Anything could've happened on his travels, if you'd like to wait for the news."

Lilac was done waiting. She couldn't sit in that chair any longer awaiting the fate she'd accepted. It seemed everything, every decision in her life, had been decided for her, and maybe Garin had been right—it did come with the territory of her birth, and it was normal for a woman, for the betterment of others, to accept a fate she hesitated on or outright did not want.

She would soon give her hand to the emperor while stuffing down the terror of placing her fate in a stranger's hands. It was a steep price for her kingdom's protection and the likely prevention of war, but in doing so, what else was she sacrificing?

Just hours ago, she was with Garin. Straddling him, kneeling before him, *tangled* in him. She flushed at the thought of their night, unable to recall where she'd ended and he'd began. Despite it all, she wanted more; she'd been left no choice but to give her free will, monopoly over her heart and mind, to him. All things considered, that should have terrified her far more than a marriage to a powerful ruler who offered her what many royal families would have jumped at.

If she were left alone with her thoughts any longer, she would make the wrong decision and doom her entire kingdom—and Brocéliande. She needed a distraction; she would not wait on a betrothal to start on her promises to the Daemons.

"I'd rather be productive in the meantime," Lilac answered, resuming her exit. This time, John and Piper rose to their feet and followed. "If the emissary shows up and presents his contract, you'll find me in the library." They would work on the Accords together. Having a finalized draft ready ahead of time would only prove a boon when they'd turned the chest over to Kestrel.

"Wait!" She looked back to see Marguerite holding her skirts, tiptoeing daintily down the steps. "Wait."

Reluctantly, Lilac waited for her to catch up as Piper and John arrived at her side.

"I know you said no celebrations or soirees, besides your coronation," Marguerite huffed, her hands out in front of her as Henri kept his head down and helped himself to breakfast, "but I simply couldn't resist."

"Mother." Lilac froze, her voice a hoarse whisper. "What did you do? What am I about to walk into?"

"I wanted to celebrate you and your new groom. Your stand-in groom."

Forgetting her strength, Lilac yanked both doors open. They swung inward, enveloping her entourage in a gush of wind.

At the end of the corridor, a small crowd of people lined the hall, spilling into the foyer. She could tell the front doors were open by the clear daylight spilling through, lighting a most elaborate selection of frosted colorful cakes propped upon the round table and several of Hedwig's carts. Pink and cream lace adorned the room with sashes lining the banisters in swooping bows and frills.

Lilac's throat constricted. She'd have to face them. If Albrecht had changed his mind, she would have to announce she was considering other options—other options for marriage that did not exist.

"Stand tall," her mother hissed as Henri lumbered over with a piece of toast in his hand. "Poise is an underrated virtue."

Lilac felt like she'd be sick. "Poise is hardly a virtue."

"It is in our world, where most men think that is all we have to offer. Play it well." Marguerite's narrowed eyes softened, and she peered past her daughter. "The emissary is late, that's all," she shouted down the corridor.

"Mother, please," Lilac snapped, her nerves balling at her core.

Albrecht had changed his mind, hadn't he? He didn't think her proper, he'd heard of her adventures in Paimpont and Rennes as her bordering forests were scouted by France. He did not think her fit for the throne or marriage to his liege, she was sure of it.

Or, also plausible—he'd awoken at the inn and was frightened out of it. Lorietta or Adelaide would've fixed his nerves, though. Bastion at least could have entranced him out of his fear. Myrddin might've even erased his memory of ever being stabbed and nursed back to health by a horde of Daemons.

There were many, many reasons he could have stalled or changed his mind. But there were equally as many reasons why he should've been there by now. Lilac glared down that blasted hallway at the returned stares, the mouthed whispers.

There was a hand at her back. "Onward," Piper said in her ear. "Whatever happens, *you* have decided it. It is within your power, and if it isn't, for God's sake let's pretend it is."

Together, the three of them walked into the corridor, Henri and John trailing behind. Lilac led them, her shoulders pulled back, a tight, polite smile at the ready. Marguerite eyed them both, watching her daughter and the strange girl who'd returned to the castle last night with simultaneous annoyance and wonder.

The front doors had been propped open, sunlight barely warming the sense of frost in the room. Lady Gertrude and Lady Helena were among the nearest and first to greet her with a bow. Behind them were Hedwig and half a dozen of her staff surrounding the tables, and a small gathering of several other friends to the Trécessons—junior nobility from surrounding provinces, those who'd likely arrived this morning as she was waiting in the Grand Hall. She craned her neck; through the last window, Lilac could just make out a row of carriages near the unmanned stable.

"Your coachman has not yet returned," noted Marguerite under her breath.

"Perhaps he and Albrect ran into the same bad weather," Piper suggested.

Marguerite ignored her lady-in-waiting's response and strutted forward, adopting a warm smile to greet her newly arrived friends.

Several of them had children around Lilac's age. She'd played with them during her mother's other soirees; she didn't see any of them now, and wondered where they were before realizing most—if not all of them—were probably busy with their own lives, married and with families of their own by now.

"The emissary hasn't arrived yet, has he?" Helena asked, craning her neck down the hallway as if he'd magically appear.

"No, it appears he hasn't," Lilac replied, maintaining her trained smile and posture with difficulty. "But I'm sure Albrecht will be here any time now."

"What if he's changed his mind?" wondered the towering woman behind Gertrude. She was Anaelle, if she remembered correctly—one of the marchionesses from Pont Aven. Her husband reddened beside her and gratefully accepted a flute of champagne from the nearest maid.

"Who?" wondered Gertrude behind her tiny gloved hand. "The emissary or the emperor?"

"*Lark*."

Lilac shifted to follow the scoff.

There was a woman in a chartreuse kirtle lounging upon the chaise on the other side of the furthest table, just out of sight. She looked older than Marguerite despite her youthful glow and bit into the pink tart in her hand before speaking again. "If he'd changed his mind," the woman offered, "may the cause be the outrageous gossips present to greet him."

Gertrude merely rolled her eyes and angled her body away from the woman.

"I can see why either might hesitate," Helena said, then covered her mouth. "Your Majesty, I didn't mean—I-I only meant, considering everything..."

Piper had started to say something cutting as Helena trailed off, but Marguerite sighed laboriously. "Don't be ridiculous. He is on the way, I assure you."

"But what of your patriarch? Has he returned yet?" Gertrude asked.

Marguerite was taken aback. "He has not."

"And the replacement archdeacon who conducted the Lilac's accession?"

"He departed two weeks ago," boomed Henri's voice from the end of the corridor.

Someone made a sound of disapproval in the small crowd.

"Well then, who will marry her and the emissary?" Gertrude pressed. "I mean, Maximillian?"

"This is a Catholic kingdom, is it not?" Lilac couldn't help the sarcasm dripping in her words. "There are priests everywhere. Those at the chapel in Rennes or Paimpont abbey would be more than willing."

"And who will conduct the Le Tallecs' funerary rite?" asked a robust woman who clung to her husband's arm near the right-hand staircase. Unlike the woman on the chaise, this one seemed familiar; Lilac thought she recognized her but a name didn't come to mind.

The room went silent. Then it was in an uproar.

"*Funeral?*" Gretchen nearly fell over herself.

"What happened?" gasped Helena when just Lilac stood there, not denying the truth to their hysteria. "For who? All three of them?"

"Just Vivien and Armand, from what I heard," the woman answered before Lilac could respond, fluffing one of her red curls. "Sinclair is still in the dungeon here. Terrible, I know."

"Where did you hear it?" asked Gertrude.

"Yes, tell us," said Lilac, crossing her arms. "Just where did you glean this information?"

The woman didn't seem bothered much being questioned directly by the queen. "Wendel and I were passing through Paimpont early this morning and stopped for a meal at the tavern, where we overheard. What a shame."

Every eye in the room landed on her as they awaited a response. Lilac's silence was deafening. She shouldn't have expected anything different from Artus. He was probably garnering the town's pity.

"I thought since it was news in Paimpont," the woman explained, "that everyone knew."

"That is enough, Agnes," Henri said quietly.

"Agnes." By the time they turned their attention back to Lilac, she'd left Piper's and John's side and made her way to the center table. On the way, she snatched a flute of champagne from the maid she passed and peered at the small, colorful frosted cakes arranged across the lace-strewn tabletop, dappled here and there with bonbons and truffles. Various shades of pinks, blues, and violet created the shape of a flower. "I don't think we've ever met. Either way, that was not your news to share."

Agnes flushed, taken aback. "Well, I—"

"You thought since it was rumor you heard in the town, you'd revel in the satisfaction of being the first one to spread it here. At my fortress." The room was silent. "You relish in spreading it, just as word of my Daemon tongue reached the moors and coasts without a single one of my town criers."

Stunned at Lilac's reply, Agnes gave a dramatically apologetic glance at Marguerite. Henri glared in the couple's direction.

"I'm sorry," Agnes whispered to them, pouting.

"Don't apologize to her parents."

Lilac looked up from the table. To her left, Piper was red as a beet, her attention fixed out the open doors even as she addressed Agnes. Every pair of eyes in the room immediately shifted to her. "They're not the ones who've carried the burden of humiliation and public outcry."

Agnes shuddered at being addressed by Piper. "No one asked *you*."

"My lady-in-waiting's opinion is favored well over yours. It is, in fact, welcome without prompting." Lilac lifted the flute to her mouth and picked the corner cake up, one that was blue-violet, the shade of early dawn. She turned it this way and that, examining Hedwig's fine craftsmanship.

They would talk, regardless. Let her remind them, then, that the decision to accept the duty of marriage had been hers; she had not been cornered or beguiled into forfeiting her freedom. Lilac was no one's puppet, and she and her circle were to be respected.

That's what Piper was to her. Adelaide, Lorietta, and Garin. Even Bastion and Myrddin. John, Giles, and Herlinde, apparently. Those who didn't owe Lilac a moment of their time nor a shard of respect, yet she'd never felt the need to question their loyalties.

Her mother had kept the women in this room close, only to be turned on once her family was in question and the stability of Henri's power hung in the balance of their daughter's fading favorability with the kingdom. In the aftermath of Lilac's fifteenth birthday, no one had supported Marguerite. Lilac used to think they were too afraid to stand by their friend and former queen consort, but there was a sense of spite in the air now— one she couldn't possibly have comprehended as a young child.

There was power, Lilac surmised, after years of her life being made so public over an ability she could not help, in holding some secrets close and forfeiting the need for validation. Her kingdom didn't deserve it, especially those who would do no good with either truth or lie.

"There will be a funeral," Lilac said briefly, licking icing off her thumb and biting into the cake. "Armand and Vivien are both dead. Plans are to be privately arranged with Armand's father, and it will likely be held at the abbey. Sinclair remains in my custody. There was an investigation to be completed before drafting an announcement. You were supposed to be the first to hear it here, but it appears Artus had other plans." She stared Agnes and her bewildered husband down. "News of it will go out to the squares today, along with my very first decree. Won't it, John?"

Behind her, their scribe nodded. "It shall be announced in the nearest squares by this afternoon."

"Send the pigeons now," Lilac said. "You are dismissed."

John bowed and scurried up the steps. Marguerite shifted, visibly uncomfortable. Henri steeled himself, and a small approving smile bloomed on Piper's face as she tore her gaze from the open doors.

"And what of the fire?" Agnes pressed. "It seems there are a lot of them these days. In your dungeon, with two of your prisoners escaping. Then the blaze at that filthy whore house in downtown Rennes. Not that I'm sure," she added, "it wasn't warranted."

Beyond her nerves and anger, Lilac held her tongue. They'd chase her into a corner if she pretended not to know, and she refused to allow this particularly vile Agnes to think she'd chastised her into telling the truth. She popped the rest of the cake into her mouth, unbothered... and smiled, momentarily forgetting herself. *Delicious.*

She swallowed and looked to Hedwig, who stood at the corner of the table nearby, but the newly appointed Stewardess's gaze was fixed straight ahead at the door. She would feed them another partial truth—one that this time benefitted her.

"The Rennes fire has been attended to. I have handled it." Lilac reached over and plucked another flute of champagne from the plate floating to her left, bringing it straight to her quivering lips.

"Handled?" echoed a distant voice that drifted in with the breeze caressing the back of Lilac's neck. "That is hardly the term I'd use to describe what had happened last night."

Champagne spurted from her mouth onto some of the cakes and dribbled down her chin. Slowly, she turned.

So did everyone else.

Lilac spun to glimpse Giles's carriage parked just outside the stables near the others. Beside it, in the middle of the bailey, were two horses: Loïg and another brown horse—Hywell's. There were two fine travel bags hanging off their thick saddles.

A tall figure strode into the room, a dark mass of black linens, leathers, and bear fur. He didn't wait for the huffing blond fellow behind him—a panting Myrddin—or even for the crowd to fully part. He pardoned and squeezed his way to her so quickly, Lilac bumped up against the table in alarm.

Garin bent into a deep bow at the waist. He caught her fingers on his way up, just as he had on the night he'd reintroduced himself at Sinclair's camp, and pressed his mouth to the back of her hand. "Your Majesty."

Lilac pulled her arm away under his crushing stare, her head spinning as his intoxicating aroma of the dark wood engulfed her.

He stood, poised and unrecognizable in his trained posture. A black tunic and brown undershirt peeked out at his chest over black leather trousers. A long, black coat fell to his ankles, its collar lined in thick, speckled furs—and beneath that, Albrecht's satchel she'd seen in Garin's memory hung across his body, resting upon his hip.

He pressed a hand to his chest. "I am Albrecht Fistch III, but you can call me Albrecht. Behind me is Ambrosius, my valet. We would have arrived earlier, but we found ourselves stuck behind one of your carriages."

Although Garin's fur-covered chest and face flooded Lilac's vision, she could hear the embarrassment in her mother's voice. "Well? Return the gesture."

"It's quite all right." Garin offered a dashing smile in Marguerite's direction. Gertrude and Helena's faces climbed in color. "She is the queen. She needn't kneel for anyone." He leaned forward suddenly, making her entire body tense. Reaching past her, his jet black waves brushed her cheek. "Certainly not me," he whispered into her ear.

Lilac held herself from him, gripping the edge of the table with her free hand, the heel of her palm digging into the wood so hard she might bleed.

He straightened, biting into one of Hedwig's cakes. White-pink frosting lining his bottom lip. He slid his tongue along it before taking the rest of the dessert into his mouth. "Vanilla and black currant? And..." He frowned. "Almonds?"

"Walnuts," Hedwig said, smiling in surprise. "You must be well traveled."

"Why, thank you. I don't leave my country often. Maximilian scarcely allows me out of his sight."

Helena coughed. "I wonder why." Gertrude jabbed her bony elbow into Helena's ribs.

Garin pretended not to hear. "Though, I do enjoy cooking, Madame..." He extended a hand.

The Stewardess, whom Lilac had never seen flustered over anything but a difficult recipe, latched onto his hand. "Heussaff, My Lord. Hedwig Heussaff."

His brows rose. Lilac couldn't tell if his surprise was genuine. "Any relation to the Heussaffs in Dinan?"

"How do you know?"

"I've heard only great things about your family's bakery. I have an old friend who insists their lavender bread saved Paimpont from some dreadfully dry marzipan turnovers."

Hedwig chuckled, turning red. "That was all very long ago. After the Raid, most of my family had—" She paused, blinking at the floor. A hand went to Hedwig's chest while she gathered herself. "Yes, well, that was my grandmother's recipe."

Garin watched her patiently. He nodded and placed an empathetic hand upon Hedwig's shoulder. "Take your time. I'm sorry to have brought up such a difficult topic." He glanced at the doorway, where three ward bundles of beads of iron, holy water, and garlic were suspended in cheesecloth by hawthorn and iron hooks wrenched into the wall—one on each side of the entryway. "It seems these days you are well equipped against those bloodsucking vermin."

"Not well enough," Lilac said through gritted teeth.

"Fortunately, Your Majesty," Garin said, reaching into his coat pocket and pulling out something half the length of his forearm and wrapped several times in cloth. Her heart dropped as he offered it to her. "I brought this from our armory. You should remain well equipped. You never know what, or whom, might be lurking out there."

She accepted it, hand trembling. She didn't need to open it to know what it was. Lilac held it away as nausea rolled through her.

Someone tapped her arm. Piper gently took the stake, careful to handle it over the cloth as the room watched with bated breath.

"Our armory contains a small collection of stakes and other odds and ends tucked away," Henri offered stiffly from the corridor archway. "We've never had to use them and hopefully never will." When she said nothing, her father cleared his throat. "Aren't you going to thank him?"

"I don't think she's accustomed to such abrupt kindness is all," Marguerite assured Garin. "Dear? What do you have to say?"

"I think you should leave." Every head in the room swiveled to face Lilac. The words were like sand in her throat, distorting her tone. She sounded hesitant, the surefire fury she felt deep down instantly tapering off at her lips.

Unphased, Garin brought his hand to his mouth, licking a residual smear of pink frosting off his knuckle. "But I've only just arrived. And what of Hedwig's delectable treats? I cannot go without tasting *all* of them."

Helena stumbled against Gertrude, on the brink of fainting.

"Come now, Your Majesty," Hedwig said, visibly flattered but still upset. "They must stay for the feast proposed for tonight."

There was a loud *pop*, followed by the sound of raining glass upon the floor. The champagne flute had shattered in her hand. Hedwig's assistants rushed to her side, attempting to examine her. Lilac brushed them off, cradling her arm to her chest and ignoring the slight sting in her hand.

"Your parents had requested a dinner celebration to mark the emissary's arrival and your new acquaintanceship," explained Hedwig firmly. "It was to be a surprise."

He had come to safeguard the pathway to her and Maximilian's alliance —he didn't trust her to make the right choice. Garin hadn't known she'd agree to it, unless Myrddin had told him. Whether or not he knew it, both scenarios made his presence all the more infuriating.

So did needing to focus on her anger as her body began to throb.

"Cancel it," she managed, swallowing hard and dusting the glass off her fingers. She couldn't exactly fault her mother's friends for being unable to peel their eyes off him; Lilac had salivated at the sight of Garin in his black sweeping cloak and fur collar. "There will be no feast tonight."

Garin stepped back, finally giving her room to breathe. Giving *himself* room, hands flexing at his side. "A feast, you say?"

There was movement behind him, then; the crowd parted with utterances of disgust as a flash of gray—*Bisousig*—slunk around Garin's legs. Giles peered around Garin's shoulders, made broader by his cloak. The coachman's eyes widened at the array of mostly untouched treats before him, but Garin turned and shot him a look.

"Get her out of here," he warned under his breath.

Giles nodded and promptly scooped the cat up from Garin's ankles, bowing and showing himself out between the perplexed guards.

"If I may, Your Majesty." Myrddin raised his hand to speak. His glorious golden hair was cropped, falling just over his ears and framing his face. He'd gotten rid of his robes and instead wore a dusk blue tunic, unbuttoned at the chest over tight dark trousers. "Under the emperor's order, we cannot leave without presenting you with Maximilian's marriage offer. You have every right to decline," Myrddin was quick to add.

Garin swiveled back on him. Whatever look the vampire gave Myrddin shut him right up. "*Which she will not*," Garin said, his mask slipping.

"I don't understand," Marguerite said, hysterical. "She has our blessing. She was willing, eager even, for Maximilian's proposition last night when Artus—" Her fingers went to her lips as she realized what she'd said.

Murmurs rose around the room.

Garin's head snapped to Lilac. "Artus Le Tallec was here?"

Had Myrddin not mentioned the former duke's visit? Although his inquiry was no demand, his tone wrenched it from her. "He and his men were here late last night spouting several harmless threats," she answered, as the rest of the nobility listened in. Then, for everyone else's benefit, added, "Do you know him?"

Garin ran a hand through his hair, collecting himself. "I've heard of him. Before I was sent on my way, I was briefed. I understand he was removed from his position years ago, but that his family retained their titles, and that they were fairly close with yours." He observed the warning look Henri and Marguerite exchanged with Lilac and lowered his voice. "I did hear there was an incident with his grandson, though. At your ceremony the other week."

"He became enraged during the end of my accession and was arrested. He and his family were on house arrest until he ended up murdering his mother."

Garin's hand went to his temple, his annoyance dissolving. He took a deep breath, pretending to process the information. "My God. Has he been executed?" He was an infuriatingly good liar.

"Not yet. He's here in the dungeons," Lilac said matter-of-factly. "Armand came to the castle shortly after. He requested an audience just to gift me his wife's severed arm and spilled his guts all over my Grand Hall."

Her mother groaned and put her face in her hands. Henri was shaking.

Garin looked back at the crowd, who watched her with unabashed abhorrence. "His own innards?"

Lilac kept her chin up, not taking her eyes off Garin's. It was his mission to get her to wed Maximilian, just as much as it was Albrecht's—wherever he was. Gagged and bound in the cellar of The Fenfoss Inn, probably. Her parents could give their approval all they wanted. It was still the emissary's duty to make the offer or decide otherwise as a public representative of the emperor.

She was more than willing to give him just cause to reconsider, just to get under Garin's skin. She wasn't changing her mind... And if Maximilian wanted access to her ports and farmland enough, neither would he. He was the one who hired an emissary terrible at keeping confidential information in the first place, after all.

Maximilian would overlook her behavior and deliver on his promises, especially if Garin thought he could corner her to the altar.

"His very own," she replied.

There was no recognition upon Garin's countenance—only a genuine, utmost sympathy. "My apologies, Your Majesty. That must've been difficult to witness."

"It was." She gave him an appreciative smile. "Not to worry though, I've been lavishing myself."

"How so?" The corner of his mouth twitched, eyes narrowing. *There it was.* Garin crossed his arms. "Do tell."

There was a small tug within—nothing like the power of his demands, but a pull still palpable. "With extended trips to the towns and cities, shopping for new gowns and drowning my worries in mead and other..." There was a small bead of blood on her fingertip—the only visible remnant of the flute she'd smashed. She stuck it into her mouth, tasting iron. "Leisures."

The lump in his throat bobbed as Garin tracked the movement, a shadow of fury gracing his features. His voice was grating, teeth upon her throat. "*Leisures?*"

"The brothel, for instance. The Fool's Folly."

There was a collective sound of exasperation from her parents and several gasps from the corners of the room.

"We're fucked," Helena moaned under her breath, shushed by Gertrude.

"Lilac, that is enough," said her father.

Marguerite had reached for the platter next to her and held two champagne glasses, sipping from one of them and chuckling to herself, streaks of black running from her lashes through her powder.

It was the warning look Garin gave, body angled to her and full of resentment, that carried Lilac through. "The Fool's Folly is a lovely place. Strong drinks, *talented* entertainment, and rather garrulous barmaids. For instance, I overheard you could not bear to keep your excitement to proposition me to yourself," she lied for her parents' sake. "In fact, their tavern gossip is where I first learned of your emperor's impressive offerings. Unless, they no longer stand?"

A muscle under his eye twitched. She could tell his mind was racing, struggling to keep up. "Your Majesty, Maximilian's offer—and my approval —would stand, even if you were observed riding a rogue vampire in one of the frontmost alcoves of that brothel."

Marguerite spat her champagne out.

Lilac retained her composure and donned a relieved smile. "I'm glad at least in your eyes my reputation remains untainted. Especially after that dreadful fire, no?"

"What fire?" Helena mouthed. Agnes and her husband nudged each other, looking shocked to be unaware of this bit of gossip.

"The one that engulfed one of the second floor rooms last night." Lilac pretended not to notice their whispering and stared Garin down. "Who knows how it started?"

"Anything can happen when two people are being *careless*," he retorted.

Garin knew she'd never reveal his true nature or put him or the Daemons in more jeopardy. But there was nothing stopping her from dancing dangerously close. "Who said anything about two?" Lilac offered. "Why not three? Or four?"

"There is no need for these frivolous stories just because you are repellent to the idea of marriage." Marguerite plopped both empty champagne flutes on the tray, nearly toppling the maid holding it. She clasped her hands together, looking pacified despite her flushed cheeks. Batting her lashes, her intrepid gaze fell upon Garin as she steadied herself. "And *you*? Are you married, Lord Fritsch?"

Garin tore his eyes from Lilac as Marguerite slinked nearer. "I am not," he answered curtly, despite a voice like velvet. Lilac watched open-mouthed as Marguerite extended her arm. He took her fingers in his despite Henri's glare, brought her gloved hand to his mouth and planted a kiss upon it. "You must call me Albrecht. I insist."

Her mother leaned in. "I intend to by the end of the week."

Lilac realized she was shaking. She needed another drink... *No*. She needed a walk, her bed, a large cup of tea and a warm croissant. To tell Piper of all the nasty and incriminating things he'd ever done—to scream into the void. To get *away* from him.

"Do not disgrace Her Majesty that way," said Piper from behind. Her friend looked equally horrified, awkwardly holding the stake at length.

Marguerite released herself from Garin and took several wobbling steps back to Henri.

Agnes snorted into her champagne. "She does every bit of that herself."

Henri grunted, shooting Agnes a look. "But what of that witch seamstress who escorted you back last night? And the haberdashery, a-and the soot and..." The former king trailed off, glancing at the tray of champagne nearby but not reaching for any. He stared at Lilac, then at Piper. "And the blood?"

"Ah." Garin crossed his arms, belatedly understanding. "The seamstress Herlinde was part of the crowd of shopkeepers, passerby, and unscathed patrons who emerged to help evacuate everyone from The Fool's Folly. I was among them." He turned to Lilac with a pensive expression. "Do you not remember me?"

She blinked slowly at him, unsure of where he would steer her partial lies. "It was all a blur, and you do not have a memorable face at all. So, no."

He ignored her comment and continued. "Well, Herlinde was the first familiar face I saw. Earlier in the week I'd visited her after hearing of her enchanted wares and finery, and she'd sold me this lovely coat." He fluffed his fur collar. Shocked whispers erupted around the room at his casual mention of Herlinde's magic. "I spotted Her Majesty struggling and ensured she was brought to safety. Passed her onto Herlinde, who took her into her nearby shop. Of course, I didn't know she was the queen at the time."

"Thank fuck." She was beginning to feel unfortunately brazen and regretted not eating at breakfast. "I wouldn't have wanted you to feel obliged to drag me back here and leverage such a grand gesture for my hand."

Garin chuckled. "Maximilian is the one in need of leveraging. I wouldn't *fathom*..." He pursed his lips and glanced knowingly at the gaggle of giddy onlookers—Marguerite, her former court, even some of Lilac's staff. "You know what I mean."

"Fortunately, I do." Lilac cocked her head, suppressing a smile. "And you? What did you think of your stay there, Lord Fritsch?"

At that moment, Hedwig began to pile some of the cakes onto a tray atop her cart. "Afternoon tea in the Grand Hall. If anyone is interested, please follow me. At this rate, tonight's merriments will start early. Better to have the ale flowing." She marched brusquely across the foyer and into the west corridor. Henri made to follow, but Marguerite caught him by the arm.

No one else moved a muscle.

Lilac stilled, ready for whatever scapegoat he'd divulge next. Bracing herself. Daring him.

But Garin only sighed defeatedly and spoke to the room, his back to her. "What I think is, in the midst of my travels to your beautiful Bretagne for the first time, on a conquest for her queen's affection on behalf of my emperor, I got carried away. And while I might have spent my first few nights here enjoying the very *best* of what the kingdom has to offer—" He pivoted to Lilac, his forehead creasing in pity. "Fucking my way through Rennes was not the most appropriate way to deal with my nerves, I'm sure you agree. What I think, Your Majesty," he said, taking a slow step toward her. "Is that we both are two *titled* individuals who were caught in the wrong place, at the wrong time."

Lilac held her ground, but her knees shook as he approached. She'd been an idiot to try to out-humiliate him.

"We'll let bygones be bygones, Your Majesty. I won't say anything about what I have seen and heard of you to Maximilian and the rest of our court if you, nor your family's court, will say nothing outside this room about me." He gave a long, sweeping look around the room, at the crowd watching them both with bated breath, before his eyes settled hungrily upon Lilac. "Or my appetites. One word out of any of you, and Ambrosius and I traipse back to safety—but not before I send a pigeon to Vienna with news of Brittany's most scandalous queen. Who knows what would happen then?"

All Lilac had for him was an expression of conflicted hatred impossible to mask, regardless of how hard she tried. Henri and Marguerite stared helplessly at her.

Her father could sense her simmering anger, though he would never know the full reasons behind it; he locked eyes with her and shook his head minutely, begging her not to do anything that would jeopardize their path to safety.

"Then, you and your tiny kingdom might find yourselves cornered by two enemies." Garin reached out to place his hand on Lilac, but she recoiled. He only smiled, and dropped his arm at his side. "Rest assured, Maximilian's offer remains unaffected as long as your generous offer of hospitality does. I have heard nothing but great things about the Trécesson soirees and your Hedwig's fine dining. Plus," he said, glancing around, "I could not help but notice your lack of sentries. Two here in your foyer, approximately eight I spotted outside including two in the immediate vicinity of the bailey and six up on the ramparts."

"They have better use out east. I have sent a group of them to Fougères," Lilac said firmly. "They are to return after scouting the bordering towns in a show of non-violent force."

Garin examined her, lips pursing in real disapproval. "You must be careful, Your Majesty. Whether it be your former duke, the fine ladies of your mother's court" —his mercurial eyes darted to Agnes, whose face blanched — "or even the valet of the emissary sent through mountain and moor to ask your hand." Myrddin didn't say a word. "Your kingdom should be parading with guards, each one of them a watchful eye on the day a foreign dignitary visits ahead of a most imminent celebration. Especially during times of such unrest between not only your crown and another, but the enchanted forest that borders your home." Garin stepped back and glanced out the window nearest the west corridor. "You all would be shocked to find just how quickly the most diplomatic meeting can turn into a bloodbath."

Lilac remained where she was, feet planted in place. "The Daemons would never touch my guards," she said, the hatred in her voice very real, yet somehow forced. His taunting words did nothing to quell her terrible urges warring to kiss and throttle him. "Wronged as they are, they know better than to retaliate while I'm attempting to guard their homes, too."

"Do they?" Garin walked back, shrugging with his hands in his pockets. "Take a look for yourself."

Knowing he was being sarcastic, she was forced to look anyway, the muscles of her shoulders pivoting her first so that the rest of her body followed. She glanced out the open doors instead of the window—beyond the bailey, past her iron gates, and into the treeline.

Brocéliande was peaceful and still despite the clear day.

The champagne in Lilac's glass shook violently when she turned back to him.

Garin bending, propping himself up on one leg. On his knee. His throat bobbed, and he looked up at her with a solemnity she'd never seen before.

Lilac's entire body went rigid. "What are you doing?" Her heart dropped. "What do you think you're—"

"You're right." Garin's voice wavered. "This cannot wait. I can see what this is doing to you, the unfathomable stress you are under. Imagine having the backing of an army so lithe, so formidable with such unmatched knowledge of the forested terrain that you wouldn't have to worry your pretty little head about any of this."

That wasn't what any of this was ever about. Her face was almost numb with heat, but she couldn't do anything but shake her head.

Gently, Garin slipped his fingers beneath hers. His skin was warm, his hand slightly trembling beneath hers as he held it up.

"Garin," she whispered, but he cut her off.

"I know we haven't known each other long. Imagine how your subjects might regard you if you agreed to an alliance securing not only your right to defend your kingdom, but the sheer power in your capability to ward larger powers off?" His gaze ensnared hers. She couldn't look away. "By right, our alliance will allow you to retain your full sovereignty and right to your throne."

The crowd was still as the leaves outside.

"You don't want me to leave, do you?" crooned Garin. "Tell me the truth of how you feel."

Lilac's body came alive under his power. "I don't want you to leave. I want you here." Her breath and the words upon it were ripped from a place deep within. "With me."

The sadness and profound relief etched in his features were almost too much to bear. She tried to look away, tried to divert her eyes.

"Eleanor."

She shook her head and looked to the ceiling, lips pursed. *What kind of freak did this in public?*

"Eleanor, please."

His eyes were soft, his command was anything but pleading. Lilac had no choice but to look. He was reaching with his other hand into his cloak.

"Eleanor of Brittany, will you enter this marriage—" Garin pulled out not a box or ring, but a thick, very official-looking scroll tied in red ribbon.

She stared at him, her bottom lip quivering in utmost hatred, trying her best to swallow the rage that rose. The tears brimming her eyes began to spill.

"With my liege, Maximillian I of Austria, Emperor of The Holy Roman Empire?"

There was an uproar around them, sounds of relief and cries of happiness from her mother and father. The crowd began to clap.

The tears could stall no longer. Blurry-eyed, Lilac took one look at him. With hands shaking in heartbreak, she raised her flute up high.

"A toast, yes!" Henri shouted, holding his own glass up. "To Lilac and the emperor!"

The crowd followed suit, tilting their glasses toward her and Garin. "To Lilac! And the emperor!"

Lilac tipped the flute and emptied it onto Garin's head, abruptly jarring the crowd from cheers of merriment to panicked distress. She ripped her hand from his and slinked through the crowd, slamming the empty flute upon a most unfortunate flattened pastry. Hot tears blinding her, the queen marched past a shrieking Marguerite, past the boisterous giggling of Agnes and the wide, encouraging smile of the woman in the chartreuse dress, past

the scullery filled with staff prepping birds and pies for the night's feast—
and up her tower stairs.

23

L ilac had paced in front of her flickering hearth since she'd slammed the door in Piper's face, hoping her frustrated footfall would stomp out the memory of the forlorn look she'd given her —as if she were a hungry animal Lilac had left in the cold. She'd lost count of how many times she walked the length of the fireplace.

Maybe the pacing thing was something that came with a vampire type of restlessness.

When a knock finally came, she shouted that she wanted to be left alone. Seconds later, rushed footsteps echoed back down the stairwell. Piper had obliged. For that, Lilac was grateful. And yet, she found herself harshly judging the pace of Piper's descent. She'd done what Lilac had asked; she had barked her wishes rather forcefully. What else was Piper supposed to do?

But did she have to honor the request so...readily? She slowed her pacing, another heavy sob forming in her chest. She wasn't used to the help, wasn't used to the company or——or friendship.

Deep down, she felt terrible.

Calming her breathing, impossibly willing that pretty-eyed, fanged sod out of her mind, Lilac perched at the edge of her bed, staring at her sunlit balcony. Escaping again sounded tempting. She could lower herself down once more; on second thought, she could probably climb down with her newfound strength if that's how Piper had made it into her room last night. Maybe she'd spook everyone and jump—she'd probably survive since Garin had all but thrown them both off the second floor of the brothel last night. She'd survived that landing.

No, she thought begrudgingly. *That wouldn't work.*

However she got down, she'd then run into the woods and this time trail the path to the inn. Maybe she'd take Loïg and hope for the best. She could always round up the ever-helpful Giles and her horses, but her parents and guard would be at the gates faster than they could prepare the carriage.

So would Garin.

This time, the monsters she ran from no longer lurked in the shadows of Brocéliande, but sat in high places. The one roaming the castle, for instance—he was touring her domain on a pleasant afternoon stroll with her parents. Her willpower could easily be negated with but a flick of his fingers. A simple, whispered command. And he was terrifyingly fast. Lilac ground her teeth at the thought of Garin dragging her and Loïg back to the bailey, knowing better than to test him.

He would do it. He would ensure she married Maximilian if it was the last thing he did.

There was another knock at the door, this time accompanied by muffled voices. Tempted to yell again, Lilac dragged herself off the bed and went to answer. It was Piper with the cloth-wrapped stake tucked under her arm, balancing a large tray of bonbons, several filled flutes, and a bottle of champagne. Behind her was Yanna and Isabel, the latter with a basket on one arm and an oddly shaped tapered bundle tucked under the other. They hovered in the doorway this time instead of eyeing the corners of the room and lingering outside like usual.

"Sorry I took so long," Piper muttered, urgently ushering Lilac aside. Relief washed over Piper's face as she set the precarious arrangement she'd been carrying down safely on Lilac's bed. "I left to find Hedwig for the rest of the bottle and fresh bonbons for you, and on the way to your tower I discovered Ga—" She coughed. "Albrecht had cornered these two at the stairwell."

Lilac's heart fluttered. "What did he do? Are you both all right?"

Yanna rolled her eyes, her mouth pulled into a hard line. "We'd heard there had been a commotion in the foyer. Hedwig sent us to comfort you."

"We *wanted* to check on you," Isabel reassured her. "He was coming down the stairwell when we nearly ran into him. He asked us to bring you these." She handed Lilac the wicker basket and bundle—which, upon further inspection, she discovered to be a cork-stopped bottle wrapped twice in parchment.

It had been Garin at her door. Lilac swallowed her shock with an annoyed grunt. "Where is he now?"

"Both Sir Albrecht and Ambrosius are being shown to their quarters at the moment," said Isabel. "Fond as she seemed of him, Hedwig really wasn't a fan of him trying to access your bedchamber unaccompanied," she added with a giggle. "Your father will give them a full tour of the castle and grounds. You seemed rather upset, so we just wanted to make you aware."

Lilac lifted the basket lid and peeked inside. There were loaves of bread, wedges of cheese dappled with peppers and fruit, and a jar of what looked to be strawberry preserves. As expected, a subtle heat emanated from the cloth-lined interior of the basket.

How considerate of him, she thought scathingly. At least it seemed he hadn't entirely torn The Fenfoss Inn apart as he'd woken up. "And I assume my mother and Hedwig have resumed preparations for tonight's feast?"

Isabel grimaced. "The decorations are minimal and pleasing to look at, Your Majesty."

She turned away. They'd seen enough of her tears over the past several weeks. Lilac closed Garin's basket, eyes stinging as she left to place the basket on her vanity. "Thank you, both of you."

She kept the bottle, figuring Lorietta had sent him with some cider or some of her strong homemade wine, either of which she could use at the moment. Yanna and Isabel stood there, awkwardly watching Piper dispose of the cloth-wrapped stake into the bedside table drawer as if it were a large rodent.

"Do you two have plans for the rest of the evening?" Lilac grunted, twisting the cork this way and that. "You're attending my feast tonight, aren't you?"

"We won't, but we'll be on, ready to support you," Isabel said as Yanna glared distantly into the fire. "We were instructed by Hedwig to have the both of you ready, but we weren't sure if you still planned to attend."

"The celebration is for Albrecht, to ensure *his* approval. They'll be fine starting the festivities without me. If he's lucky, maybe I won't show up at all."

Piper sidled over, eyeing the bottle. "I wouldn't advise skipping the feast entirely, Your Majesty."

"You haven't changed your mind on marrying the emperor, have you?" sneered Yanna. Lilac whipped her head around, fixing Yanna with an incredulous glower. Yanna just shrugged. "We heard about it on the floor."

Lilac heaved an exasperated sigh, returning her attention to the stubbornly sealed bottle in her hands. "Of course you did." The damn cork wouldn't budge, not even with her improved strength.

Isabel was fanning herself. "I mean, how can you say no, really?"

"She's marrying the *emperor*," Yanna replied, rolling her eyes. "Not Albrecht, no matter how handsome he may be. She'd still be a fool to turn down his offer, though, or even hesitate to accept it. Her marriage will save us all."

"What would you know, Yanna," Lilac said, her speech turning to a half-growl as she gritted her teeth, twisting and tugging at the cork with all her might, "about marriage—" The cork flew off and across the room.

A dizzying rush of warm air hit her square in the face, along with a putrid scent. Heavy musk and iron, then something fermented.

Lilac jerked her head to the side and held her breath, nearly dropping the bottle as she angled the neck away from her face and thrust her arm forward, desperate to distance herself from it.

It *wasn't* cider. "Oh!"

Piper's nostrils flared and she immediately snatched the bottle from Lilac. Her eyes darkened.

"No, no no. Not here," Lilac whispered. *Gods, not here.* She braced herself, preparing to usher the other two out of the room. But Piper merely licked her lips and put the bottle to her mouth. She drank like a traveler who'd run out of water days ago, tipping her head back with desperate need. The handmaidens watched, appalled and rooted to the spot as Piper's eyes rolled back and fluttered shut, her voracious gulps punctuated by sharp gasps and moans. Rivulets of deep red dribbled down her face and neck.

Before Lilac could contrive a lie about a new type of thick, burgundy wine, Yanna merely huffed, regarding Piper with a pitying shake of her head. "You know, I thought so. Some warning that you'd hired a vampire onto your court wouldn't have gone amiss, Your Majesty."

Lilac stared at Yanna. Beside her, Isabel covered her mouth, looking like she was going to be sick watching Piper. But neither of them looked shocked, or even frightened.

"You *knew?*" spat Lilac.

Yanna cocked a brow. "Do you think we're stupid?"

Piper wiped her chin on her nightgown sleeve, oblivious of the conversation surrounding her. "Hells, that's delicious." As soon as she opened her eyes to everyone staring at her, the moment of bliss was over. Piper reddened. "Oh, fuck me."

"She *entranced* us last night," explained Isabel warily. "Next time—and hopefully there won't be one—it might be useful to entrance us to *forget*, like they sometimes do. It is not a pleasant experience."

They'd known, yet they hadn't gone running to Marguerite. Her parents had reason enough to want Piper out, and they wouldn't have batted an eye at using Piper's vampirism as an obvious disqualifying trait for courtly duties.

She would never let them.

Lilac plucked two flutes of champagne from the tray. "She is kind and a good person, and—" she glanced at Piper, who'd plopped down in the vanity chair, hands trembling around the bottleneck. "She won't do it again." She held the flutes out. "Please take these and never, *ever* speak a word of this to anyone."

"I didn't know I'd entranced you." Piper's face was the picture of humiliation. "I didn't realize it until I spoke with Lilac. I promise it won't happen again."

Yanna scoffed. "I'm sure."

"She's *new*," Lilac snapped.

Isabel accepted her flute, but Yanna refrained. "Vampires don't frighten us. Those of us who worked the Rennes nightlife are quite used to them. Although, she *is* the first we've met who can walk during the day. And you're right," she said, her scathing gaze boring into Lilac. "I know nothing of marriage. Under your leadership, perhaps I never will."

Fed up with Yanna's mood, Lilac turned to her most insufferable hand-maiden. "What are you talking about?"

"You sent my beau off to Fougères."

"Your beau." Lilac stepped back, stunned. She hadn't even known Yanna had been seeing someone. Yanna's searing resentment seemed to intensify all the more as panic flitted across Lilac's face. She'd hoped, vainly, that her momentary lapse of composure would go unnoticed. It had not. "Your fiancé is one of my guards?"

"Yes," Yanna replied. Were Lilac a vampire, she'd fear her handmaiden's pointed stare alone would have set her skin aflame. "No need to fret. He's one of the few you haven't sucked off."

Lilac's ears began to ring, annoyedly nudging the flute in Yanna's direction again. She didn't know what else to say. "You could've told me. I would have held him back with the others."

Yanna snatched the drink from Lilac. "We are in love, but I have my reservations." She glanced over at Isabel who sipped at her drink, wandering over to the sweets tray. "Marguerite and Henri just hired us. We've been here a little less than a month—we'd be stupid to pass up such positions after everything we'd been through to get here."

"The offer did sound too good to be true," said Isabel. She plopped onto the bed next to the bonbons. "They'd said you were in desperate need of companionship and had run off into Brocéliande. We felt compelled to respond. It would've given us another opportunity at employment and shelter together."

Piper seemed to have calmed; she sat cross-legged on the vanity chair, blotting the blood off the rest of her neck with a napkin. She cocked her head, her gaze flitting between Yanna and Isabel.

"I don't like the hunger in your eyes," Yanna said. "Was the wine not enough?"

Piper shook her head. "You're *sisters*, aren't you?"

Isabel drew back ever so slightly, her brow furrowed subtly as she reassessed Piper. Her surprise at Piper's accusation had washed her wariness away, and a smile crept across her face until she was beaming. "How can you tell? You're the first person who's ever guessed. We've gotten best friends. Partners, even."

Piper exchanged a shocked glance with Lilac, smiling wryly. "I don't know. I just had a sense."

"We are. So the records show."

They hardly looked related. Yanna's eyes were green as springtime, and Isabel's, the warmest brown that turned to fire at sunset. Yanna's long hair was a plain straw blonde, often tightly knit against her scalp. Isabel's was dark and thick, waterfalling just between her tan shoulders. Maybe their nose bridges and brows were a bit similar, and the way their mouth set to the left when they were trying to problem solve.

They were always together. They mirrored each other often. She supposed they bickered like sisters. They finished one another's sentences and shared across plates at supper. Still, Lilac never would've thought...but maybe that was because she knew nothing of having sisters herself.

"It doesn't matter," Yanna said sternly. "We were left at the same orphanage in Rennes twenty-six years ago. We don't make a habit of telling people. That way, we've stuck together. Most establishments don't like hiring relatives. Especially sisters."

"Especially *twins*," added Isabel.

Suddenly, she understood Yanna's reservations. Marriage for either one would've meant their separation. Traditionally, Lilac's blessing and their ceremony would've led to the termination of Yanna's contract, leaving Isabel to work there alone once they moved into their own home.

"Well, I'm glad you're both here. Your secret is safe with us, we won't say anything." Lilac could barely keep up with the twists and turns of the conversation, much less the day. "Where did my parents find you?"

Setting her empty flute down on the nearby table, Yanna looked at her sister with a fierce protectiveness. Her forehead creased, as if worried she'd said too much. "When the search parties were dispatched to look for you, your parents sent requests through the town criers. One morning, as we were getting ready for work, we noticed someone had slid a pamphlet under our door sometime the previous night."

"They were desperate to find someone," said Isabel. "We'd never seen anything like it."

Lilac laughed a mirthless laugh. It was a sound born of annoyance far more than amusement. "There were several eligible maidens who would've been offered the position outright, but it's likely they were advised by their families to stay away."

"Because of your Daemon tongue?" asked Isabel.

"Because they're idiots," answered Piper.

Lilac nodded, suppressing a smile.

"How privileged they are," said Yanna, sighing. "We left that day with our Madame's blessing. We both agreed that if either of us got the job, we'd work for a few years here while the other remained. We would earn our wages, then purchase a home together. Your father was indifferent as long as we knew how to keep your quarters tidy and entertain you. Your mother wasn't very difficult to impress at all—upon first meeting, she was delighted with us. Miraculously, she accepted *two* orphans from the brothel on the spot."

"Oh, stop it Yanna. There's nothing wrong with The Fool's Folly. We worked at the Stag's Head Inn briefly before Madame approached us. We served drinks and kept patrons in line. It really was no different. It's all simply being receptive and tending to others' needs." Isabel laughed at the shock Lilac couldn't hide. "Have you seen their apothecary? There are all kinds of goods and wares down there."

"There's an apothecary?" Lilac immediately thought of Garin and his half-conscious mention of Aimee. "I didn't see one. I just remember the crowded tavern, the alcoves, and the second floor."

"It's in their basement," Isabel said through the truffle she'd popped into her mouth. "Ask the barhand for a Moonlit Path Tea, and they'll escort you downstairs. You didn't hear it from us. It's the kind of thing people know of, but don't talk about if they're decent."

"An herbalist at the brothel," mused Piper. "How intriguing."

"She's more than that," said Isabel. "Madame is a physician. An alchemist and chef, too. It is a place of reprieve for anyone finding them-selves in need of it. It even contains a small infirmary and a disheveled library."

Yanna's ever-present scowl softened. "I first met my Gwendal there, years ago. He was fetching tea for his mother. You can imagine my shock to see him here. We reconnected and things...progressed. We were going to ask your blessing for marriage." She pursed her lips, as if considering maiming Lilac with another one of her imminent barbs. "Before France."

Lilac was flabbergasted. She barely managed to keep from sputtering as her words poured out. "Yanna, why didn't you tell me? About any of this? You would have had my permission—you have it now."

Yanna stared angrily into the fire, arms crossed. "It might be too late for that. I fear abandoning my sister for a man that might be sent off to die tomorrow. No one should have to go to war. Certainly no one from a kingdom so ill-prepared by its own royal family. It is cruel to expect. It is self-sabotage. Gwendal said it appeared the armory hadn't even been restocked or surveyed before they were sent off."

There will be no war. Lilac wanted to say it, but the words stuck in her throat. There was truly nothing consoling to offer. She could not promise it. So many depended on her, and there was no easy choice. She'd see her duty through with Garin acting as Maximilian's emissary, or possibly watch her kingdom burn under François's hand.

Garin, whose presence alone made marrying another no easy task.

Sniffling, Yanna suddenly turned and strode toward the door.

"Where are you going?" asked Piper. The sun behind her had begun to sink, setting her copper hair ablaze.

"We're leaving. I expect to be on call for you tonight, whether you two plan on going to this feast or not. I've heard this family's soirees can get exceptionally rowdy." Yanna's hardened gaze snapped to Isabel. "Put the sweets down, Izzy."

"Wait." Lilac got to her feet as Isabel reddened and gathered her skirts.

Yanna's hand was already on the knob, her emerald eyes glassy. "Your secrets are safe with us, Your Majesty. We won't dare tell a soul."

Lilac rushed to her vanity and retrieved the basket. She'd stared at it throughout their conversation with half a mind to throw it into the fire; she only hadn't because of the variety of enchantments that could have imbued the item. It had been a long enough morning. The last thing she needed was an incinerated four-poster bed to drown her sorrows in.

The sisters watched warily as Lilac reached into the basket and pulled out half a steaming sourdough loaf and handed it to Piper. Then, she handed the rest of the basket to Isabel. "If you don't find your way down to the festivities tonight, please enjoy these for me."

Isabe's eyes went wide with wonder. "It's enchanted." She held her palm over the open lid as she slipped the basket onto her arm. "Are you positive? Sir Albrecht said he brought them from town just for you."

"He is overeager."

Yanna reached into the basket, inspecting the dappled corner of rye she'd pulled out before biting into it. Her eyes widened, the most enthusiastic approval Lilac had ever seen from her. She hummed, but her lips suddenly pursed.

"What is it?"

"Albrecht said he wanted to bring you some goods from the inn he'd stayed at, but there's only one tavern inn in all of Rennes. The Stag's Head is famous for their *red*-dyed, non-enchanted baskets and linens. He couldn't possibly have been referring to The Fool's Folly. They don't bake their goods in-house, and there's not one bakery in that town that produces anything *near* this caliber."

"No one cares about food there when the drinks do all the work," added Isabel.

Lilac shrugged, her expression indifferent with effort. She could still feel the red heat of being caught creeping up her neck. "That is curious, but far from my concern."

Yanna beckoned her sister hither and placed a hand on the doorknob, shooting one last withering look at Lilac and Piper. "That Albrecht fellow is dodgy. Then again, so are the both of you."

.

24

B y the time the sky was tinged in apricot and lavender, the empty
bottle of champagne and mound of chocolates had done their job.
Lilac and Piper lay side by side before the fire in a mess of her
duvet and empty champagne flutes.

Yanna and Isabel had hesitated when she'd invited them to stay, but ultimately decided to leave with the intention of returning at dusk. Lilac
hadn't expected to find an unlikely alliance in them, of all places, though
unexpected camaraderie seemed to be a going theme for her lately. After
Piper was banished, the only female relationship she'd had was with
Marguerite. She'd had no one. This was a foreign kind of relief. Stem in
hand and overwhelmed with emotion, Lilac felt compelled to tell Piper
everything—unsolicited and probably lacking chronological order—leading
up to Garin's arrival in place of Albrecht.

Piper listened silently, mortified most of the time. At the mention of
Sinclair's attempt to rape her, Piper poured herself a glass of the apricot
wine and blood concoction Garin had given them. But she couldn't hold
her laughter at the mention of Vivien's arm being gifted by Armand.

Surprisingly, Lilac found herself laughing, too. Weeks ago, the mere
discussion of something so grotesque would've traumatized her. But they'd
seen things, *done* things that warranted a buffer between their fragile sanity

and the world they'd both been thrust into. A lawless world of magic and arcane knowledge—and the steep price paid for it.

Laughter and drinks were their buffer tonight.

Lilac had slid off the bed, Piper playfully slapping her, both doubled over at the memory of Garin on one knee in the middle of her foyer, his dark hair slicked over his eyes like a dog in the rain. At this point, Lilac began to grow emotional at the thought of him, and Piper tried to pivot by distracting her with a game of guessing the bonbon fillings by scent.

Clearly past her limit and tiring of losing to Piper, Lilac found herself curled up, staring at the flames with her head on her arm. She shivered despite the fire and her friend snoring behind her. Gods, she felt so pathetic. She *hated* him. He'd strode into her castle with the swagger of some vile god with the nerve to proposition her before everyone. There'd been no urge to obey him then, though maybe it'd been down to his wording. It was a proposition, a question, after all. Still, he'd had the gall to show up when she'd finally realized the gravity of her duty to marry. And why would he come to her if their thrall bond had infuriated him so?

Blearily, Lilac blinked at the ceiling, reminded of Myrddin's words before he'd teleported them from The Fenfoss Inn. *You'll see him again. You'll have no choice.*

He'd made sure of that. Garin was a fucking prick.

Lilac winced, rolling onto her back. There was a dull ache in her abdomen, the muscles in her back tender. She must've had too much to drink and was on the brink of giving herself alcohol poisoning. She'd been there before, though, and this time she wasn't nauseous. She swiped at the mug of water she remembered Piper acquiring for her when there were voices at the door.

"Already?" She sipped, wetting her throat.

Piper shoved the wrapped bottle away. "I'll get it."

Lilac rose to her feet, willing the room to stop spinning as Yanna and Isabel entered. Outside, the sunglow had reduced to embers beneath the trees, an encouraging breeze sweeping through the room. Feeling nauseous, she somehow held it down and made her way unsteadily to the chamber pot. When she lifted her skirts to relieve herself, her heart sank.

"Shit. *Shit.*" She wasn't due on for another week or so.

"You've come on, haven't you?" asked Piper from beyond the privacy tapestry. "Knew it."

She let out a sound of disgust, feeling most violated. "Yes. Most unfortunately." It was no wonder she was beginning to cramp. A rather genius thought popped into her head. "That's it. I've fallen ill. I cannot go. Please tell Albrecht I send my regards."

"Ill with your menses?" Yanna yanked the tapestry back. "They'll send us back up here with Madame Kemble and a hot rag. That is no reason to miss out on a feast in your honor."

Lilac scowled. "You've only known me a month. It can be uncomfortable."

"She's telling the truth," Piper interjected. "She's laid in bed for an entire day before. So I've heard," she was quick to add.

Yanna hummed. "Have you?"

"Sometimes." Lilac dropped her skirts, but Isabel was already approaching, rummaging into the pochette at her hip. "What also doesn't help is my anticipation of hosting a feast for the first time in years."

"And seeing Albrecht," Yanna added.

And Albrecht.

Isabel pulled out a small silver tin from the pochette, a ring of tiny leaves engraved on the rim of its lid. "As eager as he seems, I doubt he'd try to proposition you publicly a second time."

They didn't know a thing about Garin. Lilac held her tongue as they wiped her down. Isabel handed her the tin and taught her to apply a thin layer of the yellow-green salve to her belly and lower back. It smelled of roses and some other potent earthy ingredient. They'd learned how to craft the remedy from the innkeeper at The Fool's Folly—Madame Toranaga, who'd sent the letter and apparently also ran the apothecary. The salve was warming and didn't seem to take the pain away as much as distract her, but they assured her the effects would wax and wane before reapplication was required.

She lined her bottoms with the cloth Yanna pulled from her apron, while the handmaidens observed the flutes and several bitten candies strewn about with wide eyes. But no one said a thing about it while Lilac and Piper rummaged in the closet for gown options. A squeak escaped Isabel as she reached into the armoire and extracted a pile of material.

The kirtles from Garin.

Piper gasped, standing from the chair. "I've never seen *these* before."

"Oh, those? They were a gift from Herlinde at the Haberdashery," Lilac lied, facing the mirror. "Those are much too plain."

"*Plain?*" Yanna's eyes bulged as she stalked past Lilac. "Maybe for a grand ball, but not a feast. Look."

Lilac did—and gasped. Isabel was laying the dresses out on her bed, one by one. She could have *sworn* they were kirtles. These were ball gowns, varying in color, length, and sleeve style. Generous, sparkling material in dazzling jewel tones. Once Isabel laid them out, Lilac counted at least ten.

"These are most certainly Herlinde's work," Yanna whispered, fingering the sleeves of a muted green number with a pretty lace shawl whose patterned edges were shaped like snowflakes. "These are her enchanted dresses. Rumor is they transform length and size for the occasion and the wearer."

"You know about them?" Lilac asked. "About her?"

"Of course we do," said Isabel, not taking her eyes off the dresses. "Herlinde fashions our masks at the brothel. On occasion, Madame Toranaga has tea with Herlinde at Miss Quillrose's shop in over in Paimpont. Many of our elite courtesans and their clients shop at The Hemlock Haberdashery."

"Yes, but none of them have *ever* been able to afford her arcane garments," added Yanna. "The price for just one of these is steep. We've never even seen one of her arcane gowns, she never has them on display. They cost more than I've ever held in my pockets. She must fancy you."

"She is generous." Swallowing, Lilac ran her fingers along the sapphire dress. Expensive silk, sweeping gossamer sleeves that sparkled subtly, even in the dim light. This one was without a flared waist, the hem looking like it would waterfall to her toes.

"You must wear one," Yanna said. "You'd be stupid to let these rot in your closet."

Piper hadn't said anything. She watched from the corner of the bed, blinking at the pile of clothes.

"Piper?" Lilac said. "What do you think?"

"I've never seen anything so luxurious." She cradled her arms to her chest, eyeing a deep red dress with frills and a high neck. "Dresses so beautiful."

Isabel snickered. "If it was your intention to enchant or devastate someone at The Fool's Folly, Your Majesty," she began, exchanging glances with Yanna, "and that person happens to be here tonight, then I reckon any of these dresses will do the trick."

These gowns were so beautiful she'd be foolish not to wear one. Lilac agreed upon one condition—that Yanna and Isabel were in attendance with her and Piper at the feast, and that they each pick one of the gowns to go in. The sisters refused at first, panicked at the thought of attending last minute. It would take much too long, they'd argued, and their builds were different than hers and Piper's.

But it would take no time at all, and Yanna herself had said they'd form to the wearer. Piper had become an expert at wrestling Lilac into her dresses, and Lilac was primped often enough to know how to do it for someone else.

Yanna and Isabel exchanged dubious glances, but in the end, they agreed to at least try them on. They'd been correct about the sizing, after all.

Lilac stepped back and stared into the vanity mirror. Dressed in soft lavender, Isabel was pinning Piper's long braid into a bun and embellishing it in gold emerald pins that contrasted with the carmine gown she'd chosen. Yanna's scowl softened as she turned this way and that in the juniper dress that swept her ankles.

In their reflection, Lilac saw four women who suddenly knew each other's secrets, ready to take on a feast after spending the evening laughing and crying. She was the only one who *looked* like she'd been crying. Her deep sapphire gown with its plunging sweetheart neckline and shimmering long, bell-shaped sleeves that caught every fragment of light would serve as distraction enough.

There was no need to hide her tears from Garin. She'd gladly let him see how distraught she'd been.

Her stomach knotted. Had he truly come to ensure she'd make the right decision? Or had he come because he'd changed his mind and wanted to discuss a Daemon alliance?

Something more?

BRIAR SOMERSET

She watched her cheeks flame in the reflection while Yanna shuffled forward and added the final touches of powder and color upon Lilac's lips, matting out some of the sweat on her forehead. Just in case, Isabel handed her the salve tin from her pochette, which Lilac promptly tucked into her bosom.

There was no telling what Garin's intentions were. But tonight, she'd find out.

25

Fortunately, it didn't sound like the night of formalities Lilac had feared it to be; between Marguerite and Hedwig, it could've gone either way. Music and laughter filled the keep, floating up the stairwell as they made their way down. The prayer and speech were either foregone or they'd missed it in the time it took them to get ready and swallow the fit of nerves that overcame them as they approached the stone doors.

Yanna grasped the handle below the gargoyle. "Piper, stop that fidgeting," she snapped.

Piper forced her hands to her side, off the ribbon that cinched her waist. "Sorry. This is most uncomfortable."

Thinking of the dozens of times Piper had wrestled and bribed her into dresses in their childhood, Lilac swallowed her *I told you so* and fixed the choker at her neck, squaring her shoulders.

Isabel beamed, tucking a dark wave behind her ear. "Are you ready, Your Majesty?"

"Hardly. But I shall smile and bear it." Lilac looked over at Piper, whom she could tell was stifling the urge to tear her corset off. "We all shall."

With a nod, Yanna and Isabel opened the doors.

Four tables lined the room, two on each side of the dance floor. Food and drink filled them to the brim, with ample enough space between for seating. Hardly anyone was seated, however.

In the corner to the right of the doors, musicians played on a lute, a couple of drums, and a fine mahogany harpsichord. The dance ended as the quartet concluded their song. Every pair of eyes slowly turned to the doors, but Lilac barely noticed.

Straight ahead, seated at the table at the top of the wide staircase, was Garin. He was smiling at her from atop Marguerite's throne on the left, his pearl-white teeth glistening.

His beauty alone forced her eyes back down at the crowd. There, she spotted her parents and most of their court. Gertude and Helena, slowing in their jig, just noticing the music had stopped. Agnes and her husband, whispering fervently. Hedwig swinging a tankard in a frilly chartreuse gown. There were several of her staff and dozens of others she hadn't met or seen up close in years—prominent shopkeepers and nobility alike.

"Look," Agnes's husband murmured from the edge of the dancefloor. "Do you see how she's staring at him? How uncouth."

"Shut up, William," said Agnes. "Look at the way he stares at her."

Unable to fix any expression she might've worn, knowing she could not help the unsavory thoughts her mind threw at her, Lilac dared look again. He wore a sharp black blazer emblazoned in gold, forming perfectly to his shoulders and biceps. His hair had been styled, combed through and over, even his signature drooping curl tucked neatly into place.

Logic warred weakly against her, a gnat in her ear. She should've stayed in, people would notice. They were noticing already.

As if sensing her deliberation, Garin's eyes narrowed above his shark-like smile. Even from a distance she saw his brows quirk, challenging her. If she turned back now, he would only command her forward, leaving her to struggle awkwardly against her own body. Lilac dipped into a low curtsey, everyone gaping at the gossamer sleeves and outer layer of her dress moving like sunlight through water—a ghostly trellis both man-made and magic, gracing the floor like rainfall in reverse.

When she straightened the crowd was parting for her, a whispering, glittering sea, leaving a clear path to the steps in its wake. Then, they began to kneel. One by one. First Gertrude. Then Helena, and the maids next to her. The shopkeepers around them and her parents next, nudging each other as if forgetting themselves, utterly lost in the still radiance of their daughter. Last, William, then begrudgingly, Agnes.

The room was so silent, one could hear a feather fall.

Lilac started—there was a light touch at her elbow. It was Piper, kneeling with Yanna and Isabel behind her. "Go, Your Majesty."

"*Stand*," Lilac suddenly mouthed, dread and self-doubt gnawing their way into her chest. "Walk with me. There is plenty of seating up there."

Piper shook her head minutely and said, "He only wants you. This moment is yours."

She couldn't protest with everyone staring. Redder than ever, feeling all the eyes on her now, Lilac made her way to the front of the room. By the time she reached the bottom step, her body was buzzing with more than nerves; there was an unnatural excitement, an eagerness to be near him despite everything. By the time she reached Garin, he was standing, bending at the waist. Lilac hastily curtsied and slid past him; even as she squeezed against the table, the light brush of him against her back was enough to send currents of unwavering heat throughout her body. Lilac collected her skirts to sit when Garin clicked his tongue.

"Wait," he murmured, and her body froze. "What about your speech?"

"I was ambushed by this feast and a most unexpected visit," she replied, her smile straining. "I have not had the time to prepare a speech."

Garin flashed a smile at the sea of guests, then turned his devilish charm onto her. A twinkle in his eye and a dimpled, threatening grin that said *don't make me make you*.

Lilac sighed forcefully. "Thank you all for being here. Tonight, we celebrate our Honorable Guest, Sir Albrecht Fritsch of the Holy Roman Empire. Welcome, My Lord." There was an awkward silence. She kept her gaze on the crowd, refusing to acknowledge the feigned expression of honored shock she knew Garin wore. "Please stand."

As everyone rose from their knees, there was a low hum of dissatisfaction. Beside her, Garin was fingering the rim of his cup. "If I may?" he said to the crowd.

"No, you may not," she hissed.

"Thank you, Your Majesty." He gave her a pompous smile, one the crowd could also see; they stood close enough to each other where he could place his hand lightly at the small of her back without anyone noticing. "It is indeed my honor to represent my liege, the great Maximilian—as you know, former archduke of Austria, German King, and now, faithful emperor. The histories of our kingdoms have skirted each other for years. We have supported your great crown in strife before. Now, Maximilian extends his proposition of marriage in hopes of continuing to do so on a much grander scale."

Garin coughed in pain when Lilac's foot stamped down on the toe of his boot. His right hand instantly dropped and gripped her left ass cheek, his fingertips finding purchase in her flesh and sending violent flutters throughout her stomach before releasing her just as quickly.

She glared up at him in her peripheral, cursing the urge to lean into his hand.

Heads turned in the crowd as whispers filled the room. His announcement seemed to shock a handful of her guests who were either oblivious of the purpose for Albrecht's presence, or skeptical of it. The rest probably thought Lilac had ruined her chances of marrying Maximilian by dumping a flute of champagne on his head.

If only she were so lucky.

"His offer stands to strengthen the might of your defenses, filling any gaps that might exist in numbers and armor. As his most diligent dignitary, I behoove..." Garin trailed off, lifting his hand from her thigh and squinting into the back of the crowd. "I'm sorry, is there a question?"

A man at the back of the hall was waving. One of the shop owners, it seemed. The fellow to his right was a bit taller, pointing down at him. "He has a question!"

The muscle under Garin's eye twitched. "Questions will wait."

"No, no," said Lilac with a wide smile, beckoning them forth. "Come forward. Please."

The men shuffled through the now unsettled crowd—understandably so at the topic of war. When the pair arrived at the steps, she saw she'd been right. It was both of them, the butcher and blacksmith, if she wasn't mistaken.

The shorter one bowed. "Brient Cleaver, of Cleaver and Tallow, Your Majesty. And this is Hamon Martin, of the Paimpont Forge," he said, motioning sideways at the taller one, who nervously tipped his hat.

Lilac curtsied, politely smiling through Garin's fuming. She could feel the heat radiating from his anger. "Good evening, Brient and Hamon. What is your question?" She braced herself next for the questions on France, or perhaps on Maximilian's proposition.

"Is it true you passed a decree today, making the harm of Daemons illegal?" This drew a large round of whispers from the crowd. It was likely most of them had spent the day traveling to her castle and hadn't had the opportunity to hear her town criers' announcement. "It was a rumor we'd heard on the way here."

"It is true."

"Is it now?" muttered Garin.

"What about in retaliation?" Brient asked.

She squinted. "Are you asking me if it is permissible to harm them if justified?"

Brient and Hamon exchanged unsure glances. "Well, yes," said Brient.

"It is detailed in my decree that the unjust harm and murder of these creatures is now explicitly against royal law unless in self-defense. They will be held responsible for their actions and also deserving of a right to trial, just as any mortal subject is." Her poised smile tightened at the miffed shock on their faces. "The organized hunting of them is at all times prohibited and punishable by imprisonment or death. They are our equals. They are to be treated as such."

Unsatisfied, Brient and Hamon shuffled back into a still crowd. From the center, her parents watched, helpless as usual. But behind them, Piper and her handmaidens withheld their smiles with great difficulty. What she'd done mattered. Her first decree.

There was a sharp *clink*. Garin tapped his fork upon his glass twice, shattering the unbearable silence. "Let us applaud Her Majesty's attempts at unifying her kingdom in the midst of a crisis. Maximilian has his fair share of warlocks on his court—mostly jesters, otherwise not very useful. Ambrosius there, for example. Smoke and mirrors." He motioned at the warlock, who froze at the corner of the sweets table. Myrddin slowly turned to face them, mid-bite through a cupcake. Several people gasped and backed away from him. "Entertaining, yet not the threat you think he is. But the emperor, *he* was born a politician and raised a soldier. His impressive firepower and tactics are wholly man-made."

"I did not say they weren't," Lilac added, her tone clipped.

Garin tapped his glass again, and the crowd exchanged unsure glances. "Let us not get lost in hearsay and heresy. This night is to celebrate Her Majesty, and Her Majesty alone." He lifted the cup high and in her direction. He extended his free hand to her, palm up. Fuming, she placing her hand in his. "To the stunning bride to be! To the future Queen of the Romans!"

At first, no one said anything. There was a second of hesitation, but none more. A fist clutching a tankard shot to the ceiling. "Long live the queen!" came her father's booming voice.

"Long live the queen," Piper, Yanna, and Isabel shouted back.

By the third chant, most of the room had joined in, and glasses were raised in her direction. For the first time in years, there were enthusiastic cheers for her—ones filled with hope. For the most part, it seemed France had temporarily become a larger threat to them than the Daemons they feared.

Queen of the Romans. Lilac blinked at the crowd, stomach churning. A new, massive empire to rule when she'd barely started with the country of her birth, that which she'd sworn by birthright to protect. The thought threatened to overwhelm her. It would have, if not for Garin's presence, tethering her in her buzzing body.

At the center of the dance floor, her parents were the first to resume their dance, her mother giggling and falling into her father's chest. The quartet raised their instruments, and the rest joined in.

Garin took his seat, sipping from his water glass. Lilac held her tongue and plopped into her throne, uttering her thanks as one of Hedwig's men brought her a steaming plate.

"Thank you, kind sir," he said, when the server removed his first plate and replaced it with one that matched Lilac's: dipping lamb rib, potatoes covered in butter and herbs, and a pile of maple parsnips to begin with. But even he paid no mind; Garin was preoccupied with observing Piper, Yanna, and Isabel, who were huddled, whispering at the back of the room. Once Piper noticed Garin watching, she abruptly stopped talking. Isabel bumped into Yanna, who bumped into Piper—who proceeded to beckon them to the sweets table. Garin suppressed a smirk. "I see you discovered those fine gowns I sent you home with."

"My God. Could you be any louder?" Lilac eyed the server strutting around their table with his dish cart.

"What does it matter, now that half the town knows we were at the brothel together? It seems they don't care so long as their tender throats are saved by the emperor and their most valiant queen. Thanks to me." Garin gulped his water and slowly set his glass down, peering sideways at the way the supportive bodice clung to her chest and torso. His eyes lingered as he fingered the divots in the fine crystal.

"Thirsty, are you?"

"These days? Always." He rubbed at his chin, distracted. "You look like a work of art worth the heist."

"And you look like a scoundrel stupid enough to attempt it." Lilac squeezed her thighs together, swallowing her shock at how easily she wanted to open them right there at the table.

His lips quirked. "Lithe? Suave? Cunning?"

"Like you belong at the guillotines," she rasped. "Stop that. Whatever it is you're doing."

Garin only laughed, finally tearing his hungry eyes from her. "Herlinde is a talented seamstress, is she not?"

"She is," Lilac admitted, thankful for the change of subject. There was no protesting there. "Is Herlinde related to the Algovens?"

"She is an Algoven. She's Lori's older sister."

"Lorietta has never spoken of her before. I didn't know she had any other family in the area besides Meriam."

"That's because Lori pretends her sister doesn't exist. Herlinde is the reason the Algovens—what was left of them—relocated to Paris, where her mother was from. Then, to Brittany. Years ago, Herlinde married a powerful warlock against their parents' wishes. Like Herlinde and Lori, he was also gifted in Alteration, but known to swindle and experiment with illegal magic; they'd tried to warn her, but Herlinde went against their wishes and eloped. Her new husband thus moved into their family's manor, and in the early hours of morning, attempted to cast a spell upon his travel trunk that would create enough space to steal some of their family fortune. Instead, he blew the manor and their family into smithereens."

Lilac covered her mouth in horror.

"Only a handful of them survived: Lori, Herlinde, Meriam, and Rolf.

Meriam had gone to the village with her brother—Rolf, Lori's and Herlinde's grandfather—for the day, and returned to discover a gruesome scene—the girls cowering in the foyer, covered in grime and blood. The four of them escaped and fled before authorities caught wind of it. After receiving harsh scrutiny in Paris, they eventually ended up in Rennes, where their grandfather quietly continued his family business as a haberdasher. When he grew ill and died shortly after, the business was passed down to Herlinde, which infuriated Lorietta. It was Herlinde's fault this had happened, after all. That was what Lori thought, anyway. Still blames her for it. So, she and Meriam left to form The Fenfoss Inn in the western High Forest. They've rarely been in contact with each other since."

She thought of the cornerstone at the inn. "The inn was established in 1340. Lori and Herlinde barely look forty themselves."

"I think they've both chosen to hover around their mid thirties for now. By the time we met, she'd already altered her age for several years—which is something she and her family can do, the gifted Alterationists they are. Lori was a few years younger than my frozen age of twenty-five when I stumbled upon their property after leaving the coven. She found me on the ground covered in deer blood, writhing in agony after I'd dragged a traveler off his horse into the treeline and attempted to feed."

"And they offered you a position, just like that?"

"It was out of pity more than anything. Told them about my my biting curse, and Meriam was so alarmed, she had one of their loyal mortal customers bloodletting for me behind the counter within the hour. Neither of them had ever seen a vampire so poorly. They let me tend the bar and cleared a portion of the cellar for me. A few decades later, some twenty years ago, a sullen warlock ambled into my bar on another fateful, stormy night. I took him in and cleaned him up, just as they'd done for me. Gave him a room on part of my pay. We discovered he was a gifted Conjurer when, the next morning, I retired to my makeshift cot to find my bedchamber fully furnished. He furnished most of the tavern, too. He was talented, when he wasn't ragingly drunk." Garin pinched the bridge of his nose, an annoyed, pensive smile spreading. "Lorietta had made me her project, attempting to cure me. None of it worked. But I owe that woman my life."

Lilac blinked, imagining how startling it must've been to find a starved vampire outside their business. How happy Garin must've been to rest in a furnished room. His comfortable bed, and the faded green armchair. "The Algovens are good people."

"Deeply, profoundly good. They're the most hospitable people I know, and mildly insane to take in someone like myself and Myrddin. Even Meriam. And Herlinde isn't so bad herself, she's just like her sister but alarmingly self-centered." He clicked his tongue. "Poor things. Arrived in Paris still covered in their parents' and maids' innards."

His lovely story suddenly cut short, Lilac stopped chewing and placed her piece of bread slathered in goose liver down. She bent to spit in her napkin.

"I *know*," Garin replied through a mouthful of bread and pâte, helping himself to more. "Interdimensional magic is a fascinating subset of forbidden arcana, even for the most skilled magic folk. Myrddin already skirts those lines with his teleportation. By the way, spitting is in poor taste, Your Majesty." He patted his mouth delicately. "Not that you would know."

Lilac slammed her napkin down, suppressing the urge to vomit. "Anyway, thank you, Sir Albrecht, for the gowns and pleading to the masses for me."

Garin reached for the pretty ceramic pitcher off to his left and poured himself another cup of water. He must've impressed Hedwig—not even Lilac had one of her own. "My pleasure. Someone here had to understand the gravity of Maximilian's offer. It might as well be those who have the most to lose should France invade."

She wouldn't argue with him, not now. Garin wouldn't further ruin the night; she wouldn't allow it. Lilac watched him then skewer the end of a sausage and slice it off with his knife. "Has Myrddin given you anything for that?"

Garin chewed thoughtfully. "For what, Your Majesty?"

"For your stomach." She glanced down the length of the table, left and right. Despite it usually seating her family and its most important dignitaries, no other settings had been placed. Several bottles of spirits and boxes dressed in ribbons and lace scattered her right side of the table.

He sipped at his refilled glass. "Why, I don't know this Myrddin you speak of. My valet, Ambrosius, you mean?"

"Yes, Ambrosius."

"He did not. They decided that was quite enough magic for me. He was with me earlier, but I had him direct your band to play something more lively. Everyone would fall asleep with chansons on repeat. He must be..." Garin squinted across the floor. "Ah, there."

She followed his gaze back to Myrddin, who was now striding up to Hedwig, a huge grin on his face and a tankard in each hand. He looked handsome tonight, wearing a velvet indigo cloak, ruffles adorning his sleeves with shining silver boots.

"He's an interesting fellow." Lilac glanced around to ensure no one was in earshot. "I'm surprised he hasn't run from you."

"He tried at the inn. He didn't make it very far."

She glanced at him sidelong. "Isn't he all powerful?"

"Even someone as powerful as Myrddin is upheld by the force of arcane law. None of us are exempt." He grunted, a faraway look in his eye. "Bound by his own blood." Garin paused as an upbeat jig began. The few who'd wandered to the tables to sit and pick at the feast hopped up again. "Are you familiar with the stories?"

"The only stories I was fed were those telling me I should stay clear of the woods, or else I might be eaten."

"Not wholly a lie," he replied, drumming his long fingers upon the armrest. "Long ago, before the great kings reigned, a monstrous sea spirit visited a sorceress in her bed, impregnating her. Or, so the story went. Thus, *Merdhyn* was born. Infernal-blooded. Sorcerer and warlock, all in one."

"Is there a difference between a warlock and a sorcerer?" Lilac asked, peeling her eyes away from the veins on his hand with difficulty. "Or sorceress?"

"Yes, and no. *Warlock* and *witch* are archaic, gendered terms more than anything, but they also represent the majority group who draw power from their environment through ingredient and ritual. They might use charms, grimoires, wands, or cauldrons, as Lori does for her wards."

"And Adelaide, with her vials and tonics." She took his silence as confirmation as they watched Myrddin twirl Hedwig across the floor.

"Most, if not all, with a predisposition for arcana can do this, but warlocks and witches are limited in their requirement of these external sources of power. They spend much of their lives learning from family, or seeking outside wisdom. Until a few decades ago, only warlocks were allowed to travel away from home to hone their craft." The corners of his mouth turned down in disapproval. "On the other hand, sorcerers can both perform ritual-based spells *and* perform instantaneous magic. They draw their arcana from within, irrespective of their environment."

"It sounds like Myrddin's mother was powerful. What kind of sea spirit was his father?"

Garin shrugged. "The old wives' tales from my parents' country described Myrddin's father as a deity more than a person, but who knows? Stories passed through time are how truths grow muddled. Either way, both his parents' powers made for a hellacious combination."

"In Cinderfell, Kestrel spoke of magic as if it always existed. *Neither created nor destroyed.* What makes the sorcerers' magic so efficient? It has to come from somewhere."

"I don't know that I'd call it efficient. For one, while they have access to the same ingredients and charms that make magic for witches and warlocks possible, they're usually shit at it because, given their own powers—why train?" He ran his tongue across his bottom lip, his gaze distant as he surveyed the crowd. "It's in their blood, and that's part of the reason they're so rare. Shortly after we watched Emrys stab himself with the *Guài* arrow, Lori explained that most sorcerers are connected to an infernal powersource—a deity or artifact—through a pact that affects their entire bloodline. Or, they somehow find a way to directly procreate with a mortal vessel, as in Myrddin's parents' case."

Fascinated, Lilac stabbed one of her herb-encrusted potatoes, inhaling when a dull ache in her middle came on. Isabel's salve might be shorter lived than she'd expected. "How did he end up at The Fenfoss Inn? And why did he leave for the Jaunty Hog?"

"The inn is a place of reprieve and solace for all. I'm sure he sensed it in his time of need, just as you did. He's been an almost daily patron of mine for years. A couple decades, at least. I'm still not sure why he left. All I know is, one of the mornings I'd returned from your castle after playing priest, he was gone." He refrained from saying more, sighing, as if he'd pondered this a great deal. "He is indebted to me until further notice."

Lilac started, kicking the leg of the table in shock. It jutted forward, wood scraping against stone.

"*Modron*, behave yourself," Garin said quietly, yanking the table off the ledge of the top step. Several eyes darted to them, but by then he had already smoothed his expression, piling parsnips onto his fork.

All any onlooker might have seen was the queen and Maximilian's emissary discussing what might be the nuances of the emperor over supper. Or maybe something as simple as the weather in Vienna.

"Indebted to you, because you paid a bag of coin he owed the *Guài?*"

"Apparently so. We discovered it when he tried to run from me as I woke. I don't recall, but apparently, I chased him outside. As he tried to teleport away from me, he couldn't." He gritted his teeth. "Adelaide was kind enough to surround me with her explosions."

"Do you command him, as you do me?" A quiet dread seeped into her bones.

"No. Reluctantly, Myrddin says he will work for me until *the fates decide I've been repaid,*" Garin quoted in the warlock's sing-song voice. "Whatever that means."

"Repaid, as in doing you favors?" she said slowly.

"Perhaps." Garin shrugged nonchalantly, skewering a couple more parsnips. "He is my valet, is he not? He will perform whatever task I see fit. It didn't occur to me at the time, but having the continent's most powerful warlock at my disposal can't hurt, now can it?"

Lilac looked to the crowd, an overwhelming shawl of grief settling onto her shoulders. Not long ago, she'd imagined a scene not so different; Daemons and her subjects in the same room, existing together. There were only a few tonight, but it was a start. She never imagined her first focus would be diverted to avoiding a war they were not prepared for. She never imagined giving her hand to Maximilian would be the only way.

Lilac did not want to think about the emperor or Vienna. Nor war, nor France. Nor Brocéliande's most powerful warlock working for Garin.

"That's why you've come here."

Garin placed his glass down, swallowing his mouthful before shooting her a quizzical look. "I don't know what you're talking about."

"Repaying you would reinforce your intention. Ensuring I go through with this marriage, sign Maximilian's contract, wouldn't it?"

Garin sighed laboriously. "What else was I supposed to do with my time now that you are my charge, down to your very blood? Someone had to keep an eye on you. You've already jumped to releasing a Daemon decree of your own on the day of my arrival. Admirable, although it seems you've already lost two important potential supporters—those who'd supply rations and weapons to your meager army in the case that François decides to forge his way through Maximilian's army." Lilac followed his gaze to the floor. Brient and Hamon were nowhere to be found. "You're fortunate it didn't enact the consequences of Kestrel's deal."

"I had to," Lilac seethed. "Artus is alive and well, enough to come to the castle to threaten us. He is a threat to you and the others as much as France is to all of us."

Garin snorted. "He knows a drawn out death awaits him the moment I catch him alone."

"What's next, then?" she pressed, tired of his games. "Beyond my marriage? Deciding for me when it is time to meet the emperor? Having Myrddin teleport me there? Having him alter my memories as you see fit?"

A deep chuckle was his only answer, causing Lilac's pounding heart to skip painfully. Was he always this cruel, or had their thrall bond made him such? How could Garin find it funny at all that she was being cornered into making the most important choice of her life?

"What do you expect from me once this is all over; once I've given you and everyone else what they want?"

His smile faded uncharacteristically, as if he somehow hadn't considered these things.

"What happens when I must answer to him? Go to see him?"

"Those aren't requirements Maximilian has set for you. The wedding is by-proxy. He couldn't even bother to spare a week and a half of his time to travel to marry you." He raised his brows suggestively. "It works in both of our favor, does it not?"

Lilac snorted. "What makes you think you'll have access to me? You don't trust me to do right by my kingdom, as you've made clear at the brothel and this morning. Even as I try to consider all possibilities, I am told my strategies are wrong, that England will not help us—"

Some of the water dribbled from the glass as he brought it to his mouth. "England?"

"I am told that I mustn't continue standing for the Daemons that made this throne worth fighting for, all for my public image and favor. I *will* ensure their safety, whether or not they stand with me against opposing forces. I will ensure it because they are my subjects, as are you." She felt a stab of pleasure as he clenched his jaw. "You are not my council. She is." Lilac looked toward Piper, who'd relocated their little huddle to the nearest table off to the left. "They are." The two sisters giggled together, glasses of wine in their hands, but Piper stared distantly at the quartet, picking at her nails.

She was listening in.

"And?" Garin said. "What does your daywalker think of all this? Of your thrall bond? What does she advise you?"

"You don't want to know what she thinks."

His mouth tightened. "I am her sire. She's entitled to her opinions, wrong as they may be. Ultimately, her nature will force her to fight for what is best for me. And what is best for me is what keeps you safe."

"Piper's loyalty to me, and mine to her is a tenuous bond I would not test. Don't underestimate the power of friendship." With a friendly smile, Lilac touched his bicep lightly for the sake of anyone in the crowd watching. "You might've come here to ensure my marriage, but she will fight tooth and nail for my right to choose."

"You really think that's why we're here?" He laughed, and several pairs of eyes drifted their way. Garin paid them no mind, propping a foot up on the table leg and boxing her in. "If it came down to it, I'd have this entire room laid siege in minutes, the emperor's ring on your finger in the blink of an eye. Guillaume is just outside; don't think for a moment I won't summon him. I don't need Myrddin's help to usher you to the altar for Maximilian, not when you are my thrall." His fangs suddenly glinted between his lips. He passed a hand over his face, exhaled, and took another sip of his water. When he spoke again, his fangs were gone. "While I do pride myself on being one of your *rare* loyal subjects, do not forget I am first a vampire— one most shocked to find a hawthorn stake being pulled from my back as I was thrown from the nightmare of becoming your regnant against my will. So shocked, in fact, that in my thirst-driven stupor, all I could think of was finding you."

"It's our thrall bond. You knew this would happen."

"No one knew any of this would happen," he snapped. "It started *before* the bond was even completed. Before last night. If I'd known—"

"You wouldn't have saved me." It was what he'd been too cowardly to admit at the inn.

"I would have saved you no matter what it took." A flash of heated anger crossed his face. "That is what should scare you more. You don't understand, I was *blinded* by my need for you. I was desperate—a wounded animal willing to crawl to the basin. There was not a thought in my mind but you. And your maddening scent. The pattern of your pulse follows me like a haunting melody."

The current of their conversation had changed as quickly as the shifting need in his eyes. Lilac was vaguely aware of Myrddin in the middle of the dance floor, entertaining the gathered crowd with a handkerchief and disappearing coin. Her mother's shrieking laugh was heard in the distance, but those noises were muffled, as if a veil had been draped over their table.

No one paid attention as she watched him with a mixture of longing and disdain.

Garin exhaled, unfurled his clenched fists, and placed them on the table. "This changes nothing."

"No, it doesn't," Lilac agreed. "I have made a choice." She resisted the violent urge to reach out and touch him, as if her body begged her not to say the words. "For myself. For my kingdom."

"You seemed undecided this morning." The intensity in his expression faltered forcibly. He turned to his plate again, the movement of his hands forced as he tore into the turkey leg with his teeth. "It is not the first time I've had a drink thrown in my face, but I'll admit it's the first time it's happened while on one knee."

He had some nerve to appear taken aback by her response. "You expect me to believe you, on your knees—*that* was on behalf of Maximilian?"

He chewed, unphased. "Rest assured, my being here is not some valiant effort to save you from the fate of your marriage, either."

"Good. Because it is what I want." Lilac watched Garin's face, still at her half-hearted lie. He paused over his plate and placed his fork down, but did nothing more. It didn't matter that she'd made the decision at the peak of her anger at Garin's urging, under the pressure of Artus's threats. It was a lie meant to maim Garin. He would not toy with her. Lilac would not allow it.

Maybe one day, when she overlooked the kingdom from some stained-glass window in Vienna, after making the trip there and back, discovering what it was to rule between two kingdoms, two crowns—*two hearts*—she too, might believe the lie. She would pretend, existing in the balance of folly and poise. She and the emperor did not have to get along. They could be cordial, and she could make various demands as his bride, couldn't she?

Maximilian would have his mistresses to pleasure him. That was a given. And she would have...

Lilac found herself fighting back furious tears.

Garin could not be her paramour. He ignited more fury and passion in her than any lover would. But she would not beg. She was done abandoning herself.

He was silent, nodding once.

"My hand will be his, and so shall my heart. You have made it clear I have no other choice. I refuse to be backed into a corner, or to ask you for an alliance that will never come. I have only ever entertained the prospect of marriage in the context of love. Despite everything I've come to reconsider these past few weeks, it is this belief I shall stand by."

"Do you think you will come to love Maximilian?"

Would she? Could she?

The cruel answer contrived in her moment of fury stuck in her throat. "He at least will not make me feel like my love is something to bargain for. At least his conditions are straightforward and uncomplicated."

"Splendid," Garin replied, despite the wicked edge to his tone. "Shall I have Ambrosius retrieve the marriage contract now?"

"It is *his* family I shall bear," Lilac pressed, driving her reluctant point home like a stake into Garin's chest, spitting the words as if she could convince herself they were true. "His crest, his monarchy, his children." Lilac leaned over the chair arm, her breath ghosting his cheek. Garin turned his head to her as if he could not help it, his challenging glare daring her closer. "At least this man, whom I've never met a day in my life, has offered to fight for me. My hand and my kingdom. It seems it is the very least I can expect from him. This is what you wanted for me, after all."

Lilac was nearly in his lap. Her pulse throbbed in her ears—her throat, between her thighs, and in her clit. Everywhere else she felt that inescapable heat.

Barely thinking straight, she sat back. Garin made to follow, but she placed a single finger against his chest. "So, why are you here? What more could you possibly want from me?" Her voice dropped to a viciously sultry, sarcastic whisper. "What do you want so badly that you'll willingly risk all of your scheming and hard work?"

His gaze pierced her chest like a barbed arrow. "I want to feel your pulse beneath my tongue, Eleanor."

Heat charged her core with a desirous ache. She winced and swallowed a whimper, muscles tensing at the fire that flooded her—just as the sound of the room came rushing back.

"*Lilac?*"

26

That voice. It was familiar. Dreadfully so.

She hadn't noticed him, didn't know how much of their conversation he'd heard, but by the nervous smile on his face, it didn't appear he'd heard a word at all. A gentleman in a deep red coat embellished in silver filigree and buttons stood before their table, his hands clasped behind his back as he folded into a rigid bow.

He blinked and frowned as he took her in, as if just noticing her ruddy face. Lilac wiped her nose and offered him a wide, frantic smile. The newcomer's eyes flickered over to Garin, who greeted him with a murderous glare.

"Rupert! What a surprise." Lilac stood and gave him her hand, desperately forcing herself to think of anything but leading the guard from the old coat closet to her bedchamber a year ago, tonguing him deeply with one hand down the front of his trousers and a bottle of claret in the other. Rupert was a decade older and well-liked among the ranks. He was sweet, at least kind enough to keep his mouth shut about the things they did, and hadn't been released by her father—to her knowledge. But the last time they'd snuck off was the last she'd seen of him. "W-where have you been?" she stammered. "You weren't sent to La Guerche with the rest?"

"No. I've, erm, actually been on leave. Traveling out west. Le Conquet is quite beautiful this time of year." Rupert kissed her hand as she studied him. She hadn't known their guards to simply take leave. "I returned several days ago."

"Everyone just departed under Father's watch," Lilac whispered, taking her seat. "France has been scouting out east. There's been a skirmish or two. Nothing large-scale yet."

"So I've heard. I stopped through Paimpont on my way," he added.

"Then why are you here?" she demanded, Garin's words echoing in her pounding ears.

Rupert laughed, thrown by her intensity. "Lilac, I—"

"You have addressed her by her name twice now," Garin interjected. "Her pet name, nonetheless. She is your queen and you are her foot soldier, are you not? You will address her as *'Majesty'*."

Rupert leered at him, as if offended by being addressed by someone who appeared younger, but stopped at the look on Lilac's face. She shook her head minutely, so he bowed instead. "Your Majesty, I honor my duty. That's why I'm here, I hoped to catch the others in time."

"You're leaving, then?"

"At dawn," Rupert confirmed. "The armorer briefed me upon arrival."

No one should have briefed him without Lilac's or Henri's knowledge. Seething, she looked out at the floor; her father was swaying, sandwiched between her dancing mother, a shit-faced Helena, and giggling Gertrude. He didn't seem suited to attend to any business matters after touring the castle with Garin.

Displeased, Lilac studied Rupert and wondered where he'd acquired such a fine coat. "And what of your armor? Your weapons?"

"I'll acquire them from the armory before my departure," he said with a dismissive wave of the hand.

Garin leaned forward. "Has there been an escalation?"

"None that were mentioned," Rupert responded, then curtly redirected his attention to Lilac. "When I heard there'd be a feast, I knew I couldn't miss the opportunity to congratulate you. I didn't mean to interrupt, but I couldn't bear the thought of letting the night pass without asking you for a dance."

Immediately Lilac felt lightheaded, a crawling heat radiating off to her left—from Garin. "That's kind. I'd love to share a dance with you, but you remember those silly fraternization laws." It might be entertaining to watch Garin squirm, but she wouldn't chance it for Rupert's sake. Plus, she wasn't done interrogating the vampire. "I'm afraid I must refrain."

"Ah, well yes. That's the thing." The guard turned to look at a woman perched on the corner of the table where Piper, Yanna, and Isabel sat. She was the one who'd laughed as Gertrude and Agnes had commented on Albrecht's lateness in the foyer earlier. She had a kind, round face, her plump cheeks and eyelids dappled high with a wash of peach, her hair tucked high in a playful bun over a chartreuse chiffon gown.

The woman gave them a coy wave before courteously returning her attention to Piper.

"My mother Emma is a countess from Vannes."

"The Countess of Vannes?" Garin said, tearing his simmering gaze from Rupert and craning his neck.

"Yes."

Lilac stuffed down her skepticism. "I've never seen her at any of my mother's parties. Nor you."

"My mother was not often invited to socialize. Not after having a child with a commoner."

"Oh." She was probably one of the court-adjacent women, never truly in Marguerite and Henri's circle. It had been years, she could've easily forgotten. That still didn't explain why he was at her feast. "I had no idea."

"It's perfectly fine." Rupert shook off her apology, nervousness clouding the handsome, boyish way he smiled.

Garin was studying the guard; she could feel it without looking at him.

"One dance couldn't hurt," Garin offered. "Now that it's been made clear he isn't some lowly guard."

"I couldn't." She glanced at him sidelong. "I wouldn't want to leave you alone, My Lord."

"I'll survive." Garin sat back, cozying into the throne. "Maximilian will not mind. Go ahead, Your Majesty." She glared, but Garin only gave her a generous smile, cocking his head toward the dance floor. "I insist."

"I couldn't possibly—"

"Dance. For me."

At his last words, Lilac stood abruptly, as if tugged up by strings. Heart pounding, she pushed her throne back with one hand, causing several pairs of eyes to drift to her. Even Rupert blinked at her willingness. "You know what? I shall."

Fighting the pull of Garin's demand would only draw attention; gritting her teeth and cursing him to the lowest circle of hell, Lilac obliged, allowing his power to tug her away. Garin bowed his head, lips pursed as stood to make room for her to pass him.

Seething, Lilac joined Rupert at the top of the stairs. She placed her hand upon his, feeling Garin's gaze burning the back of her neck as they descended.

She wouldn't let him instruct her again, not in front of everyone. Lilac pulled Rupert past her friends and Emma, toward the quartet and the warlock. Myrddin still stood near the musicians, chuckling and sharing a slice of cake with Hedwig. It appeared he hadn't noticed the commotion at their table, or her approaching; upon spotting them, the warlock's eyes grew wide.

She didn't know what she was doing—hadn't had enough practice for a partner dance without humiliating herself. The only consolation was that Rupert's movements were no better; he was stiff in his attempt at rhythm.

"Help," she mouthed, her hand lifting to rest upon Rupert's shoulder.

Finally realizing Lilac wasn't gracing the floor of her own accord, Myrddin skittered forward and whispered something to one of the musicians. To her horror, they brought out a stringed instrument, the ones on either side of him readied their drums, and before she knew it, her body was moving.

Rupert stifled a yelp as her foot came down on the toes of his boot.

"I am so sorry," Lilac said, straining against every movement. This was not the kind of *help* she'd had in mind.

He readjusted his grip on her upper back. "Usually it's customary I take the lead, Your Majesty."

Her muscles were already burning. The song Myrddin had requested was drum-heavy, the vibrations of the string instrument coursing through her body like an unending pulse. Maybe if she kept talking, he wouldn't find her movements so suspicious. "Sometimes, one might find it beneficial to let the lady take the lead. Don't you think?"

"I suppose." Rupert looked dubious. "Have you not learned the dances?"

"The *pavane* and *almain* are boring." She owed him no explanation, growing more annoyed with every jerky movement her body made. "I'll have you know, even if it seems that I don't know what I'm doing, it doesn't mean I cannot lead well. That I will not learn to, with time."

She caught Piper, Yanna, and Isabel staring; Lilac shot them a warning glare before launching herself out, extending her arm and nearly swiping the champagne flutes off a passing server's tray. Lilac shrieked with the wind knocked out of her as she twirled back into poor Rupert, who coughed when she landed against his chest.

"You're right, Your Majesty." He cradled her cautiously, as if handling an awkwardly large vase. "Your dancing skills are truly astounding."

She couldn't keep at this all night. Lilac looked over to Myrddin; he gave her an enthusiastic thumbs up as Hedwig watched with her hand over her mouth.

All the while, Garin watched from his perch. His expression was unreadable at first. Did he think it was funny? Was he bored? Why would he have her dance with Rupert, a noblewoman's bastard son, in front of everyone? It was just a dance, that much was true. And this was her feast. But what was the point?

The corners of his mouth quirked upward, his bored, darkened eyes on Rupert. He'd wanted to embarrass him. Garin was *jealous*.

Lilac would dance for him, indeed.

"Slower," she directed the quartet. They exchanged glances and did as they were told. The melody and pacing of the song instantly slowed, becoming much more sultry. The guests around them gasped in delight. Lilac stopped fighting, letting the pounding of the drums and surging of the string instruments wash over her. She spun and wrapped her arms around Rupert's neck, stepping so close she could smell the dates and honey on his breath.

He stiffened but didn't pull away, setting his fingertips lightly on her hips. The positioning felt off; their bodies didn't fit well together, not like hers and Garin's did. He was a beanstalk of a man, at least Garin's height, with little to no coordination himself.

Lilac said nothing and swayed, trying to enjoy the music while ignoring the eyes on them. She gently led him into a circular step, biting her lip to conceal her shocked smile. The more she acted willingly, the pressure of Garin's command lessened.

"This is much better," Rupert sighed, relief also flooding his face as he fell into her rhythm. "I thought that would last all night."

"You wouldn't know anything about lasting all night," Lilac shot.

He immediately shut his mouth. They swayed, not terribly offbeat. When they rotated, she couldn't help but look over Rupert's shoulder at Garin. His expression was unreadable again.

Good. The bastard was the one who encouraged her to take the dance.

Rupert was watching, too. "You'd think with the way he's looking at you, that *he* was your emperor."

Lilac turned her back to him. "He is merely protective."

"Over someone he's just met?"

"Of Maximilian." Lilac refused to elaborate further.

They fell into an empty silence then. Rupert's gaze kept flickering over her shoulder until she finally turned to see what he was staring at. Myrddin stared at the floor, seeming to concentrate much too hard on the story Hewig was telling.

"Ambrosius?" Lilac leaned in. "Is that why you pulled me away for this dance?"

Rupert made a sound between a cough and a snort. "What? No."

"You should go talk to him." She tried to steer them in Myrddin's and Hedwig's direction, but Rupert tugged them back.

"Stop it. I don't know him. I've passed him in the halls a couple times today, we've exchanged greetings. That's it."

"He's a warlock. A kind and talented one, at that," she offered, just in case he hadn't heard Garin earlier. "His name is Ambrosius."

"I know." He nodded, stealing a glance back again. He said nothing more on the matter, but flushed heavily.

"So," she said, changing the subject for him. "People like you usually don't serve the castle guard this way. Never as sentry or foot soldier, anyway."

"It was something I wanted to try at the time, and I preferred not to enter at a higher rank, just in case. I left last year in the autumn."

They made another rotation; Garin had not lifted his eyes from her.

"Skirting your duties, are you?" she teased.

"I was not often on duty even while I worked here."

Her face fell. She instantly wished she hadn't brought it up. They both looked away, and she tried not to think of pumping his cock in her palm. *Prick.*

"And you went to Le Conquet then?"

"No. I only spent a month there and just now returned." He paused and frowned, as if he struggled to recall. "I left when the tides became unpredictable. It happens sometimes with the turn of the season, but it seemed an unprecedented phenomena. Unusual for this time of year. Everyone in the town was in a sour mood because the waves affected their angling."

"So what did you do before then?"

"I thought about finding my father, learning more about him. He works in one of the towns, according to mother. Won't tell me who he could be, or if he's even alive." Rupert looked down, eyes shifting. "So instead, I returned home to our estate. I spent many of my younger years traveling and two years before that at the university in Paris. Lately, I've been considering going back. I think I'd like to work in administration. Maybe here one day."

"That is unlikely." Lilac offered him a bitter smile. "You'd best wait until the tensions ease before returning to Sorbonne. Otherwise, there are several institutions in the German lands, Austria, and in Urbino."

Rupert's brows shot up. "You know of them?"

"Yes, Rupert, I do," she said curtly. "I suspect many other women know of all the institutions where men are allowed to study freely, and from which we are barred. I was fortunate to have a governess and tutors. Other well-read women are not so lucky, when they ought to be. Having a non-royal parent sounds freeing, though," she added, hoping to lift Rupert's spirits. "To have one foot in the world of nobility, and one to give you a sense of normalcy."

Rupert made a face. "It can be. It is also burdensome. For one, not having a title when it would probably benefit me. Give me guidance on some grand purpose in life. Mother could take a husband at any time, rich or poor, yet I'd still be her bastard son." His head turned, and he sighed. "And here she comes."

Lilac untangled herself from him to find Emma striding toward them.

"Your Majesty!" The countess stopped much too close and leaned in to press her cheek against Lilac's. Despite her brown hair flecked with gray, her demeanor was lively and youthful. She smelled of pears, precariously balancing a champagne flute in one hand as she curtsied. "Emma Mènard, of Vannes. Pleased to meet you."

"Rupert's told me all about you. We're friends from when he worked here," Lilac added, returning the curtsey.

"And I've heard much about you." Emma motioned at her, marveling at the way her sleeves caught every fragment of warm, muted light. "And that gown. One of Herlinde's pieces?"

Lilac stole a glance at Garin over Emma's shoulder. He was looking directly at them. "Yes. It was a generous gift from a friend."

"It's a shame Vivien isn't here to see it. Would've ruined her mood to see a Daemon-made dress on the floor. Rest her soul, and good riddance."

Rupert only ran a hand over his face. "Not here."

"What?" The countess swilled her drink. "She was a terrible person born into serfdom, and still when she was raised with her parents' restored ranks. She deserved to stay a servant."

Lilac never witnessed anyone of noble rank voice such discontent with the Le Tallecs or Ermengardes. "I was blindsided by Vivien," Lilac said quietly. Her family's underlying strife with them had been made public after her accession, but it still felt taboo to admit. "What made them reinstate her parents? Do you know?"

The countess gave a sly shrug. "Good behavior on her parents' end. They even left for a weeks' long retreat to the *Armor* before resuming their duty on your grandfather's court. We all thought they were being banished, but they returned one day from Douarnenez and were welcomed back into their old quarters like nothing had happened. Vivien then had her first taste of a life of nobility and hungered for the status that came with it. And more." She squinted, rifling through her memory. "She loved spreading the rumor she'd heard from her parents about how your ancestor is the reason her family hadn't been married into the monarchy."

Lilac's forced smile faded. "I'd *love* to hear this rumor."

"Of course you would." Appearing to love the gossip, Emma looked around, ensuring no one was listening. "Toward the end of the War of Succession, this kingdom saw many moving parts. There was a respected duke then, Geoffrey of Penthievre, whose family resided in what is the Le

Tallec manor now. He had an only son, Alor, who was troublesome in his youth, but began training to spearhead the king's armies when Geoffrey fell ill. He became a fair constable at the king's right hand. Alor oversaw many, but there was a particular group of soldiers he trained himself, mostly stowaways and young men who were orphaned by the war. He and his group of men were unstoppable until they met their fate."

"They were killed by vampires." She didn't know what possessed her to say it. Maybe it was the fascination over everything. She was tired of glossing over the real histories, once overwhelmed by everything she was taught under either systems of intentional or accidental ignorance—the truths she was left to find on her own. Reddening, Lilac pulled a flute of champagne from a passing tray and sipped from it, hoping it would calm her nerves and help the dull ache in her lower back.

To her relief, Emma raised her own glass. "My," she chuckled, impressed. "You know your history."

In the Trevelyan farmhouse, Garin had told her all about Laurent's attack that had cost his company their lives. Only a few were spared. "I had a good tutor. How did you know about the vampire attack?"

"Before he died, my father worked for your grandfather as an archivist and was interested in the histories. Studied it at Sorbonne. The nature of Alor's last company's fate is not widely known. The battle was documented as an enemy victory, but Father said there were records of their camp being found littered with mutilated bodies, the snow streaked with red. By the time they were discovered, most of them were unidentifiable. Alor left behind a wife named Katella. At the time, your ancestor, the king, was betrothed to an earl's daughter from France." She gave a wry smile. "Guess who she was?"

She shook her head in disbelief. "An Ermengarde."

Emma hummed in confirmation. "But the king instead became smitten with Katella after Alor's death and called off his engagement with the earl's daughter, forfeiting not only a high-profile marriage, but a chance at a strengthened relationship with the French crown. They were married within a month. After Geoffrey died, the duchy was then passed on to the Le Tallecs."

Fascinated, Lilac peeked up through wisps of her hair; Garin's chin was resting on his knuckle, his eyes trained on his plate. *Did he know?*

A prominent vein bulged at his temple, and she thought she saw his jaw flex. He no longer looked like he was enjoying her being down there with Emma and Rupert.

Alor had been *his* constable.

"Enough of her." Emma had followed her gaze to the table, then looked this way and that. Half of the crowd had dispersed to the feast tables and were chattering amongst themselves, the ale flowing freely now. Myrddin, Piper, Yanna, and Isabel swayed nearby to the pleasant song floating from the stringed instruments. "He doesn't look like a man from Austria."

"*Mother*," groaned Rupert again, but she ignored him.

The way the countess looked at Garin was unsettling. "What do you mean? What does he look like?" Lilac tried to appear dismissive. "A Frenchman? A Breton?"

Emma leaned in. "My mother was a frivolous spirit at heart. Naturally she was devastated when father passed, but she was so young and never thought to let this stop her from enjoying herself. Shortly after, there was a friend she invited over. He was at the manor a couple of times after meeting him on her official travels. He had perfect manners, spoke several languages, and even played noddy and piquet with my sister and I once." Emma dipped a finger into her flute and dripped it onto her tongue, and winked. "Mother had fine taste in her friends. You two know, don't you? *Friends?*"

"My God," said Rupert, slipping his arm in Lilac's and tugging her away. This time, she was thankful he did. "That is far too much. Goodbye, Mother."

"Oh, you're no fun," Emma laughed. But she waved them along, fanning herself.

Reeling, she allowed Rupert to drag her to the middle of the floor. She positioned herself so his back was to the head of the room, putting Garin right in her sight. She could barely stand to look at him, Emma's words still haunting her—but she did so, anyway. Garin's shoulders were quaking with laughter, his lips pursed together.

The same irksome jealousy she felt at the brothel flooded through her. She shouldn't have these feelings—especially not one wishing to dunk kind Emma's face in the cider bowl for merely telling her the story of how Garin might've bedded Rupert's grandmother.

This was stupid. He'd been with others. Adelaide and the like.

Lilac tried to hide her pout and secured her arms around Rupert again. He settled his arms carefully on her upper back.

Who could blame Rupert's grandmother, honestly? Garin was unbearably charming and an excellent lover. He was almost too good in bed, like there wasn't another care in the world but the person in front of him.

She gritted her teeth. That person *needed* to be her. She wiped at her brow and refocused.

Rupert was speaking again. "And the truth is, I pulled you away for a dance because I had a question regarding my area of study."

"Oh." Lilac was barely paying attention anymore. Garin's stare would burn a fucking hole in her forehead. "Go on, let's hear it, then."

"Where I might find your scrivener?"

This snapped her out of her haze. "You mean our scribe?"

"Yes."

"Why?" She wasn't comfortable with him roaming the castle while off duty, nor chancing him finding John in the library, where her notes were still off limits. "Do you require something to be notarized?"

"N-no, not at the moment." His hand went to the back of his neck. "I'm not sure there exists anything to sign. I wanted to ask him for clarification on something."

Lilac stopped swaying and removed her hands from him. "What do you need?"

He shook his head. "It's really nothing. It's more a question for him."

There was movement over Rupert's shoulder; Garin had stood. He was leaning over to the right of Lilac's throne, peering at the bottles of alcohol that had been gifted to them.

"My scribe is busy tonight," she insisted. "What is it?"

Defeated, Rupert wiped his lip and stuck his hands in his coat pockets. "There was a young family I came across in Le Conquet. They were staying at the local tavern-inn after losing their home in a fire, but would soon run out of the funds to maintain their shelter. Just outside the town, there is an unoccupied property of the husband's great aunt, who'd recently passed on."

Lilac looked at him like he was crazy. "And you need this resolved right now?"

Rupert's cheeks flushed, but he quickly collected himself. "Given the nature of my path of study, I offered to help them. At the university, I was told I'd gain the ability to notarize paperwork after my completed third year."

"You have no current jurisdiction to do so since you've only completed two." She could tell where this was going and disliked feeling like no one trusted her to make the right decisions—from weighing war with marriage, to a petty inheritance matter. She could handle advising a property transfer. Lilac glanced up at Garin. He was pouring himself a cup of the wine he'd picked: a swan-necked amber glass bottle with a paper label. He brought the mug to his lips, his throat moving with an unusual eagerness as he tipped it back.

"Normally the head of their duchy would handle something like this," Lilac answered. "Unless there was an issue with the natural process of property inheritance. Don't they know homes are passed by will through male relatives first?

"That's the issue, Your Majesty. The husband is his aunt's last surviving relation, male or female, but he wasn't named in her papers. Either she wasn't prepared or didn't intend to name him at all. It was an untimely demise."

"That's a shame. Then they have no immediate right to the property. Vacant properties eventually go to the owner of the fief—its presiding earl or baron." Lilac couldn't remember who was in charge in Le Conquet; the coast was littered with smaller towns, making their administrations more difficult to keep track of than those inland. "The home belongs to the head of the duchy until the property is redistributed to them by the magistrate's contract—or sold to someone else. The family you mention is welcome to bid for the home."

"That is a shame," Rupert replied, but his brows floated above his twinking eyes, which shifted to the door, then back. "I'll see to it that they're notified."

This was common knowledge, nothing he'd need John for, and something she shouldn't have had to explain to a third-year university student. There was something familiar about the shift in Rupert's eyes, the wiggle in his peppered brown beard. Lilac couldn't place it, and was about to ask when she felt a sudden tug in her chest. She looked up at Garin and felt her body react before she even registered the way he looked at her.

Mug in hand, he lounged back in the chair. His shoulders were relaxed, his eyes anything but bored or even amused.

They were hungry.

Her chest prickled with heat. She couldn't tear her gaze away when Garin ran his tongue against his bottom lip, wiping the dribble of wine away. She couldn't help but think of placing herself upon the spread before him.

Through the heat and pull of his magic, even she knew it was a bad idea.

Rupert was staring at Garin. Then he turned to her, an expression of slight alarm on his face. "Your Majesty?"

"Shut up." Lilac barely heard him over her own heartbeat. She didn't register the musicians exchanging confused glances and halting their instruments, the entire room freezing to watch them. All she wanted was to be in Garin's arms. To sit in his lap, straddling him and the throne, her throat exposed, dress drooping.

She wanted to comfort and be comforted—to be cured from this dastardly spell put on them both, even if doing so meant accepting a most wicked fate. She imagined him fucking her with his teeth inside her again until she cried out, wanted to nuzzle into the spot where his neck met his shoulder and taste him, a flood of his own memories pouring out. To know him, the story of his mother and the secret apothecary under the brothel, the one that helped women.

Lilac took a step toward the table, her body flooding with warning adrenaline.

"Your Majesty." Piper was suddenly there, shouldering Rupert out of the way and beaming with wide, alarmed eyes. There was a sharp pinch on her forearm.

"*Ow*," Lilac snapped, yanked from her trance. The rest of the room came into focus. The only ones moving were Myrddin, precariously picking his way through the crowd along the right-hand wall, and Yanna and Isabel who made their way over from the desserts table. Disbelievingly, Lilac watched the warlock stride up to Garin, gripping the vampire's arm and jolting him from his unruly stare.

When Garin's hungry gaze finally snapped onto Myrddin, the pressure left her body. Emotion poured into the hole his stare had drilled into her.

Whispers erupted in the Grand Hall.

"How are you doing, Your Majesty?" Piper said under her breath, gripping Lilac at her elbow. "What can I bring you? A stiff drink? A warm croissant? A bucket of ice to dunk your head into, perhaps? Anything to stop the both of you from eye-fucking each other across the ballroom."

She exhaled, desperate to compose herself. She *needed* to get away from him, even if for a moment. A breath of air from his pull, lest she go to him. Lest she give in.

"It's time for a trip to the washroom." Lilac tugged Piper to the doors. She curtseyed before the tittering crowd and then rushed into the corridor, Yanna and Isabel tagging close behind.

GARIN

Whoever gifted Eleanor this wine should be sent to the gallows, or perhaps a dull guillotine. The taste was strange: bitter, then sweet, the savory lingering on his tongue—no combination of fruit he'd ever had. He didn't consider himself a slave to the bottle by any means, but it usually numbed his thoughts when his instincts were raging. It was why he indulged after every pub brawl he'd broken up, every close encounter he'd had with the Le Tallec hunting troupe, to douse the fire of his adrenaline. It was why he sipped Lorietta's heaviest scotch when he'd asked Lilac to supper on the night they'd met, so she might not preemptively become *his* supper.

He'd downed half the fucking thing, but it wasn't enough to dull his senses—nor the scent of her bleed, which made his gums throb. He might've felt himself getting drunk, but Garin was still desperate to bury his face between her thighs.

The only thing that remotely helped was fantasizing about smashing Rupert's skull in.

Garin was the one who had ordered Lilac to go with him out of spite; he knew he'd regret it the moment he'd spoken the words. It wasn't her fault, yet he couldn't help the visceral anger that bloomed from watching the bastard walk her down those steps, away from him. He'd watched them dance, their bodies awkward yet unsettlingly familiar around one another. They'd conversed with sweet Emma, both their faces red.

It was really none of his business, Garin told himself repeatedly. Lilac was the queen—a free woman, and he wasn't the type to build a cage around her.

Throat burning, he unwillingly remembered who he'd become under the influence of the Dragondew Mead, and the pulsing music that had filled the halls of The Fool's Folly. That wasn't him. The completion of their bond had even granted him a strange relief in at least dampening that frightening hunger for her—and the violent voracity that came after drinking from someone who wasn't her.

It was why he'd encouraged her to take the dance with Rupert. Deep down, he'd wanted to know what it would be to watch her with another. To test himself, to know beyond the shadow of a doubt that he could stomach it.

Therein, Garin discovered, lay the problem. It changed nothing. He didn't begrudge Lilac for taking the dance. He adored her just as much, desired her all the same. He did, however, find the mental image of tossing Rupert out the window for touching what was *his,* rather comforting.

His stomach growled, his heart aching in its slow, heavy beat. Most of all, he envied Rupert the ability to converse with Lilac about trivial matters so casually, without the lingering bloodlust or worry over an uncertain future.

What did that feel like?

What was it to be human? Twenty-something years with warm blood and a quick-beating heart had not been enough to answer this question. He'd been too preoccupied with throwing himself at the distraction he'd found in Alor's group of misfits.

Come to think of it, his discomfort had begun at the countess's unexpected mention of the duke's son. He'd glared in Lilac's direction, but all he saw was Bastion lying in the blood-streaked snow. The bodies of the other friends he'd lost to Laurent.

For decades he'd struggled with the change, unable to accept what he had become. There was a period he had fucked and drank his way through the boroughs, reveling in many of the firsts the throes of war had stolen from him. Finding The Fenfoss Inn was his solace, his second chance. There, he devoted his endless time to rediscovery, learning and clinging to anything that reminded him of the humanity lurking deep beneath the surface: Their garden, his fae-rooted plants. Assisting Lorietta in her kitchen, indulging when he simply couldn't help himself—which was often, for his friend was the best chef he knew. Nighttime strolls, which most recently led to Lilac's balcony. Staring at the forest that had become his fiercely protected home, face basked in moonlight.

Garin prided himself on the person he'd worked on becoming. He was a good man, or at the very least a chivalrous one.

Their thrall bond had undone all of it.

He thought the wine would help quell his anxiety, if not his unending hunger for her. He'd never been more wrong.

Jaw clenched, Garin watched Piper approach Lilac. Her handmaidens were close behind. They were going to leave. *Lilac* wanted to leave. Good. She was safe, especially with the redhead as much as he hated admitting it. The two had their own unique bond, whether they sensed it or not.

She was in good hands. He'd made a mistake in coming, but he'd left himself no choice—

"Should I go after her?"

Garin nearly gave himself whiplash from how quickly he turned on Myrddin. He hadn't even heard him approaching. He yanked his arm from the warlock's grasp. "Shhh," he spat, watching the doors swing shut and listening.

"I'm going to ruin everything," Lilac was sobbing in the echoed chamber of the corridor. The thud of her heart had quickened. Her ungraceful footfall stomped left, toward the washroom.

"You won't," said Piper. "We won't let you."

"I will. I *will*. It is what I do. This is my fault, I've enthralled myself to him. There are duties I am expected to uphold that I cannot stand by—not with him here. I—" She broke off in a chest-heaving sob. Lilac was panicking. Garin's fingers twitched, itching to lace themselves between hers. "I never wanted to in the first place, Piper. None of this is what I wanted."

"I promise we'll discuss this later," Piper reassured her, sounding like she was speaking out of the side of her mouth. "Another time. Not *here*."

Her handmaidens struggled to keep up.

"Enthrall?" The soft, pixie-like voice of the kind-eyed brunette.

"Be quiet, Isabel," the sterner one, Yanna, snapped.

Guilt and fear threatened to overwhelm him. Gods, he wished to turn off his hearing and heightened senses, block out their voices entirely. He shut his eyes as if it would help.

To his surprise, it did. Sort of.

"Even good acquaintances will have their disagreements," Henri was chuckling.

"Dear, you're red as a beet," slurred Marguerite. "I'm sure it's fine."

"Disagreements?" It was the unpleasant red-haired woman from the foyer that seemed particularly fond of challenging Lilac. "She's been dancing with Emma's bastard son in front of the emperor's emissary. She's more than crossed him. Doomed our entire kingdom, I reckon."

Garin's eyes snapped open. *He'd have none of that.*

"A jig, maybe," Garin called out, sounding unsure and strangled. Several people who weren't already discreetly watching turned their attention to him, commenting on the emissary having too much to drink.

Henri made a noise of agreement and motioned at the band, and they began an upbeat jig, drowning out the voices. Garin was grateful. He couldn't stand to hear Lilac upset, or what she might confide to her friends —because he knew, in his darkest hour, that he would do anything to appease her. That he'd fight tooth and nail to remain in her life, protect her, even if she wished otherwise.

I have made a choice. Her words were carved into his throbbing skull. He didn't blame her. He was supposed to want this.

"Shall I intervene?" pressed Myrddin.

"Piper's there. There's no need." Garin tugged at his collar, fingers fumbling as he unbuttoned it. He was sweating. Had he drank too quickly? Alcohol usually hit him immediately—it did all vampires—yet all it had done was worsen his anxiety and make his stomach churn. The fire in the hearth behind them seemed to grow brighter, the heat even scorching the back of his neck. "Hell," he grumbled, shrugging out of his fine coat from Herlinde and letting it fall to the floor. He'd paid in blood for it but he couldn't bring himself to care.

"Here, why don't you have some more." Myrddin leaned over him to snatch the pitcher, stumbling back. Disbelievingly, he tipped it over his palm. A single drop of burgundy spilled out. "You drank it all? Already?"

"I had to," Garin managed, trying to distract himself from the nagging burning in his throat. The punishing urge to follow Lilac. Hunt her down. "The illusion on that blood worked perfectly. I didn't know it was possible. It'll be revolutionary for...for—" The room began to spin slowly. Garin gripped the armrests.

He was glad Myrddin sent him out with his own pitcher under the glamor of water. He could hardly concentrate on what Lilac had been saying without imagining sweeping her hair back and sinking his fangs into her. He'd made a clear mistake that morning; despite how badly he wanted it to be true, maybe she wasn't safest in his presence after all.

Myrddin scanned the room, starling when his frantic gaze falling on the half-full wine bottle. "Where did you get that?"

Garin couldn't be bothered by the warlock's pedantries. "If anyone goes to check on her, it will be me." He made to get up, but slammed back down onto the throne. Reddish brown rope had appeared out of thin air, securing his wrists over his sleeves to the armrests.

"The bottle," Myrddin said with a warning glare. "Where did you get it?"

"There," Garin breathed, cocking his head to the boxes and bottles piled to their right. "Marguerite said we could help ourselves. They're gifts from the attendees." His stomach and throat were on fire. Garin's hands balled into fists as he strained against the triple tied hawthorn rope.

"Put those fangs away," growled Myrddin.

"I can't." He was losing control. He inhaled through his nose, willing himself to calm. His fangs throbbed against his lips, his feet and hands itching to move. "I can't help it."

Garin looked worriedly out to the crowd, but no one was paying attention.

"I see that look," Myrddin said. "You'll only hurt yourself—hurt others —if you get out of that chair."

The warlock was right, and Garin felt it, too. Although his hunger since saving Lilac had morphed into an unending yearning for her blood, it was nothing compared to the feeling that plagued him now.

It was unnameable, a grief that took his breath and made time stand still. Garin ached to hold her in his arms.

He shut his eyes, imagining Maximillian and his beloved in front of a crowd of hundreds in Vienna. At a podium, surrounded by flowers and attendants, and everything he could not give her, leagues and leagues away from him.

Garin opened them to his clenched fists lifting from the chair, the last of the rope dissolving in a fiery cloud of light and ash that didn't burn him. Despite Myrddin's shocked cry, he stood. There was an animalistic sound of despair that rumbled deep in his chest, drowned out by the gasps and whispers from the crowd below.

Disgusted with his thoughts and desperate to shake them, he snatched the neck of the bottle. Myrddin barreled into him, barely moving Garin at all; the warlock's hand latched onto the neck, twisting this way and that. Garin lifted it to his mouth and managed to take a few mouthfuls before he allowed Myrddin to wrestle it from him.

"I said let," Myrddin snarled. "*Go.*"

The moment the warlock finally plucked it from his grasp, he was gone. The warlock, and the bottle. Garin blinked—and so was everyone else.

The Grand Hall was empty. He rubbed his eyes when night began to leak from the high windows, dripping down the gilded walls, the darkness of the sky expanding across the ceiling in a slow-spreading blaze. Like a map held to a torch.

"Myrddin," Garin stammered, willing his eyes to adjust. He stumbled forward, expecting to catch himself upon the dining table. Instead, his hands found rough wood. As he tried to push up, they sank through the decay.

Marveling at the pieces of bark on his upturned hands, Garin staggered to his feet. Before him was a wide, moss-covered log. The crowd beyond was gone. In its place, a placid lake scattered with enormous lily pads the size of Lorietta's rugs.

Gnarled white trees surrounded him and the lake, a copse of particularly dead ones crowding the bank he stood on, as if urging Garin toward the water. What little leaves remained clung to branched fingers, rattling softly in the stale air. It smelled like decay and the faintest hint of smoke, but he couldn't detect any in the cloudless sky scattered with stars.

"Myrddin! What game are you playing?"

A strange male voice answered out in peril—a rattling groan sending chills down the length of Garin's back.

Garin whipped around. "Kestrel?"

A shuffling came from behind him. *Something* was crawling out of the trees. Garin's entire body tensed, his chest vibrating with a low growl. The last of his bravado.

It was—

An old man. Or, at least the remnants of one, dragging itself forward on his arms. Wisps of gray hair clung to the top of its head, face gaunt as if the life had been sucked out of it, the light gone from its shadowed eyes. The skin and meat of his arms and torso clung to its bones, some of which shone white in the in the dappled moonlight. A tattered shirt torn to shreds hung off its shoulders, along with several strands of something dark and wet.

Seaweed.

"Pascal," it rasped through rotting teeth, its monstrous voice enveloping Garin in frigid air. "You haven't aged a day."

Garin stumbled back, tripping over the log and landing on his ass in the mud. "I am not Pascal." The animosity in his voice shocked him. Garin righted himself, his gums throbbing, joints aching to spring away or fight. "Stay back!"

The creature approached the log, considering him. "Then, who are you?" It eyed Garin's teeth. "*What* are you?"

Was this yet another specter sent by the faerie king? Was it here to collect his debt because they hadn't brought the chest yet? Kestrel had been the one not responding to Bastion's letters.

"Who are you?" it demanded again.

Garin's throat bobbed. He'd be foolish in answering, especially if it was a creature from the Low Forest. Who knew what such a creature would do with this truth? But the words were wrenched from him. Monster. Man. *Vampire.* "I am Pascal's only child. Garin Trevelyan."

The creature smiled knowingly, its teeth shockingly straight and intact for something so...so rotted. Despite the light breeze, the seaweed and its hair swung in slow motion, side to side, as if bound to the tide. It started forward again, dragging itself through the shadow-dappled forest floor. It broke through the rotting log, the soft wood seeming to wither on contact.

"Come. Let me see you."

He certainly would not. Garin's calves strained—but his feet wouldn't budge. They were sinking into the mud. Surely he was dreaming. The surrounding trees croaked in warning, their shadows following the creature. The stench of decay and brine rose, choking Garin as it neared. Its face finally emerged from the darkness, cast into moonlight.

The creature's eyes had been partially eaten from their sockets. Barnacles were embedded into its skin like large boils, but even past the skin and sinew, its features were unmistakably familiar. *Familial*. It slowed to a halt. "My, my. You look—"

"Don't," Garin snarled. He'd heard it all his human life. He didn't need to hear it again, not from this ghoul.

The log behind it had collapsed into a steaming pile of sludge and seaweed. "I appear tonight as a husk of my mortal being, but rest assured, I exist beyond this form. I have been here, watching. Listening. Much like the forests, the Breton sea is one. More tumultuous, deceiving than the others—she is powerful, and all-knowing." It lowered its voice to a croaking whisper. "A force to reckon with, and I have been slave to her since the day your father slipped me off his boat."

Garin ogled. No one else had been aboard the small boat Pascal and Aimee sailed from Cornwall to Brittany. No one had ever mentioned—

There was a quiet splash behind Garin, causing both him and the creature to jump. He turned and saw nothing but soft ripples spanning the surface near the bank. When he looked back to the corpse, his eyes were filled with moisture. Garin scoffed and wiped it away on his sleeve.

"Your physical resemblance to him is uncanny," sang the creature, "but you are very different, aren't you?" A smile began to grow on its hideous face, a twinkle forming in its eye. "You are more careful after observing your father's tendencies. An academic with a heart for others, one who happened to pick up a sword when it had never been your dream. Almost as if destiny had aligned."

"War was never my destiny." The things Garin had done with his own hands and blade never seemed to haunt him as much as they did his peers, but not because he was heartless. By the time he got to the battlefield, he'd learned how to numb himself against violence.

Bastion was always an angry child after being separated from his merchant parents, and brawling at the old Paimpont orphanage became his forte. It was why Alor had often paired them both. Garin was able to skirt the grief until he became a creature of the night, until bloodshed was no longer an option, but a need. Then, everything caught up to him.

"It was a choice I'd made for survival. Out of loneliness and greed," Garin said quietly.

"It was a choice you made, nonetheless."

The creature cocked its head then, reminding him of Pascal when he'd started interrogating Garin on Aimee's whereabouts after she'd started working at The Fool's Folly. Aimee had told Pascal she'd started helping at the bakery they often visited, and Garin kept his mother's secret. Pascal was never truly convinced, and the kind baker's family was generous to keep her ruse. The questions began whenever his mother was away.

"Survival and destiny often feel one in the same. Perhaps one nudges you toward the other, no?" The creature shifted on its haunches, the sound of its bones cracking pulling Garin from the memory. "Still, it didn't stop you from pondering what your life could've been had you not gone to the duke's son's tent, though."

Garin's lip curled over his fangs, but he was at a loss for words. The thing had no right to be so invasive—this was blasphemy. How could it have known? Thees were things he'd never told anyone. Private, personal truths he'd willingly plastered over his bleeding heart with other trauma. His hand went to his chest, gripping the dark fabric there.

"It consumes you, doesn't it?" said the creature. "Just as it did Pascal. That heart is but a slow-beating echo of what life could have been for you. With your mother's heart and wit, you would've made a fascinating politician or orator. Or, would you have had a thrilling career in botany, like him? Had you not picked up that sword, what would have become of Garin Austol Trevelyan? A husband? A doting father? A respected citizen, at the very least." It blinked slowly—one eyelid more delayed than the other. "But, had this monstrous fate not found you, you would not be standing here before me today."

"You know nothing!" Garin spat.

"No. Perhaps not." The creature didn't so much as flinch at Garin's outburst. "But I do know you've been reading." Its empty sockets bore into him. "I know you discovered a certain passage that struck your interest as you sat, contemplating your life choices upon her balcony. That it led you to seek yet another Daemon-authored book in your witch friend's collection detailing the matrimonial tendencies of your species, when you had never bothered to know before. Odd, isn't it?"

Garin had no answer, feeling stripped bare as the dead blood that coursed slowly through his veins rushed to his face. Lorietta's book on vampire politics was long gone. "I was curious," he muttered.

"I bet you were." The creature let out a hack of a knowing laugh. "Ever the wanderer and researcher. Just like your father."

Reeling, Garin lunged forward and snatched the creature by its rags, looking it in its non-existent eyes. "My father's research was in vain, more important to him than anyone else. He chased fairy tales, mistaking magic for miracle, seeking an island kingdom of faerie folly and—and allowing it to drive him to ruinous obsession, a-and—" He was stuttering. Garin never stuttered. "My mother found her purpose in helping women, and it infuriated him. Father was so bitter, he wanted to report their apothecary to the authorities. Pascal's work was selfish, he never aimed to benefit anyone else but himself." He'd never voiced his disdain for Pascal this way, not out loud. "At the very least, my purpose now is much greater than anything I once considered important. I am nothing like him."

The creature remained silent.

Trembling, Garin dropped it to the floor. "What do you want from me? How did I get here and *how* do I return to the castle?"

The creature gave a pitiful sigh and shook itself off, as if aware there was nothing Garin could do or say that would harm it. "If it is any consolation, none of this is accidental. My son's greed set your fate into motion even before you were born. Go where the current pushes you, my boy. Fighting it will only bring destruction."

His fate was not botany nor the blade. Lilac's sweet face and saccharine smile flashed across Garin's mind.

Fury engulfed his fear like a torch to oil. It was the same knee-buckling anger that rose after discovering his mother too late, the same rage that drove him to forge a note requesting Pascal's immediate assistance at one of the battlegrounds rumored to anticipate an ambush. Garin went to Alor's tent immediately after—before his father's body was even identified, and before the magistrate could come knocking to discuss the inheritance of the farmhouse.

Assaulted by memories he'd long buried, Garin staggered back. "Pascal has nothing to do with the man I've become except ensure I am nothing like him. You are *not* Loumarch. He'd said you were buried at a chapel in Cornwall, that the sickness took you before their departure."

The creature laughed again. "Better that than admit he didn't want to care for an aging father whose mind had failed him. Especially when it became clear their boat had drifted off course from Roscoff, and that rations were slim." A fat worm crawled out of his left eye socket then—and a long, thick tongue darted out of the hole that was his mouth, sucking the worm in. It then chewed, squelching loudly.

Garin was done wasting time. He had to find his way back to Lilac. He'd send the corpse back to where it belonged. As he swung his foot back, a powerful hand seized his ankle, yanking his standing leg from beneath him.

His head slammed onto the bank, half his face in the mud. Gasping, the last he saw was his grandfather's rotting face twisting in astonishment before two hands pulled—dragged him down into the lake. He kicked and thrashed once submerged, fighting to see where the bubbles went as they leaked from his nostrils, but his eyes stung in the murky water.

He pried the bony fingers off his ankle when another hand clamped down on his shoulder. Garin managed a better grip on that one—he reached back and yanked, and when his fingers slipped, the Morgen's hand latched onto his face, pushing him down. He scraped it off, shoved its wrist into his mouth and bit down, tearing off its entire hand. The water around him vibrated, erupting in frenzied hisses and black-green blood; with one powerful kick, Garin pushed himself toward the glimmer of moonlight finally visible above.

Spitting water and dirt, he lurched his arms forward with all his might and paddled toward the nearest gigantic lily pad, hoisting himself up. He glanced back. His grandfather sat watching him, his ghastly expression unreadable.

"What do you want?" Garin asked again. He wiped his face uselessly on his soaking sleeve, knowing there were tears there. "What do you want from me?"

A muffled chorus of laughter shook the lily pad Garin stood on. Several orbs of dim light flashed in the murky depths. Their warning—a beautiful display that had led countless to their doom. He wouldn't be the next. He bent his knees and sprung to the nearest lily pad, nearly missing and pulling his leg up, just before a bony arm shot out at it. He kicked it back into the water.

"*Live!*" Loumarch shouted from the shore as Garin scrambled to his feet.

He wiped the hair out of his eyes and rose, preparing to leap off before one of the Morgen slithered onto the edge of his, her mouth gaping over rows and rows of glistening teeth. She was particularly long; her gaze particularly hungry. A crown of thorns sat upon her head above a trail of green-blonde hair. Instead of lunging for him, she slithered back into the water, causing a wave to rock the pad he stood on. Garin teetered to the back edge and ran, launching himself into the air and landing on his feet this time.

"Especially ferocious, you are. Do you know what we do with immortals like you?" came the Morgen's sultry voice, vibrating in his skull. "We drag you to the bottom, tether you in strong vines and iron chains, and pick, pick, *pick* at you until there's hardly any meat left on your bones. Then, if you've regenerated, sometimes after months, we'll do it again. When we tire of you, we leave you to drown repeatedly. You all succumb eventually."

There was sloshing behind him. She was getting closer. The next one was further than Garin could jump.

"*Live!*" the ghoul of his grandfather croaked once more.

Garin bent to center his gravity as the lily pad shook. He lashed out, snarling and swiping like a feral animal at the Morgen's head, which popped up playfully, its rows of teeth hungrily gnashing.

"I'm already dead," he snapped, his broken voice carrying across the water. "I'm a man who didn't die when he should have died. I've been dead a long time."

His grandfather's next words reverberated in his bones as the morgens' had, shocking him. "There are days, years that might feel like it. But you are a vessel of magic and knowledge. You are *not* dead, my boy. Not when you have so much life ahead of you."

The morgen bucked beneath him, and he stumbled forward, barely catching himself. Garin made a running jump for the next lily pad—and as he landed in the water just short of it, two hands clamped onto his shoulder, shoving him down into the dark. They grabbed at him, yanked his clothes; when one pair of hands released him, two more latched on, pulling him down.

He didn't need to breathe, but his human instincts were begging to kick in as panic filled him. Water in his lungs would render him just as unable to fight as any mortal would've been.

Live, the husk of Loumarch Trevelyan had said.

Chest burning, Garin glanced up at the moon through the sloshing water, finally stilling against the straining fingers digging into his mouth, ears, and nose—beneath the stands of white hair wrapped around him like a writhing tomb. Maybe it *was* a creature Kestrel sent to communicate with him, just as he'd possessed Hywell. Maybe he'd dreamt this all.

Or had the arcana of this ancient land sunk its teeth into his grandfather, too?

Suddenly the water shook, bubbles and hisses surrounding him. Garin found himself free, his arms shielding his face from a blinding light that lit the sky. An explosion of warmth cast the surface aglow, radiating from something—someone—above him.

When he broke the surface gasping, he expected smoke to fill his lungs. Yet the night air had never tasted so clear.

Standing upon the nearest lily pad at the center of the lake, was a person.

It was Lilac, and she was on fire.

She was *shrouded* in it: flames encased her, an especially bright fireglow concentrated in her eyes, her lips, at the tips of her hair, and in the vortexes that encased both hands. Unbound, her whipped in a vortex of ember around her, the ends of it also fraying in flame. Her body was glistening and entirely bare, dripping in sweat.

She was burning. She was paralyzed by the pain.

"Lilac!" he thundered. Fangs burning, his weak heart thudding harder than it had in centuries, Garin frantically sloshed toward her, unfettered by

Morgen or any of the lily pads that seemed to be making way for him across the pond. He wanted to douse her. He wanted to shield her from the night and unsuspecting eyes—she was probably cold. His own teeth had begun to chatter. "I'm coming!"

He wouldn't lose her, wouldn't dare come close to anything like it again. He'd slit his wrist upon her mouth, allow her to take of him with her blunt teeth, heal her from the inside out like he should have when she was broken and bleeding in his arms.

Anything to keep you here, right here in front of me.

Even if it meant breaking every rule, even if it meant their hierarchy invalidating anything she felt for him. Garin didn't care about some ancient law that sought to discourage what he felt for her, were he ever forced to become Lilac's sire.

No force on earth could do that.

When he was close enough to feel the heat of the fire that consumed her, he realized it was blood that ran over her bare breasts, down her legs, dripping between her fingers visible within the flames. She wasn't burning, nor was the plant beneath her. She was...she was *laughing*. Lilac's head tipped back, a look of ecstasy etched upon her delicate features, the airy sound of her giggle whooshing out like the embers rising into the night.

Then, there was a shriek. Garin tore his gaze away just in time to see two Morgen lunge out of the water, slither onto the shore, and grab Loumarch by the shoulders. He didn't struggle, didn't make a sound as they dragged his frail body toward the lake.

Instead, the old man—the remnants of him—used the last of his energy to call out to Garin once more. "I will find you again, my boy!"

The rest of his words were lost to the lake as they pulled him beneath the surface. His grandfather had no chance, he was already a dead man.

There were more nights than Garin cared to admit where he'd pondered the unthinkable. That perhaps, a mass grave beneath a blood-stained glade or the watery depths was where he, too, belonged. He was an abomination, a rudimentary ghoul exhumed from the dirt at the cruel expense of magic—just like Loumarch. Just like that *thing* that possessed Hywell.

He was a half-dead creature nipping at the heels of the living.

BRIAR SOMERSET

But tonight, contrary to those ruminations, Garin Austol Trevelyan wanted to *live*.

The Low Forest rumbled, an echo of death and the indescribable dark power that had driven his father mad. Bubbles appeared where Loumarch and the Morgen had gone down. They moved toward Garin faster than he could possibly swim, waves cresting in their wake.

Those hands grabbed at him again and pulled him under despite his scratching and thrashing. He struggled to climb onto her lily pad, but she didn't seem to hear him. Water rattled in his chest as Garin pried their brittle hands off his shoulders, his muscles seizing.

He was fatigued. He needed blood. He needed *her*.

She blinked in surprise and looked down at him, her cerulean eyes scrutinizing and bright. "Garin?" Bewildered, she extended a bloodied, flame-covered hand.

He grabbed it, hoisting himself up with the last of his strength, relief and fear flooding him. Garin wept at her feet, pressing her palm to his cheek and kissing it front to back. Much like the faerie fire, it didn't singe him, instead filling him with the golden warmth of reassurance. Of safety and—and love. Lilac wound her soft fingers into his hair, her thumb brushing his forehead. He felt her shift, craning her neck to peer behind.

Garin looked back. The Morgen were gone, the lake just as serene and eerily still as he'd discovered it. They were gone. She'd done it.

Before him, Lilac shone like a torch among violet twilight. She was his deity, and whether she wished him to suffer or worship, punish or be punished, Garin would do it. It was one in the same, as long as he lived to serve her.

She was moving again; this time she bent to his hear. "Garin Trevelyan," she whispered.

Her voice. It sent tingles down his spine, soothing him against the frigid night. "Yes, Your Majesty. Anything."

There was a sharp pinch at his shoulder. Her nails dug into him, and not particularly in the way he was fond of. "Control yourself," she snarled, her mouth brushing his earlobe. "Everyone is watching."

Everyone.

Warm light flooded his vision, no longer focused on her but throughout the entire room. They were barely in the Grand Hall doorway, the doors splayed open. Piper and her handmaidens flanked Lilac, the three of them eyeing him in terror. The redhead bristled nearest the queen, jaw clenched tight, her hands balled into fists.

He was dry everywhere but inside the front of his pants, and he knew immediately it was not urine.

Lilac had not been rubbing his head; she had one hand braced against his forehead while the other clamped down on his shoulder, shoving him away. *His* hands were up her skirts, gripping her soft inner thighs, his lips just inches from her mouthwatering—

Garin pried his fingers off her. He didn't dare move otherwise or glance behind him. He couldn't bear to.

There was the clanking of armor, then. Several armed guards had crowded behind the girls, gathering out in the corridor. It sounded like a dozen more waited behind him, as if they'd been summoned in from the courtyard.

Lilac's voice cracked across the still room like thunder. "Nobody. Touch. Him."

"Your Majesty." There was a pair of footsteps skirting across the floor from the front of the room. Panting, Myrddin was at their side in an instant. Tucked under his arm was the amber wine bottle. "It seems it was this wine that made him act. He'd been drinking it at the table, it sat among the gifts. It is—" He peered at the label. "I can't tell. Maybe a fine claret." Myrddin sniffed at the bottle mouth, then tipped it over his palm. A faint pink liquid pooled there, which he tongued, then brought to his mouth to slurp. A round of disgusted groans made its way through the crowd. "*Mmmm.* A claret steeped with mushrooms."

"How do you know?" someone called out. "About the mushrooms?"

"Isn't it obvious?" When no one responded, Myrddin rolled his eyes.

But the warlock was right. Those cold sweats, nightmarish hallucinations, were the symptoms of a particular mushroom. The *Amanita muscaria*—or, the fly agaric. Garin was familiar because his father once warned him against putting them in his mouth—both fae-rooted and mortal variations—when he'd laid his foraging goods out on their dining table.

Garin himself had spiked Sinclair's sacramental wine with the fae-rooted variety just weeks ago.

"The scandal this will cause," Marguerite slurred. "Is someone out there trying to poison dear Albrecht? I-I mean, my dear daughter?"

"Poison?" Myrddin scoffed. "Unlikely. Not unless they were trying to poison her with temporary reprieve and a wicked good time."

"I feel fine. More than fine, in fact," Garin managed, desperately willing Myrddin to shut his mouth. His jaw hurt from clenching his teeth. His shirt was drenched in sweat, and he'd begun to shiver.

"See? It's often enjoyed recreationally. We warlocks enjoy it from time to time."

"He needs to see Madame Kemble," Lilac said. She hadn't moved from her spot or retreated, her body stiff.

Garin's mouth went dry. He craned his neck up at her. "No, I do not."

Lilac's concerned frown flamed into anger. "Look at yourself and tell me you don't. You're not well."

"Well, you did pour a glass of champagne on my head upon arrival."

Gasps filled the room. Marguerite began to utter a prayer before Henri shushed her.

Lilac's eyes narrowed, the sweet pout of her lips tightening. The room grew hazy as her pulse quickened, the natural aroma of her skin invading Garin's senses as blood pooled beneath it. "And you had your hands up my skirt just moments ago. I think we are even. You will be brought to my infirmary. That is an order."

His throat bobbed as he swallowed. *What was she doing?* Why would she want him examined? Garin laughed, trying to downplay his heating temper. "I'm sorry, Your Majesty, but my fealty is to Maximilian, and him alone."

Without removing her eyes from him, Lilac reached under her skirts and whipped out her blade. That glistening, inherited dagger.

"Lilac, no!" Henri shouted.

Garin froze amidst the startled shouts from the crowd. There was a flash of silver. He shut his eyes and braced himself for the pain—but the pressure was light.

Lilac's cool blade came to rest flat on his left shoulder.

"If you hadn't consumed the wine, I would have," she said, loud enough for the room to hear. "Thank you for saving me from a most humiliating fate. I hereby grant you knighthood under the Breton crown. *My* crown. Effective immediately."

Gaping, Garin stared up at her. She was mad. Utterly mad.

Henri was suddenly at their side, extending a shaking hand to him.

Reluctantly Garin accepted, allowing the former king to hoist him up. They looked at each other, exchanging bewildered glances before Garin was finally forced to glance at the room.

Behind them, two dozen guards held their weapons at the ready. The dance floor had been mostly cleared; off to the side Rupert was the center of attention, holding his temple. Emma pressed a cloth napkin to her son's head, chiding him under her breath for getting involved.

"You." Garin jumped when Lilac stepped to him, her breathing uneven. "Your fealty is now to me so long as you are here." She nodded to the guards behind him. "Take him to Kemble. Now."

28

Only at Piper's urging did Lilac wait for the castle to be rounded up. She could barely sit still while her friend tugged a brush through several knots in her hair. The queen warily handed her the dagger, which Piper dutifully tucked back into her bedside drawer, right next to the cloth-wrapped stake.

Just as Lilac considered changing into one of her sheer nightgowns, a knock came at the door—then it banged open. It was the barely sobered pair that was Yanna and Isabel, clinging to each other to announce that they'd seen off all the guests who'd made the day trip for Albrecht's feast. Everyone else being hosted on the first floor was being put to sleep by Ambrosius.

Alarmed with that last bit of news, Lilac left the sisters with Piper and bid them all goodnight. Out in the stairwell, a faint singing—Myrddin's voice, not terribly off-tune—could be heard floating up from the first floor.

"This is a lullaby for the castle,
Where hearthflame and shadow do tussle
In deep sleep, you'll take flight,
Through this chaotic night,
Otherwise, may your posterbeds rustle..."

The infirmary was located next to the library at the rear of the northern wing, directly above the armory. It was a square room lined with beds along the back wall, with privacy curtains separating them into makeshift rooms. Lilac had mostly managed to avoid it throughout her upbringing, save a couple trips here and there for scrapes and bad hangovers. And the one evening, upon returning from the Le Tallec estate, for the fever that must've deluded her into besting their boy at the blades, and shoving a boysenberry tart in his face.

When she dashed around the corner huffing, past the library and into the dim hall, a stern voice shook her.

"Is he worth the trouble?" Madame Kemble stood behind her in the dark, barely visible by the dim light of the torch at the start of the hall near the library door. She regarded the queen dubiously, balancing a cup of what appeared to be a cup of milk on a thin, biscuit-lined saucer in one hand, and a plate of bread in the other.

"I wanted to check on him," Lilac said, steadying her breathing. "How is he?"

"Resting." Kemble looked behind her. "But I think you should know something."

Her stomach knotted. "What is it?"

Kemble ushered her down the hall to the infirmary door and unlocked it. Lilac half expected to see Rupert there as well, but it was only Garin, she assumed, in the lefthand far corner—the only cot with its privacy curtain drawn.

The nurse leaned against the doorway, glancing at him apprehensively. "His pulse is terribly slow. He's been in and out of sleep."

"Oh." Just as Lilac had expected. "That's not good, is it?"

"In itself it's not a concern, but I am worried. He's vomited all the food he's eaten today, been retching on an empty stomach, but..." Kemble stepped aside, pointing at a bucket that sat just inside the door.

In that bucket, Lilac quickly discovered, was what looked like a mixture of vomit and black sand.

"Internal bleeding, but you'd never tell by his presentation. He's not terribly pale, and is at least somewhat coherent. He muttered something about toadstools when your father brought him by with the guards. He hallucinated and is a bit weak, which is typical for toadstools. Bleeding in the stomach or esophagus isn't a noted symptom, however. I'm not able to confirm it because his valet apparently finished the wine," Kemble seethed, lowering her voice. "Either way, I must have an answer if news of tonight reaches the emperor. Albrecht is our guest, under our care. There *will* be questions. "

"Albrecht is right," Lilac was quick to say. "I would trust him. Turns out he's well-researched in Botany."

"I want him in bed for the day. Hopefully all that retching got rid of whatever was left of it. He will improve once it is out of his bloodstream." Kemble glanced sidelong at her, then at the closed curtain. "My next thought was bloodletting just to be sure, but when I brought the scalpel out, he stirred. Started talking in his sleep."

Lilac's heart began to race. "What did he say?"

"Mostly nonsense. Several incoherent demands. Fresh air, something to eat. I told him he certainly wouldn't be taking a stroll through the rose garden until he was better, but the rest I could accommodate." Kemble sighed, placing her hands on her hips. "I am glad you're here, Your Majesty, or I might've had to send for you."

Throat constricting, Lilac couldn't peel her gaze from the curtain.

"Sir Albrecht wouldn't stop asking to see you, and only quieted when I told him I'd see what I could do." Kemble held out the plates. "You wouldn't mind bringing these to him, since you two seem well acquainted?"

"Oh." Lilac accepted them, swallowing her surprise. "Of course."

Kemble ambled into the room and disappeared into Garin's curtain, only to return with a wide-mouthed golden vase. "He's still snoring." She held the vase out for Lilac to see, but the queen leaned away, stomach already turning. "After feeding him, I was going to cycle out my leeches in the bailey."

"I'll make sure he eats." Lilac stepped into the room as Kemble exited.

"Go on then." Kemble stopped just outside the doorway. "My leeches aren't the brightest things, but they never fail me when it comes to finding a vein. Tonight, they couldn't stay latched long enough."

"That is *so* odd." Lilac turned to nudge the door with her foot, but Kemble lingered.

"I also might have to replace my scalpel," the nurse commented thoughtfully. "Or sharpen it. After slicing him, I bent to retrieve my cup, when I suddenly could not find the wound. Curious, isn't it?"

They exchanged glances; Myrddin's lament had stopped.

Lilac nodded. "This evening has been altogether strange."

"A strange evening, indeed. And it won't be the last, Your Majesty." Kemble placed her hand on the doorknob. "I'll return soon. *Very* soon." Narrowing her eyes, the nurse slipped out. "*No*," she could be heard saying before it had clicked shut. There was a faint *meow*. "Shoo, leave my patient alone—*who* let this bloody cat into the keep?"

Sweet Bisousig had found her way into the castle. Hopefully, so did Giles for some warmth and a full meal.

Once the door was shut, Lilac strode across the room and yanked the curtain open.

Garin was curled on the cot, shivering under a thin white blanket despite the the hearth on the eastern wall. His eyes were shut, knees tucked into himself. He looked like he was having a nightmare.

She placed the plates down on the shelved cart at his bedside and sank into the chair Kemble had left. Lilac placed a hand upon his knee. At her touch, he jerked awake. One eye popped groggily open, and upon laying it on her, he shot up in bed.

"Madame Kemble," he called, rubbing the back of his head. "It's happening again!"

"*Shhh*." Lilac glanced nervously at the door. "It's me."

Garin opened both eyes and squinted, groaning. "Ugh." He leaned against the pillows stacked two-high. "The room is atrociously bright."

She turned to slide the curtain shut—and as she did, Garin retched all over the floor.

"Sorry." He attempted to wipe his mouth on his sleeve. "I suppose this is your clever way of seeking revenge?"

"You think *I* put those toadstools in your wine?"

"No," he said, wincing as he attempted to reach the bottom shelf of the cart, which was stacked with rolled clothes. "I mean, making me—making Albrecht—your knight."

She bent to grab it for him. "I had my blade on *your* shoulder. You were the one I knighted. Thus, you answer to me."

"Oh? And by that logic, is this also how proxy marriages work in your kingdom?"

Lilac did her best to ignore his question as she mopped the gritty liquid.

She then grabbed another cloth and dipped it into the steaming bucket of water Kemble had left against the bed.

"You don't have to do this," Garin said, watching her squeeze the excess liquid out.

Cautiously, she brought the damp corner to Garin's chin smeared in partially digested blood. He recoiled, hand darting for the cloth.

Lilac was quicker. "I know," she said, holding it just out of reach.

Reluctantly, he dropped his hand into his lap, somber eyes tracking her fluid movement as she brought the cloth back to his face. "So, did you fight off Kemble to get in? Or did you have Myrddin spell her?"

"I didn't have to. She was going to find me for you."

Regret crossed Garin's face. "What did she say?"

"Just that you were talking in your sleep, asking to see me."

His jaw tightened beneath her dabbing fingertips. "What happened in that ballroom?"

"You were hallucinating," Lilac answered too calmly.

He looked at her. *Through* her. "I will not demand it from you."

"That's a promise you've broken before."

"I need to know how I hurt you," Garin insisted. "Or anyone else."

There was no gentle way to describe the violent chill that had ripped through her just as Yanna finished helping her change. Lilac's body reacted seconds before she'd heard any of the commotion; she'd darted out of the washroom without explanation. She'd raced down the corridor to the sounds of screams and shouting, and flung open the doors to see Garin surrounded by guards. He was on his hands and knees, crawling across the dance floor while others helped Rupert off the ground behind him, the bastard son's temple and mouth bloodied.

Garin had then released an animalistic growl and lunged for her, nearly knocking her over—*would* have if she didn't have her thrall strength.

"You left the table after shoving Myrddin aside," she said, working to keep her voice steady. "They said you'd flipped Rupert on his head because he tried to intervene on your way to the door. I'm not hurt at all." She removed the cloth, noticing he was clean.

"Not hurt." Garin's dubious laugh was cold. "I was at your feet like a mongrel. My hands were up your dress—"

"You were unsettled and wanted to find me."

"I *wanted*," he confessed, "to dig my fingers into the plump flesh of your things. To spread your legs and nuzzle my way to your bloody cunt, feast on you in front of the entire room. I wanted—" Garin stopped himself, nostrils flaring. He looked down. "I don't remember much after Myrddin yanked the wine bottle from me. I came to as I knelt before you."

Silence followed, Lilac's shame and desire poorly masked, given the raucous thudding in her chest. She sat back in the chair, careful not to make any sudden movements. "What did you see when you hallucinated?"

His eyes lingered on her throat for a brief moment before looking away. "A blur of foliage, water, and flame. Details were muddied. I was in the dark and desperately had to get to the light, that's all."

He was editing, she could tell. But she wouldn't pry. It wasn't the time. "There was no one but Rupert harmed. I had my guards inspect the rest of the gifts with Father. They seemed undecided whether to consider it a crime. I advised them to let the issue lie with all the pending celebrations." She lowered her voice. "Was it a Low Forest toadstool?"

"No. I would've been stuck in my hallucination for weeks if it was. Like Sinclair," he added darkly. "You would've had to put your stake in my back."

Lilac laughed abruptly, taken aback. He must've been feeling better; it was very like him to joke in the face of danger. "Never."

He didn't return her smile. "The toadstools infused into that wine were indeed not fae-rooted. Myrddin was right, it's not a poison, but that doesn't seem to matter between regnant and thrall, given the unique effect of *any* influence—mortal or magic—that befalls us. You saw what happened with the Dragondew Mead."

"But there were those women outside your room, who wanted you just as badly."

"It wasn't the mead that caused them to act that way. Likely, they'd had a taste of being from during sex before, and wanted to experience it again. That, coupled with the mead, is a high in itself." His laugh was empty. "But *you* were the one willing to break down my door and tear another woman out from beneath me, weren't you?"

"You were the one who commanded me to you," she seethed, reddening. "It was the first time I felt your pull."

Garin frowned, as if he had more to add to the matter. But he only said,

"If ever necessary, if I am ever past reason, you *will* drive that stake through me."

Lilac refused to think of the cloth-wrapped stake in her bedside drawer. She'd never use it on him. "I don't know who'd be brazen enough to send that bottle of wine here."

"Well, let's think. You're in no short supply of those less than fond of you who'd consider it an amusing joke," Garin growled. "Have your guard investigate discreetly. I'll deal with the culprit when they're found."

By now, her vision had adjusted to the dimness of the makeshift room of curtains. He looked tired, purple-gray shadows under his eyes. Drained, even as he regarded her in morbid fascination.

Lilac tossed the cloth aside. "You need to eat. You're unwell."

"Thanks." Garin looked pointedly at the plates she'd brought him. "I'll sleep it off."

"Did you bring any blood from the inn?"

"Yes, several bottles. Lori spelled them to keep for a few days. I can go back for more when needed, but those are tucked deep in Myrddin's travel chest. Where is he, anyway?"

"I just heard him downstairs, probably in the northern corridor. I suspect he was singing them to sleep. He was the one who told me he'd handle things and advised I come see you." She'd last seen him in the foyer after he'd escorted her and Piper back out the western corridor. "I could go get a bottle for you."

"*No*," Garin said before she could get up. A small gasp erupted from Lilac's throat. Her thighs burned just as she felt her knees lock, her bottom pressing firmly into the chair cushion. Eyes darkening at the startled gasp that erupted from Lilac's throat, he froze, self-assessing. "I'm not hungry at the moment," he added softly. "I'm sorry."

Granted, there was none of the calculated voracity that had marred his countenance at the brothel, but Garin didn't look *not* hungry.

"Your hesitation is understandable after everything at The Fool's Folly," she offered. "But you should eat something."

"I've had plenty," he chuckled dryly. "You are simply my preference."

"*Oh.*" Lilac forced herself to think of anything but the sear of his fangs: pastries, *Bisousig*, the cool breeze upon her balcony... The sickening heat of

The Fool's Folly. *Shit*. The wide set of apothecary shelves across the room. "And mortal food will only make it worse."

"Madame Kemble already tried feeding me an apple. I gave her fair warning it wouldn't stay down—and it didn't. Along with the rest of Hedwig's lovely supper."

He needed sustenance. His hunger would catch up to him sooner or later. "I saw Kemble's bucket. Everything you threw up."

"I wouldn't dream of taking it from you, not by biting you. Vampires cannot be glamored. Not even by Myrddin." Curiosity crept into his expression, his slate eyes dancing as he leaned forward. "Have you ever touched yourself while bleeding?"

The low growl of his dropped voice scraped across Lilac's spine. "What?" she spat, aghast. "No. *No*."

"It might help." Garin shrugged, his mouth tilted. He didn't even attempt to hide his morbid fascination. "Have you had someone else do it? That Rupert, perhaps?"

She hadn't *wanted* it, but she'd be lying through her teeth if she said she hadn't considered it before tonight—especially after meeting Garin. The thought of something so obscene was repulsive. Distracting. She lifted her chin as her haughty voice wavered. "I haven't with Rupert." And just because she'd climb onto Garin's stupid, smug face the moment he suggested it, she flusteredly added, "And I won't with you. I told you at dinner, I belong to Maximilian."

Reminded, Garin ran his tongue over his teeth and nodded curtly, the hunger fading from his eyes. "I understand wanting to abstain for your new king of a husband."

"Emperor."

His lips pursed. "Right."

Lilac clenched her thighs together, infuriated. Even through her bleed, she could tell how wet she'd grown. As her regnant, he knew *precisely* what his presence did to her. The hungrier Garin was, the more of a menace he'd be. The more intensely she'd feel everything—this lasting loathing and longing. How was she supposed to hold herself from him, conduct herself, when his very presence edged her into temptation?

She eyed the scalpel and empty cup Kemble left for his bloodletting.

Garin remained silent when she stood, plucked the scalpel from the tray, and nervously held it over her wrist. The blade was long. It could do real damage to herself if she sliced the wrong way. He shifted, tossing the blanket off, dangling his legs over the side of the cot so he could sit up to watch her.

He was wearing a different pair of brown trousers Kemble must've given him.

"As emperor," Garin said, clearly unable to refrain from talking himself into a deeper hole, "Maximilian is allowed to have several beautiful mistresses at his disposal, before your marriage ceremony and after. But one public word of *your* infidelity, and you're done for. To the gallows for Lilac Trécesson."

"Eleanor of the House of Habsburg, thank you," she corrected. "Though, I wouldn't put it past you to be the very one to tell him of our trysts."

A vein popped at his temple, his fingers flexing at his side. "*Trysts*. Your new husband would loathe knowing it's taken me no time at all learning the nuances of your body—how to soak you without laying a finger on you—in a way that would take him the entirety of his short, miserable lifetime."

The wave of heat that hit her nearly caused her knees to buckle. "Just hours ago, you were singing his praises in front of everyone. Not so fond of Maximilian at the thought of me riding him, are you?"

Garin closed his eyes, struggling to compose himself. "He is a fine leader and excellent commander. He will make a proper husband."

"But is he a good man? Will he make an excellent lover? It's anyone's guess." She reveled in Garin's envy, trailing the scalpel teasingly along her skin. "I suppose I could always keep you around for that once I let him believe he's deflowered me."

"*Bleed yourself already*."

Her arm yanked of its own accord, the prick of pain at the base of her palm registering belatedly. She'd missed her wrist. Scowling, Lilac dropped the scalpel and hovered her palm over the cup of milk.

Together, they watched the red stain the cream in blotches. Red flowers in the snow.

"You're just afraid of what you'll lose," she whispered, hand stinging, "when I willingly follow through with what you wanted all along. You didn't consider how jealous this would make you."

"You are my thrall. I *wanted* this for you, your kingdom's safety and security above all else. I lose nothing, not when you are mine." He looked down at his hands. "You act as if you had a choice."

There was scorn in the undercurrent of his words; Lilac bitterly wondered if Garin had ever truly thought her marriage through. If it had even crossed his mind that their marriage might sentence Maximilian to a fate worse than death by Garin's own hand because of his very nature. And what he felt.

Lilac had seen him angry. She couldn't imagine what his jealousy might look like. Maybe, there was a part of her deep down, that yearned to find out.

"I do have a choice." She brought her face inches from his, stroking his cheek with her bleeding hand and leaving a small smear of herself on him. Lilac dragged her thumb over his pursed lips, just as Kestrel once had. "And that choice is Maximilian. *He* will be my husband. From now on, you will not take of me what I willingly give to him."

Garin's jaw tensed, eyes filled with disdain. He remained still as Lilac brushed her mouth against his—slid her tongue along his bottom lip, tasting her own blood. She trailed her free hand up his bloodstained thigh, reveling in how tight the front of his trousers had grown.

He only spoke when her fingertips graced the outline of his erection, irritation and threatening desire sweeping his expression. "You wouldn't want the emperor knowing you've come all over *my* cock, that I've had my hands tangled in your mouth and hair. Especially while you've been bleeding." He shook his head, his face brightening a bit. "The thought might drive him to madness. To throw himself onto a blade, or off a cliff."

"Oh?" Lilac straightened, her lower back spasming. "Is that what craving me makes you want to do?"

His glare up at her was a command in itself. His irresistible cologne filled the room, beckoning her. Lilac gasped when her muscles tugged her back toward him; there was no fighting it.

She braced her hands on his shoulders, but before she could climb into his lap, Garin's head snapped to the door—and his grip on her will vanished.

Hastily, Lilac pushed off of him and lunged for another cloth, mopped the mess she'd made on his face, then wrapped it twice around the crook of

Garin's elbow, tying it into a tight knot. The milk in the mug had turned an alarming shade of pink; she picked it up and shoved it at Garin, then pressed a piece of bread into his palm. Lilac held her bleeding hand against the fabric of her dress and yanked the curtains open just as the mechanical sound of the door unlocking came.

Madame Kemble appeared in the doorway. Her scrutinous gaze fell upon Lilac sitting on the chair—and Garin sipping his milk and munching on a piece of bread.

"Did you bloodlet him for me, Your Majesty?" Kemble said, sounding startled.

"I instructed her," Garin replied through a mouthful.

Lilac expected him to further his lie, to mention that his parents were herbalists and medics. But he continued chewing, saying nothing more.

Her gaze flitted between the both of them, landing last on Lilac. "I wanted to come by to check on you. Make sure you were still breathing."

"She at least hasn't poisoned me further." Garin offered a feeble smile. "I'm in good hands."

Kemble squinted. Lilac wondered if the nurse also sensed what she could, if she could smell the heady mixture of smoke and wood hyacinths hanging thickly in the air.

Whatever Kemble sensed, she decided against mentioning. "I'll be back," she muttered, face bright pink.

She closed and locked the door.

Breathing hard, they sat in silence. Lilac kept the pressure on her hand until the bleeding stopped. Smothering her desire proved more difficult now that they weren't egging each other on. She leaned back into her chair, willing the aching tenderness in her abdomen to subside.

Garin took his time with the rest of his meal, eating with his eyes softly shut, moving on to the biscuits when he finished his bread. Lilac picked at her nails, watching the way he savored each bite—his tongue sweeping his lips, the bob of his throat. The inhuman swiftness of his large hands that emerged whenever he wasn't masking his true nature.

Garin swallowed the last of it, swigging the rest of his blood-infused milk and finally glancing up at her appreciatively. "Thank you."

"You're welcome." It was oddly comforting to watch him eat. "I thought my blood might make it easier for you to stomach."

"I never thought of it. We'll see in a few hours, but I already feel better." He bit his lip. "I suspect crafting such a concoction would be even too nauseating a task for Lorietta. If I asked, Meriam might finally ask me to leave." He placed the mug upon the sauce, the hunger in his eyes replaced with a wanton curiosity. "You handled it well."

"The blood?" She shrugged. "I spent the other night covered in it. Drinking it, fucking you while covered in it. By this point, I think I'm immune."

Garin laughed—threw his head back and chuckled, his fangs exceptionally shiny in the dim light. He then sighed and looked down at her hands, where her nails dug into her palms.

"You're in pain," he observed.

"If you can call it that." It was monthly, some days worse than others. Tonight she could barely stand the sensation of the fabric rubbing against her nipples. She could feel every strand of hair grazing her face, the heat from the hearth intensifying everything and making her restless. "And you're still hungry."

"I appreciate you noticing. It is of my own volition, I assure you."

She stood from her seat. "For me."

"For you. Always for you."

Without hesitation, Lilac seated herself on his right thigh.

He stiffened, his hands fisting into the blankets.

Noticing his reaction—well aware she was being unreasonable considering the boundary she'd just set—Lilac reddened and made to stand. But Garin's arms shot out and wrapped around her waist, pulling her leg over his side until she was straddling him.

"At The Fool's Folly, in that room, my instincts to protect you were infiltrated by a yearning and confusion I'd never felt before. It was a hunger that did not wish to end, nor destroy. It wanted to own. Devour. I'd never been more afraid. It nearly overpowered me."

Feeling his length rock-hard against her inner thigh stole her breath. "Nearly?"

He chose to ignore this. "From the moment you sought refuge at the tavern, you have consumed my every waking thought. Whether in disdain, anger, admiration—or something else entirely. It didn't take you enthralling yourself to me to do that." His gaze dropped to the blood pooling at her cheeks. "It's as if I'd never known desire before I met you, but I am glad for it. You rouse a fire in me I thought I'd lost long, long ago. So, regardless of our time together, the chaos that follows, or whose kingdom you belong to, I can only hope you feel the same. That you find a lifelong, steadfast ally and—" The muscle under his eye twitched. "And *friend*, in me."

Lilac regarded him in pity, suppressing a cruel laugh. She rocked forward, savoring the stifled groan that escaped his lips when she rolled her body against him. He shuddered beneath her when she lightly raked her nails along the back of his neck. He was a vampire, barkeep, knight—but still *very* much a man. His head began to fall back in ecstasy, and she wanted nothing more than to run her tongue along the divots in his collarbone, up the delicious side of this throat.

She pointedly glanced down at his flexed arms on either side of her. "Is this what friends do, Garin?"

"*Modron help me.*" Growling, he shifted his hands—which had been gripping the meat of her ass—back onto her waist, lessening the pressure of his touch. "I don't want to undo what little trust you must have left in me."

Lilac felt her fury slipping from her fingers. She couldn't forget Garin's scathing demands at the inn, or his anger at realizing their thrall bond. She couldn't forget his preemptive betrayal. His cunning and lies. "I think you're wrong. I think you care very little for the trust I have in you."

"Then why are you in my lap? What is it you want—and will you please stop riding me over my trousers before answering?"

"For you to help me," she blurted, as if he'd pulled the truth from her. She was almost ashamed. His touch, his tone, his breath on her throat turned her irritation too easily into impulse. "We can help each other."

Understanding slowly crossed his face. Then, warning. "You said you belonged to the emperor. Rightfully so."

"I said, you will not take of me that which I give to him. My body and heart will be his upon our vows," she said, repulsed by her own trembling words. "But as your thrall, my blood remains yours to take. However you wish."

Disbelief marred his careful expression. "You've thought on it? You've changed your mind this quickly?"

"There's little to think about."

Whatever *he* was thinking, Garin held his tongue—with great effort, it seemed, by the way his jaw remained flexed.

It was clear he wouldn't move. Or at least make the first one.

Lilac took his face in her hands, stroking his cheek reassuringly as she bent to him. Their mouths met, softly at first. Then, she engulfed him. Her hands went into his hair, her tongue tracing his bottom lip before pushing past it, scraping one of his fangs. She smirked into the pain as their mouths filled with warmth and the taste of iron.

"Your blood comes secondary to you," he groaned into her mouth. "I want *all* of you."

The weight of his words was nearly enough to make her take her slip her dress off right then and there. Her insides felt like they were on fire, her thighs spasming, the pain melting into mounting pleasure, desperate for release. But she held firm, even as his tongue explored her—even as his lips moved to her jawline.

Garin's breathing grew heavy as he found her throat, his fingers raking her dress up the sides of her thighs.

"My blood is yours. Nothing more," Lilac panted. "We all want things we cannot have, remember?"

He released a soft laugh against her skin at the memory of his taunting at The Jaunty Hog, and kissed his way to the hollow of her collarbone. Garin sucked her flesh into his mouth. She gasped, holding him tighter to her—but Garin broke off.

"All too well," he muttered, his fingers forming a light collar around her throat. "Do you think your wedding gown will cover this if I get carried away?"

Recalling the dress Herlinde had promised her and Garin marking her neck at his farmhouse, Lilac growled, pushing at his chest. She slid off of him and onto the cot. In one swift motion, he was on the floor, kneeling between her legs. Cursing him, she slid her tongue into his mouth again. She lifted her chin and encouraged him to her throat, all care and caution blunted by the burn of her skin—and the thought of his mouth bringing ecstatic relief.

Garin pulled away. "Things we cannot have."

"Tell me what to do," she demanded. She didn't know precisely what she wanted or what she was offering him—or at least, how to ask for it without shame and incredulous desire. Lilac only knew she needed release. Wanted her vampire to bring her to it, to whatever end. "Please."

His eyes were wild. She watched him rock back onto his heels, his fingers curled as if it pained him to remove them from her.

"Lay back on the cot," he instructed, voice hoarse.

Lilac obeyed, for once moving faster than the force that shifted her bottom to the center of the mattress.

He then got to his feet, towering over her. "Slide your dress down."

All too willingly, she removed the sleeves from her shoulders and shimmied out of them.

Garin's throat bobbed as she bared her breasts for him. "Further."

She slid her thumbs into her dress and peeled it down, savoring the way his pupils widened as the material reached her navel. Everything she'd said just moments ago was meaningless, meant to hurt him and protect herself. Her mouth watered at the thought of slipping him out of his trousers and—

"Stop." Garin nodded, satisfied with her half-bare torso. Then, he turned on his heel. He stalked out of the makeshift room of curtains, toward the glow of the hearth.

"Garin?" Lilac crawled to the edge of the cot and made to get off, but her muscles seized when he spoke again.

"Stay there."

There was the sound of pouring liquid. Then, clanking iron.

Frustrated, she yanked away the curtain dividing Garin's cot and the next. He stood with his back to her at the apothecary desk on the right of the hearth. Dozens of rows of shelves were stacked upon each other above a long station, with tools and cups to Garin's left, and bottles of various liquids to his right.

He was peering into the collection of cups and containers, and plucked out a granite mortar and pestle. "Rose. Typical."

Lilac strained to hear him as he continued to mutter to himself. She tried to shift off the bed, curiosity getting the best of her—but his power held her there, so she sank back onto the mattress.

Garin held something small and grey over his shoulder while pulling open one of the larger drawers at the bottom. Isabel's tin. "I didn't know you visited the apothecary that night."

"I didn't. One of my handmaidens, Isabel, gave it to me tonight before the feast."

"Isabel." He sounded like he was only half-listening. Concentrating, Garin pocketed the tin and grabbed a handful of what looked to be dried flowers and dropped it into the mortar. He fell silent, searching again, and opened another smaller drawer up top—sniffed, then took a pinchful. He did this again with the drawer under it, and a drawer on the opposite end, then got to grinding it down. "And how did your Isabel procure this salve?"

"She made it. She and her twin sister Yanna used to work at The Fool's Folly before coming here."

At this, Garin pivoted to shoot her a look of concern. "They're young. I didn't know they were taking on apprentices."

"Yanna and Isabel were orphaned in Rennes before they began working there." Lilac watched him pound the herbs down, the veins in his hands prominent as he gripped the stone. She squeezed her thighs together. "Then my parents announced they were seeking potential handmaidens while the kingdom searched for me. They travelled to the castle, where my mother hired them right away."

Garin's brow furrowed, but he swallowed whatever he was going to say. "Your parents assigned you a pair of fine handmaidens."

"They've turned out to be worthy friends," she agreed, waiting for him to explain just what it was he was doing.

But he only turned and took the mortar to the kettle hanging over the hearth. Garin lifted the steaming lid with a cloth and tilted the pulverized herbs in, down to the last crumb. Then, he finally faced her, leaning against the desk with his arms crossed. His neatly placed hair from supper had retained its tousled bounce; Lilac's heart skipped a beat when he brushed it back.

"What?" he asked.

"I can't believe my eyes. Are you making tea?"

"I am." He lifted the tin from the desk and sniffed at it. "Rose, wormwood, mugwort."

"All I could sense was rose."

"I personally don't care for the taste. Its healing effects are also far too subtle for my liking, but some insist on throwing it into their concoctions." His lips twitched, but he said nothing in response to that. "This was her tea recipe. She made it all the time for herself at home and taught it to the owner of The Fool's Folly when I was young."

Lilac watched him in awe, swallowing her several burning questions about Aimee. "She worked at the apothecary, didn't she?"

"Sometime after my mother began helping those in town with minor ailments, rumor quickly spread that she was a healer, the daughter of talented physicians across the channel. The brothel's Madame at the time approached us one day at the market. Cornered us in the old bakery for her expertise in medicine." Garin took a porcelain mug from a stack at the back of the desk, stacking a round sieve on top. "She specialized in helping women with various ailments. Wanted and unwanted. She needed my mother's help in perfecting her methods."

"It sounds somewhat different from what your father did. He researched, didn't he?"

His laugh was rough. "You could say that." Swiftly, he unhooked the kettle from the rack that supported it and poured the steaming liquid over the sieve. He collected the covered tin before returning to her, mug in hand.

Lilac scooted back, supporting herself on her arms against the pillow as Garin perched onto the side of the bed.

"I would've guessed the salve recipe, either way. Our sense of smell is extraordinary when it's not hindered by a thrall bond waiting to snap in place. For instance, tonight I can tell which ingredient your loyal hand-maiden had forgotten. Pennyroyal is most potent and will relieve abdominal cramping caused by menses, swiftly and efficiently, by soothing the muscles of one's uterus." He cocked his head, considering. "I can tell when it's about to rain."

"I can do that, too." She enjoyed this version of Garin. It was one she'd never truly seen. Unguarded and free, safe enough to tell her about his family and brag about his abilities.

"I can tell," he said, placing the mug onto the tray and walking his fingers up her shin. "That you're on the first night of your bleed. I thought I might've sensed it last night based on your taste, but blood was everywhere." He shrugged. "I was too distracted to ask."

Lilac's smile faded as she struggled to keep her eyes off of his full lips.

"I can tell you were caught by surprise. Stress can bring it on early, or cause delay. You've been under large amounts of pressure lately and are in need of much reprieve. Relief." Garin slid his hand over her hip, leaning over her. Boxing her in. "Which, normally I'd be more than happy to provide you. But I'd consider myself a monster if I didn't warn you of my potential disservice."

"What disservice?"

"Helping you in the way you suggest will naturally drive you to offer yourself up to me, either your throat or your body, one consequently leading way to the other, given the bond you chose to enact with me."

Her irritation only made her want him more. "You are the one who first suggested it."

"I did no such thing."

"You asked if I'd ever touched myself during my bleed, immediately after we discussed you feeding. You said you didn't want anyone else's blood."

"It was a simple question. I did not infer anything you didn't already know: that I'd topple kingdoms for your blood. All I said was, as it stands, that I will not bite you." He pursed his lips, an animalistic smile on the brink of breaking through. "If anything was amiss, your carnal human mind filled in the gaps for you." The ghost of his smile then vanished. "You have made it clear what you are comfortable offering me, and what you are not. I am grateful for all of it and do not wish to cross those boundaries with you." His words were genuine, making the hunger in them all more saccharine.

Lilac swallowed thickly. "Then don't cross them."

"As you've noticed is not so simple. With our thrall bond, it is better to avoid me sinking my teeth into you, *or* taking it by other—" His eyes sank appreciatively to her throat, lingering over her breasts, then lower— "Other means. Unless you decide you want me in all the ways I wish to devour you, because that is what it will inevitably lead to. I'm sure you've noticed how painstakingly easy it is for those lines you've precariously drawn to become blurred. Fortunately for you, I am honored to do it whether I am your husband or not."

"That's never stopped you before," she said, her head pounding. "The true honor is having my hand. Which, you do not."

Something—amusement? Disappointment?—flashed behind those

probing eyes. "Maximilian wouldn't be pleased with any of this, would he?" His look turned patronizing, but it seemed forced. "My sincerest apologies, Your Majesty."

"Don't flatter yourself. A hot towel and a croissant would be just as satisfying, if not more."

Even as he rasped a chuckle, the teasing faded from Garin's expression. He leaned in and planted a kiss on Lilac's forehead, murmuring against her skin. "For now."

Lilac jumped; two slicked fingers slid below the peeled lip of her dress and undergarment. She couldn't help the soft moan that escaped when he swept them from her navel to just above her pubic bone.

"It will help ease your pain, as promised," he said, scooping another dab of Isabel's concoction and taking her by the hand, prompting her to lean into him.

She pressed her face into his shoulder, savoring her cheek rubbing against his barely-there stubble. Garin's forest cologne made her head spin, his hair tickling her forehead as he kneaded intentional, firm circles along the base of her spine.

Held the mug between them when he pulled away. "And this will help you recover from last night. The past week, really." He watched her bewildered expression turn suspicious as she inspected it. "Nothing to put you to sleep. Nothing to rid you of memories." He took a sip himself. "See?"

Lilac accepted it. The temperature was perfect; rose was the most overpowering note. She made a face but drank, anyway. "It could use some honey," she commented when she was over halfway done.

"Honey kept in apothecaries is usually infused with something else, and I didn't want to mix it with anything—certainly not more *Amanita muscaria* —on the off chance." Garin cleared his throat and reached into his pocket, removing a drawstring bag. "I'd left the inn in a hurry, but I've been meaning to give this to you."

Lilac swallowed the rest of the tea and placed the mug down. The bag rustled when she took it into her palm. She put it to her nose and was immediately brought back to The Fenfoss Inn. "Hawthorn berries."

"Yes," he said with an impressed smile. "They're dried, so they'll keep a long time. I was going to give them to you along with the stake this morning, but thought better of it after sensing your seething disdain for me."

"Lorietta served me hawthorn berry tea the first night I sat at your bar."

He smirked. "Ah. I thought I'd smelled that on you. I wasn't sure with the amount of gin she'd added."

"I should've finished it before sitting down with you," she replied teasingly. "Could've used the extra drink."

"Apparently Lori thought so. She saw me rush out of my station after Meriam led you upstairs to your room. I went into the kitchen and snatched a bottle of blood to take with me into my chamber, and chugged it there. I don't think she'd ever seen me do that just to interact with a mortal patron, so she was right to be concerned for you. Hawthorn berries aren't harmful to us like its cursed wood is, but they're said to temporarily lessen the effects of a vampire's entrancement in mortals."

Oh. She had no idea Lorietta was trying to protect her. Lilac looked down at the bag, skepticism marring her foolish spark of hope. "You're... allowing me to opt out of Marrying Maximilian, and handle France on my own?"

"I did not say that."

She knew better than to get her hopes up. "Does it even work for thralls?"

"Against the will of other vampires, yes, it should. Against me, I'm not sure. But I'd like you to have it, regardless."

Lilac wasn't sure why this unexpected, seemingly generous offer of his unsettled her. She shook her head slowly. "Why?"

Garin laughed, then frowned when she didn't join in. "What do you mean, why? The same reason I wanted you to have the hawthorn stake. With the berries, you might be able to control any vampire's affect on you. Bastion. Piper...*Casmir*. With the stake and your newfound strength and speed, our playing field becomes a tad more even." Garin stared at the bag in her hand. Then, back up at her, incredulous. "They're for you. For your protection."

"But you are still faster and stronger than me," she said dubiously.

"Of course, any defense against me is advisable. You must understand, the tether you invoked is immense."

"Exactly. Which is why you're doing this to make yourself feel better about using what I had to do to survive you, to your advantage."

Garin's mouth fell open. Irritation smothered the shard of guilt she might've glimpsed. She pulled her dress back up and donned her sleeves. "We both know you'd never let me approach that alter with so much as a hint of hesitation, much less denial. I am no less anyone's pawn because you've given me these things."

"Might I remind you, retaining your agency does not negate your monarchy or personal duty."

"Marriage isn't the only way a monarch can fulfill it!"

Garin glared warningly, nostrils flaring.

"I never wanted my freedom from you. I wanted the freedom to *choose.*"

"What do you think the bloody berries are for, Eleanor?" he whispered angrily. He moved quickly; one moment he was sitting next to her feet, and the next, her hands were in his. "This thrall bond you've enacted has stripped me bare. Each delicious laugh and scowl of yours, each time I taste of your body, your blood—" Garin's fingers traced the bouquet of veins adorning her inner wrists, like a scrupulous chiromancer hoping to find himself in her future. "Are scorched into my memory, drawing me further from doing the noble thing. *Someone* has to. The gods themselves know you are a selfish and desperate creature, too led by your heart to go against what it tells you."

Realization sunk like an anchor in her chest. Perhaps she'd deserved it. She'd spent the last few days ill, destroying a brothel, and drawing decrees of her own while her kingdom faced annexation. She publicly refuted an offer most in her situation would leap at, and still had a chest to deliver to the mad faerie who'd sent a revenant for it.

Enthralling herself to Garin might've been one of the worst missteps of her life, but at least it had been *her* decision. She had chosen it, the act of selfish defiance—of survival—even if made in delirium. And so, too, was accepting the terms of her duty.

"It is Maximilian who has propositioned me, sent an emissary to find me—the very one you wanted so badly to be kept alive. Yet where is he, Garin? In your room, bound and gagged? On a ship, voyaging to the New World?"

He said nothing.

"*I* deserve to be chosen, too. And the emperor has done just that."

Fuming, she adjusted her skirts, shoving her way to the edge of the cot. "Tomorrow will be another long day. I must—"

"*Stay*." The gravel in his voice left her no choice. Her muscles would've seized with or without his spell over her. Her breathing hitched when his hand found hers, his thumb brushing her knuckles as if the motion soothed him. "It is my last request tonight."

She eyed the pouch, feeling Garin scoot back to give her more room.

"Please," he whispered.

"I shall," she said, her rump remaining on the cot because really, she had no choice. "But at the cost of your comfort."

"You underestimate your effect on me. Your presence is wholly torturous."

She turned slowly to him. "Your stake and hawthorn berries are useless. They won't protect me from a life never truly my own." Garin was studying her, looking more wary than remorseful. Every bit lost as Lilac felt. "But that will not stop me from reveling in the fate that has befallen me."

He gently released her hand and nodded minutely.

Permission. She should have left, should've retreated to her tower...but what was Garin's permission but a wish granted?

Lilac angled her shoulders away from him and settled onto the pillow. Kemble might open the door at any moment and discover them together, but those worries felt distant when the only thing that mattered—to her dismay—was him.

He curled around her gently, hesitant in his movements, as if she were a thing that could be so easily broken. He cleared his throat when she pressed her ass into him. Garin didn't touch her further, but brought his nose to her hair, inhaling. "I am a moth to a flame, willingly consumed. You are my every waking thought. My relentless undoing."

She couldn't bring herself to leave. He should've known that. Maybe he *did*, and the offer to allow her to leave was, just as the hawthorn berries and stake, to make him feel better about everything.

The spell of deep sleep threatened to wash over her, then. Her eyes fluttered shut as she felt the blanket being pulled over her, tucked around her.

"Then become undone," Lilac whispered into the veined forearm that curled beneath her head, tugging her body against him. "How selfish of you to crave something never fully yours."

29

L ilac peeled herself off of Garin's chest. The room was hot, the
hearth blazing as if someone had stopped by to stoke the fire.
She sat up for a moment, stretched, and brushed the hair out of
her eyes, disoriented by fragments of dreams—of dark dalliances and
roaring tides she could barely remember.

A towering ballroom. A shimmering soiree.

Careful not to wake him, she slid off the cot. She watched Garin nuzzle
into the impression of her head on the pillow; thankfully he didn't move
when she settled the blanket back onto his shoulders. He shivered despite
the warmth, the dark hair on his forehead matted in sweat again. She'd
never seen him perspire this much.

Lilac tossed the bloodied cloths into the fire before picking up the
pouch of berries. She opened it and dropped a pinch of them into her
mouth. *Bitter*. She grimaced, closed the drawstring, and tucked it under
her arm.

There wasn't a guard in sight outside the door, but they only patrolled
the second floor on occasion and didn't sit watch like the sentries did on
the first floor or ramparts. She marched straight up to her tower and
wondered just what spell Myrddin might've cast to settle the castle, or if
they'd needed it at all after the night of debauchery. She contemplated

finding the warlock, updating him on Garin's health. Maybe she could share her plans with him. His advice or magic might be helpful, in hindsight.

Ultimately, she decided against it; she wouldn't be able to get to the guest quarters without drawing attention to herself. She couldn't risk it.

Lilac pushed the door open to find Piper snoring on the rug in front of the fireplace with one of the duvets from the linens trunk. She nudged Piper's shoulder and ushered her to bed. Piper startled awake and refused at first, but when Lilac insisted she wouldn't possibly be able to go back to sleep, the vampire groggily obliged and settled into the far edge of Lilac's mattress facing the balcony doors. Outside, the sky was cast in deep violet. The castle would be awake soon.

She padded to the chamber pot to clean herself and realized she didn't feel any pain. The cramping was gone, her bleed slightly lighter. Stunned and pleased, she went to her armoire, plucked out a nondescript maroon dress—the last of Herlinde's unworn garments—and changed out of her fine gown, laying it on the linens trunk to be cleaned. She slid her dagger garter onto her thigh, the pouch of berries down the front of her chemise, and slipped out the door.

Once on the second floor, she took the first right before the library, into the hall of bedrooms. The handmaidens' quarters was the first door; she rapped on it as quietly as possible and was met by Yanna.

"What?" Yanna swept her fringe out of her eyes, blinking in the dim light of the torch around the corner. Upon realizing it was Lilac, she dipped into a startled curtsey. Isabel's sleepy babbling could be heard from within the dark room. "It's the queen. Go back to bed. What's the matter, Your Majesty? Where's your candle? Where's Sir Albrecht—and why are you in the dark?"

"I need a favor—a discreet favor. I need you to wake my scribe, John."

"At this hour?"

"And Riou, the cartographer. I'll need him." Lilac was fully awake now, her racing thoughts muddled with the memory of Garin's arms around her. "And the standing armorer. We haven't had an official Master at Arms since Armand's injury."

It hadn't occurred to Lilac in her youth how odd it was that the duke at the head of her father's armies had been rendered useless, and how that issue *still* had been eclipsed by the widespread fear of her Daemon tongue.

Since then, the role had changed hands several times under Armand and Henri's orders, and would've remained so until Sinclair took his father's spot.

"And how do you expect me to find him if you don't know who he is?"

"Both Riou and John will know where to find the presiding armorer. I need all three to meet me at the library before dawn. Now is preferable." She tapped her foot while Yanna rubbed her eyes, finally awake enough to make sense of Lilac's ludicrous requests. "Well?"

"Where's Sir Albrecht?"

"Resting in the infirmary. He isn't to be bothered. Please, Yanna." Lilac did not appreciate the dubious frown Yanna gave her. "What's the matter?"

"If he's in charge of all your weaponry, he might already be on his way to La Guerche. Either that," Yanna added at the utter rage spreading on Lilac's face, "or he's sent a large supply of more weapons."

"How do you know?"

"Isabel and I stayed behind last night. Piper had us help clean and listen for more trouble while she went upstairs and made sure you were safe. We overheard some of the staff chatting, saying they earlier saw various boxes, arrows, and shields being carried out through the bailey. They were loaded into a single carriage that departed."

"By whom?"

Yanna shrugged.

"With *my* coachman?"

"I'm not sure. It was a quick ordeal." Yanna looked unsettled. "You didn't sanction this."

Lilac felt sick. Shaking her head, she made it halfway down the hall before Yanna called after her.

"Is everything all right, Your Majesty?"

"It will be."

Huffing, she burst onto the landing above the double staircase, ready to address the pair of guards flanking the entry—but they weren't there. Those guards never made rounds. What was happening? *She* was ultimately the last and final say. At the very least, she should've been notified of any change, certainly of any movement of weapons. Had no one trusted her?

More concerningly, had they emptied her castle's armory? They wouldn't be able to defend themselves against France without resources.

Lilac's mind raced as she tromped down the stairs. Should she rouse her father? Should she call a meeting for the remaining guard?

She ducked into the hall behind the stairs, passed the old coat closet, and turned the corner. Several doors to the guest suites flanked the left, while the armory sat on the right. The stern gaze of the person leaning against the armory door made her freeze. Her eyes adjusted quickly; she recognized him as one of her father's higher ranking guards.

One of Renald's men.

He frowned at the sight of her, leaning away from the door and bowing at the waist. "Your Majesty, I've never seen you out of bed so early."

She didn't bother returning the gesture. "Are you the head of my armory?"

"No, I'm Ciel. I've been stationed here temporarily. You never know with all the guests present, and that disturbance last night at your party."

"Fine. I need to talk to him."

"Inwold isn't here," he said curtly, crossing his arms.

"Well, where is he?"

"He's been summoned by your men out east. Left last night to bring more weaponry and supplies to them."

Lilac stared, unsure whether to believe Ciel. She hadn't expected him to tell the truth, yet he hadn't offered up more details. If they'd brought more weapons to the La Guerche, who wielded them? Was there an increase in foot soldiers she hadn't been alerted of? Had her father tapped the local militia after her last order of accounting for all eligible men? If this were the case, things would then be shifting in her favor.

Something about the way the guard watched her told her asking him these questions would lead nowhere. "I don't recall giving that order."

Beneath his thick beard, his lips curled in a way that infuriated her. "I don't recall you giving *any* order," said Ceil. "What I do recall is your absence most days, whereas your father has been left to handle France."

Lilac held her tongue—the fire it wanted to spout, anyway. "I'm here now. I am handling France. I want access to my armory."

Ciel stopped rubbing his mustache. Lilac stepped forward and tried the knob. It was locked.

"Did you hear me?"

He looked intentionally bored, as if he were holding in a laugh. "It will be handled when you've wed the emperor, won't it?"

She pulled back and looked him in the eye. "Why were weapons moved? In support of our and Maximilian's forces? In advance?"

Ciel said nothing, his expression stone.

"Let me in. That is an order."

He stepped in front of the door and pressed a pitiful hand to his armored chest. "Your Majesty, I took an oath near twenty years ago when your father and Armand were in their prime. This was before the kingdom was awash in a fear of strange tongues, and it was made apparent your mother would never bear a good-willed son to lead—"

Before the next word escaped his lips, Lilac's palm was wrapped around his gullet, pressing him firmly against the wood. His hands pried at her, nails raked at her dress and skin, but his strength was no match for hers. Adrenaline pulsed through her, made her feel alive; mesmerized by his struggling, Lilac watched his pale face turn purple as he begged for his life. Or, attempted to.

"Open the door," she breathed into his ear.

"Here, you bitch—" Ciel gurgled, and his shaking hand sank into his pants pocket. A *clank* reverberated as he dropped the single rusty key onto the floor.

Lilac bent to retrieve it, yanking him with her—her fist on his windpipe so he couldn't scream. She stuck it in the keyhole and twisted.

The armory was well-lit by two torches on either side. Lining the wall were racks and racks of swords, iron shields of various sizes. On another wall, armor, and the next, bows and buckets of arrows and spears. Several were missing, but not all. They'd taken more than enough to supply the men that had departed, but there were still plenty for the remaining guard. It didn't look like boxes and boxes of *anything* were moved, like her hand-maidens had overheard.

Heart hammering, she eased the door shut, when Ciel twisted free from her grasp and made a run for it. His screams weren't screams, so much as muffled retching noises as he scuttled down the hall, tripping and falling once.

Tremendous strength in her calves coiled and sprung, catching her off guard as she jolted forward, too clumsy with her uncanny speed. "Ciel! Ciel, stop!" Horrified, Lilac watched the guard careen around the corner to the left, causing him to slow a bit. She'd catch him there. Lilac rushed him and managed a tighter turn, ready to leap onto him, and—

There was nothing. No one was in the foyer. It was silent save for the crackle of the hearth. Lilac straightened and kept to the shadows of the hall, sticking close to the wall to her left.

"Ciel," she whispered. "Come ou—"

A hand wrapped around her mouth and waist, tugging her into the darkness. The closet door shut quietly in her face, the hand over her mouth slipping off before she could bite it. Lilac whirled with her fist in the air.

Her captor caught it.

"Your reflexes are increasingly impressive." Garin pressed his lips to her closed fist before she wrenched it from him.

"What are you doing here?" Lilac demanded, nauseous with rib-pounding adrenaline. She couldn't see a thing, turning around and banging her elbow onto some protruding fixture on the inside of the door—probably a low coat hook—beneath the garment hanging over it. "Ow!"

"*Shh*," Garin hissed. "Could you be any louder?"

"What are you doing in here?"

Garin stopped to listen; whatever he was hearing, she couldn't make any of it out. The castle was still silent, probably nursing their hangovers in their private quarters. "The better question is, how did you know this closet was here? The door blends in so well with the walls, I almost didn't see it before this bloke turned the corner."

The room reeked of sweat and ale. "Gross."

"You're the one who crushed his windpipe. He wouldn't have been able to speak. Or breathe. Or enjoy any of Madame Hedwig's delicious confections ever again."

"You could've eaten him."

"I'd rather not chance it. I don't know what it would do to my eyes."

"If it's from a dead body, wouldn't it be the same as drinking bottled blood from a donor?" Lilac blinked, willing her vision to adjust. As it did, she could make out Ciel's wide form slumped against the wall on the corner of the bench that lined the closet.

"From a limb, yes. From a corpse, I'm not so sure."

Lilac looked around; the old stone room had been mostly emptied since the last time she'd hid in it. There was a box there, a stack of parchment on the upper shelves. A long garment hanging beside her on the back of the door. It was narrow, barely wider than a chimney, though it soaked none of the heat from the hearth on the other side of the hall.

"This is my family's old coat closet," she explained. "It was part of the original keep, built four centuries earlier. My grandfather had since fashioned a newer coat room for guests closer to the servants' quarters near the scullery. When I was younger, this was one of my hiding spots for whenever Piper was tasked with putting gowns on me. And when we played hide-and-seek."

"It seems that hasn't changed." Garin's smile was audible. "You must've given her hell. I'll bet she never found you in here."

"A better hiding place," she continued, side-eyeing him, "was my father's study."

Garin's smile slowly faded, his brows knitting together. "That's ludicrous. This door is basically hidden."

"You've been there, haven't you?" Lilac crossed her arms, rubbing them for warmth. "I saw it in a vision."

He gaped, looking shocked but not the least bit guilty. "I thought you saw yourself stab Albrecht."

"I did in the brothel. But when I bit your hand in your room, at the inn..." she trailed off as she watched it click in his eyes. "I recognized my father's desk anywhere. What were you looking for? Was it the vampire manuscript you left near my balcony?"

He laughed nervously, like a boy caught in a lie.

"Piper discovered it and showed me."

Garin sighed. "Edith Menard."

"Who?"

"Lady Edith, Emma's mother, brought me here. Don't look so shocked; I heard every word of you and Emma chatting her mother's business up in front of poor Rupert." Garin looked around, as if deciding whether to seat himself on the bench. He remained standing. "She and her uncle were part of the group of nobles who came to help Paimpont in the week after the Raid. They had come to claim Emma's father's body."

As told in her books, there had been a committee of her grandparents' court and adjacent circles who went to provide aid in the days after. "You were there."

"Someone had to come wash the blood from the streets." He stared past her. "After a few days, I joined one of their evening efforts hoping to see Adelaide again, listening for any news of planned consequence. I met Edith as she exited The Jaunty Hog."

Lilac's look of wonder quickly churned into disgust. "Edith's husband was just killed in the Raid, and you *fucked* her?"

"We were both grieving," Garin said, scowling. "And no, at least not right away. While her uncle brought his brother's corpse back to their town, she was ordered to spend the next evening in attendance at the Ermengarde trial. I would've entranced her, but I didn't need to. Told her I was the cousin of a shop owner in Rennes and offered to accompany her. She was glad to have me. By her extension, I was invited in."

He'd entered the keep after Lilac's accession ceremony, but she'd assumed her father had invited him in with the rest of the clergy.

He'd been searching her grandfather Francis's desk—not Henri's. "*You* attended the Ermengarde trial?"

"As a guest, and I didn't stay long enough to learn much of it at all." He rubbed at his chin, and she could tell it wasn't exactly a fond memory. "In truth, I wasn't there for the trial, nor for Edith." He stepped closer. "No one can know this. Laurent promised me not to tell."

"I won't."

"The night of the Raid, I was more than cross with Laurent. He was a self-assured leader, level-headed, ruthless only when required. He was a father, friend, and brother to many of us, in a way my own never demonstrated, nor even Alor. I admired this in him, and so to order an attack like this even at the faeries' suggestion was entirely uncharacteristic."

"Did you ever suspect it was more than a suggestion from Kestrel? Faerie ether, maybe?"

"It crossed our minds, but no one ever asked. We were taught to obey. I went to Laurent the morning after the Raid with many questions, still covered in Adelaide's family's blood. I and several others in our coven were concerned about the retribution that would surely rain down on Brocéliande from your grandfather and his men. It was silent at the castle, and they hadn't yet sent a legion of guards to burn our forest to the ground."

"My grandfather never did, did he?"

"We were spared. It turned out they'd been busy dealing privately with Vivien's parents and France's presence when the Raid transpired. When I went to Laurent, Kestrel was there in our meeting room. They already had answers for me, vague as they were." He absentmindedly reached above Ciel's corpse's head, trailing his fingers along the bricks.

Lilac gasped. "He went back to Kestrel for help?"

"He had no other option. Kestrel cannot lie, and in good faith he pulled up a map and unraveled it upon our table. He performed a tracking spell in front of our very eyes—a red leather-bound book details the fate of the arcane kingdoms. Of Brocéliande, Huelgoat, and beyond. According to him, it was, and perhaps still is, located in this very castle. He said he didn't know where, that the map couldn't give us specifics. I figured it wouldn't be difficult."

It sounded awfully vague. Most of the shelves in her library were filled with earth tones and bound stacks of parchment. "I've never seen it before."

"I doubt you have. In the week after your ceremony, I searched your room. Your chapel. Your library at night. Every shelf. Every loose brick."

Lilac frowned. Her Accord notes and other paperwork were kept there. "I've kept it locked."

"I got your guards to unlock it for me. I didn't pry much." But his brows rose. "*Increased taxation for nobility to fund schools, infirmaries, inns, and orphanages, to include Daemon-run establishments,*" Garin quoted. "I was impressed."

"Could Kestrel tell us more?" Her mind raced. "And has anyone heard from him yet?"

"Myrddin said he'd deal with it today. I'll likely need to delegate its delivery to Bastion. I made it clear before I left that I wasn't comfortable with any of us bringing it straight to Cinderfell. I'd love to ask Kestrel about it, if he ever answers us." He scoffed. "Ungrateful prick."

"Okay." She didn't know what to say, stunned into silence. "So? Have you found it? The book, I mean."

"No," he answered curtly.

"And so..." She waited, expecting there to be more to his story. Garin said nothing. "So you searched my grandfather's office on the night of the Ermengarde trial. You didn't look in our library or anywhere else back then? That's it?"

"No. I left that night, though Edith and I kept in contact for a short while after that."

It was hard to believe that was the end of what happened with the red book—also, that he'd waited fifty more years to look for it again, on the off chance he'd ever returned to the Trécesson castle. He'd never mentioned it to her until now.

It was unlike Garin to give up, but the intensity of his stare killed her curiosity.

"You're cold," he observed, shrugging out of his black coat lined in gold filigree. He draped it over her.

Lilac clamped a hand to her mouth to smother a cry of surprise and pressed herself against his chest. Warmth enveloped her entire body once the coat rested on her shoulders.

"Herlinde sent me with a few garments that would emulate mortal body heat, since mine waxes and wanes depending on how recently I've eaten."

Marveling, Lilac reached for his hand. When he pulled it away, she stroked her fingers along the hollow of his cheek, the defined structure of his jawbone. With the heat of the garment quickly fading, his skin was nearly as cold as the room.

"You need to eat. Something more than milk and bread." Lilac couldn't hide her enthusiasm, yanking her sleeve up her forearm.

"So desperate to feel my fangs inside you." He bent his head and pressed his mouth to her inner wrist, flooding her body with a painful thrill. "Should my pitiful disguise falter for any reason, you'll have more blood on your hands than we'll know what to do with when I walk out of this room, eyes red as the fringe of dusk."

"But my blood doesn't turn your eyes red," she finally said.

Garin laughed. "All mortal blood does."

"Then why are yours gray now when it's only been a couple days?"

"Myrddin and Lorietta suggested it might've been a one-time occurrence after the completion of our bond."

He seemed satisfied with that answer. Whether they'd genuinely thought that was what had happened or, for some reason, wanted to

"I'll open the armory for you," Myrddin was saying, his voice back in the hall. "Stand back now!" A loud blast shook the room; shouts were heard as dust rained down on them.

Lilac licked her lips, unable to tear her eyes from Garin's wrists—the veins popping there and the way he grunted as he strangled the knob. If he jostled it more, he'd make too much noise and they'd be discovered. Or, the handle might come off.

Suddenly, she couldn't bring herself to care about being locked in a closet with a starving vampire. All she could focus on was the thinness of her kirtle. How easily he could bunch it at her thighs and access her.

More footsteps sounded outside, and shouting. There was her father's alarmed shout among some of the staff. Doors were opening in the hall, Gertrude, Helena, and Agnes chattering groggily.

Agitated, Garin lifted and flexed his fingers, seeming unsure of where to put them. "I've never met someone more bent on tempting their own fate, or—"

Lilac reached for him before she knew what was happening. She swallowed thickly and fumbled with the clasp of his belt. A desolate sound rasped from Garin's throat. It wasn't protest—and not quite alarm, either—as she slipped her hand down the front of his pants.

Unsurprisingly, he was already hard.

"Or?" She arched against him, kissing his neck, sucking his flesh lightly into her mouth. The tip was deliciously wet; Lilac smeared it down his head.

"Or going out of their way to chase after it." He groaned deeply. "Have you no semblance of self-preservation?"

"I am bound to you." Every tremble her touch elicited from him felt like a trophy. "You won't hurt me. You are no stranger to longing."

His laugh was cruel. "Longing is a tragically subdued term. *Desire* comes close." Garin's lips parted when Lilac leaned over and released the glob of saliva that had been collecting at the mere thought of him in her mouth, slicking his cock in it.

His head fell back, his hands curling into claws at his side.

"Desire plagues you, doesn't it? You cling to your restraint," she said, stroking him slowly. *Too* slowly. "Like a raft at sea."

"It is to your benefit, I assure you."

"Has blood always reigned over you so easily, Garin? You're determined to fight for my sovereignty, yet your hunger thwarts your resolve. You lean on your slipping humanity to convince yourself you're making the right choice."

"It's our thrall bond that's done that," he said tightly. "Not blood. Not my failing restraint. I *know* I've made the right choice."

She couldn't take her eyes off his mouth. She wanted to kiss him, even as it seemed he might devour her if she got any closer. "I'm sure you believe that, seeing as you betrayed me in order to do so."

"Gladly, if it meant your kingdom continues to know peace." His deliciously trembling breath ruffled her hair. "I've seen even the most primed brigade backed by England's finest archers march into a field and return with less than a fourth of its men. I know what a losing battle looks like. I refuse to have you at—" His breath hitched. "At the center of it."

"You've never seen me at the helm of an army." Lilac stroked him at what she hoped was a tortuous pace. She almost stopped fisting him there, but savored the ravenous disdain on his face far too much. She sank her fist to the base of his cock and squeezed her fingers around it. "I refuse to stand by while my kingdom remains unprepared. Who knows, we might need it the day your restraint snaps. You couldn't even stand the thought of me doing this to Rupert without wanting—"

Garin brought his mouth to hers. His kiss was soft and pleading, yet possessing as he claimed her. She tasted his anger, relief cooling her burning face.

It was delicious.

His dick twitched in her palm. "Put me in your fucking mouth," he rasped, low and soft against her lips.

Hungrily savoring the way his face twisted, Lilac braced herself against the wanton pull of her muscles, straining against it. "Say *please.*"

"Stop if it doesn't please you, Lilac, but I'm going to come if you don't stop touching me that way." His hand shot down and gripped her wrist, stilling it when she giggled and failed to heed his warning. "I can barely control myself, and nothing but magic will open that door. You don't know what you're doing."

Failing to stifle another sultry laugh, she allowed Garin's command to wash over her. Partially. She sank onto her heels and dragged the tip of her tongue against the base of his head, smiling up at him. "Stopping would not please me." Lilac tipped her head back and rubbed him, mixing his precum her thickened saliva, coating it over her lips. Garin's throat bobbed, and his hand fell away from her to clench one of the limestone bricks. "And I know *exactly* what I'm doing."

A low growl escaped Garin's lips when she nipped lightly along the bottom of his shaft and finally took him in.

"You look unexpectedly exquisite with my dick in your mouth, Your Majesty." He stroked her cheek with his thumb before trailing his hand toward her scalp.

"Hands *off*."

He reluctantly obliged, detangling his fingers from her waves with an incredulous, almost pained scowl. As terribly as she could *feel* he wanted her, the grip of his will seemed weaker the more she leaned into her own pulsing hunger.

Lilac's eyes were wild with fervor as she took him in. What was that look of his? *Want? Fear?*

Fear sounded better.

A shocked—and pleased—whimper erupted from her throat when he began thrusting into her mouth, as if he couldn't help himself. The first two times were gentle. Probing. Garin stopped himself, wrestling his need back under control.

How delightful it would be to tug him back out from it.

Lilac wrapped her hands around his thighs and raked her nails into him, pulling him deeper until she gagged.

Garin bucked and groaned in warning—and shot all over her tongue.

Lilac savored every last drop, never breaking eye contact. She rocked back on her heels, absorbing his stupid, dumbfounded glare.

Speechless, he held a hand out to help her up, but she rose on her own, daintily wiping her lips. "I assume that was an adequate distraction," she said as he refastened his belt. It was a shame; how she would've loved to ride him on that bench. "At least, it was for me. I suppose it's good practice for whatever we need to do to tide your urges over."

She felt him stiffen when she slid his coat off and reached around him, draping it around his shoulders.

"Tide me over?"

"Yes. When I'm Maximilian's."

"You are far from a distraction. Especially from my urges." His jaw tightened against the saccharine kiss she planted upon his cheek. "You are the sole cause of my suffering."

"That is all I'll be to you when I'm Maximilian's wife, isn't it?" She stepped back and regarded him with all the malice and curiosity of a fool taunting a starved lion with a piece of steak. "A distraction for your blood-lust. A vessel for your pleasure."

Garin was silent, his fury palpable.

They hadn't heard anything for a while; perhaps everyone was so hungover from the feast, they'd gone back to bed. Swallowing against the fading satisfaction and rising bitterness, Lilac turned to try the knob again. *Shit*—the door didn't budge. Garin began to chuckle, sounding even more chilling in the dark.

Lilac whirled to see him him reaching for her, jerking her arm out of the way and swiftly replacing it with her blade. She laid it against Garin's Adam's Apple, tilting his chin up.

"You are deliciously fast," he said with a deep laugh.

She pressed the blade harder against him. "You might command my will, but my touch is still mine to give. And when I do... it won't be because you demanded it. It will be because I chose to ruin you with it."

"Come to me."

So much for those hawthorn berries.

Lilac's body reacted immediately. The force of his command was so powerful it took her breath away, causing her to fall against him. Garin caught her at the elbows, dodging the haphazard slash of her blade. He plucked it out of her grasp and bent, gathering her skirts to place it neatly back into her garter, his fingers scrupulously lingering at her outer thigh.

"It would be a tortuous, most painful affair," he breathed, straightening, "if you chose to ruin me upon these benches."

"Go to hell."

Garin's eyes, softened by his laughter, were pools of muted starlight as he pulled her into his arms. "Your body and blood are my distraction, only as salvation might reprieve a man plagued by his own melancholy. The way it might remind him of the beauty of sunsets, and the smell of baking bread, and good things on the horizon. You are the veiled specter in the night, haunting my dreams each time I close my eyes." He swept Lilac's left hand into his and pressed his lips against her fingers. "And the relief of golden sunrise. There is nothing human about what I feel for you, Eleanor, yet you offer yourself to me like a fool. As if I have not considered taking you far, far away from here. Where crooked kings cannot touch you."

She should've been alarmed by how quickly her rage succumbed to desire, despite the evident warning in his words. She should detest that there'd be reasonable temptation if he ever offered such a fantasy.

But Lilac leaned into his embrace, inhaling deeply the scents of juniper and firewood.

His confession was an ax in her chest, his words the deadliest of poisons.

"They deserve a monarch who will fight," she whispered. But her conviction was already weakened, by spell or by the heart. It was anyone's guess.

Garin bent to her ear—her hand in his, his other palm pressed to the small of her back as if they were afforded the surreptitious privacy of the center of a bustling dancefloor. "By the time I made the decision, you wouldn't have a choice."

The door swung open, the top cracking off its hinge. Wide-eyed, Piper stood there with a large half-full cart at her hip, the one maids used to collect soiled laundry.

Sound flooded the tiny closet—sound they should've heard from inside. Worried voices and footsteps. Lilac wiped at the moisture in her eyes.

"What do you mean, no one knows where she is?" came her mother's shrill voice in the distance. "First Henri, now her?"

"She called a meeting in her library," replied Yanna, sounding apprehensive. "They'd been waiting for some time, so I thought I'd ask. I'm sure she's fine."

"Not to worry," Piper called out, jostling the cart violently toward their door. "I found her."

Immediately understanding, Lilac pushed Garin aside and lifted Ciel's corpse from the corner bench. She shoved it at Piper, who dumped it into the laundry cart, tugging and piling the garments over it.

"What is all that noise?" Marguerite poked her head around the corner, blinking into the dim hall. "Oh, thank heavens." Her gaze lingered on the girls before darting into the closet. She gasped. "Are you all right, Sir Albrecht?"

Garin's hand was pressed to his mouth, which remained shut. "I'm fine," he said behind it, unable to dislodge the hunger in his voice.

Even her mother heard it; Marguerite's eyes widened. Whispers erupted in the room beyond.

"He's still feeling *very* under the weather," Lilac said hastily. "He is not himself. After his bad reaction to the wine."

"He was supposed to remain in the infirmary," Madame Kemble shouted over the second floor bannister.

"The leeches made him squeamish. All that blood."

At first glance, to anyone who didn't know *what* he was, Garin might've appeared seasick, or as if he'd had one too many boysenberry tarts. But there was something else there in the shadows beneath his eyes—a lingering hunger perceptible in the clench of his jaw, the way his hands were balled fists.

Lilac found Garin's hand, but he resisted when she made to lead him out of the closet. She looked back with a glare she hoped was reassuring, squeezed his wrist, and firmly led him out.

Marguerite retreated from the hall to make room for them, eyeing their interlocked fingers with silent incredulity. Half the guests staying on the first floor had spilled out of the northern corridor into the foyer. Several maids from the scullery room peeked into the hallway to their left, each holding their breath as their gazes fell first upon Lilac.

Then Garin.

Her mother and Piper trailed them into the foyer, where several of her staff waited. Yanna and Isabel were there, Yanna's eyes wide and apologetic. Helena and Gertrude were on the other side of the door, nudging each other, looking panicked. Emma was still in her nightgown, glancing distantly out the stained glass window.

Lilac led him to the center, feeling stripped bare. She would try. She *had* to try.

"So, what were you doing together in the closet?" Agnes stood behind them, leaning arms crossed against the center table. There were streaks down her cheeks that cut through her powder, eyes rimmed in black, as if she'd been crying.

Lilac held firm, fighting to hold the baroness's amused gaze, feeling every other pair of eyes on her heating face. Her kingdom deserved its own defenses—and more imminently, a queen who fought no matter the outcome. Regardless of the ring on her hand. Such gall demanded a monarch who did not care what others thought.

Garin managed to remove his hand from his face. "Not to fret, she was showing me—"

"I am sleeping with him, Agnes, if that is what you're inferring." Lilac sighed, shooting a sidelong glance at Marguerite—and Henri, wherever he was. A quick sweep around the room told her he wasn't there. "In true Trécesson fashion."

Her mother's face reddened further as Agnes let out a high-pitched giggle. "Hold your tongue and have some decorum for once."

Although Garin said nothing beside her—she didn't know what his expression was because she wouldn't dare look at him—she felt a violent jolt of adrenaline, so strong it made her nauseous.

His displeasure. Lilac dug her nails into his arm. The sensation passed as quickly as it came on, but she felt her face blanch.

"You're not coming down with an illness, too, Your Majesty?" Kemble leaned against the railing looking down on them.

"No," she snapped. "I'm not."

"Wait." Helena fidgeted with the frills on her day gown and glanced down at their hands. "So, you two aren't at odds with each other?"

"What she means to ask is," said Gertrude hastily, "you *are* still considering the emperor's offer, aren't you? Despite last night."

"I haven't yet denied the motion." A wave of hopeful, half-concerned whispers spread through the crowd. "Unless specified otherwise. And if any of you want our kingdom to be spared, you won't say a thing." Lilac turned to Marguerite. "Is Father still recovering from last night?"

"He departed with several guards to assess the situation out east," her mother answered reluctantly.

Lilac's heart dropped—it was an answer she wasn't expecting. Garin remained expressionless. "He went there himself? So soon? Has there been any change in status?"

"None confirmed," Marguerite said, straightening a little under Lilac's rigid tone. "We didn't receive an active update from them yesterday, so he wanted to see it for himself ahead of your ceremonies. He will be back in time. It is only a day trip, I made him promise."

"Did he leave with Rupert? He mentioned last night that he'd leave this morning for the battleground."

"No. Your father took a moment to gather his men and armor. He just left."

"Rupert seemed in a rush and brought no guard," added Emma, wringing her hands.

Marguerite nodded with surprising reassurance. "I assume they will catch up with him, though, Lady Emma. The armorer wasn't around, but Ambrosius opened the armory for them before leaving."

"Blew it up, you mean," muttered Agnes, sniffling.

"Where did Ambrosius go?" Lilac looked to Garin, who remained silent. Maybe he'd gone to deal with the chest.

"I don't know, he didn't say. What I do know is that Rupert has departed and Henri took a quarter of the remaining guard with him." Marguerite's lip quivered. "Your ceremony is in two days. Our country is on the brink of war. Yet our keep remains defenseless."

Not for long, Lilac thought.

"I must attend this meeting," Lilac said. "It is important." Hedwig was peeking around the corner of the kitchen wall, smiling when the queen turned to her. "After last night, perhaps our guests would enjoy retiring for tea and breakfast in the Grand Hall?"

"Gladly, Your Majesty." Hedwig bowed before disappearing into the scullery.

"Meanwhile, Albrecht will retire to his quarters."

"On the contrary," Garin said, slinking his arm from her grasp. "I'm going to step outside to find my valet. I'd imagine he's walking the grounds."

"But you need rest," Lilac suggested.

"I'm plenty rested."

"And to *eat* something."

Garin returned her warning smile with one of his own. "Believe me, I am well sated."

"Fine, My Lord." Her fingers flew to her mouth. The agreement was lifted from her lips by his magic, shocking her. It wasn't even an outright command this time. She gritted her teeth, glaring daggers at him.

One could hear a pin drop as Garin dipped into a reverent bow and gave a quick peck to the back of Lilac's hand—a simple acknowledgement of hierarchy. No one could tell, perhaps besides Piper, that it was a gesture that made her blood sing with rage and desire.

"Madame Agnes," Garin said, looking past Lilac as he straightened. "You look rather upset."

Agnes uncrossed her arms, her scowl deepening. She wiped at the corner of her eye. "Most unfortunately."

"What's the matter?" The tilt of Garin's head was unmistakably predatory. A few of the maids retreated a couple steps, Marguerite's face went pale. "Why were you crying?"

Only Agnes seemed to think he exuded concern. "It's William. He was gone from the bed this morning with no warning, no note."

"That's odd. Has he gone off with your aid?"

"Aid?"

"Your own valet or servant."

"We didn't bring any of them. It's just us, Will and I."

Garin clicked his tongue. "That's a shame. You know, Ambrosius has the habit of wandering off when he has much to ponder. Last night my misconduct was inexcusable," he said with a small bow to the rest of the room. "Perhaps they've taken reprieve together. Gone on a walk through the grounds." He glanced back at Lilac. "I might take Madame Agnes to look for her dear William. What do you think, Your Majesty?"

Lilac leered in his direction. She would've fought harder to stop him, had it been anyone else. "Perhaps you should go together to search for them." The words were almost painful, like he'd stolen the breath from her lungs. "Some fresh air will be good for you both," she added stiffly.

Agnes shot Lilac a look of annoyance, temporarily breaking from whatever trance he had her under.

"Shall we?" Garin offered his arm and a most charming smile. Looking flattered, the baroness took it.

"Enjoy your stroll," Lilac offered, exhaling her unease. *Don't get caught.*

"I hope you have a productive meeting, Your Majesty. Don't you dare do anything rash, like start a war."

Garin ushered Agnes out the door with all the poise and posture of a true noble as his command pivoted Lilac's shoulders toward the staircase, her buzzing body following.

30

Riou removed his spectacles, breathing on them until they were fogged. Then, he took the lenses to his shirt before placing them back on his nose. "You mean two dozen." Across the table, he saw John, fidgeting with the large white feather on his quill. "She means two *dozen*, surely."

"Two hundred," Lilac said, shoveling the second handful of hawthorn berries into her mouth, ignoring Piper's disgusted open-mouthed stare from across the room. She didn't *intend* on starting a war—one could definitely argue France started it for them—but she wasn't sure what Garin's brand of Sanguine magic would consider a motion of initiation. Lilac only knew they would be ready, come what may. And she required the ability to disobey his command if the need arose. They hadn't worked against him in the coat closet, so she'd decided downing half the bag couldn't hurt.

She hummed, satisfied despite the bittersweet aftertaste. Swiping her tongue across her teeth to dislodge the berry skins, then pulled the bag shut before tucking it back in her bosom. Exchanging a glance with John, she slid off the corner of her desk and straightened her stack of research tomes and manuscripts, where a few of the Accords notes she'd left behind remained tucked beneath them.

"Two hundred destriers," Lilac repeated, pronouncing every syllable for clarity. "Half stored at the stables in Rennes and the other half here."

Riou pushed his spectacles further up. "We don't have room to house one hundred horses here. Two dozen at most. That beast your emissary rides nearly takes up two stalls. I hope you're not expecting breeds of that caliber, either." Riou took a puff from his long pipe. "If I might speak freely?"

Lilac sauntered over to John's chair, reading the document over his shoulder. "You may."

"Maximilian must be crossbreeding like hell down there. I've never seen a Freisian or Andalusian quite that tall."

"Shires?" guessed John.

"Likely not," Piper quipped. She was perched on the far end of the table, finishing one of the buttered croissants from the plate Isabel had brought. "From what I'd seen out the window, anyway. Huge, magnificent thing, he is."

Riou tilted his head, squinting appreciatively. "Do I know you, lass?"

"I've got distant family in farming and breeding," replied Piper, dusting the crumbs off her front. "It's how my parents know the Trécessons. I'm sure our paths have crossed at some point."

"You might agree, then. In my years of expertise, I've never seen anything quite like him. It's not an unrecognizable breed, but rather, one with distinctive features of many of them at once." Riou's dark brows furrowed, his olive complexion blanching then reddening as he rubbed his eyes. "There were rumors, less than a month ago, of a smaller fleet of similar horses. Twenty in approximation, marching behind a hooded leader north of Rennes. A shepherd saw them on a fogged morning from quite a distance and mentioned it at the Stag's Head, but by the time the local guard went to investigate, no one could find them."

"Intriguing." Garin hadn't mentioned where Loïg came from. Too distracted to orchestrate a full lie, she busied herself with examining her nails. "Perhaps they were Maximilian's, for his court. They were headed southeast, I presume?"

"No, the shepherd said he saw them travelling west. There was no movement of weapons or anything else, just the horses. It wasn't enough to pursue further."

"They were probably for breeding or show," said Piper quickly. "I've heard Krenn Farm has some availability in their stables."

"Perfect." Lilac's eyes widened. "We'll store them to capacity between Rennes and the castle. Any overflow will be housed at Krenn Farm. If necessary, I'll see that our treasury funds a stable extension for them."

Riou had nothing more to refute. He stared at the queen, his thin lips pulling into a ghost of an approving smile.

John stuck his nib between his lips, staining them. He licked the ink away. "Your language is standard, erring on the side of extreme politeness. There's still no promise their king will agree."

"We stood beside him for decades. We are known, public allies." Lilac pointed at the short shelf nearest them. "Any number of those tomes, will tell you when, and how. Which battles. How many won, and how many lost."

"Understood. He might not send destriers like the one outside, or those seen mobilized out west. He'll likely send his smaller stock. Coursers, or Rouncey. Even if he does have the horses to spare and is willing to help, he and his court will have to consider what the implication of perception might be. They can only keep a fleet of two hundred horses sailing across the channel so secret." John's eyes flitted across the parchment again. "I'm only advising that we do not count on it."

He was right. What Riou had said last week about England's direct involvement bringing unnecessary consequences—the possibility of France considering it an act of aggression—remained true. They'd have to be careful. She'd have to prepare for denial.

"Send the request. Two hundred as soon as England can provide them. It is my order." Her chest grew tight as she stared her duty in the eye for what felt like the first time. The possibility of entering war and the uncertainty that laid in their dependence on sole ally protection. The rising tensions, both in the east and in her heart. The pressure of Garin's teeth and fingers upon her throat. It was paralyzing.

But it was *thrilling*.

By the looks on her court's faces, they felt it too. There was nothing more to object.

John stood and slid the parchment across the table to Riou, along with his quill and inkpot. Riou said nothing, mouth tight as he scribbled his signature on the first line. Then he slid it to Lilac and handed her the quill.

She lifted the parchment, reading it over once more.

To the Most Excellent Lord Henry,

With great reverence and utmost faith in our longstanding friendship, I, Eleanor Trécesson of Brittany, send this letter requesting the purchase of two hundred warhorses. My plea for your assistance comes after reassessing our inventory upon inheriting my father's monarchy. It is of utmost importance we remain prepared for any annexation attempt by neighboring realms. Please respond at your earliest convenience. My treasury will await your correspondence. Your most generous aid will only strengthen our favorable bond, one I hope to maintain in the years to come.

Given at the Château de Trécesson on the Eighteenth Day of the month of May in the year of our Lord, one thousand five hundred thirty-two.

There. Nothing too specific, in case of interception. Nothing inflammatory.

Lilac nodded, placing the nib onto the parchment and moving her fingers, her signature marred by her trembling hand.

Fare thee well as I fare,

Eleanor Trécesson.

She slid it to her left in front of John, who signed the very bottom in his tight scrawl, notarizing it just next to his elaborate stamp.

He stood, wiping his brow and rolling the parchment into a tied scroll. "Is there anything else before I go, Your Majesty?"

"Maximilian's contract, perhaps?" murmured Riou.

John glared at him, but he looked just as apprehensive.

"Albrecht and I are getting to know each other well. His sovereign's offers sound entirely promising. The decision will be made in time for my ceremony." She gave John her hand, and he pecked it. Before he released her, she gave his palm a slight squeeze. "Have faith in me."

Have faith in me, she'd said. It was a loaded request. What reason did they have to trust her with their lives? They had reason to be nervous as they appeared. She'd never led an army before, never had a father who fronted one... or ever led by virtuous example, really.

But kings didn't need virtue to win a war, and neither did she.

Lilac had also never married. Didn't know what it was to be betrothed with a man of her own choosing, didn't know what it was to be a wife, and was never allowed to attend anyone else's wedding ceremony. She didn't know what it was to fall with child, the seed to be sown.

But she *had* fought and negotiated before, for her own life and those of others. If she could do it in Cinderfell at the mercy of Kestrel, wherever he was, defeat his revenant, overcome a carriage accident and somehow absorb some of Garin's powers, enthralling herself to him...

If she survived Garin's hunger and desire—*whatever lay beyond desire*—then none of that mattered. Then, there was hope.

"Remain discrete. Find our best pigeon and have my treasury ready."

John clutched his quill and ink box to his chest in horror. "Your Majesty, this kind of correspondence should be hand carried. There is too much risk in delivery by pigeon."

"How would flight carry more risk than a person travelling by horse and boat? We have perfectly reliable birds in our loft," Lilac argued. "Hand delivery will take weeks; the bird is much faster."

"The thing is, anyone suspicious could hunt it down and we'd never know. Your family's messengers are quick," Riou reassured her. "They'll journey discreetly to the northern ports on horseback and find a merchant ship. There are several departures a week, if not per day."

"Whether your plea is heard depends on your letter's delivery, Your Majesty," John added. "I advise you to weigh—"

"I'm not asking either your advice or permission. Send for my horses by air." She held their gazes, forcing herself to exhale slowly. This would be far easier with magic.

John dipped his head. "Very well," was all he said in reply. He scooted his chair back, rose, and shuffled to the door, tipping his hat to Piper on his way out.

Riou stood and strode around the table to meet her. He took Lilac's hand as she offered it, and squeezed gently, his mouth set in a hard line. Then, he continued toward the exit.

"You both have good reason to doubt me."

Riou stopped in his tracks.

Lilac's chest ached with the ghost of humiliation. "I know who my father is. I'm also aware of the negotiation skills of my grandfather and the desperation of my mother. I know my family's history, my reputation, and that there are those in our kingdom and beyond—in human and Daemon realms—who move to use these things against me. But I know who I am," she said quietly. "I am learning her, just as I'll learn my role here. I have many reasons to doubt myself, but I am confident in my resolve."

"Start next with the forge," he directed brusquely, turning to her. "Hamon is one of the blacksmiths working closely with Inwold. He specializes in other types of weapons, but he'll craft for you for the right price. He might be hesitant at first. He was once close with Armand—but he is loyal to your father. He will listen to you."

There was no question both Hamon and Brient were Le Tallec loyalists. They had attempted to question her new Daemon law in front of everyone, but weaponry was her most logical next step. The Sanguine Mine was extensive, a never-ending maze of vestibules, central rooms, halls, and tunnels. Garin had mentioned burning corpses and their dead at the pyre, but she never saw one outside; could he have meant a furnace? She *had* spotted a chimney in the main room before Garin led her to his bedchamber. Old mines often accommodated smelting, or at least held the resources to do so on-site.

There'd been a weapons rack in Garin's room there. Sword after sword displayed like trophies, a small armory on its own. "I'll discuss it with Inwold when he gets back. Whenever that is."

Riou's head tilted. "Back from where, Your Majesty?"

"La Guerche. The battlefield outside it." Her certainty faded when his peppered brows furrowed. "With the others. He was summoned east. You weren't aware?"

Stunned, Riou blinked. He ran a hand through his blond hair. "I wasn't made aware, no. To the battlefield? Why would he be summoned away from here when he's in charge of *our* armory? This is unacceptable." He made his way toward the door once more. "If we don't hear from Inwold, wherever he is, then I will send a pigeon to the encampment or engage Hamon myself."

"Thank you, Riou." Perhaps Inwold hadn't communicated his summons with anyone—it seemed unlikely this was unintentional, though. If he'd told her father, then maybe it inspired Henri to go and observe.

Riou had every right to be cross; he was their cartographer, after all. He hadn't signed up to do Armand's or Henri's job. But he dutifully bowed. "Mademoiselle Allard. Your Majesty."

When the door creaked shut, Lilac looked at Piper. She was still staring after Riou.

Piper hummed contemplatively into her next bite of croissant. "Interesting."

"*Riou?* He could be your father. Older, even." A pastry flew through the air. Lilac's hand shot out, catching and smooshing it in her fist.

"So could Garin. A few generations back."

Fighting the urge to make a very obscene gesture, Lilac bit into the pastry, savoring the dark red jam oozing out. From her bosom, she retrieved the bag, untied it with her teeth, and added the rest of the berries to what she was already eating.

"All that bravery and standing up to men must have you starving," Piper retorted. "And Riou just smells familiar, is all."

"That's weird." Lilac licked her fingers and tossed the bag onto the table. "Who does he—"

There was a pop and violent *woosh* of smoke in the far corner, across from the door. Then a thud, causing the nearest bookshelf to teeter.

Two figures emerged from the dissipating vortex—Myrddin first, smoothing down his dark robes. Bastion was behind him, straightening the bookshelf he nearly knocked over. Lilac could only tell who it was by the mess of sandstone hair; colorful patchwork shawl of some sort graced his shoulders. He tossed his hair out of his hazel-green eyes and pulled the large shawl over his head, skittering back out of the strip of sunlight pouring in through the floor length window behind Lilac.

She darted forward, wanting to help him, but when she reached the end of the table realized he wasn't burning. Not his face, furiously and incredulously peeking out of the hood the shawl formed, nor his exposed hands—one of which clutched what looked to be a dull red pendant encased in silver hanging from a cord around his neck.

"See?" Myrddin panted, punching the air. "I told you it would work!"

"That is *not* what you said." Bastion looked utterly terrified. "You said you were 99% sure."

"You never know with anything purchased from the *Guài*. Especially if it is stolen."

Lilac swiveled her head toward the warlock. "Wait, *that's* what you stole from them? That amulet is what Garin repaid them for?"

Still catching his breath, Myrddin held up a finger. He placed both hands on the table and closed his eyes, letting the sunlight illuminate his profile. "The Veiled Garnet," the warlock breathed, "is an amulet that casts a cloaking spell of night upon its wearer. Allows vampires to daywalk artificially—or for anyone else magic or mortal to reap the benefits of dusk, at any time. They said they'd sell it to me for very cheap. In hindsight, considering what it does, a bag of coin was a good deal indeed." He chuckled under his breath, finally opening his eyes. They were filled with pensive amusement. "It didn't seem so back then, so I bought it from them with another *Guài* purchase I'd made a few centuries back. The Coins of Conjuring." Myrddin rubbed his hands together and opened them to reveal a small, lumpy burlap pouch. "You pay with them, then spell them back into your pocket."

"You protected me," Bastion shouted from the shadows of his shawl, huddling against the wall. "With a bargain item?"

"It was a good sale! Even twenty years ago." The pouch vanished with a puff of smoke and a shake of Myrddin's fist. The warlock sauntered over to Bastion and snatched the end of the shawl. "It was crafted by a gifted bloodsmith and there can only exist *one* amulet at a time. It still works. See?"

As Bastion shouted in protest, Myrddin yanked it off—exposing him. Bastion's face twisted murderously, but nothing happened when his body was bathed in the wall of morning sun.

He opened his mouth, but there was a flash of red and emerald across the room. Bastion was knocked off his feet, his head cracking against the wall.

Piper was on him, swinging, her green gown strewn about. She landed a third punch before Lilac got to them. With his back to the floor like an overturned turtle, Bastion refused to fight back—or perhaps couldn't—and was focused on blocking his head instead.

"Get your mongrel *off* me!"

"Stop it, Piper." Lilac scooped her arms around Piper's waist and moved to lift her off of him, but Piper's fist only cracked a fourth time on Bastion's jaw and swung back, landing hard on Lilac's shoulder. Enraged, she yanked with all her might, finally prying Piper from him. "Not... *here!*" She stumbled back and dropped Piper.

Bastion's ears and lips were bloodied when he sat up. Lilac jabbed a finger at the head seat closest to the window, then Piper. "There. Now." She then placed her hand on the chair back nearest her and jutted her chin at Bastion. "You, here."

Bastion stood, dusted himself off, and sneered at Myrddin the whole way to the chair. He plopped into it, cursing under his breath.

"You've had that amulet all these years," panted Lilac, her muscles burning as she looked up at Myrddin, "and you could've given it to Garin."

"So that he could've *what*, Your Majesty?" Myrddin's blond brow shot up. "Gone on a daytime stroll? Tended the garden out front? Left to seek you sooner? There is a method to every form of madness that befalls me." Beneath his levity, there was something else brewing—a lingering darkness in the way he leered at her. "I cannot *help* it."

"Can't help what?" scoffed Bastion.

"The method, nor the madness." Myrddin exhaled and spoke slowly, his expression filled with regret. "Being pursued by the *Yao Guài* and having my tenure stripped at the Sanctum, I decided to do something I'd never tried before and took on a drastic new appearance."

Lilac almost felt sorry for him. "How long did you live in your glamor?"

"It was not a glamor, Your Majesty. It wasn't quite an illusion. I *aged* myself."

They all stared blankly at him.

"But you're immortal, are you not?" asked Bastion.

"It was an artificial acceleration of time I inflicted upon myself. I'd always wondered what I might look like if ever damned with the curse of growing old, had I not stopped my physical aging in my thirty-fifth year. I intended the effect to last me a bit, soon discovering that the ailing symptoms of being in your eighties are far from pleasant. I'd tried to turn back but discovered my tragic dilemma when I found my magic was heavily reduced; my arcana dwindled down to that of a simple warlock."

"You couldn't draw from your own power," said Lilac in wonder. "That must've been horrible."

"It was," he said scathingly. "Worst of all, I couldn't access any of my *things*. I store most of my valuables and attire within a large trunk, which now sits in my room at The Fenfoss Inn. I couldn't access the depths of it while in my aged state, as it refused to allow me access. I never offered

Garin the amulet because I could never *get* to it—until the day I was able to turn myself back with the enchantment stripping spell imbued in that arrow."

"Perhaps the *Guài* could have helped you, had you not stolen their amulet in the first place."

Unmoved, Bastion pouted from his chair. "If there's only one amulet in the world at a time, how is *she* doing *that*?"

Across the table, Piper's murderous glare never left Bastion, her eyes backlit by the window's golden light.

"No one seems to know," said Lilac, rubbing her temples. "Seeing as there's only one amulet, consider yourself fortunate. I'd have ripped it off your throat to give it to her."

"Just in case another squabble breaks out," Myrddin said, chuckling nervously. He raised his finger; there was a *pop*, another cloud of vapors, and a flash in the corner of the room. The door to the library glowed violet just as the closet knob downstairs had. "As I was saying," he continued, starting to pace the length of the table, "the Veiled Garnet is an amulet I procured from the *Guài* twenty years ago for the College of Restoration at the Ambleside Sanctum in Douarnenez. An extension of the Ambleside Academy up in Brest," he explained with a nod at Lilac and Piper.

Lilac had heard the Sanctum mentioned before. By Lorietta or Adelaide, she was sure. "Are mortals aware of these institutions?"

"Select few. Those who can be trusted to do clandestine business with magic folk. The majority are unaware, thanks to College of Illusion out of the larger institutions in St. Malo and Mont Saint-Michel. When all else fails, memory erasing spells help." Myrddin pivoted and threw a pensive smile in her direction.

"Like the one you cast on Lilac?" Piper's eyes bore into the back of the warlock's skull.

He whirled on her. "Precisely, though no magic comes without cost and it will never be done upon her again—Garin's made sure of that." Myrddin turned back to Lilac and Bastion. "The Sanctum is smaller, reserved for novice magic users and mages; there are mostly studies and arcanists' rooms, sleeping quarters, and a dining hall. A forge and the rotunda housing their library. I held a position there after centuries of serving on several kings' courts. I retired as their lecturer shortly after I obtained the

Veiled Garnet for the School of Restoration at the Sanctum. I uh... it was more useful in my own hands."

"Adelaide said they come through every third century to sell their wares, and that their last visit here was in 1340," said Lilac. "How did you steal it from them twenty years ago?"

"Indeed, 1340 was their last *market* pilgrimage through Brocéliande. Fateful day." Myrddin placed a finger on his pursed lips. "As for that amulet, I obtained it in the summer of 1512 when they'd arrived by special request of the School of Restoration at the Ambleside Sanctum." He hummed, counting on his fingers. "They were also here at the end of our War of Succession, in the spring of 1365. The Hundred Years' War still raged elsewhere in Europe, but the *Guài* were witnessed on the edge of the Low Forest surveying our damages after the fires."

"They're business people, first and foremost." Everyone slowly turned to Bastion, whose hooded hazel-green eyes remained fixed on the window —on the sunlight pouring in. His head was tilted up slightly, allowing his pale, freckled face to absorb as much warmth as remotely possible. "A few centuries ago, *Guài* caravans were dispersed widely over Asia and the north, travelling frequently and selling various arcane goods."

Bastion had been alive—*human*—the same time Garin was. He'd also been recruited and fought alongside him under Alor's command, just under two hundred years ago. Lilac found this particularly fascinating, glancing at the Histories section across the table. "The *Guài* traded on the Silk Road."

"I thought that was obvious," muttered Myrddin under his breath.

"Alongside my family." Bastion shifted forward, leaning against the table. "Black powder, parchment, and silk. My brother and I spent months at a time travelling with them. I was thirteen when my father suggested expanding business to Europe after an unforgivingly harsh winter. They searched for a caravan willing to take our products with them for a portion of the profit. The *Guài*, who regularly purchased powder from us, were quick to offer. My mother was hesitant to trust them with our earnings, so the *Guài* countered with an offer for us to travel with them. They restored our cart and generously stored our goods in their carriage—which, by the way, was far more spacious on the inside than it appeared." Bastion scraped his teeth along his bottom lip, deep in thought. "We then departed for Rome from Xi'an."

Xi'an. Lilac knew it well. A powerful capital and trading city in its own right. "China to Rome, then back. That must have taken years."

"Not with their flying oxen." Bastion smirked at the incredulity written on their faces, but his smile quickly faded. "I never made it back. I was thirteen when we left. Fourteen by the time we were caught in a severe storm traveling through the desert. The rain was relentless. We couldn't exactly stop; there were many others trying to clear the mountain pass. My parents made me jump into the *Guài* carriage. They were about to pass my brother over and secure our valuables to join us so we could all take flight, but Georgie was scared. My father tried to chase him around our cart, and —" He looked as if he'd continue after taking a shuddering breath, but with a little shake of his head, said, "The *Guài* will travel extensively, east to west, every three hundred years. But they'll make exceptions outside their market schedule for various reasons. Various customers, or collaborative journeys."

Something—a creeping feeling—tugged at Lilac's subconscious. Nagging at her.

"Bastion has tried shaking the chest," Myrddin commented. "There doesn't seem to be anything in it." He frowned and craned his head at Bastion, who was sniffling and wiping his eyes. "Are you all right?"

"I could do with a throat to sink my teeth into, but seeing as the only eligible one in this room has enthralled itself to Garin, I'll pass."

"I'll rip that thing off your neck before Garin lays a finger on you," said Piper.

Lilac shot a warning look at Piper and turned to Bastion. "I assume Myrddin filled you in on last night's incident?"

"He did." Bastion's scowl returned as he wiped the drying blood off his chin, the scratch wounds from Piper already gone. "Intentional, from the sound of it."

Myrddin made a sound of disagreement. "I told you, it was toadstool-infused wine. People create that at home. If someone wanted to poison or harm Her Majesty, or anyone else in this castle, they could've done much worse. *Would* have done much worse. Even without magic, there's Belladonna, Water Hemlock. Various natural poisons... the list goes on."

"Yes, but one can do much more with mild poisons if the goal isn't murder. You could aim to make someone sick to make a point. Or create a diversion." Bastion's voice dropped to a whisper. "Have you considered Kestrel? Not like he's particularly fond of any of us."

"I doubt it," said Lilac. "Kestrel is loud with his deliveries. He loves his letters and bouquets. He sent a revenant in my envelope, remember? He would've used any of the fae-rooted flora at his disposal."

Bastion quieted then, his eyes widening—perhaps in surprise at the mention of Garin's research. Lost in thought, Myrddin silently fiddled with his mustache.

"Speaking of, Garin said you'd look into what to do about the chest today."

"Kestrel hasn't responded to our letters noting his chest's retrieval, or those proposing us getting it to him," interjected Bastion. "The hawthorn trees are empty, void of response. We've sent several letters. From two separate locations."

"Several, as in how many?" Lilac asked.

Bastion and Myrddin exchanged glances. "Once after the chest was obtained, and twice daily since the morning Garin sent you home. Before dawn, and once after nightfall," answered Myrddin. "The letters *are* going through the hawthorn channel. We just aren't receiving any responses."

Piper uncrossed her arms. "Is there any way the letters might be getting intercepted?"

"No," said Myrddin. "The faerie channels are tightly protected by their unique portal magic."

"Is portal magic the same thing as interdimensional magic?" asked Lilac.

Myrddin cast another surprised glance Lilac's way. "Yes. One of the most complex capabilities in Alteration, nearly impossible to manipulate or interfere with. Dangerous when practiced at a whim, or by someone inexperienced. The witches have double checked the trees on our end. They're healthy and secure." The warlock tapped his chin. "Either end of the channel can be destroyed, a tree cut down or burned, rendering the other side useless. But if that happened, we'd know, because our letters wouldn't have gone through at all."

A sense of unease coiled itself around Lilac's throat. She wondered if the lack of correspondence was unusual for the faerie king or not. "Maybe he's busy. He did send a revenant to deliver his request."

None of them said anything. Piper bit at her nails.

"Then you will deliver it," she directed at Bastion.

It was like Lilac had slapped the perpetual scowl from his face. "To Cindefell?"

"To Cinderfell."

Bastion slipped out of his chair and shuffled across the floor. The sight of him grovelling was pleasantly distracting; before she knew it, he was sweeping her hand in his. He managed to press his lips fervently to it several times before she tried to yank it away. But he held on. "Your Majesty, there must be some other way. Garin and Myrddin will go! It will be grand, and I can stay here with you." He fingered the encased gemstone with his free hand, holding it up in the light. "With this amulet, I'll protect you."

Lilac stepped back, pulling him into the beam of sunlight. Bastion winced and released her—then scowled when nothing happened to his uncovered hands. "Likely, when the sun still makes you flinch." She extended a hand, and the vampire begrudgingly took it, righting himself. "I need *someone* to bring the chest to Kestrel. Garin is my emissary."

"And now, one of her knights," Piper said, crossing her arms and savoring the look of shock on Bastion's face.

"Garin isn't going anywhere *near* the Low Forest," Lilac confirmed.

Bastion looked helplessly at Myrddin.

"As much as I'd love to help, I cannot," the warlock said. "Garin gave me clear instructions to watch over her." He angled his head toward Lilac. "Your Majesty, when would you expect Bastion to leave?"

"Today. We shouldn't prolong getting the chest to Kestrel with my approaching coronation day." She failed to mention the wedding—the words failing to form. "Bastion's amulet will protect him from any sunlight that might otherwise undo his existence, so long as it stays on his neck. It will be more than enough."

"So kind of you," Bastion spat. "So kind of you both. Let's send the big, bad vampire traipsing into the den of faeries."

"Perfect. It's settled then," said Lilac, pressing her fingers together. "Then you can ask Kestrel, straightforwardly, if that generous bottle of delicious wine was a gift from him. He won't be able to help himself from admitting it was he who thought of such a grand gesture. If he dances around the answer, it was him."

"And what will you have me do if it is?"

Lilac chewed on her lip. She thought of the sheer terror she felt fighting and running from his revenant. Not even she would want to put Bastion through that. "Nothing, I suppose. But it is important we find out."

The vampire remained quiet.

Myrddin had begun to stroke his beard.

"Something is bothering you, too," Lilac said to the warlock. "What is it?"

"Besides the imminent danger of going to Cinderfell without a fae escort?" Bastion growled.

Myrddin silenced him with a glare. "Kestrel, King of the Court of the Valley, asked you specifically to bring this chest to him? Was there any confirmation of *whom* the Yao Guai might've been delivering the chest to when the accident occurred?"

"No," she replied slowly. "But I think Kestrel's wish to obtain it trumps anyone else's need for a measly chest. They offered it to us without question."

"Did he request you hand-deliver it to him?" asked Myrddin.

Lilac considered the night of the failed Accords meeting and couldn't quite recall. She'd been rightfully distracted. "All he said was that we were to retrieve the chest from the Midraal Market and bring it to him. He never got to say *how* before he—I mean, his revenant—grew violent."

"But he didn't specify a journey to his manor in the Low Forest? That is what I'm asking."

"No. Once the revenant took over Hywell's body, the communication with him ended. He said the deal was made in blood as he died in that fire, and then he was gone."

"Lovely," said Bastion. "So that settles it. We don't go. Garin has his way with Lilac and we all get on with our lives."

Piper shot up from her seat, knocking her chair back. Before Lilac could stop her, Bastion lunged sideways and yanked her into a headlock.

Lilac gasped as the wind was knocked out of her, and somehow managed to twist and jerk out of Bastion's grasp. Once free, she craned her arm around and snaked her fingers against his scalp, slamming Bastion's head upon the desk and holding him there. Or, attempting to.

He nearly bucked her off, but Lilac's fingers stayed curled into Bastion's long sandstone hair, taut against his skull. Marvelling at her own strength, she laughed—until his hand shot out, fingers snapping around Lilac's free wrist and squeezing. She yelped when he twisted his hand.

"I should have let you die in that room," Bastion rasped. "Should've let Garin have his way with you."

"Actually," said Myrddin, chuckling and only sounding mildly alarmed, "she got herself out of the brothel. And he wouldn't have killed her. It would take a dark and unholy magic to *force* him to allow that to happen."

"Shut. Up," Bastion breathed against the tabletop, Piper frozen near the window with the back of her chair in her hands like she was getting ready to swing. "Any one of you move a muscle, and I'll snap her forearm in half. She might've inherited an ungodly amount of our speed and strength, but it is yet only a portion. She still has the body of a human. A *shell* of mortal life. And she is just as delicate, just as easily broken."

"Let go of me," Lilac snarled, yanking away from him, still refusing to let go of his head.

Bastion dug his nails into her flesh. "I'll—"

"*Stop!*"

A *pop* sounded, followed by a gust of wind that violently ruffled Lilac's hair. A deafening silence followed, as if all the air and sound in the room were sucked away.

She gasped when she cleared her eyes. It was unlike any of his spells she'd witnessed before; the warlock was surrounded by several books knocked off the shelves by the wind—two on the floor, one was *frozen* midair, blown open on its way down. Several of its pages were impossibly suspended mid-fall, their corners quivering in the dying breeze.

Myrddin's arms were raised, his hands projecting a cannonball-sized *thing* of swirling mist, shards of gold, mahogany, and gray just inches from his chest. A reflection of the library pulsed in a frenzy within the floating sphere—the same muted colors of the room, anyway.

The pain at her arm from Bastion's grip had subsided; Bastion's face and unruly hair had frozen, too, wrenched in a furious snarl.

Stunned, she shimmied her arm out from his grasp. "What have you done? What kind of magic is this?"

"A kind you don't want me using," Myrddin said warningly, his expression stoic. "Something only I can do. It is a beacon of arcana, enacts all kinds of consequences, good and bad." He lowered his voice. "But I *will* use it if it means saving you and that disastrous vampire. Beyond your kingdom's immediate future, the very fate of our arcane world relies on—"

There was a gasp. "Look!" Piper was very much *not* frozen, her face pressed against the floor length window.

Myrddin turned and blinked in disbelief. He trailed Lilac over to Piper, bringing the hovering ball of smoke and fragment with him. "Does magic just roll off her body, like rainfall on a goose? Meanwhile you, Your Majesty, soak it up like a sponge."

Outside, the swaying canopy of Brocéliande was still. *Completely.* More than it ever was on dry, windless days.

But that wasn't all Piper had noticed. Up and to the right, just past her tower balcony, an unfamiliar black bird with extravagant olive wing markings hung in the sky.

Frozen, like everything else.

"A lone Cormorant," Piper whispered in wonder. "What's it doing so far inland?"

"Oh, marvellous." Myrddin cocked his head for a better view beside Lilac. "Why, would you look at that? Yes, that is rather strange. An ample distraction for this kingdom going to shit!"

Both Lilac and Piper turned to look at him.

"Each and every one of us has a role to play." His brilliant blue eyes flitted threateningly between them, first landing on Piper. "No more picking fights." Then, on Lilac. "No risking your lives. Not yet."

"Bastion was her kidnapper and abuser. He deserved at least *three* of those punches she landed," said Lilac, sneering at his spinning ball. "Garin might've brought you, but you have no authority over us. It sounds like he's made it crystal clear to you *what* your role is in securing my sovereignty."

To this he said nothing, solemnity gracing his golden features.

"I'll do what I have to. Your interference isn't needed. What do you think I was doing before the two of you broke into my library?"

Myrddin's mouth twitched as if he wished to say more. But he simply brought his hands together. The mystical sphere was gone—and the lone cormorant soared north, past the window in the foreground of the rustling trees.

There was a *thud* behind them.

Bastion was on the floor, barely catching himself on the edge of the desk. He stood again, glancing around the room and snarling when he finally discovered them by the window. "I have no idea what's going on anymore. What I do know, is that *I've* been with the witches and those aggravating trolls. None of them think travelling to Cinderfell is a good idea. I've left the same letters to the Fair Folk in two separate trees, every day," Bastion reiterated, spreading his arms. "No response. Is that not odd to any of you?"

"What's odd," quipped Piper, "is that, out of all of you—witches, korrigans, and other vampires—no one has found a way to deliver this chest for Lilac."

"Wait," interjected Myrddin as Bastion grumbled. "No, he has a point. You vampires and even we have always communicated with Kestrel this way, at least since he came into power as a young faerie centuries ago. By leaving notes in the hollows of Brocéliande's or Huelgoat's hawthorn trees. Then, either he or the bluejays retrieve them."

"Does it hurt?" Piper glanced sideways at Bastion.

"Sometimes," Bastion answered. "Not if we're careful."

"Hawthorn, or the Fairy Tree to the Old Faith. It is one of the oldest tree species in the world, posing a danger to various Daemons, including vampires. But they're not the only tree connected to the Fair Folk," Myrddin said. "The Court of the Valley has hidden entrances all throughout Brittany. Kestrel likes to craft his in the trunks of wide and sturdy trees. If you're invited, you're approached by his guards, who escort you to one of their nearest portals."

"There's one an hour or so east of the Sanguine Mine." A shudder passed through Lilac despite the warming sun on her back. She looked over to Bastion, but he was staring at the ground, looking extremely unsettled by the notion of going to Cinderfell.

"That tree his guards brought us through," he said. "The one they set on fire. How could I forget?"

"Faerie fire," said Myrddin.

Lilac gasped as a *brilliant* thought struck her. "Can it transport items instead of people?"

"By their law, visitors must be escorted. But with a lone chest..." The warlock's forehead creased. "The willow should transport the chest to the

Court of the Valley. All it takes is a hawthorn arrow shot through the hole to ignite their fire. I'm not sure that it will work, but we can try."

"Wonderful," said Lilac. "And if Bastion is that afraid, then you can go with him."

"Ah. That I'm afraid I cannot do. Garin has ordered me to watch over you here. That is the only specific command he has given me, and I am not to break it."

"Then the redhead can come."

Piper hissed, affronted. "That's not my name."

"Fine. The *other daywalker* can come."

"You can't expect her to—" Lilac's shrill voice died at the look of hesitation on Piper's face. She fully expected her friend to decline. "Oh. Do you *want* to go?"

"With him? No. But I haven't fed in days," Piper admitted quietly. "Hedwig's meals have been sustaining me since before I arrived. I'm just afraid of slipping into that hunger again."

"Do you feel the hunger now?" asked Lilac, as both Bastion and Myrddin studied them.

"I mean, I could always eat, but it's been a bit worse today. I had two servings of eggs this morning off Hedwig's cart, tea, and a few pastries. Still feeling a bit peckish. I assume it's time for me to find some soon."

Myrddin's hand passed over his face.

"*What?*" Bastion spat. "But you completed your transition. You bit Lilac."

"The hunger was bad then. And it isn't now. I *do* drink it, I just don't crave it that way."

Bastion looked to Myrddin. "But what does she mean, she doesn't crave it? If she's not bound by a curse like Garin was, then what's wrong with her?"

Myrddin was scratching his beard. "I'm not sure anything's wrong with her, though she does exercise the will of ancient vampires. Maybe someone centuries and centuries old, like Garin's friend Casmir."

A string of expletives flowed under Bastion's breath.

"Nothing is wrong with me," Piper snapped, scowling at Bastion. "That hunger I felt at the beginning was pure instinct and not at all driven by taste, by the way. Compared to the slop you had your henchmen feed me at the mine, I suppose human blood is edible."

Bastion's hands went into his hair. "*It's what you're supposed to eat.*"

"Are you so sure?" Piper jabbed a thumb at Lilac. "Hers tastes like rotten milk on a summer's day. Don't really remember what her blood tasted like the first time in the forest, or before that, with the man in the vestibule. All I remember was that everything was cold and dark, as if a ghoul had draped itself upon the room. I was neither here nor there." Her face fell at the memory, gaze distant. "Blood was the only vibrant thing there, but I can't imagine it tasting as good as anything Hedwig's made."

"*Garin* doesn't seem to think so." Lilac pressed a hand to her chest, affronted. "And his tastes like figs and honey to me, yet I am not sustained on it."

"Because you are not a vampire." Bastion just stared at both of them in disgust, then directed an exasperated glare at Myrddin. "She isn't one, is she? *Modron*, I'll throw myself upon a stake."

"No, she certainly is not. But Ambleside would love to have a good look at them both."

Lilac threw her arms up. "No one is going to Ambleside. You two will drop the chest off at the willow tree. You are to return with a report as soon as you are done." She pressed a finger into Bastion's chest. "Watch over my friend. She mustn't drink from anyone's vein—you can either bleed them, or entrance them to do it for you. There are crossbows, hawthorn arrows, and blades at your disposal in my armory. Myrddin can at least teleport you there."

"Likely not, Your Majesty. There is a sizable hole in the wall where your armory door once was, remember?"

"Why can't you just teleport the chest?" asked Bastion. "We'll babysit the queen. Then no one would have to take the journey."

Myrddin snapped his fingers—and the amulet Bastion had just stopped fidgeting with shot into the air, straining against its string. The vampire gasped, reaching for it, but Myrddin pulled the amulet further. "That is quite enough. Your brother was reserved with the way he described you at the tavern. And it's thanks to my debt to *him* that my power reserves are draining much quicker than they usually are. Even going to the inn to fetch Bastion was taxing, when these distances usually don't phase me." Myrddin waved a hand; the amulet fell into Bastion's palm, where he clutched it to his chest.

"Is it because he's assigned you to chaperone me?" asked Lilac.

"That is what I suspect. Any extensive travel that sets me apart from you might exhaust me. Garin would kill all of us if I took you with me, away from your fortress without his permission—and he'd find a way to *keep* me dead. I don't want to find out what happens or where I end up if I exhaust my arcana reserves before I've rebuilt my stamina. I'll teleport your friends outside the gate. Within the treeline, even. Lorietta has to have some sort of armory besides her wand and tonics—I suggest you stop there first."

"Fine," shot Bastion, casting an irritated glance at Piper. "She'll make do with bottled blood. I can't wait to hear what Garin thinks of her. His first sire, preferring bread and eggs. His own thrall, enjoying the taste of *his* blood? Abominations."

"Thank you." Relief washed over Lilac. She clasped her hands together at Myrddin. "I'll make sure you get a private room here and that you're well attended to after all of this." As his eyes brightened considerably, she frowned. "Speaking of Garin, where is he? Did he end up running into you? Is he resting in his room now?"

"Resting?" Myrddin blinked rapidly. "I'm not sure. I haven't seen him."

It was like the breath had been knocked out of her. Lilac froze, already feeling a wave of panic cresting.

"I'm sure he's fine," said Piper, despite glancing nervously at the door.

He very well *might* have been fine; knowing Garin, he was probably surrounded by Marguerite and her friends downstairs, spoon feeding them a detailed story of how Agnes had alarmingly departed the grounds in search of her dear husband.

But she couldn't ignore the insidious dread burrowing into her chest— the nagging feeling that something was wrong. Or amiss. "Garin's missing?"

"Now, now," said the warlock, "don't go jumping to conclusions. Just because you haven't laid eyes on him, doesn't mean he's gone *missing*."

"You remember what happened the last time you lost sight of him?" Her shaking fingers dug into her palms. "He said he'd look for you in the courtyard. Left through the foyer doors. I assumed you'd ran into him before retrieving Bastion."

"All is well," said Myrddin, beckoning Piper and a wary-looking Bastion closer. "I teleported from the bailey to the inn shortly after discovering you two. Garin might still be outside. I will keep an eye out."

"You will bring him to me if you see him," she snarled.

He nodded, looking uncharacteristically unconcerned. "He's bound to be around." With a wink, he extended his arm to Piper. "Ladies first. Go on, then."

Piper pursed her lips, glancing hesitantly at Lilac.

"You'll be safe with them. I promise. I'll have their heads if anything happens to you."

"You're a direct extension of Lilac," added Myrddin. "*Garin* will have our heads if anything happens to you."

The moment Piper placed her trembling hand on him, Myrddin clamped his other palm onto Bastion's shoulder.

In a blur of color and smoke, the trio was gone; Piper's delicate scream immediately cut off.

The outline of the library door flashed violet as soon as they were gone. Wasting no time, Lilac strode across the room and jerked it open.

There was a shriek.

Marguerite stumbled into the room, knocking the door open. A flurry of voices could be heard downstairs, fading as her mother stepped in and softly shut the door. Pieces of her hair stuck out from beneath her towering wig, chest heaving as if she'd been running. "Good God, what on earth are you doing in here? Alone?"

Lilac steadied her. "Were you waiting outside?"

"Yes. I sent Yanna to get you when Riou and John came downstairs, but she said the door was locked. Not even the key would open it." Marguerite fanned the air, the stemmed glass hooked in her other hand sloshing pale cider at their feet. "Why does it smell like the chapel in here? Did you have John run a private Liturgy for you?" When Lilac tried to sidestep her, Marguerite swung the glass dramatically before sipping from it, sweeping her back.

"*What* are you doing?"

Marguerite merely motioned to the scrap parchment and croissant tray left over from their meeting. "What did you need Riou for, anyway?"

"He knows the land. He's the closest thing I have to an informant.

What does it matter to you? The armorer isn't here and neither is Father." Lilac's ears were burning, the panic of needing to find Garin clashing with her mother's nerve to corner her for interrogation. "Were you listening in? Eavesdropping is an offense in our kingdom."

Marguerite only laughed. "Prosecute me, then. Your father is preoccupied with his whims as he's always been. I've done my due diligence in raising a single daughter. I—" Her mother trailed off, swaying and clutching the glass to her chest. "Whatever. Excommunicate me. Banish me, so that kind Sir Albrecht might whisk me away to Vienna."

"It is the morning after a long night for everyone." Lilac plucked the glass from between Marguerite's fingers. "The least you can do is behave yourself."

"Oh, please. Henri has spent many a night out among gamblers and wastrels. If my daughter can set some whores on fire, I am allowed a moment. Hedwig made it a point to lavish us in the courtyard." Marguerite glanced over her shoulder at the closed door. "And I should advise you the same."

"They are not whores. And they weren't set on fire." Lilac eyed Marguerite carefully. "Albrecht's been very kind. He was apologetic about last night."

"I'm sure he feels rightly forgiven, if not overly welcome. Did he at least enjoy himself at the brothel?"

Lilac's face climbed in color.

Marguerite adjusted her shawl. "I am not here to cast stones. In this peculiar, extravagant life we're born into, romance scarcely crosses paths with duty. There are futures we see for ourselves that never come to fruition because the monarchy holds greater plans, and so it is for our own sanity that we might learn the byways of law and expectation. I figured that out at a pitifully young age. Even then, they took what I most wanted."

Lilac looked around, unsure of what to say. Her body was itching to move. "What was it?"

Marguerite wiped regretfully at her face. "It was a stupid whim. A pair of Spaniel pups showed up at our door one day, and my mother said we should keep them. So, we had beds made, bowls crafted. They even slept at the end of my bed. But in the winter, when Father returned from an excursion with Francis, he insisted they'd never allow them. He managed to convince me, because the Le Tallecs oversaw our manor, that we'd answer to them if the furnishings and floors were ruined. So, I put them out in the snow." Marguerite regarded her daughter with an irked scorn. "That old coat closet? *Really?*"

"Maybe you do need this." Lilac handed Marguerite back the half-full glass. "I'm sorry, Mother. About your pups. I had no idea."

"That hardly surprises me."

Her mother had never been the type to give softness, not to her husband nor her daughter. It seemed she was also bad at receiving it. Neither had she been the type, now that Lilac thought about it, to show affection toward animals. The summer that the family of cats sought refuge in their bailey, Marguerite had refused to lounge in the courtyard, citing the feline infestation as the reason. Maybe she was a dog person.

"You were not one to speak of your childhood."

"And you were never one to ask," Marguerite said curtly. With that, it was clear whatever she had come to tell Lilac no longer mattered. The frost in her demeanor had returned, her cheeks and nose exceptionally red as she turned and adjusted her shawl. "Now, if you'll excuse me."

"Mother?"

Marguerite made a sound of impatience. "I haven't got all morning. And neither do you."

"When love and duty don't align—"

"Which, they won't." She gave Lilac a warning glance. "And I said nothing about love."

"If *romance* and duty don't align, but one's heart calls out for both, and there is no way to reconcile them... then, what does one do?"

Her mother gave a hapless shrug. "I am no fortune teller, Lilac."

Lilac grabbed the doorknob before she could escape. "But I am your daughter, and you've lived half a life that I have not. It's been your prerogative to strictly govern my education and deny me horse riding and self-defense lessons hoping to save your own minor reputation. It was never for me. It's no secret that you detest the attention I have drawn." Lilac swallowed, so irritated she couldn't cry. "You might even hate the unfair circumstances that brought you to a life as consort, seeing how you and Father tolerate each other. You married into a life I was born into; I did not ask for it any more than you did. The least you can do is pretend to *relate* to me, or or that you care."

Marguerite's scowl burned brighter with every word. Lilac thought she might strike her, but her mother's expression faltered. "I do not lack the tact, the etiquette, and poise you do. I don't have your stubbornness, or your gall. I was a girl who had everything and was promised a lavish life, willing to sacrifice anything to maintain it. *Anything.* You're willing to lose it all in order to stand up for those creatures. You hesitate on the path of convenience presented to you that other monarchs would jump at. How could I possibly relate to you?" Marguerite's bleary eyes turned piercing. "Which one scares you most? Choose that, and brace yourself for the consequences like I failed to. Life is filled with heartache, Lilac. Use some of that idiotic selfishness you *did* inherit from me to your advantage, hm?" She swatted Lilac's clammy fingers off the knob. "Now, if you'll excuse me, I've got a garden party and a game of cricket to oversee. Oh, and please deal with that obnoxious witch seamstress of yours. She's making a mess of my foyer as we speak."

31

The front doors were once again propped open to the daylight with two new guards flanking the entry. Just outside, there was a bright white carriage adorned in what looked like vines of real ivy, goldenrod, and dog rose growing around its frame.

Garin was nowhere in sight; Lilac could see as much as she gripped the railing overlooking the foyer in rising panic. In the middle of the room, was Herlinde. Her backside, anyway. The front half of which was stuck inside a spacious trunk nearly double the size of the round table it sat next to.

Descending the stairs with Marguerite, Lilac saw four sizable wooden chests piled at the foot of the other staircase.

"Where is it, you swine?" Herlinde's voice was muffled. "We're on a tight schedule."

"I warned you about using me as storage," rasped a disembodied voice, sounding as if it were on the verge of heaving. It was decidedly male, human, and *not* echoing in Lilac's skull as the lingua arcana would have. "Especially after all that work you put me through last night."

Lilac gasped when they reached the bottom. The witch's aproned rump stuck out the trunk, her front resting upon a long, wide, carpet that lolled out of the chest, creating what looked like a tapered hall runner—all the way out the door. One guard pinched the bridge of his nose and looked like he was on the verge of passing out, while the other had clamped a hand over his mouth.

There was the sound of glass shattering, making her jump.

"Oh my," Marguerite squealed in horror, her cider spilled among the shards on the floor.

A tongue. It was a giant tongue.

Herlinde heaved herself out, brushing her curls aside. They appeared to be damp. "Oh, hello again, Your Majesty. Told you I'd be back." She did a partial curtsey with her arms still deep in the trunk, her elbows resting on the lip. "Queen Mother, don't think I didn't see you scurry upstairs at the sight of us."

"I am—" Marguerite tripped over herself as she backed away into the western corridor. "Much, *much* too drunk for this."

Lilac had scuttled back against the door. She desperately looked to the guard beside her—the one who'd broken into a cold sweat. Then, she cocked her head at Marguerite. "Would you please?"

"Gladly." Without another glance, the guard shuffled toward her mother, holding his arm out.

"Wait! Don't you wish to see what I brought you?" Herlinde called, motioning at the boxes in the corner. "There are several wigs and gowns there. Some for Mademoiselle Phoebe as well."

"How thoughtful." Marguerite laughed disbelievingly and gave a little shake of her head. She made to turn, but stopped, fiddling with the trappings on her dress. "What of the others?"

"The others, Madame?"

"Yanna and Isabel, Lilac's handmaidens. They're entertaining our guests in the courtyard as we speak and have proved useful. Certainly more so than that *Phoebe*." She spat the name as if it left a bad taste in her mouth. "My daughter shouldn't have to continue lending her hand-me-downs to them if it isn't necessary, that's all."

"Mother," Lilac snapped, unable to take her eyes off the enormous, dripping appendage.

"Not to fret." Herlinde fought a smile, exchanging a quick glance with Lilac. "There's enough there to go around for now. Share them with whom you'd like—it's the rest of my current inventory. They aren't all enchanted garments, but I did have Freidrich fix each of them with a basic sizing spell since we learned I wouldn't have the time to fit all of you today."

By now, Marguerite was retreating halfway into the hall, dragging the guard with her.

Before Lilac could apologize, the trunk rattled, its mouth opening wide above Herlinde's head. "You could've brought any other trunk."

"We didn't have the room," argued Herlinde, leaning into its opening once more. "My customer specifically requested a full wardrobe of *only* enchanted garments."

"Please forgive my mother's atrocious manners." Lilac glanced outside. Although no one manned the gate across the yard, several guards could be seen marching in pairs now. Her heart fluttered, relief flooding her. They were probably under Garin's orders. "Also, I never placed an order for enchanted garments."

"Oh, I wasn't referring to you. And it's quite all right, Your Majesty," said Herlinde, fishing around. "I've been working with Marguerite for a while on those shipments. I suppose I should've disclosed in the beginning of our acquaintanceship that I was a witch. I didn't think it mattered when I agreed to import her wigs from Paris. She was my most esteemed customer, until now."

"*Heuuugh*—too far," the trunk retched. Despite it speaking, what truly did Lilac in was the little angry jig it did on its four-pawed feet painted in tarnished gold. "*Watch the uvula!* And they're *my* customers, too."

"And just what will you do with coins? Bank notes?" With an exasperated groan, Herlinde crawled out, plucking a cloth towel off the back of her apron and wiping some of the clear slime—*saliva*—that covered her head and forearms. She smoothed her hair and eagerly grinned at Lilac. "Just received a note this morning. We've got a wealthy buyer to meet in a few days. That is, we'll be meeting the impressive export ship this buyer has arranged to bring my goods *to* her. They say they're able to pay in the tender of my choosing, that they'll have bronze coins and paper money. Silver dollars from Spain. Anything I want."

Lilac's eyes narrowed. There it was, the tug at her subconscious again— so subtle, she wouldn't have noticed if she weren't already on edge, hoping for any sign or hint that Garin was near. "Who is your buyer? Are they Daemons? Faeries?"

"We don't know. They didn't bother with a signature or other details. Understandable, for the size of their order." Herlinde was about to dive back in, but the trunk rattled again.

"Let me," it said, a tinge of annoyance in its peculiar voice.

Lilac's further questioning was lost as she watched the tongue jerk. It began to slowly roll itself in from the tip. "Who is that?" Her hands went to her mouth when the trunk swallowed its tongue whole, like a carpet in storage. "*What* is that?"

"It's her husband." A boy wearing a mischievous grin emerged from the carriage and jogged up the shallow steps. He was a child, probably no older than fourteen. Curls of strawberry blond hair fell into his round face, which he dusted out of his fawn brown eyes as he stopped beside Herlinde. "Already done, Madame Herlinde? That was quick."

"Not yet. Friedrich has misplaced our parcel."

"I have not!"

Herlinde ignored her trunk's adamant reply. "Your Majesty, this is one of my assistants, Ozzie. His brother is at home recovering from a violent illness he had the other night."

Lilac held up a hand, pressing the other to her temple. "I'm sorry. I'm— wait. That trunk is your *husband?*"

Herlinde scoffed. "My *ex*-husband."

"We are still married," Friedrich spat.

"We haven't gotten around to annulling it yet, but I for one was never eager to bring him king's bench. I call him my ex-husband because he's no longer a person."

Lilac looked upon Friedrich in horror, somehow deeply bothered that something with such a disproportionately large mouth and tiny feet lacked eyes. She remembered Garin's story at his feast. "You turned him into a chest?"

"No, he did it to himself in an unfortunate accident. I was forced to bring him along when we fled our homeland."

"They do work well together, at least," offered Ozzie.

"He helps me with my dress craft, I dust cobwebs off of him every few weeks. It is a fine business exchange."

There was a choking sound then. Friedrich was coughing. He shuddered, his lid shutting then bouncing half open. He shut again—and when he opened a second time, the lid flung all the way back. Out flew a large bundle wrapped in cloth, secured with a thick white ribbon.

It landed right in Herlinde's arms. "There we are!"

"Swell!" Ozzie grinned. "Is that Her Majesty's wedding gown?"

"It is. A pair of lace gloves and a veil to match." Herlinde handed the bundle to her eager assistant. "No one unfolds it or takes it out of its package until your wedding day. Understand?"

Lilac's throat was dry, a surge of nerves and mixed feelings leaving a too-bitter taste in her mouth. "Herlinde, how were you able to craft this in time?"

"I've been doing this for many years. I come from a long line of haberdashers and dressmakers alike, gifted in Alteration and other minor branches of magic. We've helped everyone from royalty to neighboring townsfolk, and specialize in making others feel their very best on any occasion. Plus, a little magic doesn't hurt."

Lilac watched in awe as Herlinde rummaged again in the now-silent Friedrich. "I don't know what to say. How much do I owe you?" John was nowhere to be seen outside. "I'll have my treasurer contact you."

"Nonsense." Herlinde yanked out another bundle of material and unfolded it. "A dear friend of mine told me this belongs to you."

Lilac made to object but trailed off. It was a wrinkled blue kirtle, the one she'd left in her cell in Garin's bedchamber at the Sanguine Mine.

"Now that I've got your measurements jotted down at the shop, I can craft any fineries or armor you might need. Any at all, once we return from our coastal excursion out west, that is." She winked at Lilac and laid the kirtle atop the bundle in Ozzie's arms.

Out west.

Her kingdom's most frequented ports were out of the northern towns. She supposed popular trading routes shifted every year; nothing about that was out of the ordinary. There could be some out west with the changing seasons, perhaps out of Brest or one of the bays. But warmer weather afforded a diversity of trade routes north this particular time of year, didn't it? The reduced risk of sea ice at the docks made for optimal conditions.

And really, none of that mattered for someone ordering a wardrobe overhaul of enchanted garments from the Hemlock Haberdashery. The order must've been extensive if Herlinde was willing to hand all her premade pieces to her friends and Marguerite, and accept nothing in exchange for a custom made wedding gown. Likely, they were a *private* client hiring a contracted maritime merchant.

And what other naval trader not sanctioned by her or her father would boast various kinds of tender? Paper money was rare, a foreign commodity of distant kingdoms.

Lilac stared at Herlinde, then her trunk of a husband, several things clicking into place at once.

"Very well. No time shall be wasted." Herlinde returned Lilac's look with a friendly smile and craned her head. "Do you have anyone who could take these up for you?"

"We will." They turned to see Yanna and Isabel emerging from the western corridor. Their hair escaped their buns in frazzled tendrils, their faces bright pink from the sun. "Her Grace sent us in to see if you needed help."

"We have heard so much about you," added Isabel before Yanna elbowed her.

"Ah, some of Madame Toranaga's friends!" Herlinde's eyes brightened. "I recognize you."

They both smiled and curtsied.

"Have you seen Sir Albrecht?" Lilac blurted. "Outside, anywhere?"

Isabel shook her head. "We've only been in the courtyard assisting the others with a game of cricket."

Herlinde poked Ozzie, who then handed the bundle and dress to Yanna. "Yes, where is this emissary, Your Majesty?"

"Now that you mention it," Yanna added, "I haven't seen him all day. Not since this morning, when he left with that horrid Agnes. They were searching for Ambrosius, weren't they?"

"Agnes the Baroness?" Herlinde eyed Lilac sidelong. "Where would they have gone off to?"

Isabel's fingers went to her mouth. "You don't think they've—"

A loud bang startled everyone, causing them to jump. It sounded like it came from the rear of the keep, near the northern wing. The guard at the door started forward, but Lilac beat him to it.

"Stay," Lilac commanded, leaving Yanna clutching her wedding gown,

Isabel clutching Yanna—and a rightly concerned-looking Herline and Ozzie frozen in place. "All of you."

Without explanation, Lilac took off. There was something wrong, she could feel it. Because she couldn't feel *him*, his closeness—his pulsing proximity she'd grown used to. In his confirmed absence, the dread in her chest had only worsened.

There were shouting and footsteps, then; Yanna was there, panting, Isabel close behind and glancing nervously back at the foyer. Herlinde could be heard speaking urgently, presumedly to Ozzie or the guard—or the several members of her staff probably roused from a mid-morning nap.

"I told you to stay," Lilac said hurriedly.

"What are you going to do, fire us?" Yanna peered at the doors in scrutiny. "What was that sound?"

Nothing seemed out of place in the corridor—save for the person-sized hole leading to the armory—until one of the guest quarters on the left burst open. Myrddin stumbled out, a thick trail of smoke billowing behind him.

He looked startled to see her, his hair flat against his head and his robe hanging half off, as if he'd been in a wind tunnel. "Your Majesty, thank goodness, you—"

Lilac shoved him back into the room; she hadn't meant to do it that hard, but his body flew several feet into the air before landing near the hearth.

"*Lilac*," Yanna shrieked, trailing her into the double guest bed chamber. "What's gotten into you?"

"Vampires," Myrddin wheezed, clutching his chest. "Specifically, a volatile one that transferred some of his power to her the moment she enthralled herself to him."

Yanna's disgusted gasp was lost to the distant, echoing sound of Marguerite's and her friends' laughter.

Lilac leaped forward, pouncing upon Myrddin before he could sit up again. "I need your help," she begged, the front of his robes in her fists as she turned back to the bewildered sisters. "Leave. Lie for me. Tell them that all is well and Garin's been in his chamber recovering the whole time, that we're tending to him."

"*Garin?*" Yanna said, refusing to move. "What is a Garin?"

Isabel remained in the hall, terror stricken upon her face; the voices grew louder, Herlinde's blending in with the rest.

Lilac cursed herself. "Albrecht, I meant to say. Sir Albrecht. Please, do this for me."

Yanna stomped toward the door and shoved the bundle and dress into Isabel's arms. "Go. Now, Izzy."

Isabel blanched but nodded, departing with an uneasy glance.

Then, Yanna shut the door, sliding the lock in place and slowly pacing to the opposite side of the room. She didn't say anything else, didn't prod further, but it was painstakingly clear she would not leave.

The room was simple, similar to the handmaidens' quarters but more spacious; it consisted of a hearth in the center wall, and simple wooden beds against the far left and right sides of the room, storage trunks at the foot of each. Garin's bed on the right was made, but the blankets were slightly dented in the center, as if he'd laid there contemplating without the intention of sleep.

Myrddin's was a mess of covers, a pillow hanging halfway off the bed. There was a garment on the floor that caught her eye, crumpled beneath his own velvet cloak hanging on the end post. Lilac wouldn't have paid it any mind, but she recognized the red blazer from last night.

"*Rupert?*" She hadn't noticed Myrddin had shimmied from her grasp.

He turned the color of the coat. "The night was stressful. It was a one-time thing," the warlock stammered. "You don't... you don't fancy him, do you?"

"No, of course not."

"If you did, Garin would have his way with him, anyway," he said, seeming eager to steer from the topic of him and Rupert. "Especially with how this bond has changed him."

"Where is he?"

In answer, the warlock's eyes flitted over her shoulder to Yanna. "Your servant, Your Majesty."

"My name is Yanna," her handmaiden snapped, tromping over. "And you should answer Her Majesty."

"Leave," Lilac said, whirling on her. "I don't need your help."

"It looks like you do. You're interrogating Albrecht's valet. You threw him across the room." Yanna sneered at both of them, her panicked countenance still so lethal that Myrddin flinched. "*Who* is *Garin?*"

"He's the leader of the Brocéliande vampire coven, to whom your queen enthralled herself just nights ago. He is also your emissary." Myrddin pressed a hand to his chest. "And I am Myrddin. Still a warlock—a warlock and sorcerer, technically."

Whatever answer Yanna had anticipated, this didn't seem to be it. Her hands shot to her face, anger more than shock flitting across it.

There was a *pop* and overwhelming aroma of black powder, especially pungent this time—the outline of the door burning bright violet before fading. "*Just in case*," muttered Myrddin.

Yanna's voice was scarily quiet. "Was there ever a proposition from Maximilian? Was my Gwendal always doomed?"

"Yes, there was an emissary sent from Vienna to proposition me." Lilac reluctantly faced her, fuming and guilt-ridden. "The truth is, Gwendal was doomed the moment he decided to join the guard of an incompetent king and his corrupt men. It will remain so unless I am allowed to intervene. Otherwise, they all volunteered for their certain deaths." The room was silent, the castle outside eerily still. "Do you feel better knowing the truth?"

Yanna swallowed, her eyes brimming with moisture. "I-if Garin is acting as emissary, then where is the man Maximilian sent?"

"I—"

Myrddin chuckled, motioning vaguely. "At the bottom of the Argent River, the meat picked off his bones by now."

Slowly, Lilac turned to him, eyes wild. Whether he was serious was anyone's guess; she didn't put anything past Garin at this point.

The warlock shrugged, but Lilac gripped him by the robes and slammed him against the wall beside the fireplace. "*Where is he?* Garin, where is he?" Her hand found his throat.

"I don't know!" Myrddin gargled.

Lilac slipped her dagger from her skirts. "Tell me."

Yanna let out a disgraceful sound of protest, rushing over to them. "You're crazy, let him go—"

"Where?" Lilac snarled, pressing the flat edge to his throat.

"I came to tell you," Myrddin hissed, "that he wasn't outside. I couldn't
—*find*—*him*."

"Then you'll bring me to him." She angled the blade, nicking his collarbone and drawing blood.

His lake blue eyes bulged in fear. "You know I'm immortal. I come
back, every time."

Lilac brought her lips to his ear. "It'll take you a while if I slit you at the
middle and start roasting your innards over that fire."

"Fair." Myrddin gulped and spoke hurriedly. "I brought Bastion and
Piper to the edge of the path, watched them disappear into the treeline. I
had a look in the bailey then, and couldn't find him. Cast a quick tracking
spell and my Lacewing tugged me east. But I can't teleport—"

Lilac plucked the blade from Myrddin before sinking it into his neck,
warmth spreading across her fingers; as she withdrew the dagger and
stepped back, some of the blood splattered her chest and chin.

"*Fuck this*," Yanna screeched, and there was the jiggling sound of the
doorknob being strangled. "Help me! Let me out!"

"Garin was right. You..." Myrddin sputtered on his blood, wheezing,
gripping his neck and cursing until he dropped to his knees. "Are a
marvelously ruthless creature." Then, he went pale and fell face first onto
the stone floor.

Within seconds, his body stopped convulsing altogether, a large pool of
red spreading rapidly beneath him.

"Is he really dead?" asked Yanna, trembling.

Lilac nudged his shoulder with her boot, once. Then twice. She wiped
the warm blood drops from her face and resheathed her dagger. "Not for
long."

"*God*. Oh gods, help me," Myrddin gasped. His back finally inflated,
rising as the warlock sucked in a sputtering breath. "You." He turned his
head to sneer up at them. "Really?"

Lilac bent and gripped him by the collar, lifting him all the way to his
feet. "Take me to him. Now."

"How, when I don't know where he is? He didn't tell me anything, only
to keep watch over you."

"You said that when you teleport into a building or structure, you can only teleport to a person's location. Doesn't it work that way regardless of where he is?"

"I can only do it with certainty when I'm sure my tethered person is at that location, or in that building. The world is much too vast." His hand ran over his face. "Your Majesty, it's harder for me to do if I don't know *where* he is—there's no promise we'd end up at his side. We could end up on the rooftop of a neighboring establishment, or in the middle of someone's hearth in the next town over. We could land in a volcano, or worse—become separated."

"I'll take the chance. I believe in your magic, however it works. I believe in you."

He glanced at her in incredulous warning. "Out of all the terrible decisions you've made, that is by far the worst one."

Lilac hated the desperation that had overcome her. She could be wrong this time, but she hadn't been the last, when she'd found him trapped by his own hunger at the brothel. The pull was undeniable. Garin needed her—needed help. She felt like she'd explode if they didn't go.

Lilac gritted her teeth and released him. "Fine. I'll leave on foot."

"You will *not*."

There was a knock at the door, causing Yanna to jump and scuttle further into the room, her hands clamped over her mouth.

It was her mother. "Lilac!"

Another knock. A guard's rough voice this time. "Open the door!"

Myrddin began to whisper frantically, a forlorn prayer to the arcane gods that had long abandoned him. "Modron, help me, I am surrounded by beautiful, terrifying women and a vampire who would delight in painting the trees in my blood for all of eternity if this goes wrong."

Heart shattering her ribcage, Lilac held her hand out, bracing herself for the unpleasant sensation.

Myrddin grimaced, true doubt in his eyes. There was pressure at her palm, and the floor disappeared from under them as they were whisked away in shadow and smoke.

They stopped spinning, and she went careening sideways. Lilac splayed her arms out in front of her, only for her shoulders to slam against something rough and wide. She landed back on her ass, her head and shoulder knocking against Myrddin.

"My god," she groaned, fixing her skirts and shoving off him. They were outdoors—in the shade, a cool breeze whipping around them, bringing with it a strange, unpleasant aroma.

Against her, Myrddin was dead still. Her heart dropped. *Had he been knocked unconscious?*

"Lilac?" Myrddin's voice came from off in the distance.

Dizzy, Lilac staggered to her feet. Something was wrong, very wrong. They were in the woods, illuminated by the deepening sunlight of approaching dusk.

Panting, the warlock emerged from behind a birch trunk not twenty paces away, coughing and dusting himself off as he approached her. "That was much further than I'm used to."

Then, he froze as he laid eyes on Lilac.

No, at her feet. She glanced down at the shoulder she'd landed against and nearly lost her footing. Her stomach roiled, threatening to loosen itself.

It was a pile of bodies—a torso, remnants of its head scattered nearby. Another beside it, his head intact but his torso crumpled in on itself.

She opened her mouth to scream, but was cut off by a high-pitched wail.

It was Yanna.

Lilac stepped out from behind the tree. They were several yards inside the treeline, the grass within and outside the forest border *littered* with bodies. Human bodies—armored corpses—maybe thirty of them, scattered among the bluebells stained in red. It looked like thirty, though there were probably more.

French and Breton alike, dead or on the verge of it.

Most of them were of the opposing party, some headless with a clean cut while others still had their heads intact but their throats and ribcages had been ripped open. Lilac put a hand to her mouth, speechless in her horror.

Yanna had moved; she was several feet away, crouched just in the shadows, picking her way over the bodies. She sobbed as she touched some of them, the ones with her guards' plain uniform of leather and metals. Trembling, Yanna sniffled and grabbed one that laid face down, shifting to turn him over.

"Yanna," Lilac said, her own voice a broken sob as Myrddin watched helplessly, his fingers intertwined above his head.

"Gwendal," called Yanna. "Oh, Gwendal. Please, please…" She shook her head vehemently and heaved—the dead man flopped over, an oozing *bullet hole* in his forehead. Yanna cried out in a mixture of horror and relief at the sight of his features, stumbling back into Lilac. She caught Yanna under the arms and steadied her.

The forest edge overlooked a lush, grassy knoll covered in casings and blades among the wildflowers, guts, and blood. Between the bodies lay scattered swords and muskets, some still in-hand.

muskets.

They were a new advancement. Her father had a couple prized pieces in their armory that he'd used for hunting last winter—one, a gift from one of his earls, the other from a foreign king, but her own armies were never supplied with them.

A pair of hands clamped onto her shoulder and mouth; Lilac struggled against the warlock's hold, but he held tight as she clung to Yanna, who'd slumped into shoulder-tremoring sobs in Lilac's arms.

"*There's someone still here,*" whispered Myrddin, tugging them back into the shadows.

He was right. There was rustling near, on the outskirts of the treeline— and more noise, she realized, between her own labored breaths. Voices and rustling. The restless whinny of horses and clomping of hooves.

Someone was shouting in the near distance.

"Albrecht!" It was Henri. Her father's broken voice, somewhere between a somber moan and a wail. "*Albrecht!*"

Lilac's heart thundered in her ribcage. Yanna turned her head to them, her eyes terrified and questioning, but Lilac slowly shook her head.

Henri's calls were met with silence.

"He left, Your Grace," said someone else. One of their guards. His voice shook so hard, Lilac could barely understand him. "Was that Maximilian's emissary?"

"Yes." A quiet sob from her father. "Yes, it was."

"He was—w-was a monster—"

"He spared us," Henri spat, sounding broken with disbelief. "*Saved* us."

"Are you all right, Your Grace?" asked another guard. "Did you get hit?"

"No. No—get off of me!"

There was another beat of silence, followed by labored breathing.

Then, the second voice again. "He got shot, didn't he?"

"Twice," said Henri. "It didn't stop him."

"*Ma Doue*," said the first guard. "Thirty men. Just like that."

There was a muffled sound—a high-pitched moaning at Lilac's feet, making all of three of them jump. It was one of the two bodies, presumably the one with its head still intact. Blood soaked the ground beneath their boots; the sound wasn't a cry for help. It was the last broken sound his body could manage. A cry begging for the end.

There was movement, closer now. "Hello?" one of Henri's guards fearfully called out. "Do you hear that?"

"Can you glamor us, Myrddin?" whispered Lilac. "Make us invisible?"

"Not with them this close. Not with them already looking this way. Plis, I feel my arcana growing fatigued. I don't want to waste it if I have to get us out of here fast."

Lilac looked down and spotted the rapier handle her heel rested against. She grabbed it, prying the handle from the man's still-warm fingers. He whined again at her touch, this time louder. She held her breath and placed the tip against the middle of his back, forcing herself to think of the chateau courtyard and sitting upon the warm grass with Piper, counting the ducks and clouds as she exhaled—and sank the blade into him. All the way through.

His moaning tapering off.

Despite the abrupt ceasing of the man's wailing, it didn't seem anyone in her father's party was willing to go see what it was.

"Don't mind the dying. Say nothing of this," Henri demanded. He sounded nearby, just outside the trees. "*Nothing*. Understood?"

The other voices murmured in agreement.

Henri grunted, and she knew from the sound he had mounted his horse. "We'll head back and arm the castle. Mark it, the forests just northwest of Montfort-sur-Meu on the map."

"Yes, sir."

Henri cussed into the wind. "Barnabaz, ride into town to warn them, then head to Rennes and do the same. Right away. Cadwethen and I will go back to the castle, where we'll ready the ceremony and send word to Austria."

Lilac's stomach dropped. Her ceremony wasn't for another two days. More guests would start arriving between tomorrow eve and the morning of her coronation.

"But what of the festivities?" said Barnabaz.

"Has she officially accepted?" Cadwethen asked, sounding shocked.

"It doesn't matter. François will eventually send more and more of his men."

"Sir," Barnabaz said. "Might I rally the towns' militias? I can direct them to the castle."

"There's no time. I imagine these soldiers were headed for Rennes with an ambush planned. Paimpont is next. Then, the chateau—then, the coast. They won't stop. We only have enough time as it takes for them to realize their leading frontline have been torn apart. We don't have enough bodies to protect the towns, *and* aid in our preparation. They'll have to hold their own."

"Maximilian won't send his men for us until Lilac is married," said Barnabaz gruffly. "It'll take weeks."

"I *know* what he will and won't do. What matters is that she is his husband—the moment it happens, that and that alone should be enough to dissuade him from advancing. And she will accept his hand if I have the last say." There was a brief silence; the afternoon was mild, but Lilac shook as the finality of her father's affirmation rang through the trees. "Well? Let's not stand here and twiddle our thumbs. We must fortify the castle and alert the others."

"And what of the vampire, Your Grace?"

The three of them waited with bated breath as Henri considered. "He is the least of my concerns," he finally grunted. "For all we know, he and his warlock are on their way back to Vienna. I—I don't know." His voice dropped so low, Lilac strained to hear. "There will be no more public word of Lilac's marriage, the timing of her ceremony or lack thereof, until the ink is dried on paper and any oath is spoken. Do you understand me?"

"Yes, sir," they answered in unison.

"Good. Onward."

Then, they were off.

No one dared speak a word; Lilac's shoes were soaked in warm blood, and they didn't move a muscle until the sound of Henri's and Cadwethen's voices and the pounding of hooves were heard no longer.

She peeked around the trunk and watched her father and his companion gallop past the distant dip in the hill.

"We have to find him," Lilac said, picking her way over the corpses, wiping her brow and probably smearing Myrddin's and the stranger's blood further. "Garin's injured."

"He will heal, as he does from all mortal wounds," said Myrddin lightly. "Your Majesty, shouldn't we return to meet your father?"

She glanced over her shoulder, leading them out of the trees. "He needs our help. Something's not right."

They emerged, overlooking a vast swath of hilled moor. The sun would set soon, and while Myrddin's magic could surely take care of lighting, they had no indication of where Garin was. According to Henri, they were just outside of Montfort-sur-Meu; Rennes was directly west. Paimpont and the bulk of Brocéliande were just beyond that—a few hours' travel southward on a galloping steed.

Garin was probably headed back in that direction, but there was no way to be sure. Dread tore at her insides. She'd never felt so lost. With France encroaching, they needed to find him. They needed to move.

"Can we try again? Can you teleport one more time?"

Myrddin gave Lilac a worried grimace. "I can try, but it may not work and it definitely won't feel good. I haven't teleported this many times in a day, let alone the week, for a *very* long time. I'm afraid of throwing us even further off path without ample rest."

Sniffling, Yanna faced the moor, her hands shielding her eyes from the dying sun. "Is that... Albrecht's horse?" She frowned. "Garin's horse?"

Lilac spun. Galloping at them at full speed—surely faster than she'd seen any steed move—was Loïg. As he neared they exchanged glances; Yanna nervously backed out of the way and Myrddin watched, open-mouthed.

Loïg slowed to a trot, then came to rest before them.

It looked like an apparition, shrouded in a layer of dark mist floating just above his coat, following him with every movement.

"Mother Modron," Myrddin cried.

Loïg dipped his head, bowing before them.

"This is my horse. Garin gifted it to me for my birthday." Breathless, Lilac couldn't help but laugh out loud, moisture welling in her eyes. "I can't believe you're here," she whispered. Cautiously, she reached a hand up to stroke the steed's snout; the moment her hand made contact, the dark mist lessened in the fading sunlight. He was not an apparition, but she was certain, more than anything, that he was magic.

Loïg remained kneeling, as if encouraging them to mount.

Incredulous, Lilac rounded Loïg and stepped into the stirrup, lifting herself onto him gracefully. She held a hand down for Yanna, who stood frozen in place, watching the horse warily. "He's safe. I promise."

Yanna looked like she didn't know whether to sob or laugh. She wiped her eyes and turned back to face the field of bodies, hesitant. "He isn't here. His body isn't here."

"He must be safe, then," Lilac said reassuringly, hoping it was true. "You will be reunited with him. We *will* find him, but for now, I can't leave you here. I won't."

With one last parting glance, Yanna scowled and crammed her foot in the stirrup while taking Lilac's hand. She cursed violently under her breath as she made herself comfortable behind her.

"Did you summon him for me, Myrddin?" Lilac asked as Yanna held her hand out to him.

"No, but I think you did." Myrddin cocked his head and slowly, with his hands out as if to show the creature he was harmless, made his way to the back. "Where did Garin say he got this horse again?"

"He didn't."

Myrddin grunted dubiously as he lifted himself with both of their help and settled in behind Yanna.

Mesmerized, Lilac ran her hand along Loïg's striking black mane, the strange dark ether rising off of him swirling at her fingertips in the deep afternoon sun. "Where did you come from, and how did you know where to find us?"

"Whatever it is, it's tied to you. Do you even know how to steer a horse? Magic, or no?" Myrddin asked.

"I don't." Garin must have mentioned it to them. Her heart sank, but adrenaline pulsed through her now. She would either learn or figure out a way. "Do you?"

"Why would I need to learn if I've been able to teleport my whole life?"

She ignored him, a glimmer of hope spreading through her as she stroked the horse's mane and down to the intricately woven and sturdy saddle. There was a thick rope attached to his face.

Yanna sighed loudly. "Take the rein just there. Bunch it loosely in your fists. Just there... good. Now, squeeze him with your legs."

Lilac did as she was told.

"Harder."

She did, and nearly lost her balance as Loïg sped up; Myrddin shrieked and held onto Yanna, who grasped for Lilac's middle.

"Whoa," said Yanna, and he eased his pace.

Despite everything, Lilac found herself laughing. She was doing it. Lilac pulled on the reins with her right hand, and Loïg easily pivoted that way. She tugged left, and he did that, too.

Myrddin let out a disgruntled sound as Lilac steered them in a wide, perfect circle atop the knoll. "Why, you're a natural. Garin said you'd need childrens' lessons—how are you doing this?"

"I don't know," shouted Lilac. "I feel I could use some practice. He seems a very mild-mannered, if not completely agreeable, horse."

"For *you*. Garin could barely pet the thing without it trying to take his fingers off. I think you of all people would appreciate knowing vampires are not regenerative and do not grow back any of their appendages."

Loïg snorted, braying as he shook his head back and forth, his regal onyx mane rippling in the wind.

"I wonder..." mused Myrddin as they trotted along in the zig-zag path Lilac drove them into. But he remained quiet, not bothering to tell them what it was he wondered.

"Anyone can ride a horse. It doesn't mean a thing if we don't know where we're going," said Yanna impatiently.

Myrddin began shuffling inside his pockets. "I could whip up a tracking spell if he just slowed down."

There was a tug at her navel again—and not an unpleasant one this time. It was subtle, like a tap on the shoulder. Instinct settling her gut. Lilac leaned toward Loïg's twitching ears. "Bring us to Garin," she whispered, straightening when the wind picked up.

Leaves began to skitter along, dancing forward from the treeline. Some of them were splattered in blood.

Loïg whinnied. Then, they were off.

She screamed and scrambled for the saddle, Yanna and Myrddin cursing and holding on for dear life.

This was the way, back toward Paimpont and the High Forest. She could feel it. Garin had *just* been there. He was alive and near.

Loïg's quick canter turned into a gallop, and all they could do was brace themselves as he took off down the grassy knoll, away from the embers of sun and toward the trees beyond.

32

GARIN

Garin ran west as fast as his feet would carry him in the dying light. He paid no mind to staying hidden—not so much as a single tree shrouded his path. The summer evening air ghosted his palate as he panted through his strides. With each sharp breath, he tried to catch the scents of the butcher or fromagerie, any aroma pointing him toward Paimpont.

The bloodied rapier he'd snatched from one of the bodies and the baldric it hung from jostled at his back. It was nothing like the mildly irritating rattle that came with riding horseback; on foot, each step bounced the blade high enough to deliver bruising smacks against his shoulder. It was an awkward, cumbersome affair, especially with the unconscious armored man he carried on the other.

He'd fled the castle grounds after hastily shoving Agnes's corpse headfirst into one of the rain-filled troughs at the rear of the bailey. No one seemed to patrol the northern gate; it was surrounded too closely by Brocéliande. They'd find the baroness, eventually. Hopefully before she began to decompose.

It hadn't taken much to subdue or entrance her, just a few compliments on her skin-tight bodice and the way her deep auburn curls framed her face in his crooning tone, and she was out like a light. Garin had intended to go into it with pleasant conversation about the weather, but her being unconscious worked well, too. He'd also intended on letting Agnes live, but without the distraction of small talk, thoughts quickly arose of the most hateful way the woman spoke to Lilac.

And so, he just kept drinking. There was a certain thrill that came with doing it in public, tucked away just out of sight while basking in sunlight. He'd even tilted his head back and imagined being at the shore.

He'd then rinsed out the tankard he'd repeatedly bled her into and placed it into her hand. An unfortunate case of too much cider—and, ironically, too little water—in the blazing sun would do that to anyone.

At the front of the bailey, he'd asked one of the passing guards to bring Giles some food; they hadn't had one of their late night sit downs in a couple weeks, but one effect of the prolonged entrancement, Garin had noticed, was that the old priest often forgot to feed himself.

This morning, though, Giles looked surprisingly well. His cheeks were plump, eyes filled with vigor in a way Garin had never seen as the priest lounged in his seat with Bisousig curled his lap. The cat had stretched and pushed herself against Garin's outstretched hand before leaping down and scenting his calves with her little rotund body.

What an insufferably cute creature of misfortune, he'd thought, just as Lilac's anxious scribe burst out of the keep, scroll in-hand. When Garin approached, John muttered about being on his way to the lofts, after which he lamented his critical doubt in the queen's insistence on sending an urgent letter to the King of England by bird.

Garin had held out his hand, pointedly nodding at the parchment John was holding. John passed it to him without question.

His throat had tightened as he'd read the letter, his widening eyes and the fury behind them the only meaningful response he could muster as words failed him. *How had he not known Lilac would attempt to fight the battle on her own?* He'd briefly considered intercepting the note himself, but that consideration was cut short by the clomping of hooves in the distance.

FRUSTRATED, GARIN HAD INSTRUCTED JOHN TO CARRY ON WITH WHAT Lilac had had the *nerve* to request, then climbed the only manned lookout at the gate, took one look at the rider trotting down the path on an unmarked Arabian horse, and then entranced the alarmed guard next to him to fire three clean arrows into the newcomer.

After unseating the rider from his mount, Garin had leaped down and snatched the nondescript horseman's satchel. It hadn't been the Trécessions' usual courier; he could at least tell that much.

Garin had stopped Ivon nearly every day since Lilac had ascended the throne. Some days, there were no letters for her at all, but he'd made it a consistent point to check. On the occasions there were messages for her, few, if any, were ever of any importance. Congratulations on her ascension, a sympathy note or two wishing for Sinclair's swift recovery, all manner of the innocuous drivel favored by the upper echelons.

With those, he'd unentranced the messenger, then sent him on his merry way.

In the week after her ceremony, Garin had fielded several offers for Lilac's hand, and one non-marital business alliance that did *not* please him. None of them did, in hindsight. *At all.* They displeased him so greatly, in fact, that he'd shoved them into his pocket and burned them at his hearth over a bottle of scotch and blood when he got home. He'd told himself it was the right thing to do. And, at the time, it was.

It had only taken him a moment to skim the letter before he was off, bounding through Brocéliande in a northeasterly direction and fighting every firing nerve that told him to turn around, march up those stairs, and *stay*.

But he had to go. To see for himself that France was making a real play for the Breton crown. Why else would Maximilian send the letter he did? Earlier kings had toyed with the idea but never tested it; they might've overtaken the duchies earlier if it weren't for the war that had spanned a century.

Whatever the cause, France had decided the turmoil surrounding Eleanor inheriting her father's kingdom presented a chance to try again. *Cowards*, Garin thought. Little did François know, she was a force on her own, fueled by others' doubt in her and a developing love for her subjects who, in his opinion, did not deserve it. Necessity sharpened her wits; she wasn't above using the blade, bribery, or magic to get what she wanted.

Maximilian was so confident in his offer, he'd sent an emissary to proposition her directly. His decision was *brilliant*. So unsettlingly so, that the waves of relief that had washed over Garin upon learning of it were tainted with a fetid, foaming worry—albeit one that could at least wait to be addressed. Not one king or prince had offered for her to keep her sovereignty the way Maximilian did. Not one of them offered her kingdom their unfaltering protection. He could at least respect the emperor for that.

But then, the queen had to go and enthrall herself to him. The envy he'd intended to drown with the bottle and bury under the code of chivalry was frothing over, and there was nothing Garin could do to stop it.

Garin ran back west through the moors now, cursing the injuries that slowed him. The metal bullets in the meat of his bicep and thigh were lodged deeply enough that his body couldn't heal over them, or so it seemed. The worst of the bleeding had stopped, but each stab of pain that surged with every step strangled his breath. He needed help. He needed blood—blood from the vein. He needed that blasted Madame Kemble. Or Lorietta, or Adelaide. Maybe not Adelaide—she'd too gleefully attempt amputation. He was far away from anyone who could help.

Far from Lilac.

Long ago, he'd vowed to never again interfere with the affairs of mortal nobles, refusing to participate in another war that ravaged so many lives for the pithy honor of rulers who spurned the poor and arcane alike. Tonight proved love made fools of even the most hardened hearts.

Garin slowed to catch his breath as he finally approached the border of the Low Forest on his left, the pale gnarled trees making way for the lush canopy that made up the High Forest. The man's quiet heartbeat was slowing, the rush of his blood struggling to keep up.

He groaned, trying to wipe his hands on his pants. He would have liked to clean himself before arriving at the farmhouse, but there was nothing he could do without a nearby creek that would wash the blood off his hands. Going for a dip in the Morgen-infested Argent was not an option. Blood, innards, and flesh matted his hair and congealed under his nails.

He was drenched in the aftermath of his destruction, and with the guard dying on his shoulder, he had no time to spare.

He hadn't been travelling long after leaving the castle before he caught sight of a group. From what Garin could gather from downwind, there were three men: the former king and two heavily armed guards. He'd trailed them quietly past the moorland and hills, to a forest just north of a small village.

Garin had sensed the enemy even before Henri and his guards had started charging.

He should've let the old king die, but doing so would only encourage François further. He was too stricken with alarm at the possibility of French troops west of Rennes, and acted without thought. The moment Garin heard the first musket being loaded, he knew he'd break his vow to himself.

The soldiers stopped firing when he'd lunged in front of Henri, upon realizing the person their poorly-aimed shots *did* hit showed no signs of slowing.

Garin laid waste to the entire encampment in seconds. Most of Lilac's soldiers there were already dead; it seemed a dozen of them had broken off from their group to scout, and had been ambushed by François's men.

Those who lay on the ground appeared either quite dead or well past the point of no return on the path to it. It came as quite a surprise when a feeble croak burbled from one of them.

"*Yanna.*"

Garin had recognized the name—it was one of Lilac's handmaidens. Her friend, if he could call her that. Without thinking, he'd picked the guard up and slung him over his shoulder before retreating from Henri and his guards.

Garin managed to rouse the man for questioning, but he didn't stay conscious for long. He was just coherent enough to tell him he'd been one of the troops Lilac and her father had sent east. Exhaustion began to take the man as he'd finished his answer, and he'd slumped, unconscious once again, onto Garin's shoulder.

Since news of the skirmishes had broken, Garin had considered travelling to the bordering towns to witness the fights himself. He likely would have gone, had he not been commanded to do Kestrel's bidding and nearly lost Lilac in the process.

Even in his second life, Garin had never killed so many at once. His skin tingled, the muscles of his jaw clenched and twitched, poised to snap. The urge to tear and maim and bite warred with his fraying self-control, setting his teeth to grinding. He'd been careful to avoid the latter until his business at the castle was finished, but he yearned to revel in blood *he* spilled. Feel it running through his powerful fingers and taste it on his tongue, pumping from hot flesh.

He wanted to do it again.

His legs shook as he found a copse of trees to rest under. He placed the man down, being exceptionally gentle with his head and propping his feet up on a fallen log. Then, he wiped his fingers off on a clean patch of his blood-soaked shirt, so as not to stain the letter past legibility.

He slipped it from his pants pocket and read aloud the words that prompted him to leave Lilac's castle in the first place.

"*Dearest Eleanor*," Garin whispered, eyes flying across the parchment so quickly he had to double back at the near-illegible scrawl. "*As it stands, my informants believe François's generals are moving to encroach upon the settlements along your eastern border. Your safety is of great concern to me. Given the difficulty France's location between our kingdoms poses to the task of traveling to you, the chances of me retrieving you myself are decidedly remote.*" Garin scoffed, shaking his head in simmering disbelief. "*I have impressed upon Albrecht that the acceptance or denial of my offer must remain your choice, and it is my hope he is conducting himself accordingly. When and if our union is made with my dear friend in my stead, please send a pigeon right away. As you can understand, my men are prepared to defend your kingdom once our crowns are joined, but not a moment before. Once I receive word, I shall dispatch a fleet of carriages and an army to aid in your defense, and provide any additional accommodations required for your court of up to ten. We stand at the ready.*

It is my hope to see you very soon.

Warmly Yours,

Maximilian."

What little blood flowed through Garin's veins rushed to his head. This wasn't the plan. It hadn't been in his offer. Maximilian, send a *carriage* for her? A fleet of them? What a fool. He'd draw attention. He'd put her at risk.

Part of him knew there was no need to panic. Wherever his forces gathered to start their journey—Vienna, most likely, but it hardly mattered now—there was no way they'd make it, *through* France. Not unless the emperor sent several hundred soldiers to escort them. At that point, the effort would prove fruitless. The terrain was treacherous enough for a small contingent of troops moving discreetly. For an army of that size? One that would be so easily detected?

Impossible.

For now, François's men weren't focused on monitoring France's western borders. They were stealthily positioning themselves along the easternmost forests of Lilac's kingdom, readying for more attacks. Right where Maximilian's people would have to move through. But even if they did make it through France and Brocéliande, they'd have to go through Garin to take her away.

Surely not... Surely there was another way.

His breathing grew labored, his head suddenly light at the thought of Lilac boarding a carriage to be driven through France's enemy territory to Vienna. Garin's gums throbbed, every nerve in his body fired at the thought of *his* thrall—the woman who, in another life, would be *his* bride—becoming a prisoner of war because a cowardly emperor, her *betrothed*, couldn't be bothered to risk retrieving her himself.

Just months ago, Lilac was merely the woman whom Laurent had held on a pedestal, whom his well-meaning sire had warned everyone to watch. Besides considering every now and then how lovely it would be to stroll into the castle and hold her at the end of a blade until Henri agreed to end his cruelty to Daemons, Garin hadn't paid Lilac a single passing thought. To him, she was the hidden girl who could speak to Daemons, nothing more. Before she'd entered his tavern, he hadn't *wanted* to think about the Trécessons or their castle.

When he'd learned her identity at Sinclair's camp, he'd craved her fear. He'd wanted to make her submit, pay for her parents' crimes ten times over. Then, she'd jumped into the Morgen-infested Argent River. Wildly unexpected. And thoroughly intriguing. It had stirred in him the instinct to covet his prey. It was then, he first realized, that the Trécesson princess was not some spoiled heiress who deserved to suffer.

She was his reckoning in the flesh.

It had all been bloody downhill from there. Her parents and their ilk had made not the slightest effort to understand those such as Garin, let alone the world they lived in. Yet, there Lilac had been, badgering him with questions about that very thing. About the creatures in it. About him.

His hunger for Lilac's blood, his craving for her company, became all the more difficult to ignore after Kestrel had set them on a path of fate together at Cinderfell. Garin well understood his duty and the nature of what he'd become. His early yearnings for her were natural, but he hadn't expected the overwhelming urge to ensure her wellbeing. To befriend her and make her laugh. He hadn't expected the need to protect her with his life.

He hadn't expected any of *this*.

Whatever the reason, nothing mattered now, save the unbreakable, diamond-hard certainty in his heart that no one could love her, treat her, protect her like he could. By the time she'd foolishly enthralled herself to him, their bond had only made ignoring what he'd begun to feel for Lilac an utterly futile task. She was bound to him now, in ways she did not understand. He even struggled to comprehend it.

In Garin's days as a fledgling, Laurent had briefed him on the throes of romance and vampirism—told him, as it had proven to be true, how cumbersome and even deadly it could turn in the hands of a creature who wielded such an unnatural lust for the living.

For ownership and grasping, gnawing possession.

He'd known for decades the vampiric matrimony was something he'd refuse to entertain, much less ever pursue. He'd known without the shadow of a doubt he'd never do it to Lilac after skimming the pages of that blasted vampire manuscript at the castle—and what little he'd bothered to read of *The Histories of the Lasting Night* before chucking it into the Argent after the accident, when Lilac laid bleeding from the inside out. It had shook him to his core.

He then knew he'd made a mistake. He had a name for the Sanguine matrimonial rite: the Blood Vow. Something he could research, pour over. Allow to consume him like flame to straw.

He would never subject anyone he cared for to it, much less the woman he loved. Much less the last and *only* woman he'd love.

But he also knew, deep down, the heart-rending truth.

Lilac is the only woman I'd ever offer that to.

Garin crumpled the note until it was pulverized in his fists, opened his hand, and let the pieces scatter to the wind. He hoisted the man back onto his shoulder and pivoted south.

33

GARIN

The sky was awash in blood by the time he entered the Paimpont farmlands from the north. He emerged from the trees, storming to his destination, blinded by rage. A warm breeze struck him the moment his view was clear of leaves and branches. It carried with it a most peculiar bouquet of scents: The refined, perfumed rosewood and walnut woodcraft from the castle. Polished hawthorn.

Lilac's little friend, Rupert.

Garin was delirious from his hunger, and the pained throbbing of his limbs only thickened the fog settling in his mind. He had considered— several times—stopping to bleed the unconscious man into his mouth. It would have been a convenient snack. *Revitalizing.* And it wasn't as though the man would've noticed; he wasn't waking anytime soon. If ever. Why waste the blood? What was left of it, anyway. But Garin had pushed on.

For some deeply vexing reason, his desire to get the man some sort of help won out over his thirst. The man would bleed out without the proper care—which Garin had reluctantly concluded did *not* involve further exsanguination for the purposes of slaking vampiric thirst—and if he'd belonged to Lilac's handmaiden, it was just as well, if rather bothersome, that seeing to this soldier's recovery should fall to him. There was nothing for it but to carry that responsibility out now. At the very least, he could finally get the man off his damned shoulders. Maybe then he could see about getting back to the castle. He was eager to return.

Frowning, he looked down on his parents' sloping land. Through the red-orange haze of dusk, he wasn't quite sure *what* he was viewing. Garin's feet carried him down the hill, through barren wheat fields. Many, many summers ago, they had been lush berry patches tended by an old neighbor, Mrs. Botrel. She'd pick from them to make fruit baskets and had gifted several to his mother through the years. But for a few more enduring features nearby—an oddly shaped rock formation, the gentle, familiar hill it sat upon—the fields were just as he'd left it.

The rear windows of his home were aglow. Normally, the bales of hay and loose stacks yet to be bundled would have obscured the light coming from inside. Not tonight; they'd been moved to the right of the house, sitting to his left. It looked like dirt had been loosened. Garin frowned. The scene resembled preparations for a harvest. Behind the house, though?

Rearranging the farm was common enough practice. But if that was what they were doing, they were doing it months too early.

And... celebrating it?

Laughter and jeers carried through the open window, accompanied by the clinking of glasses.

Two large rugs of some sort swung on a beam in the wind, just beyond the garden. Garin slowed and rubbed his eyes, squinting. Large sacks? Something to dry? Or ferment, maybe? Animals? Pelt?

Garin stumbled, nearly toppling over as the ache in his thigh flared. He groaned and caught himself as he fell to his knees, narrowly avoiding landing flat on his face. His arm burned under the weight of the guard. Dragging himself to his feet, he made his way down the hill, slowly, lest the silhouette he was casting draw unwanted attention.

As the pang of realization hit him, disbelief was the only thing that kept him going.

A pair of horse drawn carriages were parked on the opposite side of the house, one appearing to be a storage cart, and the other, a commoner's carriage.

He approached the makeshift gallows just to the right of the front windows and placed the man down between the nearest hay stacks before removing his baldric—then his coat. Fingers trembling, Garin laid it upon him, covering the man from the breastplate down.

Wordlessly, he slipped Sable out of her noose, hoisting her gently. Her body was slightly warm, but her heart was still.

Memories of returning from the apothecary assaulted him, making him shiver uncontrollably. Garin's mother had asked him to meet her there. She hadn't shown.

Unlike Sable's, Aimee's body had been deathly cold by the time Garin discovered her.

He blinked the memories away and placed the old woman on the swaying grass, laying the back of his hand against her neck to confirm what his other senses had already told him. Then, he removed Jeanare, laying him alongside his wife.

There were several farms here; his was the smallest and most cramped, flanked closely to the south and to the west by larger properties. Yet, none of the residents had come to Sable or Jeanare's aid. They hadn't noticed—hadn't heard the fight they must've put up.

Humans were selfish creatures by default. But—but *how could no one have heard them?* How could no one have noticed them? Bodies, swinging in the wind.

Haunted, Garin stroked Sable's cheek once more, squeezed Jeanare's limp hand, and staggered to his feet.

There was a man watching from the doorway, his face illuminated by two oil lamps, one on each side of the railing.

"Come to join our festivities?" asked Artus.

Garin strode up the porch steps and braced himself against the pillar.

Artus stood there, unarmed. No weapons, no stakes. Behind him, the house was *crowded* with people, men and women alike. Twenty at least, most of them recognizable from his hunting troupe at The Jaunty Hog. They were in his parlor, slipping in and out of the west wing. In his pantry and kitchen, spilling into the entry hall behind him. They'd even broken into the buttery, several of them passing bottles and stoneware around.

Garin's voice was barely audible. "What have you done?"

Unconcerned, Artus squinted past him at the bodies in the grass. "They were marked for investigation weeks ago when the head of Henri's guard went missing. This was the last house Renald reportedly checked."

"You *murderer*. You don't have the grounds to investigate."

Just then, a pair of familiar faces emerged from the west hall, snickering until they laid eyes on Garin. Brient doubled back at the sight of him and nudged Hamon in the ribs, but Artus held a finger up. They quieted, but remained to watch.

"Oh, the irony. With my son gone and grandson wracked with hysteria, you'd be surprised by what grounds I do hold."

"They were innocent!" Garin snarled. "They had the right to due process under Trécesson law."

"Not if we found evidence of past doubt. On the same night Renald disappeared, there were reports of a brush fire on the hill out back." Artus reached into his back pocket and held out three blackened pieces of jewelry. A brooch and two heavy rings, one on a chain. "My men found this on a partially burned corpse in a nearby shallow grave. His family identified him that way."

"That doesn't mean they were guilty."

"And how would you know? You didn't *know* them, did you, vampire?"

At this, everyone within earshot went quiet. "Vampire, sir?" stammered Brient. "But t-that's the emissary."

Artus leaned against the doorway, cocking his head back at the town butcher. "Emissary?"

"The emissary that's come to proposition Lilac for the emperor," said Hamon. "The one that caused the commotion last night, remember?"

Artus's eyes narrowed, darkening with recognition. "The vampire is a creature of eternal pretense, my friends. A thinly veiled shroud, masquerading as many things. A good man. A faithful citizen, loyal friend. A devoted and capable lover, even." He pointed a trembling finger at Garin. "He is none of those things, but a cursed mockery of life. Certainly no one important. Not man, nor emissary."

Garin marched into his house—or, tried to. His face cracked off of thin air.

Artus watched gleefully as Garin growled, using his palm to straighten his nose. Brient and Hamon laughed, stunned. Several others began to murmur nervously behind them, but Artus shushed them. "We're safe. See?"

Garin retreated several steps and hurled himself at the open door. His shoulder slammed against the solid, invisible force. Heaving, he grabbed the frame of the door, and a fistful of wood came away easily, but his fingernails scraped against the invisible barrier when they reached the perimeter of the house. He pulled his hands away; some of his nails cracked to the bed.

Garin roared and stuck them in his mouth.

Calmly, Artus returned the jewelry to his trousers and reached into his coat pocket. He pulled out a faded piece of parchment, folded at the middle.

Even if he'd never laid eyes on it, Garin knew what it was before Artus even began reading.

"*On this day 1338, under the Chief Lord of the Fee, His Majesty John IV of Brittany and Duke Geoffrey de Penthièvre, this property at the northwesternmost corner of the Paimpont Farmlands falls under the ownership of Pascal Trevelyan of Cornwall.*" Artus looked up, his eyes twinkling. "Funny little parcel I found just outside the Jaunty Hog. Picked it up off the street after witnessing a couple ruffians get thrown out into the square."

The crowd behind him gathered. Garin's stomach knotted, dread poisoning him. He'd forgotten all about the envelope Sable had slipped him when they'd first left the inn, and had been too distracted with suppressing his fury after watching Lilac nearly get mauled to death by that revenant.

But this didn't make any sense; he didn't understand—he'd had access to the property all these years, hadn't he? He'd had it when he and Lilac had taken shelter there. "Physical possession of the deed doesn't mean anything."

"Ah, but it does when there is no heir named. All this time, the deed remained on the premises, likely within your father's belongings."

Pascal's box beneath the floorboards.

"By the time this farmhouse's first set of owners died," Artus continued gleefully, "the deed was never signed by their son. The magistrate never possessed the property, as it should have been. Many things were missed during the ongoing war, you see. So, all these years, whether or not it as it was occupied, it belonged to its inhabitants, but remained under the original family's name because of these administrative matters so *poorly* tended to. Until today, after falling vacant due to the most unfortunate circumstance. With no apparent heir, this farmhouse now belongs to the owner of the fief." He turned the parchment toward Garin to show him a fresh stamp and scrawled signature at the bottom, just below Pascal's. "And that owner of the fief, boy, is me."

There was once a time Garin wished to return to his property, before realization of what he'd become had fully struck him. He'd returned one evening, years and years later, when curiosity got the best of him. It was that summer evening he'd met Adelaide, then stayed far away after he'd murdered her family in the parlor.

Garin blinked. All that *blood*.

What would Lori and Adelaide think of him now?

"What's wrong?" Artus's insufferable voice broke his reverie. "All those years antagonizing us and nothing to say for once?"

"Armand is dead and Sinclair was denounced. So were you."

"Poor Francis was so eager to get rid of me over our misunderstanding that he only removed me from his court that night."

"It was no misunderstanding," Garin snarled. "You know what you were trying to do."

"And what would you have cared of it?" Even as Garin towered over him, Artus's gaze was effectively condescending. "Have you ever asked yourself that?"

He remained silent.

"Francis demanded I leave the castle, but no one stripped me of my title on paper. He told me he could not stand to see me, but deep down, he must've known executing me or anyone in my lineage would become a *very* public affair, giving France another one of many reasons to engage in a war that would inevitably crush his puny kingdom. So, he merely banished me. Quietly and swiftly." His smile grew knowing. "You remember that fateful night, now, don't you?"

Garin refused to allow the unbearable memory of the eve of the Ermengarde trial to resurface. He stepped to the door, placing his palms flat against the threshold. "You have no claim to my parents' land, Artus."

"Oh, but I do. It is your own law that prevents your entry. I am but a man." Artus chuckled. "A man you cannot get to. The magic speaks for itself." He stepped back into the house, hardly hobbling as he'd pretended to at the Jaunty Hog. "How funny, the very magic that keeps your unnatural heart beating."

The crowd parted for someone shuffling through, then. Bog appeared, eyes glassy, shoving Hamon aside. The tavern owner stumbled and grinned at the sight of him; a bravado, Garin could tell, from Bog's hammering heart. His fangs began to throb. How he'd love to stoke that sweet-smelling fear.

Someone else bumped into Bog from behind, followed by the sound of shattering glass.

"Sorry," the man muttered, emerging next to him.

He was nearly a foot taller than Bog. Broad shoulders and an irritatingly open if not aloof demeanor despite the familiar way his eyes shifted from the murmuring crowd, back to Bog for nervous approval.

Just like Bog's did to Artus.

"You clumsy shit." Bog reached up to slap him on the head, then kicked aside the pieces of the glass Rupert had been carrying.

Rupert was dressed in poorly fitting armor, a dull broadsword at his hip. His determined grimace turned cold at the sight of Garin. Then, seeping realization as his gaze trailed down Garin's body, landing on his blood-soaked sleeve and pant as Bog and Artus watched in silent amusement.

Aloof as Rupert appeared, the recognition in his eyes shifted unexpectedly to alarm. He began to stutter under Garin's heavy-lidded haze. "Erm, he's bleeding. Perhaps we should let him—"

Brient slapped a hand over his mouth. "Don't you dare."

"Oh, that is the last thing you would want to do," said Artus. "Fortunately for us, I'd have to be the one to invite him in."

"But he is in evident distress," Rupert suggested.

Garin's lip twitched. *What a righteous prick.*

"Yes, and blood is the only thing that will soothe him," snapped Bog.

Garin found himself only half paying attention to the bickering that spread throughout the crowd. Rupert was strangely hard to convince of Garin's vampirism for a Daemon hunter's son. He supposed his neutral eye color made it hard to believe, but if they only *knew* how difficult it was to kill with his rapier and hands while his parched mouth ached to be flooded with blood...

Someone was shifting around in the house, lighting the west hall hearth. Garin's vision only sharpened in the deepening nightfall, each and every vein within eyesight painstakingly visible and audible to him. So many to choose from.

There was a crash; Brient had pushed Bog's shoulder, so Bog shoved Brient into the vase table in front of the very window Garin burned his arm through just weeks ago. The scuffle knocked some of the broken pieces of glassware onto the porch.

"You idiots," a sharp-voiced woman shouted from the back of the parlor. "But *how* will we leave for the hunt if he's standing there?"

"He's trapped us," stammered Hamon.

"He has not," shouted Artus. "So long as we're in here, no vampire can enter."

"He is a wolf outside a rabbits' den. We're done for."

The hunt. He could've guessed as much. Garin stared at the familiar wide base and long stem that had rolled to his feet. The pair of his parents' engraved wedding flutes were the most prized things they'd owned. Adelaide's family and Sable and Jeanare had been gracious enough to leave them in the aged aumbry in the kitchen, still visible at the back of the northern hall.

His composure shocked even himself. The result of the pain eating away at his sanity, no doubt. The last fragment of his resolve.

Rupert was staring at him while Bog and Artus continued to argue with the crowd.

"I know you," Garin crooned. He allowed the hunger to seep through his voice, though he wasn't sure it was a choice at this point. His tone was familiar, warm—the very one he'd used to lure a victim away from the crowds when he and Bastion would prowl the towns. "We met the other night, didn't we?"

As Rupert nodded, all Garin could think of was him, trying—and failing—to control Lilac's unruly rhythm. From the table, Garin had eventually combatted his jealousy by eyeing his favorite sweet spot at the base of Lilac's throat, her dizzying scent made all the more intoxicating by her anger and humiliation as they'd traversed the floor.

Right side. Plump blue-green veins.

"Don't listen to him." *Finally*, a delicious drop of fear in Artus's voice.

"Handsome. Strong jawline. Poised stance." Garin shrugged, swallowing the saliva that had accumulated. "The bold walk of a Lord in his own right. A potential knight, one worthy of the favor of the queen."

The bastard had his grandmother's high cheekbones; they reddened as he dipped into a shallow bow. The contusion on his temple was still visible. "We did, My Lord."

"Get him out of here, Bog." A sheen of sweat frosted Artus's forehead. Perhaps he'd realized they could keep a vampire out of its own home all they wanted, but they'd eventually run out of sustenance.

If Garin hadn't had an alliance to secure, he would've reveled in waiting them out. He'd circle the house several times, allowing them to watch from the windows. Maybe he'd climb his mother's trellis, perch quietly onto the roof, and pounce on the first mortal foolish enough to believe he'd left. He'd drink his fill, drag their remains to the porch. Rinse and repeat. He knew, too well, the horrors of waiting for death to come—for the ghosts of his past to catch up to him.

He waited for the gods to smite him, but instead, they'd sent a destroying woman who brought him to his knees. He supposed it was one in the same.

"Let's go, son." Bog tried to insert himself, slipping his arm through Rupert's. "It's not safe."

But Rupert remained in place.

"Right, because taking him on one of your Daemon hunts is? Under *your* wing?" He remembered Rupert's gaze dropping when he'd mentioned his father to Lilac. Garin crossed his arms and glanced between them. "Is this... your first time meeting? Have I interrupted your dear family reunion?"

"I reached out, finally," muttered Bog, seemingly to no one in particular.

Rupert frowned down at him. "I happened across your bar."

"I reached out from across the bar," he replied, far too drunk for a chance at a coherent thought. "Decided my boy was old enough to join in. He came all this way for me."

Garin scoffed, actually affronted. He shouldn't have been surprised. "So he lied to the queen about his duty."

"I was told I'd become Junior Armorer if I brought her the wine and pried about property inheritance law," Rupert blurted, blanching when Artus shot him a deadly glare.

Garin didn't know which was more ridiculous, believing the unspoken rules of vampirism care about a kingdom's shifting legalities, or the thought of Rupert working anywhere near the armory.

Bog spun, relinquishing the battle of tugging Rupert back down the hall. "*I* gave him armor and a weapon. I have prepared him. He is to lead us."

Artus balled a fist and sent it into Bog's ribs. "Shut. The fuck. *Up*."

"Against me?" Garin scoffed, despite the alarming notion of a group this size on a Daemon hunt. "He wouldn't stand a chance. None of you would, but especially him."

Rupert stiffened near the hallway entrance.

"But you *knew* that. He's an academic. Sorbonne, straight into the castle guard after years of travel? No training or experience? Come on, he's too broad for his armor. He's not even got the right scabbard on."

"What are you on about?" Rupert growled, though he thumbed the strap at his chest.

"You were trying to lead Eleanor with your left hand on the dance floor. That's why you looked like the blind leading the blind. Your left hand is dominant."

Rupert snarled to hide a grimace. "Your point?"

"Your scabbard hangs on your left. You'll have to switch hands or draw with your right, already a costly second in sword combat. That blade there is at least two decades old, if not older than yourself, and hasn't been sharpened in years." Garin passed a hand over his face; he might've actually felt bad for him, had he not played a willing part in Artus's ploy against the queen. "How trained were you in Renald's guard?"

"I received six months."

"Of swordplay? Or a hay bale?"

Rupert didn't answer. Evidently.

Garin stepped back from the threshold, licking his lips. "And that, gentlemen, is what happens when a kingdom operates on the belief that its greatest opponent is a community of species they've worked relentlessly to oppress. Now, you've got a new generation of men unprepared for battle against your own kin."

His comment seemed to strike a soft spot for Artus. "We are not underprepared for either," he spat, as his crowd began to murmur. "Don't listen to him!"

"Why train the towns' militias when annexation under your neighboring crown would grant your and your daughter-in-law's families a place in their court? Especially when you had a hand in Eleanor's downfall. You, stripped of your duties in your time as duke. The Ermengarde scandal and your son's failed role as head of their army? No one noticed all the while, because your family succeeded in turning everyone's attention toward the forests. The Daemons were to blame for their fears and strife. Then, your spineless grandson grew of age. And you knew you had one last chance."

The scum didn't even bother denying it. Garin's accusation didn't seem to rile or shock anyone in the crowd, either. Bog and Rupert remained dead silent.

"*You* are unprepared for France because you were born a traitor, weren't you? And so with Armand and Sinclair. And now that the queen has decided to—" Garin broke off with a shuddering inhale, for the very thought of her at the altar still stole the breath from his lungs. "She has decided to marry Maximilian. What will you do? With knowledge of this potential new alliance, do you think France will bother sparing you? Or your little inn? Or your family's estate?"

Finally, moisture began to well behind Artus's eyes. But it was not enough.

"You're grasping at straws. Did you plan to win the king's approval by the prize of your hunt? He's your only hope, because half the town and forest know by now that your queen has been safe, and shall remain safe in my arms. In my bed."

"You are nothing but her pawn." Artus lurched forward and spat a glob at Garin's feet. "You are nothing. You think she'll make you an equal?"

"I don't want a crown, Artus. I want her." Garin looked pointedly at Rupert, ignoring Artus's murderous glare. He felt almost sorry for Emma's son, for what a spineless father he had—not the fact his dick had been in Lilac's mouth. "That sword and scabbard they gave you would not only hinder your ability in battle." Rupert's trousers were expensive, well-made, and lacked pockets. No other weapon sat on his baldric. "They haven't armed you with one bit of hawthorn, have they?"

Rupert shook his head slowly, helpless as realization sank in.

"You're their sacrifice, Rupert."

Fear flashed across the bastard's face.

Garin exhaled, letting his tensed shoulders droop and his gaze to sharpen. He felt the ancient, Sanguine Magic buried beneath his skin begin to work its way to the surface. "You don't want this. You don't want this life, Rupert. Come to me."

"No!" cried Bog, sobering, watching his son's eyes glaze over.

"I'll have him drag you out, too," Garin snarled at Bog under his breath. He locked eyes with Rupert once more and smiled disarmingly. "Come, friend," Garin commanded, "and use your mighty blade on anyone else who stands in your way."

Lip trembling, Bog jumped at Rupert. His hand went straight for the hilt of Rupert's sword, but Rupert was faster; his son whipped the blade out and slashed at him.

Garin marveled at the clean gash, that stunning shade of ruby dripping from Bog's fingers, leaking onto the floor. Rupert had done so with precise skill under his entrancement, lurching back with a perfect arch of the sword. With his *right* hand, even.

Bog sank against the wall; his wrist and several fingers cut open. As he screamed and the blood spilled, the burn at the back of Garin's throat and the twist at his core increased. Bog was lucky, *so* lucky he was on the other side of that barrier.

"Mathias! Lorenzo!" Artus shrieked, shrinking back as Rupert stalked past.

His long legs brought him forward, through the door and into the night. Garin met no resistance when he plucked the blade from his hands, nor when he gripped Rupert by the back of his shirt, spinning him. He was trembling.

Mathis and Lorenzo had emerged, watching from the hallway, but they'd seemed sobered enough to notice the grim realization of being under a vampire's will.

"Well?" shouted Artus as Bog sniveled beside him. "Don't just stand there!"

"What do you want us to do," shot Mathias, "wrestle him from the brute?"

"I'm not going out there." Lorenzo rubbed his still-bandaged shoulder.

It seemed Brient and Hamon had taken their places following the aftermath of the troupe happening upon the ogre camp west of The Fenfoss Inn, but even the faithful butcher and blacksmith couldn't be found when Garin surveyed the crowd.

He whipped out his rapier and pressed it against Rupert's throat. "Give the deed to me, Artus."

He waited expectantly for Bog to shuffle over and wrestle it from him, but the tavern owner remained against the wall.

"Artus," Bog stammered. "My boy."

Artus's eyes burned with an inhuman hatred. "Do it!"

Garin readied the blade, adjusting the hilt in his palm. He should. The bastard was going to be a waste of a life on their Daemon hunt, and he was now.

He'd make a far better dinner. Garin tossed the rapier aside, peeled his collar down, and—

He heard it before he felt it: the whizz through the air, then the searing pain shooting down his arm. Garin staggered as the arrow landed in the dirt behind them. It only had grazed his bicep, yet the violent jolt of pain mere inches from his bullet wound rocked his entire body.

An archer stood in the hall sandwiched between Artus's bodyguards, clinging to her longbow. Garin immediately recognized her as the elderly woman who'd sat across from him and Lilac at The Jaunty Hog.

"Put it down," Garin demanded from over Rupert's quaking shoulder.

"Do as he says, you old hag," Rupert sobbed.

She ignored their pleas, her weathered fingers fumbling over another hawthorn arrow. "I know you," she said, sneering at Garin. "You killed my neighbor during the Raids. I saw you run out of this house, you coward! My best friend and her family," she cried. "You killed the Fangs."

There was no sense in denying it. Garin swallowed and nodded, guilt still proving secondary to his own fear. "If it's any consolation, one of their daughters is still well and alive!"

The old woman let out a hideous snarl and raised her readied arrow at them.

Garin cursed his burning arm. *"Forgive me, Laurent."* He brought own hand to his mouth, shredded the inside of his wrist, and muttered, "Sorry, mate."

Then, he slammed his bleeding arm to Rupert's blabbering mouth. The bastard kicked and bucked; the arrow whistled through the air, and Garin's injured leg shook against the force that hit Rupert square in the stomach. Through Rupert's rattled wailing, Garin couldn't tell if he'd ingested any of it.

Just as he was about to drop him, a second arrow hit them in rapid succession; Rupert's groaning cut off abruptly as he went limp. Garin lost his footing, and they both tumbled down the porch steps.

He heaved Rupert's body to the side, where he rolled into the dirt, eyes glassy and open, mouth twisted in pain. It was Garin's second time seeing a dead vampire. Those who died by the stake instead of sunlight looked no different from other bodies, he'd learned from Laurent, who rested in the crypt at the Mine. Their fangs remained protruded, their bodies perfectly preserved forever to rest in peace—or, for a most unlucky grave robber to discover.

But Rupert hadn't had the time to wake up and complete the change by drinking from a human, even if he had swallowed some of Garin's blood. Rupert would not rise again with the second hawthorn arrow that protruded from the middle of chest.

Garin shifted to his knees—and gazed up the length of the next arrow, aimed this time by Bog. The tavern owner's hands shook, looking too small for the longbow; there was no way Bog was a better shot than that impressive old hag—she must've had decades of experience fending off her crops and livestock, probably joining in on Daemon hunts from time to time. But with the alarming pain spreading throughout his body, he felt too winded to run.

There was something very wrong. The wrist he'd bitten into moments ago had already healed, but his arm and leg were struggling to expel the bullets like they should have. He'd expected it would take some time, but instead of slowly healing, he was growing weak.

"He's injured," Artus was murmuring. "Do it, Bog. What are you waiting for?"

Garin looked up at the deepening sky and thought of Lilac. Her warmth that he wanted to wrap himself in, her soft hair and skin. Her angelic face and those taunting dimples he yearned to kiss.

Her uneasy, lumbering cadence of footfall and sharp voice, clear as night.

"Get away from him!"

There was another *whiz* over Garin's head, and the sound of a bow and arrow clattering onto the porch. Bog flew back into the crowd, one arrow sticking out of his face, and the other out of his shoulder.

Screams erupted from the house. There were hands yanking Garin before he knew what was happening, and Myrddin mumbling behind him.

On either side of them, Yanna and Lilac held longbows at the ready, their next arrows already nocked.

34

GARIN

Lilac's hands shook violently, her expression unreadable. Garin could tell she'd been crying, likely from seeing Sable and Jeanare's bodies.

A quick glance told him they'd remained untouched, and the soldier he'd carried from Monfort-sur-Meu was still snoring, concealed in the middle of the hay bales. The door to the storage carriage down the hill was open, the horses snorting under their breath.

What was she doing here? Why would Myrddin allow this?

Panting, Garin struggled to steady his breathing, righting himself upon Myrddin. He grabbed the warlock by the arms, causing him to yelp.

"Why are you here?" Garin snarled, an overwhelming surge of want and new hungers flooding through him, unbidden.

Myrddin scoffed. "She slit my throat!"

"This wasn't supposed to happen! You were meant to protect her!" Garin's fury boiled over. He snarled, lunging at Myrddin—but a searing flash of violet burst from the warlock's chest. Agony lanced through Garin's hands, surging up his arms like fire. He cried out, staggering back as blistered skin bubbled across his palms, only to shimmer and slowly begin to mend before his eyes.

Artus was laughing. "Come to arrest me, little queen? You and your servants?"

Two arrows soared through the air—one from Yanna stuck inches from Artus's head into the doorframe, while Lilac's flew into the house, also narrowly missing Artus but actually hitting someone else in the arm.

If it was Lilac's first time wielding a longbow, she was a natural; impressive, in fact.

There were screams and yelps of pain, but Artus hushed them with a garbled command.

"I've come to do what my grandfather and father didn't have the nerve to," Lilac said, her hair whipping around her face.

"I would think twice about that." Artus's gaze flickered to Garin before boring tauntingly into hers. "Your own guard was ready to kill more Daemons than enemy forces by the look of your armory. Armand convinced Henri to have more made after Lilac went missing, but that section has always existed. And you had no idea, did you?"

"In a kingdom built upon oppressing its most vulnerable communities? I should have guessed."

"When Rupert walked into The Jaunty Hog, all too proudly discussing his decision to return to Renald's guard, we knew the perfect opportunity had fallen into our lap." Artus chortled himself into a coughing fit. "Just before the town crier called us to the square to announce your stupid decree? It was too perfect."

Lilac made a noise of disgust, glancing down at Rupert's lifeless corpse. Its glassy eyes reflected the moon above. She scrunched her face full of fury and approached him, reaching for the arrows in his chest.

Garin tutted, smothering the shallow stab of jealousy in his chest. A scrape, really. "The arrows stay in him."

She froze, straightening once more. "You sent him," Lilac snarled at Artus.

"And that God awful wine," Garin was quick to add, imagining the sheer joy of draping the blabbering imbeciles in the fallen duke's innards.

"We all heard *you* enjoyed it," replied Artus. "Bog's son proved himself useful after all. While everyone rushed to watch you humiliate yourself, Inwold had his men transport most of the hawthorn weaponry in the Trécesson armory." Artus looked back down the hall at a tall, hulking fellow skirting the corner of the parlor. The man said nothing, reddening and trying to shrink into the crowd. Artus laughed and turned a scathing eye toward Lilac. "It was meant for her. While I'd hoped it would make her delirious enough to forestall or have Maximilian forfeit their marriage entirely, what it did to you turned out to be as useful."

Knowing it was all intentional—that he had missed it—made Garin see red. His lip curled over his fangs. "An adverse reaction could have killed her."

"Oh, one could only hope."

Garin had never wanted more badly to put his hands on someone. To tear into them with his bare fingers. When he started for the house, the rest of the crowd scuttled into the back rooms. He limped past Yanna and Lilac all the way to the porch. He stumbled on a divot in the dirt, barely catching himself in time on the railing.

Myrddin was at his side to help him, but Garin growled in warning, and the warlock backed off. He righted himself, shuffling up the last two stairs.

In the doorway, Artus was waving the deed like a festival prize. "Come quickly. Even as the mongrel of the house, I think it only fair you witness the moment it is gone from your family name." He held it teasingly under the torch at the base of the stairwell that led up to his childhood bedroom in the attic. "Imagine, decades' worth of toil and tears. A sacrificing voyage across the channel to escape sickness. Safety from the plague, I'd imagine."

An overwhelming rage swept over Garin when Artus tilted his head knowingly.

"A journey like that will test anyone's character. Your mother struggled with melancholy, didn't she? I'm sure scorning your father for pushing his own dad out of their boat when it had started taking on water did not help, either. They were only minutes from shore."

Garin was beyond response. He thought of his hallucination. Of Loumarch being dragged back under by the Morgen.

No one had ever told him.

"Although he was not her own father," Artus continued, "she often got on with him quite amicably. She appreciated his insights and humor as someone raised by strict physicians, long dead."

Wiping at his eyes, Garin startled at the brush at his side; he hadn't heard Lilac approach him. She enveloped his hand in hers, twining her fingers between his and rubbing the back of his knuckles as they itched to tear into flesh once more. Rage, sweat, and heat radiated from her, only driving his aching need to taste her.

"She despised Pascal for it," continued Artus, loud enough for everyone to hear, "even as your parents turned from trying to sell their crops to harvesting illegal flora at the edge of the Low Forest. Your father, anyway," he added with a look of disdain. "Your mother was not better by any means, murdering unborn children. But the straw that broke the camel's back was when your father tried to pawn you—"

"*Enough*!" Garin shouted. He never wanted to hear about his father again. How could Artus have known these things? "What dark magic is at play here?"

Lilac remained silent beside him, but he could hear and *feel* her heart thrumming away.

Artus regarded them curiously, taking notice of their intertwined fingers. Sighing, he tucked the deed beneath his arm and reached back into his pouch. He fished out a palm-sized book—tattered brown leather with purple stitching at the binding. Swirling leaves and flora were etched into the leather with a fine-tip knife.

Garin's mouth went dry. It had been *years* since he'd laid eyes on the tattered journal Aimee would occasionally scribble in before bed. When he was small, he'd curl up behind her in their cramped room, the sound of the fire and his mother's quill soothed him to sleep on nights Pascal was out foraging..

The last time he'd seen it was after her burial at the abbey. He and Pascal had walked home in the snow that evening; not a word exchanged between them after thanking their neighbors at the parish for their condolences at her funeral. Not even a quarter of the church had been filled, and most of them were nuns from the convent. As his father hung the kettle, changed clothes, and threw a tangled clump of jewelry—two necklaces and Aimee's ring—on the table, Garin watched from the doorway.

Pascal had last withdrawn her journal from his coat last, tossing it next to the jewelry.

"Tuck this in the envelope at the back of your mother's book," he'd demanded, his expression cold.

He remembered wondering why Pascal hadn't buried these things with her. Knowing his father, he'd probably spent the night before the funeral pouring through it. It felt like a hostile violation of privacy.

"What do I do with it?" Garin had asked. The last words spoken to his father.

"Get it out of my sight," Pascal had snapped. "I never want to see it again."

Garin had done what his father asked of him with shaking hands, barely able to touch his mother's accessories. He'd just shut the aumbry door when Pascal Trevelyan shouldered his medic bag and walked through the door without another word, and took their only horse to the battlefield Garin had assigned him to with the forged note he'd written.

Artus frowned, lingering on a page a little over halfway through, then glanced up. "Her last entry was in autumn of 1354. You had just turned fourteen and she couldn't believe how much you'd grown." He flipped through the rest of the book, finding empty pages. "That's it? Did she end up getting apprehended by the Church? Did your father finish the job?"

Seething, Garin gently loosened his hand from Lilac's and all but lunged at the door. He grunted at the pain shooting up his leg and placed both palms flat against the threshold. "Give it to me."

"No. No, I don't think I will." Artus shut Aimee's journal and nudged Bog's body with his toe. "If I'd known all it took was a musket to slow you down, I would've put one to your skull ages ago."

"I'll shoot an arrow through yours if you don't give that book to him." Yanna stood off to their right, just beyond the porch. The girl's longbow was angled expertly at the door.

With a withering glance back, Artus strode down the hall toward the parlor.

"Artus," Garin called out. He couldn't bring himself to beg.

The old man slowed, watching the hearth cast eerie shadows upon the trembling crowd. There were murmurs amongst them, discussion of finding a way out. Jumping out the windows, climbing up to the second floor. If they'd be able to run fast enough with his apparent injury.

When Garin said no more, Artus stepped into the parlor and tossed the deed into the hearth.

A tinny ringing began in Garin's ears when the room burst into an uproar, every nerve in his body alight with the sound and scent of so much fear.

"What are you doing, Artus?" cried Brient.

Mathias began to shake. "He'll come in, now, won't he?"

"Silence! *Look*." Artus motioned to the door—at Garin, still tensed against the threshold, peering hungrily into the cage they'd put themselves into. "Now that there's nothing for him to sign, he will not enter this house as long as my bloodline lives. That is a feral animal, and this is the fool-proof cage we've put ourselves in to prepare for our hunt, just in case something like this happened." Artus strode to the aumbry at the back of the hall, opened it, and placed Aimee's journal upon the top shelf.

"But what happens now?" asked the old woman archer.

"We wait him out."

"But the sun doesn't affect him," Hamon pointed out.

"No matter," Artus growled. "Someone will come and put a stake in his chest come daylight. We will hunt another day, and his little coven will fall apart without their leader."

They'd have sent Rupert into Brocéliande first. He was inexperienced, and the only one seeming to wield a blade, which would do nothing against the coven. Even the most clumsy fledgling driven by hunger would have overpowered Rupert in an instant.

Everyone else who was armed held bows and hawthorn arrows stolen from the Trécesson armory. They'd have him walk ahead and planned to attack from a distance. Rupert was meant to draw Garin's coven out. Then, the troupe before him would've ambushed his vampires.

Successfully.

A loud *bang* pulled Garin's attention; Artus dusted his hands off after slamming the aumbry shut with a violent kick. "If you want your whore mother's journal so badly," he said, returning to the front of the house, "then you can come and get it yourself."

All the speech in the room melted into a dizzying cadence—shouts of protest, incredulous shouts of hysteria. A cacophonous, rapturous high washed over him, wave upon wave, mounting upon the unrelenting pulse of pain and hunger. Garin's home echoed with the staggered rhythm of dozens of heartbeats, bags of blood ready—*begging*—to be spilled.

"Garin," Lilac said into his ear, her voice determinedly calm as she pressed her body against his, squeezing his hand. He blinked. "Listen to me. They're done, all of them. They will be apprehended and hung in the street by tomorrow, I'll be sure of it."

Artus cackled behind her. "By you and what army?"

"That one," said Myrddin quietly, followed by Lilac's sharp inhale.

A deep, distant rumble of hooves pummeling the ground cut through the crops. Garin froze—then turned to see a small army of Trécesson guards galloping up the hill, weaving and bobbing between the patches of farmland and from behind the parked carriages. Torches danced, littered among at least twenty others wielding bows and blades aimed at his house.

Yanna yelped and scuttled nearer to the porch.

How this was possible, Garin did not know—nor did he have the energy to find out.

Artus began to laugh, a choking, broken sound as those in the parlor behind him fell silent. "Corruption! Blasphemy!"

The sound of the queen's slamming pulse drowned the sound of Artus's shouting. He hadn't noticed it growing louder—and the night certainly hadn't quieted—but it was all Garin could hear. Lilac craned her head before him. Her cheeks were stained with the salt of tears, eyes bright with concern. She reached up to stroke Garin's face reassuringly, but Garin shook his head as his hand rose to envelop hers. He squeezed her hand in warning and swiftly removed her palm from his face; it wasn't her fault. She didn't know he was fighting the urge to heal himself by plunging his fangs so deeply into her that it would frighten her.

"Guillotines," she whispered urgently, almost crooning as she tugged him away from the house. "A torturer." He could tell by her scent that her body was beginning to react to whatever it was he felt. "Whatever you see fit to punish them, I'll rearrange it."

"They won't get that far," Garin replied through his teeth, his body unfamiliarly rigid against hers. "I won't allow it."

"But we have to leave," she argued, glancing down at his body. "You're hurt, I need to get you to the infirmary."

"Kemble would never treat a vampire. Not one looking like this."

"She *has*. Just unknowingly. Kemble will treat whomever I ask her to. I'll notarize your paperwork for this property myself." When he didn't answer, she said, "It's the journal, isn't it?"

Garin's hardened gaze remained on the aumbry.

Lilac spun for the door—toward Artus—but Garin shot his arm out and snagged her waist, tugging her against him.

"Don't think about it," he said softly into her ear. Her pulse went haywire in his arms, and Garin forced his mouth away from her delicate neck. "Stand down."

Outrage sparked in her eyes.

"Down the steps. Stand down and *stay* there." Garin turned toward the house, unable to watch as her body raged against her instincts and dragged her down the steps; her fingernails had raked across his shoulder, sending a dangerous surge through his muscles and loin. She joined Myrddin at the base of the stairs.

Garin stared at his feet.

It had been so long. Bitter memories stained the place, lifting from the floorboards like creeping ghouls. Tendrils of time and past had tugged at him the first time he'd visited with Lilac. Tonight, they had him by the throat.

He saw himself, scrawny and helpless, pulling Aimee's body from the kitchen and into the yard. He'd cradled her cold torso to his chest, shouting, waiting for help to come because he'd refused to leave her, cursing the way he'd dawdled for a pastry and cup of milk from the bakery on the way home from the brothel after the Madame told him there must be some sort of mistake: Aimee wasn't working that evening, and might've simply experienced a spell of forgetfulness when she'd asked Garin to meet her there.

Unlike the fantasy he'd painted in a heroic, almost boring lie for Lilac, his childhood—what little he'd allowed himself to scrape from the surface of his muddy memory—wasn't exactly something to preserve. His parents' screaming matches they thought they'd hidden well behind the paper-thin walls, and Pascal threatening to report Aimee to the Church.

It was painful. It hadn't made him stronger, or better. Time alone hadn't healed him.

This farmhouse hadn't been Garin's home in many years, if ever—not in the way The Fenfoss Inn had become. Bast, Adelaide, the Algovens. Not in the way that Lilac was. There was no use in mourning ghosts, not when his future was paved with them.

Not when Garin promised Loumarch he would live.

Flashes of unwelcome memory assaulted him: the witches' uncertainty surrounding Lilac's survival, pouring over that book as he'd sat at her bedside and *hating* what he'd read as he monitored her every pause in breathing, every irregular heartbeat.

Lorietta begging him to reconsider as he mounted Loïg and dragged Myrddin with him, pleading Garin to simply tell Lilac the truth about what he'd done. As if there was any easy way to explain why Albrecht was being picked apart at the bottom of the Argent, along with Lori's copy of *The Histories of the Lasting Night*. Garin had thrown it in, hopeless, wholly convinced there was no other choice—that *he* could never be her choice, with or without the threat of France.

Then, watching Lilac awkwardly sway with Rupert at the feast, trying to distract himself from the thought of massacring half the room to steal the dance.

Fool, he thought aggressively, regarding his empty hands that wished to tear, maim, and—and hold. *The moment you let your walls dissipate, the fangs of love impale you.*

"Garin," came Lilac's voice, a hymn to his ears. "Come to me. Let us leave."

She stood next to Yanna, who'd shifted her body protectively closer to her friend, arrow still aimed. Myrddin hovered behind them both, glancing occasionally over his shoulder at the guards.

Oddly, not one of them had uttered a single word since their arrival.

The corner of Garin's mouth quirked. He peered back at the aumbry, then hummed to himself, lifting the nearest flickering oil lamp from the porch railing as he made his way down the steps. "Goodnight, Artus."

"What? Where are you going?" the fallen duke spat.

"To be a proper gentleman and see a woman to the altar."

"You, a gentleman?" Artus tutted, chuckling in pity. "France will reign. A formidable army does not matter when one's neighbor has a flaming arrow aimed at their window. They will conquer, and I'll rejoice in soon seeing the day your queen is overthrown and hung from the gallows once Maximilian realizes she is not worth the resources. I tried to finish the job at the castle, that fateful eve of our meeting."

Garin stopped at the last step, refusing to allow the memory of that night into focus. Still, his body remembered for him. The world began to slowly spin, and he grasped the bannister for support. Lilac was there, straight ahead. Her arm was outstretched, those generous, round eyes beckoning him further.

He swallowed, desperate to wet his parched throat. Lilac. Eleanor. She was so—so good. So warm. She was patient and full of vigor; everything he was not. He'd go to her, collapse into her arms, and nuzzle his face into her warm, nectared hair. He'd sink to his knees and—

"They'll drown your parents' farmland in flame, just as they will your precious forest. Though, if I'd have known this was your home, I would have taken the honor upon myself years ago."

Garin's fist tightened around the lamp's handle. "Then let me help you."

There was a flash of realization in Lilac's enlarged pupils, just before Garin whirled and flung the oil lamp straight at the torch above Artus's head.

It shattered. Oil and flame rained down upon Artus's face, engulfing his entire head.

The entryway burst into flames immediately after, fire rapidly spreading wherever else the oil had splashed—down Artus's torso, the coatroom door, into the hallway.

There was a scream and sound of shattered glass; someone leapt through the slow-spreading flames in the hallway and had thrown the table vase out the window to the right of the door. Garin started toward the man lowering himself out, but an arrow stuck in the escapee's back before his feet hit the floor.

Although Yanna wasn't in sight, Garin could hear her shouting around the back. Lilac had taken her friend's place; she'd picked up her bow and quiver again, her exquisite face wrought in a smoldering concentration. He watched her chest rise, then fall, as she loosed the next arrow into a second escapee's chest.

Everyone was either abandoning the shelter of the structure to evade the fire spreading throughout the halls, or trapping themselves further into the bowels of the house. Garin could see his bedroom door up the stairs was wide open, probably filled with those who forgot smoke rose. It would choke the breath from their lungs if the flames didn't eat through the dry beams quick enough. It was an old house, after all.

Myrddin watched the blaze from the path as if in a trance, flames reflected in his somber eyes. Lilac shook with fury, alternating between shouting at those climbing over each other to escape and cursing through gritted teeth, pulling hawthorn arrow after hawthorn arrow out of the quiver slipping off her shoulder.

She'd shot five in under a minute despite her fumbling fingers and awkward stance.

The door frame was a halo of holy fire, both warding and beckoning, bits of it breaking away in charred ash. Without another glance back, he strode up the porch steps and into his doorway.

The threshold was no longer.

The roar of the fire and the wails of the dying drowned out Lilac's and Yanna's shouts at the escapees; they remained amply distracted. Artus was gone, or Garin at least didn't recognize him in the immediate pile of dead near the entry. He covered the lower half of his face with his hand out of habit and began to move.

As expected, the fire devoured the front of the structure first, climbing upward faster than it spread outward. Black smoke filled the hallway; he winced and batted as the flames grazed him, the heat shockingly not searing so much as it was bothersome. He'd never walked directly into fire, but the sensation at least momentarily distracted him from the throbbing in his limbs.

He held his apology as he stepped on bodies, over those begging for their end. Fire seemed a shitty way to go, but so was an arrow through your body or a creature with an iron grip sucking the life out of you. They'd dug their own grave.

Fangs dripping, eyes stinging, Garin walked with his arms out beside him, fingers trailing the wall until he emerged into the kitchen, the parlor to his right. A wide sweep of his hand and the hollow *thump* of aged wood it hit told him he'd reached the aumbry.

The smoke was a little thinner here; someone had broken the back window, but Yanna was out there, snarling threats and continuing to shoot arrows. He fumbled for the handle, throwing the door open and knocking several glasses over, shattering them before the book was in his grasp.

He swallowed, real tears beginning to fall as his hands grazed his mother's handwriting. Garin flipped to the back and felt the small leather envelope—snarled and stuck his fingers inside. Empty.

BRIAR SOMERSET

The fact that the Adelaide's family and Sable and Jeneare had kept the aumbry as it was shocked him, and filled him with a dangerous hope. Maybe it had fallen out. Just as he reached further into the aumbry, knocking his hand into the far corners, there was a sharp stab of pain at his back.

Garin roared and dropped the book, blinking into the smoke; he spun and swung, and his arm made contact with a body. Artus grunted before him, his entire face charred, grasping blindly around Garin's torso for the hawthorn stake that had impaled him. The old man snarled and shoved Garin against the aumbry, trying to drive it further into him.

"No!" Fighting to keep conscious, Garin lost his footing and felt the stake inch into him as he slid down the front of the cabinet. Just as his vision began to go and felt his mind slipping, there was a shriek and a *thump*; someone else grabbed him—someone strong and full of vigor. The painful pressure at his back and cloud of stupor that began to seep over him lifted, and Garin heard the stake clatter across the room.

"Come on," shouted Lilac over the roar of flames. Coughing into her shoulder, she hauled him to his feet and threw his arm over her shoulder. She dragged him toward the now flame-covered hallway, retching and gasping for air.

He allowed her to pull him, but not before instinct had him tugging her back, sweeping his arm across the floor. He didn't find Aimee's journal and there was no time to look—but his fingers did find purchase in something else soft and brittle. Garin grabbed onto it, dragging it along over the piles of smoldering flesh.

The screams had become one with the creaking timber as the blaze spread throughout the east hall and second floor. A deafening groan shook the building. Lilac looked up at the ceiling, ducking and shielding her petrified face when embers began to rain down.

With all his might, Garin lunged for her, wrapping his free arm around her waist, pulling her down the hallway and out the door.

They stumbled together into the night and down the porch steps, collapsing onto the sodden earth. A crashing roar sounded behind them.

The Trevelyan farmhouse was gone.

35

L ilac stared up at the sky, blinking the stars and smoke into focus as her muscles seized against the ground. Her lungs burned, and it was painful to breathe; scowling, she turned her head and spat into the dirt. She could feel by the biting breeze at her feet and shoulder—despite the thick layer of soot that coated her skin—that part of the hem of her dress had been singed off. She sobbed once and gritted her teeth against the tremendous ache that resonated throughout her body. Miraculously, nothing *felt* raw; if she'd sustained burns anywhere on her legs as Garin had, the adrenaline was enough to dull the pain.

By the time she found the strength to try to sit up, Garin was crawling away from the spot where he'd landed beside her—back toward the flame-swallowed porch that was no longer. He, too, was covered in soot, his shoes gone and one pant leg partially burned through, streaks of dark blood left in the dirt behind him.

"Garin," she croaked as he pulled himself off the floor, cursing how convenient it would be to have even a smidgeon of the power he held over her. She coughed and scanned the grass for any sign of the bow she'd flung aside. "If you take one more step toward that house I'll shoot you myself. Garin, I order you to stop!"

At that moment, Yanna rounded the corner of the house and took one look at him nearing the blazing porch. She exchanged a look of fury with Lilac before dropping her bow and quiver. "Not again," Yanna growled, striding straight for him.

"Yanna, no!" Lilac pushed through the ache in her joints and had barely staggered to her feet when there was a gargled yelp.

Garin had his mouth to Yanna's throat.

Lilac froze. An unruly, apple-green rage stuck like a stake into Lilac's chest, nearly smothering her fear for Yanna's life.

Nearly.

"Get off of her!" Lilac demanded, tugging Garin's head away with a fistful of his hair, wrapping an arm around his chest. "Let her go, Garin, she'll die!" Lilac pulled with all her might, but even with her thrall strength, it was no use.

He only grunted and shifted his grip.

"Help me." Whimpering, Yanna bucked and cursed both Lilac and Garin—but he clung to her so tightly at the throat and around the waist that the veins in his forearms bulged. His breaths between gulps were so loud, Lilac could hear them over the roar of the fire and Yanna's bellowed gasps.

She staggered back and swallowed, sick with a burning envy she couldn't help. This was her friend. It was her friend—*and she didn't care*.

Of course, Myrddin was nowhere to be found. His illusion of guards had disappeared along with him.

"Get—him—*off*," Yanna thundered, her voice furious as it was hitched. "Get your stupid, oversized leech off of me, or I'll haunt your children's children to the grave!"

The thought of Yanna's body, limp in his arms, flashed through Lilac's mind. She ran her tongue across her lower lip. Would it be so bad to let him have her? He was hungry, after all. Whatever pleased him. It couldn't be Lilac feeding him. Not now. Not with the way he looked at her, touched her, craved her. He might—

"*Lilac, please!*" Yanna's pained sob pierced the night.

Blinking the vision away, Lilac dropped to her knees and frantically ran her fingers through the grass. Her knuckles brushed against a solid shaft; she grabbed it, leaped up, and slashed it hard under Garin's shirt. It skidded along the skin of his back, just above his trousers.

Warmth pooled over her fingertips. Lilac clung to the arrow and scuttled back.

Garin released Yanna with a roar, blood dribbling down his front. It was everywhere. He began retching and coughing, confusion marring his anger while he spat what was left in his mouth into the dirt. He wiped at his red-stained chin and whipped around.

"*No.*" Garin wiped his mouth, his ruddy, blown irises shrinking as they flew over her. "No, no, no—"

"It wasn't me," she whispered, placing her hand on his cheek.

He slowly turned to Yanna, who stood there trembling. "I'm sorry. I—"

A loud *crack* echoed across the fields, sending startled nightingales soaring into the sky before Yanna stomped off.

Garin's hand went to his cheek where she'd slapped him. "She's still bleeding," he murmured when Lilac stumbled from his side, stalking toward Yanna.

What was wrong with her? She was so willing, more than willing, to sacrifice her handmaiden to him.

Her throat tightened, thinking of the two girls standing outside of Garin's room at The Fool's Folly. How they'd sacrificed their friend to sate his hunger enough for him to want to bed them.

She'd been so fixated on her and Myrddin's mission, fucking him seemed far from her thoughts until the moment she slit her though. But now, it was more than envy. Something deep-seated—an arcane wrath that strained against any attempt to grasp at logic. She slowed in the middle of the path, realizing her hands had been balled into fists.

"Let him heal you, Yanna," Lilac managed, nauseous at the thought of his tongue on her.

"No," Yanna screeched. "Stay the *fuck* away from me, the both of you!" She gathered her skirts into her fist. Holding the bunched outer hem of her gown against the wound at her throat, Yanna staggered toward the nearby pile of hay stacks that sat between Sable and Jeanare and the farmhouse.

Lilac turned back to urge Garin to help her, but he'd already left. His back was to her—he was approaching the porch again.

No, something in *front* of it.

He was so disfigured and crumpled, Lilac hadn't noticed him there.

Several feet away, Artus lay face-up, his charred lips gaping to swallow rattling breaths, his torso quaking but otherwise still.

"You." Garin sank to his knees beside the old man, slipping his arms beneath his head and shifting him further away from the fire. If she didn't know better, she'd have thought Garin was attempting to save him.

The blaze before them burned brighter, the last of the west hall collapsing in on itself. Lilac retreated and was forced to shield her eyes and face against the blast of heat, but Garin remained oblivious to the embers flung at them, his hands flying over the old man's body. He was *searching* him. Armand's breast pocket, the leather pouch. Then his trousers and even under his shirt.

"Where is it?" His snarl was barely audible, a treacherous sound ensnared in bile and venom. He coughed and spat into the dirt beside Artus's head. "What have you done with it? Where is—" As if belatedly realizing Artus was incapable of answering even if he'd wanted to, Garin broke off and grabbed him. He shook him violently by the shoulders, hard enough to bounce the back of Artus's skull off the ground.

A heavy growl of frustration leaked from Garin's lips as he dropped him, fingers curled. He hung his head, chest rising and falling in a scattered rhythm. Without warning, he brought a heavy fist down on Artus. *Through* his skull. Lilac jumped and covered her mouth.

He did it again, upon Artus's chest. Then, into his ribcage.

Over and over and over again.

Lilac wanted to move. Her legs burned against her will, her fingers itching to slip down the front of her gown, but she couldn't bring herself to do any of it. She couldn't divert her gaze or shut her eyes, or even retreat to prevent her feet from being further covered in the gore that splattered with every hit. The raw agony with which Garin moved petrified Lilac. There was nothing stealthy or lithe about him as he pummeled Artus's remains into the earth.

He was the force of falling night in the flesh.

Lilac licked her lips, enchanted by the melodious sound of his fist squelching, shattering Artus's bones.

"For this kingdom," Garin grunted to the pulverized corpse between punches. "For my mother." He lifted his fist high once more. "For the love —of my—life."

Before she knew it, her legs carried her forth. Reflexes steady, Lilac caught his wrist when it raised again.

Garin startled, face twisting up at her in anguish. Lilac couldn't do anything but nod in silent reassurance, hot tears suddenly clinging to her lashes.

What was this overwhelming feeling that crested over her? *How* had she swung from the violent urge to rip Yanna out of his arms, to picturing letting him have her friend until her heart stopped beating—to this? It was more than sadness, more than the exhaustion of walking through flames to drag him out of his burning home.

It was loss—the four closed walls of a shrinking room. Regret and torture. She was so filled with grief, she couldn't gauge the exact reasons for the weight behind it.

All she knew was that it was crushing, the pit in her stomach heavy and hollow at the same time.

It was as if she and Garin were tethered by barbed arrows on two ends of a taut chain. An unwavering connection. The more she recoiled, tried to pull away—the more viscerally it dug into her, bleeding her.

Lilac gripped his hand and closed her eyes, willing the sensation to pass.

Instead, grief barreled into her—a feeling she knew by name, but never before at this intensity. It was an inhuman devastation that stole her breath: the farmhouse, mounds of blood-splattered snow, and all the could've-beens that had ever kept Garin up at night, soaked into her conscience. She could *taste* it, his bittersweet, aged melancholia.

It was an ancient knowing; she *felt* memories she couldn't see, loved people she'd never touched, and scorned those she'd never met.

"Enough," Garin said softly, the plea rumbling from deep within his chest, and she wondered if he felt what she did, too. If he'd witnessed her lifetimes unfurling like the petals of spring—the slow, silent churn of summer into autumn—the ghosts of her reluctant reverie dancing with the earthbound ghouls of his.

She tried to yank her hand from him, but Garin held it firm in an iron cradle, his eyes otherworldly garnets glowing in the moonlight. Blood and saliva dripped from his ash-stained mouth as he knelt before her.

He said nothing, pressing his lips to the back of her hand.

Why would he do this? What had brought him here? Why had he gone to

Montfort-sur-Meu? Just to reaffirm what the scouts had been reporting to her father?

Henri had witnessed Garin in his wrath. But if he hadn't, Henri and his men would've been three more bodies to the bloodbath.

"I am not myself tonight," he whispered pleadingly against her skin. An echo of his words at The Fool's Folly, yet there was no threat behind them. "I put you in danger, risked your life. I was not thinking. I should have known your disobedience would win out in the end. You are my thrall, after all."

Lilac wanted to strangle him—would've struck him, had she not decided Yanna's heavy slap had been enough. "My disobedience saved your life."

"As if yours wouldn't have been made uncomplicated by mine in the first place."

Jaw set, Lilac crouched and leveled her tearful, intent gaze with his. "You have never been more yourself," she ground out. "I would've followed you into that fire, with or without your spell over me. Your command won't always best my will, I can promise you that for as long as I live." Ignoring the rage that shadowed his desperation, she swept the hair from his forehead, along with the layer of sweat that mixed with the soot there. There were no words cutting enough to express the sickening swell of relief and anger at finding him in time.

The only thing Lilac could bring herself to say gripped her throat in an unrelenting vice of terror. "Garin," she began. "I—"

"Found some!" Mryrddin thundered from over her shoulder. She released Garin quickly, wiping at her eyes to see the warlock trudging up the hill—an enormous ball of something dark and glittering hovering above him. Myrddin cocked his head at the neighboring farms down the hill behind him. "Stole it from the troughs!"

It was water. A giant, spinning sphere of it, larger than the house itself.

Lilac hurriedly hoisted Garin to his feet, tugging him away from the porch. They watched, stunned and open-mouthed, as Myrddin twisted his outstretched hand, then extended it. The ball of water floated ahead and fell upon the house, immersing them in an enormous cloud of smoke and steam.

Garin snaked an arm around Lilac's waist and held her to him—just before a wall of water slammed into them. They remained upright, but she felt him teeter and dig his heels into the mud.

"Myrddin," he sputtered. "When I get my hands on you!" He peeled her off, gripping her arms and assessing her body, forcing gentleness into his voice when she could tell he wanted to scream. "Look at me. Are you hurt?"

She shook her head vehemently, not quite able to speak. She was unscathed, too busy scanning Garin herself. There was a stream of dark red flowing from his intact pant leg with the last of the drainage. His shirt was in pieces, whatever was left of it hanging halfway off his torso—a jarring reminder of the rippled leanness his tunics often masked, his skin smooth beneath the ash and stain. All the burns he'd sustained—she'd *seen* his leg on fire in the house, though he hadn't seemed to notice—had already healed over.

The leaking, half-visible wound on his right bicep and the one on his left thigh, however, had not.

Lilac glanced down at her soaked gown, trailing her fingers along her bosom and exhaling in relief. Her gaze dipped to the blood-tainted water. Then, at his fangs glistening temptingly in the moonlight. "Are you?"

He tore his eyes away from her throat, sliding them to Myrddin. "You idiot. What was that for? The house was already gone!"

"We couldn't leave a fire that size burning at the top of the hill. I glamored your parents' property the moment we'd arrived, but it's not the same as Lorietta's wards. Onlookers can still smell smoke billowing from your chimney. It's a wonder their guards aren't storming up here." Myrddin dusted his hands and placed them on his hips, surveying the damage. The entire second floor of the house had fallen in on itself. All that was left was a grim mess of wet cinder and charred brick of the crumbling chimney. "I must admit, I do envy those water mages."

"There's a creek just there." Garin cocked his thumb over his shoulder at the strip of grass before the field met the trees. "You didn't have to drop twenty troughs on it."

"You didn't have to run into a burning house."

Garin's rebuttal was cut off by a heart-rending screech.

Yanna was crouched over by the haystack near Sable and Jeanare's heads, chunks of hay flung into the air as her arms flailed. "Gwendal? *Gwendal?*"

Myrddin was already at her side, heaving unsuccessfully against the large bundle. A burst of purple sparks short from his palms on the third go, causing part of the haystack to burst into flames. Myrddin cussed and hurriedly batted them out.

Garin began to stalk across the path.

Matching his stride, Lilac stared at the red dripping from his soaked pant leg as they approached Yanna. Garin didn't seem the least bit alarmed if he noticed. "What did you do?"

"I tried to help him," Garin replied stiffly. "One of your men."

When they approached, Lilac shouldered the hay bale; it was heavy, but nothing that would crush her. Yanna fell upon the man laying in the dirt as Lilac gave a final shove, the hay bale rolling off and bounding to a stop at Jeanare's side.

Garin immediately went to Gwendal's head, shifting his hands beneath the guard's shoulders and hooking them under his armpits. He gingerly tugged him out from the shadow of the other haystacks and nudged Myrddin aside, placing a hand against the guard's neck.

Gwendal was a broad-shouldered fellow, strikingly handsome from what Lilac could see of his face, though he was barely recognizable with all the blood leaking from his mouth. It was splattered over his cheeks and drying in his thick black beard. His helmet had fallen off or had been removed at some point, eyes half open and bleary; she could only tell he was still breathing by the faint click behind his breastplate.

"Give him space," Garin demanded, and she and Myrddin went to crouch at Gwendal's head, leaving Yanna to sob at his feet. Garin's fingers flew across the guard's shoulders, first his left, then his right, breathing heavily. He moved down Gwendal's arms next, loosening strap after strap, then shifted to his legs, unfastening the remaining belts beside Yanna. "Remove his gorget and pauldrons. And his gauntlets."

Lilac's muscles twitched as she glanced up at him in urgency, hands hovering hesitantly over the metal piece at Gwendal's throat.

"Do you need a primer in everything?" Yanna sighed, rubbing her nose. "That neck piece, just there."

"And his shoulders and hands," Garin instructed. "Trust yourself." Just like that, Lilac began to remove the plates expertly—even if she'd never done it or seen it done a day in her life. "That's it now. Well done."

Yanna turned her head and leaned away from Garin. "Do you control her?"

"He merely advises me," said Lilac.

"That is a gross underestimation." Annoyance colored Garin's tone. "It is temporary—*will* be temporary."

"He guides her," Myrddin interjected, coughing into his robe. "And the queen just so happens to find his advice *extremely* persuasive."

"You aren't helping," Garin said between his teeth, plucking Gwendal's leg plates off. "I tried to save him." In the middle of removing the last plate, Garin exhaled sharply. Yanna gasped in horror—a pool of thick blood spilled out of the cavity of his armor onto the grass. "He was among those wounded in the skirmish. I heard him calling your name," he said to Yanna. "It appears he's been shot or stabbed in the inner groin. I'm afraid he won't make it." Garin bowed his head and held out his hand to her. "I'm sorry."

Yanna stared at Gwendal, silent tears catching the moonlight as they clung to her lashes, plopping onto her reddening cheeks. She didn't take Garin's apology, nor his palm. "Whatever it takes."

Garin's brow knitted. "What?"

"Save him," Yanna snapped, her softened gaze for her lover turning cold once it landed on Garin, then Lilac and Myrddin. "Whatever. It. Takes."

"I cannot. Lilac is already my thrall. I won't risk any more complications with sharing my blood and what its magic might bring."

"But you can," Lilac insisted, thinking back to his explanation on the way to find the Midraal Market. It felt like eons, another lifetime ago. "You can only have one thrall at a time."

"Yes, by the typical workings of Sanguine law. But you know as well as I that nothing about our bond has been typical."

"Fine. So sire him," said Yanna.

"It is not that simple." Garin passed a hand over his face. He glanced over his shoulder, then back at Gwendal. "I sired my first fledgling the night I brought Lilac to the Mine. I've barely been there to govern her, much less my own coven. I haven't been back in weeks."

"Save your self pity," Yanna said, her fists balling in the dirt. "Gwendal is resourceful and intelligent. He's good at the stone, used to apprentice for Hamon Martin before realizing Hamon participated in Armand's Daemon hunts. Resigned and came to the castle shortly after. He'd be a worthy asset to your—your coven." She couldn't get the words out without breaking into tears. "He can't leave. He can't leave me."

"If you don't want him, then he'll join my court alongside Yanna," said Lilac. "And her sister, Isabel."

"Do not say a word of it to anyone," Yanna snapped at Garin and Myrddin, wiping at her cheeks. "Nobody knows we're related."

"There's no guarantee he'll be the same person after he's realized what happened to him." Garin's gaze was distant, focused on Lilac's hand resting protectively on Gwendal's shoulder. "*Any* siring must be handled responsibly. Vampirism is not an out for anything, especially with how destructive a fledgling can be in the wrong company."

"Don't look at me that way," said Lilac. "I've been handling yours *more* than responsibly. Piper spends most of her day reading books and strolling the grounds. She eats grapes and croissants and chases the ducks in the courtyard pond. She's revolted by blood, especially mine."

"She's—" Garin pinched the bridge of his nose and shook his head. "Nevermind. I don't want to know."

"My point is that she has been just fine with us. And so will he."

"Piper?" said Yanna. "Piper, as in, Piper Krenn? The banished handmaiden?"

Lilac shifted onto her heels, brushing off the stab of irritation. "You know of her?"

"We all heard what happened. Years ago, news of it made rounds. Even in the orphanage and brothel. Some said it was a rumor meant to detract from the shifter who was executed." It seemed Yanna wanted to say more, but at the look on Lilac's paling face, she quieted.

"She's real. Both of them were. Phoebe Allard is Piper—*our* Piper. Her appearance was altered a bit when Garin sired her weeks ago. Before then, she was imprisoned by the vampires after my parents exiled her, leaving her to travel home without a carriage or protection. On the way, she was taken by Garin's Second-in-Command, Bastion, and his men."

"Do your parents know?" Garin already looked doubtful, lost in thought. "Have they suspected she's returned?"

Lilac thought back to Henri's reaction the first night Piper had arrived, and her mother's abrasive irritation with her. "No," she lied.

Garin's brows rose, but all he said was, "I'm not surprised."

"I will say, Mademoiselle Krenn's will is quite free for a recently sired Sanguinarian," Myrddin added. "Lilac has not been so lucky."

"I am his *thrall*. Not his sire."

Garin glowered at her and Yanna. "Neither of you will house a newborn vampire in that castle."

Myrddin had righted himself as they'd argued. He stood with his arms crossed, watching the steaming pile of smoke and carnage that was the Trevelyan farmhouse, his fingers moving minutely in the air, drawing odd shapes.

"Stop your prayers and spells, warlock," snapped Yanna. "He's not dying. Not tonight." She lashed out and grabbed Garin by the shirt. "Save my fiancé."

He looked down at her fist, nostrils flaring. "You don't know what you're asking for. You could never imagine the life you're demanding of him. For yourself."

"I don't have to imagine. I see what the two of you have." Yanna glared at Lilac, then back at Garin. "You fooled no one at the castle. You hide your vampirism more skillfully than what you feel for her. Everyone saw it at the feast, even before you went mad. Did Piper tell either of you?"

"Tell us what?" Lilac looked to exchange a nervous glance with Garin, but his eyes were turned toward the floor.

"The things he said as he made his way across the floor? Snarling, seeking his wife."

Lilac's chest flushed. "No, she hadn't."

"No one said anything. Conveniently." Garin's seething glare rose to Myrddin.

"It is *her* blood Gwendal is willing to die for," Yanna insisted. "He cares for Lilac and her cause, even her family—even those of them who deserve the gallows. And now that I know she is your thrall, vampire, I know you're *nothing* without her."

Garin fell silent as he gently plucked Yanna's fingers from his collar, grimacing and eyeing the crusting blood upon her throat.

"Save him," Lilac urged. "For her. Please."

He exhaled—but dragged himself over, plopping down on the other side of Gwendal's head. "For you, and only you," he said softly, his breath a sharpened blade across her flesh. "Her blood is on your hands if he loses control. Her heartbreak is yours to bear if he turns her. You *will* be there to comfort your friend when she is sorely disappointed in what comes of this."

"Gladly," Lilac replied. "Especially since she has generously comforted my tears over you."

Wordlessly, Garin lifted Gwendal's head onto his lap. The guard's amber eyes widened with the movement, a rich flicker of life behind them even as tears leaked from the corners. Garin slid a short knife from the baldric that sat at Gwendal's waist, and Lilac and Yanna watched in horror as he swiftly slit his wrist and hovered it over Gwendal's partially open lips.

He dropped the blade and propped Gwendal's mouth open wider with his thumb. "Welcome to the Lasting Night, my brother. Apologies in advance for, well, everything."

Gwendal began to sputter and choke on the amount of blood dripping into his mouth.

"Turn him on his side," Yanna suddenly burst, watching from between her fingers. "He'll choke!"

"That *is* the point," said Myrddin.

Gwendal's rasped breathing quieted. So did his gurgling on Garin's blood.

"Oh, Gwenny," Yanna sobbed, rubbing his shin.

"Well?" Lilac slipped her hands off of Gwendal's shoulders, picking at her nail beds. "What happens now? Is he dead?"

"Not yet." Garin scooped the knife at his side and rose it high, sinking it into Gwendal's chest, drawing eruptive screams from Lilac and Yanna. "Now, he's dead."

36

With a sickening squelch, Garin yanked the blade from the battered guard and tossed it aside. "It'll take up to three days for your Gwenny to awaken."

Lilac crawled over to Yanna, who actually allowed the queen to embrace her.

She was trembling like a frightened hare. "He will wake, won't he?"

"I nearly asphyxiated him with enough of my blood. I'd say he's got a good chance."

"And what of him?" Myrddin nudged a finger at the twisted body laying just beyond the charred remains of the farmhouse. "How long will it take *him*?"

Not Artus. He was nearly flattened into the earth.

"Rupert?" Lilac wiped at her eyes. She'd been too distracted to scrutinize him before, or even remember he laid there, off to the right of the porch. Maybe she hadn't wanted to, especially since learning he'd been working for Artus. "He's gone."

"And he's no vampire," said Garin curtly.

"But he's on the verge of it, isn't he?" Myrddin pressed, striding over to Rupert.

Garin would never—ever— turn Rupert, especially knowing he'd touched her. Well, it was Lilac who'd done most of the teasing and touching. She expected Garin to deny it just as quickly as he had Myrddin's first inquiry.

Instead, Garin didn't answer.

Lilac froze mid-pat, Yanna still sniffling into her shoulder.

Myrddin bent to stroke the matted hair from Rupert's forehead. He gazed quietly into the corpse's frightened, open eyes, then looked up at the endless night they stared into. "You pitied him, even if for a moment, didn't you? You saw something in him, so you tried. You wouldn't have, otherwise." Myrddin straightened. "Isn't that why there's a hawthorn arrow in the middle of his chest? Because you changed your mind?"

"I used him as a human shield. That's why that arrow is there." Garin winced, rocking onto his haunches before rising to his feet. "There's also one through his stomach, marking him definitively dead." His fingers flexed at his side, for a second it looked as though he meant to stride toward her and Yanna.

Lilac's muscles involuntarily tensed, her arms curling protectively around her friend.

Myrddin squinted, scrutinizing Garin's tender movements. "Are you unwell?"

Garin stopped to fix the warlock with a withering glare. "I've been *shot* in the *arm* and *leg*, Myrddin. Of course I am unwell."

"But are you not healing? Perhaps some of Lorietta's magical pottage would help. Or, more readily, some of your beloved's blood from the vein," Myrddin added from the corner of his mouth.

"You and I both know why that is a bad idea right now." Garin began to stalk toward Myrddin with a lethal grace in his step that Lilac had never seen before. Like a ghoul, his boots made no sound as he slinked up the hill. "Forgive me, if it takes me a tad longer to recover from the ammunition lodged deep inside my body, by weapons no pea-brained mortal should ever have in their possession in the first place. I doubt the ancient, unholy arcana that made me what I am ever considered cannons and gunpowder artillery. Especially in violent, colonizing hands." He came to a halt, glaring down at Rupert. "He is a useless bastard's son. Whatever I tried was done in a moment of weakness. I have no need for him."

"You might not." Myrddin stood his ground over Rupert's body, his probing eyes darting over Garin's shoulder to Lilac. "She will need allies within her courts. Your coven serves you well. Now that she's enthralled to you, they will serve *her* well. Still, they are foot soldiers, scouts, swordsmen and archers of a bygone era. With everything to come, her Majesty will need those able to pass as human and Daemon, maintain their ranks and exist between worlds as creatures once did long, long ago. She'll need those able to defend, sleuth, and assess—she could stand to hire shifters onto her court, too. Our glamors don't work on you in the same way they do others whose physiologies bind to illusory magic."

"What do you mean, *'with everything to come?'*" Lilac asked. It had sounded both warning and plea.

Myrddin shrugged in a helpless gesture, his face scrunched, as if the mere thought of telling her caused him great pain.

"What my queen *needs* is a court she can trust," Garin bit back, his anger growing more volatile with every word. "Furthermore, she needs none amongst her rank so willing to bed the traitor." His laugh was chilling when Myrddin's face fell. "That's why you want him back so badly, isn't it?"

"Garin, stop it," Lilac objected. "That's cruel, even for you."

Garin spun on her, his lips curled warningly over his fangs. "You cannot possibly defend him."

"There's no way Myrddin could've known."

"He has done enough tonight. Bringing you both here, putting you in danger." Garin's chest rose and fell unevenly, his breath shallow. "I ordered him to watch over you, protect you against any harming hand. My own or otherwise."

"His duty may be to you, but Myrddin's will is his own. Just because he has not done it your way, doesn't mean he has disobeyed you. At least he has the freedom to do so." Garin flinched. "You will never hurt me."

"You think—" Garin laughed, a ridiculing sound, just as a patch of clouds moved across the moon. This had seemed to strike a deeper chord of fury in him. "You think I am incapable of hurting you?" The clouds had shifted across the moon, casting them into the shadows, but she could feel it—his eyes combing her face. A lover's caress as he spoke slowly. Intently. "You are mine. You made sure of that. Mine to protect. Mine to covet. Mine to break."

She swallowed, Garin's fixed gaze a noose around her neck. He was shifting, morphing into something and someone else entirely—yet not wholly unfamiliar. The brothel had been but a glimpse of his depraved hunger, hadn't it?

"I thought you were an open book before. Simple to read, most amusing to digest. Spread too easily upon my fingers. Now that we're bound, I've come to realize my hold on you is directly related to my appetite."

Lilac didn't dare budge, despising the way her body was already reacting —the heat creeping up her throat, stinging her cheeks, surging between her thighs.

"Look at you. You register the threat in my words, yet still struggle to hold yourself from me. I can sense it now, just what this does to you." His head tilted, craning toward her. "I hear your heart thudding away, I can feel your clit jumping at the sound of your name on my tongue. Doesn't it, Eleanor? Your Majesty. Lilac." The last word he spoke nearly broke her will. "*Princess.*"

She was her kingdom's beloved ermine caught in a snake's trance, coiled tightly between muscles trained to kill with nowhere to run—not that she even wanted to.

The minute movement of Myrddin caught her eye. Over Garin's shoulder, the warlock was inching back towards Rupert.

Myrddin put a slow finger to his lips.

"I taste you on the wind," Garin muttered. "It is gut-wrenching how sinfully I crave you. Your laughter is the sound of cathedral bells—the scent of your hair, the sun warming me through the high windows. Your body, the pulpit. All I want to do is kneel, and repent, and drink of your wine, and sin, and *sin* again, until there is little left of the monster I've become."

Lilac dug her nails into her palm so hard, she started to bleed. She raised her chin, simultaneously acknowledging Myrddin's message. "You miss it, don't you? You miss your mouth on me, my arousal coating your lips. Your fingers slicked in me." She cocked her head—a very Garin-like gesture. She hoped he recognized himself in her. "You go without the taste of this pussy for three days, and you've already lost your mind? Shame."

His smile then grew vicious, and she could've sworn his eyes glinted in the dark. Garin's head fell back, mouth opening in a plea of silent laughter as he gripped his chest.

At that moment, the clouds parted.

Yanna gasped.

Lilac would've run for the trees, then, if not for every bit of instinct telling her being chased—*hunted*—would certainly have made it worse.

With his face basked in the moonlight, Garin's features were illuminated. *All* of his teeth were fangs, some whose point came at a lethal slant —some, more jagged than others, his canines still especially long in comparison. Sharp nails had sprouted upon his lengthened fingers, his already-huge hands enlarged.

Blinding need boiled her blood, stronger than the fear that chased it painfully through her veins. She imagined tackling him, pushing him back and riding his mouth, her fingers twined through his luscious black hair until he sank his teeth into her.

She wanted to nip at his throat and make him bleed. "Your bark is stronger than your bite."

"*No*," Yanna whimpered frantically, sidling up to her. "Are you fucking crazy?"

"I do miss it." Garin wiped his chin across his forearm. He was *drooling*, his voice a deep moan that may as well have been two of his thick claws up her skirts. "Oh, gods, I do. More than you'll ever know." His eyes darted onto Yanna, who hid behind the curtain of Lilac's hair. "Though, the taste of your sister was almost—*nearly*—close enough."

Lilac's hungry smile fell.

All the excitement left her body in the whoosh of air expelled from her lungs, her chest caving in until it ached. This time, the pang of raw jealousy at the fresh memory of his fangs in Yanna clanged with something far more primal.

Lilac turned to Yanna through her heated, already blurry vision; her handmaiden's blonde hair was silver in the moonlight, framing her face. Yanna was too busy glaring daggers at Garin, tears already streaming down her plump cheeks.

"Don't listen to him," Lilac said, grasping at her own sanity. "He's trying to get into your head."

"Me?" Garin pointed at himself, his claw pricking his chest. "No. No, not in the way I've buried myself into yours."

Lilac slinked her fingers between Yanna's, just in case she ran to fight

BRIAR SOMERSET

him. Or worse. She thought of her castle—her throne. "My father never told me—"

"You think your father would have half the mind to tell you if he'd fathered any more children? He can barely handle one." Garin chuckled, nostrils flaring in their direction. Lilac and Yanna took a step back. He brought his hand to his mouth, running his tongue along a blood-crusted finger. "You taste of each other." He cocked a brow, licking his fingertip and lips as if cleaning himself after a jam tart. "Your blood, at least. And you both smell of Marguerite. There's often a resemblance there between siblings." A certain darkness shadowed his expression. "From what I can tell, you smell and taste nothing of Henri," Garin added, with a pointed look at Yanna. "Lucky you."

Lilac stared at her in disbelief. *How? How, and when?*

Did Marguerite know? Had either of them known? Was that why they came to work for her—in her home? Piper had sensed it first, between Yanna and Isobel. How had she known without drinking from them?

Adelaide's face abruptly interrupted her train of thought. The witch's ochre eyes were ablaze with terror—along with the pale, round visage of another young woman. A girl no more than the age of ten with the same pin-straight black hair as the witch, her eyes rolling and half shut. Red flecked across her cheeks and mangled throat. Two bodies slumped over each other in the background.

Lilac rubbed aggressively at her face, desperate to rid herself of the unwelcome memory. *His* memory. "Stop it."

"You sick fuck." Yanna shook Lilac by the shoulders, and her vision vanished. "Leave her alone!"

"Believe what you will." Garin shrugged. "And, while your second request is far beyond my control... if you want, I'll sample your dear Isabel, just to be sure. And your mother. Delicious, beautiful Marguerite, perfuming herself, wearing her hair tall—not a stray lock upon her throat. Baring herself for me without even realizing it. I'm sure she wouldn't mind."

Truth or lie, he really was a monster. Cruelty and hunger came too naturally to Garin. Maybe it was him; maybe it was everything he'd been through, his vampirism—perhaps both—but it was always in him in the end. His thirst had brought it out, their thrall bond worsening it. She should've known.

That was why it had upset him so much.

"Touch them and I'll stake you myself."

Garin's smirk faded at Lilac's threat. He remained expressionless, running his hand over his face. Despite the hunger that filled them, his eyes were tired. "You have no idea what any man, mortal or creature, is capable of when he is hungry enough."

"It is still no match for a woman's wrath or determination." Lilac squeezed Yanna's hand. "We rode Loïg here."

Rapt fascination crossed his face. "You... rode him here?"

Lilac suppressed a more vulgar response, scorning the way his incredulity around this fact seemed to center him. "We all did. He's rather agreeable."

Behind Garin, Myrddin had turned back toward the house. The violet currents between his fingers were there again; they began to smoke once he resumed drawing shapes in the air.

In a matter of seconds, a violet teardrop-shaped ball of flame the size of a fist floated from the steaming remains, bobbing toward Myrddin and Rupert. It hovered between them for a moment, then sank silently into the earth just next to the corpse's head.

Rupert's body began to glow, an outline of arcana shrouding his form, just bright enough to see in contrast with the deepening night.

"He trotted right into the trees just there and vanished in a veil of black smoke, just as quickly as he'd arrived," added Lilac, pointing back west toward the castle. "That is no typical horse."

Yanna wiggled her hand from Lilac's, eyes bulging at the sight behind Garin. "Is—"

Lilac elbowed her in the side.

"That doesn't make sense. There's no way all of you rode here that quickly. It's at least half a day's ride from the chateau nonstop, even along the most direct route. Even slower with an encumbered steed."

"Myrddin teleported us to the battlefield outside Montfort-sur-Meu."

"To be fair, she would not take no as an answer," Myrddin said, eyes widening frantically at Lilac.

Garin whirled back on him, just as Rupert's body ceased glowing.

Fuck. "*I* commanded him to." Lilac stepped forward, shrugging off Yanna's hand that went straight to her arm. "I cornered him."

"She's strong, Garin," Myrddin stammered. "S-she's yours, she takes after you. She'd gleefully keep slitting my throat if she had her way—"

"You teleported them *where*?" Garin roared, stalking toward the warlock.

"The battle was already over, you all were gone. You saved my father's life." Lilac spoke hurriedly, realizing her grave mistake. "Garin, wait, Myrddin has been a tremendous help!"

Garin ignored her shouts. There was a explosion of spark and flame at his feet.

"Center yourself," Myrddin shouted. "Remember who you are!"

"I *know* who I am," Garin snarled back, his voice drenched with desperation. "I've spent the last two weeks in shock over the discovery of that very fact. I have never been more painfully aware of who I am, and what this curse had made me." His claws grasped at his bare chest. "A slave to time. And my violent, dastardly heart. I have no choice but to obey."

"You're going to be all right!" Myrddin held his hands out, backing away from him and Rupert's still body. "You're gravely injured, and I don't want to hurt you. Doing so will only endanger the queen." He lurched back and dodged a swipe of Garin's outstretched hands.

"I'll kill you!"

Lilac's muscles seized against her will; she strained to move, to help, but her legs had grown impossibly heavy. "He's been a guide to us both! He's your patron, you've served him all these years at the inn. He's your friend."

Garin snarled and launched himself onto the warlock.

"He is my council," Lilac thundered. "Myrddin...what is your family name?"

"*Wyllt*! Myrddin Ambrosius Wyllt!"

"Myrddin Abrosious Wyllt, I hereby assign you to my royal council, to aid me in...in Diplomacy and Magic." Lilac jumped; a floating scroll materialized in a puff of smoke before her very eyes, a huge peacock's quill suddenly in her right hand.

"Only if you mean it," Myrddin gargled, Garin's hands around his neck.

Lilac shakily put the nib to the parchment, with no time to read the neatly scrawled text. "He is at my behest and protection, Garin! As are you." She finished her signature, and the quill and scroll vanished into thin air with a puff of smoke. "I order you to unhand him!"

Garin was way past reason; his fangs gnashed at Myrddin, who stumbled back, toppling them both. They rolled. The warlock had a clumsy sort of strength of his own, punching and clawing at Garin's face until Myrddin gasped out in pain.

Garin's mouth was latched onto his neck.

She had to act quickly; Rupert as a vampire sounded like a nightmare, their brief tryst aside. He was aloof and privileged, he'd willingly worked for Bog *and* poisoned her. But Myrddin did say in her library that there was a method to his madness. She had to believe there was reason beyond him fucking Rupert for wanting to save him so badly. Such, that he was willing to brawl Garin for it. There was no time to question it.

With all her might, she lunged for the corpse and stuck her foot onto his shoulder, yanking the arrow out of his belly. She tossed the arrow aside and pulled the remaining one from his chest, the head catching onto meat and bone before it came free from his chest cavity.

There was a yelp of pain—Garin's entire body flashed violet before he was thrown into the air, off of the warlock, rolling several yards down the knoll.

Lilac made to run after him—she couldn't help herself—but Yanna's arm linked with hers, yanking her back.

"Good thinking." Myrddin sat up, wiping his own blood from his face, staining it into his beard. The gaping wound at his throat closed before their eyes. "Keep her from him."

"What did that scroll do?" Lilac pressed, desperate to distract herself.

"Formalities." Myrddin waved an unconcerned hand, pulling himself to his feet. "Just some fine print binding me to you. My duty, that is. I thought I was going to have to beg."

"Magically binding?"

"Now, I did not say that." Myrddin wagged a finger. "Mostly, being amongst your ranks protects me from him." He jabbed that wagging finger at Garin, stirring in the dirt.

She considered Kestrel and his deals. Surely striking one with a warlock wasn't any better. "But what do I owe you?"

"Me? Nothing. I want nothing more than to see you to greatness. The both of you."

She had no reason to trust him explicitly, but for now, he was the most powerful person in their vicinity. Despite all the grief he'd given the vampire, he'd never once crossed Lilac.

At least she wouldn't be the first ruler he'd served. "Fine."

"It is more than fine, Your Majesty. It is done as dusk."

Garin sat halfway up, arms darting out toward his thigh, moaning. "My —" he started to cry, but he leaned over to retch. Thick, black ichor poured from his mouth.

"Don't, Your Majesty," Myrddin said sternly, as if reading her mind.

"But he needs me." Lilac's entire body turned rigid at the sound of his wails, despite the urge to drop to her knees and feed him from her throat. It was as if even the muscle and bone Garin had previously commanded strained against her every attempt to ensure his well being. "He's hurt."

"Not mortally," replied Myrddin. "Not yet. We've got to get him inside. To the castle, away from the public."

A primal fear struck her.

"Don't even think about it." Yanna whipped her head toward Lilac so fast, the last of her hair flew out of its braid. Her hand tightened around Lilac's wrist, nails digging into her in panic. "Are you delusional? With him looking and—and speaking like *that*? After everything he just said? The tongue of the devil, mouth of a hell hound on him." Yanna shuddered. "Last night at the feast, I'd understand. Right now, he looks like a demon who crawled out of hell after devouring everyone there. You're not going anywhere *near* him."

Yanna wasn't wrong.

Garin's hair was a nest of branch and leaf, the leftover ribbons of his shirt singed all the way off after Myrddin had shocked him. His already-large ears, she hadn't noticed before, tapered into little points, the tips sticking out from his jet black waves. His muscles coiled under the layers of dried blood leaking from the glistening, gaping hole in his arm as he tensed, grinding his sharpened teeth against the pain. The tip of his nose to his chin was stained in the burgundy he'd gulped down from Yanna and Myrddin—fangs covered in the tar-like bile he continued to vomit.

If he never looked more a vampire at the brothel, then he was monstrous tonight.

She'd never seen anyone so beautiful.

Indeed, deluded Lilac would remain if it was her flesh that sated him, her voice that soothed him. Her blood that drew him like a beast desperate to lap at her beckoning tide.

"Your sister is right. He needs your blood, but he musn't access it freely. He is momentarily too volatile for that."

The wind picked up, ruffling their hair. Lilac reached up to pick a bramble from her mess of frazzled blonde hair. The eve was mild, but Lilac had spent the most of it trembling. She didn't now, with her hand in Yanna's. She thought of Isobel, and Piper.

She and Isobel were older—*six years* older than Lilac. Her mother had been young, maybe only two or three years Lilac's senior when she'd birthed her.

"Did you know?" Lilac's voice cracked, unable to mask the heaviness of the night.

Yanna's laugh was scornful. "You think we've come to you on purpose. You think we've come to beg for status. For safety."

"You would not *have* to beg. You have been immediately elevated to my court." She almost broke a smile at the look of disbelief on Yanna's ruddy face. "When I'd mentioned it before, it was an offer." Lilac nodded at Gwendal, who was still unmoving. "Now it is an order."

"I don't believe it," was all Yanna said in response, her expression growing dubious and cold once more. "We are not Marguerite's daughters. Our mother is a stranger unto us. The same with our father. It's always been me and Izzy. Just us, and only us. That's the way it was meant to be."

"Whether it is true or not, my request remains. You, Isobel, and Piper. My friends, Lorietta, and Adelaide, at The Fenfoss Inn. Even him." She looked to Myrddin. "We were meant to find each other."

Myrddin was silent. He hadn't shown an once of surprise upon Garin's revelation; if he felt any at all, it did not show.

"Did you?" Lilac asked him, knowing he'd immediately understand her question. He was a fortuneteller, bound by the truth.

"I have an eye for many an occurrence, both large and small. Sun and moon, reconciliation and reckoning. But I cannot see into the past. What I do know, is that you are correct in that regard, Your Majesty. You and Mademoiselle—" He glanced questioningly at Yanna.

"Galvan."

"You and Miss Galvan were destined to find each other, as is true with many special friendships. Piper is lovely, but it will be helpful to surround yourselves with those not unaffected by Garin's arcana." Myrddin picked a patch of dried blood out of his beard. "Regarding your thrall bond, you might find your penchant for unfettered obstinance an unexpected boon."

"He seems to be worsening," Lilac whispered, as if Garin wouldn't be able to hear her. She wasn't sure the vampire bothered paying attention, with all the retching he was doing. "Nothing's a match for Garin's will."

"Not with his deepening hunger, as you've seen, no," agreed Myrddin grimly. "But with the way your body reacts to magic, either absorbing or deflecting it entirely as we've seen with the *Guài* disillusionment charm, I'd be intrigued to see what happens when your gall meets any other form of arcane resistance against him." His brow arched, almost as if the thought amused him. "Tonight you'll find Garin's powers, usually dormant outside of your thrall bond or any active entrancement, more violent in their effects."

"Is that why he looks like that?" Yanna asked.

"Yes. He's taken the form of one of the ancients. A Strigoi."

"*Strigoi*," Lilac repeated, letting it roll off her tongue. Myrddin hadn't seemed shocked by this, either. "Did you know this would happen when you sent me to enthrall myself to him?"

"I did not anticipate it, no." Myrddin pursed his lips, studying Garin—the animalistic way he was sprawled, arms out, expelling the last of the tar-like blood from his stomach. "It is a possibility, when regnants are kept from their thralls. Forced to abstain from their bodies and blood for an extended amount of time, they turn into walking ghouls. More like the undead. Stronger. Hungrier. More swollen."

"Garin's not swollen," Lilac managed, horrified.

"I did not say *where*."

"But I haven't fed him or—or done any of that since the night at The Fool's Folly." She was incredibly red, her chest flushing. "But that was mere days ago."

"What do you mean? You sucked his cock this morning in your closet," added Yanna, throwing an arm up. "Does that not count for anything?"

Myrddin shot Yanna a stern look. "It usually takes much, *much* longer for a vampire to turn into a Strigoi. There's no set rule, though it's usually weeks. Months, even. And by then, the vampire has descended into such a frightening state—into something so depraved and unjust in its ways—that whomever is keeping the thrall from it will often return it to them. And the thrall will make no easy captive, either." Myrddin's eyes darkened. "Most of the time, if they're not closely monitored, it is the mortal thrall who won't survive the separation. It's almost never the thrall holding *itself* from their regnant," he added, regarding Lilac knowingly. "That, I know, is unheard of."

"In that way," Lilac said slowly, processing it all, "it sounds like Strigoi are often created."

"You'd be correct in your astute assumption. Strigoi are rare extremely rare. I don't know if there's ever been a recorded sighting in all of Brittany. Or even your neighboring France." He stifled a incredulous laugh. "They're commonly seen in the countries where the vampire governs feely, alongside or maybe even over the human populace. There are such communities across every continent, as I've witnessed in my travels. In the eastern, mostly Romanian sect, the Strigoi serve among Sanguine elites as guards or court to the Doyen. There, they reside in remote castles or manors overlooking their villages. They're created, then kept in a perpetual state of hunger during times of war or anticipated battle, their thralls held from them in iron and blessed hawthorn cages until they've carried out their purpose or task."

"Then what happens?" Yanna asked, picking her nail beds raw.

"Then, the Strigoi is rewarded with their thrall. I would not call this specific reconciliation a reward for the thrall, though," said Myrddin, grimacing. "It is often a very violent reunion. When the vampire in question is needed for duty once more, their thrall is stripped from them again. Then, the process begins all over."

Lilac's stomach was in knots. She thought about the passage in the vampire manuscript she and Piper had read. "Is the Doyen a clan leader?"

"Yes. Garin is the Doyen of the Brocéliande vampire coven after Laurent, although I'm not sure Laurent ever applied the same terminologies. Garin certainly does not. He was very informal in his ways, more focused on the family he created. Great leader, he was, for someone so young and inexperience. Garin's transformation into a strigoi was likely accelerated by his intense hunger for you, made worse by drinking Yanna's blood. That's not even counting whatever ails him that prevents those injuries from healing."

Lilac eyed Garin's gaping arm and thigh, the pant leg soaked through in water and blood. Not even the magic of his strigoi transformation had healed him. "Is this permanent?" she asked under her breath.

Myrddin did not answer right away. He pursed his lips, then blew a breath out. "Some say Sanguine magic is a branch of underdeveloped arcana on its own. Some say it is an adjunct form of Necromancy. I think it can stand to be studied more, which is what I'd been pushing for at the Ambleside Sanctum when I decided to flee with the amulet I'd given Bastion. Either way, much like Necromancy, it is a volatile, poorly understood type of magic. No," he finally replied. "He should revert to his humanoid form after he's had you."

"*Had* her? Are you joking?" blurted Yanna. "He'll kill her."

Myrddin's shrug was slow and apologetic. "She'll have to sate him one way or another, Mademoiselle Galvan. It can be done carefully. They've done it before. The queen is stronger than she knows."

Lilac's ears began to ring. Yanna and Myrddin's arguing should've sobered her, cleared her mind enough to push against the raging urge to serve him.

All she could think about was his fangs teasing the crease of her inner thigh.

Garin sat up, panting through every tender movement as he staggered gingerly to his feet. "You prick," he rasped, wiping the filth from his lips. "What did you do to me?"

"It's temporary. And you did it to yourself," said Myrddin, matter-of-factly. "This is what you get for drinking from an incubus-born warlock. My blood is meant to render any attackers or potential devourers useless."

Lilac much disliked the way Garin's hands trembled. "What's wrong with him? Besides the obvious."

"His gifts of speed and strength remain encumbered, but for how long varies. He was already weakened. Drinking my blood just made him easier to handle."

Garin bared his teeth and made to charge Myrddin, but cried out instead, stumbling forward. "*Argh*, my leg!"

Lilac broke free of Yanna's grip just as she released her, and before she knew it, she was striding toward him—she *needed* to help him if no one else would. Myrddin's shout preceded a flash of white-violet that blinded her, a blast of heat singing her front.

Ears ringing, her world went dark.

SHE THOUGHT SHE MIGHT'VE FAINTED. MAYBE SHE HAD. ALL WAS QUIET —but as quickly as the silence came, she could hear rushed conversations and shouting around her, felt the slowly returning ache of her joints as she was jostled about.

The faint susurrations grew louder. Her hands lowered instinctively and grasped at the earth at her sides, steadying herself.

"Easy now," Myrddin said, nearing. "Let her sit, regain her bearings."

"You were the one who nearly blew her up," Yanna snarled from above her. "I wouldn't have let her go if not for that *lunatic*. I am of the queen's court, not a vampire's snack!"

"It was required for him to turn." Myrddin was hovering over them, slipping an arm under Lilac's. Together, they helped her to her feet. "We'll have Minerva get you a bandage and you'll be back to your courtly duties in no time."

"What about Gwendal?" Yanna asked, pressing her skirts to the other side of her neck.

"He will awaken. This one was instant because I brought him back to life. My unique contribution in Necromancy—tugging souls back from the precipice of the void, and replacing them with another. I've only performed it once before, for one of the Old Kings. The recently expired soul of a first-degree relation is required to bring the dead back."

Lilac blinked the remnants of light away to see a large blackened circle of earth mere feet away.

　　　　BRIAR SOMERSET

There was a new voice giving stern orders. "Be *still*. This is for Lilac's safety."

Rupert was awake. Garin's back was pressed to him, head locked in the new vampire's grasp. Rupert's opposite arm held Garin's hands behind his back. He was entirely helpless, swinging his leg back to meet Rupert's shins. But he was a fledgling—unimpeded, unlike Garin was. He was stronger, faster with Myrddin's blood still in Garin's veins. The blows that would've otherwise broken Rupert's kneecaps did hardly anything at all.

"Keep her name out of your mouth, you ungrateful traitor." Garin's head whipped this way and that in the tight vice that was the crook of Rupert's arm, teeth gnashing. "When I regain my strength, it's over. I'll shove a stake through your heart, make a roast of you upon the pyre, and scatter your remains for the wolves to feast upon!"

"I *am* grateful," Rupert muttered quietly, alarm flashing in his eyes. "I owe you my life. But I must protect Her Majesty. She saved me."

"Let me—go—"

"Do not," Myrddin warned. "I highly advise against doing anything he tells you in this state."

His struggling barely moved Rupert, whose gaze darted down at Garin, then back up at the three watching with bated breath. "Is this going to happen to me?" he said, over his fangs.

"The teeth and ears?" Lilac asked. "Or the momentary weakness?"

"Either."

"Don't enthrall anyone," Myrddin retorted. "And keep your fangs out of my neck. If you can help yourself, that is."

Just then, Garin buckled at the knees and thrashed, lunging in Lilac's direction. She stumbled back into Yanna; Garin had broken free for a second before Rupert tackled him to the ground, pinning his arms behind his back again.

Teeth gritted, Lilac marched forward, ignoring the warnings of Myrddin and Yanna. Rupert watched warily as she approached, securing his hold on Garin. He was breathing heavily, staring past her at the house and avoiding her gaze.

Jarring as it was to see him spiraling out of control under the claw of his hunger, it was almost worse seeing Garin defeated.

She knelt, placing her hand upon his cheek. "If you want me," she whispered, "in all the ways you crave, then you will let us help you."

He didn't move, didn't snap his teeth at her, just inches from her wrist. Heart pounding, Lilac nodded at Rupert, and allowed him to hoist Garin up.

"Careful." Myrddin put his hands out in warning, beckoning her and Yanna closer. "Easy. Easy, now. Gather in."

"Get us to the castle. Bring us to my infirmary."

Yanna made a noise of protest. "But what about Gwendal?"

"You are *not* bringing them to the castle," Garin panted, nearly incoherent. Drool dripped from his mouth. "You—" But he stopped speaking and snapped his head up at the house.

Two figures approached from the rear of the smoking pile, dressed in a variety of hats, light armor, and tattered gauntlets.

Lilac immediately recognized them from the vestibule at the Sanguine mine.

"Garin." The woman shaded her eyes from the moonlight as thy neared, as if the dark allowed her to see better. They widened when they fell upon Rupert's hold on him. And Garin's face, nearly inhuman. "What in the seven hells did they do to you?"

Garin's voice cut through the night. "Stand down, Isolde. Walter. You remain in the presence of the queen."

They took one look at Lilac and lowered themselves to their knees. Shock crossed their faces when she responded with a deep bow.

"Your Majesty. My Lord—we smelled smoke and wanted to investigate," said Walter. "Further down the path we thought we'd heard your voice. We came right away."

Myrddin glanced down the knoll, toward Paimpont. Chimneys smoked, windows and torches flickered, pinpricks downwind. He turned toward the farmhouse and waved a hand.

A gust of wind rattled the grass and haybales, just as it had when the *Guài* had broken their ward around the scene of the carriage accident.

Rising to his feet, Walter removed his cap. "Sir."

"There was another skirmish out east," Garin managed, wiping his dripping mouth on his shoulder. "Bastion's told you about them, hasn't he?"

"No," said Isolde, "but we'd heard about it through the korikaned.

Blitzrik's kept us informed. I've kept several patrollers close to your inn, for good measure. They're safe. We're all safe, My Lord."

Garin dipped head into a grateful bow, falling silent.

"This is Yanna." Lilac motioned to her right. "She's one of my Ladies-in-Waiting."

Isolde's nostrils flared in their direction. "Is she a fledgling?"

"*No.*"

"No, but he is." Lilac looked over her shoulder at Rupert. "And so is he." She pointed at Gwendal's body.

Walter glanced at Garin. "One of her guards?"

"He was the only survivor in François's most recent attack. Garin brought him here."

"Take him to the mine. Ensure his first feed, keep it ethical," said Garin. "Oversee it, and provide the *volunteering* donor extra rations. When this is all over, we're going to discuss freeing them—but not a moment before," he warned. "They've given years of their lives to the coven under Bastion's order. Under mine, we will protect them, cater to them as our own."

The vampires exchanged glances.

"He belongs with her," Lilac said with a softened glance at Yanna, who'd begun to tear up again. "Take care of him."

Isolde went to Gwendal without another word, scooping him up and propping him carefully over her shoulder. "You will see him again," she told Yanna with a small, fanged smile. "I promise."

"And the house?" Walter asked, eyeing the wreckage.

Garin blinked blearily up at it. "It is a house. Nothing more."

Isolde and Walter moved toward the trees with no more than a parting glance at Garin and Rupert. Lilac took Yanna by the wrist and tugged her toward Myrddin, Rupert, and Garin.

For once, the world was somber and still as the trees and smoldering house began to spin, and the ground dropped from beneath their feet.

⚘ 37 ⚘

Kemble shrieked, knocking her chair back from her desk.

Lilac shoved Myrddin and Rupert off; they landed on the floor next to her with a thump. Yanna had landed on the cot to her right closest to the door.

Garin was the only one already on his feet, already prowling across the room; his limp didn't slow him one bit. Myrddin's hand flew up from the tangle of limbs between the cots; the infirmary door was instantly shrouded in its violet glow, filling the room with the scent of sulfur as it sealed shut.

That didn't stop Garin from trying.

"Open it." He slammed his body against the door. Dust rained down from the doorframe. "I said, *open* the *door*." Lilac braced herself before she even felt the inevitable tug at her navel. She fought it, curling her fingers into the thin blankets and locking her legs around the nearest bedpost as if it would stop him—until Garin's shoulders stiffened and he glanced over his shoulder. "Anyone but *her*."

Her body ceased struggling immediately, and she scrambled back onto the cot as if it were a life raft. Yanna climbed from hers onto Lilac's anyway, eagerly distancing herself from the vampire.

Garin yanked and pushed on the handle, which snapped off in his hands. It clattered to the floor when he levitated several feet off the ground. He shouted, swinging his arms and legs at the air. "Put me down, Myrddin!"

But Myrddin was still peeling himself off the floor, detangling his legs from Rupert. The fledgling rose first, propping himself against the foot of Lilac's bed; when Garin let out a territorial growl, Rupert cursed under his breath and stood erect. "I'm not touching her."

Kemble stood between her desk and the medical supply cart from the night before, arms outstretched toward Garin, the veins at her temples bulging.

"Minerva! Good evening to you, too!" Myrddin tossed his hair out of his eyes. "Nice to see you've continued your schooling, after all. Now, would you mind putting my vampire down?"

"Your—*vampire*," Kemble hissed, clutching her breast and pointing sideways at Rupert. "*That* is a vampire. He's a Strigoi—"

"I know what he is, Minerva."

"Are you out of your mind?" Kemble screeched. "A Strigoi in Brittany? In this castle?"

Garin gave a final, determined kick to the door from the air, launching himself at Kemble. She shrieked and swung her arms in a half circle, flinging him across the room. Garin's head bounced off the wall with a sickening crack, and he landed on the cot adjacent to Lilac's—the one he'd cradled her on, nose buried in her hair the night before.

He coughed and rolled onto his side, and didn't move after that.

There was a tug at Lilac's collar; Yanna's fists were wrapped around the ribbons at her back. "I see that psychotic look in your eyes. I'll put you in a headlock, too."

But Lilac's anger wasn't for Garin—not solely.

Kemble? It was like the breath had been stolen from her lungs. Had her parents known? Had anyone known? Kemble often kept to herself, but she'd sometimes have tea with Hedwig in the afternoons. Was Hedwig a witch, too? Was anyone else at the castle magic folk? Kemble's apothecary shelves hadn't seemed to hold any Fae-rooted ingredients—if so, Garin would've sensed it last night. Kemble didn't have the amber-tinged feline irises both the Algovens and Adelaide had.

Bile stung Lilac's throat. She shrugged Yanna's hand off and rose. She made her way past Myrddin, centering herself between Garin's cot and the witch. "You know each other?"

"Most unfortunately," Kemble said with a scornful glare at Myrddin.

"Minerva is a talented healer from the School of Restoration. An old colleague of mine from the Sanctum."

"And *you* are a stain upon the sanctity of the Arts."

At the foot of the now-empty cot Yanna had landed on, Rupert was rubbing the back of his neck with one hand, and fanning his collar with the other. "Is it just me, or is it sweltering in here?

"Just you," Yanna replied. "I'm freezing."

Kemble squinted over her shoulder at Rupert. "Do I know you from somewhere?"

"You were here this whole time, and not a word of it to me." Lilac's tone was cold, drawing Kemble's attention back to her. It wasn't the least bit warm, nor filled with the familiarity she would've loved to hear in her darkest hours. She knew it wasn't an immediate concern, but it was almost like she couldn't control her anger, nor her mouth. What she would've reserved for perhaps another time, or drowned in a flute of champagne and bonbons, came spilling out. "No olive branch extended on your behalf, even after Freya was found and everything for us changed."

The muscle under Kemble's eye twitched. "Your Majesty," she said, pressing a hand to her chest. "I've diligently served your family for years after being expelled from the very institution my father helped found, thanks to your criminal warlock. My loyalty's remained all the same. Why, I attended your birth."

"No discreet acknowledgement in passing." Kemble's countenance darkened at the accusation lacing Lilac's rising voice. "No motion of reassurance. The entire castle heard me crying myself to sleep some nights. You knew what it was like to be treated this way, yet you never said anything."

"That is *why* I never said anything, you stupid girl. I hid so I could be free. Sometimes freedom is not worth the pursuit." Kemble pursed her lips. She cleared her throat and smoothes her hair, then, her skirts. Avoiding Lilac's glare, she looked about the room—at her apothecary cabinet, at the empty cots. At Myrddin, her eyes brimming with blame.

Garin groaned, then.

Lilac drew the knocked-back curtains all the way. He'd rolled onto his side, facing her, his legs tucked into his chest. In contrast with the white sheets, a deep carmine had pooled around his legs and up by his shoulder.

Kemble let out a disgruntled gasp, skittering back. "Is that... is that Maximilian's emissary?"

"He is very important to us, so please refrain from thrashing him around." Myrddin joined Lilac near Garin's cot with his hands out.

"Is he dead?" asked Yanna, sounding hopeful and pulling the blanket up to her chin.

"It takes far more to kill a Strigoi. In fact, it is nearly impossible. Minerva knocked him unconscious. He might be out longer than usual because he drank some of my blood, which encumbered him," Myrddin added, for Kemble's benefit. "I wouldn't want to be the one to further handle or mistreat him, even when he's this weak."

"*Great*," murmured Rupert.

"He was shot by François's men." Lilac's throat grew tighter and tighter around every word. "It was hours ago. And he isn't healing."

"But how did this—how did Albrecht—" Kemble stammered. "I don't understand. Was it the wine?"

"There is no mushroom or tonic that turns vampires into Strigoi, Minerva," Myrddin said slowly. "Remember?"

Kemble's face blanched. She shook away whatever alarming thought that had come to mind, along with her realization. "He was obviously trying to escape this room to find his thrall. Preventing him from doing so is dangerous. I don't understand why you'd withhold him from his pet, and bring a Strigoi *here*, of all places, when our kingdom is already on the brink of..."

Suddenly, Kemble trailed off, glancing at Myrddin, but the warlock was distracted, his eyes partially shut, his fingers drawing their minuscule shapes again.

"You're not resurrecting him, are you?" Lilac asked through a stab of panic.

"*Hush.*"

The witch scrutinized Yanna—the crescent-shaped wounds on either side of her neck, the red staining her skin. Then, Lilac—pink-faced, nails digging into her palms with more than the hem of her skirts singed off. Her unscathed legs, and the way she'd perched herself just onto the far corner of Garin's bed, still close enough to reach out and touch him.

"It was my choice," said Lilac unflinchingly. "Mine alone."

"I've only worked for Her Majesty for several weeks," Yanna added from her cot. "But I feel like I've known her just as long as my—my friend, Isabel. And if there's one thing I know about the queen, it is that she would never willingly make herself susceptible to such instruction unless required."

Kemble's hand went to her hair, voice dropping to a terrified whisper. "Does anyone else know about this?"

"Well, there's us. Probably a few others close to Her Majesty," Rupert responded. He was slumped over the side of the furthest cot, shoulders angled toward the door. "More might inadvertently learn of it if you don't shut your mouth."

A low groan interrupted Kemble's scathing response.

In his sleep, Garin attempted to move his wounded leg, but winced. Lilac was at his side in an instant, lifting him up. There was a sharp intake of breath from Kemble as she righted him against the pillows like he weighed nothing at all. His head lolled forward—there was a wet warmth beneath Lilac's fingertips.

She gripped his jaw to discover his fangs coated in fresh red. "Garin," she whispered frantically, patting his cheek. There was a flash of purple light—followed immediately by a white-hot heat at her knuckles. Lilac jumped, cursing, and dropped Garin back onto the pillows. She stuck her pinky into her mouth. "*What is wrong with you?*"

"I wouldn't wake him if I were you," warned Myrddin through his teeth, apparently finished with his whispered incantation. "Not here."

A rush of heat flooded her. "Will this kill him?"

"It shouldn't, but I've also never seen a Strigoi up close before—for good reason. His injuries won't do his voracious appetite any good." Myrddin squinted. "Whatever's harming him is still inside him."

"Yes, the ammunition," replied Lilac impatiently. "We've been over that. Can you remove it?"

"Me? Not without potentially blowing his leg into smithereens."

"*I'm* not getting close enough to try." Kemble stumbled back, unable to tear her eyes from Garin's oozing wounds.

"Can't you levitate them out?"

"I can't without being able to see or visualize the bullets lodged inside him. It would take immense concentration—arcane levitation is not meant to substitute the skill of a surgeon. If I try, and it rouses him, then we're all in trouble."

"He saved my father outside of Monfort-sur-Meu." Lilac felt pathetic, like she was begging. Because she was. "He saved Henri's life, and that of two of his men."

"I'm sorry. It's impossible, yet even if there was a chance..." Kemble sighed. "Vampires might not be the sole reason we're so widely regarded the way we are, but pillaging Paimpont fifty years ago certainly didn't help. They set us back decades. I refuse," she said, chin quivering. "Vampires are no friends of mine, certainly not some primordial version of them. Unspell the door, Myrddin, or I'll flag down the Midraal Market, too."

Myrddin smiled begrudgingly down at Garin. "Actually, my score with them has been settled by that very Strigoi."

"This isn't funny. Don't you see? Does anyone understand the gravity of the queen being the thrall to a Strigoi? Once he drinks and is reverted to himself, it is just a waiting game before it happens again."

"Not if he remains fed, though," Lilac asked. "Right?"

"Once a regnant becomes a Strigoi, he is always susceptible to it if he hasn't been sated. At times more easier than others. Sanguine magic is fickle." Myrddin cleared his throat with a sideways look at Kemble. "As I've said before, if it were a branch of arcana studied more freely, we'd have far more insight on the matter than we do tonight."

"This implicates *everything*," insisted Kemble. "With France, with Maximilian. A regnant would never willingly secede its bond with its mortal for anyone. Even an emperor. Even for a king with his armies at our throat. What do you think a Strigoi would do?"

Lilac looked down. Garin's hand had twitched against hers, his thumb rubbing her knuckles—then stilling once more. She grabbed his hand, sweeping her fingers across his inner wrist. His weak, slow pulse was imperceptible now—if he even had one anymore. The only things that told her he was alive were his shallow, ragged panting and the occasional wince.

Daemon as she was, Madame Kemble was a person who'd chosen comfort over resistance for years, apparently. Lilac couldn't blame her for that and that alone, but it was at the cost of camaraderie. Solidarity. Of everything else. It had provided her the ultimately grand illusion of safety, which was a cage, much like Lilac's tower; Henri would've had her executed the moment he'd discovered her pretense.

"You're wrong, Madame Kemble. About everything. The cruelty you've once endured would've persisted, with or without their Raid. Stripping anyone of their right to exist freely, shrouding them in a society that forces them to exist on scraps of justice—all while that same society has continued to benefit from their roots and magic—makes people do terrible things. I will never blame them if the ones in charge, my ancestors and otherwise, were not held accountable, either. You were never doing yourself any better by hiding here. It does not make you strong; it does not make you safe. It doesn't make you free." Lilac squeezed Garin's palm in hers. "And you have no idea what he is willing to do for me."

The good, the bad. And the bloody.

Kemble said nothing, hesitancy and self-disgust written upon her pursed lips. But the disdain in her eyes was stronger.

"Well?" said Lilac. "You heard the witch. Get to it. Unspell the door."

"What? *Why?*" Myrddin frowned so disapprovingly, even his blonde mustache furrowed. "I mean," he stammered, glancing at Kemble, "not that I anticipated trapping you, or incapacitating you and tying you up. Certainly not with—" There was a *pop* and cloud of smoke, and a large bundle of what looked to be a chain of thick iron links and rust-colored rope materialized before him. His voice rose an octave, and he snatched it out of the air. "*Gods*—and we certainly didn't use *these* last night."

Even Rupert glanced up from his hands. He looked like was going to be sick. "For fuck's sake, Myrddin." Rupert shot up from the cot just as Kemble backed into him, causing her to fall flat on her ass. He was so pink from the neck all the way to his ears, he didn't even seem to notice; his ruby red glower was fixed upon Myrddin as Kemble scoffed in disgust, peeling herself off the floor.

"Out of my way, you beanstalk of a vamp—" She cocked her head at him. "Emma?" she screamed, shrill. "*Not Emma's son?*"

Myrddin waved his hand, and the door was outlined in a shimmer of violet once more. Kemble scrambled for the door, fumbling the handle.

She never got there.

Rupert caught Kemble in a single stride. "I'm sorry," he sobbed, the chilling sound of his apologetic grief causing the hair on Lilac's neck to stand. Yanna had already leapt out of her cot and was cowering behind Myrddin.

"I'm so, so sorry." Rupert petted Kemble's hair and clamped his hand over her mouth to soften the blood-curdling screams that cut off when he yanked her head back and feasted on the front of her throat.

If anyone couldn't tell he was a fledgling on account of his pompous demeanor and poor coordination, they'd know by his bite. It was messy— blood was everywhere. After he'd adjusted his mouth twice on her with Kemble crying and wrestling herself from him, it began to spray all over the cots and floor.

All that red.

Lilac stared as it stained her shoes. *What a pretty color.* The way the fire-light from the hearth across the room illuminated it, pools of ruby—the color so deep and thick, not even sunlight could break through.

"Lilac, look out," cried Yanna.

She tore her gaze away. Garin was sitting up, transfixed on the commotion before him. The adrenaline that instantly flooded her body was a beacon of distress, something that called out to him. He swiveled his head to her, a purely predatory movement.

For once, the vice of self-preservation snapped into place, throttling her; Lilac scuttled back, but not before Garin's hand clamped around her wrist, digging his talons into her forearm. She yanked anyway, successfully freeing herself on the second tug—and tumbled backwards into one of the poles supporting the beams of linen curtains.

Every one of his fangs were visible when he slid off the bed and lumbered toward her. It seemed Myrddin's blood was still in his system, but she wouldn't be the one to test it. Lilac quickly untangled herself from the thick material and clambered over the next cot, but her stomach lurched when his thick fingers wrapped around her ankle and yanked. She slammed back down onto the cot then the floor as he dragged her back under the divider.

"I need to taste you." His inflection, his hulking shoulders, the girth of his clawed fingers creeping up her thigh toward her ass tugged every inch of her heated flesh toward him.

She flipped over and flung her hair out of her eyes, tossing the remainder of the curtain off. A flash of regret suddenly crossed his part-human features, the traces of monster flickering.

Garin lifted his hand, nails dragging down her cheek and the line of her jaw, sweeping her hair off of her throat. The scuffle beyond the curtains raged on—Kemble's screaming and the crashing of glass along the apothecary wall, now—but Garin took no notice. He snaked his arm around the small of her waist, pulling her under him.

Maybe Strigoi were vampires with their veneers melted away, any pretense of humanity shriveled off, for he was a monster in the flesh. He was the throbbing appetite of night unending. He wanted her blood; she wanted to play the strings of his dark heart and watch him come further undone.

The urge had snaked its way under her skin, a voracious acid eating at her will.

"I must have you," Garin said, gazing upon Lilac as she would a table-length feast. "I am sorry."

Lilac gripped his jaw and tugged his face toward her; brought her lips to his tapered ear and ran her soft tongue along his lobe. His shoulders shuddered against her.

"I'm not," she whispered, twisting her fingers into the curtain hem and yanking. The beam snapped—and several iron poles came crashing down on them, one narrowly missing her. Another struck the back of Garin's head.

He snarled and dropped her.

Lilac scrambled out from under him and crawled toward the room. She barely dodged an amber bottle Kemble threw at Rupert and the violet flames and smoke that exploded at his feet, dashing for the door—upon which there was a light set of rapid knocks. She quickly pressed her shoulder against it when the knock came again.

"Hello?" It was Isabel. "Is everything—"

"Don't come in." Lilac pressed harder against the door when she felt the doorknob jingle.

"*Your Majesty?*"

There was a crash; Garin burst out of the curtains, tearing down the remainder of the beams. His gaze locked greedily upon Kemble, cornered and chased by Rupert. He bent his legs, readying to pounce, when Isabel knocked and spoke again. Louder this time.

"Let me in," she demanded. "Where is my sister? Is she all right?"

Garin spun toward the door—to Lilac—and lunged. She shielded her face and threw herself to the side.

There was a heavy *thud*.

Across the room, Yanna and Myrddin had detangled themselves from the curtains.

The door swung open. Isabel took one look at the scene before them—Yanna, covered in blood and bite marks, Rupert's satisfied, heavy gulping from a finally surrendered Kemble in the corner, and Garin, bloodied, shirtless, and sprawled on his side, his hands bound at his front by thick rope and chains.

Her handmaiden uttered a squeak of terror and turned to leave, but Lilac grabbed her arm and tugged her back in, slamming the door. "See? Yanna is fine."

"Define '*fine*,'" Yanna snapped.

"You'll heal her, Isabel." Lilac pointed at the askew apothecary shelves, shockingly calm as she gave orders. "Feel free to help yourself to Kemble's supply, since it doesn't look like she'll be needing that any longer. Yanna's lost a bit of blood, too."

Myrddin helped Lilac hoist Garin to his feet. Garin winced, avoiding their gazes, but he didn't resist.

Isabel fell silent, looking like she'd be sick as she clutched her pochette.

"Yanna will explain," Lilac said softly, offering the kindest smile she could muster. She began plucking supplies from the cart that had been shoved against the wall, bundling them into a linen cloth and tucking it in the crook of her arm.

Yanna's glare bore into the side of her skull. "How *much* do I explain?"

"As much as you want."

Isabel kept her eyes on Garin as she sidled over to her sister. "What *happened* to him?"

Garin's head hung low, but she could tell he was coherent. Centered, at least in the moment. He was completely still, despite the prominent veins in his arms.

His wrists and hands had broken out in a violent rash against the hawthorn rope.

Yanna drove an elbow into Isabel's side. "He was shot. Isn't it obvious?"

She knew it wasn't what Isabel had meant. Lilac slipped her free hand under Garin's arm and led Garin toward the door. "He's injured, and I'm going help him."

Yanna made a noise of warning protest. "But where do you think you're going?"

"To my bedchamber. I'm going to extract the bullets." There was no reaction from Garin but a slow blink at the floor. "My father will return with his men soon, and the castle will be in disarray after what they've witnessed."

"You don't want to do it here?"

"No," said Myrddin sternly. "You wouldn't want that."

Yanna immediately grew red and swallowed whatever her rebuttal was going to be.

"Won't it be dangerous?" Rupert had placed Kemble's body down next to the hearth and covered it halfway with a spare blanket from the shelf. He was in the middle of cleaning his mouth with a damp towel when he noticed Isabel and bowed. "I mean, dangerous for you?"

"Are you going to do it, then?"

Rupert said nothing more.

"Wait." Myrddin stopped and snapped his fingers. Another bundle of thick leather and metal appeared before them, this one smaller—the chains, also thinner. He plucked it from the air and pressed it into Lilac's arms.

There were several pieces—three, from the looks of it. Two identical types of chains, and the third... The leather strap on *this* restraint was doubly thick. Wide, too. She frowned, alarmed, turning it this way and it this way and that. There was a piece of leather about the size of her hand, supported by belts on either side, and a round linen pouch sewn onto one of the surfaces.

She looked up, wide-eyed at Myrddin. She shoved it back at him, vehemently shaking her head.

"Come, Rupert," Myrddin sighed, beckoning the fledgling.

He did as he was told. Still, Garin did not flinch, nor fight, nor seethe when Rupert stood by him, taking him by the arm as Myrddin got to work.

Myrddin held the wide piece of leather and its pouch toward Garin's face. Garin's nostrils flared when the pouch neared; he gagged, but Myrddin prodded him in the shoulder. "This is for her," he said quietly. "Open up."

To her shock, he obeyed. Myrddin hurriedly began working the chain at the back of his head.

She forced herself to look; her gaze stilled upon the contraption that framed his somber eyes. "A *muzzle?*" She turned to Myrddin, an inexplicable rage turning her breaths shallow. "What is wrong with you? He needs my help, not more restraint."

"Oh, but he does." The warlock clicked the last of the three chains together. The leather covering Garin's face wrapped around his chiseled cheekbones and cupped under his chin, and she couldn't help but think it would only provoke him further. Myrddin pointed at Garin's covered mouth. "To prevent him from biting. There's a sack of hawthorn powder propping his mouth open, so if he tries, he'll choke on that first and knock himself unconscious for a few days. Of course, we can't have that." He held up the pair of thinner chains. Each had a padlock attached to the end. "Self-binding restraints." He looked at them and frowned—then sighed roughly. Myrddin quickly closed his eyes and began to mutter under his breath, drawing shapes in the air. Another puff of smoke, and there were more in his hand. "There you go. Four more, six total."

"Where are you finding these? Conjuring them from?"

"From my room at the inn. Illusion, of course, is my specialty, but I'm good enough to Conjure from locations within close proximity, or my personal belongings. It's just a matter of being able to visualize the item." He handed the bundle of chains to Lilac. "Throw them or place them. They'll work on their intended target. They'll also fortify the object they're bound to, to a limit."

She'd be sick. Boils had broken out across Garin's forearms, his hands curled into fists against the persisting pain, like they had been at Sinclair's camp. Surely his own talons were bleeding him further. Daemons weren't meant to be restrained, not like this. "This is unnecessary and cruel."

"Cruelty would be allowing his hunger to overwhelm him when he's drowning in it," Myrddin warned. "He will thank you later. Use them. They'll at least hold him as long as he's under the effects of my blood."

Jaw clenched, she snatched them from him. "How long do I have?"

"I never stuck around long enough to know. Best not find out." He last handed her a rusted key. "Keep him bound until after the last of the ammunition is removed. I'll be here. I need my rest if I am to come to your aid."

"I need you to alert Riou and John about the carnage we've witnessed. Piper and Bastion will be arriving soon—they are both to be allowed inside. And we should call for the guards to prepare." What little guards were left, anyway. Most of them were slain because she and her father both had failed them; while there were boxes and boxes of stolen hawthorn weaponry she and Yanna had discovered in Artus's carriage at the farmhouse—from stakes, to blades, to arrows—her own men were grossly underprepared in comparison with France's developing armory.

"I'll do it," Rupert offered.

Myrddin spared him a skeptical glance. "Do you feel better, Sir Rupert?"

He reddened. "I do."

"Good. Your kind does no one any favors by being martyrs when it comes to the appetite." Myrddin's eyes darted to Lilac. "You'll first aid Her Majesty and Sir Garin to her tower. Then, you'll secure the castle and stand watch. Her decree will protect you."

Rupert's chest inflated before Lilac added, "Be mindful of the sunrise. You're allowed to be here, by the way. You belong among us."

Myrddin took her hand. Garin said nothing. "Assuming that was the first wave of Francois's men, it will take them hours to dispatch more of them. If Garin killed them all, there were no scouts to immediately report back to Francois's leaders. You have time; I will make sure of it. Do you understand?"

In answer, Lilac shifted her supplies to one arm, taking Garin's in the other. She glanced up at Rupert. "Make sure the coast is clear for us."

"Wait." Yanna trudged over, dragging Isabel with her. "Wait. We're coming."

"No." Isabel dug her heels into the floor, shrinking away from Garin. "We can't."

"We must help. You would do it for me, wouldn't you?"

"Yes, but—"

"Then you'll do it for her."

❧ 38 ❧

No one said a word as Yanna and Isabel prepared her bath. This time, Rupert had done the filling. After they showed him the furnace room next to the infirmary, he filed in and out with two buckets while they filled the tub with rose petals and fragrant oils, lining the table at its side with cloth, towels, and a nightgown from one of the boxes Herlinde had brought.

It seemed, without a single word of explanation, that each of them understood one thing: Lilac's mission to save Garin required some preparation.

She stood in the doorway clutching the bundle of supplies, running the key through her fingers and desperately keeping her eyes off his bare, bloodied torso.

To no avail.

Garin sat in her vanity chair with his back to the hearth, wrists still bound together on his lap as he expertly avoided her gaze. He was no longer wincing in pain; she couldn't tell if it was because he wasn't forced to put pressure on his wounded leg, or if it'd been a convincing act all along, but he seemed perfectly content to watch Rupert, Yanna, and Isabel over his shoulder in the mirror's reflection.

And although it was something he couldn't help, his silence unsettled her more than anything else; she could *feel* his impatience behind the mask of bored amusement.

When the tub was just over three-quarters of the way filled, there it was —the familiar tug behind her navel. The nudge of encouragement for her to near him.

She didn't dare look up. She didn't have to. Every inch of her body registered the beckoning—a warm, unexpectedly friendly invitation at first. Wordless but palpable, though she could almost hear his voice.

I won't hurt anyone, certainly not you, he said—or so she imagined. His voice even echoed. She was exhausted and running on too little sleep. *You're nervous, I can feel it. Just as I can feel your desire for me.*

Lilac stared down at the grooves in the wood, at the fox and bear pelts adorning the floor. Curiosity skirted the argument bubbling up in her tight chest. Whether it was the creeping madness of exhaustion or another obscure effect of their bond, it was convincing. She shifted the supplies under her arm and lifted her hands to her ears.

I can feel them burrowed in deep, Garin groaned, his voice slipping deeper into her thoughts like silk drawn over a blade.

Seething, Lilac looked up. Garin's hands had remained in his lap. He was still transfixed on Yanna and Isabel fussing about and tidying the room; part of her suspected they were reluctant to leave her alone with him. Part of her knew they were eager to soak in every last juicy detail of their interaction.

Despite her best efforts, the sound of his voice was clear as the night outside.

They're hawthorn, of all things. At least, that's what I suspect. Not fire, nor silver, but shrubbery. Can you imagine? I'm being murdered from the inside out by an aggressive sort of landscaping.

Lilac froze. It was no wonder he wasn't healing. "But how are you conscious?"

Believe me, I wish I weren't.

"Did you say something?" asked Yanna, jolting her from her thoughts.

Lilac glanced around the room, fanning herself. "Where did Rupert go?"

Yanna and Isabel exchanged nervous glances and placed the pillows they'd been fluffing.

"He just left," Isabel answered. "He said Marguerite was curious about the commotion on the second floor. He's dealing with them now."

This pain—gods, it's exquisite. I've never felt anything like it. Garin wheezed a laugh. *Come. Closer.*

She could feel herself breaking into a cold sweat. Lilac wiped at her brow and took an involuntary step toward him, wobbling when she tried to stop herself.

"Are you all right?" Yanna approached, hesitant. "You look like you're going to faint."

"Please leave."

Isabel skittered toward the door instead. "Of course, Your Majesty."

"What? No, we can't just leave her."

I'm going to die like this, stretched thin between torment and desire. Garin's voice turned cunning. *That's what you want, isn't it? To watch me break?*

In silent indignation, Lilac stood her ground. She'd need to get within dangerous proximity in order to remove the bullets; she supposed she was safe with his mouth and hands secured. Still, something warned her to wait until she was alone to—

Eleanor Trecésson, if you don't remove this godforsaken muzzle from my mouth, you'll regret the next time I get my hands on you. You'll beg to be bled. I'll lap it up from you in places you've never dared imagine—

Lilac's body lurched forward, but she used the momentum to stride past Garin and march over to the opposite side of her bed, while Yanna and Isabel watched from the doorway with their mouths open. She yanked her bedside table drawer open and plucked out the long bundle Piper had earlier deposited there, just when Garin's power took hold of her once more. She skittered back, just catching herself on the bedpost.

The key stilled in her right hand; she leaned over and stuck it into the tiny padlock on his wrists. The moment his hands were free, he made to stand, but Lilac shoved him back into the chair, put her foot on his chest—and *kicked*. Garin and the chair went skidding across the room. She flung the handful of Myrddin's chains toward him; he snapped back to the chair, his wrists bound to the armrests.

His snarls were drowned out by Yanna and Isabel's shrieks.

"What is going on up there?" her mother could be heard saying, followed by Rupert's rushed explanation. They heard Myrddin's voice too, followed by Emma's. She sounded shockingly calm for a mother who probably just discovered her son's Daemon transformation.

"*Go*," said Lilac, placing the bundled stake on the vanity next to her supplies. "And don't wait outside."

"Didn't plan to." Yanna glared at Garin and took Isabel by the wrist. "If you hurt her, I'll light you on fire myself." The door slammed shut.

It was silent as soon as they were alone. He worked to slow his breathing, the cut of his jaw tight as he took in her soot-covered body. His blood covering her skin, the gashes and burned holes in her clothing.

Lilac cautiously closed the space between them; there was no use pretending she wasn't afraid when he could hear every sound her body made. Tonight, her desire consumed her fear whole.

"How did you speak to me with your mind?" No response, but the skin at her throat heated. "How did you know you could do that?"

Garin merely blinked up at her, as if he did not know the answer himself.

"What else can you do with your Sanguine magic?"

His brows knitted in confusion.

Bullshit. Lilac padded over to the edge of the steaming tub and peeled the remains of her dress up without warning.

She bent over slowly, taking her time snaking her undergarments and blade garter down her leg. Lilac smiled at him over her shoulder—he didn't notice, his eyes were glued to her ass—and placed her still dagger on the table, pleased her bleed had lightened considerably since having Garin's tea.

She pulled her dress over her head and let it drop, stepping in and savoring the scalding heat on her skin. She hadn't bathed in a couple of days. Washing her sin away, only to do it all over again—do it worse—was a welcome, dark ecstasy.

"You're much more depraved in your head than you lead on, you know." She ran a cloth down her neck, slipping it between her breasts. Rose petals swirled and stuck to her skin, one to her nipple. Lilac flicked it off. "Is it always like that for you?"

Garin's sigh morphed into a growl; he turned back to the mirror.

She dipped her head, massaging the soot and oils from her scalp—imagining him regaining his strength. Breaking out of that chair and joining her. Taking her forcefully in the water—cracking the wall of her tub further as effortlessly as it had crumbled in her hands. "Or is it a show you put on?"

When no answer came, Lilac pressed her back to the tub wall nearest him as she had at his farmhouse, suddenly feeling very naked and vulnerable in his chosen silence. It was only in the middle of lathering her face, eyes shut against the suds, when his voice echoed again.

Every day requires a mask. A show, you see. It's born from necessity, not folly, and I fault no one who does the same. I suppose it is less so when I am in your company. I am wholly myself here. You pry it out of me.

Fight the urge to face him she did, Lilac didn't need to. She *felt* him. The whisper of a touch—fingertips waltzing up the column of her spine, cupping the curve of her throat. Whatever this feeling was, she wanted to drown in it.

"You are thirst incarnate," she whispered. "Night on the fringe of dawn, never quite breaking the horizon."

I come as the thing you made me. An appetite persevering.

"Are you always so hungry? I couldn't imagine living with it." The question was meant to be taunting, but it came out all wrong—tender, and laced with her own selfish agony. "I learned to make myself small after witnessing my father's cruelty at work, haunted by Freya's murder and my own complicit existence. While I was never good at going unnoticed, I was great at running and acting in my own favor." Her throat bobbed; she was unable to stop herself from vomiting the words. "I am no victim. I am an instrument."

Garin said nothing—thought nothing—while Lilac looked down at her reflection.

"By the time I escaped, I was so disgusted with myself, I wanted to claw my way out of my skin. I'd willingly tear my flesh from my own bones just to free myself of what I'd become and the life I'd inherited. The things I'd allowed." Tonight, she saw herself clearly. The haunting glint in her wide eyes, the fevered flush in her cheeks, waves of her hair clinging to her shoulders like a damp shroud told the tale of a woman who no longer feared the cost of her desires. For better or worse, she knew what she sought—and what she'd surrender for it. "I'd never before known hunger that made me want to crawl into someone else's."

You are a cataclysm forged in fire. The tug that came behind her navel was gentler, this time. A weary welcome, and not a command. *Come to me if it pleases you. Save me if you wish. Or ruin me whole.*

Lilac stood and stepped out hearthside, letting the fire dry her back as she toweled off her hair. Garin's eyes returned to the mirror to watch her, softening against the reflected flame.

The nightgown Yanna had left for her was a pretty set; cream and sheer when she picked it up—transparent when Lilac slinked it over her head. The second piece was a comfortable undergarment that hugged her belly and hardly covered her ass. She donned her garter and dagger.

Garin's palpable gaze trailed her all the way to her vanity, where she plucked the bundle of tools and stake from her dressing table, brought them over to her bed, and laid them out—along with the key. She surveyed her weapons of choosing: Gauze, a pair of forceps, a scalpel, and a long piece of hammered metal with a small, hooked end.

She unfurled the stake, and her breath caught. It was embellished, whittled down to smoothness and etched in intricate knotted patterns. The handle came to a head, the ermine symbol of her kingdom etched at the very top, along with an L.T. just below it. That end was so shiny, it had to be covered in some sort of resin. Lilac turned to him questioningly.

His eyes were bright over his muzzle. *What do you think?*

"You think this impresses me?"

My carving, at least. Impressed with my hands, you might be, but it's been years since I've honed this skill.

"I'll never use it on you," Lilac said simply, but tucked it under her arm anyway, point facing away from him. She slipped the pair of forceps off the cloth.

Garin might've been stable, but he was still bleeding all over her chair. Was it even possible for vampires to bleed out? He'd been trickling blood for hours now. He diverted his gaze as she bent over him.

Lilac inspected his leg first. There was a deep wound in the middle of his left thigh, inches above his knee. The edges around it were already dark, but she couldn't see much else with the material in the way and the fire on the wall. She needed more light.

"Hold still."

Garin's eyes bulged; he shook his head and grunted in protest when she tucked the forceps under her arm, gripped the sides of the chair, and tugged, jerking him and the chair across the room and towards the hearth. With every scraped vibration, he winced, cussing into the leather.

"Sorry," Lilac said, wincing herself. "I'm so sorry."

He was panting again, eyes no longer amused but narrowed. He fell silent.

She positioned herself over him, extending her arm with the readied forceps, widening the prongs slightly as she lifted them over his thigh.

He suddenly jerked, bounding the chair back and shaking his head.

"My god," she snapped. "Don't *do* that!"

He lifted his good leg, brushing it against Lilac's outer thigh.

"Oh. Right." Lilac pulled the weapon from her opposite leg. It was still silent; Garin was hungry enough to drink, but not to kill. Supposedly. "Good idea."

She held the material of his trousers taut, adjusting her grip near his crotch and making him groan, low in his throat. She carefully slid the blade of her dagger into the hole in his pants and began to apply pressure to slice the fabric away from herself and his leg. As she did, all she could think about was the hilt pressed against her wet center; without looking up at him in case he was thinking the same, she pressed harder, sawing slightly until the material gave way. She placed her blade aside, gripped both sides, and yanked with all her might, exposing his thigh nearly up to his groin.

Lilac then retrieved the forceps once more and held them above his leg. Her hands were shaking, and it wasn't just because she was afraid of hurting him further. "Garin, you know I cannot concentrate with you staring at me like that."

When she scorched him with a warning glare of her own, he snorted.

She shoved the thin nose of the prongs into the hole in Garin's thigh.

There was a bone-curdling cry that came from behind his muzzle. He bucked again, followed by a muffled, *real*, "Take it off!"

She yanked the tool from him. "Myrddin said I shouldn't. I'm not taking it off until I pry the ammunition from you. Your mouth is far too dangerous."

There was a scrape against the threshold of her mind—one of his taloned fingers, prodding her chin up and digging into her flesh. *Take. The muzzle. Off.*

"You're going to bite me."

He held her gaze firmly. *I will not.*

Lilac's sharp laughter cracked off her high ceiling. "Did you see what you tried to do back in the infirmary?"

You are on your bleed, he thought matter-of-factly. *Your scent is everywhere, it is as if I'm drenched in you. I promise to remain perfectly merciful, as long as I am in these chains.*

She groaned inwardly. She could already feel his power creeping over her, this time a throb at her lower back. She circled him, glaring, noticing some of the chains she'd thrown had fallen to the floor; she scooped them up and fumbled with the clasps one by one. The muzzle fell into his lap, where she quickly snatched it off. Lilac tossed the horrid contraption and the chains onto the edge of her bed. Within reach.

"What do you want?" she demanded.

"First of all, you look devastatingly beautiful." Condensation slicked his face; the curl of hair that usually hung over his forehead stuck to it now. His lips curved into a polite, closed-mouth smile—admiration edged in a sly look that indicated he'd rather do nothing more than reach out and touch her. That he despised that he couldn't. "Second, I just wanted to guide those precious little hands of yours."

"You wanted me to remove your muzzle for this? You couldn't have said it through this talent you've been hiding from me?"

"I haven't been hiding anything from you. I discovered it sitting there, at your vanity. Didn't know you could hear my thoughts until your body began reacting." He shrugged. "Then again, its reacted to everything lately, hasn't it? Just think of what my bite might do."

"You sat there and imagined the things you'd say to me," Lilac replied, ignoring her burning ears. "How pathetic."

"You'd be surprised. I do it quite often. There are a lot of things I'd say to you but can't."

She shoved the stake at him. "Tell me what to do or I'm putting that contraption back on."

Garin's pupils grew, his grin salacious as he cocked his head toward the bed. "There is a tool there. The long, thin piece of metal. You'll *carefully* insert it into the wound. You'll hit the bullet, and that's how you'll know how far to insert the forceps so you're not prodding around in there and shoving it deeper."

Lilac nodded, retrieving the long tool with the tiny hook at the end.

"Maybe the one in my arm first? It's not nearly as painful."

It wasn't a demand; he'd been careful about his words so that it wasn't an order. She did as requested, positioning herself above him once more. A shudder passed through him as she brought her face near and examined his bicep; it did seem a lot more shallow.

"You've done this before," she said, hoping to distract herself from the pressure of his eyes on her.

"Why do you say that?"

"You know what to do. And the pain to expect."

"We saw the use of hand cannons, or the *arquebus*, toward the middle of the Hundred Years' War. Alor refused to issue them, and so did the king. I've never touched nor trained with one of those abhorrent weapons. Neither had any of the men I've led." His lip lifted into a soft snarl. "But I have extracted my fair share of bullets. The ones that were removable, anyway."

Now that he'd finally stopped squirming, she sucked in a steadying breath and inserted the fine tip of the hooked tool into the wound on the exhale. It was hard to see with all the blood that oozed out. The end of the tool hit something solid, causing him to wince. This wound was much shallower, maybe just over a knuckle deep—one of her knuckles, she noted, peering sideways at his massive hands, which were clenched over the armrest. Lilac lifted the tool slowly, straightening and placing it back onto the cloth.

"Maybe," he choked, and it looked like he was holding himself against the back of the chair. "Maybe put the muzzle back on now."

She approached with the forceps this time. "Tell me about him."

"About what?"

"About Alor." Without warning, Lilac lowered the head of the prongs into him; they were wider, and had to hit the raw meat of his arm in order to grasp anything. He groaned, the sound sending a wave of heat through her thighs. "Emma told me a bit about him," she said breathlessly. "I take it you heard."

His knuckles paled against the armrests. "I'd gone to see him at the tents outside his estate when they were home on a short reprieve. I sent my father to act as medic for another battlefield with a forged letter maybe a week before. They were ambushed on the second day."

"I take it he didn't make it," she said quietly.

"No," he answered, but there was no grief behind his eyes. "Alor and Laurent were fathers to me·more than Pascal ever was—eventually. At first, Alor told me I was much too young, but I'd pointed out he himself was barely old enough to lead a kingdom into war. He argued Geoffrey wasn't made for it like he was." Garin laughed, and his dimples flanking the rows of fangs made her breath catch. "He was right. Mid-thirties, talented leader, and a barren wife, or so we thought."

"What does that mean?"

"Katella married the king and fell pregnant with his son just after Alor had gone missing. It was a quick affair, but she was wrought with grief. She refused to address it publicly. Rumor had it, Alor had left her a note telling her he couldn't live with himself after everything he'd witnessed. But Bast and I knew the truth."

He ground his teeth; Lilac had inched the head of the forceps further into his wound.

"You told me he'd gone to kill himself before completing the change."

"That's... right." He exhaled roughly. "I've heard it's hard to do."

His fists were clenched so tight, she feared the chains would pop off of their own accord. "Did Alor and Geoffrey reside in the Le Tallec estate?" The forceps caught the end of the bullet, then slipped off, causing him to snarl; he turned his head away from her to do so, and Lilac took another deep breath as she repositioned the prongs.

"Back then, it was the Chateau de Penthièvre," he breathed, "and I prefer to recognize it as such today, though my newfound abhorrence for them makes it almost impossible to see it as much else. The king back then wanted Alor to take anyone tall enough to wield a sword and bow, ride a horse, but the duke's son was eventually willing to make exceptions—especially for me and Bastion, who never left my side after I saved him from being impaled by the new recruits. He was shorter, then. Two years my junior."

The prongs closed around the bullet, and his breath hitched. Lilac lightly placed her hand reassuringly on his bicep, feeling it flex—then relax —at her touch. "Did he know your parents?"

"He knew *of* them. Alor knew I was Pascal and Aimee's son. My mother was an acquaintance of his wife's—they'd met briefly before, at The Fool's Folly."

"Katella was a customer of your mother's?"

She'd glanced up at him, somehow shocked yet another peek into his incredible but brief human existence—accidentally yanking the prongs out. He jumped at her sudden movement and, likely, the pain, his legs kicking out involuntarily. The chair skidded back, almost toppling him over. She caught and steadied him before quickly scuttling away.

"*Fuck!*" Garin cussed in a roar, the word tapering off into a low groan that felt like hands gripping the small of her waist as the wound upon his bicep began to close before her very eyes.

Lilac opened her hand. The object in it was multicolored and marbled, but she couldn't tell much else. It was covered in his blood. She went to dip it into the still-warm bath and held it up in the light; it was smooth and round, coated in a thin, clear layer. Inside was a crude swirl of metal and dark wood.

"Iron and hawthorn." A wave of nausea roiled through her. She turned it over and over in her hand, picturing the armory cart left on the hill below Garin's property, where they'd gotten the bows and quivers filled with arrows.

Garin straightened. Blood from his leg covered the seat and dripped onto her rug. "Those fucking bastards."

"It's covered in glass." Lilac tapped it with her nail, each plink a deafening sound in the still air. "That barrier must be what kept you conscious."

"Let them come," Garin growled. "I'll finish each and every one of them."

"You won't. Not now that we know they have guns, and this kind of horrid ammunition."

She teetered, stomping past him to deposit the bullet onto her mantle, far away from him. Her letter would make it to King Henry, and they could send their horses, but Garin wouldn't have any part in it except for training new recruits. She wouldn't allow it. Her own men would have to fight, as they should've all along; François's army posed an even greater threat to her Daemon populace than burning Brocéliande to the ground.

Except, there was no time. His men were already outside her bordering fortresses, waiting with cannons and guns filled with weaponry poised to destroy all of Garin's coven if they so pleased.

She rounded his chair, interrupting his string of curses. "Your leg. Now," she demanded, snatching the long hooked tool again and positioning herself. She kneeled and spread his legs, lowering the prongs into Garin's thigh. The shaft of the hooked tool sank *much* deeper than it had in his arm. He inhaled sharply when it hit the bullet—roughly half its length down—and she withdrew it.

Totally focused, fueled by pure panic and rage, Lilac slid the forceps in, widened it infinitesimally, and grasped the end of the bullet. When she did, Garin lunged at her, his jaws snapping in her direction.

Startled, she yanked away, squeezing the bullet in the prongs as she fell back on her ass—the tool ripping out of him. Lilac shrank away from the murderous expression that shadowed his features, dropped the piece in her hand, and hastily washed it off.

When the water ran clear, a mess of glass and iron sat in her palm.

The bullet had *broken* in her grasp—half remaining in his muscle.

Slowly, she looked up at him. Garin glanced desperately up at her, his hunger and rage battling for his sanity. It was a wonder he was still seated.

"I'm so—"

"Don't," he panted, begging when she stepped closer. "Go get Myrddin. Or Rupert. Don't come near me."

But there was no time. Raw hawthorn was lodged in Garin's body, along with the broken glass, both cutting into him. He looked green. He might not be breathing when she returned to the room.

Garin's eyes began to cross, saliva dripping from his twisted mouth.

Heart pounding, core throbbing, Lilac stumbled forward and placed herself in his lap. She used her ankles to sweep his legs open, spreading them to make his wounded thigh available to her.

Garin resisted for all of two seconds. Then, his nose found the curve where her neck met her shoulder, and he inhaled like a man starving. "Lilac," he rasped, voice cracking. She could feel the tremble in his frame, the way he barely held himself together. "I can't. Don't—holy *shit*." The words barely held form, broken and entirely unconvincing.

But she didn't stop. *Couldn't*. His need was a command on its own. She ground over his hardening cock—of her own accord or his simmering ache, she did not know—but Lilac pressed against him, offering warmth, and blood, and something that no longer had a name or held shape.

"*What are you doing?*" he growled helplessly, claws curled.

"Saving you," she managed.

His answer was a sharp tug against her scalp. Fingers down her throat. "You'll be dead before you have the chance."

Lilac stilled in his lap.

For a heartbeat, neither of them moved. Then she slid to the side, trembling and perching herself on his good thigh. Her pulse was frantic with his hot breath, sharp fangs inches away from her neck. But her fingers were steady.

In her left hand, the hawthorn stake gleamed; she'd plunge it into him if he tried to attack her. In her right hand, she hovered the prongs of her forceps above the angry wound.

Garin's eyes were slow to rise, still rimmed with hunger. But hers held.

"Trust me," Lilac whispered, gritted her teeth—and hesitated before sticking the tool back in. If she'd broken the bullet, the pieces might be too minuscule to grab without repeated injury. She swallowed, dropped the forceps, and without warning—inserted her small finger into the wound. It grazed something hard—not bone. She grimaced, and Garin hissed against her skin, teeth scraping but not breaking as she dug deeper, and finally found the next large piece. Even his blood and muscle seemed repelled by it, and she managed to get her nail around it to scrape it out, to his most intense displeasure.

Lilac breathed through the stab of heat at her core—a punishing pain of want.

There it was. Glass, hawthorn, and a dull metal in two crumbled shards on her palm. She made sure before letting it fall to the floor.

She was about to get up, retrieve the key to undo his shackles so she could feel his hands on her—

But the wound remained open and oozing. Confused, she swept the flaps of his trousers aside and peered closer. Was there more? Smaller pieces she'd missed? She wiped her hand across her front, ready to try again.

Then, Garin gave his next command, his breath against her hair. A single word, this time laced with conviction and unfaltering desire. "Still."

She froze against him, her body instantly slipping under his spell. Securing her in place.

"Did you know this would happen when you enthralled yourself to me? Did you know that I'd need to feed more than the average vampire does?" Instinctively, she sidled closer, further onto his lap as his arms flexed on either side of her. "That all it takes is a simple injury for me to morph into something that can no longer wait the three days it takes before the discomfort sets in? I did not. Not until tonight."

A strangled whimper of surprise rose in her throat at the fury in his voice. She shook her hair off her neck, encouraging him further; he didn't bite, so she shifted in his arms to better see his face. It had barely been three days since their bond had formed. "But you've fed."

"Bottled blood dulls the ache for a few hours," he agreed. "But my supply is gone. I even had Agnes. She tasted as bitter as her tongue. Your sister was delicious, yet all I could think of was you. Each time I try to sate myself, I find myself hungrier than the last."

Lilac swallowed hard, past the stab of jealousy at the reminder of Yanna. "I thought that stopped when I enthralled myself to you."

"It softened the burn. Took the edge off the hunger. The rage." Garin's gaze dipped to her throat. Her breath caught. "It didn't cure my desire, but left it to rot." His nose brushed the side of her throat. "I can always take it from someone else. Choke it down. But I've come to understand, to my utter dismay, the blood I prefer has become the blood I need. *Yours*."

Her legs were stuck; she couldn't bring herself to move. She'd intended to feed him—looked forward to it, even—but she needed to heal him. The pain was driving him mad, further into the monster that would rejoice in draining her.

Lilac lifted the stake and held it above his thigh, ready to shove it into him—an unconscious Garin would be easier to deal with as she pried any remaining shards of hawthorn out of him.

He tsked, and suddenly her wrist was frozen, too. Garin chuckled at the sight of the stake clutched in her clammy palm. "But your blood is not all I hunger for, Your Majesty." His mouth found the corner of her jaw. "And I can sense you need the same."

Garin adjusted himself beneath her; Lilac gasped. She could've imagined it, but his thick erection felt *swollen* against her. He leaned back, giving her a wider seat. "There. Now, spread your legs for me, Your Majesty."

There was no resisting him. She did as she was told, leaned into his request—and stifled a whine at the feel of his cock beneath her ass. Lilac instantly reddened when she caught their reflection in the mirror; a faint mark of pink was visible between her thighs, staining her undergarment. She diverted her gaze, blood flooding her face.

"You're stunning, Eleanor," he murmured. "The picture of smoldering power. Look at yourself, for your own pleasure if not for mine. I want you to watch as you come for me."

Her eyes snapped back to him in their reflection; he lounged back, watching her intently. Appreciatively. They shifted down to his bound arms —then, immediately, to her still-risen hand. The stake clutched within it. "You want me to fuck myself with this?"

"My heart's desires are plentiful and dark, Your Majesty, but I cannot form a single thought past the ache that's been wafting off of you since you'd decided to make yourself mine." Garin's taloned fingers drummed upon the armrest. "What I *want* is to watch you stretch yourself over the instrument I prepared for you to drive through my heart."

"I am—" she corrected once more, her own conviction comically bare— "Maximilian's."

"That," he groaned, grinding himself under her, "is where you have me wrong. See, that's the thing I've learned, against my better judgement, about Sanguine magic. As your regnant, my allegiance to you is unwavering. I could rally my coven against you. Despite my excellent strategy, I'd somehow ensure my own kind would fall one by one, before a hair on your head was harmed."

She fought him—but only on the surface. Her own will was no freer than his. Lilac watched as her hand obeyed, lowering with quiet precision.

"This bond of ours doesn't care who we were. Not the woman whose hand was promised to an emperor with endless armies. Not the heir of a starving, morally inept kingdom. It doesn't care about crumbling treaties, or the wars we'll lose."

His eyes flicked downward, sharp and assessing, as Lilac drew the stake up beneath her nightgown, mechanical—deliberate—even as she resisted.

"It cares only for *you*," Garin said flatly. "And now, it's hollowed you out.

Turned you into something else entirely." He chuckled. "That poor guard—what did you call him? Ciel? The way you crushed his throat with your bare hands did something to me. Made me tingle."

"I don't regret it," she said harshly, to combat the horror of the memory of how good his windpipe giving way under her fingers felt.

"Precisely. Our thrall bond has made you cold. Exacting. Just like me." His brow rose. "And for that, I cannot fault you."

Her hand shook there—the blunt tip resting against her clit over her undergarment as she resisted.

It stilled when he clicked his tongue. "You're right—bring that stake closer, would you?" She felt him cock his head, and her hand drifted the stake up to her mouth. He straightened, his breath hot on her ear. "Spit on it."

Seething, she did as she was told, growling and wiping the glob dribbling down her chin on her thin sleeve.

"There we are. Carry on."

Rage and heat flooded her. "I'll kill you."

"How about this, Your Majesty," he countered, his dimples reappearing at the challenge. "If you strain against your own innermost urges one more time, I'll have you baring that soft, pulsing throat for me whether you beg for it or not. And I won't be gentle."

This command was the last her will needed. The last link, before her chain of restraint snapped.

She rocked into him, carefully using her other hand to pull her undergarments to the side. "But I'm still bleeding," she whispered, her face flooding with heat.

"You're far too composed for someone *actively* losing a war within herself," he murmured, the curve of his mouth brushing her ear. "If you think I give a fuck about a little blood, then you're sorely mistaken."

Lilac's lips parted—the silence stretched when she slid the blunt tip of the stake into her cunt. She breathed, inching it in. Her disgust mixed with waves of pleasure, dissipating altogether into her own hunger as her head fell back in pleasure. "You're foul."

"Oh, I *know*, Your Majesty," he rasped, his own teasing lilt giving way to a groan as she felt her pussy clench around it. She pulled the stake out—then thrusted it back in. "Deeper. Good."

She did it again, and again, until she did it on her own accord. It made her hips grind against him. Watching herself writhe in the mirror felt dangerous and unhinged; Lilac locked eyes with him—this time her gaze was wholly predatory. Garin looked like he was about to come himself, eyes nearly rolling back.

"Look at you," he said, his breath hitching at the friction of her ass over his trousers. "The way you arch your back, tilting your head just so. Leaning into me, as though your body already knows what your pride won't admit."

Any flashes of horror or shame she might've felt went as quickly as they came. Lilac let her head fall back, pressing into him and panting in heavy ecstasy—shuddering when she fucked herself so hard, she began to pant Garin's name.

His teasing stopped. So did his shallow breaths that came in time with the rhythm of her pleasure. The moment Lilac quieted, another wave of ecstasy hit her, with a searing pain that made her cry out, startled.

"Sorry," he lifted his mouth to sputter drunkenly against her throat, before sinking his teeth back into her. He didn't sound sorry at all.

The sensation was unlike anything she'd ever felt. His bite was rough, and possessive—and although she could feel the blood pumping out of her, she didn't tire. At least, not yet, or if she did, she didn't notice; the surging pain at her throat was countered by a steady, pulsing warmth between her thighs. Somewhere between fingers and a vibration, it was a cresting wave. The feeling built, and built at her throat and clit, until the bloodied stake clattered to the floor, and her hands snaked into his hair, pressing him closer. He groaned into her, causing her to fracture and thrash.

Lilac shut her eyes. It was not a feeling she *ever* wished to relinquish. She hated him for it.

Garin jerked beneath her, and the chains securing his wrists suddenly clattered to the floor. His jaw then shifted angles, his fangs cutting deeper as she opened her eyes to him rising from the chair, cradling her.

The knot at her center not only unfurled, but caught fire.

✣ 39 ✣
GARIN

He placed Lilac down gently on the bed, sweeping the displayed bundle of tools out of the way.

Garin was reeling. The pain in his arm and thigh that had driven him to the point of delirium was finally *gone*, his strength instantly returned.

He was a new man. One, prisoner to an ancient hunger that had drawn out a side of him that had seemed to frighten and allure Lilac simultaneously. He could think clearly now, to his resurfacing chagrin; he could smell the dew outside, and the dried yew crackling away in the hearth. All tainted in the earthy, sweet aroma of her intoxicating bleed, but her veil had at least lifted enough for him to realize what was in front of him.

Lilac blushed and attempted to clean herself with the cloth he'd knocked aside.

And it all came barreling into him at once—the ring of the shots on the battlefield, losing himself in the gore of its aftermath. The sheer horror in Henri's and his guards' eyes in realizing Garin had been shot and did not collapse.

The farmhouse—the swinging bodies of Sable and Jeanare. His coven and its newfound members. Aimee and Pascal.

Maximilian's letter.

His gut finally twisted. Garin was no man. He was a mere vampire, suddenly painfully aware of the passage of time. The way it slipped through his fingers like sand.

Garin did not want to think about the politics threatening to break them apart and burn his forest down, nor the insufferable emperor who now claimed her future. He wanted a repeat of whatever the fuck just happened. He wanted more than that. He wanted her again and again, in the way only monsters could want.

He wanted forever from a human woman who could barely afford a week. She'd be married in less than two days.

He could still taste her—not the taste of blood, but of her essence—still feel the ghost of her heartbeat hammering against his mouth in the moments he'd held her too close, kissed her too deeply; first in the grotto, and then at his farmhouse, when she'd opened up *beautifully* for him.

It hadn't been a feeding those times, but his body had trembled like it was. His hunger curled inside him, vicious and relentless.

And yet, after everything, she'd trusted him... even as he had carved the path that led her straight into Maximilian's hands.

This was the cost of his restraint. Of pretending to be anything other than himself. Lilac would be wed by-proxy to the Holy Roman Emperor—a gilded cage cloaked as diplomacy, meant to keep France at bay. Meant to keep her and her family breathing.

Garin had lied to her. Forged the letter from the count in hopes of facilitating a meeting with Lilac and her parents, knowing Maximilian's offer was too good to pass up. A throne across Brittany and all of his empire in exchange for her bloodline, her autonomy. But... her own people had already turned on her once. How long until they did it again? A queen without reverence was one subject to rebellion, wasn't she?

They do not respect her, whispered the distant voice of reason, his once-clear logic now smothered beneath thirst and guilt. How easy it had been for Lilac's own subjects to stage a coup against those she wished to protect most. Who would they have struck next? The castle? Her?

The thought made his blood boil. He'd been too distracted at the inn and at the castle, lost in her pull. He'd nearly missed the large-scale

Daemon hunt that would've swept across the High Forest. *He*, who was supposed to guard them from those things. Now that Maximilian's court had gotten wind of France's movements—the quiet advances that even the Daemons hadn't caught—the emperor wanted Lilac to travel to him, through enemy terrain.

A cold chill prickled Garin's spine. He didn't trust Maximilian with his own court, much less her. But he'd been the one who had condemned the one he loved to a cage because he couldn't trust himself with her blood.

But wasn't it already too late? She was already bleeding for him. Wet for him.

They don't revere her like you do, another voice said then, not the voice of a well-meaning cherub on his shoulder, but something darker, *older* than the woods itself, coiled deep within. It was the thing that allowed him to reach into her mind.

It wasn't reason. It was nothing that resembled it. This was his instinct. Hunger.

Mine, it growled. And she heard it, too.

Distrust flashed in those sparkling, bitter eyes—but it wasn't stronger than the want that lingered at the upturned corners of her mouth.

She was going to be the end of him. The end of the world.

He dug his nails into her plump hips, dragging her to the edge of the bed. When Lilac instinctively tried to cover herself, he snaked his fingers beneath her undergarments and pulled them off, dropped to his knees, and bit her inner thigh.

Her body went rigid, but not in protest. Of course not.

Your blood is mine, his hunger rejoiced.

Lilac whimpered as he pulled from her, swallowing thickly and digging her heels into the mattress. Hit after hit, her blood sang to him. He nearly sheathed his fingers in her, but stopped himself in time.

Talons, he'd have to remember. He had not turned back into the man he at least thought he'd resembled—yet, the queen at least appeared unrepulsed by it.

She was holding her breath, resisting him and the orgasm that threatened to break her yet again. *Gods, he didn't even need to touch her or be pumping inside her to drive her over the edge*. His hand slipped up to wrap around her left breast, tenderly cupping and squeezing, thumbing her nipple before he withdrew his fangs, tongued the messy crescent he'd left and felt her flushed skin smooth over.

Lilac's chest shuddered before she let out an involuntary gasp that made his entire body coil with pleasure. Garin pulled back and shifted her legs to rest over his shoulder.

Your pussy is mine. She writhed before him, her mind registering the words.

Then, he parted her. He sucked her clit lightly into his mouth and moaned against her; he'd tasted her blood and arousal together at The Fool's Folly, but *this* was a delight. A forbidden treat. His.

Lilac's hands rose. If she pushed him off, if she asked him—hells, even if her heart began to thrum in all the wrong ways—he'd promptly step away. He'd resist, chain himself if he had to.

But then her nails raked into his shirt, gripping him closer as she began to pant. She was *enjoying* it.

This was terrible. This was dangerous. Warning and his distant logic-turned-panic began to war with his instinct. Lilac was his thrall. In a traditional vampire court, it was her call to feed him, pleasure him, but it was he who needed to protect her.

She was... She was someone else's wife, for fuck's sake.

He should—

Lilac's entire body gave a violent shudder, and she finally jerked away from him, unhooking her legs and pushing herself up. *There.* She was done —maybe self-preservation had actually clicked, albeit weeks belated, for her. Lilac would fight him, and that would bring him back to center.

Instead, she wrapped her hands tighter into his hair and tugged him up. She rose at the elbows and kissed him over his pursed lips—his ruddy mouth dripping with her bleed and come—pressing herself *into* him with such force, he pulled back to look down at her.

Your lips are mine. He couldn't help himself. The thought came, unwarranted and irreverent.

Her eyes blackened at the scrape of his insidious thoughts against the threshold of her mind. What was this creature that wanted him *back* in such violence?

"Are you certain?" Garin said hoarsely, rising over her.

Lilac brought her lips back to his. "Never more."

Her leg shifted, brushing against his inner thigh, sweeping across Garin's groin as she cupped his face. He smoldered at her touch—

Then, he was airborne.

❧ 40 ❧

The moment Garin landed on his back on the center of the bed, she tossed the chains at his head—one by one. They each snapped to their respective bedposts, his wrists secured in place.

He blinked, glanced at both his extended arms, and began to laugh. His deep, arousing chuckle tapered off when she leaned over him and fingered the drawstrings at the top of his trousers. Lilac kissed him deeply; he seemed reluctant to let her into his mouth at first, as if worried she'd forget to be gentle around his fangs.

Garin was exactly right; she sliced her tongue on his razor-sharp front teeth, gasping at the sharp pain... but it quickly dissipated. His tongue, sweeping over hers, healed the gashes instantly. This seemed to rouse the monster in him; Garin's voice rumbled, a heavy vibration at the back of her skull.

Bleed for me, he begged, voice tight. *Just a little. I'll make it worth your while. There's no song sweeter than the way your heart races for me.*

Lilac gasped against his mouth in breathy surprise and did it again, losing all sense of her own safety; she straddled him and ground herself over his trousers, cutting herself and kissing, rubbing her clit with one hand until she couldn't stand it anymore.

Her fingers found his waistband and yanked it down, freeing his cock. Garin's teeth and ears were not the only things that had transformed.

Mine, his voice echoed in her mind again, this time taunting.

"Let me rule," she whispered, crawling back, taking his thickened head into her mouth. She choked, dribbling down it.

Garin cussed, his head lolling back. "Fuck, Eleanor," he panted. "That feels so good."

"Let me do this," she repeated determinedly, working him from base to tip, coating it in her saliva. She willed her lust to win out over the fragment of hope that seemed to carve its way into her throat. "We can do it together, can't we? Without Maximilian. King Henry will send us his horses. I've sent him—"

"I know you have," he said tightly. His smile grew at the triumph that faded from her eyes. "I sent John on his way and instructed him to follow your orders. To deliver your request your way."

Garin propped himself up on her pillows to watch her rise, then slide onto him slowly. Lilac's breath hitched at his size probing at her cunt. Politely, he said nothing; his apprehensive grin grew teasing when she barely held back a shuddering moan.

Mine, came the voice again as he filled her. Louder. Somehow closer.

That delectable throat is mine. Your unbelievable body. Mine.

Mine.

Mine.

Mine, for all of eternity.

Lilac winced and straddled him, eliciting a low hiss from deep within Garin's chest. She reached up and placed her hand around the curve of Garin's throat, tightening her fingers around the sides. His smile only widened as she stretched herself slowly around him. "Then, ask."

Something like warning flashed across his features, his jaw clenching through his glorious grin of fangs.

"If I am to be yours," she managed, moaning around the throbbing swell of his cock. "It is *your* name I shall bear. Not his." She rose, then sank, stifling a whimper. "That's what you want, isn't it?"

Something broke in him at the same time her will splintered. Lilac leaned back, her hand sweeping against the crumpled duvet for the key to undo his shackles, desperate to feel his claws against her flesh.

But Garin yanked his hands free—snapping them in a single movement—and molded them around her hips. He shifted his feet and plunged himself *up* and into her, causing Lilac to fall against him.

His fingers traveled up her back, shredding her nightgown completely down the middle.

Garin's mouth found her breast without effort; his tongue flicked against her nipple, sucking and teasing. She writhed against him, alarmed at the brush of his fangs against her tender breast, but he only shifted her, biting into the curve of it and moaning against her burning flesh.

It stung badly, but she only leaned into him.

He gulped deeply, thrice—lashed the gash with his tongue—then lifted his head from her bosom.

"Don't you understand, Eleanor?" he growled into her ear, each painstakingly slow thrust punctuated with restrained fury, his nails biting into the silk over her thighs. "You could wear the crowns of dozens of empires, take kings to your bed and birth entire dynasties, and still—*still*—I would bleed for you. Nothing you do, no one you fuck, no child your bear nor no kingdom you lead could unravel what you've sewn into me."

Relieved, heartbroken tears began to spill at his words—and his enormous cock stretching her. Her breath hitched, her hair sticking to her face, nails digging into his shoulders to pull him closer. Deeper. She wanted him to fill her and *fill* her.

Garin didn't stop.

"Tell me you're mine," he rasped, the request both an oath and a curse. He looked up at her, his own eyes filled with a weighted grief and self-disgust. "Even if it shouldn't be true—should never be uttered outside this room. Even if it damns us both. Please, tell me."

"Yours," Lilac managed, savoring his long strokes, his arms around her. She was exactly where she wanted to be. "I'm—"

There was no warning—Garin snarled under her and sheathed himself deep, cussing into and kissing her collarbone; at the same time, Lilac came over him, her body convulsing, clenching, pressing in sweat and heat and remnants of soot against his bare, chiseled form.

She collapsed over him, and he pulled her in close, his claws threading her hair.

"I may belong to the kingdom," she breathed into his chest. "To an emperor, even. But the parts of myself I squander and hold close. I want more than anything to share them with you, Garin."

He kissed the top of her head twice before speaking again. "Urging you toward Maximilian, the idea of you marrying a great and powerful leader, those were not betrayals," he whispered gently. "Not in my mind. Because in the marrow of my bones, every godforsaken night I've walked to your tower and climbed those stones to watch you sleep, I've known that I'd guard you—*love* you through peace or bloodshed. Through every victory gained and every soldier lost." His throat bobbed. "And there will be losses, Eleanor. Many."

She turned her face toward him, eyes brimmed with moisture and heat as she rested her chin on his chest. "You didn't just urge me, Garin. You *manipulated*. You orchestrated my marriage to Maximilian like a commander planning an insidious siege."

"It was my mistake." The words were rough. "Even before our thrall bond was sealed, I feared what it might become—what *I* might become—if you ever mirrored what I felt."

"Why are you afraid of this? Of us?"

Garin shifted himself against the pillows and pulled away enough to look at her. Truly look at her. As she rose on her forearms over him, his eyes reflected the firelight in the vanity reflection, combing over her hungrily—desperate to soak her in.

As if summoned by her hammering pulse, the flames surged in the hearth next to them.

"What I feel isn't love, Eleanor."

She pushed off of him, sitting up. Her face was *filled* with blood. Her cheeks, her ears—even her pounding throat, were stained in the shade of berry that made his eyes darken.

"Not the way mortals understand it. Know it. This is *obsession*. And you should be afraid of what I'd do to keep you, if what I've already done isn't proof enough." He grasped her hands before she had a chance to pull them away. "Maximilian is not for you, despite how hard I've tried to convince myself. Your kingdom, Brocéliande—they need the defenses more than ever, anything beyond the meager army your father and those Le Tallecs left you. *Your* safety comes before everything else to me. Everything. Even before truth." This was a truth that evidently ate him alive. Burned him to admit. "There's a part of me, Eleanor—a part I keep buried, deep down—that would do terrible things to ensure it."

Her pulse would shatter her ribcage, want and horror existing there together.

There is no cost too great. For me. What, then, are you to pay?

It was what he'd meant at the inn. He'd known it even before she'd enthralled herself to him. There was no tempting a fate already sealed in blood.

"You speak of my safety as if it were yours to guard in the first place." She took a breath—measured, but bitter. "As if I haven't lived for this crown, tarnished it, bled for it more than anyone alive or dead."

Garin merely shook his head. Slowly, as if he couldn't believe the horrid things he'd done. "If you ever find yourself pondering," he murmured, taking her hand in his and pressing it to his lips, "whether in this kingdom or the next, this life or the after—know this: I am yours till my last breath, and whatever lies beyond. A ring is too mortal a signet to bear in the name of the breadth of what I feel for you." His eyes were distant—wistful—and she knew his thoughts were in a different time and place. "If ever the day comes I do own the privilege of placing one onto thine hand, it will be wrenched from my blood and yours, on arcane soil. Tragedy making us whole." A sad, bitter smile touched his mouth. "No king shall bar your name from my lips. No crown shall hold you from me."

"Do you really think I don't see you for what you are, Garin? You think I don't understand what it means to say yes to you?" Lilac's throat tightened. "It would ruin my reputation with Brittany. It would end my relations with several allies, including the one offering us a way out. And still, I'd—" She reddened, giddy with the hope lacing her impossible words.

Garin leveled his gaze with hers. "You want to be my wife, Eleanor?"

The proposal was laced in cruelty and hunger, sounding more a dare than a solemn offer, yet Garin made no attempts to hide his burning curiosity. He didn't blink. He waited patiently, brows slightly raised. Too calmly.

Lilac gritted her teeth. It was what she wanted, wasn't it? More than anything. Slowly, she placed her hand in his, lips parting to answer, when Garin's head suddenly snapped toward the door.

A sharp bang at the door made them jump.

"Of *course*," Garin muttered, releasing her.

"Who is it?" she whispered, knowing he was already listening.

He said nothing, fuming and padding to the door. She licked her lips, watching his rippled back move in irked stealth for a moment before rising.

"Wait," she hissed, already across the room rummaging in her boxed wardrobe from Herlinde. Lilac fished out another dress—this one cream, sleeved, and most certainly solid. She tugged a leather waist belt out and scrambled for the bundle of burned gown beside the tub, ears burning. Reeling.

Lilac straightened and threw him a towel from the table; Garin hastily wrapped it around his waist as she donned the belt and tucked the book into the pouch at the front.

The moment he undid the latch, Bastion burst in with a bundle of what looked like stationary in his arms. Piper and Adelaide promptly followed, and last—Myrddin, huffing and out of breath as he stumbled in and shut the door behind them.

Piper gasped. Adelaide's ochre eyes widened at the sight of Garin. "What the *fuck* happened to you?"

"Well?" demanded Garin, ignoring them as Bastion strode straight to the vanity. "Did you do it? Where is the chest?"

"Delivered." Bastion swept his hand across the desk, knocking perfume bottles, jewels, and trinkets onto the floor as Myrddin sealed the door with a spell.

"What do you think you're doing?" Lilac shrieked, stomping over.

Bastion bared his fangs in a vicious growl and slammed a quill box onto the table, unfolding the piece of parchment tucked under his arm. Myrddin and Adelaide lingered by the door, looking shaken as Piper and padded over to the tub to sink to her knees and splash her face.

"Sign this." Bastion jabbed his finger at the document, where an elaborate gold and red seal was stamped at the top. "I'll run it to Maximilian myself if I have to."

Lilac stared at the lengthy document packed with tight scrawl, then back up at him. Bastion looked like he'd walked through a firestorm himself; his cloak was singed at the sleeves, his hair sticking up at odd ends with twigs in them. "What happened?"

"Sign it!" he bellowed, snatching her by the wrist.

Garin was between them, his fist clamped over Bastion's jaw. "I will dislocate your skull from your body," he breathed, slamming Bastion back against the vanity. "Do not talk to her that way. She's not signing anything unless she chooses to."

"She will if she wants her kingdom and Brocéliande to have a chance at survival."

"The French have laid siege to Rennes, starting with their chapel," said Adelaide urgently. "There's been report from the magic folk. Lorietta and I were about to be on our way here to inform you, when those two showed up for some blood." She pointed a black and silver talon at Bastion and Piper. "Lori's downstairs helping your chef with preparations."

"And? Have they retaliated?" Lilac asked, her stomach crawling.

"They're protecting their own. Using charms and wards where warranted, mostly over the businesses and the orphanage. Many don't want to expose themselves."

"They'll only intervene if it seems their militia is overwhelmed," added Bastion. "For now, they're watching from the shadows."

"Already." Garin swore furiously under his breath and shoved Bastion aside. "How many?"

"Two dozen. Maybe more."

"It's likely they thought it was where you might hold your ceremony, Your Majesty." Piper toweled her face off.

Lilac gripped the edge of her vanity bruisingly, her vision swimming as she stared at the crest at the top of the scroll. She couldn't even bring herself to read it. She didn't need to. The sigil alone, Maximilian's black eagle over a golden shield, was declaration enough.

A symbol of union, of domination. Of inevitability.

"The contract is preliminary," Garin advised behind her, as if he heard her pulse racketing in her chest. "It is the ceremony that officiates it, for the public and church records' sake."

"What do you think they're doing downstairs?" Bastion glared accusingly at them.

Garin's eyes flashed dangerously. "They're setting up for her wedding?"

"Everyone is scrambling. They're going to marry her, then crown her immediately after. Ceremonies have been postponed, the ball canceled, and arriving visitors are being turned away far down the road."

Lilac's heart slammed against her ribcage. *Preliminary*, Garin had said. A word meant to reassure her, but it landed like an iron anchor upon her chest. The ceremony would make it real, rushed or not.

"What of my father?" Lilac asked, mouth dry. "He and his men?"

"They're downstairs briefing the guard. Arrived just after we did."

Garin nodded cautiously. "You told them, I assume?"

"I *had* to." It must've been difficult for Bastion to address Henri alone. "I had Piper bring me to him, I had no choice. That's when they began setting up for the ceremony—the entire castle's been notified." His lip curled in disdain toward Lilac. "Rupert informed your parents you've returned and are safe in your tower, but there's only so much time that will buy you."

"Time," Myrddin commented with a faraway look, "is a strange and fickle thing. There's never enough of it, is there?"

"Where are the others?" Garin pressed. "The coven?"

"The inn's been secured. As for the vampires, I've sent some of them to monitor Rennes, mostly to keep watch over France's movement as they're likely to travel in the evenings," Bastion said brusquely. "The others are at the Mine. It would be foolish to expect them to stand in for Lilac's lack of soldiers. They don't have a means of protection for battle in the daylight." He glanced at Lilac, exhaling. "But they are ready to stand by her in the night."

Hope swelled with guilt in her chest. "I won't have them fight for me. Not with their hawthorn ammunition." Lilac looked at Garin. "But I don't understand, why didn't we hear anything?"

"I placed a temporary two-way sound spell over the room," Myrddin muttered, eyes flicking toward the door. "It's safer this way. Especially during a feeding."

"Safer?" Bastion's scoff was menacing. "None of us are safe. *This* is what happens when you invoke a thrall bond. We're one misstep from full-fledged war, and you set yourself on fire for her."

"Bastion," Garin warned.

"No. You let me speak." Bastion turned on him. "The leader of the only real defense we have against an enemy we haven't faced in decades, is tethered to a queen whose marriage is supposed to save us. You didn't just enthrall her—you fell in love with her." He glanced at Lilac. "Or is it the other way around? Does she pull the strings now?"

The flames in the hearth hissed in the silence that followed. Bastion's gaze followed the sound and caught onto something. He moved—past Piper, toward the hearth. When he straightened, he was gripping her bloodied stake.

Garin's face shifted, his barely tethered mask slipping. He lunged.

Bastion caught him, arm twisting viciously around his neck, and forced him to his knees. "Make her sign it," he growled, pressing the tip of the stake against Garin's back. "Maximilian's marriage contract. End this madness, before it guts us all."

Across the room, the fire continued to crackle like a warning; Lilac heard nothing but the sound of her own blood roaring in her ears. Garin's hand, offered to her just moments ago, still hung in question. A gesture of noble surrender. Of defiance.

"Lilac," Bastion barked. "*Now.*"

The weight of her crown was heavy enough to break her spine. Her voice was cold as frost. "You would rather see me sold for safety than at your brother's side," she said, fully aware of how selfish she sounded. "Signed away like a treaty."

"I would rather see you alive, for fuck's sake," Bastion spat. "I would rather see Brocéliande stand."

"Do as he says, Lilac," Garin ordered.

With no time to react, her arm moved of its own accord, snapping the lid off the long box back. She unscrewed the lid to the inkpot.

"The moment it is complete," Bastion said, "François's men will be encroaching on Maximilian's betrothed's territory. The moment you are married, and they are made aware, France then involves itself in a direct altercation with the Holy Roman Empire."

"I understand how this works," she seethed.

"Then sign it."

"If I may," Myrddin interjected, stepping forward. "Garin and Your Majesty, if I could just have a word?"

"Not now," warned Garin.

"Do as he says, Lilac," urged Adelaide, a half-sob.

Piper neared. "She deserves the right to choose."

Her heartbeat was so loud, it drowned out their voices. Her muscles strained, weakly resisting she picked up the quill. "Wait," she panted. "I want to read it first."

"Go ahead." Garin's voice was taut. Measured. "Read it. Then sign the contract."

The parchment kept rolling; she spread it out between her sweaty palms, the words barely legible with the tears that stained it.

THE CONTRACT

This Indenture, made the twenty-eighth day of April in the Year of Our Lord 1532, between the Most Noble and Serene Lady, Eleanor of Brittany, Sovereign Queen of Brittany, through the hand and consent of Her appointed proxy, Lord Henri Trécesson, on the one part, and His Most Imperial Majesty Maximilian the First, Holy Roman Emperor, Archduke of Austria, King of the Romans, through the person and authority of his appointed and sworn proxy, Count Albrecht Fritsch the Third of Vienna, on the other part:

Whereas it hath been mutually agreed by treaty and sealed consent between the Royal House of Brittany and the Holy Roman Empire, that a matrimonial union shall be entered into by Lady Eleanor and His Imperial Majesty Maximilian, with all solemnity and binding force, to the end that peace may be established and amity strengthened between their realms, especially in light of the reported increasing hostilities by the Kingdom of France:

It is therefore covenanted and confirmed that lawful proxy shall contract the aforementioned marriage, in full accordance with the customs of the Holy Church, and shall be held in full force as though both sovereigns were present in-person.

And furthermore, for the advancement and securing of this union, Her Majesty Queen Eleanor doth bestow, as her royal dowry to His Imperial Majesty, the following entitlements and grants:

i. *Unfettered access and usage rights to all royal naval ports of the Kingdom of Brittany, including but not limited to: St. Brieuc, St. Malo, the Channel, and the western Bay of Douarnenez for purposes of both Imperial defense and commercial passage;*

ii. *Exclusive trade rights and privileges along the eastern and southern routes through Brocéliande's harbors and overland passages, extending north to the Channel and allied maritime territories;*

iii. *Primary levy and purchase rights upon the agricultural yields of the Breton crown demesnes, including grain, flax, honey, and seasonal harvests, with exemption from tolls customary to foreign powers.*

And it is agreed that, these privileges, being given with mutual consent, shall endure for the natural lifetime of the union, and shall be renegotiated upon the death or abdication of either party.

Moreover, it is hereby expressly stated and confirmed that Her Majesty Queen Eleanor shall retain, in perpetuity, full sovereignty and right to rule over the Kingdom of Brittany as Queen Regnant, free of vassalage or subjugation to any foreign crown, including that of her consort; nor shall she be bound to take residence in Vienna or any other Imperial court, save by her own sacred volition. Furthermore, in the event of war, invasion, or any attempt at forced annexation of the Breton realm, His Imperial Majesty Maximilian shall be obligated, by oath and by arms, to render military aid and the full muster of his forces in defense of Her Majesty's person, lands, and throne.

In witness whereof, the aforementioned proxies, being empowered by their respective sovereigns with full right, writ, and seal, have enacted this marriage by proxy in lawful form, and have set their hands to this indenture in the presence of witnesses noble and learned, upon or after the day and year first above written.

Signed:

Reichskanzler Ulrich von Trapp zu Salzburg

Imperial Chancellor of the Empire

Gräfin Margaretha von Hohenberg

Countess of Hohenberg, Lady of the Inner Court

By the Authority and Eternal Will of His Imperial Majesty, Maximilianus Primus, Holy Roman Emperor, King of the Romans and Archduke of Austria, I, Albrecht, Count Fritsch, do hereby stand as His Imperial Proxy in this sacred and unbreakable union with Eleanor of House Trécesson, Daughter of the *Armor* and *Argoat*.

By my hand and solemn oath, I bind both houses, sealed this 28th day of April, Anno Domini 1532, at Hofburg, Vienna.

Albrecht, Count Fritsch

Imperial Proxy and Voice of the Emperor

❧ 42 ❧

And where was *she* in that long line of acknowledgments? Of demands? Her kingdom would be secure. But what of her?

Lilac turned her head toward Garin, just slightly, but it was enough to feel the way the air had shifted between them, charged and thick. Hesitation had turned to urgency, and she wasn't just backed into a corner—she'd been shoved into it.

Garin stood there, watching; he analyzed and listened in the silence, the way he always had despite his transformation.

Hers. He was hers.

And she was undeniably his. But what other choice was there, when the only path in front of her that ensured the safety of millions, ended with another man's ring on her finger and hundreds of eyes witnessing her union?

Regardless of their loyalties, mortals and Daemons alike deserved a queen who not only fought, but who understood the weight of sacrifice.

But Lilac deserved...

Swallowing, Lilac wished the thought away, a tear rolling down her cheek for the echo of hope that had taken shape as something sharp, its edges piercing her heart.

Her hand stilled over the parchment. Straining. Waiting.

You are deserving of a burning and steadfast love. Garin's voice was a soft, echoing thunder. *Especially from yourself.*

I deserve you, she thought timidly. But it was the truth.

I will follow you wherever you go, as flame to shadow. As shadow to night.

The ink had pooled at the tip of the quill, leaking heavily like blood. Her signature would secure peace for Brittany, strength against France... perhaps her own legitimacy in the eyes of man and creature.

I love you, Lilac thought, a trembling prayer from the depths of her blood-bound soul.

When her hand began to move, a sudden and viscous wind whipped her hair into her face, slipping the heavy parchment out from beneath her quill. She grabbed for it, but the scroll flew over her head, tumbling and twisting through the air—straight into the hearth.

"What are you doing?" Adelaide shrieked, looking towards Myrddin.

His hands were open, framing the swirling ball of fragment and mist again. His eyes were aglow with white light.

"*Tempus Glaciem,*" he boomed, and shoved his palms toward the sky, floating the ball high above his head. The sphere turned as bright as his eyes—

Then, it exploded.

An invisible force shocked the room. She shielded her face, losing her balance against the magic that emanated from the blast. Lilac swayed; the wind had died down as suddenly as it had started. The hearth was a blurred rectangle of light across the room when she blinked, willing her vision to readjust.

A racketing sob escaped her chest. It was all she could manage.

Garin kept a wary eye on the stake still clutched in Bastion's hand as he staggered to his feet. Bastion was still as a statue, unmoving, his face twisted in dumbfounded confusion toward Myrddin. Adelaide was mid-stride in the warlock's direction, her cascade of black hair billowing behind her, hand shoved wrist-deep in the pocket of her black dress.

Even the flames in the hearth were motionless.

Piper slid off the edge of the bed, waving a hand in front of Adelaide's face in wonder.

"Now that I have your undivided attention," said Myrddin, the light in his eyes fading. "I thought I'd introduce you to someone who I believe has been attempting to reach out to you from beyond the gloam, Your Majesty."

Garin groaned. "Marvelous. And at no less dire a moment."

"What is a *gloam*?"

"An unofficial term for the realm of the fae Your Majesty. Your presence is requested as well, Sir Trevelyan," he added, inclining his head at Garin. Then, with a weary sigh at Piper—"And you, my mystery of daylight-made-flesh, shall remain at my side."

Lilac's eyes narrowed while Garin cast a distant glance through the balcony doors toward the still forest below. "Does the entire world halt each time you do this?" she asked.

"No. Especially not for as long as I'll need you this time," he scoffed. "Do you know the cost of such a spell?" But Myrddin considered it, tapping his chin. "The whole world. It might be enough arcana to *unmake* me. A tempting idea... No, what I've done here is far less dramatic." He turned, voice suddenly grave. "Currently, we dwell within a pocket of time, carved from the flow. To our own senses, the world has frozen, but in truth, we are simply removed from it—ghosts walking unseen, unfelt. Time presses on without us, until we rejoin her raging current."

"You mean the *four* of us?" Piper asked, glancing sideways at Lilac.

Myrddin's smile was thin. "If it pleases you."

"Return us," Lilac commanded, her will ironclad as unease settled into her marrow. "Rennes is burning. Others will follow."

"Oh? So eager to sign that contract, are you?"

"The one you destroyed?" Garin said quietly. He wrenched the stake from Bastion's hand. "I saw it fly straight into that fire. *Someone* is going to have to explain to the emperor just what happened to his long list of demands."

Myrddin simply dusted his shoulder. "That was not *my* doing."

"Whoever wishes to speak with us can wait," insisted Lilac.

"No." Putting a finger up, Myrddin's pleasant demeanor turned instantly threatening. "No, it cannot."

He would not budge; that much was clear, cryptic as he'd insisted on remaining.

"What matters right now is our ceremony," Lilac said. "The public oath itself. That François's men see I've become Maximilian's wife."

She hadn't heard him approach; she blushed as Garin swiped the handle of her dagger on the towel at his waist before slipping it into a high sheath at her right hip that looked like it was made just for stakes.

Jaw clenched, Garin looked like he was going to be sick. "Keep that at your side."

Myrddin motioned at her. "Your Dawnshard, too."

Garin looked up. Lilac's hand went defensively to the outline of her dagger, pulling up her skirts and extracting it carefully. "What did you call it?"

"The Dawnshard," Myrddin said, eyes flicking to the blade with a mix of irritation and something like fondness. "The name of your weapon. Keep that thing in its sheath. Magic folk and arcana wielders might recognize it if they're well-traveled, but they'll likely *feel* the weight of what you carry, regardless."

Realization hit her through a surge of panic. "*This* is what my family had stolen from the Fair Folk, isn't it?" Myrddin remained silent. "But Kestrel's seen me with it."

"It doesn't matter," Garin said roughly. "You won't be giving anything more of yourself to that fucking faerie. We owe them nothing."

Lilac hesitated; there was only one other loop on the belt—much too wide, as if it were made for a broadsword. But Garin just nodded at her, and she slid the dagger and its sheath in. The leather snapped right to it, molding snugly. "It's useless, anyway," she said dubiously, just in case they were mistaken. "It's not very good at killing anyone and *keeping* them dead. I should probably replace it with something else from our armory, if you haven't blown the interior to bits."

"Some weapons were never forged for battle in the first place, Your Majesty."

"So," Garin interjected, "Bast and Adelaide are dashing out of the room to report to the crowd downstairs that the queen and her Strigoi have vanished into thin air, along with Albrecht's warlock?"

"If they haven't already, then yes." Myrddin twirled his finger, and a black bundle appeared in a puff of smoke. It flew across the room, hitting Garin square in the chest. "Here's one of the ensembles Herlinde sent you along with. Put it on. I don't think the queen's summoner in particular would appreciate her bringing a nude Strigoi along. Especially you."

"What—"

"Just do it, Garin," Myrddin snapped.

Piper joined Lilac as Garin brought the bundle to the far corner of Lilac's bed to change. The thought of him undressing again drove a distant ache in her chest.

They slipped into an awkward silence, broken only by the soft rustle and *click* of Garin's gear. *Dawnshard.* Knowing her dagger's name gave it a strange, unexpected weight. Lilac fingered its jewel-encrusted hilt, marveling at the intricate patterns crafted over its fine silver alloy.

"There was no *answer* from the Fair Folk," Piper commented.

Lilac turned her head slightly, distracted by Garin's outline in the corner of her eye. She dared sneak a peek at him as Piper spoke; despite the turmoil of the evening, he fixed her with a molten grin displaying *all* of his fangs, disappearing into the shirt he pulled down over his head.

Her insides melted, and her mouth began to water.

"The Fair Folk," Piper said again, prodding Lilac in the side, "did *not* answer."

"Right, sorry. But Kestrel received the chest?"

"Yes." Piper's mouth tilted. "I assume so. The faerie fire consumed it, and then the tree—the actual willow tree—burst into flames. Do you not think it unusual?"

She did, but perhaps Kestrel had decided he was simply done

Myrddin's giddy laughter echoed near the doorway as he staggered back.

Both of them looked up and gasped to see a vivid blue light puncturing the space beneath her door. A thick seafoam mist began to swell through.

"Good heavens," the warlock whispered.

"I *know*," said Garin; Lilac glanced back to see him angled away, adjusting himself down the leg of his dark trousers below a fitted black shirt and silk vest. "That's what Lilac—" He broke off, looking up to see the mist consuming the room.

He leapt over the bed in one swift move, fumbling to button his pants. Garin positioned himself between Lilac, Piper, and the mist, but Myrddin simply opened the door.

The entire stairwell was illuminated in mist, the light seeming to emanate from downstairs. Lilac was about to ask whom—or *what*—dared summon her and Garin on her apparent wedding day, but a low sound cut through the thick, damp air.

A moan—a male voice. It was a wet sound that made her hair stand on end.

Myrddin seemed to be enjoying himself far too much; his poorly withheld grin broke when Garin spoke.

"*You* were the one behind my hallucination," he said under his breath. "My dream."

Confused, Lilac placed a hand on Garin's heaving chest, attempting to calm him in case he lost control again. "What dream?"

"Yes," Myrddin simply said. "What *dream*, Garin? I'd take care to remember, time revolves around us all. It doesn't stop for anyone, not even the well-meaning immortal. With Rennes on fire and the emperor awaiting good news, I wouldn't want to waste too much of it, if I were you."

THE DESCENT FROM THE TOWER FELT LONGER THAN IT EVER HAD. THE narrow staircase spiraling down to the second floor keep and eventually the scullery, had seen many different versions of her—angry, forlorn. Heartbroken and brave. Tonight, it saw her descend in silence, the leader of a small but mighty pack: the queen, her warlock, her vampire knight, and her handmaiden.

Some nights, Lilac could hear the wind howling against the tower's exterior like a warning. Tonight, everything and everyone was dead still, silent, save for the moaning that came at odd intervals, but didn't seem to be an imminent threat otherwise; at least, Lilac hoped so, seeing as Myrddin had encouraged her not only to lead the troupe, but to follow the sound.

Garin stiffened, his nostrils flaring; this put Piper on alert, too. The vampires stalked closely at the rear.

She approached the second floor, where there a crowd of people gathered around something, or someone; upon closer study, Lilac saw it was Yanna and Isabel flanking her mother, slumped against the railing, one hand clutching the bannister while the other bunched in the silks at her chest. Marguerite's eyes were stained in black, her rouge washed from her face stained in tears. Kemble had emerged from the hallway with a bucket and cloth, and Rupert stood on the wall beside the library entrance, wringing his hands. By his side was Emma, with her hand wrapped around her son's waist, looking like she'd been briefly crying. He held her hand in his, as if rubbing it in reassurance.

It all felt eerily surreal, all of them cast in a sickly blue-green hue, like she was in a dream herself; Garin took her by the hand and tugged her along, steering her onto the landing, down the last leg of stairs.

The scullery at its base looked like a war zone itself. Cooks were at the ovens, and other staff scrambled in and out of the kitchen it opened up to, as if grasping for any sense of normalcy in a period of such uncertainty. They ducked and dodged plates and trays that hung precariously in the air, it seemed, save the sweaty hands they balanced upon; while the food smelled delicious, nausea roiled through Lilac at the sound of the wailing growing louder and louder the closer they drew.

"Don't touch that," Garin muttered to Piper, who'd reached out for a teetering croissant.

The kitchen corridor then opened into the heart of the keep. Torches flickered, dimmed by the enchantment, flanking the open front doors.

It was dark out, the moon obscured by the heavy clouds. Guards swarmed the bailey, fully dressed in their battle armor—several of them making wild gestures with their hands, their arms casting elongated shadows across the floor and ancient stone.

The sound was growing closer, even as she'd halted; it was approaching them too. Sickness and nervous heat crawled from her middle to her limbs; Lilac slipped her dagger out, holding it at the ready.

"Still think it's useless?" Myrddin muttered.

A hand shot out for the hilt; Lilac whipped around and slashed, but Garin caught her wrist mid-swing. He let out a low whistle and fixed Lilac's grip on it, facing the blade down and back toward her, forcing her arm down at her side.

"Like that," Garin instructed, his breath hot on her ear. "You don't want to impale yourself."

As they moved through the inner bailey hall, which ran adjacent to the west wing corridor, Lilac felt the pulse of *something* drawing them forward. It wasn't magic, exactly. Older than that.

They strode in the direction of the chapel and Grand Hall, where the preparations for her coronation and wedding were being made—or not made. Shrinking closer to the castle structure, Lilac peered through the floor-length window.

Henri was there at the corridor junction, to the right of the main entrance, just outside the cross section of the north and west corridors. He was mid-toast, next to an apprehensive-looking Riou with a couple of their guards. John stood next to them, quill suspended mid-word.

"Onward," Garin whispered.

"Where did that sound go?" Piper spun.

"I'm not sure," said Lilac, her hand gripping the dagger tight. "Better we find it than it find us."

Moments later, they finally emerged into the courtyard. Everything was obscured by a heavier layer of mist there—it was lush with hedges and short trees, but not a single fern could be seen poking out of the fog. The light seemed to be coming from *within* the courtyard itself. A faint bubbling and something else—*a voice?*—could be heard; it was muffled like the rest of the party had been at Albrecht's feast.

The fog was an enchantment. A veil.

"*Tempestas Minor*," Myrddin said, sweeping his hands aside, and the fog began to clear. At the same moment, the clouds above opened to the moonlight, pale and full above the castle walls. The stars sparkled and wheeled across the sky overhead, unfrozen by Myrddin's spell.

In the center of the courtyard, surrounded by flagstones and thorned rose-bushes and lilac hedges, was the pond she and Piper would spend their summers lounging beside. Its quiet surface bubbled at the center, illuminated with blinding white light from below. She was reminded of the glowing orbs the Morgen had given off when they'd swam beneath her, circling her. Taunting her.

The family of ducks usually inhabiting the courtyard were frozen at the pond's edge, eager to escape, the water gently lapping the heels of the last.

Lilac took a slow, steadying step onto the grass—and that was when they heard it.

Movement, and a moan. Tremoring, low. Filled with fear.

They all turned at once.

"It's *him*," Piper said, her voice thick with terror. "Oh my God."

He was pale, mottled, and damp. His blonde hair hung in slick clumps across his brow, his once-fine clothes, dungeon rags. His hands rose before him, reaching out like someone spotting a mirage. His blue eyes were glazed, unfocused at first. Then, they locked onto Garin, then *her*—familiarity slow to form but quick to snap into place.

"You," he managed, blood staining his gums above yellowing teeth, his lips dry and cracking. "How does it feel to reap everything my family has sown, you traitorous whore."

Garin immediately sank onto his haunches, a snarl ripping from his throat, but Lilac was quicker. She gave way to her reflexes, everything about that night barreling into her like stone meeting stone—

The estate. The letters—the countless, *relentless* letters sent after he'd thrown his tantrum about not besting Lilac at wooden swords. Encountering him again with his hand up an unwilling maid's shirt near the chapel on the eve of her fifteenth birthday, and it being the very reason she'd gone downstairs to the kitchen and met Freya in the first place.

Watching him brand Garin across the face with his flame-steeped sword.

His hands clawing at her body thrashing in the dirt, violently forcing her legs open with his knees—

She charged through, shoving Myrddin aside and readying her dagger— she didn't care if it didn't kill, stabbing him repeatedly would bring her *much* joy—and sank it into him all the way to the hilt, until they were body to body.

They were close enough to kiss.

Sinclair's expression stilled. Then, his mouth opened, his eyes rolled back to the whites—and dark smoke poured out of his throat. His body began to tremble and hiss.

Horrified, Lilac glanced down at her hands.

The dagger was gone. In its place an onyx hilt laid with rubies and glowing firestone. She put her foot against his chest and yanked it out.

Sinclair fell to the ground in a thud, his chest cavity still smoking with the smell of burnt flesh.

Out came a double-edged blade, its fuller laced with haphazard patterns of crimson and magma—pulsing ember that moved beneath its reflective surface like molten stone. The metal itself wasn't nearly as bright as the alloy of its former shape, as if it were cloaked in starlight itself.

Her hand shook, but she didn't want to drop it and risk setting the castle ablaze. Lilac slowly turned—Garin's mouth hung open as he watched her. Piper cowered behind him, and Myrddin stood there with his arms crossed, looking pleased and only a little surprised. "Fascinating," was all he remarked.

"What is this, Myrddin?" Garin demanded.

"It holds many names—Dawnshard to the Anglo-Saxons. *Pòh Chyu Jé* in its commissioned tongue of origin. Tanvalan, most commonly, in our own language of the Old Isles."

"Tanvalan," Lilac mouthed, turning to the warlock.

"A fire blade," Myrddin said simply.

"Have you known this whole time? A weapon like that is dangerous in the wrong hands," Garin hissed.

Mesmerized, Lilac watched the sword begin to crack; starting at the tip, the molten patterns grew, began to swallow it whole, until the glowing red crept toward the hilt.

She yelped and dropped it. Its dormant form, glistening and bright silver, landed upon the grass.

"The Dawnshard transforms in times of dire need for its wielder, otherwise merely vibrating in warning when those with deadly intent are nearby. Its victims will never perish of its own accord." Myrddin motioned to her. "Do those look like the wrong hands to you?"

"So it's always glamoured?" Lilac asked, the blade somehow heavier at her hip now.

"Not glamoured," Myrddin answered with the ghost of a smile. "Simply changed. A magical metamorphosis, wrought by the catalyst of fate. Sometimes, it's an ornate paperweight most will mistake as a thing of beauty. Sometimes, it is an arcane blade tempered with phoenix fire. Most of the time, it's simply a guiding light—protection from the most fatal danger. Only its true, rightful owner can summon its power at will."

Their attention was pulled by a louder sloshing, then. Lilac's heart stilled as the bubbling at the center of the lake began to spread.

Garin gazed nervously at the water. "Get us back, Myrddin. *Now.*"

The light itself remained stationary, but the movement expanded outward—waves and bubbles—until the entire lake came alive. She skittered forward and snatched the Dawnshard, sliding it back into her sheath just as water sloshed onto the bank.

"*Whose blood has been spilled?*" echoed a booming, wet voice, bouncing off the bailey walls, both within her skull—and without.

The four of them backed slowly away from the mouth of the pool.

Lilac shot a terrified look at Myrddin, who ushered her forward.

"*Tell him,*" Myrddin prompted through his teeth.

"Tell who?"

"*Whose blood has been spilled upon my doorstep?*" said the voice again, even louder this time.

"The marquis," Lilac stammered. Myrddin motioned for her to proceed as Garin stared at the lake's surface, face pale. "Once a nobleman's son, betrayer of the Breton crown. Rapist. Colonizing sympathizer. A Le Tallec," she threw in, not knowing how specific the mysterious entity required the information.

The frothing tide stopped its slow ascent up the flat bank, pausing for a second. "A *Le Tallec?*" it spat.

"Yes," Garin confirmed, appearing at Lilac's side. "The youngest and only heir."

Sinclair's body lay still smoking, off to their left.

"Marvelous. What a treat," the voice thundered, and the bubbling began again.

"A *treat,*" Piper echoed, shuddering.

"Go on then." Myrddin was basically rubbing his hands together. "Give him to the Bugul Noz."

Lilac froze, a chill sweeping her body. She *had* heard of the Bugul Noz. He was a thing of their childhood folklore. A Breton deity—an omen, a shepherd of the shadows. Some said it was a benevolent monster, terribly ugly in its appearance but a friend to lost travelers.

"He's waiting." Myrddin gestured emphatically toward the water. "The Bugul Noz is a *guardian*, not a guide. To know its secrets—to access its library beneath the earth—you must pay the toll. One body per visit, unless otherwise stated."

"What if we don't want to access its secrets?" Garin growled.

"But he is persistent, and wishes to share them with you," Myrddin said. "Or so I assumed, since the bubbling at the pond began moments ago. The Bugul Noz is an old—albeit distant—acquaintance of mine. I've never visited his collections, but I've heard they are grand. And he does send the nicest and most thoughtful letters. Like the owner of the Dawnshard, and much like Bastion's Veiled Garnet, there can exist only one Bugul Noz at a time," he added curiously. "They are solitary creatures, not by choice. Why don't you pay him a visit?"

"What other collection does he own?" asked Piper with a skeptical frown. "Corpses?"

"Never you mind." Myrddin ushered her back with a sweep of his robes. "Piper and I will remain here, watching over the pond. If anything goes amiss, I'll draw you back myself."

"But what about the ceremony?" Lilac asked, glancing back at the gates, and the front of the bailey. "Rennes, my outlying marches. What about Brocéliande?"

"They'll hold their own." Myrddin glanced toward the pond, its surface already darkening. "They have to. The Daemons will hold the enemy back —if they so choose—and your mortals will see just how much they could stand to uphold the treaty Francis put in place. No matter what happens, you two will be safe, at least. Our existence in the gloam tends to... bend. There, we exist *alongside* the mortal realm. But not amongst."

The gloam.

Lilac didn't much feel like finding out the consequences of ignoring the Bugul Noz's summons, especially with Kestrel's silence to address when her wedding business was over.

She'd also be an idiot to turn down another second spent with him. Another adventure awaiting.

Garin's eyes found hers and held them, as if searching for something. Despite his rigid posture, his brow softened in reassurance. "Nothing will touch you. Not tonight, not while I'm with you." Without another word, he bent and hefted Sinclair's slack, dripping corpse into his arms. The marquis's limbs swung, and the dark stain of charred rot dribbled from his middle, down his fingers into the moss.

The moment Garin's boots touched the water's edge, the pond began to churn.

Shivering, they waded in, Lilac behind him, until the water was at their thighs—then, Garin dropped Sinclair's body. Slowly, Sinclair floated out to the center of the pond where the remaining light had begun to grow warmer, like the color of flame; he sank quickly, the folds of his loose rags flowering outward before he disappeared entirely.

The surface went still. No ripples. Just silence, as if the pond had drawn in a breath.

Then, one by one, the lilies began to float outward, making room—a ring around the perimeter of the pool. From the center, a circular mouth of gray stone parted beneath the water, resembling an oddly shaped well with an opening before them. The water began to flow toward it, away from the entry, creating a path and revealing a staircase that spiraled down to the light.

"It has begun," said Myrddin from the bank. Piper watched apprehensively beside him.

Lilac peered down into the newly opened passage. It smelled of salt, iron, and candle smoke. Of leather and parchment, and knowledge long buried.

She grabbed Garin's hand, feeling his stiff form relax just a bit. "Then let us descend."

43

T he door closed behind them with a sigh. The air was different here, not cooler but older. Thicker. The way Brocéliande smelled after rainfall.

Lilac and Garin stood in an enormous, circular room boasting a high, alabaster ceiling carved with gilded cherubs and other strange creatures not glimpsed in any sort of cathedral she'd seen. Torches lined the room, but so did several balls of blue-white light, floating throughout the shelves as if they were wandering patrons themselves. Several arches and pillars of the same pristine marble that made up the floor could be seen leading into different rooms and wings through the initial columns of shelves.

The sanctum they stood in offered shelf upon shelf of tome, folder, and scroll. Stacks of loose papers sat off to their right, beside boxes she assumed they'd be sorted into. The left bore shelves filled with heavier, thicker books, dyed in an array of deep jewel tones whose spines were inscribed with emblazoned script. Bottles of dry ingredients peppered the shelves sparingly, along with the occasional skull—human and animal.

What spanned before them was no mere library, Lilac realized, inhaling deeply the aromas of aged leather and worn parchment.

This was an *archive*.

There was rustling at the head of the room; directly across from the foot of the spiral staircase, there was a worn oak desk. A stack of papers floated, thumbing through and rearranging itself.

A low rumble warning began in Garin's chest as his hand found hers, and the papers jumped—then put themselves down. "Oh, my. My apologies," said the same voice that had rumbled up from the pond—quieter and more bearable this time. It no longer echoed in her skull.

There was a clang of metal, and a man appeared in front of the desk. Sort of.

The creature that stood before them seemed half-something her anglers might bring back from a long seafaring expedition—and half-human. Pale, green-blue skin, palm-sized fins and gaping gills that flanked his cheeks, right where his ears would be. Long gray hair hung down to its mid back with twigs and moist seaweed tangled in it. Lilac swore she'd spotted an orange piece of coral—yet, his features were clean cut, sharp and probing. He was strangely, oddly handsome.

Standing at nearly Garin's height, it regarded them with saucer-sized, bulging, toad-like eyes at the front of its face above a wide mouth—with several rows of wide, jagged teeth, not like a vampire's fangs but a shark's.

Just like the Morgens'.

The creature shrugged further into an oversized brown coat that had seen better days and placed a thick banded circlet with emeralds encrusting each spire down on the desk, and folded into a brisk bow. Lilac swore she could hear his bones creak, despite his nimble movements, like a fish in water.

"Welcome to my library," he said, speaking with a distant yet familiar accent. A *mortal* one. "We'll keep this quick and simple, won't we?"

Lilac had heard the legends, which said the Bugul Noz had once been a guardian of sacred groves, but grew too lonely, too monstrous in its mourning to show its face. Some, according to her father, had said it walked after nightfall, weeping for those who strayed from their paths. Others would claim it stole memories to preserve them from the rot of passing time.

She'd never heard of it living underwater—in the courtyards of castles, *hers* nonetheless. But Lilac believed the last part now.

"This place is..." Garin trailed off, breathless as he gazed up at the ceiling. "Has it always been here?"

The Bugul Noz smiled at him, unsettlingly wide. "Astute as always, my boy. Her Majesty's little lake is but a door. You sense that this is not of the world—your world, anyway. The many ponds and waterways of *Breten* are accesses to my library and what lies beyond—with an invitation, that is. I don't get much company."

Garin snorted, but the sound was tight. He stiffened beside her. "I can't see why."

"It's been a while—several decades since I've seen anyone, actually." The comment was forlorn. "But I have a feeling that'll soon change." The Bugul Noz rubbed his slimy hands together. "And you two are most certainly invited, esteemed guests of mine."

Lilac grabbed the hilt of her blade—but a low rumble shook the marble floor.

At the center of the atrium, a pale statue rose from the floor. It was covered in moss and roots—a half-nude woman adorned a towering, brittle crown. Iridescent scales covered patches of her body, and her hair had been meticulously carved in a way that captured the essence of the motion of it underwater, billowing out from behind her.

It *looked* like stone, but something about it pulsed faintly.

Its hands were open in front of it. On it sat two small tomes—one bound in a deep red bark-colored hide, its clasp etched in gold. The other was a green leather book.

It looked familiar, though she couldn't place where she'd seen it.

"Your wedding gifts," he sang. "Two books in your favor."

"We aren't—" Lilac exchanged a reddened glance with Garin.

"We don't need your books," Garin said curtly, eyes fixed on the statue's offering. "No one asked for them."

"And I requested the company of the Breton queen and her vampire. I wasn't expecting a Strigoi, yet here we are." The Bugul Noz turned back to Lilac and offered a kind smile. "I collect books, letters, passages of experience etched in time and tome, everything one can read that is lost to the Breton sea, from the Channel to the seas *ouest*. The Argent River, lakes, marshes. Ponds," he added, looking extremely proud. "Oh, come on. It is merely a gift, and what one chooses to do with a gift is entirely up to fate herself, is it not?"

Garin exhaled in frustration. He marched forward to snatch the books, but another presence stirred, and the base of the statue began creaking. Beneath the altar, before their very eyes, the roots unfurled to reveal an inscription that had been grown—not carved—into the moss itself.

No truth is dredged without the tide taking its due.

No memory is opened that a forest does not mourn.

For every truth, an heir must drown.

"Drown?" snarled Garin.

"This is an age-old inscription. You mortals and once-mortals take everything with such weight. *Relax*. Let the tide guide you, as you've allowed it to guide you here."

"*You* summoned *us*."

"All the same. The ancient waters brought you here. Your truths await."

Lilac finally found her voice, hand still on the Dawnshard. Nothing arcane ever came for free—the Fair Folk taught her that. "What do you want in exchange?" The Bugul Noz's eyes sparkled. "What must we offer?"

"Smart girl." The creature tilted its head. "Well, nothing much. Just... the weight of your blood, the very thread of your line. The memories that root you, deeper than the ones you hold in your conscience, but ones bound to your soul." He chuckled when they exchanged another alarmed glance. "Each tome you take shall cost you one ancestral remembrance. One loss, one forgetting. You'll keep these memories for yourself, of course... maybe even learn something new of yourselves, and each other? This is as much of a gift to you as it is to me, wouldn't you say?"

Lilac stared at the altar, then at the creature, instantly thinking of Freya. Piper's gaunt face at the Mine's vestibule. "Why would you demand that?"

Solid as it was, the library creaked.

"Because this place remembers too much, Your Majesty," the Bugul Noz replied. There was a grief, a contorted heaviness to his words. "And you mortals remember far too little."

"What are you playing at?" Garin stepped forward. "What's your ruse?"

"Nothing. I am the guardian of memories scorned. Lost. I find—and do not lose—what is precious. I keep it safe here." His eyes narrowed at Garin. "Even from you. I've been trapped here for a couple centuries, you see, and am prisoner to the archive. I simply enjoy seeing the world for what it is today, and take great pleasure in the visceral *human* experience. Or inhuman. I can't afford to be picky."

"Fine," said Lilac, silencing Garin's glare of protest. "And as soon as it's done, we're leaving."

"*With* the books," the Bugul Noz said. "When you're ready, step up to the statue and introduce yourselves. One at a time."

The chill in her lungs felt ancestral. Bracing herself, Lilac stepped forward—but Garin made an unsettled sound.

"I'll go first. Get Myrddin if anything happens."

"I will." She pulled her blade from its sheath, and the Bugul Noz's breath hitched.

But then, Garin began speaking. "I'm Garin Austol Trevelyan, of—" He gestured vaguely—"no house worth mentioning. Born to lines of botanists, physicians, and lavender farmers. Brother of nettles, and dragged reluctantly into immortality. Cornwall forged the roots of my blood, the battlefields of Brittany saw it spilled, and the forest fermented it. I'm now Doyen of the Coven Brocéliande, heir of the Sanguine Mine, north of the High Forest... which sounds impressive, until you meet the vampires who reside there." Nothing happened. He glanced back at Lilac, then at the Bugul Noz, who waited patiently beside the statue. "What I lack in pedigree, I make up for in persistence, poor decisions, and a working knowledge of the blade, tavern tap, and arcane soil."

The shelves shivered. Every root, every branch upon the statue creaked in ancient fervor. A sound like wind rushing through dead canopies passed overhead, but there was no breeze. From the farthest shelves, something gave a slow, longing groan.

And then the room went dark, the only source of light were the white-blue spheres that floated to the outlying shelves.

Lilac could still feel herself—bite her lip, grip her dagger—and sensed the room and Garin and the Bugul Noz near. But everything was entirely dark... until a scene began to play before their very eyes.

There was a man before them, sitting across the way beside a stone mantel and oakwood floors illuminated by a dim hearth, which cast menacing shadows upon his sharp profile.

He was tall, Lilac could tell even as he sat rigidly in a chair she recognized—faded green leather, though it was a touch more vibrant here. He scrawled in a book, cross-checking the parchment splayed out onto a small table next to him. The floor was covered in bits of soil and freshly potted plants, some of them glowing—some moving about in their pots.

A sharp rap came at the door. He sighed laboriously, folded the page, placed his book and quill down, and went to the door down the familiar hallway. The scene moved to follow him, like the perspective of a lone spectre in the night.

He opened the door to a hazel-eyed woman with black hair that fell in waves around her plump face. She stuck a finger in his face, and he moved out of the way, merely turned back down the hall as she began to speak, low and harsh, not bothering to shut the door to the snow outside.

"You didn't do it," she said, trailing him. "Tell me you didn't do it."

The man sighed and turned. "Calm down, Aimee."

An echoing slap sounded throughout the room. He put a hand to his cheek.

"Tell me you didn't write that letter to Madame Toranaga."

Toranaga.

Next to the hearth, Aimee's face was the picture of horror. She clutched her round belly. "You told her I'd been laboring overnight, didn't you? I've said to you no such thing. I walked into the room today with a tub and laboring tools ready. He can't come early. It'd be weeks early—and—" She shook, eyes brimmed with angry, knowing tears.

"Shame," he said dryly. "I promised to pay her handsomely to take him out of you. Told her it was urgent."

"What is wrong with you?" she breathed. "That is my *friend*. She would never—never do that to me." Tears streamed down Aimee's face. "Tell me this isn't about those faeries, Pascal—"

He lunged, knocking a vase over and pinning her wrists to her side as she cried against the wall. "You're fucking selfish," he spat. "Do you know what this could do for us? We haven't been able to grow anything for months now."

"Because all you do is obsess, and obsess over those plants." She shoved him off, strode to the pots, picked one up and flung it across the room—

Before it shattered against the wall, seafoam mist filled the air once more. The memory was gone.

GARIN WAS SILENT, BUT LILAC COULD FEEL THE RAGE EMANATING from him.

The Bugul Noz hummed loudly in awkward disapproval. "That wasn't the one I wanted. Let's try this again."

THE MIST THINNED TO REVEAL A DESK COVERED IN ORGANIZED STACKS OF parchment, quill boxes, and a stack of dried pastries on a plate pushed to the side.

Henri's desk. Except his was usually askew and littered with tankards.

An arm rummaged through the drawer before them before sliding it carefully shut.

"Shit." Garin's voice, low and barely audible.

There were footsteps and voices outside the study. The scene shifted up to the rest of her father's study. Again, much too neat.

"She's with child," chimed one—male. There was the sound of metal, something like clinking armor. "Surely he will let them off easy."

"I don't know." A second voice, female. "Francis is a kind king, but François's men are here."

"This is true. His kindness tonight would look too easily like pandering weakness."

The footsteps passed the study; Garin moved out from behind the desk, slipped out the door, and into the dark western tower. Distant, echoing voices floated throughout the keep. The clanking of dishes and hushed whispers of gossip.

He passed the rooms on the left Lilac recognized as spare rooms for her parents' court, leaving the king and queen's chamber behind as he rapidly descended the steps, barely a sound to his footfall.

Garin broke into the empty second-floor keep and peered down into the foyer. No one was there save the guards flanking the front doors; one was dawdling, loosening the straps at his shoulders. The other had his head back against the wall.

The scene shifted, as if he'd descend the foyer steps—when there was another sound. One beyond the castle chatter.

The sound of a strange wheezing. Then, a cough, high-pitched and wet. It was an infant.

The scene blurred, jostling and churning her stomach. Garin was suddenly in her tower, his vision bright despite the dying embers in the fireplace. Her four-poster bed was not there; near the hearth, in the center of the room, was a lone crib—and a figure standing above it, a bundle in its arms.

"*No.*"

The man's head snapped up, face twisting in shock beneath his dark blonde brows and slicked mop of hair. His familiar icy eyes narrowed. "Erm, yes? Can I help you?"

The infant's wheezing continued, but he seemed in no rush to help it.

Garin strode toward him, causing the man to retreat. "What are you doing? Who are you?" The man stumbled back, tripping over a wooden toy.

"Give the child to me," Garin demanded, his voice laced with panic.

The man shrank away. "N-no, I was—"

A fist shot out. Bones crunched, and the man screamed. "Guards!" he roared.

Lilac immediately recognized the way he sobbed and demanded justice after doing something vile.

The sound of the infant's labored breathing was louder now—and the scene shifted down to show the purple face of a child, one not several months old. Its cerulean eyes bulged, lips turning blue.

Garin swore and stuck a trembling finger into its mouth and began to scoop globs of saliva out, along with pieces of something deep purple and leaf-green. He bent on one knee, turned the babe over upon his thigh, and firmly—*urgently*—began to rub its back.

"No. No, come on," Garin whispered as Artus moaned and crawled toward him. "If you touch me, I'll break your other leg," he snarled. "Touch him or his bloodline ever again and I'll end your life."

"Halt!" There was a pair of guards at the door. They froze at the sight of the bundle in Garin's arms.

The guard's next cry for help was cut off as Garin raced for the door and shoved his way through, knocking them down the steps and leaping over them, armor and blades clattering down the stairwell behind him.

"Help," Garin cried, the anguish in his voice piercing the room.

Lilac swallowed and wiped her tear-stained face.

He ran, past the alarmed scullery maids, past the roused entry guards and foyer, and into the west wing hallway. The four guards that flanked the door to the Grand Hall already had their weapons at the ready.

They'd begun screaming at him.

"Is that—"

"It's the prince!"

One of them stepped forward. "Put the infant down! Now!"

Garin didn't stop. He lifted the child in both arms, shielding it from their approach.

The guard who ran the sword through him gasped, staggering back, realizing it hadn't injured him at all. Garin reached down, yanked the dripping sword from himself. It clattered to the floor. "I need to speak to the king and queen," he said urgently, patting the babe's back. "He's been poisoned!"

The guards scattered away, horrified, as Garin tried to push through with the young prince in his arms.

"Please," Garin shouted. "Anyone, help!" He kneeled again; the infant's body lolled across his lap, and he began working again, rubbing and patting furiously.

The Grand Hall doors opened, the sound of frenzied alarm breaking through. "Handle them," came a stern, clear-cut voice.

"But—" started one of the shaken guards.

"Go. Now."

The eight of them filed into the Grand Hall, leaving Francis alone with Garin.

The king said nothing, only kneeling and watching, wide-eyed, as Garin massaged and prodded Henri's back. Finally, Henri coughed, producing two whole berries that plopped onto the floor.

His lips were still pale, but he'd begun to breathe again. Garin lifted him to his chest and patted several times until the babe began wailing again. Hands shaking, Garin then rose to his feet and tenderly placed him in Francis's arms.

There was another commotion, then—Artus, sobbing in the foyer. Other guards clambered and whispered fervently behind him.

"Vampire," Artus wailed. "There is a vampire here! In the castle—help! *Anarchy is at our door!*"

Reeling, Garin staggered down the southern corridor, toward the chapel.

"Wait!" The king had started after him. "Who are you?"

But Garin turned and snarled warningly. "Belladonna," he choked, the fading panic thick in his voice. "It was Belladonna. Deadly Nightshade."

Garin stumbled away, out the door, barrelling through the rows of diplomatic carriages adorned with the red and blue Grand Royal Coat of Arms, over the gate, and toward the treeline.

44

A hot, sickly breeze swept the circular room. Two of the torches flanking the statue flared to life, their flames sputtering against the stillness. On the altar, the topmost book began to glow, its light slow and pulsing, like a heartbeat.

Even the Bugul Noz sounded unsteady. "Thank you," he murmured. "That one is yours."

Garin didn't speak. He strode forward in silence, lifted the glowing red book from the altar, and turned away from the statue. He sank onto one of the stone benches lining the sanctum, tucked the book into his vest pocket, and dropped his face into his hands.

"Where did you get it?" Lilac asked quietly. *He'd been searching for it.*

"It came to me, as with everything here. I did not seek it," the Bugul Noz said, sounding tired. "Just after the war, His Majesty, John the Gentlehand, had thrown it into the courtyard pond in a fit of rage one night. It's been calling out to you these past few weeks.

"What is it?" Garin's voice was a scrape against their throats—a nicking blade.

"I don't know," he said wistfully. "I myself cannot read any of the closed books or journals here, not until they're reunited with their original owners, or those who can use them most. Even then, I'm not privy to the information unless someone decides to share it with me. I'm stuck with the unbound letters, manuscripts, and whatnot." He tapped his head with a sad smile. "Memorized most of them."

A strange, unnatural stillness had fallen, thick and heavy. Even the pair of torches seemed to hush their flames. Garin's fury, moments ago barely restrained, had been swallowed whole—as if the chamber itself demanded silence.

"You're next, Your Majesty."

"Do it if you want to," Garin interjected, releasing a handful of his hair. "*Only* if you want to. If not, I'll get us out of here."

The Bugul Noz's eyes bulged in protest, but Lilac stepped up the statue, glaring up at the woman, raising her chin and sheathing the Dawnshard.

Her eyes fluttered shut and spoke from within. Deep within.

"*I am Eleanor Trécesson, daughter of a house that fears its own blood.*" The words reverberated in her own ears, skull, and bones. "*Queen by blood and burden. Daughter of Henri, who named me 'Lilac' for the softness he invented to make sense of me. A softness he yearned. A flower—fragile, sweet, blooming in spring.*"

Her voice sharpened, but didn't rise. "*But the season of my birth is the only soft thing about me. He never understood that lilacs root best in ruin. That they bloom in silence, and thrive in the abandoned soil of crypts as well as castle hedges. He named me gently because he could not bear the thing I was becoming.*

"*I speak now not as a bride, nor as a daughter, but as the blade he tried to silence in moments when love was rationed like breath. I was given fire before I was given choice, and tonight I carry both.*"

THE WOMAN RAN THROUGH THE COBBLESTONE ALLEY, EVEN AS NO ONE chased her.

Her turnshoes splashed through puddles fouled with soot and slop, her too-large cloak flaring behind her. The eve was dense, thick with mist dulling the sound of her slamming footfall.

Somewhere, far behind, the abbey bell tolled midnight.

She didn't hesitate, not when the alley twisted unnaturally, not when the shadows bent in directions they shouldn't, or when she thought she saw one of her husband's castle guards lurking in the fog.

Not even when the crooked sign appeared ahead of her, exactly where it should've been—above the warped door adorned in peeling red paint.

The Fool's Folly.

The jester carved into the sign grinned wide, its remaining eye whittled to a jagged hole. It was watching over her. Judging. The Folly never forgot the Fool's whims.

Even those done in the dark.

She pulled the wool hood over her head and entered without knocking. The brothel's warmth hit her—cheap perfumed heat and candlelight, bodies pressed close in shadows, laughter rising and falling like the waves during a full moon.

At the bar on the far wall, she spoke the words without ceremony. "Moonlit Path Tea."

The barkeep didn't flinch. A deep scar crossed his face, curling like a smile that hadn't belonged to him; his amber eyes flashed orange. He polished a glass that didn't need cleaning and nodded toward the hallway behind the bar, just as she'd been advised by the tea maker in Paimpont years and years ago.

She'd been here many times before, up to just a few *months* before, for a simpler sort of tea. Yet it hadn't felt simple at the time.

Behind the curtain, the air cooled. The hallway narrowed into a short stairwell carved into the earth. The candles lining the walls burned blue, flickering in the absence of wind, their flames bending toward her as she passed. She descended quickly, though her breathing had changed—shallow, strained.

Above, the brothel throbbed with noise and sin. Before her—below—the silence thickened like the air.

The apothecary walls were ancient stone. Shelves flanked the room, heavy with jars filled with pressed flowers, floating organs, silver dust that moved in circles without wind. Herbs hung like trophies—dried, curled, and beckoning. A cauldron sat at the center of it all, bubbling with something that smelled of burnt cloves, satsumas, and rusted iron.

The woman tending it wore a blood-red robe, her back hunched slightly from her long years bent over the brew. Her face was pale and smooth tonight, untouched by time, her probing amber eyes deep set and shaped like fine almonds.

She stepped into the chamber, her voice too loud in the quiet. "I need to see Aimee."

The robed woman turned slowly, her eyes reflecting the candles but showing none of her usual fire. "It's been a while, Katella." Her watering gaze flickered down to her womb. "I take it her teas have worked for you and the king?"

"It's urgent, Madame Toranaga," Katella pressed, her words rushing out. "I cannot keep it."

"I see." Madame Toranaga merely twiddled the gold tassels at the end of her robe. "Your wedding night was last month."

"And it has been two cycles without my bleed," Katella said.

"Breathe, dear. John might be generous, but you are worried about upsetting him. Is that right?"

Katella nodded, the lump in her throat growing.

"Kings are permitted to keep their bastard children all the time. Surely you can ask."

"It is not a bastard child."

Madame Toranaga crossed her arms, skeptical. "Come, now. Who was it? A friend? A farmhand?"

She blanched and shook her head.

The witch's eyes narrowed. "Then *how?*" Madame Toranaga demanded.

"I don't know." Katella's voice was barely a whisper. "I thought it was a dream, a pleasant dream—"

"He died in the attack," the witch whispered, suddenly tugging her back to the door. "In the ambush. Alor is dead, Katella. Stop being ridiculous, you're doing yourself no favors by being here. Say nothing about this. He is *dead*, you hear me?" She shook her at the arm. "Dead."

Katella sobbed, and she reached into her cloak pocket, producing a crinkled piece of parchment. "I should have stayed awake, comforted him, assured him it was going to be all right."

Madame Toranaga's eyes danced fleetingly across the paper. She didn't even finish it before crinkling it and stuffing it back into Katella's palm, shutting her eyes against the words she consumed. "You were never here," the witch breathed. "I will not end the king's pregnancy."

Katella shook her head fervently. "But you don't understand. It's not—"

"I understand enough, Katella. In doing so, I'd put my entire business and the girls in jeopardy—I'm sure you understand." Madame Toranaga drew near. "If I get word you tried to end it yourself, I *will* come after you."

Katella tried to resist, but the witch was strong. She cried and begged, until Madame Toranaga gripped her by the shoulders.

"It's early on enough. Tell the king's physicians the child came early, that's all. It happens often. More than you think." She brought her porcelain face near. *"Burn that letter."*

Katella's crying stopped, and despair took over her darkened features. "But you help women like me all the time."

Madame Toranaga shot her a dangerous look. "Those are not women like you."

"But—"

The witch left her a moment, disappearing into the array of low shelves that lined the northern wall. When she returned, she pressed a small book —*the green one*—into Katella's hands. "Hold your head high, keep your mouth shut, and never, ever repeat this to anyone."

Madame Toranaga shoved Katella back into the darkened hallway and slammed the door in her face.

BLINKING THROUGH HER TEARS, WIPING AT HER FACE, LILAC WAITED TO be thrust back into the sanctum.

But she remained there in the silent dark, the cries and desperate bellows of her ancestor's pleas ringing out into the desolate pit of memory. Fear filled her, and she violently rubbed at her eyes, only to open them to...

The foyer. *Her* foyer.

Sunlight streamed in as bright as day, and there was a small crowd at the open doors.

A round-faced young girl flanked by a man and a woman stood outside.

And in front of her was another child, with her back to Lilac. Shorter. Younger. Auburn brown hair and a crooked stance, as if she couldn't wait to leave whatever dull conversation her parents had roped her into for formality's sake this time.

"What do you say, Lilac?" said Henri. His hair was lush and brown, leaving no gaps atop his scalp.

"Maybe she's not ready," Marguerite crooned, inspecting her manicured nails. "Perhaps this was a poor idea."

The girl's parents exchanged silent glances, then looked to Henri.

"Nonsense," he laughed, twirling his mustache as he did when he was nervous. He bent to the girl's height and placed a hand on her shoulder. "You're going to come live with us next week, understand? You can visit with your parents every turn of the season if you wish. You and Eleanor will be fast friends."

The girl's face lit up spectacularly, but fell when Marguerite said, "You will serve her. That is it."

Her parents ushered her back out, toward the awaiting carriage. Hedwig scurried in, and scooped up the girl with brown hair, who'd covered her ears with her parents' bickering.

"How would you like to bake a pie with me, young lady?" Hedwig said, with a playful poke on the belly.

Young Lilac went away happily in her chef's arms, her own wrapped around Hedwig's neck.

But Lilac—the one who'd weathered both time and memory—remained in the middle of the foyer.

"What was that?" said Henri, turning on Marguerite furiously and motioning for every guard in the room to leave. "You will not speak to her that way."

Marguerite stepped to him, her voice low and angrier than Lilac had ever heard it. "I shall speak to her as I please. Do you truly believe I welcome the bastard echo of your infidelity, wandering these corridors like a prancing ghost?"

Henri's hand rose, brushing his brow, as if trying to press the truth back into his skull. "You agreed—"

"I *said* she would not be cast into the gutter," Marguerite cut in. "Not left to rot in the streets. Not *abandoned*, as I was forced to abandon my own." Her throat bobbed, her eyes glistening. "Twins, Henri. Torn from me, at my father's command. I have never seen their faces. Riou scoured the records for me. And you have never been any help." She shrugged, silent tears falling. "Never."

"And what," Henri snarled back, his expression twisting. "And if we found them, then what? You'd bring them here? Filled this castle with three crownless girls with nothing to their name, surround and overwhelm the one with the timid voice and anxious hand, and call that mercy? Would they be gift to our daughter? Each a persisting monument to what I failed to sire?" He motioned around the foyer. "No boys? No *men?*"

Heartbreak flashed across Marguerite's face. She sniffled. "Let Agnes take Piper, then, Henri."

"Agnes will leave Piper for dead," Henri warned. "Or worse."

"She is no better than me." Marguerite turned for their tower stairs, her skirts dragging behind. "She will know no kindness from me under this roof. She won't find warmth here. Not from me." She looked back once, over her shoulder. "And you? You think there's anything in *you* that resembles warmth or love?"

❧ 45 ❧

The library shifted, rumbling from within. The floor lurched, and she teetered sideways. Garin snagged Lilac by the waist, tugging her close and smearing her tears into his shirt. "It's all right," he murmured softly. "Tell no one."

She nodded, too shocked to form words, unable to process fully what they'd just seen.

"Out," said the Bugul Noz behind them, his sticky wet fingers on Garin, shoving them toward the door. "And tell no one what you saw."

Garin's voice cracked louder, like a whip over her shoulder. "What is this? What have you done?"

"Something wakes. Older than memory." The Bugul Noz looked back, into the further recesses of the archive. "Get *out*. Hurry, my boy."

Cracks laced the marble beneath their feet and shelves trembled, loosing several books that clattered to the floor. The statue at the heart of the sanctum began to bleed dust and blood from her eyes.

A lone splinter threaded through her.

Lilac didn't wait—she ran for the green, glowing tome that pulsed in the hands of the altar. As she reached for it, the ground gave another lurch, slamming her to the ground. She scrambled to her feet, elbows and knees stinging, but Garin pulled her up by the arm and tugged her out.

"I believe you dropped that one earlier, Garin," the Bugul Noz shouted over the noise, moving to grab the book for them—but he hissed, snapping his smoking hand back. The green book remained upon the crumbling statue.

The creature bounded forward and shoved them toward the passage, trails of bubble and froth already creeping under the door.

"I'll see you again. Get you the book. Be ready to run," the Bugul Noz urged. "Or swim."

Before they could ask, the door opened—

And the flood followed. A rush of cold, blinding pressure swept them out—a wave that seemed wary of the sacred space of the creature's sanctum of lost knowledge—and swallowed them whole. They were submerged and tugged violently up like ragdolls.

Lilac broke the surface in the courtyard pond, sputtering against the cold, the water warmer than the frigid night and screaming they emerged to.

Time had resumed. They'd rejoined the current.

There were shouts, and sounds of steel clashing against stone, horses neighing. The courtyard rang with chaos. Lilac coughed hard, spitting up water and still clutching the green tome, the Dawnshard still sheathed but vibrating wildly at her hip.

"François," Garin shouted behind her, kicking and steering them to the slope, shoving her onto the bank and rising to his knees. "They're already here."

Soldiers in red, blue, and gold uniforms surged at the outer gate before them, jeering into the bailey between the bars. Her guards stood against them, blades at the ready, holding the line. More of them were on the ramparts, firing arrows straight down like harpoons. Four large cannons were pointed outward from the embrasures, haunting in the moonlight as more ammunition was wheeled out on carts from the armory entrance.

Loïg had broken free from the stable and was prancing warningly back and forth behind the rows of weapons.

Garin took Lilac's hand, and they were off toward the entrance. "Don't look," he said. "Keep your eyes on me."

Just inside the foyer, they barreled into someone, sparks of violet flooding their vision.

"Garin—Your Majesty," Myrddin said hurriedly, picking himself off the floor. "I was coming to get you. Everyone's ready in the chapel."

"But the gate," Lilac said, forced to look back; she had to. Those were *her* men. Several of François's soldiers had spotted and recognized her, pointing and laughing at her ridiculous soaked frame.

Garin growled and shoved her behind him, and they immediately fell silent at his appearance in the torchlight.

They turned toward the west wing corridor—

But then the screams started, louder—not from within, but from the field beyond the wall.

Lilac squinted, and her vision swam.

Shapes blurred in the shadows of the early morning. Faster than human. Several figures, four, maybe five—moved like wraiths through the crowd. They tore through the French front line with surgical cruelty, pulling men away into the fog, blood splattering onto the gate and turrets.

Muskets began to crack in the air.

They'd been *saving* their guns for the Daemons. The vampires.

"No—*NO!*" Garin screamed, lunging back at the door, but Lilac and Myrddin snatched him by the back of his vest and held firm. "Stand down! Retreat! Bastion, where are you—pull them back!"

But Myrddin took their arms, pushing them both toward the chapel. "Inside, the both of you. *Now.*"

Just then, another figure came jogging toward the entrance, right at them. Garin's head snapped hungrily, and Bastion put his hands up. "Jesus *fuck.*"

"Where've you been?" Garin snapped.

"Having a nice shit in the outhouse—what does it *look* like I was doing? Grabbing your priest. Who else can marry her?" He was soaked in blood— surely not his own, his mouth was clean—Giles slumped, unconscious, over his shoulder. The Veiled Garnet glowed in the torchlight on his chest. "They'll hold the gates, but only until dawn breaks."

"The French are using hawthorn bullets," Garin said, chest heaving.

Several maids' eyes widened as they parted way for them, scurrying around the queen and her odd party as they turned into the hall.

"They know," Bastion said. "They know."

THE CHAPEL WAS DIM AND TREMBLING WITH DISTANT ARTILLERY. HALF adorned with flowers and finery, a corner of the room strung with banners and garland—as if their decorators had fled the scene mid-pin-up. Guests sat rigid in the pews, wet from fog and terror, partially dressed, eyes wide and teeming with unanswered questions.

Henri and Marguerite's former court were among them. Helena and Gertrude.

No Agnes, nor William.

The tea and spice maker, Madame Rillrose, and Madame Toranaga sat near the front, watching solemnly.

Across from them were Adelaide and Lorietta, dressed in black silk and chiffon, sitting next to Rupert and Emma.

In the frontmost row sat Yanna, Isabel, and Piper.

Marguerite and Henri stood near the altar, Henri's face pale. Marguerite's, unreadable.

Bastion marched to the front and slumped Giles into the pew, then jogged to the back of the church. There was a plink, the sound of metal wrenching, then stone splitting; he returned with one of the fonts of Holy Water attached to part of the brick that held it, and splashed it straight into Father Guillaume's face.

"*Don't you touch the butter!*" the priest shouted, snorting and jerking awake. He blinked up at everyone. "Oh. What's going on?" He spotted Lilac, shivering in Garin's arms. Henri and Marguerite, glaring in their direction. His gaze stilled on Garin. "What happened to him?" he asked. "And where is my Bisousig?"

"It doesn't matter, priest," Bastion snapped. "Read from the scripture there." He nodded his head at the scroll and Bible next to it. "Just do your job and no one gets hurt."

"They," Myrddin offered, swirling his hands and producing a square red box, and an enormous crown upon a pillow, "are getting married. And Lilac will be crowned."

Not bothering to correct him, Garin left her side and took his place at right of the altar, soaked, eyes darkening. Lilac joined him, and gave him a small smile. Her bottom lip wouldn't stop quivering, not just because of the frigid air soaked into her wet clothes.

But instead of returning it, Garin's hands shot out and gripped hers, squeezing, as if it were the last thing on earth he needed to feel.

Giles cleared his throat. Garin released her hands and forced his down at his side.

He stood at the altar and began the rites, voice slightly trembling as he began. "*In nomine Patris, et Filii, et Spiritus Sancti.*" He eyed the crowd. Bastion's eyes narrowed threateningly, so he continued. "We are gathered here under God's Holy Church to solemnize the marriage between the noble Lady Eleanor Trécesson and His Imperial Majesty, Maximilian, by his most trusted proxy, Sir..." Father Guillaume glanced sideways at Garin, who was still fuming. "Garin—"

"Albrecht," Henri corrected from his seat behind them.

"Sir *Albrecht*. Let the vows now be spoken, by God's grace and under the seal of Heaven."

As Father Guillaume spoke, Lilac remained reeling. Those memories she'd witnessed of Garin's, feeling like an unwelcome intruder into his most private family past—memories woven into his bloodline, as the creature had said, now inextricably wound into the threads of her mind. As hers, with him.

The memory of her ancestor, Katella... The dim apothecary that held centuries of secrets within its perfumed walls.

Lilac glanced down at Garin's hands balled into fists, unseeing, her thoughts flickering like candlelight back to the library—the strange, hidden sanctum filled with lost archives. The Bugul Noz, a not-so-hideous Daemon who had shown them kindness without demand.

Whatever it had been—the gloam, a Daemon realm, some fraying border of dream and memory—Lilac found herself wondering what it would be like to walk those echoing halls again. With Garin, never alone.

Twice usurper, Kestrel had called her.

A breath caught in her throat, something jagged and strange—a laugh, or perhaps the beginning of a sob. She stifled it, swallowing the noise as a whisper brushed against her senses.

Piper. In the front pew, shoulder to shoulder with Isabel.

Her friends. Her *sisters*.

Both smiled at her—gently, fiercely—while Yanna smirked, casting the occasional scowl toward Bastion and Garin. Nonetheless, they *saw* her. Perhaps, that was the duty of a sister. Knowing the grief and heartache one carried, and loving her all the more for it.

Piper leaned ever so slightly toward her, lips barely moving. "Breathe, Your Majesty," she mouthed. "You look beautiful."

The tension in her chest cracked, just a little. The grief and fury didn't leave her, but for one breathless moment, it softened. They were with her. And she was not alone.

Garin cleared his throat, low and sensuous. His jaw remained tense, unnaturally still as Father Guillaume rushed on. For a fleeting moment, she thought his lips looked too pale without her blood staining them.

He had not looked her in the eye since the rite began.

"Garin," she whispered. "We don't have to do this."

His eyes lifted slowly, and she saw it then—the faint ring of deep burgundy around his garnet irises. The strain in his working throat. The tremendous effort it cost him to remain composed.

"It is already done," he said hoarsely, leaning in. "You were about to give your word on paper, as I have pushed for."

"Your brother had you on your knees with a stake at your back," she countered.

"This is my own doing. I will never forgive myself. I—" He stopped, as if the words were physically caught. "I will not shame you before the altar, Eleanor. You mean too much to me. Your decision is your own. I will not be the one to corner you, command you, nor fight you. Whatever your decision is, I will live with it."

Garin was right. The decision was hers—had to be hers. France was already at her gate. Once they broke through, they'd storm their way through to her. If they could not reach her, they'd go after more of her towns. Her farmers, women, and children... the most vulnerable.

Father Guillaume rattled off before them, intoning his script. The scent of frankincense and myrrh grew cloying. Lilac's pulse, anxious and galloping, filled the air like a drumbeat.

Suddenly, Garin flinched.

"Repeat after me, Sir Albrecht," Father Guillaume said solemnly, beginning to dictate. "I, Albrecht, by the solemn authority vested in—"

He trailed off as Garin interjected, his expression nearly a scowl, "Vested in me as lawful proxy for His Imperial Majesty Maximilian, *do* take thee, Eleanor Trécesson, to be his wedded wife, before God and this Holy Church."

Lilac stared at him in wonder. He'd researched. He'd memorized the vows.

He continued, unflinchingly holding her gaze. "I pledge, in his name, to *love* thee, to honor thee, and to *cherish* thee, in sickness and in health, for better or for worse, so long as my life shall endure."

Garin slowly, reverently, dipped into a low bow, and caught her left hand on the way up, just as he had the night his true identity had been revealed to her. "By this vow, he binds himself to thee in Holy Matrimony, according to the rite of our mother Church."

Myrddin released the red box into the air, and it floated smoothly over to them. In the crowd, Lorietta shook her head as Adelaide grinned appreciatively. Marguerite was clutching at her necklace so tight she might strangle herself.

Garin opened the box and pulled out a shining gold ring—a large inlaid pearl, set between emeralds and diamonds.

Father Guillaume cleared his throat with a knowing smile at Lilac. He slowly closed the book. "Have you written your own vows, too?"

The small crowd flinched at the drum of artillery outside in rapid succession—two steady bangs, back to back. She glanced out the high windows. Just as the sky began to brighten, they'd fired the cannons.

Rupert suddenly stood and bowed, before striding quickly toward the corridor exit.

"Hey," Henri murmured. "Where do you think you're going?"

"He's a vampire," Marguerite snapped, as the door swung shut.

"So am I," said Bastion from the empty front pew, opposite her sisters.

Lilac's parents grew quiet.

Piper raised a steady hand, her fangs protruding. "And me."

Henri's ruddy face blanched.

Garin was distracted, staring down at the ring, his face expressionless as Lilac began to speak.

"Brocéliande whispered to me before I could speak the language of our courts. I inherited the Tongue of the Old Faith, the Arcana Lingua that binds me to Brocéliande and the creatures within her."

Not a sound was made. Not even from her parents. Garin's gaze had drifted from the ring to her hands, stilling there.

"Today, I take the hand of an emperor I have never touched, whose voice I have only read in decrees and never heard. By proxy, through blood, through duty, and *not* desire—I am bound to him." She let her hardened gaze fall upon Garin, where it softened. Lilac spoke to him—through him. "I do this not for love, but for the bones of a kingdom too fragile to stand alone. For those who need a voice, my voice, to be heard.

The room was still. Silent, as her words echoed in the chamber of the chapel.

"Let it be known, I do not offer my heart, for it is no longer mine to give. What I offer you is my loyalty and my sovereignty, which will remain. I bind myself to the empire—not the man. So, let the Old Gods mark it. Let your false prophets rejoice. Let Brocéliande forever remember this day."

With unsteady hands, Garin plucked the ring from its holder; it began floating again, and Myrddin tugged it away. He held it before her but waited expectantly. There was a ghost of a teasing chuckle there. His eyes were kind despite their shade of garnets, and his brows rose expectantly.

"With this vow," he murmured under his breath, his dimples taking her breath away.

Right. "With this vow," she repeated.

"I bind myself to him."

"I—" She swallowed tightly. "Bind myself..."

Garin waited for her to finish the sentence. When she did not, he continued, brows knitted. "In holy wedlock, as ordained by our Lord Jesus Christ."

Lilac choked, suddenly blinded by her tears. "I—" She shook her head, unable to finish. "Just put the fucking ring on, Garin."

"Are you sure?" His hands fell immediately. "Let me—"

She cut him off with a glare. "Do it."

He dipped his head, held his breath, and took her left hand in his.

With reverent restraint, Garin—her regnant, her friend, her great love —slid Maximilian's ring onto her second-to-last finger.

46

The shouting beyond the walls sounded throughout the chapel, a persistent reminder of the cost of her own selfish cause. Lilac couldn't tell whether they were winning or losing. Garin's face remained stoic as he listened, his eyes glazed over.

It was a solemn and quick affair. There was no ceremony for the crowning. No row of bishops to kiss her hand or congratulate her. No cardinal to bless her. Only the hanging silence of a chapel filled with strained reverence, and her aching knowledge that every step forward, for herself or her kingdom, had come at a price.

Father Guillaume and Henri stood on the step above her.

The crown loomed, heavy and foreboding, lowering onto her head like a chain clasped shut. And still, she remained standing.

Lilac didn't falter, nor faint. The applause through the room was quiet, as if everyone felt her heart breaking.

No one realized Garin's hunger until it was too late.

His hand trembled, and he stared down at it, confused. Then, his arm lifted—and he reached for her. She thought he would caress her face, but he kept going... and gently lifted the crown from her head.

He was merely shaken. Lilac hushed everyone who made a disapproving comment and extended a hand to him—to her crown—but he jerked his shoulders back, just out of reach.

"Garin?"

"*No,*" Garin hissed, curling into himself, staggering away as if her touch would burn him. He dropped the circlet, which clattered against the chapel stones. "It's the hunger. Kestrel's deal—"

He snarled, clawing at his head.

Dread tore through her. She yearned to help him, to calm him, but every part of her screamed to run. "But the chest was delivered!" Lilac stepped forward, pale in the sputtering torchlight. "Garin, talk to me—please."

Everyone shot from their seats and began backing away, freezing when Garin's head popped back up, tracking their movement.

He shrank away from them. "Bast," Garin croaked, low and deep. "The chest."

"We—we sent it off in the faerie fire," Bastion said, fingers twitching toward the blade at his side. "I swear."

"We did," Piper cried. "It vanished like you said it would!"

Henri and Father Guillaume stumbled back toward the altar, while Marguerite was already halfway up the organ's woodwork, skirts hiked, hair wild.

Garin snapped his head up at her, and his eyes were no longer human. Deep crimson bled into them, twin pools of bloodshot hunger. His fangs split his mouth in a snarl too wide, too ravenous to resemble anything human at all.

Yanna and Isabel surged forward, but he turned and *growled*, a deep, guttural sound born of curses and carrion, and it rooted them in place. "Help her," he said in a voice no longer his own, "and you will be slain."

"Get back!" Lilac shouted, throwing a hand toward the doors. "Leave us! Go!"

The human attendants needed no convincing, and fled toward the corridors and courtyard. But then, the castle groaned, rooting them in place. Low at first, like something ancient stirring in its sleep.

Then a *rumble*. Dust sifted from the rafters. Cracks spider-webbed across the chapel's eastern wall, toward the back facing the courtyard.

A section of the wall exploded inward. No screaming or artillery could be heard—just the sound of the world crumbling. Stone shattered, just when a large wave surged across the flagstones, toward the pews.

Garin stiffened as Lilac shielded herself, the stench of sea filling the chapel and mingling with the heady incense.

Wind howled through the breach, thick with the reek of brine and rot —and through it stepped a tall figure with billowing, unbound hair. She was wet and naked, her lower half below her navel sinewed with pale-green skin wrapped in opalescent scales that shone purple and green.

She was laughing, the sound a nightmarish tide—and in a dripping, clawed hand, she held a shuddering mess of hair and coral, limping, straining to walk alongside her.

The Bugul Noz.

"I'm sorry, Your Highness," he was whimpering, voice paced with pain. "I—I won't do it again."

"Well," she purred, ignoring the creature, her melodic intonation catching Garin's attention. "You've all made *such* a mess."

She flung the Bugul Noz aside, and he hit one of the pews with a sodden thud, sliding to the floor, crumpled and twitching.

Garin turned to look over his shoulder, his garnet eyes disinterestedly catching the sea witch's gaze before returning to her—but Lilac was already moving, driven by something deeper than instinct.

Her blood sang, her thrall's strength *surging* through her veins. If Garin was made stronger, faster—hungrier—through the curse of Kestrel's deal... then so was she. Her limbs were not her own. The bond between her and Garin—the magic that chained her soul to his appetite—snapped taut like a wire and pulled.

Lilac ran, faster than human feet could ever carry her. She ran toward the outdoor opening just past the sea witch, but the bitch put her hand out, teal claws inches from her face as Lilac skidded to a stop.

"I don't think so. Your owner's that way, mutt."

Lilac snarled and careened right, tripped over the old candelabra sitting in the corner and vaulted, slamming against the choir loft. Pain lanced up her side, but she climbed, feral and unthinking, her fingernails scraping, gouging into the brittle wood.

She was no longer herself. She hadn't been in a long time, not fully. *This* was a taste of it. This was what it was to let hunger drive her.

The thrall in her—whatever fragment of Garin's cursed blood burned up inside her—dragged her up the beams like a creature born to fight and flee. She scrambled higher, effortless and sobbing, eyes wild, until she reached the rafters above the altar.

Garin snarled below, eyes locked on Lilac, his claws flexing. Bastion, lurking in the pews, suddenly launched himself toward him—but he was caught midair and flown backwards toward the altar, landing at Yanna and Isabel's feet.

A thick wooden pole from the chapel rubble was embedded in his chest, blood leaking from his mouth. Piper grabbed him, dragged him up the stairs to the front of chapel where everyone else cowered, and yanked it out.

In the wreckage of the wall and courtyard, the sea witch watched the chaos unfold, dusting her hands, eyes half-lidded and amused. She strode forth slowly as water lapped at her heels. "Oh, my darling," she cooed to Garin. "Albrecht, was it?"

"Garin," he managed distractedly, blinking up at the queen.

Flames of green jealousy ignited in Lilac's chest.

But by the time the sea witch spoke again, the hunger had consumed his expression once again. "Morwenn. Pleasure." She tutted, studying him unabashedly. "A *Strigoi*, in the flesh. I was not expecting this—expecting you. My, you really do ruin everything you touch."

Lilac crawled forth, snarling down, her own blunt teeth bared. "Leave him alo—"

She'd slipped.

Lilac caught herself, clinging to the beam, breath ragged and limbs aching. Dust and old incense thickened the air as she hung above the altar, the chapel yawning beneath her. She swung a leg to pull herself up, but the wood began to splinter under her bare hands; she cussed, shifting her grasp, when an old, rusted nail slashed her wrist.

She winced and forced herself to look down, warm splatters of her blood hitting her cheek.

Garin stood motionless below, positioning himself, letting the drops stain his face. His claws flexed at his sides; horrified, Lilac glimpsed the struggle in him, the fraying edge where his mind ended and the monster began in watching her fight for her life.

He closed his eyes for a moment, and dragged his hand across his cheek, slipping his fingers into his mouth.

Garin moaned, a sound of desperate ecstasy.

Morwenn stepped lightly over the rubble, following him. "Are you truly going to let her hide from you like that? Strong Strigoi like you, what a shame. Your beautiful little thrall, all tangled up in borrowed strength and fear?" She turned up at Lilac and smiled with snide amusement. "You can run, girl, but you won't get far from what's already been inside you."

Garin's breath caught. Lilac saw it in his face, his smoldering decision. She swung her leg again, catching it on the rafter, finally hoisting herself up.

And then—he leapt.

With a growl, Garin kicked off from a toppled pew, his claws sinking into the stone pillars. He climbed expertly up the height of the chapel wall. Each movement was smooth and utterly silent, save the groaning wood under his weight once he reached the rafters in front of Lilac in a matter of seconds.

Henri was shouting. Marguerite's cries echoed through the broken chapel.

Lilac skittered backward along the rafter beam, heart thundering.

Garin perched like a gargoyle, red eyes burning.

She hissed like an animal in warning. "Don't come closer."

"I cannot stop myself," he said softly. "Stop running."

Her fingers were so sweaty and slicked in blood, they would've slipped from the wood behind her if not for her thrall strength. "You have to fight it, Garin."

"Listen to me," he said, and she wondered which part of him was speaking. "I want you. I *need* to chase you. If you stop—if you let me reach you—there will be nothing left of me to hold back until you are finished."

"Then why would I stop running?" she snarled.

"Because," he said, rising to his feet with perfect balance. "You can *fight*."

Lilac was on her feet in a flash, wobbling violently, using her arms to steady herself. In one swift motion, she unsheathed the Dawnshard and slashed at him from a distance, almost willing the blade to open.

"That won't do anything," he rasped. "It won't kill me."

"I'm not *trying* to kill you." Lilac stepped forward, slashing again; Garin's hungry gaze only grew more amused, more terrible.

"You have to."

Rage boiled within. She would not—not in a world of magic and medicine and things she never would've fathomed possible. There *was* another way. She'd find it.

"A puny dagger," Morwenn chided below, and Lilac deliciously envisioned severing her head with it.

Alas, the Dawnshard remained dormant, silent as it had been all these years. Lilac's balance was getting better, her body quickly adjusting; she lunged again, the blade gleaming in the dark. Just when she thought it would hit him, Garin jumped over her, landing behind her with regal grace.

His weight still rocked the beam; Lilac shrieked and turned just in time to see him snatch the hilt from her grasp. He wielded it expertly, lancing and twirling it in the air.

"You used your Dawnshard because you knew I'd come back. I'd only wake with renewed resolve to find you, track you down." Lilac's mouth went dry at his warning as Garin's ravenous eyes dropped to her hip. His head tilted, a predatory demon savoring the memories of the cursed body it inhabited. "If there is a next time, I'm going to fuck you myself and make you *scream* my name on the hilt of that thing."

And I'm going to shut you up, she thought furiously, snatching the stake from its sheath and adjusting her grip, *hating* the way Garin watched her.

"Thumb between your forefinger and middle finger," he sang out, still somehow filled with the insufferable need to teach. His lips quirked when Morwenn's giddy laughter rang out in the pit again.

Lilac readied the stake.

"You can do it," Garin coaxed through the challenging gleam in his eyes. "One stab, and you'll finally be free."

She bared her teeth and struck him, slashing, carving through the air instead of stabbing. It made contact with his shoulder, searing the skin under his ripped shirt. Smoke lifted from it.

He winced. The muscle beneath Garin's eye twitched. "That is *not* how you use it."

Lilac slashed again, too easily catching his forearm. She watched the

wound at his shoulder close up. The one at his arm, deeper, followed slowly.
"You're holding back!"

"I intend to lose," he admitted easily, loosely fingering the blade, tossing
it between his nimble fingers and keeping it out of reach.

"You took my dagger, so this was the only chance I had at survival."
Anger billowed through her. "You left me no choice."

Lilac was close enough to land the blow. Instead, she held the stake over
the edge of the beam. Early sunlight from the nearby stained-glass window
caught on the iron-banded shaft, casting a long shadow across the rafters.

This was a game they both could play.

"I've a talent for that, haven't I? Leaving the ones I love with nothing
but terrible choices." Garin's cruel grin disappeared. "But no, *this* is how I
would do that." His eyes flashed dangerously, ablaze against the dawn. She
glimpsed something like regret there. "Eleanor, I command you to drive
that stake through my heart."

Lilac stood there, panting. Bracing herself, ready to drop her weapon
and—

And what? And die? She never expected it to happen here—in a church
of all places. Not at the meager age of twenty, like this, atop a rafter, spar-
ring the one she loved. How woefully poetic.

But as her fingers shook with the weight of her only option... nothing
happened.

"Do it."

There was no urge to fight against. Lilac's eyes widened. *The bag of
berries.*

As if reading her mind, a look of fury overcame Garin.

She immediately dropped her gaze, feeling his intense eyes probing
hers, fingering her mind for a chance at entrancement. "I won't," Lilac said
to his boots. His long, nimble legs. "I will not. You deserve to *live*, and love,
and be loved, Garin." He stalked toward her, walking her back toward the
front of the church. He opened his arms wide, bearing his chest. The lump
in her throat nearly choked her. "You deserve good things, *we* deserve more
time—"

Her heel slipped; Marguerite sobbed below.

But Lilac caught her balance. Barely.

"Fight me when I am unable to do it. I'd never be able to live with myself if I let anything terrible happen to you. But I'd burn this entire world and the next down if your demise was by my own hand—*please*, Lilac," he crooned, chest rising and falling as he neared. Saliva dribbled from his chin, his pupils blown wide in hunger. Tears were falling past the tips of his boots. "If you love me... do it for me. For us. Put me out of the misery of fantasizing about your blood—all of it, running through my fingers, so much of it spilling into my mouth that it chokes me. This is not what you want, Eleanor. Look at me, what I am. This is not the future you deserve."

"You said I deserve a burning, steadfast love," she whispered fiercely. Unflinching. Her gaze rose to him, boring into him. "Try as I might, I cannot imagine one as deep or piercing, or as corrupting as yours." Lilac leaned in, watching his eyes drop to her throat. "Ache for me, Garin. I am yours everlasting. I am bound and I am *willing*."

Her dagger shook in his hand.

As if fate itself drove her, Lilac grabbed for her blade—the blade itself.

"No!" He yanked it back, slashing her.

Hissing, she let go in time to preserve all of her fingers, but it was enough to slice her—soak her front and forearms in blood. Garin collapsed *into* her, his hunger taking over his need to kill her, just as she wanted.

Lilac made to sink the stake into his shoulder, his stomach—anywhere *away* from his heart—but he was too heavy, and his fangs had latched onto her arm.

She lost her balance, and they both tumbled off the beam.

✖ 47 ✖

When Garin felt the warmth of sun on his face and his beloved's perfumed hair against his chest—her full weight against him —he knew he'd either gone to heaven, or had been dragged into the deepest pits of hell.

And when he felt the liquid ecstasy trickling onto his arms, he wished he'd never left that sanctum with her. For a pocket full of time, thousands of books, and the odd creature that now lay snoring in a crumpled heap just feet away, he didn't know what he'd give.

They'd rolled and tumbled. That was all he'd remembered from their quick, unpleasant descent. Lilac grappling for her dagger in his grasp; red clouding his vision, his stomach lurching.

The way her sweet flesh gave way between his new, sharper teeth.

Garin slid Lilac's body off of him, and reached for the dagger handle, ready to yank it out of her back and watch her chest inflate.

But he winced, his hand knocking wood. Garin sat up, watching his raw knuckle heal over, smoking in the ray of sunlight piercing the high window.

Lilac's eyes were glassy, an expression of brief shock contorting her face as she stared back at him, unseeing, her head twisted in his direction. Red leaked lightly at the front of her damp gown, and at the crescent of fang marks he'd left on her forearm, but it was *pouring* from her back, pooling rapidly beneath her.

He crawled and yanked it from her, then flipped her face-up.

Why? his logic and hunger snarled within, anger and confusion merging into an ungodly wrath, slamming into him all at once. *Why had this happened, why had Kestrel's curse gripped him the moment she'd been crowned?*

Garin tore his wrist with his teeth and let his blood flood her mouth.

Breathe, he thought desperately. It was all he could think, even with the nearing measured footfall of that blasted nuisance sea witch. *Breathe. Choke on it. Sputter.*

"Come on," he muttered through his teeth, slapping her face. Gods, it was still warm. Still pink and warm. She would live, walk among his kind. He would rather her fall out of love with him, walk by his side as his fledgling than lose her—that much was clear as dawn.

But his blood only pooled at the back of her open mouth, spilling out.

"Come. *On.*"

There was another set of footsteps, then. Henri knelt behind him, sniffling.

"She's gone, son."

Son. Garin spun, clutching the hulking git by the front of his white silken robes. He was hardly moved—the drunkard should have been on his arms and knees, begging the Old Gods for his daughter back.

"This is your doing," Garin hissed. "And if she were to marry—" The words caught in his throat. "If she were ever to marry me, she'd take *my* name. Join my forsaken bloodline. I would have taken her far from this cursed place. Far from *you*, if not for her reluctant duty to the very honor you squandered." His voice dropped to a growl. "I am no son of yours, and never will be if you could not stand to love her in the first place."

Garin stood, passing Morwenn and dragging Henri by the nape of his neck. He strode straight toward the group huddled at the chapel's far end, his gaze hardening on the priest, who'd broken down in the corner and was sobbing quietly. "P-please, Sir Trevelyan," he cowered. "Spare them. They know not what they do."

"They know exactly what they have done, Father." He roughly dropped the old king and tilted his head up. He glowered at Marguerite, still perched on the organ like some cowardly bird. Her friends and former court cowered beside her. His eyes lingered for a moment on Edith Menard's daughter. He tipped his head and turned away. "Ostracized, for *language*? I should tear your throats out where you stand. You have no idea what *else* she's capable of. She is much, *much* worse than she leads on."

He turned back to the open chapel. They didn't deserve his broken, cruel eulogy for the woman who was the world to him.

Lorietta and Adelaide stood against the far wall. Adelaide clutched one of her glass bottles, frenzied liquid gold inside. Lori locked eyes with him, offering a gentle smile filled with sorrow yet reassurance.

He forced himself to look away, shame boring into him. His friend had seen enough of the cruelty and carnage he was capable of.

Beyond, the wounded watched from the chapel's broken edges—guards and servants peeking through crumbled stone, limbs poorly bound, expressions wary. A few sat bleeding in the dust of the bailey, too weak to stand. Others simply stared, as if waiting for orders that would never come.

It was quiet beyond. There was no more movement at the gate.

He stalked down to Lilac's body like a lion refusing to waste its spoils— and caught the glimpses of Lilac's sisters off to his right, gathered in the dim light just beyond the ruined choir rail. Isabel, her soft eyes alert and unreadable. Yanna, shoulders squared, one hand on her twin's shoulders as she returned his gaze in loathing—and Piper, her face withdrawn, fixed on him with something like mourning.

They huddled close together, silently watching.

He couldn't bring himself to look at them long. It had been *his* hand that reached for something he should never have touched in the first place. His hands trembled—not with fear, but with the ache to tear something apart. To bleed the world back into balance. But there was no other enemy here.

Only the ghosts of what once was, and the monster who made them.

Garin sank to his knees, almost refusing to touch her. He couldn't bring himself to feel Lilac's skin cold—colder than his

"*Lilac*," Morwenn mused, singing her name. She circled them with slow, liquid grace, her strange shoes clicking, echoing off the walls with each step. There was something eerily familiar in her stride, slow and elegant. Intent. "Feisty little one, wasn't she? Your queen, Eleanor. Your own curse, in and of herself. Trepid, yet more consuming than your bloodlust."

"*Speak her name again and I'll cut your tongue from your mouth, witch.*"

"Sorceress," she corrected. "Water mage, to be exact. Necromancer reigning."

His lips spread into a threatening sneer. "I don't care *what* or *who* you are."

"For now." She smiled. "There he is, the monster behind the mask. I imagine your lovers prefer you angry. Thirsty."

Garin didn't even hear half of whatever the fuck she was saying. He glanced around, combing the room for the blasted warlock. Where was he —where had he been?

Did death work the same for thralls? Was this truly the end? He was going to be sick.

Morwenn stepped closer. Water curled around her feet. "I've an offer. A request I think you'd find quite appealing."

Garin's head slowly lifted. "Bring her back to me, and I'll do anything for you."

A maelstrom of irritation flashed behind her eyes, the color of swirling cognac in the sun. She looked down at Lilac, whose hair was backlit by the sun. A dark, smoldering auburn, made richer after the *Guài's* disillusion-ment arrow had struck her hand. Embers stained in the crimson rapidly spreading beneath her.

Eyeing him, Morwenn tossed her own long hair, golden brown as if the sun itself were imbued in its hue. Her sunburned pale-green throat smelled of the western shores. "It is not an exchange I offer, but—"

"She cannot do it," Myrddin was stepping through the cliff-sized hole in the wall. "Do not deal the queen's life with her." Part of his blue robes and pants were singed off, still smoking. In his hand, by the scruff of its neck, was the plump gray cat.

Behind him, Loïg neighed concernedly like a hulking shadow. They stepped into the hall, then, Myrddin, into the chapel.

Morwenn made a sound of relief. "Oh! Duchess, there you are."

"I found her hanging by her tail from a rope about halfway down the flagpole," Myrddin muttered. Bastion busied himself studying the carvings in the ceiling.

"And you are?" Morwenn asked, eyeing the newcomer with cautious fascination.

Most of the warlock's ire had faded, leaving deep shadows under his eyes. He ignored her question and strode straight over to Garin, regarding Lilac as he spoke. "The vampires have extinguished much of the efforts at the south gate. They had armor on, for the most part," he added, for Garin's benefit. "Gwendal the fledgling helped them obtain it from the recently abandoned forge."

Yanna choked a delirious laugh from their corner, Isabel violently shushing her.

"They retreated at dawn—I told them about The Fenfoss Inn. They should be there now."

"Meriam must be thrilled," Garin said numbly, but gratefully. He reached out and gripped Myrddin's hand in a firm squeeze, and shook. "And the rest?"

"Injured, shaken. No losses of the coven from what I've seen, but there are a mixture of Breton and enemy bodies scattered outside, more the latter than the former. They can't seem to find Kemble." He blinked slowly, intentionally, at Garin. The rush of the night, the crippling hunger and raging lust that shook him, all felt like a distant, blood-soaked nightmare. Rupert was safe in the shadows, even as his mother remained. "So Hedwig is tending to them."

There was movement at the back of the chapel. "We'll help," muttered Adelaide, also unable to take her eyes off the queen's form.

"Go," Garin said, his voice rougher than he'd intended.

They left for the opening, toward the courtyard. "There's a ward over the castle," Lori said when she passed. "It's not ancestral, and only lasts as long as I'm here physically here, but outsiders would see no difference. I've covered the corpses, too."

"I'll reinforce it with my own protections, but that will deplete all of my arcana." Myrddin coughed into his smoking sleeve, and the witches hurried toward the main keep. "It will take me a bit to recover from that, and I'm afraid I'll prove useless to you and—" The warlock's throat bobbed, and his eyes darted down at Lilac.

"You are never useless," Garin said, his voice unintentionally rough. A pang of guilt hit him. "You've been an invaluable help, and friend." He felt terrible for the next question he'd ask. "How long will that take? Your recovery."

"For a spell that size? Three moon cycles."

Just then, the cat spun and scratched Myrddin in the face; he swore and dropped it.

Bisousig—*Duchess*—pranced right past Morwenn's waiting arms, over Lilac's lifeless body, up the steps and into Father Guillaume's arms. The warlock swiped the wound off his face, and the priest scooped him up, cooing.

"*Well.*"Affronted, Morwenn put a hand to her chest and squinted, just noticing Loïg munching on a piece of kelp she'd trailed in.

"What do you want?" Garin demanded. "What is your offer?"

"The Isle of Ys has risen again," she said simply, smiling at the instant recognition that flashed across his face. "The sea has given it back to me, my island kingdom—my drowned jewel lost to the abyss. I've been shackled to this plane for several decades, but Ys has been lost to the sea for far, far longer than that. It was broken into pieces by my father's hand; he stole them, scattering them far and wide across the kingdom in his attempt to flee his failures." Her suddenly glassy eyes drifted up to Bastion, then to Myrddin. Then, back down—with dripping disdain—onto Lilac. "I come not as an enemy, but as a petitioner. A hopeful ally to your cause. I need help exhuming my beloved kingdom, rebuilding from ruin and rubble."

Garin blinked, warm tears forming, the rush of his slow heartbeat flooding his ears.

"I've already found a lovely clothier, but now I need to find someone to forge its bones. To hammer steel where coral grows. I seek a blacksmith."

"I cannot help you. I'm the reigning Doyen of the Brocéliande Vampire Coven," Garin replied coldly.

"Well, yes. I've heard *so* very much about you." A slow, salacious grin curved her lips. "You and the queen have already met *Me Maouezed-Dour*—my Belles of the Deep. My teeth beneath the tides."

At the mention of the Morgen, Garin's face blanched, his mask of composure faltering.

"When I was finally torn free from the forty-odd years I'd spent trapped in the godforsaken prison of your mortal realm—really no better than nine-hundred or so years sealed under the sea—" she continued, her tone darkening, "they were the first to speak of you two. The vampire and his princess, scrambling through Brocéliande together. They'd tried to trap you for me, knowing my reckoning was near." She swallowed. "Before that? Only fragments. Glimpses. Memories snagged, just beyond the veil. But now I can rebuild."

Garin said nothing, heard nothing she said. Finally, he brought himself to bend and brush his knuckles against Lilac's hand.

It was cold. Garin began to tremble against the slow-burning ache that would consume him, the need to tear into something—someone. He'd do it if he didn't soon hold her, feel her pulse hammering back to life.

But the sea witch kept talking. "I imagine you're quite the bladesmith. You have a smithing station in your Sanguine Mine, don't you?"

"I scarcely used it. My skills are rudimentary," he lied.

But Morwenn gave him a knowing smile. "I should travel through the Argent, pay them a little visit. Find someone else willing."

He bared his teeth, fear and disbelief striking him even deeper. The Isle of Ys was legendary—a folktale. A thing of legend.

Then again, so was he.

"Leave them be," he snarled, straightening.

"My Duchess has kept me well-informed, you see." Morwenn watched Garin pick up the dagger that had clattered near Lilac's blood-soaked head. "My dark creatures would relish working alongside an esteemed soldier such as yourself. A *daywalking Strigoi*," she commented, assessing, "stuck in his form because... I'm guessing his own thrall is a prude?"

Garin slowed halfway up the steps. His nostrils flared. "She gives me everything and more."

Morwenn's brow rose.

"And I don't care what you need."

"You will. François might be dissuaded from advancing for the time being, at least from launching into full-fledged war now that he'll see your Daemons are openly, publicly on Lilac's side. But what of Maximilian? With an empire that large, I doubt such frailties would not discourage him so easily from pursuing her hand."

His head was pounding, his hunger pulsing to life once more—not for her body, not even distinctly for her blood. Certainly not like the overwhelming tide of urges to end her life, as the opposing end of Kestrel's deal had demanded.

He wanted *her*. Wanted her for himself.

And Morwenn was regrettably right. France would leave them alone for the time being, but *someone* would come knocking, or snooping eventually. Lilac would not be the one to answer.

"You've got nothing left here but ghosts."

Slowly, tiredly—fondly—he hummed in disagreement. "I have her."

Henri remained sitting in the middle of the floor, clutching his hip where he'd fallen. The others had remained, too terrified to move from their spots. He kneeled so they were face to face.

Then, Garin bowed reverently, his forehead nearly touching the floor. "I have to do this."

Henri began to sputter, to tear up, to beg. His arm rose to cover his face.

"I have to. Your life given will save her. It will bring her back; I've seen it done before. Your daughter is not lost. She is fierce and unyielding, willing to listen and learn. To grow. Eleanor is meant to lead, with or without a crown. She'll make a great leader one day." Garin swallowed, glancing back at the chapel ruins. "Somewhere, for the kingdom wise enough to trust her. She will."

Henri was quiet for a long moment. His eyes, heavy with grief, no longer wavered. Then, with surprising strength, he reached for Garin's hand and folded his weathered palm over it.

"She already is," the old king replied. He gave Garin's hand a rough shake, the tremble in his beard betraying what his voice refused to. "Take care of my daughters. All of them."

Garin's only answer was the tightening of his grip, and the promise in his silence.

"You won't come back from this, Your Grace," warned Myrddin over Garin's shoulder. The warlock's fingers were moving feverishly, his eyes softly shut. "The dagger won't bring you back if I exchange your soul for hers."

Henri offered a small smile, but his gaze was fixed on Lilac. "I know."

The old king's nails dug into Garin's hand as he skewered his heart.

It was instant, the life in his eyes fading immediately. Garin yanked the Dawnshard from him, and Henri slumped back onto the granite.

Marguerite turned away, into the organ. Piper watched with wide eyes while the twins held her, as if they knew what wasn't yet spoken.

Myrddin whispered in an unknown language, and Garin watched, fascinated, as a ball of brilliant *orange* flame lifted from Henri's chest. The warlock inhaled sharply.

"What?" Garin asked, panic rising. "What's wrong?"

"This is the third time I've performed such a spell, and I've never seen a soul flame that color." Myrddin guided the flame over the altar, down the steps, and over Lilac.

"A life taken for exchange is one thing," said Morwenn dryly, rooted in her spot near Lilac's feet. "A life willingly given is another entirely."

"Holds a different type of weight. Magic," Myrddin agreed.

The flame sank into her chest, and her entire body came alive in an outline of warm light before fading.

Garin rose, her dagger still dripping with the old king's blood. "I will be your blacksmith, Morwenn." Morwenn's head popped up. "*With* conditions."

"As expected."

Just then, there was a shifting behind him; Marguerite had climbed down from her perch. She strode past Henri's still-warm body and went to Lilac, kneeling and scooping her daughter's head into her lap despite the blood soaking the fine material of her gown.

Marguerite sobbed once, brushing her hair off her face.

"Lilac will—" He was cut short by an indistinguishable sound between a sob and gasp of pain.

The queen was upright.

L ilac sat up to stare first into the eyes of her mother, whom she'd never seen cry, except for the night her *arcana lingua* was discovered. Then, she locked eyes with Garin standing over Henri's lifeless body, her dripping blade hanging loosely in one hand.

All her incandescent rage and anxiety returned as fragments of memory, flashing through her mind. Numbly, unthinking, Lilac pulled herself off the floor, off her crying mother—she didn't even know how the bloodied stake ended up back in her hand—and charged.

Garin's incredulous, sun-laced smile and the way he opened his arms as he strode to meet her only infuriated her further.

Lilac pressed her thumb over her pointer and middle finger wrapped around the hawthorn and aimed for his shoulder—but Garin sheathed the Dawnshard and dipped, dodging the point. He scooped her up in a chest-breaking embrace.

Unable to help herself, she leaned into him, furious tears streaming down her face. He smelled of a bluebell wood, of the summer hyacinths peppering the glades, and the iron-tinged rush of the Argent. Of dark and ancient magic, and an existence foreboding.

He was everything she ever wanted, the darkest parts of herself in the flesh. He brought them out of her.

Garin slowly released her, planting his lips upon her forehead as his fingers found her wrist—gave it a quick squeeze, causing her to drop the stake—and pinned it behind her back. He kissed her, just deeply enough to make her mother look away, and found her other hand.

There was a quick *clink* of metal, then. Much too fast to be mundane.

Lilac looked up at him, and he, down at her. She pulled at the iron and hawthorn chains binding her wrists. They tightened magically—painfully—cutting into her skin.

"I will be your blacksmith," he said, glancing over her shoulder. "I'll come to Ys."

Lilac slowly turned. The sea witch, Morwenn, stood there silently, watching them—watching Garin—with too thin-lipped a smile.

"You will *not*," Lilac breathed furiously, her mind and memory muddied. He would not be going to wherever or whatever *Ys* was.

But Garin shushed her. "Hold your tongue while I do the negotiating, please," he said quickly.

Lilac tried to argue, but no sound would come. Whatever countereffect had taken hold on her upon the rafters, berries or otherwise, had vanished.

"Oh, I do love a rift. Alas, that irreverent, cantankerous thing is not your wife," Morwenn offered playfully, eyeing Lilac unabashedly. As if she were an animal. "That is not *your* ring on her finger, is it?"

"I will come." Garin didn't so much as blink. "But let this be clear: Lilac —whether my mistress, my fiancée, my wife, or the nice village baker who once overcharged me for bread—is coming *with* me."

"No need for the violence, vampire." Morwenn dismissively examined her long, teal talons. "I can see perfectly well what she is to you. Though, I should warn you both, that in the realm of the Fair Folk and of every creeping, clawing thing you can imagine," she added, explaining very slowly for Lilac, "any relationship between Daemon and mortal are considered... irregular. At best."

They're not accepted in our world, either, Lilac thought bitterly. Kestrel had once given them a similar warning. She yanked her arms against her constraints, unable to fathom an arcane island—one led by the likes of Morwenn.

"As a human, your pet cannot exist there as your public counterpart—as anything other than your subordinate. She will *never* be seen as an equal. Most definitely not yours." Morwenn shrugged, turning away.

Garin's shoulders began to steadily, noticeably rise and fall.

"Granted, I cannot help nor regulate what goes on behind closed doors. In my centuries imprisoned underwater, I, too, have fucked several of my servants out of pure boredom. Or pity." She eyed Lilac, something like ravenous admiration crossing her serpentine features. "I'd say it surprises me she's lived to tell the tale, but I've seen her strength. And her speed. She must make for an entertaining blood slave." At Garin's murderous glare, she stuck her bottom lip out. "Do you have her convinced that what you have is something more?"

Fuming, Lilac descended the steps. Doing so was harder than she'd ever imagined with her hands tied.

I will not go as a servant, she thought at him, boisterously as possible. *Not yours.*

Would you rather be hers? he growled, claws against her mind. "Eleanor is mine. Whether they choose to acknowledge it or not is irrelevant. She will be my hand at your forge."

"I'm not seeking apprentices."

"Funny. *I* am."

The sea witch ignored this and merely turned, producing a glistening conch out of thin air.

As she put it to her mouth, Garin spoke again. "Lilac's court will accompany us. That is my last and final demand."

Morwenn followed his gaze to the huddling group. Yanna, Isabel, and Piper froze, an array of emotions crossing the terror on their faces.

Lilac would never intentionally subject them to whatever Garin had just agreed to. But... what was left for them at the castle?

And what of Maximilian? John and Riou would likely aid in the administrative declining of his offer—wherever they were. If they were alive. But what then? After such a public affair, what if her decision angered the emperor to the point of seizing them with the very army he'd promised in exchange for her hand?

The thought of bringing them along for whatever Morwenn had in store was terrifying, but the thought of being torn from them was far, far too much to bear.

What will they do there? Lilac glared at him questioningly. It seemed he hadn't thought that far. *I will not be the cause of their suffering.*

You need them just as much as they need you, he snarled.

You were the one who offered your services!

Garin faced her, fuming. He didn't say a word—but her throat tightened, and her knees nearly buckled with the unnatural wave of terror and want that flooded between her legs. *Do you think she was asking?*

"No," Morwenn said after a second's deliberation.

Garin's defensive anger hit Lilac like a blast of frigid air. "They're her courtiers and attendants. She is still royalty here."

Myrddin stepped forward. "If I may, Lady Morwenn," he said, voice even with diplomacy. "Their presence may be of some benefit. She is human, after all. Would you truly wish your wretched sea-born things preparing her bath? Dressing her? Touching her? Feeding her?"

Lilac growled in her mind, but Garin quieted her with a brush of his knuckles on hers.

Morwenn regarded the warlock. "And you are?"

If she'd truly been buried beneath the sea for centuries, if time had eroded her name from every living memory until she'd been reduced to a folk tale... it made sense she wouldn't know his identity.

His eye twitched slightly, but he folded into a *deep* bow. "Myrddin Ambrosius Wyllt. I am Her Majesty's advisor in Diplomacy and Magic."

"I see," Morwenn murmured. Her smile didn't reach her eyes as they turned slowly, gleefully, onto Lilac. "You want me to bring her servants and a pet wizard, too."

"Warlock. Sorcerer," Myrddin corrected.

A harsh growl erupted from Garin's throat. "*Be quiet.*"

"*And* a Strigoi, wrapped duly around her finger, rather than her throat." Morwenn studied Lilac, the room that stood behind her in silent wonder. "How bizarre."

"She does not come alone," he repeated, the threat in his voice thick.

Morwenn laughed softly. Her tone dropped like a knife into water. "You mistake my hospitality for weakness, vampire. You both come freely at *my* mercy. I will not house human courtiers, or any flailing handmaidens clutching onto a blood slave's skirts. This is no diplomatic visit. This is our reckoning."

Without warning, she pressed her lips to the conch, puffed her cheeks —and blew. The sound was like a foghorn, a slow and steady moan that rattled the timber above, shaking her to her core and sending any perching fowl who'd decided to roost in the aftermath of their duel, flocking from the structure.

It sounded like a cry for help, a summoning for ships filled with the dead.

It might as well have been.

Even Myrddin looked panicked, his eyes bulging as the floor began to rumble, the wet pebbles bouncing. Everyone but Morwenn backed towards the walls and the cracked opening leading into the courtyard.

Just when she thought the earth would open up and swallow them all, the same seafoam mist that had infiltrated the castle with the Bugul Noz's invitation began to rise from the floor.

The conch's final note echoed like the dying breath of her chapel. The sharp stench of brine filled the air, seeping into her lungs before she realized what was happening.

This was a *portal*.

"No!" Lilac shouted, lunging for her sisters. They dashed past the altar toward her, Bastion and Giles shouting—but Garin was faster. His arm snagged around her waist, and he lifted her off her feet as the fog engulfed them quicker than she would've been able to escape it. She felt the ghost of her mother's fingertips against her cheek, then Garin's steady arms around her before the world fell away.

THERE WAS NO SCREAM, NO WIND NOR WEIGHT TO THEIR FALLING. ONLY an overwhelming sense of dread and being dragged down, down—down through a deep, long silence. Through cold, across moors and towns, in the liminal dark.

Then—salt. Lilac gasped, the breath knocked out of her, the taste of it on her lips and the crash of waves below. The smell of kelp and brine thrashed in the wind, fluttering her hair back. She stared disbelievingly at the vast swath of turquoise beauty—at the hiss of tides colliding with cliffs, the bones of the world cast in blinding sunlight.

The coast. A corner of her kingdom she'd heard of many times, but never experienced herself.

She sat up, groaning, eager to soak in more of its beauty despite the pressure of warning in her chest. She had landed hard on a mixture of cool stone and warm sand, silted and damp beneath her stinging, scratched palms. Her chains had broken in the fall, it appeared; she stretched and moved her wrists stiffly. The fog was gone, and something about the way the breeze howled and scraped across the granite under her told her they were very, *very* high up.

Elbows bleeding, knees scraped, Lilac shifted on all fours and peeked over the nearby edge. Her stomach dropped. Just an arm's length away, pristine aquamarine waters trickled in their gentle swell below the jagged cliff edge, footed by a too-small beach shrouded in sea spray, bramble, and peculiar bushes of purple petals and round, blue flowers.

Garin lay beside her, chest rising, coughing as he stirred. He let out a strangled shout and shot to his feet—and was met face-to-face with a hulking shadowed figure whose teeth bared in his periphery.

He yelped and stumbled back, but Lilac caught him, dragging him away from the cliff's edge with more strength than grace.

It was *Loïg*. Under him, Bisousig threaded herself between his hooves.

Lilac seized Loïg's reins and tried to tug him toward firmer ground, when Morwenn emerged from behind the horse's massive flank. In her arms, she held the limp but stirring form of the Bugul Noz. Without a second glance, the sea witch made her way to the cliff's edge, where she dangled the creature's body.

"No!" Garin reached for her, but it was too late.

The Bugul Noz fell gracelessly into the sea, landing with a plop before a wave rolled over him.

"He did nothing wrong," said Lilac, the sheer height of the cliff making her dizzy. Garin gripped her arm.

"The sea is his cursed home. He'll return to Ys, where he will be properly dealt with." Morwenn eyes glittered, shards of shell in wet sand. "This is where I leave you both. You've got your steed with you, I see. How convenient." She smiled toothily at Garin, her rows of teeth covered in algae. "That explains the one missing from the cavalry I summoned."

Garin stiffened.

"Unfortunately, they're inseparable from their tamers. I would've taken him back, but he'd be useless to me. Now, he's yours. You'll need him where you're going."

Lilac narrowed her eyes, the salt-wind tugging her hair across her face. Her grip tightened on the reins.

"You'll make your way down to the beach," Morwenn continued, gesturing toward the jagged descent behind them. "My galleon will collect you there and bring you to Ys."

Lilac dared peek over the edge again. "There is no galleon."

"It's coming," Morwenn replied. "Just as fate does, sometimes slow but impossible to outrun."

"No." Garin's jaw was set. He uneasily eyed the waves tumbling over the base of the cliff. His voice was low and ragged as he mounted Loïg with ease. "Let's go." He held a hand down to her.

Lilac didn't need his Sanguine magic to obey. She gave him her hand, and he pulled her up, sitting her in the wide seat before him. "What are you doing?"

"We're going home," Garin said decidedly. "Back to the High Forest. I've changed my mind."

Morwenn tilted her head as she stroked its snout. Loïg whinnied at her, stomping his front legs.

Garin slipped his hands over the reins and tugged them left.

But Morwenn tutted, wagging her finger before Loïg. "They're our guests, and we're going to make sure they get to the island safely. Where the rest of your brethren are."

As Garin cussed and tried to tug to the right, Morwenn calmly bent, and straightened with Bisousig in one arm, kissing the struggling feline on the head. The cat swiped, and the sea witch narrowly dodged it; Bisousig then turned in Morwenn's arms and reached—for them, for Garin, cater-wauling loudly.

Ignoring this, Morwenn tossed her hair over shoulder, baring herself, and sauntered past them, trailing her free fingers over first Lilac's calf, then

Garin's. It didn't look like it, but Morwenn's skin was *ice*-cold. Clammy, like a corpse at the bottom of a cave.

As Garin clawed her off, dread festered within Lilac's very bones. Her dreams of high cliffs and rocky shores—the towering, glittering palace with its twisting turrets like sea glass she'd witnessed in her slumber... those raging tides. They had been waking nightmares.

Below, the waves had begun to crash against the cliff, tremendous walls of barrelling water. The skies above darkened, and there it was again—the thick blue fog rolling in, obscuring the horizon.

"You're rather fond of soirées, aren't you, Your Majesty?" The sea witch's deep, husky laughter rumbled from behind them. "Hurry up, then. You won't have all day, and the ride to the island is several hours." She tilted her head at Garin. "You and my brother are our esteemed guests, and my dark creatures are *so* looking forward to welcoming the representatives of the High and Low Forests."

Something began to nag, *pull* at Lilac's subconscious again, stronger than fear. This had all gone wrong. The chest—Kestrel's silence.

The revenant.

The stories were *wrong*; this was more than a wayward princess left to drown. Morwenn was worse—was shaped by time, eroded by the forces of the sea. She was older than the Breton thrones, older than the skewed bloodline of Trécesson heirs.

"We're leaving," growled Lilac forcefully. She grabbed the reins and tugged herself, but her loyal horse seemed entirely ensnared in Morwenn's gaze.

"I'm afraid the poor Strigoi is afraid of a little water, my dear Morvarc'h," she cooed. "I thought that was an old wives' tale."

"*Morvarc'h?*" Garin snarled. His arms snagged around her, creating a protective cage, and together they scrambled to dismount—but it was too late.

With a tap on his rump, Mowenn sent Loïg galloping toward the thin edge of the cliff. Garin contorted his body to throw them off to the side, but the reins they clutched came to life, latching onto them, securing them into place on the saddle.

The creature leaped, sending them plunging toward the crashing maw of sea below.

EPILOGUE

I've been cursed to walk this earth for 192 years—193 in early November, but who's counting? Any poor sod who's ever crossed paths with me will tell you that there are an unreasonably high number of things that irk me to the high heavens. It began in my childhood: slow, misting rain—I prefer drenching storms, a sprinkling of thunder and lightning, if you will. The feel of the coarse wool coats Aimee made me wear on our market day trips down to the Paimpont bakery run by the Heussaffs in the winter.

As I got older, it was the clanking of the armor we were forced to don, and—understandably—the cries of dying men. But eventually I grew numb to it, as one does when he is subjected to continuous war for a decade of his youth. Many of us did.

When I was turned at twenty-five, I found the feeling returning tenfold. Sensation fed into my anger, which then fed into my hunger. Years later, the inn brought me great reprieve, and the Algovens seemed unbothered by my need to interact minimally on my shifts, and looked the other way when I'd slink down to my cellar room where I'd rot, a bottle of blood in my hand, until the next evening. Even on the tavern's most raucous nights, it seemed being among Daemon folk—not even necessarily other vampires—was different for me. Soothing. Calming.

Reassuring, almost—and on my darkest days, when the memories refused to quiet, I'd sit and ponder if I was ever meant for the human life I scarcely truly missed. Of the childhood that came to me in eye-blurring fragments.

And then, the princess walked in, and everything changed. Like the fates themselves were calling out to me, a burning beacon of change and reprieve. It was as though everything warm and good in the world stood right in front of me, in the form of a rain-soaked woman making a mess of my floor.

I'd banished the thought of making a mess of *her* immediately from my fucked up mind.

Last night I was hardly myself, either. Shards of the evening unfold: sitting at the card table with Bast, Myrddin, and that loathsome Casmir. Drinking. Betting. Gambling, and running to Rennes, feeling as free and as caged and scared as I've ever felt.

That thumping, sweaty mass of writhing bodies that drove my senses wild. And the queen—the queen in her mask, smelling of magic and dusk and Myrddin's black powder, and her blood that sings out to me. Centers me.

And that dripping, sweet cunt that leaves me breathless and drives me over the edge all over again.

Last thing I knew, I was in an alleyway, and the next, I'm chasing the warlock down the stairs and out the door. Adelaide nearly took my eye out with one of her exploding bottles, but Myrddin didn't manage to get very far from me, either. It seems that we, too, are tethered in a way.

At the moment, I am blinded by the sensations of a red lust and ravenousness, locked in a most intimate embrace and whispering sweet nothings to the soft, white linen canvas before me.

"*Die already,*" I snarl, hardly aware of the enormous repercussions of what I'm doing—of just *how* important the man beneath the pillow I'm holding taut is.

But he's got a lot of fight in him, probably from all the magical pottage Lorietta's been feeding him the past week.

His hands scramble for purchase over mine, gold rings adorning them— and a palm slams at the locked bedroom door for the umpteenth time.

"Don't do it," Lori snaps. "Remember yourself, Garin. You'll cause more trouble than you'll solve."

Then, Meriam. "I don't know. Maybe a mortal death in our walls would be good for Daemon business, after all."

"*Not the emperor's emissary*," Lori screeches.

Adelaide bursts out laughing. Of course she does.

But I couldn't stop myself if I tried. My mood's already inexplicably soured from the thrall bond that's snapped into place, and the bloodied blur of the night. My dick is still ragingly hard, my mouth watering at the thought of kneeling for my queen.

And my hands, as they move to murder—they shake, desperate to feel Eleanor again. Desperate to feel the swell of her ass against me, desperate to hold her fingers in mine. Sweaty at the thought of her at the altar with anyone else.

What an infuriating, idiotic mistake I've made—and will continue to make. Because it is the right thing to do, the chivalrous thing to do.

But for now, I am blinded by the inescapable, cemented knowledge of two things: the first, the force that drove me to chuck *The Histories of the Lasting Night* into the Argent. Stumbling upon the knowledge that vampire-human marriages unsanctioned by the arcane powers are strictly outlawed, and would put a magical bounty upon their heads. Surprising? No.

Infuriating? Absolutely.

Ancient law or not, I'd raze kingdoms, traverse treacherous seas to keep her.

"Garin, if you stain my walls in the Imperial emissary's blood, you will *never* be allowed back, mark my words."

Lori has a point. She abides by Francis's treaty—at least that part of it—and wrath hath no fury than a witch scorned... I should know.

I lift the pillow from Albrecht's ruddy face and yank him up by his shirt. He fights me again, sputtering through blue-tinged lips, but I'm doing him a favor. No one wants to see the wrath that might come on Lilac's wedding day, especially if I'm forced to keep my distance from her. Yet again, I'd be the worst kind of wedding guest imaginable.

I swing the door open, to the witches' shocked faces, and gently excuse myself between them. Lori is screaming at me; Meriam has decided to stay out of it, though I've never seen her more uncomfortable. Adelaide watches warily from the bottom of the staircase, and most of the Korikaned in the tavern are instantly hushed by Bast and Casmir.

I break out into the night. Early morning? I'm not sure.

The git sobs at my side, begging for his life. Poor thing, he didn't ask for this. He's the messenger—Maximilian's proxy. None of this is his fault.

But I drag him to the edge of the Argent, just under the window Lilac jumped out of in order to escape me that lovely, fateful day. I drop to my knees, the lapping water soaking my trousers, and shove Albrecht's head face-first into the slow-moving river, bubbles and his frantic scrabbling frothing from beneath.

The rage surges through me, out of me, my mind clearing just a bit as my uneven breath steadies. The blinding bloodlust remains, but this is better than nothing.

Better him than the emperor, right?

I stand and float his body to the middle of the Argent, where two pairs of hands snatch him by the legs and yank him under. He disappears without a sound, until a lone pale-green head pops up above the surface, her eerie eyes glowing in the dim light of Brocéliande. She waves in gratitude, and I nod before turning my back on her, shuddering.

The door swings open as I trek up the bank. Out stumbles Giles, followed by Myrddin. Blitzrik and Ra'arak watch from the windows, their button noses pressed against the fogged glass.

"Ready the carriage and the horses, please," I grunt. "Myrddin, get your things."

The warlock is mysteriously *much* too chipper to be caught in the middle of all this; without further clarification, he disappears into the inn without a word. Giles also obliges, humming a hymn that's supposed to be solemn to himself. It's chipper, upbeat, and I can't help but feel a stab of dread-filled hope as Bisousig slinks around my ankles, purring loudly.

Bastion ducks his head out, wary of the soon-rising sun. "Where are *you* going?"

"Where do you think I'm going?" I say. It might be my fault the emissary is no longer, but Lilac will not be kept waiting for the meeting I myself had organized.

The second thing is that, by vice or virtue, Lilac is my queen. *Eleanor of Brittany*. Not only do I kneel for her with unwavering reverence.

There remains a steady truth, unavoidable and unsettling as fate itself:

I've fallen in love with her, Dear Reader. It is a simple, nonsensical fact. Against my better judgement and rudimentary sense of self warring with the thing I've become—both are in agreement. *It is her.*

The one my thirst burns to covet. The one the man in me, buried beneath decades of vine and sinew, yearns to serve. And cherish. And hold, in sickness and in health. In this life and the next.

There is no other choice but to go to her, I decide, as Myrddin lumbers out with two travel bags.

Hunger does things to a person, you see. Need skirts reason, logic is no longer a boon, and may the end always justify the means.

Disastrous and unholy as it sounds, although it is my ultimate wish for Eleanor to be safe in the arms of any powerful ruler with the resources to ensure her kingdom's safety—

At the end of all this, it'll be *my* ring on her hand.

AUTHOR'S NOTE

Writing *Disillusioned* was like digging through wreckage with my bare hands. It is a love letter for the eldest and defiant daughters, those condemned for feeling deeply, loving messily, and wanting more.

It's a story steeped in vampire myth and Breton legend, but at its core, *Disillusioned* is a discussion about hunger. The need to be understood and wanted as you are, bleeding and torn open.

What parts of yourself do you save from the ruins, and what do you leave to rot?

This is the tale of a reluctant monarch and the vampire who aches for her—not just her blood, but her rage, her gall, her mind. We navigate class, patriarchy, neurodivergence... the joy of finally being seen and finding the people *meant* for you. It's for anyone who's ever exhumed themselves and glimpsed something ruined yet powerful in the mirror.

Thanks for reading this sequel. It means more than you know.

With fierce love and dirt under my nails,

Briar Somerset

ALSO BY BRIAR SOMERSET

Disenchanted

Disillusioned

ACKNOWLEDGMENTS

Writing a sequel is a strange kind of alchemy. No matter how well you think you've prepared yourself on the quest to write the imperfect follow-up to your Dark Fantasy debut, there's always a rogue stranger in the dark, with too many fangs and a glint in their eye.

Or, maybe there are *many* of them, each with a bit of wizened advice to share.

Shayne, Chantal, Amanda, Michael, Cindy, Jessica, Alyssa, Erica, and Loni: You first believed in *Disenchanted*, even as *Disillusioned* carved a different path. Your support has meant everything to me.

To my editors, Olivia, Jessica, Erica, Diksha, and Zachary: thank you for helping me reshape this sequel and letting it bleed where it needed to. We worked on tightening things, but I still ended up with an insane word count. Apologies, I won't (will) do it again.

Krys, Daniele, and Zachary: It was your friendship and endless talent that inspired me to forge on when my sequel drafting process felt particularly difficult. Hearing my characters speak truly changed everything about the way I think about them and tell their stories. Thank you for breathing life into them.

Diksha and Erika: I'm honored and privileged to work with you as my PAs. Thank you for help, honest feedback, and guidance in everything from prep, to marketing, to release. You're the best.

Alex and Isobel—you both are the reason I was able to put so many grueling hours into this project. I owe you both a drink—or several—the next time we're together.

Tim, my sweet sounding board and chaos sponge: Thanks for listening to my rambles about vampirism, feeding me, and loving me through every groggy midnight rewrite. I wouldn't have been able to do this without your encouragement and support.

And to my readers... thank you for letting me lure—I mean, *guide*—you even deeper into Brocéliande and the magic world beyond the shoreline. This leg of the journey was bound to be heavier, bloodier, but you stuck with me and came along anyway. I'm grateful for you.

I swear there's light ahead. Maybe.

ABOUT THE AUTHOR

Briar Somerset is an emerging author of Medieval Dark Romantasy. This is the second book in the A Lay of Ruinous Reign Series.

Somerset is a Filipino-American vampire girl and enjoyer of fantasy RPGs, scalding cups of tea, and jotting down maladaptive nightmares of an arcane sovereign and a fanged botanist-barkeep with a voracious appetite.

In all facets of her craft, she enjoys exploring the ominous—*disenchanting*, if you will—undertones of history, romance, and the arcane.

www.ingramcontent.com/pod-product-compliance
Lightning Source LLC
Chambersburg PA
CBHW030737030726
47497CB00001B/12